# FROM THE PAGES OF
## *MAN AND SUPERMAN AND THREE OTHER PLAYS*

"People are always blaming their circumstances for what they are. I don't believe in circumstances. The people who get on in this world are the people who get up and look for the circumstances they want, and, if they can't find them, make them."

(Mrs. Warren's Profession, page 62)

"What is any respectable girl brought up to do but to catch some rich man's fancy and get the benefit of his money by marrying him?——as if a marriage ceremony could make any difference in the right or wrong of the thing!" (Mrs. Warren's Profession, page 65)

"Do you think that the things people make fools of themselves about are any less real and true than the things they behave sensibly about?"

(Candida, page 144)

"God has given us a world that nothing but our own folly keeps from being a paradise." (Candida, page 145)

"All the love in the world is longing to speak; only it dare not, because it is shy, shy, shy. That is the world's tragedy." (Candida, page 150)

"Man can climb to the highest summits; but he cannot dwell there long." (Candida, page 176)

"I'm only a beer teetotaller, not a champagne teetotaller. I don't like beer." (Candida, page 182)

"The worst sin towards our fellow creatures is not to hate them, but to be indifferent to them: that's the essence of inhumanity."

(The Devil's Disciple, page 244)

My conscience is the genuine pulpit article: it annoys me to see people comfortable when they ought to be uncomfortable; and I insist on making them think in order to bring them to conviction of sin.

(Shaw's Epistle Dedicatory to *Man and Superman*, page 302)

"We live in an atmosphere of shame. We are ashamed of everything that is real about us; ashamed of ourselves, of our relatives, of our incomes, of our accents, of our opinions, of our experience, just as we are ashamed of our naked skins. Good Lord, my dear Ramsden, we are ashamed to walk, ashamed to ride in an omnibus, ashamed to hire a hansom instead of keeping a carriage, ashamed of keeping one horse instead of two and a groom-gardener instead of a coachman and footman. The more things a man is ashamed of, the more respectable he is."

(*Man and Superman*, page 345)

"I had become a new person; and those who knew the old person laughed at me. The only man who behaved sensibly was my tailor: he took my measure anew every time he saw me, whilst all the rest went on with their old measurements and expected them to fit me."

(*Man and Superman*, page 368)

"In the arts of life man invents nothing; but in the arts of death he outdoes Nature herself, and produces by chemistry and machinery all the slaughter of plague, pestilence and famine."

(*Man and Superman*, page 438)

"It is not death that matters, but the fear of death. It is not killing and dying that degrades us, but base living, and accepting the wages and profits of degradation. Better ten dead men than one live slave or his master."  (*Man and Superman*, page 442)

"Marriage is a mantrap baited with simulated accomplishments and delusive idealizations."  (*Man and Superman*, page 453)

"An epoch is but a swing of the pendulum; and each generation thinks the world is progressing because it is always moving."

(*Man and Superman*, page 464)

# Man and Superman and Three Other Plays

## GEORGE BERNARD SHAW

*With an Introduction and Notes*
*by* JOHN A. BERTOLINI

*George Stade*
*Consulting Editorial Director*

**BARNES & NOBLE CLASSICS**
NEW YORK

𝓑

## BARNES & NOBLE CLASSICS
### NEW YORK

*Mrs. Warren's Profession* and *Candida* were first published in 1898, *The Devil's Disciple* in 1901, and *Man and Superman* in 1903.

Introduction, Notes, and For Further Reading
Copyright © 2004 by John A. Bertolini.

Note on George Bernard Shaw, The World of George Bernard Shaw, Inspired by the Plays of George Bernard Shaw, and Comments & Questions Copyright © 2004 by Fine Creative Media, Inc.

*Man and Superman and Three Other Plays*
ISBN 1-59308-067-0
LC Control Number 2003109511

Produced by:
Fine Creative Media, Inc.
322 Eighth Avenue
New York, NY 10001

President & Publisher: Michael J. Fine
Consulting Editorial Director: George Stade
Editor: Jeffrey Broesche
Editorial Research: Jason Baker
Vice-President Production: Stan Last
Senior Production Manager: Mark A. Jordan
Production Editor: KB Mello

Printed in the United States of America
QM
1  3  5  7  9  10  8  6  4  2
FIRST PRINTING

# GEORGE BERNARD SHAW

Dramatist, critic, and social reformer George Bernard Shaw was born on July 26, 1856, into a poor yet genteel Dublin household. His diffident and impractical father was an alcoholic disdained by his mother, a professional singer who ingrained in her only son a love of music, art, and literature. Just shy of his seventeenth birthday, Shaw joined his mother and two sisters in London, where they had settled three years earlier.

There he struggled—and failed—to support himself by writing. He first wrote a string of novels, beginning with the semi-autobiographical *Immaturity*, completed in 1879. Though some of his novels were serialized, none met with great success, and Shaw decided to abandon the form in favor of drama. While he struggled artistically, he flourished politically; for some years his greater fame was as a political activist and pamphleteer. A stammering, shy young man, Shaw nevertheless joined in the radical politics of his day. In the late 1880s he became a leading member of the fledgling Fabian Society, a group dedicated to progressive politics, and authored numerous pamphlets on a range of social and political issues. He often mounted a soapbox in Hyde Park and there developed the enthralling oratory style that pervades his dramatic writing.

In the 1890s, deeply influenced by the dramatic writings of Henrik Ibsen, Shaw spurned the conventions of the stage in "unpleasant" plays, such as *Mrs. Warren's Profession*, and in "pleasant" ones like *Arms and the Man* and *Candida*. His drama shifted attention from romantic travails to the great web of society, with its hypocrisies and other ills. The burden of writing seriously strained Shaw's health; he suffered from chronic migraine headaches. Shaw married fellow Fabian and Irish heiress Charlotte Payne-Townshend.

By the turn of the century, Shaw had matured as a dramatist with the historical drama *Caesar and Cleopatra*, and his masterpieces *Man and Superman* and *Major Barbara*. In all, he wrote more than fifty plays, including his anti-war *Heartbreak House* and the polemical *Saint Joan*, for which he was awarded the Nobel Prize. Equally prolific in his writings about music and theater, Shaw was so popular that he signed his critical pieces with simply the initials GBS. (He disliked his first name, George, and never used it except for the initial.) He remained in the public eye throughout his final years, writing controversial plays until his death. George Bernard Shaw died at his country home on November 2, 1950.

# TABLE OF CONTENTS

# THE WORLD OF GEORGE BERNARD SHAW AND HIS PLAYS

1856  George Bernard Shaw is born on July 26, at 33 Upper Synge Street in Dublin, to George Carr Shaw and Lucinda Elizabeth Gurly Shaw.

1865  George John Vandeleur Lee, Mrs. Shaw's singing instructor, moves into the Shaw household. Known as Vandeleur Lee, he has a reputation as an unscrupulous character.

1869  Embarrassed by controversy and gossip related to his mother's relationship with Vandeleur Lee, young "Sonny," as Shaw was called by his family, leaves school.

1871  He begins work in a Dublin land agent's office.

1873  Shaw's mother, now a professional singer, follows Vandeleur Lee to London, where they establish a household that includes Shaw's sisters, Elinor Agnes and Lucille Frances (Lucy). Shaw's mother tries to earn a living performing and teaching Vandeleur Lee's singing method.

1876  Elinor Agnes dies on March 27. Shaw joins his mother, his sister Lucy, and Vandeleur Lee in London. Although he tries to support himself as a writer, for the next five years Shaw remains financially dependent on his mother.

1877  Shaw ghostwrites music reviews that appear under Vandeleur Lee's byline in his column for the *Hornet*, a London newspaper. This first professional writing "job" lasts until the editor discovers the subterfuge.

1879  Shaw completes and serializes his first novel, *Immaturity*. He works for the Edison Telephone Company and later will record his experience in his second novel, *The Irrational Knot*. Henrik Ibsen's play *A Doll's House* premieres.

1880  Shaw completes *The Irrational Knot*.

1881  He becomes a vegetarian in the hope that the change in his diet will relieve his migraine headaches. He completes *Love Among Artists*. *The Irrational Knot* is serialized in *Our Corner*, a monthly periodical.

1882  Shaw hears Henry George's lecture on land nationalization, which inspires some of his socialist ideas. He attends meetings of the Social Democratic Federation and is introduced to the works of Karl Marx.

1883  The Fabian Society—a middle-class socialist debating group advocating progressive, nonviolent reform rather than the revolution supported by the Social Democratic Federation—is founded in London. Shaw completes the novel *Cashel Byron's Profession*, drawing on his experience as an amateur boxer. He writes his final novel, *An Unsocial Socialist*.

1884  Shaw joins the fledgling Fabian Society; he contributes to many of its pamphlets, including *The Fabian Manifesto* (1884), *The Impossibilities of Anarchism* (1893), and *Socialism for Millionaires* (1901), and begins speaking publicly around London on social and political issues. *An Unsocial Socialist* is serialized in the periodical *Today*.

1885  The author's father, a longtime alcoholic, dies; neither his estranged wife nor his children attend his funeral. Shaw himself never drinks or smokes. He begins writing criticism of music, art, and literature for the *Pall Mall Gazette*, the *Dramatic Review*, and *Our Corner*. *Cashel Byron's Profession* is serialized in the periodical *Today*.

1886  Shaw begins writing art and music criticism for the *World*. *Cashel Byron's Profession* is published.

1887  Swedish dramatist and writer August Strindberg's play *The Father* is performed. The Social Democratic Federation's planned march on Trafalgar Square ends in bloodshed as police suppress the protesters; Shaw is a speaker at the event. His novel *An Unsocial Socialist* is published in book form.

1888    Shaw begins writing music criticism in the *Star* under the pen name Corno di Bassetto ("basset horn," perhaps a reference to the pitch of his voice).

1889    He edits the volume *Fabian Essays in Socialism*, to which he contributes "The Economic Basis of Socialism" and "The Transition to Social Democracy."

1890    Ibsen completes *Hedda Gabler*.

1891    Ibsen's *Ghosts* is performed in London. Shaw publishes *The Quintessence of Ibsenism*, a polemical pamphlet that celebrates Ibsen as a rebel for leftist causes.

1892    Sidney Webb, a founder and close associate of Shaw, is elected to the London City Council along with five other Fabian Society members. *Widowers' Houses*, Shaw's first "unpleasant" play, is performed on the London stage.

1893    Shaw writes *The Philanderer* and *Mrs. Warren's Profession*, his two other "unpleasant" plays. The latter is refused a license by the royal censor because its subject is prostitution; as a result, the play is not performed until 1902. *Widowers' Houses* is published.

1894    Seeking a wider audience, Shaw begins a series of "pleasant" plays with *Arms and the Man*, produced this year, and *Candida*, a successful play about marriage greatly influenced by Ibsen's *A Doll's House*.

1895    Shaw writes another "pleasant" play, *The Man of Destiny*, a one-act about Napoleon, and drama criticism for the *Saturday Review*.

1896    Shaw completes the fourth "pleasant" play, *You Never Can Tell*. He meets Charlotte Payne-Townshend, a wealthy Irish heiress and fellow Fabian. The Nobel Prizes are established for physics, medicine, chemistry, peace, and literature.

1897    *Candida* is produced. *The Devil's Disciple*, a drama set during the American Revolution, is successfully staged in New York.

Shaw is elected as councilor for the borough of St. Pancras, London; he will serve in this position until 1903.

1898   Shaw writes *Caesar and Cleopatra* and publishes *Mrs. Warren's Profession* and *The Perfect Wagnerite*. His first anthology of plays, *Plays Pleasant and Unpleasant*, is published. He falls ill and, believing his illness fatal, marries his friend and nurse Charlotte Payne-Townshend; his wife's fortune makes Shaw wealthy.

1899   *You Never Can Tell* premieres. Shaw writes *Captain Brassbound's Conversion*.

1900   The Fabian Society, the Independent Labour Party, and the Social Democratic Federation join forces to form the Labour Representation Party, which is politically allied to the trade union movement. The party wins two seats in the House of Commons. *Captain Brasshound's Conversion* is produced. *Three Plays for Puritans* collects *The Devil's Disciple*, *Caesar and Cleopatra*, and *Captain Brassbound's Conversion*.

1901   Strindberg's *Dance of Death* is completed. The Social Revolutionary Party, instrumental in the Bolshevik Revolution, is formed in Russia. Shaw writes about the eternal obstacles in male-female relations in his epic *Man and Superman*, which he subtitles "A Comedy and a Philosophy." He also publishes *The Devil's Disciple* and sees *Caesar and Cleopatra* produced for the first time.

1902   A private production of *Mrs. Warren's Profession* is staged at the New Lyric Theatre in London.

1903   Shaw publishes *Man and Superman*. *The Admirable Bashville* is produced.

1904   *John Bull's Other Island* premieres in London.

1905   Shaw writes the play *Major Barbara*, through which he attempts to communicate many of his moral and economic theories, including the need for a more fair distribution of wealth. It is produced this year, as is *Man and Superman*. In New York City, *Mrs. Warren's Profession* is publicly staged for the first time. Oscar Wilde's *De Profundis* is published posthumously. The Sinn Fein party, dedicated to Irish independence, is founded in Dublin.

1906    The Labour Representation Party wins twenty-nine seats and shortens its name to the Labour Party. Henrik Ibsen dies. Shaw's *The Doctor's Dilemma*, a satire on the medical profession, is produced.

1909    Shaw writes *The Shewing-Up of Blanco Posnet* and the one-act farce *Press Cuttings*, both banned by the royal censor.

1910    Shaw writes *Misalliance*, which he compares to Shakespeare's *The Taming of the Shrew*.

1912    He publishes *Misalliance*, and his satire *Androcles and the Lion* is staged for the first time.

1913    A German language version of *Pygmalion*, another satire Shaw wrote in 1912, premieres in Vienna.

1914    With World War I imminent, Shaw publishes a polemical antiwar tract, *Common Sense About the War*, which provokes a popular backlash and public denouncement. *Pygmalion* is produced for the first time in English.

1917    Dejected over the war, Shaw writes *Heartbreak House*.

1919    *Heartbreak House* is published in New York.

1920    The canonization of Joan of Arc gives Shaw the idea for a new play. *Heartbreak House* is produced in New York.

1922    Shaw publishes five linked plays begun during the war under the title *Back to Methuselah*, a dramatic work that begins in the Garden of Eden and ends in the year A.D. 31,920.

1923    Shaw writes *Saint Joan*, which is produced and hailed as a masterpiece.

1924    *Saint Joan* is published.

1925    Shaw is awarded the Nobel Prize for Literature for *Saint Joan*. He donates the prize money to fund an English translation of the works of August Strindberg.

1928    Shaw publishes his nonfiction *The Intelligent Women's Guide to Socialism and Capitalism* and writes *The Apple Cart*, a dramatic comedy set in the future.

1929   *The Apple Cart* is produced.

1931   Shaw visits Russia, where he meets Josef Stalin and Maxim Gorky. He completes the play *Too True to Be Good*, which explores how war can undermine established morals.

1932   *Too True to Be Good* is staged for the first time.

1933   An international celebrity, Shaw makes his first trip to America. *On the Rocks* and *Village Wooing* are produced.

1934   Shaw writes the plays *The Simpleton of the Unexpected Isles*, *The Six of Calais*, and the first draft of *The Millionairess* during a cruise to New Zealand. *Simpleton* is produced this year.

1938   *Geneva*, a play that imagines a successful League of Nations, premieres.

1939   Shaw writes *Good King Charles's Golden Days*, which is produced this year. He wins an Academy Award for the screenplay for *Pygmalion*, over which he exercised tight control.

1943   His wife, Charlotte, dies after a long illness.

1947   Shaw completes the play *The Buoyant Billions*.

1948   *The Buoyant Billions* is produced in Zurich.

1949   Shaw's puppet play, *Shakes Versus Shav*, is produced.

1950   George Bernard Shaw dies on November 2 from complications related to a fall from a ladder. He bequeaths funds for a competition to create a new English alphabet based on phonetics rather than Roman letters. The competition, won in 1958 by Kingsley Read, results in the Shavian alphabet.

# INTRODUCTION
# THE HIDDEN SHAW

Bernard Shaw's reputation as a writer was controversial in the last decade of the nineteenth century and remains controversial in the first decade of the twenty-first. No writer, however, would want to carry the current state of Shaw's literary reputation. It is, at least for the moment, at as low an ebb as Poins's linen shirts were according to Prince Hal. Shaw's plays were at one time revived regularly in London and New York, but they have now become rarities. Worse, star-actors do not push to play the lead roles. Hollywood types may take a break from receiving multimillion-dollar salaries for playing whatever the public wants to see in order to rededicate themselves to the Art of the Theater by appearing comparatively gratis in an O'Neill or Chekhov revival, but they seem uninterested in Shaw. Whether their shyness with Shaw proceeds from an inability to speak the sculpted rhetoric of his longer sentences or from discomfort with the politeness of his language, the effect is the same: They do not play him and he does not get played. Even the wonderful Shaw Festival in Canada has cut the number of Shaw plays it produces each season from three or four to two. There has not been a film of a Shaw play since *Great Catherine* in 1970. Nor has American television shown a Shaw play since the Rex Harrison *Heartbreak House* (1986), preceded by the Peter O'Toole *Pygmalion* (1983).

In academe, the situation is bleaker still. Most of the commonly used anthologies of drama that once automatically included Shaw in the modern canon have dropped him (while retaining Ibsen) in order to include multicultural contemporary plays, or have replaced Shaw with Oscar Wilde, as if the two were interchangeable. Fewer colleges offer seminars in Shaw; indeed, some English departments do not even bother to include his plays in their drama courses—that is, when they deign to teach dramatic literature besides Shakespeare at all. Yet he seems still to be read, if the major bookstore chains are any indication, for on the ever-dwindling number of shelves they devote to plays other than those by Shakespeare, Shaw continues to jostle in among the twenty-or-so other playwrights for a respectable number of inches of shelf-space.

The decline in Shaw's literary reputation and theatrical popularity proceeds from varied causes, but there are three major ones. Contemporary audiences and readers are used to explicit treatments of sexuality, so that Shaw's reticence in this regard makes him seem outdated, suitable only for the graying crowd. Not that Shaw's plays do not quake with sexual subtext and symbolism—they do—but nothing is explicit, nothing denoted, and all the sex receives ferocious comic treatment instead of the usual transgressive representation in so much contemporary drama. The worldwide failure of communism in the late 1980s, and the revelations of the murderous and massive abuses of human rights it produced, makes Shaw's life-long devotion to socialism—and especially his naive acceptance of the rosy picture of itself the Soviet Union presented to him during his trip to Russia with Lady Astor in 1934—seem somehow corrupt, or at least stupendously idiotic. But Shaw was not the first, nor will he be the last writer with a huge public profile to look at political situations and see more what he wants to see than what is actually there.

The third cause for the decline in Shaw's popularity is the explicitness of his stage directions. In our era, when the director and the production concept—meaning the director's and actors' "creative" reinterpretation of the play's meaning to fit their view of the world, morality, and politics, as opposed to the author's views—have dominion, Shaw's elaborate stage directions are inhibiting. Shaw believed that directors and actors who wanted to convey ideas and views that differed from the author's should feel perfectly welcome to write their own plays, but not to undermine his carefully wrought way of dramatizing his ideas: There is a difference between finding new things in the text and putting them there yourself with your own hands. In truth, though, anyone who has rehearsed and performed Shaw's plays knows well the practical value of his stage directions, based as they usually were on Shaw's own experience of directing the first performances of the plays, working out the stage business, seeing what needed to be made clear to an audience. His stage directions are rather like a film director's use of the camera to tell the story. Shaw uses the stage and everything on it, including the actors' bodies, faces, movements, and clothing, to tell his story. The adverbial indications as to how lines should be delivered ("*aggressively*," "*gallantly*") are not as ubiquitous as they seem; they mainly aid readers who are not actors themselves, but they also rescue actors from the danger of misinterpretation.

Theatrical fashions change; new generations of actors appear; discredited ideas gain currency again—and Shaw too may yet rise from his present supine condition. He certainly should because he is worth reading and seeing and hearing. Arthur Miller, who in his twenties read a lot of Shaw, was once asked what attracted him to the playwright. Miller replied: "Laughs. The irony of his plays. Terrific style and stylishness. And his ability to handle ideas—which I think is unapproachable" (*Conversations with Arthur Miller*, 1987, edited by Matthew C. Roudane, p. 274). One can see why a playwright like Miller, who by his own confession could write pathos easily, would admire precisely these qualities of Shaw's writing for the theater: humor, comic irony, stylishness, and the interplay of ideas.

Along with the best comic playwrights, Shaw has a gift for stage humor. He is a master of the running gag, as in *Candida*, where Burgess successively finds every other character to be mad. Shaw can turn anything to wit, including gallows humor, as in *The Devil's Disciple*, in which General Burgoyne presides over Dick Dudgeon's trial for treason and their exchanges turn into a duel as to who can be more wittily urbane and "gentlemanly" about the execution of the latter. The result is one of the most genuinely hilarious discussions of capital punishment.

Above all, Shaw has an uncanny instinct for how much discussion of ideas an audience can take before it needs comic relief. The debate on the purpose of Life in *Man and Superman* (in the third act, "Don Juan in Hell") shows that instinct working at its peak. The Commander, in the midst of refuting Don Juan's criticism of the Devil, takes the latter's name in vain, and then suddenly stops with the thought that he may have inadvertently offended the Devil. His sincere concern elicits from the Devil a most deferential exhibition of largesse in allowing the Commander to use his name whenever he needs it. The Devil, man of the world that he is, even turns the Commander's moment of embarrassment into an opportunity to display his devilish good manners by suggesting that he regards the use of his name "to secure additional emphasis" as "a high compliment to me." When people apply the term "high comedy" to Shaw, this is the sort of thing they mean, and they are quite right. But behind the "high comedy" lies the substantial implication that good manners can be used by the Devil as well as by anyone, perhaps even more cleverly, and for not such innocent ends.

## MRS. WARREN'S PROFESSION

*Mrs. Warren's Profession* was written in 1893, published in 1898, but not performed until 1902, and even then privately. Its first public production in New York in 1905 resulted in the actors' being arrested, for one of the play's two main protagonists was a prostitute and a procuress, and therefore in violation of stage censorship. It was Shaw's third play, his last play written after the pattern of Ibsen's plays, and his first masterpiece. The two plays that preceded it, *Widowers' Houses* (1892) and *The Philanderer* (1893), paid special homage to Ibsen: the former by imitating Ibsen's dramatic structure (one based on the gradual revelation of a hidden transgression from the past that has been poisoning the characters' present lives), the latter by having as its setting the Ibsen Club, a place where the members, who are advanced thinkers, can express their advanced thoughts and also romance one another.

Shaw was a socialist, and therefore a severe critic of capitalism, from his reading of Karl Marx and other economists of the 1880s. *Widowers' Houses* made a socialist point that *Mrs. Warren's Profession* would reiterate—namely, that as we all participate in capitalism, whether we like it or not, none of us can have clean incomes, meaning incomes that do not at some point or in some way derive from the exploitation of other people's labor. As a consequence, it does no good for one participant to point to another and call him villain; Shaw believed it was the capitalist system that needed to be transformed, and by everyone. In keeping with that principle, Shaw does not assign villain status to any of his characters in *Mrs. Warren's Profession*, not even the woman whose past transgression—prostitution—is the Ibsenite secret from the past that comes back to affect the characters' destinies.

Instead Shaw crafts a series of ambushes for the audience, leading us to sympathize with one character in the first act only to reveal something in the second act that discredits that sympathy. One of the great theatrical pleasures of watching *Mrs. Warren's Profession* with an audience is to feel its sympathies seesawing between Mrs. Warren and her emancipated daughter, Vivie, who represents "the New Woman" of her era. As act II begins, Vivie, who has never met her father and has just finished a distinguished academic career at Newnham, the women's college at Cambridge, prepares to challenge her mother's authority over her, particularly her mother's plan to live with her daughter and, in Lear-fashion, set herself on Vivie's "kind nursery." She bases her challenge on her mother's secretiveness about her past, so her mother reveals the secret, which is that she has been a prostitute and made the money that supported Vivie from that profession of prostitution. Vivie is only cowed, however, when her mother explains the circumstances in which she chose to become a prostitute. Mrs. Warren explains that she saw her half-sister die of lead poisoning after working "in a whitelead factory twelve hours a day for nine shillings a week." Meanwhile, Mrs. Warren's older sister, Liz, had left home only to return after a time fashionably dressed and with plenty of money. Liz advised her younger sister not to let other capitalists exploit her good looks for their profit, but to become instead a prostitute like her and maintain her self-respect by making her own way, free of exploitation by others. Vivie is impressed by her mother's tale because of the gumption she displayed and particularly by her apparent lack of shame, which seems to Vivie like a kind of integrity. The curtain falls on Vivie's admiring her mother for her strength of character ("you are stronger than all England") and on the procuress Mrs. Warren's bestowing "a mother's blessing" on her daughter. It is one of the most strikingly odd and ironic curtains in British drama because the audience does not know quite what to think or with whom to side. And because Shaw believed the primary purpose of drama was to stir people out of conventional thinking and automatic assumptions so they would think for themselves, such a state of unease and discomfort suited his purpose perfectly.

The play's ending similarly disallows the audience a complacent position. Vivie renews the struggle with her mother until she learns that her mother has not renounced her "profession" and yet pursues the image of respectability. Not being able to stand her mother's hypocrisy in this regard, which to Vivie signifies a lack of integrity, she breaks with her mother finally and fully in a scene of compelling conflict in which every line between them contains a bullet wrapped in an irony.

The final phase of their confrontation begins with Mrs. Warren appealing to her daughter on the basis of duty and justice, and as she does so Shaw directs that she fall back into her dialect "*recklessly*," as a way of showing the emotional pitch she has reached, in which she is no longer in control of what she says or feels. But she errs when she invokes Vivie's daughterly duty. Such an appeal, based as it is on convention, will not sway the hardheaded Vivie. Mrs. Warren's other appeal, "Who is to care for me when I'm old?" makes it seem as if she only supported Vivie so she would have a prop for her old age. But when she adds that she kept herself "lonely" for Vivie by letting go all of the girls who had formed an attachment to her, she hits the audience right in the heart, though she touches Vivie not at all. Quite the opposite: Mrs. Warren's regression to her native accent (according to Shaw's stage directions) jars and antagonizes Vivie. Another dramatist might have made Vivie melt a little at her mother's self-denial, but it is precisely Shaw's strength and originality that he does not and instead has Vivie firmly repudiate her mother's assertion of her daughterly duty.

Mrs. Warren then shifts to a more aggressive tactic. And by her economic vocabulary, Shaw shows how capitalism marks every aspect of human relations: She accuses Vivie of "stealing" an education from her mother, and avers that instead of sending Vivie away to school, she should have brought her up in her own house. As if correcting her mother's grammar, Vivie says, "[*quietly*] In one of your own houses," reminding her with devastating insult that she is a procuress. This is too much for Mrs. Warren, and she begins to separate herself from her daughter by referring to Vivie in the third person: "(*screaming*). Listen to her! listen to how she spits on her mother's grey hairs! Oh, may you live to have your own daughter tear and trample on you as you have trampled on me. And you will: you will. No woman ever had luck with a mother's curse on her" (p. 102). Here Shaw deliberately invokes King Lear's curse on his daughter, Goneril, for driving him from her house, in which he likewise refers to his daughter in the third person though she is present: "If she must teem, / Create her child of spleen, that it may live / And be a thwart disnatured torment to her . . . that she may feel / How sharper than a serpent's tooth it is / To have a thankless child" (act 1, scene 4). Though this allusion is ominous in so far as it predicts Mrs. Warren's being driven away by her daughter, it also begins to betray the presence of comic and ironic elements. For example, Mrs. Warren invites an invisible audience to "listen" to how Vivie "spits on her mother's grey hairs"—a mixing of the aural and the visual, not unlike Bottom's proclamation in *A Midsummer Night's Dream* that "the ear of man hath not seen . . . what my dream was" (act 4, scene 1). The simultaneity of authentic tragic emotion and the faintly ridiculous is deeply Shavian (even though it derives partly from the Ibsen who wrote *The Wild Duck*).

Shaw augments both the tragedy and the comedy in Mrs. Warren's next speech to her daughter by having her invoke Heaven (the only time in the play she does) to forgive her for only doing *good* to Vivie. Such irony—her asking Heaven to forgive her for doing good—marks the moment as Shavian: Just when the pathos of the scene reaches tragic proportions, when the mother-daughter bond's being violently severed produces the proper tragic awe, Shaw chooses just this moment to have Mrs. Warren become ridiculous by exhibiting a shocking misapprehension of the circumstances in which Heaven normally forgives people. Shaw compounds the tragicomedy of the intense moment—the climax of the play, really—by having Mrs. Warren invoke Heaven again: "From this time forth, so help me Heaven in my last hour, I'll do wrong and nothing but wrong" (p. 103). A detached observer might have pointed out to Mrs. Warren that the people Heaven usually helps in their last hour are not those who have done nothing but wrong during the period preceding their last hour.

The closest analogue to such an unsettling mixture of comic and tragic registers, perhaps, would be found in *The Merchant of Venice* when Shylock reacts to his daughter's rejection of him, when she elopes with Lorenzo and steals her father's money (act 2, scene 8). Shylock cannot seem to make up his mind about which is the greater loss (or betrayal), his stolen ducats or his deserting daughter, Jessica: He seems to feel both keenly and to be unaware of the irony of such an economy of emotion. Likewise, Mrs. Warren's sorrow and anger at what she feels is a betrayal by her own daughter seem to stem more from the disappointment of her hopes that Vivie would be the prop of her old age than from the loss of her daughter's affection and companionship, particularly since Mrs. Warren was quite generous in providing materially for Vivie, but quite stingy with maternal care and time. After all, Mrs. Warren had a business to run and so could not be a mother; and now Vivie has her own business to tend, doing actuarial calculations for a woman lawyer, and so cannot be a daughter. Justice has an ironic sense of humor.

Shaw's final stage direction in the scene, Vivie "*goes at her work with a plunge, and soon becomes absorbed in her figures*" (p. 103) maintains the perfect ambiguity with which Shaw presents the reunion and re-separation of mother and daughter. If we find Vivie hard-hearted, like Lear's daughters, and Mrs. Warren a pitiable and cruelly rejected weak figure, we must ignore her mother's lifelong egoism, her regarding her daughter as a financial investment against the loneliness and enfeeblement of old age, and above all, her ridiculously contradictory invocation of Heaven's aid in her vow to do nothing but wrong henceforth. If we find Mrs. Warren a monstrous parody of maternity, and Vivie's self-emancipation a liberation from her mother's oppression, we must ignore how Vivie severs all intimate human connections (her suitor, Frank, and her mother) in favor of turning herself into one of the drowned numbers in her actuarial calculations ("*goes at her work with a plunge, and soon becomes absorbed in her figures*"). No choice is made easy: The cost is laid out nakedly for each reader to gauge and decide its worth. Vivie does liberate herself, but was it worth the cost? The play began with Vivie alone on stage, lying in a hammock while reading a book and making notes; it ends with Vivie alone, sitting at a desk, having read a final note from the suitor she has rejected, and making notes again. In between, she has reunited and re-separated from her mother. Is she now a grown-up, independent, liberated woman? Assuredly, yes. And yet . . .

To its would-be censors, Shaw's play was about prostitution; to Shaw's socialist friends, it was an indictment of the capitalist system; to readers and playgoers of the twenty-first century, it is still a play about costs, but not in the sense of capitalism's profits and losses. Rather, it teaches the lesson that everything, even reputed social progress, comes at a cost, sometimes at the cost of humanity.

Shaw's distinctness as a playwright in *Mrs. Warren's Profession* is not exhausted by either his mixture of comic and tragic tones, or his evenhanded, if not downright ambiguous, presentation of both sides of a given issue; his distinctness is also defined by his bold and unsettling (not vulgar or obscene) treatment of sexuality. There is a momentary yet extraordinary sexual tension in the opening of the second act between Mrs. Warren and her daughter's suitor, Frank, a tension that Shaw presents as arising on the instant and subsiding as quickly and spontaneously as it arose, just as such tensions rise and fall in life, without specific impetus and without furtherance. As Frank helps Mrs. Warren take off her shawl, Shaw's stage directions indicate that he gives "*her shoulders the most delicate possible little caress with his fingers.*" Mrs. Warren, while continuing her idle conversation with him, glances "*back at him for an instant from the corner of her eye as she detects the pressure*" (p. 47). Interestingly, when Shaw revised the text for a subsequent publication (and after more experience with staging his plays), he changed the stage direction to an action more readily detected by the audience: "*gallantly giving her shoulders a very perceptible squeeze.*" A camera could easily convey the action and its significance in the earlier version, but on stage the new formulation would be more clear to the audience.

As the scene progresses, what began as a silent, subtle exchange of sexual signals between Frank and his girlfriend's mother becomes something more than mere naughtiness. Frank continues to flirt with Mrs. Warren by asking her to take him with her to Vienna, by teasing her with his playacting, and by using his wooing voice on her until finally he makes a cheeky remark that provokes her to pretend "*to box his ears.*" So far the bantering, though odd, seems not too far beyond the playful and harmless. But then Mrs. Warren looks at his "*pretty, upturned face for a moment, tempted. At last she kisses him and immediately turns away, out of patience with herself*" (p. 48). What motivates her to do this? Sexual competition with her Cambridge-educated daughter? An aging woman's impulsive attempt to assert her continuing sexual attractiveness? A momentary surge of sexual appetite? This moment is genuinely Shavian because of its fidelity to the suddenness of human impulse and the mysteriousness of human motivation.

As rapidly as the impulse arises in Mrs. Warren, it subsides and changes into half-hearted regret: "There! I shouldn't have done that. I a m wicked. Never you mind, my dear: it's only a motherly kiss." (The spaced lettering in "a m" was Shaw's way of telling the actor where the accent should fall in the delivery of the line.) Her self-reproach would be more convincing if she did not quite relish her own misbehavior so much, which relish the emphasis on "am" enacts. But even more Shavian (or ironic) is her use of the word "motherly" here. Her kiss is "motherly" only in the sense that Jocasta's kisses to Oedipus were "motherly." And her "motherly" kiss utterly undermines any "motherly" claims she makes upon Vivie in the final scene of the play. Shaw's characters are complex and contradictory, and he gives them a moment-to-moment life on stage that is as unpredictable and funny and disturbing as that of anyone you are likely to meet on the planet Earth.

*Mrs. Warren's Profession* would be the last play Shaw would write in Ibsen's mood, meaning a play in which Shaw almost always compresses his humor into irony and allows darker human impulses to dominate the more genial ones. For example, Frank woos Vivie by playing a fantasy-game with her in which the two imagine themselves as the Babes in the Wood covered with leaves. What Shaw would later convert into the ridiculousness of human romantic impulse he here makes ironically sinister: The Babes in the Wood of legend were young brother and sister orphans whose bodies, after the two children were abandoned in the Wood and starved to death, were covered in strawberry leaves by the birds. Frank's invitation to Vivie to get covered with leaves, therefore, suggests that their potential sexual relations would be a perverse death for Vivie. But Shaw simply did not have the gloomy Norwegian's relentless appetite for unrelieved irony and darkness, though he admired the depths of human nature Ibsen's genius allowed him to reach.

# CANDIDA

After *Mrs. Warren's Profession*, Shaw's next four plays, including *Candida* (completed in 1894), more truly expressed his individual nature, personality, and idiosyncratic view of life. Shaw would later group *Mrs. Warren's Profession* (written in 1893) with *Widowers' Houses* and *The Philanderer* as "unpleasant plays." He grouped *Candida* with *Arms and the Man* (1894; a satire of war as a force inimical to romance and sexuality), *The Man of Destiny* (1895; a one-act play about Napoleon's involvement in a romantic intrigue), and *You Never Can Tell* (1896; Shaw's response to Oscar Wilde's *The Importance of Being Earnest*) as "pleasant." In 1898 he published these works, in two volumes, as *Plays Pleasant and Unpleasant*.

Like most socialists, Shaw had difficulty recognizing or acknowledging evil in this world—beyond the capitalist system, that is—and the world he creates in his "pleasant plays" is largely devoid of evil and tragedy, though not of sorrow or seriousness. Shaw's turning away from a preoccupation with evil and death (because neither can be helped) meant turning toward the comic spirit that insists the most important thing about human beings is not that we die, but that men and women are sexually attracted to one another, get married, and produce children—a process Shaw found a boundlessly fecund source of humor.

However, in the author of *Candida* one may find still the author of *Mrs. Warren's Profession*, but as if after a conversion. Where *Mrs. Warren's Profession* presents George Crofts as a palpably repulsive "capitalist bully," *Candida* portrays Candida's prosperous father as a genial if scoundrelly businessman. The former acts the villain; the latter plays the comedy figure. With that shift, the banishment of outright evil, the play's weather system becomes Shavian rather than Ibsenesque. Where Mrs. Warren's "motherly" kiss of Frank provoked wonder and revulsion, Candida's embodiment of young motherhood *is* her sexual attractiveness. And that change makes all the difference in the play's atmosphere, which is not unpleasant but pleasant. Shaw has not abandoned seriousness, but he has become more his true self, expressing his serious ideas through the genre that suited his personality and temperament, comedy, just as Molière had before him.

Candida is the wife of a Christian socialist parson, the Reverend James Morell (pronounced "moral"), the mother of three children, and the object of amorous worship by high-strung eighteen-year-old poet Eugene Marchbanks, who enters the Morell household as an invader, unconsciously intent on winning Candida's affection away from her husband. Eugene's contesting of Morell's right to his wife tests the apparent happiness of the marriage, for the reverend finds himself wilting when the young poet imputes smug dullness to him and implies that his wife sees what a fool he is and despises him for it. And he becomes genuinely perturbed when she says something that seems to confirm Eugene's implication. The final scene in the play, in which Candida solicits bids for her care from her two wooers, is one of the most suspenseful in dramatic literature, for Shaw has cunningly made us care equally for each of the three actors in the contest so that we do not see how to choose. How Shaw resolves the impasse, the paradox according to which Candida makes her choice, I will leave the reader to delight in discovering.

I suggested earlier that in moving from *Mrs. Warren's Profession* to *Candida*, Shaw had moved into a different weather system, from a frosty-ironic Ibsenesque climate to a more balmy and clement Shavian one. Nevertheless, Shaw did not discard the Ibsen influence altogether, for in many ways *Candida* responds to Ibsen's pre-feminist play *A Doll's House*. When at the end of Ibsen's epoch-making play, his heroine, Nora, walks out of her home and leaves behind her husband and children—in order to fulfill her duty to herself as an individual, to get experience, and to decide for herself what she thinks about life, religion, and morality—she slams shut the door of her house of illusions, her doll's house, her unreal life. Shaw was so impressed by Ibsen's courage in making his dramas out of his characters' struggles with the major social and moral issues of his time that he wrote the first sustained critical examination of Ibsen's plays both as works of art and as social criticism, *The Quintessence of Ibsenism* (1891).

*A Doll's House* particularly made its mark on Shaw not only for its bold critique of the restricted roles of women inside the typical respectable middle-class marriage but also because of what Shaw noted as its technical innovation in the art of play-making. For Ibsen, having set up an elaborate situation involving financial fraud and blackmail, does not resolve the crisis in the usual manner, with suicide, but with a discussion between the husband and the wife. Shaw knew that he wanted to do his own version of Ibsen's critique of modern marriage, and *Candida* was it. But in Shaw's version the modern husband suffers as much as the wife from unreality in a marriage based on illusions. Candida reveals that her husband's public success as a forward-thinking socialist preacher has come at a cost to the women in his family—his mother, his sisters, and his wife—all of whom have guarded him from the quotidian bothers, worries, and responsibilities of life, so that he may win glory and be worshiped in the public arena, a truth the young poet had intuited. Shaw suggests that Morell is as much of a doll living in a doll's house as any wife. But the revelation does not lead to his exiting the house. Instead the young poet slams the door on domestic solace in favor of pursuing the adventure of his life into the unknown region of poetic ambition. And there Shaw leaves the play poised between the two values of domestic love and a poet's destiny. The play celebrates but separates the two realms. And they will not be brought back together until several years later in *Man and Superman*.

Shaw bases the separation on a mystery, each realm's unknowability to the other. The final stage direction tells us that after Eugene leaves, Candida holds out her arms to Morell and *"they embrace."* But then Shaw adds a direction only for the readers of the play, *"But they do not know the secret in the poet's heart"* (p. 190). Of course, no audience has this stage direction available because it cannot be acted. The secret in the poet's heart is a secret between the playwright and the reader. It is Shaw's invitation to the reader to imagine the separateness of the realm of the poet, the line he follows out into the un-known night of poetic creation, the mystery of that craft, while the couple's realm is the circle their arms trace, their embrace, the mys-tery of marriage. Shaw subtitled the play "A Mystery" for a number of reasons. One reason was that he intended Candida as his equiva-lent to the Virgin Mother of medieval and Renaissance paintings. An-other was because in the Middle Ages a mystery play was a play that celebrated one of the many mysteries of faith—for example, how a virgin could also be a mother. Such plays were sponsored by one of the town guilds of craftsmen—that is, men who had mastered a par-ticular craft or mystery, such as wheelmaking.

A quarter century after the play was written, some students at Rugby wrote to Shaw in order to discover the secret in the poet's heart. Shaw wrote back to them—he was always kind and consider-ate to children, as childless people like himself so seldom are—invit-ing them to submit their theories. Their proposals, charmingly articulated, ranged from the cliché that Eugene wanted to put "an end to his miserable existence," to the ridiculous suggestion that Eu-gene planned to come back after Morell was dead, to the imperti-nent, "There is no secret, and it is only mentioned for the purpose of puzzling the reader." Shaw was much amused and replied in a mock lament for the vanished spirit of Rugby. He dubbed all the proposals "wrong" and "pure sob stuff," except for that of the "soulless wretch" who called the secret "a spoof secret." He explained patiently that he meant the poet to be going to meet his writer's destiny, into the night where "domestic comfort and cuddling" have no place. He ends by deferring his authorial authority: "It is only my way of looking at it; everybody who buys the book may fit it with an ending to suit his own taste." So he returns the play to the realm of mystery again.

But the secret in the poet's heart is not the only mystery in the play. In truth, it is full of mysteries of all sorts, most of them revolv-ing around Candida's character, motivation, and inner life. How is it that Candida's father, Burgess, speaks like an uneducated man with a thick local accent (which Shaw phonetically reproduces), while Candida herself talks grammar and speaks beautifully with no discernable accent? Why does Candida love and marry such a foolish man who knows himself so little? When she becomes so distracted while listening to Eugene recite his poetry, is it because the poetry is jejune or because she cannot really appreciate the poetry? Who imagined a spiritual resemblance between Candida and Titian's Virgin of the Assumption and hung an autotype of her on the wall in homage to Candida? What does Candida mean when she says to her husband that if she knew she would prevent Eugene's learning about sexual love from a prostitute by teaching him herself, she would do so as willingly as she would give her "shawl to a beggar dying of cold"—that is, if her love for her husband were not there to restrain her? (After hearing Shaw read the play aloud, Shaw's socialist friend and co-founder of the Fabian Society, Beatrice Webb, called Candida "a sentimental prostitute.")

Many have fallen under the mysterious spell of Shaw's idealized virgin mother, the epitome of womanly grace in strength, simultaneously both a husband's fantasy figure of a wife and a boy's Oedipal dream-mother. Indeed, Vladimir Nabokov fell under her spell, for though he found little to value as literature in modern drama, he made an exception (in his essay "The Tragedy of Tragedy") of "Shaw's brilliant farces, (especially *Candida*)." No doubt its depiction of an amorous affiliation between an eighteen-year-old poet and a thirty-three-year-old married woman particularly engendered admiration in the author of *Lolita*. The playwright who succeeded Shaw in dominating British theater during the 1940s and '50s, Terence Rattigan, named seven Shaw plays as the most popular with general audiences, *Candida* coming first—not surprisingly, since *Candida*'s taking male weakness as such a focus makes it Shaw's most Rattigan-like play. And in the 1950s American playwright Robert Anderson wrote *Tea and Sympathy*, which is in effect a version of *Candida*.

# THE DEVIL'S DISCIPLE

In his still pertinent 1936 essay on Shaw in *The Triple Thinkers*, Edmund Wilson suggests that while Shaw's political ideas were "confused and uncertain," he was always "a considerable artist." And like any fine artist, Shaw never could leave a theme or situation until he was satisfied that he had painted it from every interesting angle. So it is that the basic dramatic situation of *Candida*—an apparently comfortable marriage between a clergyman and his attractive wife upset by the intrusion on the domestic hearth of an unconventional outsider—replicates itself in *The Devil's Disciple* (1897), but with a major shift in period and place (to the American Revolution and New England), and with various adjustments in the postures and positions of the three protagonists. For example, the clergyman, Anthony Anderson, has married a handsome but considerably younger wife, Judith, who unconsciously longs for a more romantic connection to a man. The titular hero, Dick Dudgeon, unwittingly fulfills her unrecognized desire: When British soldiers arrive to arrest Anderson in his home for the capital offense of rebellion against the crown, Dick substitutes his neck for the Parson's in the noose. But due to a last-minute rescue of Dick from the scaffold by his rival, Minister Anderson, now transformed into a militia captain, Dick's heroic self-sacrifice comes to naught, and Judith keeps with her newly attractive husband.

Shaw subtitled the play "A Melodrama," to make clear that he was both employing and making fun of the conventions of the genre. The hero of such a melodrama attains his heroic stature precisely by going to his death for the sake of another (or for the other's wife, with whom the hero is secretly in love). But Shaw gets to eat his cake and have it too by mocking the conventions of melodrama, yet exploiting their capacity to thrill and please: While he allows his hero to offer himself in sacrifice, he precisely prevents his hero from actually sacrificing himself. When the heroine, Judith, visits Dick in prison, under the assumption that out of love for her Dick is sacrificing his own life to help her husband save his, Shaw also prevents her from having the satisfaction of hearing a declaration of his undying devotion to her—indeed, she gets a denial and then an evasion, which she misinterprets as love, much to the comic delight of the audience. Best of all, as Martin Meisel points out in his *Shaw and the Nineteenth-Century Theatre*, while traditionally the ne'er-do-well hero of melodrama, no matter how much of a scalawag and delinquent he is, has a sentimental reverence and loving soft spot for his dear mother, Shaw makes clear that rebellious Dick and his bitter, hard-hearted, puritanical mother heartily hate one another. (The otherwise excellent 1959 film version with Kirk Douglas failed Shaw only by giving Dick a visible pang of regret when his mother is forced to leave her home by the terms of her husband's will.)

Shaw's concerns in *The Devil's Disciple* extend further than the playful upending of generic expectations. When it was published in 1901, Shaw grouped it with two subsequent plays, *Caesar and Cleopatra* (written in 1898) and *Captain Brassbound's Conversion* (1899), and called the volume *Three Plays for Puritans* (1900). He did so because the three have a number of elements and aspects in common. All are set in contexts where empire clashes with native resistance: the American Revolution, the Roman conquest of Egypt, and the British presence in Moorish Africa. (Shaw does not, however, sentimentalize or reduce these clashes to melodramatic struggles between wicked oppressors and saintly colonials: He subjects both groups to humorous and ironic treatment.) All three plays culminate in trials in which the distinction between judicial vengeance and true justice is at issue. Shaw also used the colonial context as a metaphor through which he could explore the borderline between adolescence and adulthood. Indeed, all three plays involve a young man or young woman's conversion to adulthood through a confrontation with an adult who has great power, beauty, charm, or maturity.

What lends *The Devil's Disciple* its genuine distinction is that it plays with the theme of the Double (which probably explains why Alfred Hitchcock once thought of turning it into a film). The alliterating names of the twin protagonists, Dick Dudgeon and Anthony Anderson (the name—of Teutonic/Scandinavian origin—means "other son" or "son of another") signal their doppelgänger relationship: Each embodies an unrealized aspect of the other's inner self. Despite his defying King George and apparently breaking all conventions and rules, Dick Dudgeon has the impulse to sacrifice himself and to care for others that marks a born minister. He also finds himself mysteriously drawn to the integrity of Minister Anderson's hearth—and perhaps envies the minister his wife's "most ungodly allowance of good looks"— when he visits the minister's home. Anthony Anderson meanwhile finds himself instantly converted to a man of action when he learns that the British soldiers came to his home to arrest him and not Dick Dudgeon. Shaw contrives the action so that Dick Dudgeon puts on the minister's coat when he is arrested just as Anderson will then wear Dick's coat when he leaves to join the rebel militia. Shaw said that all his plays were in one way or another about conversion. Here the man of action becomes passive in allowing himself to be arrested while the man of peace goes to war in order to save his double. Shaw modeled the way the theme of the Double is embodied— in an exchange of coats—on the similar transaction between Sidney Carton and Charles Darnay in *A Tale of Two Cities*, written by one of Shaw's favorite authors, Charles Dickens. Indeed, so intentional was this allusion that posters for the early productions of the play closely resemble posters for the contemporaneous standard theatrical version of the Dickens novel, renamed *The Only Way*.

But Dick Dudgeon and Anthony Anderson are not the only doubles in the play. The minister's protected and foolish wife, Judith, has a counterpart in the genuinely suffering serving girl, Essie. Judith misunderstands her attraction to her husband and therefore has to undergo a trial of authentic suffering in which her conceptions of goodness and badness are painfully transformed. Essie's instinctive and immediate attraction to Dick is exactly the impulse within Judith that she rigorously suppresses. Shaw points out how Essie represents Judith's repressed self by systematically paralleling the two women's struggles with tears. Each of the three acts ends with Essie in tears; and these three episodes surround episodes in the second and third acts when Judith breaks down crying. In the first act, Judith tries to convince Essie that she should not ever mention Dick's name or admit him into her presence. Judith likewise tries to prevent her husband from leaving her alone in their home with Dick. All the episodes of crying involve anxiety over Dick's safety, and with each woman he alternately approves the tears or orders that they be stopped. In observing these parallels, we see Judith gradually become more like Essie, and therefore more her true self.

Though Shaw's female characters cannot have the same impact on contemporary audiences that they had in his time—when Robert Louis Stevenson read Shaw's novels, he remarked to his and Shaw's friend, William Archer, "I say, Archer, what women!"—they nevertheless receive remarkably sympathetic and individualized representation in the plays. And so does the cause of equality for women, but never in the agit-prop way. An episode from *The Devil's Disciple* illustrates the point. Shaw presents Dick's mother, Mrs. Dudgeon, as a rather unpleasant and unsympathetic character: a hypocritical puritan who has suppressed her own romantic and sexual desires for the sake of respectability and propriety with the result that she is bitter, bullying, unkind, reproachful, and even cruel to those who come within her power—Essie, for example. Yet Shaw uses Mrs. Dudgeon as the vehicle to make the point that the legal system always favors men and therefore treats women unjustly. Mrs. Dudgeon's husband leaves their house and land to his son, Dick, which means that if she wants to stay in her own house, she would be living in the house of a son she can no more stand than he can stand her. To his wife he leaves an annuity of fifty-two pounds a year. At the reading of the will, she complains bitterly at the unfairness of this disposition of property, especially because, she claims, her husband had no money of his own when they married and she brought him a marriage portion that he now uses for her annuity. She asks if she has any legal redress, and Lawyer Hawkins replies that she has none because "the courts will sustain the claim of a man—and that man the eldest son—against any woman, if they can" (p. 236). Thus does Shaw highlight the law's systemic bias against women in favor of men, but note that he does not allow the audience or readers to click their tongues complacently at a social injustice with easy sympathy for the victim. The victim is unsympathetic and pointedly so. The will is poetic justice, but social injustice. And Shaw's whole strategy bends to make us separate principles from personalities, so that we must think for ourselves about the principles, and not just ride the hobbyhorse of our personal prejudices. In short, it is the difference between dramatic art and propaganda.

## MAN AND SUPERMAN

Though Shaw's initiation to sex did not come until comparatively late in life, at age twenty-eight, he made up for lost time by subsequently juggling several amorous relationships, some active, some epistolary—a state of affairs reflected in *The Philanderer*. He finally married an Irish millionairess, Charlotte Payne-Townshend, in 1898. Various biographers say various things about the sexual status of the marriage—that it was abstemious by agreement or that it began with relations but continued without them. My own opinion is that no one knows or can know the truth of it and, as the saying goes, whereof we do not know, thereof we cannot speak. What we can say is: After Shaw's marriage, he wrote *Man and Superman*, a play about sex and marriage that is full of the charm of sexual attraction between men and women, and the play makes that attraction palpable on stage.

It took Shaw a year to write *Man and Superman* (1901: published, 1903; performed 1905), and well it should have, even for a man to whom, as Clive James said, writing must have been like breathing. For Shaw attempted in this big-in-every-way play to enter the arena with Dante's *Divine Comedy*, Milton's *Paradise Lost*, Shakespeare's *Hamlet*, and Goethe's *Faust*, to give an account of the cosmic purpose and destiny of the human species, and to do so through the traditional form of comedy—that is, the story of a couple's overcoming the obstacles to their marrying—but raised to the status of epic drama. In itself that is a comic idea. But Shaw means it seriously: He subtitled the play "A Comedy and a Philosophy." Actually, it expounds the philosophy of comedy, which is that human beings have a justification for being alive, and that justification is striving to understand themselves so they can change into something better. The long-range means of development is evolution, but the short-range means is marriage or procreation. A man and a woman seek one another out as sexual partners, whether they realize it consciously or not, so that together they can produce a superior child. Evolutionary instincts push particular males and females together, in spite of parental, social, tribal, religious, political, or any and all artificial barriers, including personal friction between the couple, because their future child wills itself to be born healthier and smarter from them. Shaw was not a Darwinian evolutionist; he preferred Lamarck's more poetic vision of evolution, that evolution follows from a creature's will to survive and change itself in response to its environment. Shaw the optimist about human destiny found Darwin's vision of will-less adaptation too bleak because it was too mechanical. (Currently science tells us Darwin was right and Lamarck was wrong, but then Shaw's view was always more a faith than a theory, though he himself called it science.) Shaw called his own version of evolution the working of the Life Force within us, driving us to think more so that we can be more than we are now. Comedy was an ideal means for Shaw to propound his view of evolution because comedy always ridicules people for behaving mechanically, inflexibly, unyieldingly, or Darwinianly, whether in thinking or doing. Comedy defines humanity as flexibility. Only in heroic tragedy do people die for unbending principles, and receive approval for doing so.

Comedy as a genre was ideally useful to Shaw from two other angles. It allowed him to synthesize two traditions from dramatic literature: the Don Juan tradition, and the tradition of the battling couple. To take the latter first: The protagonist and antagonist of *Man and Superman*, John Tanner and Ann Whitefield, descend directly from Petruchio and Kate in *The Taming of the Shrew* and from Benedick and Beatrice in *Much Ado About Nothing*. That is, before the couples finally give in to marriage, they spar and argue, insult one another, struggle against their fates, flirt with and charm one another as much as they exasperate and terrify one another—like most couples. In addition, Shaw drew upon several "gay couples" (as they were called) in post-Shakespearean plays: Mirabell and Millamant in Congreve's *The Way of the World*, for example, and Sir Peter and Lady Teazle in Sheridan's *The School for Scandal*. Shaw borrows different elements from these couples but renovates the tradition by making the woman the avid and determined pursuer in the love chase and the man the unaware and apparently unwilling prey. Shaw cited Rosalind in Shakespeare's *As You Like It* as a model for his heroine as an aggressor in courtship, but he also intuited that a woman chooses a man for the kind of children he will father and for the kind of father he will be, and that goal makes her pursuit transcend the personal.

The Don Juan tradition served Shaw well. The legend of Don Juan combines two apparently unconnected motifs. Don Juan is a man attractive to and attracted by many women whom he feels compelled to seduce. Don Juan also invites to dinner a stone Statue of an outraged father he (Don Juan) has slain in a duel, and receives in return an invitation from the Statue to dine with him in Hell. When Don Juan refuses to repent his wickedness, the Statue drags him to his damnation. The motif of the seducer anxious to spread his seed as widely as possible (insuring the survival of his genes) connects itself to the motif of damnation in that both motifs are concerned with the issue of individual mortality and immortality, with an anxiety about the future. So it is that Shaw presents us with John Tanner, an apparently anti–Don Juan, a man who believes himself not made to marry, a man who believes Ann Whitefield has designs on his best friend, Octavius, but not on himself. Yet he also does everything a male can do to impress Ann Whitefield with his qualifications for fatherhood. And in the course of the play, though he runs away from her, he comes to understand when she catches him that there is such a thing as a father's heart as well as a mother's, and that he has one and therefore must marry Ann—for, as Benedick says when he capitulates to love, "The world must be peopled."

In the detachable third act of the play, known, when it is performed separately, as "Don Juan in Hell," John Tanner, having fled to the Sierra Mountains in Spain to escape Ann's pursuit and capture of him, dreams of himself as Don Juan debating with the Devil whether he (Juan) should stay in Hell or move to Heaven. Doña Ana and the Statue of her father are the audience and sometime participants in the debate. Hell, it turns out, is not unlike the world we all know—a place where people love beauty and romance, seek pleasure, and pursue happiness, and deceive themselves about reality when it interferes with such goals. The Devil is the promoter of Hell as a paradise where the aesthetic reigns supreme. Heaven, by contrast, is the place where the Real reigns, where people work to make life more intensely self-conscious. After a seventy-five-minute discussion that is by turns witty, profound, hilarious, and dizzying about the purpose of life and the operation of the Life Force, about whether Man is primarily a creator or destroyer, about the roles of romance and sex in marriage, Don Juan finally argues himself into leaving Hell and heading for Heaven. The Statue looks upon this decision with regret since from his perspective Heaven is "the most angelically dull place in all creation." But Doña Ana does not; she is inspired by Don Juan's decision and goes off in pursuit of "a father for the Superman." Through his dream Tanner tells himself that by marrying Ann he will make his contribution to "helping life in its struggle upward." Once he understands that he can marry, Shaw's new Don Juan seeks not a personal genetic immortality through the seduction of many women but the evolutionary improvement and immortality of the species by marrying one woman and becoming a father.

Shaw's plays are full of ideas, ideas of every color on the spectrum from dangerous to preposterous, from wonderful to thrilling, and, as

Jacques Barzun says, it is never a question with Shaw of agreeing with all his ideas but of being moved by the vision. It is a vision that is always a play of contrary ideas, and therefore a mirror of life itself—ideas dramatized always with graceful wit, genial humor, and fearlessness, but also with the great feeling and emotional fervor that comes with thinking that life, and how it goes, and where it is headed, matter. Not for Shaw the despairing gaze into the abyss—laughter, rather, and the imagining of hope.

---

JOHN A. BERTOLINI was educated at Manhattan College and Columbia University. He teaches English and dramatic literature, Shakespeare, and film at Middlebury College, where he is Ellis Professor of the Liberal Arts. He is the author of *The Playwrighting Self of Bernard Shaw* and editor of *Shaw and Other Playwrights*; he has also published articles on Hitchcock, Renaissance drama, and British and American dramatists. He is writing a book on Terence Rattigan's plays.

# MAN AND
# SUPERMAN AND
# THREE OTHER PLAYS

# MRS. WARREN'S PROFESSION

# PREFACE
## MAINLY ABOUT MYSELF

THERE IS AN OLD SAYING THAT IF A man has not fallen in love before forty, he had better not fall in love after. I long ago perceived that this rule applied to many other matters as well: for example, to the writing of plays; and I made a rough memorandum for my own guidance that unless I could produce at least half a dozen plays before I was forty, I had better let playwriting alone. It was not so easy to comply with this provision as might be supposed. Not that I lacked the dramatist's gift. As far as that is concerned, I have encountered no limit but my own laziness to my power of conjuring up imaginary people in imaginary places, and making up stories about them in the natural scenic form which has given rise to that curious human institution, the theatre. But in order to obtain a livelihood by my gift, I must have conjured so as to interest not only my own imagination, but that of at least some seventy or a hundred thousand contemporary London playgoers. To fulfil this condition was hopelessly out of my power. I had no taste for what is called popular art, no respect for popular morality, no belief in popular religion, no admiration for popular heroics. As an Irishman I could pretend to patriotism neither for the country I had abandoned nor the country that had ruined it. As a humane person I detested violence and slaughter, whether in war, sport, or the butcher's yard. I was a Socialist, detesting our anarchical scramble for money, and believing in equality as the only possible permanent basis of social organization, discipline, subordination, good manners, and selection of fit persons for high functions. Fashionable life, though open on very specially indulgent terms to unencumbered "brilliant" persons ("brilliancy" was my speciality), I could not endure, even if I had not feared the demoralizing effect of its wicked wastefulness, its impenitent robbery of the poor, and its vulgarity on a character which required looking after as much as my own. I was neither a sceptic nor a cynic in these matters: I simply understood life differently from the average respectable man; and as I certainly enjoyed myself more—mostly in ways which would have made him unbearably miserable—I was not splenetic over our variance.

Judge then, how impossible it was for me to write fiction that should delight the public. In my nonage I had tried to obtain a foothold in literature by writing novels, and did actually produce five long works in that form without getting further than an encouraging compliment or two from the most dignified of the London and American publishers, who unanimously declined to venture their capital upon me. Now it is clear that a novel cannot be too bad to be worth publishing, provided it is a novel at all, and not merely an ineptitude. It certainly is possible for a novel to be too good to be worth publishing; but I pledge my credit as a critic that this was not the case with mine. I might have explained the matter by saying with Whately,* "These silly people don't know their own silly business"; and indeed, when these novels of mine did subsequently blunder into type to fill up gaps in Socialist magazines financed by generous friends, one or two specimens took shallow root like weeds, and trip me up from time to time to this day. But I was convinced that the publishers' view was commercially sound by getting just then a clue to my real condition from a friend of mine, a physician who had devoted himself specially to ophthalmic surgery. He tested my eyesight one evening, and informed me that it was quite uninteresting to him because it was "normal." I naturally took this to mean that it was like everybody else's; but he rejected this construction as paradoxical, and hastened to explain to me that I was an exceptional and highly

---

*Richard Whately (1787–1863), Anglican archbishop of Dublin.

fortunate person optically, "normal" sight conferring the power of seeing things accurately, and being enjoyed by only about ten per cent of the population, the remaining ninety per cent being abnormal. I immediately perceived the explanation of my want of success in fiction. My mind's eye, like my body's, was "normal": it saw things differently from other people's eyes, and saw them better.

This revelation produced a considerable effect on me. At first it struck me that I might live by selling my works to the ten per cent who were like myself; but a moment's reflection showed me that these would all be as penniless as myself, and that we could not live by, so to speak, taking in one another's washing. How to earn my bread by my pen was then the problem. Had I been a practical commonsense moneyloving Englishman, the matter would have been easy enough: I should have put on a pair of abnormal spectacles and aberred my vision to the liking of the ninety per cent of potential bookbuyers. But I was so prodigiously self-satisfied with my superiority, so flattered by my abnormal normality, that the resource of hypocrisy never occurred to me. Better see rightly on a pound a week than squint on a million. The question was, how to get the pound a week. The matter, once I gave up writing novels, was not so very difficult. Every despot must have one disloyal subject to keep him sane. Even Louis the Eleventh had to tolerate his confessor, standing for the eternal against the temporal throne. Democracy has now handed the sceptre of the despot to the sovereign people; but they, too, must have their confessor, whom they call Critic. Criticism is not only medicinally salutary: it has positive popular attractions in its cruelty, its gladiatorship, and the gratification its attacks on the great give to envy, and its praises to enthusiasm. It may say things which many would like to say, but dare not, and indeed for want of skill could not even if they durst. Its iconoclasms, seditions, and blasphemies, if well turned, tickle those whom they shock; so that the critic adds the privileges of the court jester to those of the confessor. Garrick, had he called Dr. Johnson Punch, would have spoken profoundly and wittily, whereas Dr. Johnson, in hurling that epithet at him, was but picking up the cheapest sneer an actor is subject to.

It was as Punch, then, that I emerged from obscurity. All I had to do was to open my normal eyes, and with my utmost literary skill put the case exactly as it struck me, or describe the thing exactly as I saw it, to be applauded as the most humorously extravagant paradoxer in London. The only reproach with which I became familiar was the everlasting "Why can you not be serious"? Soon my privileges were enormous and my wealth immense. I had a prominent place reserved for me on a prominent journal every week to say my say as if I were the most important person in the kingdom. My pleasing toil was to inspect all the works of fine art that the capital of the world can attract to its exhibitions, its opera house, its concerts and its theatres. The classes patiently read my essays: the masses patiently listened to my harangues. I enjoyed the immunities of impecuniosity with the opportunities of a millionaire. If ever there was a man without a grievance, I was that man.

But alas! the world grew younger as I grew older: its vision cleared as mine dimmed: it began to read with the naked eye the writing on the wall which now began to remind me that age of spectacles was overtaking me. My opportunities were still there: nay, they multiplied tenfold; but the strength and youth to cope with them began to fail, and to need eking out with the shifty cunning of experience. I had to shirk the platform; to economize my health; even to take holidays. In my weekly columns, which I once filled from a Fortunatus well that never ran dry or lost its sparkle so long as I pumped hard enough, I began to repeat myself; to fall into a style which, to my great peril, was recognized as at least partly serious; to find the pump tiring me and the water lower in the well; and, worst symptom of all, to reflect with little tremors on the fact that my magic wealth could not, like the money for which other men threw it away, be stored up against my old age. The younger generation, reared in an enlightenment unknown to my childhood, came knocking at the door too: I glanced back at my old columns and realized that I had timidly botched at thirty what newer men—Rudyard Kiplings, Max Beerbohms, Laurence Irvings* and their contemporaries—do now with gay confidence in their cradles. I listened to their vigorous knocks with exultation for the race, with penurious alarm for my own old age. When I talked to this generation, it called me Mister, and, with its frank, charming humanity, respected me as one who had done good work in my time. Mr. Pinero wrote a long play to show that people of my age were on the shelf; and I laughed at him with the wrong side of my mouth.

It was at this bitter moment that my fellow citizens, who had previously repudiated all my offers of political service, contemptuously allowed me to become a vestryman†—me, the author of "Widowers' Houses"! Then, like any other harmless useful creature, I took the first step rearward. Up to that fateful day I had never stopped pumping to spoon up the spilt drops of my well into bottles. Time enough for that when the well was empty. But now I listened to the voice of the publisher for the first time since he had refused to listen to me. I turned over my articles again; but to serve up the weekly paper of five years ago as a novelty—no: I had not yet fallen so low, though I see that degradation looming before me as an agricultural laborer sees the workhouse. So I said "I will begin with small sins: I will publish my plays."

How! you will cry—plays! What plays? Let me explain.

One of the worst privations of life in London for persons of intellectual and artistic interests is the want of a suitable theatre. The existing popular drama of the day is quite out of the question for cultivated people who are accustomed to use their brains. I am fond of the theatre, and am, as intelligent readers of this preface will have observed, myself a bit of an actor. Consequently, when I found my-

---

*Laurence Irving (1871–1914) was a biographer and the son of famous actor-manager Henry Irving.

†Elected member of a local city council; Shaw represented St. Pancras, London, from 1897 to 1903.

self coming across projects of all sorts for the foundation of a theatre which should be to the newly gathered intellectual harvest of the nineteenth century what Shakespear's theatre was to the harvest of the Renascence, I was warmly interested. But it soon appeared that the languid demand of a small and uppish class for a form of entertainment which it had become thoroughly accustomed to do without could never provide the intense energy necessary for the establishment of the New Theatre (we of course called everything advanced "the New": vide "The Philanderer"). That energy could only be supplied by the genius of the actor and manager finding in the masterpieces of the New Drama its characteristic and necessary mode of expression, and revealing their fascination to the public. Clearly the way to begin was to pick up a masterpiece or two. Masterpieces, however, do not grow on the bushes. The New Theatre would never have come into existence but for the plays of Ibsen, just as the Bayreuth Festival Playhouse would never have come into existence but for Wagner's Nibelungen tetralogy. Every attempt to extend the repertory proved that it is the drama that makes the theatre and not the theatre the drama. Not that this needed fresh proof, since the whole difficulty had arisen through the drama of the day being written for the theatres instead of from its own inner necessity. Still, a thing that nobody believes cannot be proved too often.

Ibsen, then, was the hero of the new departure. It was in 1889 that the first really effective blow was struck by the production of "A Doll's House" by Mr. Charles Charrington and Miss Janet Achurch. Whilst they were taking that epoch making play round the world, Mr. Grein followed up the campaign in London with his "Independent Theatre." It got on its feet by producing Ibsen's "Ghosts"; but its search for native dramatic masterpieces, pursued by Mr. Grein with the ardor and innocence of a foreigner, was so complete a failure that at the end of 1892 he had not produced a single original piece of any magnitude by an English author. In this humiliating national emergency, I proposed to Mr. Grein that he should boldly announce a play by me. Being an extraordinarily sanguine and enterprising man, he took this step without hesitation. I then raked out, from my dustiest pile of discarded and rejected manuscripts, two acts of a play I had begun in 1885, shortly after the close of my novel writing period, in collaboration with my friend Mr. William Archer.

Mr. Archer has himself described how I proved the most impossible of collaborators. Laying violent hands on his thoroughly planned scheme for a sympathetically romantic "well made play" of the type then in vogue, I perversely distorted it into a grotesquely realistic exposure of slum landlordism, municipal jobbery, and the pecuniary and matrimonial ties between it and the pleasant people of "independent" incomes who imagine that such sordid matters do not touch their own lives. The result was most horribly incongruous; for though I took my theme seriously enough, I did not then take the theatre more seriously, though I took it more seriously than it took itself. The farcical trivialities in which I followed the fashion of the times, some flagrant but artistic and amusing examples of which may be studied in Mr. Pinero's "Hobby Horse," written a year later and now familiar in the repertory of Mr. John Hare, became silly and irritating beyond all endurance when intruded upon a subject of such depth, reality, and force as that into which I had plunged my drama. Mr. Archer, perceiving that I had played the fool both with his plan and my own theme, promptly disowned me; and the project, which neither of us had much at heart, was dropped, leaving me with two abortive acts of an unfinished and condemned play. Exhuming this as aforesaid seven years later, I saw that the very qualities which had made it impossible for ordinary commercial purposes in 1885, might be exactly those needed by the Independent Theatre in 1892. So I completed it by a third act; gave it the far-fetched mock-Scriptural title of "Widowers' Houses"; and handed it over to Mr. Grein, who launched it at the public in the Royalty Theatre with all its original tomfooleries on its head. It made a sensation out of all proportion to its merits or even its demerits; and I at once became infamous as a dramatist. The first performance was sufficiently exciting: the Socialists and Independents applauded me furiously on principle; the ordinary play-going first-nighters hooted me frantically on the same ground; I, being at that time in some practice as what is impolitely called a mob-orator, made a speech before the curtain; the newspapers discussed the play for a whole fortnight not only in the ordinary theatrical notices and criticisms, but in leading articles and letters; and finally the text of the play was published with an introduction by Mr. Grein, an amusing account by Mr. Archer of the original collaboration, and a long preface and several elaborate controversial appendices in the author's most energetically egotistical fighting style. The volume, forming number one of the Independent Theatre series of plays, is still extant, a curious relic of that nine days wonder; and as it contains the original text of the play with all its silly pleasantries, I can recommend it to collectors of quarto Hamlets, and of all those scarce and superseded early editions which the unfortunate author would so gladly annihilate if he could.

I had not achieved a success; but I had provoked an uproar; and the sensation was so agreeable that I resolved to try again. In the following year, 1893, when the discussion about Isbenism, "the New Woman," and the like, was at its height, I wrote for the Independent Theatre the topical comedy called "The Philanderer." But even before I finished it, it was apparent that its demands on the most expert and delicate sort of acting—high comedy acting—went quite beyond the resources then at the disposal of Mr. Grein. I had written a part which nobody but Mr. Charles Wyndham could act in a play which was impossible at the Criterion Theatre—a feat comparable to the building of Robinson Crusoe's first boat. I immediately threw it aside, and, returning to the vein I had worked in "Widowers' Houses," wrote a third play, "Mrs. Warren's Profession," on a social subject of tremendous force. That force justified itself in spite of the inexperience of the playwright. The play was everything that the Independent Theatre could desire—rather more, if anything, than it bargained for. But at this point I came upon the obstacle that makes dramatic authorship intolerable in England to writers accustomed to the freedom of the Press. I mean, of course, the Censorship.

In 1737, the greatest dramatist, with the single exception of Shakespear, produced by England between the Middle Ages and the nineteenth century—Henry Fielding—devoted his genius to the task of exposing and destroying parliamentary corruption, then at its height. Walpole, unable to govern without corruption, promptly gagged the stage by a censorship which is in full force at the present moment. Fielding, driven out of the trade of Molière and Aristophanes, took to that of Cervantes; and since then the English novel has been one of the glories of literature, whilst the English drama has been its disgrace. The extinguisher which Walpole dropped on Fielding descends on me in the form of the Queen's Reader of Plays, a gentleman who robs, insults, and suppresses me as irresistibly as if he were the Tsar of Russia and I the meanest of his subjects. The robbery takes the form of making me pay him two guineas for reading every play of mine that exceeds one act in length. I do not want him to read it (at least officially: personally he is welcome): on the contrary, I strenuously resent that impertinence on his part. But I must submit in order to obtain from him an insolent and insufferable document, which I cannot read without boiling of the blood, certifying that in his opinion—h i s opinion!—my play "does not in its general tendency contain anything immoral or otherwise improper for the stage," and that the Lord Chamberlain therefore "allows" its performance (confound his impudence!). In spite of this document he still retains his right, as an ordinary citizen, to prosecute me, or instigate some other citizen to prosecute me, for an outrage on public morals if he should change his mind later on. Besides, if he really protects the public against my immorality, why does not the public pay him for the service? The policeman does not look to the thief for his wages, but to the honest man whom he protects against the thief. And yet, if I refuse to pay, this tyrant can practically ruin any manager who produces my play in defiance of him. If, having been paid, he is afraid to license the play: that is, if he is more afraid of the clamor of the opponents of my opinions than of their supporters, then he can suppress it, and impose a mulct of £50 on everybody who takes part in a representation of it, from the gasman to the principal tragedian. And there is no getting rid of him. Since he lives, not at the expense of the taxpayer, but by blackmailing the author, no political party would gain ten votes by abolishing him. Private political influence cannot touch him; for such private influence, moving only at the promptings of individual benevolence to individuals, makes nice little places to job nice little people into instead of doing away with them. Nay, I myself, though I know that the Queen's Reader of Plays is necessarily an odious and mischievous official, and that I myself, if I were appointed to his post (which I shall probably apply for some day), could no more help being odious and mischievous than a ramrod could if it were stuck into the wheels of a steam engine, am loth to stir up the question lest the Press, having now lost all tradition of liberty, and being able to conceive no alternative to a Queen's Reader of Plays but a County Council's Reader or some other seven-headed devil to replace the oneheaded one, should make the remedy worse than the disease. Thus I cling to the Censorship as many Radicals cling to the House of Lords or the Throne, or as domineering women marry weak and amiable men who only desire a quiet life and whose judgment nobody respects, rather than masterful men. Until the nation is prepared to establish Freedom of The Stage on the same terms as we now enjoy Freedom of The Press, by allowing the dramatist and manager to perform anything they please and take the consequence as authors and editors do, I shall cherish the court reader as the apple of my eye. I once thought of organizing a Petition of Right from all the managers and authors to the Prime Minister; but as it was obvious that nine out of ten of these victims of oppression, far from daring to offend their despot, would promptly extol him as the most salutary of English institutions, and spread themselves with unctious flattery on the perfectly irrelevant question of his estimable personal character, I abandoned the notion. What is more, many of them, in taking this course, would be pursuing a sound business policy, since the managers and authors to whom the existing system has brought success have not only no incentive to change it for another which would expose them to wider competition, but have for the most part the greatest dread of the "New" ideas which the abolition of the Censorship would let loose on the stage. And so long live the Queen's Reader of Plays!

In 1893 the obnoxious post was occupied by a gentleman, now deceased, whose ideas had in the course of nature become quite obsolete. He was openly hostile to the New movement, and declared before a Royal Commission his honest belief that the reputation of Ibsen in England was a spurious product of a system of puffery initiated by Mr. William Archer with the corrupt object of profiting by translations of his works. In dealing with him Mr. Grein was at a heavy disadvantage. Without a license "Mrs. Warren's Profession" could only be performed in some building not a theatre, and therefore not subject to reprisals from the Lord Chamberlain. The audience would have to be invited as guests only; so that the support of the public paying money at the doors, a support with which the Independent Theatre could not afford to dispense, was out of the question. To apply for a license was to court a practically certain refusal entailing the £50 penalty on all concerned in any subsequent performance whatever. The deadlock was complete. The play was ready; the Independent Theatre was ready; two actresses, Mrs. Theodore Wright and Miss Jane Achurch, whose creations of Mrs. Alving in "Ghosts" and Nora in "A Doll's House" had stamped them as the best in the new style in England, were ready; but the mere existence of the Censorship, without any action or knowledge of the play on its part, was sufficient to paralyse all these forces. So I threw "Mrs. Warren's Profession," too, aside, and, like another Fielding, closed my career as playwright in ordinary to the Independent Theatre.

Fortunately, though the Stage is bound, the Press is free. And even if the Stage were freed, none the less would it be necessary to publish plays as well as perform them. Had the two performances of "Widowers' Houses" achieved by Mr. Grein been multiplied by fifty—nay, had "The Philanderer" and "Mrs. Warren's Profession" been so adapted to the taste of the general public as to have run as

long as "Charlie's Aunt,"* they would still have remained mere titles
to those who either dwell out of reach of a theatre, or, as a matter of
habit, prejudice, comfort, health or age, abstain altogether from play-
going. And then there are the people who have a really high standard
of dramatic work; who read with delight all the classic dramatists,
from Eschylus to Ibsen, but who only go to the theatre on the rare
occasions when they are offered a play by an author whose work they
have already learnt to value as literature, or a performance by an
actor of the first rank. Even our habitual playgoers would be found,
on investigation, to have no true habit of playgoing. If on any night at
the busiest part of the theatrical season in London, the audiences
were cordoned by the police and examined individually as to their
views on the subject, there would probably not be a single house
owning native among them who would not conceive a visit to the
theatre, or indeed to any public assembly, artistic or political, as an
exceptional way of spending an evening, the normal English way
being to sit in separate families in separate rooms in separate houses,
each person silently occupied with a book, a paper, or a game of
halma, cut off equally from the blessings of society and solitude. The
result is that you may make the acquaintance of a thousand streets of
middle-class English families without coming on a trace of any consciousness of citizenship, or any artistic cultivation of the senses. The
condition of the men is bad enough, in spite of their daily escape into
the city, because they carry the exclusive and unsocial habits of "the
home" with them into the wider world of their business. Although
they are natural, amiable, and companionable enough, they are, by
home training, so incredibly ill-mannered, that not even their business interests in welcoming a possible customer in every inquirer, can
correct their habit of treating everybody who has not been "introduced" as a stranger and intruder. The women, who have not even
the city to educate them, are much worse: they are positively unfit

---

*Brandon Thomas's perennially popular farce involving female impersonation.

for civilized intercourse—graceless, ignorant, narrow-minded to a quite appalling degree. Even in public places homebred people cannot be taught to understand that the right they are themselves exercising is a common right. Whether they are in a second-class railway carriage or in a church, they receive every additional fellow-passenger or worshipper as a Chinaman receives the "foreign devil" who has forced him to open his ports.

In proportion as this horrible domestic institution is broken up by the active social circulation of the upper classes in their own orbit, or its stagnant isolation made impossible by the overcrowding of the working classes, manners improve enormously. In the middle classes themselves the revolt of a single clever daughter (nobody has yet done justice to the modern clever Englishwoman's loathing of the very word "home"), and her insistence on qualifying herself for an independent working life, humanizes her whole family in an astonishingly short time; and the formation of a habit of going to the suburban theatre once a week, or to the Monday Popular Concerts, or both, very perceptibly ameliorates its manners. But none of these breaches in the Englishman's castle-house can be made without a cannonade of books and pianoforte music. The books and music cannot be kept out, because they alone can make the hideous boredom of the hearth bearable. If its victims may not live real lives, they may at least read about imaginary ones, and perhaps learn from them to doubt whether a class that not only submits to home life, but actually values itself on it, is really a class worth belonging to. For the sake of the unhappy prisoners of the home, then, let my plays be printed as well as acted.

But the dramatic author has reasons for publishing his plays which would hold good even if English families went to the theatre as regularly as they take in the newspaper. A perfectly adequate and successful stage representation of a play requires a combination of circumstances so extraordinarily fortunate that I doubt whether it has ever occurred in the history of the world. Take the case of the most successful English dramatist of the first rank, Shakespear. Although he wrote three centuries ago, he still holds his own so well that it is not impossible to meet old playgoers who have witnessed public performances of more than thirty out of his thirty-seven reputed plays, a dozen of them fairly often, and half a dozen over and over again. I myself, though I have by no means availed myself of all my opportunities, have seen twenty-three of his plays publicly acted. But if I had not read them as well as seen them acted, I should have not merely an incomplete, but a violently distorted and falsified impression of them. It is only within the last few years that some of our younger actor-managers have been struck with the idea, quite novel in their profession, of giving Shakespear's plays as he wrote them, instead of using them as a cuckoo uses a sparrow's nest. In spite of the success of these experiments, the stage is still dominated by Garrick's conviction that the manager and actor must adapt Shakespear's plays to the modern stage by a process which no doubt presents itself to the adapter's mind as one of masterly amelioration, but which must necessarily be mainly one of debasement and mutilation whenever, as occasionally happens, the adapter is inferior to the author. The living author can protect himself against this extremity of misrepresentation; but the more unquestioned is his authority on the stage, and the more friendly and willing the co-operation of the manager and the company, the more completely does he get convinced of the impossibility of achieving an authentic representation of his piece as well as an effective and successful one. It is quite possible for a piece to enjoy the most sensational success on the basis of a complete misunderstanding of its philosophy: indeed, it is not too much to say that it is only by a capacity for succeeding in spite of its philosophy that a dramatic work of serious poetic import can become popular. In the case of the first part of Goethe's "Faust" we have this frankly avowed by the extraction from the great original of popular entertainments like Gounod's opera or the Lyceum version, in which the poetry and philosophy is replaced by romance, which is the recognized spurious substitute for both and is absolutely destructive of them. But the same thing occurs even when a drama is performed without omission or alteration by actors who are enthusiastic disciples of the author. I have seen some remarkably sympathetic stage interpretations of poetic drama, from the achievements of Mr. Charles Charrington with Ibsen, and Mr. Lugné Poe with Maeterlinck, under the least expensive conditions, to those of the Wagner Festival Playhouse at Bayreuth with the most expensive; and I have frequently assured readers of Ibsen and Maeterlinck, and pianoforte students of Wagner, that they can never fully appreciate the dramatic force of their works without sensing them in the theatre. But I have never found an acquaintance with a dramatist founded on the theatre alone, or with a composer founded on the concert room alone, a really intimate and accurate one. The very originality and genius of the performers conflicts with the originality and genius of the author. Imagine, for example, Shakespear confronted with Sir Henry Irving at a rehearsal of "The Merchant of Venice," or Sheridan with Miss Ada Rehan at one of "The School for Scandal." One can easily imagine the speeches that might pass on such occasions. For example: "As I look at your playing, Sir Henry, I seem to see Israel mourning the Captivity and crying, 'How long, oh Lord, how long'? but I do not see my Shylock, whom I designed as a moneylender of strong feelings operating through an entirely commercial intellect. But pray dont alter your conception, which will be abundantly profitable to us both." Or "My dear Miss Rehan, let me congratulate you on a piece of tragic acting which has made me ashamed of the triviality of my play, and obliterated Sir Peter Teazle from my consciousness, though I meant him to be the hero of the scene. I foresee an enormous success for both of us in this fortunate misrepresentation of my intention." Even if the author had nothing to gain pecuniarily by conniving at the glorification of his play by the performer, the actor's excess of power would still carry its own authority and win the sympathy of the author's histrionic instinct, unless he were a Realist of fanatical integrity. And that would not save him either; for his attempts to make powerful actors do less than their utmost would be as impossible as his attempts to make feeble ones do more.

In short, the fact that a skilfully written play is infinitely more adaptable to all sorts of acting than ordinary acting is to all sorts of plays (the actual conditions thus exactly reversing the desirable ones) finally drives the author to the conclusion that his own view of his work can only be conveyed by himself. And since he cannot act the play single-handed even when he is a trained actor, he must fall back on his powers of literary expression, as other poets and fictionists do. So far, this has hardly been seriously attempted by dramatists. Of Shakespear's plays we have not even complete prompt copies: the folio gives us hardly anything but the bare lines. What would we not give for the copy of Hamlet used by Shakespear at rehearsal, with the original "business" scrawled by the prompter's pencil? And if we had in addition the descriptive directions which the author gave on the stage—above all, the character sketches, however brief, by which he tried to convey to the actor the sort of person he meant him to incarnate, what a light they would shed, not only on the play, but on the history of the sixteenth century! Well, we should have had all this and much more if Shakespear, instead of having merely to bring his plays to the point necessary to provide his company with memoranda for an effective performance, had also had to prepare them for publication in competition with fiction as elaborate as that of Balzac, for instance. It is for want of this process of elaboration that Shakespear, unsurpassed as poet, storyteller, character draughtsman, humorist, and rhetorician, has left us no intellectually coherent drama, and could not afford to pursue a genuinely scientific method in his studies of character and society, though in such unpopular plays as *All's Well*, *Measure for Measure*, and *Troilus and Cressida*, we find him ready and willing to start at the nineteenth century if the seventeenth would only let him.

Such literary treatment is ten times more necessary to a modern author than it is to Shakespear, because in his time the acting of plays was very imperfectly differentiated from the declamation of verses; and descriptive or narrative recitation did what is now done by scenery and "business." Anyone reading the mere dialogue of an Elizabethan play understands all but half a dozen unimportant lines of it without difficulty, whilst many modern plays, highly successful on the stage, are not merely unreadable but positively unintelligible without the stage business. The extreme instance is a pure pantomime, like "L'Enfant Prodigue,"* in which the dialogue, though it exists, is not spoken. If a dramatic author were to publish a pantomime, it is clear that he could only make it intelligible to a reader by giving him the words which the pantomimist is supposed to be uttering. Now it is not a whit less impossible to make a modern practical stage play intelligible to a reader by dialogue alone, than to make a pantomime intelligible without it.

Obvious as this is, the presentation of plays through the literary medium has not yet become an art; and the result is that it is very difficult to induce the English public to buy and read plays. Indeed, why should they, when they find nothing in them except a bald dialogue, with a few carpenter's and costumier's directions as to the heroine's father having a grey beard, and the drawing-room having three doors on the right, two doors and an entrance through the conservatory on the left, and a French window in the middle? It is astonishing to me that Ibsen, who devotes two years to the production of a three act play, the extraordinary quality of which depends on a mastery of character and situation which can only be achieved by working out a good deal of the family and personal history of the individuals represented, should nevertheless give the reading public very little more than the technical memorandum required by the carpenter, the gasman, and the prompter. Who will deny that the result is a needless obscurity as to points which are easily explicable? Ibsen, interrogated as to his meaning, replies, "What I have said, I have said." Precisely; but the point is that what he hasn't said, he hasn't said. There are perhaps people (though I doubt it, not being one of them myself) to whom Ibsen's plays, as they stand, speak sufficiently for themselves.

---

*"The Prodigious Child" (French); a scenario for music by Michel Carré, co-librettist of several nineteenth-century operas by Charles Gounod.

There are certainly others who could not understand them at any terms. Granting that on both these classes further explanations would be thrown away, is nothing to be done for the vast majority to whom a word of explanation makes all the difference?

Finally, may I put in a plea for the actors themselves? Born actors have a susceptibility to dramatic emotion which enables them to seize the moods of their parts intuitively. But to expect them to be intuitive as to intellectual meaning and circumstantial conditions as well, is to demand powers of divination from them: one might as well expect the Astronomer Royal to tell the time in a catacomb. And yet the actor generally finds his part full of emotional directions which he could supply as well or better than the author, whilst he is left quite in the dark as to the political, religious, or social beliefs and circumstances under which the character is supposed to be acting. Definite conceptions of these are always implicit in the best plays, and are often the key to their appropriate rendering; but most actors are so accustomed to do without them that they would object to being troubled with them, although it is only by such educative trouble that an actor's profession can place him on the level of the lawyer, the physician, the churchman, and the statesman. Even as it is, Shylock as a Jew and usurer, Othello as a Moor and a soldier, Cæsar, Cleopatra and Anthony, as figures in defined political circumstances, are enormously easier for the actor than the countless heroes as to whom nothing is ever known except that they wear nice clothes, love the heroine, baffle the villain, and live happily ever after.

The case, then, is overwhelming for printing and publishing not only the dialogue of plays, but for a serious effort to convey their full content to the reader. This means the institution of a new art; and I daresay that before these volumes are ten years old, the attempt that it makes in this direction will be left far behind, and that the customary, brief, and unreadable scene specification at the head of an act will by then have expanded into a chapter, or even a series of chapters, each longer than the act itself, and no less interesting and indispensable. No doubt one result of this will be the production of works of a mixture of kinds, part narrative, part homily, part description, part dialogue, and (possibly) part drama—works that can be read, but not acted. I have no objection to such works; but my own aim has been that of the practical dramatist; if anything my eye has been too much on the stage, though I have tried to put down nothing that is irrelevant to the actor's performance or the audience's comprehension of the play. I have of course been compelled to omit some things that a stage representation could convey, simply because the art of letters, though highly developed grammatically, is still in its infancy as a technical speech notation: for example, there are fifty ways of saying Yes, and five hundred of saying No, but only one way of writing them down. Even the use of spaced letters instead of italics for underlining, though familiar to foreign readers, will have to be learned by the English public before it becomes effective. But if my readers do their fair share of the work, I daresay they will understand nearly as much of the plays as I do myself.

Finally, a word as to why I have labeled the three plays in this first volume Unpleasant. The reason is pretty obvious; their dramatic power is used to force the spectator to face unpleasant facts. No doubt all plays which deal sincerely with humanity must wound the monstrous conceit which it is the business of romance to flatter. But here we are confronted, not only with the comedy and tragedy of individual character and destiny, but with those social horrors which arise from the fact that the average homebred Englishman, no matter however honorable and goodnatured he may be in his private capacity, is, as a citizen, a wretched creature who, whilst clamoring for a gratuitous millennium, will shut his eyes to the most villainous abuses if the remedy threatens to add another penny in the pound to the rates and taxes which he has to be half cheated, half coerced into paying. In "Widowers' Houses" I have shewn middle class respectability and younger son gentility fattening on the poverty of the slum as flies fatten on filth. That is not a pleasant theme. In "The Philanderer" I have shewn the grotesque relations between men and women which have arisen under marriage laws which represent to some of us a political necessity (especially for other people), to some a divine ordinance, to some a romantic ideal, to some a domestic profession for women, and to some that worst of blundering abominations, an institution which society has outgrown but not modified, and which "advanced" individuals are therefore forced to evade. The scene with which "The Philanderer" opens, the atmosphere in which it proceeds, and the marriage with which it ends, are, for the intellectually and artistically conscious classes in modern society, typical; and it will hardly be denied, I think, that they are unpleasant. In "Mrs. Warren's Profession" I have gone straight at the fact that, as Mrs. Warren puts it, "the only way for a woman to provide for herself decently is for her to be good to some man that can afford to be good to her." There are some questions on which I am, like most Socialists, an extreme Individualist. I believe that any society which desires to found itself on a high standard of integrity of character in its units should organize itself in such a fashion as to make it possible too for all men and all women to maintain themselves in reasonable comfort by their industry without selling their affections and their convictions. At present we not only condemn women as a sex to attach themselves to "breadwinners," licitly or illicitly, on pain of heavy privation and disadvantage; but we have great prostitute classes of men: for instance, dramatists and journalists, to whom I myself belong, not to mention the legions of lawyers, doctors, clergymen, and platform politicians who are daily using their highest faculties to belie their real sentiments: a sin compared to which that of a woman who sells the use of her person for a few hours is too venial to be worth mentioning; for rich men without conviction are more dangerous in modern society than poor women without chastity. Hardly a pleasant subject this!

I must, however, warn my readers that my attacks are directed against themselves, not against my stage figures. They can not too thoroughly understand that the guilt of defective social organization does not lie alone on the people who actually work the commercial makeshifts which the defects make inevitable, and who often, like

Sartorius and Mrs. Warren, display valuable executive capacities and even high moral virtues in their administration, but with the whole body of citizens whose public opinion, public action, and public contribution as ratepayers alone can replace Sartorius's* slums with decent dwellings, Charteris's† intrigues with reasonable marriage contracts, and Mrs. Warren's profession with honorable industries guarded by a humane industrial code and a "moral minimum" wage.

How I came, later on, to write plays which, dealing less with the crimes of society, and more with its romantic follies, and with the struggles of individuals against those follies, may be called, by contrast, Pleasant, is a story which I shall tell on resuming this discourse for the edification of the readers of the second volume.

(To be continued in our next.)

---

*Sartorius is a slum landlord in Shaw's first play, *Widowers' Houses* (written in 1892).

†Charteris is the title character in Shaw's second play, *The Philanderer* (written in 1893).

# MRS. WARREN'S PROFESSION

## ACT I

*Summer afternoon in a cottage garden on the eastern slope of a hill a little south of Haslemere in Surrey. Looking up the hill, the cottage is seen in the left hand corner of the garden, with its thatched roof and porch, and a large latticed window to the left of the porch. Farther back a little wing is built out, making an angle with the right side wall. From the end of this wing a paling curves across and forward, completely shutting in the garden, except for a gate on the right. The common rises uphill beyond the paling to the sky line. Some folded canvas garden chairs are leaning against the side bench in the porch. A lady's bicycle is propped against the wall, under the window. A little to the right of the porch a hammock is slung from two posts. A big canvas umbrella, stuck in the ground, keeps the sun off the hammock, in which a young lady lies reading and making notes, her head towards the cottage and her feet towards the gate. In front of the hammock, and within reach of her hand, is a common kitchen chair, with a pile of serious-looking books and a supply of writing paper upon it.*

*A gentleman walking on the common comes into sight from behind the cottage. He is hardly past middle age, with something of the artist about him, unconventionally but carefully dressed, and clean-shaven except for a moustache, with an eager, susceptible face and very amiable and considerate manners. He has silky black hair, with waves of grey and white in it. His eyebrows are white, his moustache black. He seems not certain of his way. He looks over the paling; takes stock of the place; and sees the young lady.*[1]

THE GENTLEMAN[2] [*taking off his hat*]   I beg your pardon. Can you direct me to Hindhead View—Mrs. Alison's?

THE YOUNG LADY [*glancing up from her book*]   This is Mrs. Alison's. [*She resumes her work.*]

THE GENTLEMAN   Indeed! Perhaps—may I ask are you Miss Vivie Warren?

THE YOUNG LADY [*sharply, as she turns on her elbow to get a good look at him*]   Yes.

THE GENTLEMAN [*daunted and conciliatory*]   I'm afraid I appear intrusive. My name is Praed. [*VIVIE at once throws her books upon the chair, and gets out of the hammock.*] Oh, pray don't let me disturb you.

VIVIE [*striding to the gate and opening it for him*]   Come in, Mr. Praed. [*He comes in.*] Glad to see you. [*She proffers her hand and takes his with a resolute and hearty grip. She is an attractive specimen of the sensible, able, highly-educated young middle-class Englishwoman. Age 22. Prompt, strong, confident, self-possessed. Plain, business-like dress, but not dowdy. She wears a chatelaine at her belt, with a fountain pen and a paper knife among its pendants.*]

PRAED   Very kind of you indeed, Miss Warren. [*She shuts the gate with a vigorous slam: he passes in to the middle of the garden, exercising his fingers, which are slightly numbed by her greeting.*] Has your mother arrived?

VIVIE [*quickly, evidently scenting aggression*]   Is she coming?

PRAED [*surprised*]   Didn't you expect us?

VIVIE   No.

PRAED   Now, goodness me, I hope I've not mistaken the day. That would be just like me, you know. Your mother arranged that she was to come down from London and that I was to come over from Horsham to be introduced to you.

VIVIE [*not at all pleased*]   Did she? H'm! My mother has rather a trick of taking me by surprise—to see how I behave myself when she's away, I suppose. I fancy I shall take my mother very much by surprise one of these days, if she makes arrangements that concern me without consulting me beforehand. She hasn't come.

PRAED [*embarrassed*]   I'm really very sorry.

VIVIE [*throwing off her displeasure*]   It's not your fault, Mr. Praed, is it? And I'm very glad you've come, believe me. You are the only one of my mother's friends I have asked her to bring to see me.

PRAED [*relieved and delighted*]   Oh, now this is really very good of you, Miss Warren!

VIVIE   Will you come indoors; or would you rather sit out here whilst we talk?

PRAED   It will be nicer out here, don't you think?

VIVIE   Then I'll go and get you a chair. [*She goes to the porch for a garden chair.*]

PRAED [*following her*]   Oh, pray, pray! Allow me. [*He lays hands on the chair.*]

VIVIE [*letting him take it*]   Take care of your fingers: they're rather dodgy things, those chairs. [*She goes across to the chair with the books on it; pitches them into the hammock; and brings the chair forward with one swing.*]

PRAED [*who has just unfolded his chair*]   Oh, now d o* let me take that hard chair! I like hard chairs.

VIVIE   So do I. [*She sits down.*] Sit down, Mr. Praed. [*This invitation is given with genial peremptoriness, his anxiety to please her clearly striking her as a sign of weakness of character on his part.*]

PRAED   By the way, though, hadn't we better go to the station to meet your mother?

VIVIE [*coolly*]   Why? She knows the way. [*PRAED hesitates, and then sits down in the garden chair, rather disconcerted.*] Do you know, you

---

*For emphasis Shaw used spaced letters rather than italics, which he reserved for stage directions.

are just like what I expected. I hope you are disposed to be friends with me?

PRAED [*again beaming*]    Thank you, my dear Miss Warren; thank you. Dear me! I'm so glad your mother hasn't spoilt you!

VIVIE    How?

PRAED    Well, in making you too conventional. You know, my dear Miss Warren, I am a born anarchist. I hate authority. It spoils the relations between parent and child—even between mother and daughter. Now I was always afraid that your mother would strain her authority to make you very conventional. It's such a relief to find that she hasn't.

VIVIE    Oh! have I been behaving unconventionally?

PRAED    Oh, no: oh, dear no. At least not conventionally uncon-ventionally, you understand. [*She nods. He goes on, with a cordial outburst.*] But it was so charming of you to say that you were dis-posed to be friends with me! You modern young ladies are splendid—perfectly splendid!

VIVIE [*dubiously*]    Eh? [*watching him with dawning disappointment as to the quality of his brains and character.*]

PRAED    When I was your age, young men and women were afraid of each other: there was no good fellowship—nothing real— only gallantry copied out of novels, and as vulgar and affected as it could be. Maidenly reserve!—gentlemanly chivalry!—always saying no when you meant yes!—simple purgatory for shy and sincere souls!

VIVIE    Yes, I imagine there must have been a frightful waste of time—especially women's time.

PRAED    Oh, waste of life, waste of everything. But things are im-proving. Do you know, I have been in a positive state of excite-ment about meeting you ever since your magnificent achievements at Cambridge—a thing unheard of in my day. It was perfectly splendid, your tieing with the third wrangler. Just the right place, you know. The first wrangler is always a dreamy, morbid fellow, in whom the thing is pushed to the length of a disease.

VIVIE    It doesn't pay. I wouldn't do it again for the same money.

PRAED [*aghast*]    The same money!

VIVIE    I did it for £50. Perhaps you don't know how it was. Mrs. Latham, my tutor at Newnham,* told my mother that I could distinguish myself in the mathematical tripos† if I went for it in earnest. The papers were full just then of Phillipa Summers beating the senior wrangler—you remember about it; and nothing would please my mother but that I should do the same thing. I said flatly that it was not worth my while to face the grind since I was not going in for teaching; but I offered to try for fourth wrangler or thereabouts for £50. She closed with me at that, after a little grumbling; and I was better than my bargain. But I wouldn't do it again for that. £200 would have been nearer the mark.

PRAED [*much damped*]    Lord bless me! That's a very practical way of looking at it.

VIVIE    Did you expect to find me an unpractical person?

PRAED    No, no. But surely it's practical to consider not only the work these honors cost, but also the culture they bring.

VIVIE    Culture! My dear Mr. Praed: do you know what the mathematical tripos means? It means grind, grind, grind, for six to eight hours a day at mathematics, and nothing but mathematics. I'm supposed to know something about science; but I know nothing except the mathematics it involves. I can make calculations for engineers, electricians, insurance companies, and so on; but I know next to nothing about engineering or electricity or insurance. I don't even know arithmetic well. Outside mathematics, lawn-tennis, eating, sleeping, cycling, and walking, I'm

---

*College for women at Cambridge University.

†Special final examination at Cambridge; the three highest-ranking students were called "wranglers."

a more ignorant barbarian than any woman could possibly be who hadn't gone in for the tripos.

PRAED [*revolted*]  What a monstrous, wicked, rascally system! I knew it! I felt at once that it meant destroying all that makes womanhood beautiful.

VIVIE    I don't object to it on that score in the least. I shall turn it to very good account, I assure you.

PRAED    Pooh! In what way?

VIVIE    I shall set up in chambers in the city and work at actuarial calculations and conveyancing. Under cover of that I shall do some law, with one eye on the Stock Exchange all the time. I've come down here by myself to read law—not for a holiday, as my mother imagines. I hate holidays.

PRAED    You make my blood run cold. Are you to have no romance, no beauty in your life?

VIVIE    I don't care for either, I assure you.

PRAED    You can't mean that.

VIVIE    Oh yes I do. I like working and getting paid for it. When I'm tired of working, I like a comfortable chair, a cigar, a little whisky, and a novel with a good detective story in it.

PRAED [*in a frenzy of repudiation*]    I don't believe it. I am an artist; and I can't believe it: I refuse to believe it. [*Enthusiastically.*] Ah, my dear Miss Warren, you haven't discovered yet, I see, what a wonderful world art can open up to you.

VIVIE    Yes, I have. Last May I spent six weeks in London with Honoria Fraser. Mamma thought we were doing a round of sight-seeing together; but I was really at Honoria's chambers in Chancery Lane every day, working away at actuarial calculations for her, and helping her as well as a greenhorn could. In the evenings we smoked and talked, and never dreamt of going out except for exercise. And I never enjoyed myself more in my life. I cleared all my expenses and got initiated into the business without a fee into the bargain.

PRAED   But bless my heart and soul, Miss Warren, do you call that trying art?

VIVIE   Wait a bit. That wasn't the beginning. I went up to town on an invitation from some artistic people in Fitzjohn's Avenue: one of the girls was a Newnham chum. They took me to the National Gallery, to the Opera, and to a concert where the band played all the evening—Beethoven and Wagner and so on. I wouldn't go through that experience again for anything you could offer me. I held out for civility's sake until the third day; and then I said, plump out, that I couldn't stand any more of it, and went off to Chancery Lane. Now you know the sort of perfectly splendid modern young lady I am. How do you think I shall get on with my mother?

PRAED [*startled*]   Well, I hope—er—

VIVIE   It's not so much what you hope as what you believe, that I want to know.

PRAED   Well, frankly, I am afraid your mother will be a little disappointed. Not from any shortcoming on your part—I don't mean that. But you are so different from her ideal.

VIVIE   What is her ideal like?

PRAED   Well, you must have observed, Miss Warren, that people who are dissatisfied with their own bringing up generally think that the world would be all right if everybody were to be brought up quite differently. Now your mother's life has been—er—I suppose you know—

VIVIE   I know nothing. [*PRAED is appalled. His consternation grows as she continues.*] That's exactly my difficulty. You forget, Mr. Praed, that I hardly know my mother. Since I was a child I have lived in England, at school or college, or with people paid to take charge of me. I have been boarded out all my life; and my mother has lived in Brussels or Vienna and never let me go to her. I only see her when she visits England for a few days. I don't complain: it's been very pleasant; for people have been very good to me; and there has always been plenty of money to make things smooth.

But don't imagine I know anything about my mother. I know far less than you do.

PRAED [*very ill at ease*]    In that case— [*He stops, quite at a loss. Then, with a forced attempt at gaiety.*] But what nonsense we are talking! Of course you and your mother will get on capitally. [*He rises, and looks abroad at the view.*] What a charming little place you have here!

VIVIE [*unmoved*]    If you think you are doing anything but confirming my worst suspicions by changing the subject like that, you must take me for a much greater fool than I hope I am.

PRAED    Your worst suspicions! Oh, pray don't say that. Now don't.

VIVIE    Why won't my mother's life bear being talked about?

PRAED    Pray think, Miss Vivie. It is natural that I should have a certain delicacy in talking to my old friend's daughter about her behind her back. You will have plenty of opportunity of talking to her about it when she comes. [*Anxiously.*] I wonder what is keeping her.

VIVIE    No: she won't talk about it either. [*Rising.*] However, I won't press you. Only mind this, Mr. Praed. I strongly suspect there will be a battle royal when my mother hears of my Chancery Lane project.

PRAED [*ruefully*]    I'm afraid there will.

VIVIE    I shall win the battle, because I want nothing but my fare to London to start there to-morrow earning my own living by devilling for Honoria. Besides, I have no mysteries to keep up; and it seems she has. I shall use that advantage over her if necessary.[3]

PRAED [*greatly shocked*]    Oh, no. No, pray. You'd not do such a thing.

VIVIE    Then tell me why not.

PRAED    I really cannot. I appeal to your good feeling. [*She smiles at his sentimentality.*] Besides, you may be too bold. Your mother is not to be trifled with when she's angry.

VIVIE    You can't frighten me, Mr. Praed. In that month at

Chancery Lane I had opportunities of taking the measure of one or two women, very like my mother who came to consult Honoria. You may back me to win. But if I hit harder in my ignorance than I need, remember that it is you who refuse to enlighten me. Now let us drop the subject. [*She takes her chair and replaces it near the hammock with the same vigorous swing as before.*]

PRAED [*taking a desperate resolution*]   One word, Miss Warren. I had better tell you. It's very difficult; but—

[*MRS. WARREN and SIR GEORGE CROFTS arrive at the gate. MRS. WARREN is a woman between 40 and 50, good-looking, showily dressed in a brilliant hat and a gay blouse fitting tightly over her bust and flanked by fashionable sleeves. Rather spoiled and domineering, but, on the whole, a genial and fairly presentable old blackguard of a woman.*

*CROFTS is a tall, powerfully-built man of about 50, fashionably dressed in the style of a young man. Nasal voice, reedier than might be expected from his strong frame. Clean-shaven, bull-dog jaws, large flat ears, and thick neck, gentlemanly combination of the most brutal types of city man, sporting man, and man about town.*]

VIVIE   Here they are. [*Coming to them as they enter the garden.*] How do, mater. Mr. Praed's been here this half hour, waiting for you.

MRS. WARREN   Well, if you've been waiting, Praddy, it's your own fault: I thought you'd have had the gumption to know I was coming by the 3:10 train. Vivie, put your hat on, dear: you'll get sunburnt. Oh, forgot to introduce you. Sir George Crofts, my little Vivie.

[*CROFTS advances to VIVIE with his most courtly manner. She nods, but makes no motion to shake hands.*]

CROFTS   May I shake hands with a young lady whom I have known by reputation very long as the daughter of one of my oldest friends?

VIVIE [*who has been looking him up and down sharply*]   If you like. [*She takes his tenderly proffered hand and gives it a squeeze that makes him open his eyes; then turns away and says to her mother*] Will you come in, or shall I get a couple more chairs? [*She goes into the porch for the chairs.*]

MRS. WARREN    Well, George, what do you think of her?

CROFTS [*ruefully*]    She has a powerful fist. Did you shake hands with her, Praed?

PRAED    Yes: it will pass off presently.

CROFTS    I hope so. [*VIVIE reappears with two more chairs. He hurries to her assistance.*] Allow me.

MRS. WARREN [*patronizingly*]    Let Sir George help you with the chairs, dear.

VIVIE [*almost pitching two into his arms*]    Here you are. [*She dusts her hands and turns to MRS. WARREN.*] You'd like some tea, wouldn't you?

MRS. WARREN [*sitting in PRAED's chair and fanning herself*]    I'm dying for a drop to drink.

VIVIE    I'll see about it. [*She goes into the cottage. SIR GEORGE has by this time managed to unfold a chair and plant it beside MRS. WARREN, on her left. He throws the other on the grass and sits down, looking dejected and rather foolish, with the handle of his stick in his mouth. PRAED, still very uneasy, fidgets about the garden on their right.*]

MRS. WARREN [*to PRAED, looking at CROFTS*]    Just look at him, Praddy: he looks cheerful, don't he? He's been worrying my life out these three years to have that little girl of mine shewn to him; and now that I've done it, he's quite out of countenance. [*Briskly.*] Come! sit up, George; and take your stick out of your mouth. [*CROFTS sulkily obeys.*]

PRAED    I think, you know—if you don't mind my saying so—that we had better get out of the habit of thinking of her as a little girl. You see she has really distinguished herself; and I'm not sure, from what I have seen of her, that she is not older than any of us.

MRS. WARREN [*greatly amused*]    Only listen to him, George! Older than any of us! Well, she has been stuffing you nicely with her importance.

PRAED   But young people are particularly sensitive about being treated in that way.

MRS. WARREN   Yes; and young people have to get all that nonsense taken out of them, and a good deal more besides. Don't you interfere, Praddy. I know how to treat my own child as well as you do. [*PRAED, with a grave shake of his head, walks up the garden with his hands behind his back. MRS. WARREN pretends to laugh, but looks after him with perceptible concern. Then she whispers to CROFTS.*] What's the matter with him? What does he take it like that for?

CROFTS [*morosely*]   You're afraid of Praed.

MRS. WARREN   What! Me! Afraid of dear old Praddy! Why, a fly wouldn't be afraid of him.

CROFTS   You're afraid of him.

MRS. WARREN [*angry*]   I'll trouble you to mind your own business, and not try any of your sulks on me. I'm not afraid of you, anyhow. If you can't make yourself agreeable, you'd better go home. [*She gets up, and, turning her back on him, finds herself face to face with PRAED.*] Come, Praddy, I know it was only your tender-heartedness. You're afraid I'll bully her.

PRAED   My dear Kitty: you think I'm offended. Don't imagine that: pray don't. But you know I often notice things that escape you; and though you never take my advice, you sometimes admit afterwards that you ought to have taken it.

MRS. WARREN   Well, what do you notice now?

PRAED   Only that Vivie is a grown woman. Pray, Kitty, treat her with every respect.

MRS. WARREN [*with genuine amazement*]   Respect! Treat my own daughter with respect! What next, pray!

VIVIE [*appearing at the cottage door and calling to MRS. WARREN*] Mother: will you come up to my room and take your bonnet off before tea?

MRS. WARREN   Yes, dearie. [*She laughs indulgently at PRAED and pats him on the cheek as she passes him on her way to the porch. She follows VIVIE into the cottage.*]

CROFTS [*furtively*]   I say, Praed.

PRAED   Yes.

CROFTS   I want to ask you a rather particular question.

PRAED   Certainly. [*He takes MRS. WARREN's chair and sits close to CROFTS.*]

CROFTS   That's right: they might hear us from the window. Look here: did Kitty ever tell you who that girl's father is?

PRAED   Never.

CROFTS   Have you any suspicion of who it might be?

PRAED   None.

CROFTS [*not believing him*]   I know, of course, that you perhaps might feel bound not to tell if she had said anything to you. But it's very awkward to be uncertain about it now that we shall be meeting the girl every day. We don't exactly know how we ought to feel towards her.

PRAED   What difference can that make? We take her on her own merits. What does it matter who her father was?

CROFTS [*suspiciously*]   Then you know who he was?

PRAED [*with a touch of temper*]   I said no just now. Did you not hear me?

CROFTS   Look here, Praed. I ask you as a particular favor. If you do know [*movement of protest from PRAED*]—I only say, i f you know, you might at least set my mind at rest about her. The fact is I feel attracted towards her. Oh, don't be alarmed: it's quite an innocent feeling. That's what puzzles me about it. Why, for all I know, *I* might be her father.

PRAED   You! Impossible! Oh, no, nonsense!

CROFTS [*catching him up cunningly*]   You know for certain that I'm not?

PRAED   I know nothing about it, I tell you, any more than you. But really, Crofts—oh, no, it's out of the question. There's not the least resemblance.

CROFTS   As to that, there's no resemblance between her and her mother that I can see. I suppose she's not y o u r daughter, is she?

PRAED [*He meets the question with an indignant stare; then recovers himself with an effort and answers gently and gravely*] Now listen to me, my dear Crofts. I have nothing to do with that side of Mrs. Warren's life, and never had. She has never spoken to me about it; and of course I have never spoken to her about it. Your delicacy will tell you that a handsome woman needs s o m e friends who are not—well, not on that footing with her. The effect of her own beauty would become a torment to her if she could not escape from it occasionally. You are probably on much more confidential terms with Kitty than I am. Surely you can ask her the question yourself.

CROFTS [*rising impatiently*] I have asked her often enough. But she's so determined to keep the child all to herself that she would deny that it ever had a father if she could. No: there's nothing to be got out of her—nothing that one can believe, anyhow. I'm thoroughly uncomfortable about it, Praed.

PRAED [*rising also*] Well, as you are, at all events, old enough to be her father, I don't mind agreeing that we both regard Miss Vivie in a parental way, as a young girl whom we are bound to protect and help. All the more, as the real father, whoever he was, was probably a blackguard. What do you say?

CROFTS [*aggressively*] I'm no older than you, if you come to that.

PRAED Yes, you are, my dear fellow: you were born old. I was born a boy: I've never been able to feel the assurance of a grown-up man in my life.

MRS. WARREN [*calling from within the cottage*] Prad-dee! George! Tea-ea-ea-ea!

CROFTS [*hastily*] She's calling us. [*He hurries in. PRAED shakes his head bodingly, and is following slowly when he is hailed by a young gentleman who has just appeared on the common, and is making for the gate. He is a pleasant, pretty, smartly dressed, and entirely good-for-nothing young fellow, not long turned 20, with a charming voice and agreeably disrespectful manner. He carries a very light sporting magazine rifle.*]

THE YOUNG GENTLEMAN    Hallo! Praed!

PRAED    Why, Frank Gardner! [*FRANK comes in and shakes hands cordially.*] What on earth are you doing here?

FRANK    Staying with my father.

PRAED    The Roman father?

FRANK    He's rector here. I'm living with my people this autumn for the sake of economy. Things came to a crisis in July: the Roman father* had to pay my debts. He's stony broke in consequence; and so am I. What are you up to in these parts? Do you know the people here?

PRAED    Yes: I'm spending the day with a Miss Warren.

FRANK    [*enthusiastically*]    What! Do you know Vivie? Isn't she a jolly girl! I'm teaching her to shoot—you see [*shewing the rifle.*]! I'm so glad she knows you: you're just the sort of fellow she ought to know. [*He smiles, and raises the charming voice almost to a singing tone as he exclaims*] It's e v e r so jolly to find you here, Praed. Ain't it, now?

PRAED    I'm an old friend of her mother's. Mrs. Warren brought me over to make her daughter's acquaintance.

FRANK    The mother! Is s h e here?

PRAED    Yes—inside at tea.

MRS. WARREN    [*calling from within*]    Prad-dee-ee-ee-eee! The tea-cake'll be cold.

PRAED    [*calling*]    Yes, Mrs. Warren. In a moment. I've just met a friend here.

MRS. WARREN    A what?

PRAED    [*louder*]    A friend.

MRS. WARREN    Bring him up.

PRAED    All right. [*To FRANK.*] Will you accept the invitation?

FRANK    [*incredulous, but immensely amused*]    Is that Vivie's mother?

PRAED    Yes.

---

*A stern father with life and death authority over his children; here used ironically.

FRANK    By Jove! What a lark! Do you think she'll like me?

PRAED    I've no doubt you'll make yourself popular, as usual. Come in and try [*moving towards the house*].

FRANK   Stop a bit. [*Seriously.*] I want to take you into my confidence.

PRAED    Pray don't. It's only some fresh folly, like the barmaid at Redhill.

FRANK    It's ever so much more serious than that. You say you've only just met Vivie for the first time?

PRAED    Yes.

FRANK [*rhapsodically*]    Then you can have no idea what a girl she is. Such character! Such sense! And her cleverness! Oh, my eye, Praed, but I can tell you she is clever! And the most loving little heart that—

CROFTS [*putting his head out of the window*]    I say, Praed: what are you about? Do come along. [*He disappears.*]

FRANK    Hallo! Sort of chap that would take a prize at a dog show, ain't he? Who's he?

PRAED    Sir George Crofts, an old friend of Mrs. Warren's. I think we had better come in.

[*On their way to the porch they are interrupted by a call from the gate. Turning, they see an elderly clergyman looking over it.*]

THE CLERGYMAN [*calling*]    Frank!

FRANK    Hallo! [*To PRAED.*] The Roman father. [*To the clergyman.*] Yes, gov'nor: all right: presently. [*To PRAED.*] Look here, Praed: you'd better go in to tea. I'll join you directly.

PRAED    Very good. [*He raises his hat to the clergyman, who acknowledges the salute distantly. PRAED goes into the cottage. The clergyman remains stiffly outside the gate, with his hands on the top of it. The REV. SAMUEL GARDNER, a beneficed clergyman of the Established Church, is over 50. He is a pretentious, booming, noisy person, hopelessly asserting himself as a father and a clergyman without being able to command respect in either capacity.*]

REV. S.    Well, sir. Who are your friends here, if I may ask?

FRANK    Oh, it's all right, gov'nor! Come in.

REV. S.    No, sir; not until I know whose garden I am entering.

FRANK    It's all right. It's Miss Warren's.

REV. S.    I have not seen her at church since she came.

FRANK    Of course not: she's a third wrangler—ever so intellectual!—took a higher degree than you did; so why should she go
to hear you preach?

REV. S.    Don't be disrespectful, sir.

FRANK    Oh, it don't matter: nobody hears us. Come in. [*He opens
the gate, unceremoniously pulling his father with it into the garden.*] I
want to introduce you to her. She and I get on rattling well together: she's charming. Do you remember the advice you gave
me last July, gov'nor?

REV. S. [*severely*]    Yes. I advised you to conquer your idleness and
flippancy, and to work your way into an honorable profession
and live on it and not upon me.

FRANK    No: that's what you thought of afterwards. What you actually said was that since I had neither brains nor money, I'd better turn my good looks to account by marrying somebody with
both. Well, look here. Miss Warren has brains: you can't deny
that.

REV. S.    Brains are not everything.

FRANK    No, of course not: there's the money—

REV. S. [*interrupting him austerely*]    I was not thinking of money, sir.
I was speaking of higher things—social position, for instance.

FRANK    I don't care a rap about that.

REV. S.    But I do, sir.

FRANK    Well, nobody wants y o u to marry her. Anyhow, she has
what amounts to a high Cambridge degree; and she seems to
have as much money as she wants.

REV. S. [*sinking into a feeble vein of humor*]    I greatly doubt whether
she has as much money as y o u will want.

FRANK    Oh, come: I haven't been so very extravagant. I live ever so quietly; I don't drink; I don't bet much; and I never go regularly on the razzle-dazzle as you did when you were my age.

REV. S. [*booming hollowly*]   Silence, sir.

FRANK   Well, you told me yourself, when I was making ever such an ass of myself about the barmaid at Redhill, that you once offered a woman £50 for the letters you wrote to her when—

REV. S. [*terrified*]   Sh-sh-sh, Frank, for Heaven's sake! [*He looks round apprehensively. Seeing no one within earshot he plucks up courage to boom again, but more subduedly.*] You are taking an ungentlemanly advantage of what I confided to you for your own good, to save you from an error you would have repented all your life long. Take warning by your father's follies, sir; and don't make them an excuse for your own.

FRANK   Did you ever hear the story of the Duke of Wellington and his letters?

REV. S.   No, sir; and I don't want to hear it.

FRANK   The old Iron Duke didn't throw away £50—not he. He just wrote: "My dear Jenny: Publish and be damned! Yours affectionately, Wellington."* That's what you should have done.

REV. S. [*piteously*]   Frank, my boy: when I wrote those letters I put myself into that woman's power. When I told you about her I put myself, to some extent, I am sorry to say, in your power. She refused my money with these words, which I shall never forget: "Knowledge is power," she said; "and I never sell power." That's more than twenty years ago; and she has never made use of her power or caused me a moment's uneasiness. You are behaving worse to me than she did, Frank.

FRANK   Oh, yes, I dare say! Did you ever preach at her the way you preach at me every day?

REV. S. [*wounded almost to tears*]   I leave you, sir. You are incorrigible. [*He turns towards the gate.*]

---

*Words written to a former mistress who tried to blackmail Arthur Wellesley, duke of Wellington (1769–1852).

FRANK [*utterly unmoved*]   Tell them I shan't be home to tea, will you, gov'nor, like a good fellow? [*He goes towards the cottage door and is met by VIVIE coming out, followed by PRAED, CROFTS, and MRS. WARREN.*]

VIVIE [*to FRANK*]   Is that your father, Frank? I do so want to meet him.

FRANK   Certainly. [*Calling after his father.*] Gov'nor. [*The REV. S. turns at the gate, fumbling nervously at his hat. PRAED comes down the garden on the opposite side, beaming in anticipation of civilities. CROFTS prowls about near the hammock, poking it with his stick to make it swing. MRS. WARREN halts on the threshold, staring hard at the clergyman.*] Let me introduce—my father: Miss Warren.

VIVIE [*going to the clergyman and shaking his hand*]   Very glad to see you here, Mr. Gardner. Let me introduce everybody. Mr. Gardner—Mr. Frank Gardner—Mr. Praed—Sir George Crofts, and—[*As the men are raising their hats to one another, VIVIE is interrupted by an exclamation from her mother, who swoops down on the REVEREND SAMUEL*].

MRS. WARREN   Why, it's Sam Gardner, gone into the church! Don't you know us, Sam? This is George Crofts, as large as life and twice as natural. Don't you remember me?

REV. S. [*very red*]   I really—er—

MRS. WARREN   Of course you do. Why, I have a whole album of your letters still: I came across them only the other day.

REV. S. [*miserably confused*]   Miss Vavasour,* I believe.

MRS. WARREN [*correcting him quickly in a loud whisper*]   Tch! Nonsense—Mrs. Warren: don't you see my daughter there?

---

*Commonly assumed name for a procuress.

# ACT II

*Inside the cottage after nightfall. Looking eastward from within instead of westward from without, the latticed window, with its curtains drawn, is now seen in the middle of the front wall of the cottage, with the porch door to the left of it. In the left-hand side wall is the door leading to the wing. Farther back against the same wall is a dresser with a candle and matches on it, and Frank's rifle standing beside them, with the barrel resting in the plate-rack. In the centre a table stands with a lighted lamp on it. Vivie's books and writing materials are on a table to the right of the window, against the wall. The fireplace is on the right, with a settle: there is no fire. Two of the chairs are set right and left of the table.*

*The cottage door opens, shewing a fine starlit night without; and* MRS. WARREN, *her shoulders wrapped in a shawl borrowed from* VIVIE, *enters, followed by* FRANK. *She has had enough of walking, and gives a gasp of relief as she unpins her hat; takes it off; sticks the pin through the crown; and puts it on the table.*

MRS. WARREN   O Lord! I don't know which is the worst of the country, the walking or the sitting at home with nothing to do: I could do a whisky and soda now very well, if only they had such a thing in this place.

FRANK [*helping her to take off her shawl, and giving her shoulders the most delicate possible little caress with his fingers as he does so*]   Perhaps Vivie's got some.

MRS. WARREN [*glancing back at him for an instant from the corner of her eye as she detects the pressure*]   Nonsense! What would a young girl like her be doing with such things! Never mind: it don't matter. [*She throws herself wearily into a chair at the table.*] I wonder how she passes her time here! I'd a good deal rather be in Vienna.

FRANK    Let me take you there. [*He folds the shawl neatly; hangs it on the back of the other chair; and sits down opposite MRS. WARREN.*]

MRS. WARREN    Get out! I'm beginning to think you're a chip off the old block.

FRANK    Like the gov'nor, eh?

MRS. WARREN    Never you mind. What do you know about such things? You're only a boy.

FRANK    Do come to Vienna with me? It'd be ever such larks.

MRS. WARREN    No, thank you. Vienna is no place for you—at least not until you're a little older. [*She nods at him to emphasize this piece of advice. He makes a mock-piteous face, belied by his laughing eyes. She looks at him; then rises and goes to him.*] Now, look here, little boy [*taking his face in her hands and turning it up to her*]: I know you through and through by your likeness to your father, better than you know yourself. Don't you go taking any silly ideas into your head about me. Do you hear?

FRANK [*gallantly wooing her with his voice*]    Can't help it, my dear Mrs. Warren: it runs in the family. [*She pretends to box his ears; then looks at the pretty, laughing, upturned face for a moment, tempted. At last she kisses him and immediately turns away, out of patience with herself.*]

MRS. WARREN    There! I shouldn't have done that. I a m wicked. Never you mind, my dear: it's only a motherly kiss. Go and make love to Vivie.

FRANK    So I have.

MRS. WARREN [*turning on him with a sharp note of alarm in her voice*] What!

FRANK    Vivie and and I are ever such chums.

MRS. WARREN    What do you mean? Now, see here: I won't have any young scamp tampering with my little girl. Do you hear? I won't have it.

FRANK [*quite unabashed*]   My dear Mrs. Warren: don't you be alarmed. My intentions are honorable—e v e r  so honorable; and your little girl is jolly well able to take care of herself. She don't need looking after half so much as her mother. She ain't so handsome, you know.

MRS. WARREN [*taken aback by his assurance*]   Well, you  h a v e  got a nice, healthy two inches thick of cheek all over you. I don't know where you got it—not from your father, anyhow. [*Voices and footsteps in the porch*]. Sh! I hear the others coming in. [*She sits down hastily.*] Remember: you've got your warning. [*The REV. SAMUEL comes in, followed by CROFTS.*] Well, what became of you two? And where's Praddy and Vivie?

CROFTS [*putting his hat on the settle and his stick in the chimney corner*] They went up the hill. We went to the village. I wanted a drink. [*He sits down on the settle, putting his legs up along the seat.*]

MRS. WARREN   Well, she oughtn't to go off like that without telling me. [*To FRANK.*] Get your father a chair, Frank: where are your manners? [*FRANK springs up and gracefully offers his father his chair; then takes another from the wall and sits down at the table, in the middle, with his father on his right and MRS. WARREN on his left.*] George: where are you going to stay to-night? You can't stay here. And what's Praddy going to do?

CROFTS   Gardner'll put me up.

MRS. WARREN   Oh, no doubt you've taken care of yourself! But what about Praddy?

CROFTS   Don't know. I suppose he can sleep at the inn.

MRS. WARREN   Haven't you room for him, Sam?

REV. S.   Well, er—you see, as rector here, I am not free to do as I like exactly. Er—what is Mr. Praed's social position?

MRS. WARREN   Oh, he's all right: he's an architect. What an old-stick-in-the-mud you are, Sam!

FRANK   Yes, it's all right, gov'nor. He built that place down in

Monmouthshire for the Duke of Beaufort—Tintern Abbey they call it. You must have heard of it. [*He winks with lightning smartness at MRS. WARREN, and regards his father blandly.*]

REV. S.    Oh, in that case, of course we shall only be too happy. I suppose he knows the Duke of Beaufort personally.

FRANK    Oh, ever so intimately! We can stick him in Georgina's old room.

MRS. WARREN    Well, t h a t ' s settled. Now, if those two would only come in and let us have supper. They've no right to stay out after dark like this.

CROFTS [*aggressively*]    What harm are they doing you?

MRS. WARREN    Well, harm or not, I don't like it.

FRANK    Better not wait for them, Mrs. Warren. Praed will stay out as long as possible. He has never known before what it is to stray over the heath on a summer night with my Vivie.

CROFTS [*sitting up in some consternation*]    I say, you know. Come!

REV. S. [*startled out of his professional manner into real force and sincerity*]    Frank, once for all, it's out of the question. Mrs. Warren will tell you that it's not to be thought of.

CROFTS    Of course not.

FRANK [*with enchanting placidity*]    Is that so, Mrs. Warren?

MRS. WARREN [*reflectively*]    Well, Sam, I don't know. If the girl wants to get married, no good can come of keeping her unmarried.

REV. S. [*astounded*]    But married to  h i m ! —your daughter to my son! Only think: it's impossible.

CROFTS    Of course it's impossible. Don't be a fool, Kitty.

MRS. WARREN [*nettled*]    Why not? Isn't my daughter good enough for your son?

REV. S.    But surely, my dear Mrs. Warren, you know the reason—

MRS. WARREN [*defiantly*]    I know no reasons. If you know any, you can tell them to the lad, or to the girl, or to your congregation, if you like.

REV. S. [*helplessly*]    You know very well that I couldn't tell anyone

the reasons. But my boy will believe me when I tell him there
a r e reasons.

FRANK   Quite right, Dad: he will. But has your boy's conduct ever
been influenced by your reasons?

CROFTS   You can't marry her; and that's all about it. [*He gets up
and stands on the hearth, with his back to the fireplace, frowning determinedly.*]

MRS. WARREN [*turning on him sharply*]   What have you got to do
with it, pray?

FRANK [*with his prettiest lyrical cadence*]   Precisely what I was going
to ask, myself, in my own graceful fashion.

CROFTS [*to MRS. WARREN*]   I suppose you don't want to marry
the girl to a man younger than herself and without either a profession or twopence to keep her on. Ask Sam, if you don't believe me. [*To the REV. S.*] How much more money are you going
to give him?

REV. S.   Not another penny. He has had his patrimony; and he
spent the last of it in July. [*MRS. WARREN's face falls.*]

CROFTS [*watching her*]   There! I told you. [*He resumes his place on
the settle and puts up his legs on the seat again, as if the matter were finally disposed of.*]

FRANK [*plaintively*]   This is ever so mercenary. Do you suppose
Miss Warren's going to marry for money? If we love one another—

MRS. WARREN   Thank you. Your love's a pretty cheap com-
modity, my lad. If you have no means of keeping a wife, that settles it: you can't have Vivie.

FRANK [*much amused*]   What do you say, gov'nor, eh?

REV. S.   I agree with Mrs. Warren.

FRANK   And good old Crofts has already expressed his opinion.

CROFTS [*turning angrily on his elbow*]   Look here: I want none of
y o u r cheek.

FRANK [*pointedly*]   I'm e v e r so sorry to surprise you, Crofts;

but you allowed yourself the liberty of speaking to me like a father a moment ago. One father is enough, thank you.

CROFTS [*contemptuously*]    Yah! [*He turns away again.*]

FRANK [*rising*]    Mrs. Warren: I cannot give my Vivie up even for your sake.

MRS. WARREN [*muttering*]    Young scamp!

FRANK [*continuing*]    And as you no doubt intend to hold out other prospects to her, I shall lose no time in placing my case before her. [*They stare at him; and he begins to declaim gracefully*]

> He either fears his fate too much,
>     Or his deserts are small,
> That dares not put it to the touch
>     To gain or lose it all.*

[*The cottage door opens whilst he is reciting; and VIVIE and PRAED come in. He breaks off. PRAED puts his hat on the dresser. There is an immediate improvement in the company's behaviour. CROFTS takes down his legs from the settle and pulls himself together as PRAED joins him at the fireplace. MRS. WARREN loses her ease of manner, and takes refuge in querulousness.*]

MRS. WARREN    Wherever have you been, Vivie?

VIVIE [*taking off her hat and throwing it carelessly on the table*]    On the hill.

MRS. WARREN    Well, you shouldn't go off like that without letting me know. How could I tell what had become of you—and night coming on, too!

VIVIE [*going to the door of the inner room and opening it, ignoring her mother*]    Now, about supper? We shall be rather crowded in here, I'm afraid.

MRS. WARREN    Did you hear what I said, Vivie?

---

*From "My Dear and Only Love," by seventeenth-century poet James Graham, marquis of Montrose.

VIVIE [*quietly*]   Yes, mother. [*Reverting to the supper difficulty.*] How many are we? [*Counting.*] One, two, three, four, five, six. Well, two will have to wait until the rest are done: Mrs. Alison has only plates and knives for four.

PRAED   Oh, it doesn't matter about me. I—

VIVIE   You have had a long walk and are hungry, Mr. Praed: you shall have your supper at once. I can wait myself. I want one person to wait with me. Frank: are you hungry?

FRANK   Not the least in the world—completely off my peck, in fact.

MRS. WARREN [*to CROFTS*]   Neither are you, George. You can wait.

CROFTS   Oh, hang it, I've eaten nothing since tea-time. Can't Sam do it?

FRANK   Would you starve my poor father?

REV. S. [*testily*]   Allow me to speak for myself, sir. I am perfectly willing to wait.

VIVIE [*decisively*]   There's no need. Only two are wanted. [*She opens the door of the inner room.*] Will you take my mother in, Mr. Gardner. [*The REV. S. takes MRS. WARREN; and they pass into the next room. PRAED and CROFTS follow. All except PRAED clearly disapprove of the arrangement, but do not know how to resist it. VIVIE stands at the door looking in at them.*] Can you squeeze past to that corner, Mr. Praed: it's rather a tight fit. Take care of your coat against the white-wash—that's right. Now, are you all comfortable?

PRAED [*within*]   Quite, thank you.

MRS. WARREN [*within*]   Leave the door open, dearie. [*FRANK looks at VIVIE; then steals to the cottage door and softly sets it wide open.*] Oh, Lor', what a draught! You'd better shut it, dear. [*VIVIE shuts it promptly. FRANK noiselessly shuts the cottage door.*]

FRANK [*exulting*]   Aha! Got rid of 'em. Well, Vivvums: what do you think of my governor!

VIVIE [*preoccupied and serious*]   I've hardly spoken to him. He doesn't strike me as being a particularly able person.

FRANK    Well, you know, the old man is not altogether such a fool as he looks. You see, he's rector here; and in trying to live up to it he makes a much bigger ass of himself than he really is. No, the gov'nor ain't so bad, poor old chap; and I don't dislike him as much as you might expect. He means well. How do you think you'll get on with him?

VIVIE [*rather grimly*]    I don't think my future life will be much concerned with him, or with any of that old circle of my mother's, except perhaps Praed. What do you think of my mother?

FRANK    Really and truly?

VIVIE    Yes, really and truly.

FRANK    Well, she's ever so jolly. But she's rather a caution, isn't she? And Crofts! Oh, my eye, Crofts!

VIVIE    What a lot, Frank!

FRANK    What a crew!

VIVIE [*with intense contempt for them*]    If I thought that *I* was like that—that I was going to be a waster, shifting along from one meal to another with no purpose, and no character, and no grit in me, I'd open an artery and bleed to death without one moment's hesitation.

FRANK    Oh, no, you wouldn't. Why should they take any grind when they can afford not to? I wish I had their luck. No: what I object to is their form. It isn't the thing: it's slovenly, ever so slovenly.

VIVIE    Do you think your form will be any better when you're as old as Crofts, if you don't work?

FRANK    Of course I do—ever so much better. Vivvums mustn't lecture: her little boy's incorrigible. [*He attempts to take her face caressingly in his hands.*]

VIVIE [*striking his hands down sharply*]    Off with you: Vivvums is not in a humor for petting her little boy this evening.

FRANK    How unkind!

VIVIE [*stamping at him*]    Be serious. I'm serious.

FRANK    Good. Let us talk learnedly. Miss Warren: do you know that all the most advanced thinkers are agreed that half the diseases of modern civilization are due to starvation of the affections in the young. Now, *I*—

VIVIE [*cutting him short*]   You are getting tiresome. [*She opens the inner door.*] Have you room for Frank there? He's complaining of starvation.

MRS. WARREN [*within*]   Of course there is [*clatter of knives and glasses as she moves the things on the table*]. Here: there's room now beside me. Come along, Mr. Frank.

FRANK [*aside to VIVIE, as he goes*]   Her little boy will be ever so even with his Vivvums for this. [*He goes into the other room.*]

MRS. WARREN [*within*]   Here, Vivie: come on, you too, child. You must be famished. [*She enters, followed by CROFTS, who holds the door open for VIVIE with marked deference. She goes out without looking at him; and he shuts the door after her.*] Why, George, you can't be done: you've eaten nothing.

CROFTS   Oh, all I wanted was a drink. [*He thrusts his hands in his pockets and begins prowling about the room, restless and sulky.*]

MRS. WARREN   Well, I like enough to eat. But a little of that cold beef and cheese and lettuce goes a long way. [*With a sigh of only half repletion she sits down lazily at the table.*]

CROFTS   What do you go encouraging that young pup for?

MRS. WARREN [*on the alert at once*]   Now see here, George: what are you up to about that girl? I've been watching your way of looking at her. Remember: I know you and what your looks mean.

CROFTS   There's no harm in looking at her, is there?

MRS. WARREN   I'd put you out and pack you back to London pretty soon if I saw any of your nonsense. My girl's little finger is more to me than your whole body and soul. [*CROFTS receives this with a sneering grin. MRS. WARREN, flushing a little at her failure to impose on him in the character of a theatrically devoted mother, adds in a lower key.*] Make your mind easy: the young pup has no more chance than you have.

CROFTS   Mayn't a man take an interest in a girl?

MRS. WARREN   Not a man like you.

CROFTS   How old is she?

MRS. WARREN   Never you mind how old she is.

CROFTS   Why do you make such a secret of it?

MRS. WARREN   Because I choose.

CROFTS   Well, I'm not fifty yet; and my property is as good as ever it was——

MRS. WARREN [*interrupting him*]   Yes; because you're as stingy as you're vicious.

CROFTS [*continuing*]   And a baronet isn't to be picked up every day. No other man in my position would put up with you for a mother-in-law. Why shouldn't she marry me?

MRS. WARREN   You!

CROFTS   We three could live together quite comfortably. I'd die before her and leave her a bouncing widow with plenty of money. Why not? It's been growing in my mind all the time I've been walking with that fool inside there.

MRS. WARREN [*revolted*]   Yes; it's the sort of thing that w o u l d grow in your mind. [*He halts in his prowling; and the two look at one another, she steadfastly, with a sort of awe behind her contemptuous disgust: he stealthily, with a carnal gleam in his eye and a loose grin, tempting her.*]

CROFTS [*suddenly becoming anxious and urgent as he sees no sign of sympathy in her*]   Look here, Kitty: you're a sensible woman: you needn't put on any moral airs. I'll ask no more questions; and you need answer none. I'll settle the whole property on her; and if you want a cheque for yourself on the wedding day, you can name any figure you like—in reason.

MRS. WARREN   Faugh! So it's come to that with you, George, like all the other worn out old creatures.

CROFTS [*savagely*]   Damn you! [*She rises and turns fiercely on him; but the door of the inner room is opened just then; and the voices of the oth-*

*ers are heard returning. CROFTS, unable to recover his presence of mind, hurries out of the cottage. The clergyman comes back.*]

REV. S. [*looking round*]   Where is Sir George?

MRS. WARREN   Gone out to have a pipe. [*She goes to the fireplace, turning her back on him to compose herself. The clergyman goes to the table for his hat. Meanwhile VIVIE comes in, followed by FRANK, who collapses into the nearest chair with an air of extreme exhaustion. MRS. WARREN looks round at VIVIE and says, with her affectation of maternal patronage even more forced than usual.*] Well, dearie: have you had a good supper?

VIVIE   You know what Mrs. Alison's suppers are. [*She turns to FRANK and pets him.*] Poor Frank! was all the beef gone? did it get nothing but bread and cheese and ginger beer? [*Seriously, as if she had done quite enough trifling for one evening.*] Her butter is really awful. I must get some down from the stores.

FRANK   Do, in Heaven's name!

[*VIVIE goes to the writing-table and makes a memorandum to order the butter. PRAED comes in from the inner room, putting up his handkerchief, which he has been using as a napkin.*]

REV. S.   Frank, my boy: it is time for us to be thinking of home. Your mother does not know yet that we have visitors.

PRAED   I'm afraid we're giving trouble.

FRANK   Not the least in the world, Praed: my mother will be delighted to see you. She's a genuinely intellectual, artistic woman; and she sees nobody here from one year's end to another except the gov'nor; so you can imagine how jolly dull it pans out for her. [*To the REV. S.*] You're not intellectual or artistic, are you, pater? So take Praed home at once; and I'll stay here and entertain Mrs. Warren. You'll pick up Crofts in the garden. He'll be excellent company for the bull-pup.

PRAED [*taking his hat from the dresser, and coming close to FRANK*] Come with us, Frank. Mrs. Warren has not seen Miss Vivie for a long time; and we have prevented them from having a moment together yet.

FRANK [*quite softened, and looking at PRAED with romantic admiration*] Of course: I forgot. Ever so thanks for reminding me. Perfect gentleman, Praddy. Always were—my ideal through life. [*He rises to go, but pauses a moment between the two older men, and puts his hand on PRAED's shoulder.*] Ah, if you had only been my father instead of this unworthy old man! [*He puts his other hand on his father's shoulder.*]

REV. S. [*blustering*]    Silence, sir, silence: you are profane.

MRS. WARREN [*laughing heartily*]    You should keep him in better order, Sam. Good-night. Here: take George his hat and stick with my compliments.

REV. S. [*taking them*]    Good-night. [*They shake hands. As he passes VIVIE he shakes hands with her also and bids her good-night. Then, in booming command, to FRANK.*] Come along, sir, at once. [*He goes out. Meanwhile FRANK has taken his cap from the dresser and his rifle from the rack. PRAED shakes hands with MRS. WARREN and VIVIE and goes out, MRS. WARREN accompanying him idly to the door, and looking out after him as he goes across the garden. FRANK silently begs a kiss from VIVIE; but she, dismissing him with a stern glance, takes a couple of books and some paper from the writing-table, and sits down with them at the middle table, so as to have the benefit of the lamp.*]

FRANK [*at the door, taking MRS. WARREN's hand*]    Good night, d e a r Mrs. Warren. [*He squeezes her hand. She snatches it away, her lips tightening, and looks more than half disposed to box his ears. He laughs mischievously and runs off, clapping-to the door behind him.*]

MRS. WARREN [*coming back to her place at the table, opposite VIVIE, resigning herself to an evening of boredom now that the men are gone*] Did you ever in your life hear anyone rattle on so? Isn't he a tease? [*She sits down.*] Now that I think of it, dearie, don't you go encouraging him. I'm sure he's a regular good-for-nothing.

VIVIE    Yes: I'm afraid poor Frank is a thorough good-for-nothing. I shall have to get rid of him; but I shall feel sorry for him, though he's not worth it, poor lad. That man Crofts does not seem to me to be good for much either, is he?

MRS. WARREN [*galled by VIVIE's cool tone*]    What do you know of men, child, to talk that way about them? You'll have to make up your mind to see a good deal of Sir George Crofts, as he's a friend of mine.

VIVIE [*quite unmoved*]    Why? Do you expect that we shall be much together—you and I, I mean?

MRS. WARREN [*staring at her*]    Of course—until you're married. You're not going back to college again.

VIVIE    Do you think my way of life would suit you? I doubt it.

MRS. WARREN    Y o u r  way of life! What do you mean?

VIVIE [*cutting a page of her book with the paper knife on her chatelaine*]    Has it really never occurred to you, mother, that I have a way of life like other people?

MRS. WARREN    What nonsense is this you're trying to talk? Do you want to shew your independence, now that you're a great little person at school? Don't be a fool, child.

VIVIE [*indulgently*]    That's all you have to say on the subject, is it, mother?

MRS. WARREN [*puzzled, then angry*]    Don't you keep on asking me questions like that. [*Violently.*] Hold your tongue. [*VIVIE works on, losing no time, and saying nothing.*] You and your way of life, indeed! What next? [*She looks at VIVIE again. No reply.*] Your way of life will be what I please, so it will. [*Another pause.*] I've been noticing these airs in you ever since you got that tripos or whatever you call it. If you think I'm going to put up with them you're mistaken; and the sooner you find it out, the better. [*Muttering.*] All I have to say on the subject, indeed! [*Again raising her voice angrily.*] Do you know who you're speaking to, Miss?

VIVIE [*looking across at her without raising her head from her book*]    No. Who are you? What are you?

MRS. WARREN [*rising breathless*]    You young imp!

VIVIE    Everybody knows my reputation, my social standing, and the profession I intend to pursue. I know nothing about you.

What is that way of life which you invite me to share with you and Sir George Crofts, pray?

MRS. WARREN    Take care. I shall do something I'll be sorry for after, and you, too.

VIVIE [*putting aside her books with cool decision*]    Well, let us drop the subject until you are better able to face it. [*Looking critically at her mother.*] You want some good walks and a little lawn tennis to set you up. You are shockingly out of condition: you were not able to manage twenty yards uphill to-day without stopping to pant; and your wrists are mere rolls of fat. Look at mine. [*She holds out her wrists.*]

MRS. WARREN [*after looking at her helplessly, begins to whimper*] Vivie——

VIVIE [*springing up sharply*]    Now pray don't begin to cry. Anything but that. I really cannot stand whimpering. I will go out of the room if you do.

MRS. WARREN [*piteously*]    Oh, my darling, how can you be so hard on me? Have I no rights over you as your mother?

VIVIE    A r e  you my mother?

MRS. WARREN [*appalled*]    Am I your mother! Oh, Vivie!

VIVIE    Then where are our relatives—my father—our family friends? You claim the rights of a mother: the right to call me fool and child; to speak to me as no woman in authority over me at college dare speak to me; to dictate my way of life; and to force on me the acquaintance of a brute whom anyone can see to be the most vicious sort of London man about town. Before I give myself the trouble to resist such claims, I may as well find out whether they have any real existence.

MRS. WARREN [*distracted, throwing herself on her knees*]    Oh, no, no. Stop, stop. I  a m  your mother: I swear it. Oh, you can't mean to turn on me—my own child: it's not natural. You believe me, don't you? Say you believe me.

VIVIE    Who was my father?

MRS. WARREN    You don't know what you're asking. I can't tell you.

VIVIE [*determinedly*]    Oh, yes, you can, if you like. I have a right to know; and you know very well that I have that right. You can refuse to tell me, if you please; but if you do, you will see the last of me to-morrow morning.

MRS. WARREN    Oh, it's too horrible to hear you talk like that. You wouldn't—you c o u l d n ' t leave me.

VIVIE [*ruthlessly*]    Yes, without a moment's hesitation, if you trifle with me about this. [*Shivering with disgust.*] How can I feel sure that I may not have the contaminated blood of that brutal waster in my veins?

MRS. WARREN    No, no. On my oath it's not he, nor any of the rest that you have ever met. I'm certain of that, at least. [*VIVIE's eyes fasten sternly on her mother as the significance of this flashes on her.*]

VIVIE [*slowly*]    You are certain of that, at l e a s t. Ah! You mean that that is all you are certain of. [*Thoughtfully.*] I see. [*MRS. WARREN buries her face in her hands.*] Don't do that, mother: you know you don't feel it a bit. [*MRS. WARREN takes down her hands and looks up deplorably at VIVIE, who takes out her watch and says*] Well, that is enough for to-night. At what hour would you like breakfast? Is half-past eight too early for you?

MRS. WARREN [*wildly*]    My God, what sort of woman are you?

VIVIE [*coolly*]    The sort the world is mostly made of, I should hope. Otherwise I don't understand how it gets its business done. Come [*taking her mother by the wrist, and pulling her up pretty resolutely*]: pull yourself together. That's right.

MRS. WARREN [*querulously*]    You're very rough with me, Vivie.

VIVIE    Nonsense. What about bed? It's past ten.

MRS. WARREN [*passionately*]    What's the use of my going to bed? Do you think I could sleep?

VIVIE    Why not? I shall.

MRS. WARREN    You! you've no heart. [*She suddenly breaks out ve-*

*hemently in her natural tongue—the dialect of a woman of the people—with all her affectations of maternal authority and conventional manners gone, and an overwhelming inspiration of true conviction and scorn in her.*] Oh, I won't bear it: I won't put up with the injustice of it. What right have you to set yourself up above me like this? You boast of what you are to me—to m e, who gave you the chance of being what you are. What chance had I? Shame on you for a bad daughter and a stuck-up prude!

VIVIE [*cool and determined, but no longer confident; for her replies, which have sounded convincingly sensible and strong to her so far, now begin to ring rather woodenly and even priggishly against the new tone of her mother*]   Don't think for a moment I set myself above you in any way. You attacked me with the conventional authority of a mother: I defended myself with the conventional superiority of a respectable woman. Frankly, I am not going to stand any of your nonsense; and when you drop it I shall not expect you to stand any of mine. I shall always respect your right to your own opinions and your own way of life.

MRS. WARREN   My own opinions and my own way of life! Listen to her talking! Do you think I was brought up like you—able to pick and choose my own way of life? Do you think I did what I did because I liked it, or thought it right, or wouldn't rather have gone to college and been a lady if I'd had the chance?

VIVIE   Everybody has some choice, mother. The poorest girl alive may not be able to choose between being Queen of England or Principal of Newnham; but she can choose between ragpicking and flowerselling, according to her taste. People are always blaming their circumstances for what they are. I don't believe in circumstances. The people who get on in this world are the people who get up and look for the circumstances they want, and, if they can't find them, make them.[4]

MRS. WARREN   Oh, it's easy to talk, very easy, isn't it? Here!— would you like to know what m y circumstances were?

VIVIE   Yes: you had better tell me. Won't you sit down?

MRS. WARREN    Oh, I ' l l sit down: don't you be afraid. [*She plants her chair farther forward with brazen energy, and sits down. VIVIE is impressed in spite of herself.*] D'you known what your gran'-mother was?

VIVIE    No.

MRS. WARREN    No, you don't. I do. She called herself a widow and had a fried-fish shop down by the Mint, and kept herself and four daughters out of it. Two of us were sisters: that was me and Liz; and we were both good-looking and well made. I suppose our father was a well-fed man: mother pretended he was a gentleman; but I don't know. The other two were only half sisters—undersized, ugly, starved looking, hard working, honest poor creatures: Liz and I would have half-murdered them if mother hadn't half-murdered u s to keep our hands off them. They were the respectable ones. Well, what did they get by their respectability? I'll tell you. One of them worked in a whitelead factory twelve hours a day for nine shillings a week until she died of lead poisoning. She only expected to get her hands a little paralyzed; but she died. The other was always held up to us as a model because she married a Government laborer in the Deptford victualling yard, and kept his room and the three children neat and tidy on eighteen shillings a week—until he took to drink. That was worth being respectable for, wasn't it?

VIVIE [*now thoughtfully attentive*]    Did you and your sister think so?

MRS. WARREN    Liz didn't, I can tell you: she had more spirit. We both went to a church school—that was part of the ladylike airs we gave ourselves to be superior to the children that knew nothing and went nowhere—and we stayed there until Liz went out one night and never came back. I know the schoolmistress thought I'd soon follow her example; for the clergyman was always warning me that Lizzie'd end by jumping off Waterloo Bridge.* Poor fool: that was all he knew about it! But I was more

---

*Site in London notorious for prostitutes' suicidal jumps (as in Robert Sherwood's *Waterloo Bridge* of 1930).

afraid of the whitelead factory than I was of the river; and so would you have been in my place. That clergyman got me a situation as scullery maid in a temperance restaurant where they sent out for anything you liked. Then I was waitress; and then I went to the bar at Waterloo station—fourteen hours a day serving drinks and washing glasses for four shillings a week and my board. That was considered a great promotion for me. Well, one cold, wretched night, when I was so tired I could hardly keep myself awake, who should come up for a half of Scotch but Lizzie, in a long fur cloak, elegant and comfortable, with a lot of sovereigns in her purse.

VIVIE [*grimly*]   My aunt Lizzie!

MRS. WARREN   Yes: and a very good aunt to have, too. She's living down at Winchester now, close to the cathedral, one of the most respectable ladies there—chaperones girls at the county ball, if you please. No river for Liz, thank you! You remind me of Liz a little: she was a first-rate business woman—saved money from the beginning—never let herself look too like what she was—never lost her head or threw away a chance. When she saw I'd grown up good-looking she said to me across the bar: "What are you doing there, you little fool? wearing out your health and your appearance for other people's profit!" Liz was saving money then to take a house for herself in Brussels: and she thought we two could save faster than one. So she lent me some money and gave me a start; and I saved steadily and first paid her back, and then went into business with her as her partner. Why shouldn't I have done it? The house in Brussels was real high class—a much better place for a woman to be in than the factory where Anne Jane got poisoned. None of our girls were ever treated as I was treated in the scullery of that temperance place, or at the Waterloo bar, or at home. Would you have had me stay in them and become a worn out old drudge before I was forty?

VIVIE [*intensely interested by this time*]   No; but why did you choose that business? Saving money and good management will succeed in any business.

MRS. WARREN   Yes, saving money. But where can a woman get the money to save in any other business? Could y o u save out of four shillings a week and keep yourself dressed as well? Not you. Of course, if you're a plain woman and can't earn anything more; or if you have a turn for music, or the stage, or newspaper-writing: that's different. But neither Liz nor I had any turn for such things: all we had was our appearance and our turn for pleasing men. Do you think we were such fools as to let other people trade in our good looks by employing us as shopgirls, or barmaids, or waitresses, when we could trade in them ourselves and get all the profits instead of starvation wages? Not likely.[5]

VIVIE   You were certainly quite justified—from the business point of view.

MRS. WARREN   Yes; or any other point of view. What is any respectable girl brought up to do but to catch some rich man's fancy and get the benefit of his money by marrying him?—as if a marriage ceremony could make any difference in the right or wrong of the thing! Oh, the hypocrisy of the world makes me sick! Liz and I had to work and save and calculate just like other people; elseways we should be as poor as any good-for-nothing, drunken waster of a woman that thinks her luck will last for ever. [*With great energy.*] I despise such people: they've no character; and if there's a thing I hate in a woman, it's want of character.

VIVIE   Come, now, mother: frankly! Isn't it part of what you call character in a woman that she should greatly dislike such a way of making money?

MRS. WARREN   Why, of course. Everybody dislikes having to work and make money; but they have to do it all the same. I'm sure I've often pitied a poor girl, tired out and in low spirits, having to try to please some man that she doesn't care two straws for—some half-drunken fool that thinks he's making himself agreeable when he's teasing and worrying and disgusting a woman so that hardly any money could pay her for putting up with it. But she has to bear with disagreeables and take the rough with the smooth, just like a nurse in a hospital or anyone else. It's not work that any woman would do for pleasure, goodness knows; though to hear the pious people talk you would suppose it was a bed of roses.

VIVIE    Still you consider it worth while. It pays.

MRS. WARREN    Of course it's worth while to a poor girl, if she can resist temptation and is good-looking and well conducted and sensible. It's far better than any other employment open to her. I always thought that oughtn't to be. It c a n ' t be right, Vivie, that there shouldn't be better opportunities for women. I stick to that: it's wrong. But it's so, right or wrong; and a girl must make the best of it. But, of course, it's not worth while for a lady. If you took to it you'd be a fool; but I should have been a fool if I'd taken to anything else.

VIVIE [more and more deeply moved]    Mother: suppose we were both as poor as you were in those wretched old days, are you quite sure that you wouldn't advise me to try the Waterloo bar, or marry a labourer, or even go into the factory?

MRS. WARREN [indignantly]    Of course not. What sort of mother do you take me for! How could you keep your self-respect in such starvation and slavery? And what's a woman worth? what's life worth? without self-respect! Why am I independent and able to give my daughter a first-rate education, when other women that had just as good opportunities are in the gutter? Because I always knew how to respect myself and control myself. Why is Liz looked up to in a cathedral town? The same reason. Where would we be now if we'd minded the clergyman's foolishness? Scrubbing floors for one and sixpence a day and nothing to look forward to but the workhouse infirmary. Don't you be led astray by people who don't know the world, my girl. The only way for a woman to provide for herself decently is for her to be good to some man that can afford to be good to her. If she's in his own station of life, let her make him marry her; but if she's far beneath him she can't expect it—why should she? It wouldn't be for her own happiness. Ask any lady in London society that has daughters; and she'll tell you the same, except that I tell you straight and she'll tell you crooked. That's all the difference.[6]

VIVIE [*fascinated, gazing at her*]   My dear mother: you are a wonderful woman—you are stronger than all England. And are you really and truly not one wee bit doubtful—or—or—ashamed?

MRS. WARREN   Well, of course, dearie, it's only good manners to be ashamed of it; it's expected from a woman. Women have to pretend to feel a great deal that they don't feel. Liz used to be angry with me for plumping out the truth about it. She used to say that when every woman could learn enough from what was going on in the world before her eyes, there was no need to talk about it to her. But then Liz was such a perfect lady! She had the true instinct of it; while I was always a bit of a vulgarian. I used to be so pleased when you sent me your photographs to see that you were growing up like Liz: you've just her ladylike, determined way. But I can't stand saying one thing when everyone knows I mean another. What's the use in such hypocrisy? If people arrange the world that way for women, there's no good pretending that it's arranged the other way. I never was a bit ashamed really. I consider that I had a right to be proud that we managed everything so respectably, and never had a word against us, and that the girls were so well taken care of. Some of them did very well: one of them married an ambassador. But of course now I daren't talk about such things: whatever would they think of us! [*She yawns.*] Oh, dear! I do believe I'm getting sleepy after all. [*She stretches herself lazily, thoroughly relieved by her explosion, and placidly ready for her night's rest.*]

VIVIE   I believe it is I who will not be able to sleep now. [*She goes to the dresser and lights the candle. Then she extinguishes the lamp, darkening the room a good deal.*] Better let in some fresh air before locking up. [*She opens the cottage door, and finds that it is broad moonlight.*] What a beautiful night! Look! [*She draws aside the curtains of the window. The landscape is seen bathed in the radiance of the harvest moon rising over Blackdown.*]

MRS. WARREN [*with a perfunctory glance at the scene*]  Yes, dear: but take care you don't catch your death of cold from the night air.

VIVIE [*contemptuously*]  Nonsense.

MRS. WARREN [*querulously*]  Oh, yes: everything I say is nonsense, according to you.

VIVIE [*turning to her quickly*]  No: really that is not so, mother. You have got completely the better of me to-night, though I intended it to be the other way. Let us be good friends now.

MRS. WARREN [*shaking her head a little ruefully*]  So it has been the other way. But I suppose I must give in to it. I always got the worst of it from Liz; and now I suppose it'll be the same with you.

VIVIE  Well, never mind. Come; good-night, dear old mother. [*She takes her mother in her arms.*]

MRS. WARREN [*fondly*]  I brought you up well, didn't I, dearie?

VIVIE  You did.

MRS. WARREN  And you'll be good to your poor old mother for it, won't you?

VIVIE  I will, dear. [*Kissing her.*] Good-night.

MRS. WARREN [*with unction*]  Blessings on my own dearie darling—a mother's blessing! [*She embraces her daughter protectingly, instinctively looking upward as if to call down a blessing.*]

# ACT III

*In the Rectory garden next morning, with the sun shining and the birds in full song. The garden wall has a five-barred wooden gate, wide enough to admit a carriage, in the middle. Beside the gate hangs a bell on a coiled spring, communicating with a pull outside. The carriage drive comes down the middle of the garden and then swerves to its left, where it ends in a little gravelled circus opposite the rectory porch. Beyond the gate is seen the dusty high road, parallel with the wall, bounded on the farther side by a strip of turf and an unfenced pine wood. On the lawn, between the house and the drive, is a clipped yew tree, with a garden bench in its shade. On the opposite side the garden is shut in by a box hedge; and there is a sundial on the turf, with an iron chair near it. A little path leads off through the box hedge, behind the sundial.*

*FRANK, seated on the chair near the sundial, on which he has placed the morning papers, is reading the Standard. His father comes from the house, red-eyed and shivery, and meets FRANK's eye with misgiving.*

FRANK [*looking at his watch*]   Half-past eleven. Nice hour for a rector to come down to breakfast!

REV. S.   Don't mock, Frank: don't mock. I'm a little—er—[*Shivering.*]——

FRANK   Off colour?

REV. S. [*repudiating the expression*]   No, sir: u n w e l l this morning. Where's your mother?

FRANK   Don't be alarmed: she's not here. Gone to town by the 11:13 with Bessie. She left several messages for you. Do you feel

equal to receiving them now, or shall I wait till you've breakfasted?

REV. S.    I h a v e  breakfasted, sir. I am surprised at your mother
going to town when we have people staying with us. They'll
think it very strange.

FRANK    Possibly she has considered that. At all events, if Crofts is
going to stay here, and you are going to sit up every night with
him until four, recalling the incidents of your fiery youth, it is
clearly my mother's duty, as a prudent housekeeper, to go up to
the stores and order a barrel of whisky and a few hundred
siphons.

REV. S.    I did not observe that Sir George drank excessively.

FRANK    You were not in a condition to, gov'nor.

REV. S.    Do you mean to say that I—

FRANK [calmly]    I never saw a beneficed clergyman less sober. The
anecdotes you told about your past career were so awful that I
really don't think Praed would have passed the night under your
roof if it hadn't been for the way my mother and he took to one
another.

REV. S.    Nonsense, sir. I am Sir George Crofts' host. I must talk to
him about something; and he has only one subject. Where is Mr.
Praed now?

FRANK    He is driving my mother and Bessie to the station.

REV. S.    Is Crofts up yet?

FRANK    Oh, long ago. He hasn't turned a hair: he's in much better practice than you—has kept it up ever since, probably. He's
taken himself off somewhere to smoke. [Frank resumes his paper.
The REV. S. turns disconsolately towards the gate; then comes back irresolutely.]

REV. S.    Er—Frank.

FRANK    Yes.

REV. S.    Do you think the Warrens will expect to be asked here
after yesterday afternoon?

FRANK    They've been asked already. Crofts informed us at breakfast that you told him to bring Mrs. Warren and Vivie over here to-day, and to invite them to make this house their home. It was after that communication that my mother found she must go to town by the 11:13 train.

REV. S. [*with despairing vehemence*]    I never gave any such invitation. I never thought of such a thing.

FRANK [*compassionately*]    How do you know, gov'nor, what you said and thought last night? Hallo! here's Praed back again.

PRAED [*coming in through the gate*]    Good morning.

REV. S.    Good morning. I must apologize for not having met you at breakfast. I have a touch of—of—

FRANK    Clergyman's sore throat, Praed. Fortunately not chronic.

PRAED [*changing the subject*]    Well, I must say your house is in a charming spot here. Really most charming.

REV. S.    Yes: it is indeed. Frank will take you for a walk, Mr. Praed, if you like. I'll ask you to excuse me: I must take the opportunity to write my sermon while Mrs. Gardner is away and you are all amusing yourselves. You won't mind, will you?

PRAED    Certainly not. Don't stand on the slightest ceremony with me.

REV. S.    Thank you. I'll—er—er—[*He stammers his way to the porch and vanishes into the house.*]

PRAED [*sitting down on the turf near FRANK, and hugging his ankles*] Curious thing it must be writing a sermon every week.

FRANK    Ever so curious, if h e did it. He buys 'em. He's gone for some soda water.

PRAED    My dear boy: I wish you would be more respectful to your father. You know you can be so nice when you like.

FRANK    My dear Praddy: you forget that I have to live with the governor. When two people live together—it don't matter whether they're father and son, husband and wife, brother and sister—they can't keep up the polite humbug which comes so easy for ten minutes on an afternoon call. Now the governor, who unites to many admirable domestic qualities the irresoluteness of a sheep and the pompousness and aggressiveness of a jackass—

PRAED    No, pray, pray, my dear Frank, remember! He is your father.

FRANK    I give him due credit for that. But just imagine his telling Crofts to bring the Warrens over here! He must have been ever so drunk. You know, my dear Praddy, my mother wouldn't stand Mrs. Warren for a moment. Vivie mustn't come here until she's gone back to town.

PRAED    But your mother doesn't know anything about Mrs. Warren, does she?

FRANK    I don't know. Her journey to town looks as if she did. Not that my mother would mind in the ordinary way: she has stuck like a brick to lots of women who had got into trouble. But they were all nice women. That's what makes the real difference. Mrs. Warren, no doubt, has her merits; but she's ever so rowdy; and my mother simply wouldn't put up with her. So—hallo! [*This exclamation is provoked by the reappearance of the clergyman, who comes out of the house in haste and dismay.*]

REV. S.    Frank: Mrs. Warren and her daughter are coming across the heath with Crofts: I saw them from the study windows. What a m I to say about your mother?

FRANK [*jumping up energetically*]    Stick on your hat and go out and say how delighted you are to see them; and that Frank's in the garden; and that mother and Bessie have been called to the bedside of a sick relative, and were ever so sorry they couldn't stop; and that you hope Mrs. Warren slept well; and—and—say any blessed thing except the truth, and leave the rest to Providence.

REV. S.    But how are we to get rid of them afterwards?

FRANK    There's no time to think of that now. Here! [*He bounds into the porch and returns immediately with a clerical felt hat, which he claps on his father's head.*] Now: off with you. Praed and I'll wait here, to give the thing an unpremeditated air. [*The clergyman, dazed, but obedient, hurries off through the gate. PRAED gets up from the turf, and dusts himself.*]

FRANK    We must get that old lady back to town somehow, Praed. Come! honestly, dear Praddy, do you like seeing them together—Vivie and the old lady?

PRAED    Oh, why not?

FRANK [*his teeth on edge*]    Don't it make your flesh creep ever so little?—that wicked old devil, up to every villainy under the sun, I'll swear, and Vivie—ugh!

PRAED    Hush, pray. They're coming. [*The clergyman and CROFTS are seen coming along the road, followed by MRS. WARREN and VIVIE walking affectionately together.*]

FRANK    Look: she actually has her arm round the old woman's waist. It's her right arm: she began it. She's gone sentimental, by God! Ugh! ugh! Now do you feel the creeps? [*The clergyman opens the gate; and MRS. WARREN and VIVIE pass him and stand in the middle of the garden looking at the house. FRANK, in an ecstasy of dissimulation, turns gaily to MRS. WARREN, exclaiming*] Ever so delighted to see you, Mrs. Warren. This quiet old rectory garden becomes you perfectly.

MRS. WARREN    Well, I never! Did you hear that, George? He says I look well in a quiet old rectory garden.

REV. S. [*still holding the gate for CROFTS, who loafs through it, heavily bored*]    You look well everywhere, Mrs. Warren.

FRANK    Bravo, gov'nor! Now look here: let's have an awful jolly time of it before lunch. First let's see the church. Everyone has to do that. It's a regular old thirteenth century church, you know: the gov'nor's ever so fond of it, because he got up a restoration fund and had it completely rebuilt six years ago. Praed will be able to show its points.

REV. S. [*mooning hospitably at them*]    I shall be pleased, I'm sure, if Sir George and Mrs. Warren really care about it.

MRS. WARREN    Oh, come along and get it over. It'll do George good: I'll lay h e doesn't trouble church much.

CROFTS [*turning back towards the gate*]  I've no objection.

REV. S.   Not that way. We go through the fields, if you don't mind. Round here. [*He leads the way by the little path through the box hedge.*]

CROFTS   Oh, all right. [*He goes with the parson. PRAED follows with MRS. WARREN. VIVIE does not stir, but watches them until they have gone, with all the lines of purpose in her face marking it strongly.*]

FRANK   Ain't you coming?

VIVIE   No. I want to give you a warning, Frank. You were making fun of my mother just now when you said that about the rectory garden. That is barred in future. Please treat my mother with as much respect as you treat your own.

FRANK   My dear Viv: she wouldn't appreciate it. She's not like my mother: the same treatment wouldn't do for both cases. But what on earth has happened to you? Last night we were perfectly agreed as to your mother and her set. This morning I find you attitudinizing sentimentally with your arm round your parent's waist.

VIVIE [*flushing*]   Attitudinizing!

FRANK   That was how it struck me. First time I ever saw you do a second-rate thing.

VIVIE [*controlling herself*]   Yes, Frank: there has been a change; but I don't think it a change for the worse. Yesterday I was a little prig.

FRANK   And to-day?

VIVIE [*wincing; then looking at him steadily*]   To-day I know my mother better than you do.

FRANK   Heaven forbid!

VIVIE   What do you mean?

FRANK   Viv; there's a freemasonry among thoroughly immoral people that you know nothing of. You've too much character. T h a t ' s  the bond between your mother and me: that's why I know her better than you'll ever know her.

VIVIE   You are wrong: you know nothing about her. If you knew the circumstances against which my mother had to struggle—

FRANK   [*adroitly finishing the sentence for her*]   I should know why she is what she is, shouldn't I? What difference would that make? Circumstances or no circumstances, Viv, you won't be able to stand your mother.

VIVIE   [*very angry*]   Why not?

FRANK   Because she's an old wretch, Viv. If you ever put your arm round her waist in my presence again, I'll shoot myself there and then as a protest against an exhibition which revolts me.

VIVIE   Must I choose between dropping your acquaintance and dropping my mother's?

FRANK   [*gracefully*]   That would put the old lady at ever such a disadvantage. No, Viv: your infatuated little boy will have to stick to you in any case. But he's all the more anxious that you shouldn't make mistakes. It's no use, Viv: your mother's impossible. She may be a good sort; but she's a bad lot, a very bad lot.*

VIVIE   [*hotly*]   Frank—! [*He stands his ground. She turns away and sits down on the bench under the yew tree, struggling to recover her self-command. Then she says*] Is she to be deserted by all the world because she's what you call a bad lot? Has she no right to live?

FRANK   No fear of that, Viv: s h e won't ever be deserted. [*He sits on the bench beside her.*]

VIVIE   But I am to desert her, I suppose.

FRANK   [*babyishly, lulling her and making love to her with his voice*] Mustn't go live with her. Little family group of mother and daughter wouldn't be a success. Spoil o u r little group.

VIVIE   [*falling under the spell*]   What little group?

FRANK   The babes in the wood:[7] Vivie and little Frank. [*He slips his arm round her waist and nestles against her like a weary child.*] Let's go and get covered up with leaves.

---

*An immoral person.

VIVIE [*rhythmically, rocking him like a nurse*]    Fast asleep, hand in hand, under the trees.

FRANK    The wise little girl with her silly little boy.

VIVIE    The dear little boy with his dowdy* little girl.

FRANK    Ever so peaceful, and relieved from the imbecility of the little boy's father and the questionableness of the little girl's—

VIVIE [*smothering the word against her breast*]    Sh-sh-sh-sh! little girl wants to forget all about her mother. [*They are silent for some moments, rocking one another. Then VIVIE wakes up with a shock, exclaiming*] What a pair of fools we are! Come: sit up. Gracious! your hair. [*She smooths it.*] I wonder do all grown up people play in that childish way when nobody is looking. I never did it when I was a child.

FRANK    Neither did I. You are my first playmate. [*He catches her hand to kiss it, but checks himself to look round first. Very unexpectedly he sees CROFTS emerging from the box hedge.*] Oh, damn!

VIVIE    Why damn, dear?

FRANK [*whispering*]    Sh! Here's this brute Crofts. [*He sits farther away from her with an unconcerned air.*]

VIVIE    Don't be rude to him, Frank. I particularly wish to be polite to him. It will please my mother. [*FRANK makes a wry face.*]

CROFTS    Could I have a few words with you, Miss Vivie?

VIVIE    Certainly.

CROFTS [*to FRANK*]    You'll excuse me, Gardner. They're waiting for you in the church, if you don't mind.

FRANK [*rising*]    Anything to oblige you, Crofts—except church. If you want anything, Vivie, ring the gate bell, and a domestic will appear. [*He goes into the house with unruffled suavity.*]

CROFTS [*watching him with a crafty air as he disappears, and speaking to VIVIE with an assumption of being on privileged terms with her*]    Pleasant young fellow that, Miss Vivie.    Pity he has no money, isn't it?

---

*Unstylish, untidy.

VIVIE   Do you think so?

CROFTS   Well, what's he to do? No profession, no property. What's he good for?

VIVIE   I realize his disadvantages, Sir George.

CROFTS   [*a little taken aback at being so precisely interpreted*]   Oh, it's not that. But while we're in this world we're in it; and money's money. [*VIVIE does not answer.*] Nice day, isn't it?

VIVIE   [*with scarcely veiled contempt for this effort at conversation*]   Very.

CROFTS   [*with brutal good humor, as if he liked her pluck*]   Well, that's not what I came to say. [*Affecting frankness.*] Now listen, Miss Vivie. I'm quite aware that I'm not a young lady's man.

VIVIE   Indeed, Sir George?

CROFTS   No; and to tell you the honest truth, I don't want to be either. But when I say a thing I mean it; when I feel sentiment I feel it in earnest; and what I value I pay hard money for. That's the sort of man I am.

VIVIE   It does you great credit, I'm sure.

CROFTS   Oh, I don't mean to praise myself. I have my faults, Heaven knows: no man is more sensible of that than I am. I know I'm not perfect: that's one of the advantages of being a middle-aged man; for I'm not a young man, and I know it. But my code is a simple one, and, I think, a good one. Honor between man and man; fidelity between man and woman; and no cant about this religion, or that religion, but an honest belief that things are making for good on the whole.

VIVIE   [*with biting irony*]   "A power, not ourselves, that makes for righteousness," eh?

CROFTS   [*taking her seriously*]   Oh, certainly, not ourselves, of course. Y o u  understand what I mean. [*He sits down beside her, as one who has found a kindred spirit.*] Well, now as to practical matters. You may have an idea that I've flung my money about; but I haven't: I'm richer to-day than when I first came into the property. I've used my knowledge of the world to invest my money in ways that other men have overlooked; and whatever else I may be, I'm a safe man from the money point of view.

VIVIE    It's very kind of you to tell me all this.

CROFTS    Oh, well, come, Miss Vivie: you needn't pretend you don't see what I'm driving at. I want to settle down with a Lady Crofts. I suppose you think me very blunt, eh?

VIVIE    Not at all: I am much obliged to you for being so definite and business-like. I quite appreciate the offer: the money, the position, L a d y    C r o f t s, and so on. But I think I will say no, if you don't mind. I'd rather not. [*She rises, and strolls across to the sundial to get out of his immediate neighborhood.*]

CROFTS [*not at all discouraged, and taking advantage of the additional room left him on the seat to spread himself comfortably, as, if a few preliminary refusals were part of the inevitable routine of courtship*]    I'm in no hurry. It was only just to let you know in case young Gardner should try to trap you. Leave the question open.

VIVIE [*sharply*]    My no is final. I won't go back from it. [*She looks authoritatively at him. He grins; leans forward with his elbows on his knees to prod with his stick at some unfortunate insect in the grass; and looks cunningly at her. She turns away impatiently.*]

CROFTS    I'm a good deal older than you—twenty-five years—quarter of a century. I shan't live for ever; and I'll take care that you shall be well off when I'm gone.

VIVIE    I am proof against even that inducement, Sir George. Don't you think you'd better take your answer? There is not the slightest chance of my altering it.

CROFTS [*rising, after a final slash at a daisy, and beginning to walk to and fro*]    Well, no matter. I could tell you some things that would change your mind fast enough; but I won't, because I'd rather win you by honest affection. I was a good friend to your mother: ask her whether I wasn't. She'd never have made the money that paid for your education if it hadn't been for my advice and help, not to mention the money I advanced her. There are not many men would have stood by her as I have. I put not less than £40,000 into it, from first to last.

VIVIE [*staring at him*]   Do you mean to say you were my mother's business partner?

CROFTS   Yes. Now just think of all the trouble and the explanations it would save if we were to keep the whole thing in the family, so to speak. Ask your mother whether she'd like to have to explain all her affairs to a perfect stranger.

VIVIE   I see no difficulty, since I understand that the business is wound up, and the money invested.

CROFTS [*stopping short, amazed*]   Wound up! Wind up a business that's paying 35 per cent in the worst years! Not likely. Who told you that?

VIVIE [*her colour quite gone*]   Do you mean that it is still——? [*She stops abruptly, and puts her hand on the sundial to support herself. Then she gets quickly to the iron chair and sits down.*] What business are you talking about?

CROFTS   Well, the fact is, it's not what would be considered exactly a high-class business in my set—the county set, you know—o u r  set it will be if you think better of my offer. Not that there's any mystery about it: don't think that. Of course you know by your mother's being in it that it's perfectly straight and honest. I've known her for many years; and I can say of her that she'd cut off her hands sooner than touch anything that was not what it ought to be. I'll tell you all about it if you like. I don't know whether you've found in travelling how hard it is to find a really comfortable private hotel.

VIVIE [*sickened, averting her face*]   Yes: go on.

CROFTS   Well, that's all it is. Your mother has a genius for managing such things. We've got two in Brussels, one in Berlin, one in Vienna, and two in Buda-Pesth.* Of course there are others

---

*Old spelling for Budapest; reflects the fact that the modern city was once two separate cities.

besides ourselves in it; but we hold most of the capital; and your mother's indispensable as managing director. You've noticed, I daresay, that she travels a good deal. But you see you can't mention such things in society. Once let out the word hotel and everybody says you keep a public-house. You wouldn't like people to say that of your mother, would you? That's why we're so reserved about it. By the bye, you'll keep it to yourself, won't you? Since it's been a secret so long, it had better remain so.

VIVIE    And this is the business you invite me to join you in?

CROFTS    Oh, no. My wife shan't be troubled with business. You'll not be in it more than you've always been.

VIVIE    *I* always been! What do you mean?

CROFTS    Only that you've always lived on it. It paid for your education and the dress you have on your back. Don't turn up your nose at business, Miss Vivie: where would your Newnhams and Girtons be without it?

VIVIE [*rising, almost beside herself*]    Take care. I know what this business is.

CROFTS [*starting, with a suppressed oath*]    Who told you?

VIVIE    Your partner—my mother.

CROFTS [*black with rage*]    The old—[*VIVIE looks quickly at him. He swallows the epithet and stands swearing and raging foully to himself. But he knows that his cue is to be sympathetic. He takes refuge in generous indignation.*] She ought to have had more consideration for you. *I'd* never have told you.

VIVIE    I think you would probably have told me when we were married: it would have been a convenient weapon to break me in with.

CROFTS [*quite sincerely*]    I never intended that. On my word as a gentleman I didn't.

[*VIVIE wonders at him. Her sense of the irony of his protest cools and braces her. She replies with contemptuous self-possession.*]

VIVIE    It does not matter. I suppose you understand that when we leave here to-day our acquaintance ceases.

CROFTS  Why? Is it for helping your mother?

VIVIE  My mother was a very poor woman who had no reasonable choice but to do as she did. You were a rich gentleman; and you did the same for the sake of 35 per cent. You are a pretty common sort of scoundrel, I think. That is my opinion of you.

CROFTS [*after a stare—not at all displeased, and much more at his ease on these frank terms than on their former ceremonious ones*]  Ha, ha, ha, ha! Go it, little missie, go it: it doesn't hurt me and it amuses you. Why the devil shouldn't I invest my money that way? I take the interest on my capital like other people: I hope you don't think I dirty my own hands with the work. Come: you wouldn't refuse the acquaintance of my mother's cousin, the Duke of Belgravia, because some of the rents he gets are earned in queer ways. You wouldn't cut the Archbishop of Canterbury, I suppose, because the Ecclesiastical Commissioners have a few publicans and sinners among their tenants? Do you remember your Crofts scholarship at Newnham? Well, that was founded by my brother the M.P. He gets his 22 per cent out of a factory with 600 girls in it, and not one of them getting wages enough to live on. How d'ye suppose most of them manage? Ask your mother. And do you expect me to turn my back on 35 per cent when all the rest are pocketing what they can, like sensible men? No such fool! If you're going to pick and choose your acquaintances on moral principles, you'd better clear out of this country, unless you want to cut yourself out of all decent society.

VIVIE [*conscience stricken*]  You might go on to point out that I myself never asked where the money I spent came from. I believe I am just as bad as you.

CROFTS [*greatly reassured*]  Of course you are; and a very good thing, too! What harm does it do after all? [*Rallying her jocularly.*] So you don't think me such a scoundrel now you come to think it over. Eh?

VIVIE  I have shared profits with you; and I admitted you just now to the familiarity of knowing what I think of you.

CROFTS [*with serious friendliness*]   To be sure you did. You won't find me a bad sort: I don't go in for being super-fine intellectually; but I've plenty of honest human feeling; and the old Crofts breed comes out in a sort of instinctive hatred of anything low, in which I'm sure you'll sympathize with me. Believe me, Miss Vivie, the world isn't such a bad place as the croakers make out. So long as you don't fly openly in the face of society, society doesn't ask any inconvenient questions; and it makes precious short work of the cads who do. There are no secrets better kept than the secrets that everybody guesses. In the society I can introduce you to, no lady or gentleman would so far forget themselves as to discuss my business affairs or your mother's. No man can offer you a safer position.

VIVIE [*studying him curiously*]   I suppose you really think you're getting on famously with me.

CROFTS   Well, I hope I may flatter myself that you think better of me than you did at first.

VIVIE [*quietly*]   I hardly find you worth thinking about at all now. [*She rises and turns towards the gate, pausing on her way to contemplate him and say almost gently, but with intense conviction.*] When I think of the society that tolerates you, and the laws that protect you—when I think of how helpless nine out of ten young girls would be in the hands of you and my mother—the unmentionable woman and her capitalist bully—

CROFTS [*livid*]   Damn you!

VIVIE   You need not. I feel among the damned already. [*She raises the latch of the gate to open it and go out. He follows her and puts his hand heavily on the top bar to prevent its opening.*]

CROFTS [*panting with fury*]   Do you think I'll put up with this from you, you young devil, you?

VIVIE [*unmoved*]   Be quiet. Some one will answer the bell. [*Without flinching a step she strikes the bell with the back of her hand. It clangs harshly; and he starts back involuntarily. Almost immediately FRANK appears at the porch with his rifle.*]

FRANK [*with cheerful politeness*]   Will you have the rifle, Viv; or shall I operate?

VIVIE   Frank: have you been listening?

FRANK   Only for the bell, I assure you; so that you shouldn't have to wait. I think I showed great insight into your character, Crofts.

CROFTS   For two pins I'd take that gun from you and break it across your head.

FRANK [*stalking him cautiously*]   Pray don't. I'm ever so careless in handling firearms. Sure to be a fatal accident, with a reprimand from the coroner's jury for my negligence.

VIVIE   Put the rifle away, Frank: it's quite unnecessary.

FRANK   Quite right, Viv. Much more sportsmanlike to catch him in a trap. [*CROFTS, understanding the insult, makes a threatening movement.*] Crofts: there are fifteen cartridges in the magazine here; and I am a dead shot at the present distance at an object of your size.

CROFTS   Oh, you needn't be afraid. I'm not going to touch you.

FRANK   Ever so magnanimous of you under the circumstances! Thank you.

CROFTS   I'll just tell you this before I go. It may interest you, since you're so fond of one another. Allow me, Mister Frank, to introduce you to your half-sister, the eldest daughter of the Reverend Samuel Gardner. Miss Vivie: your half-brother. Good morning. [*He goes out through the gate and along the road.*]

FRANK [*after a pause of stupefaction, raising the rifle*]   You'll testify before the coroner that it's an accident, Viv. [*He takes aim at the retreating figure of CROFTS. VIVIE seizes the muzzle and pulls it round against her breast.*]

VIVIE   Fire now. You may.

FRANK [*dropping his end of the rifle hastily*]   Stop! take care. [*She lets it go. It falls on the turf.*] Oh, you've given your little boy such a turn. Suppose it had gone off—ugh! [*He sinks on the garden seat, overcome.*]

VIVIE    Suppose it had: do you think it would not have been a relief to have some sharp physical pain tearing through me?

FRANK [*coaxingly*]    Take it ever so easy, dear Viv. Remember: even if the rifle scared that fellow into telling the truth for the first time in his life, that only makes us the babes in the wood in earnest. [*He holds out his arms to her.*] Come and be covered up with leaves again.

VIVIE [*with a cry of disgust*]    Ah, not that, not that. You make all my flesh creep.

FRANK    Why, what's the matter?

VIVIE    Good-bye. [*She makes for the gate.*]

FRANK [*jumping up*]    Hallo! Stop! Viv! Viv! [*She turns in the gateway.*] Where are you going to? Where shall we find you?

VIVIE    At Honoria Fraser's chambers, 67 Chancery Lane, for the rest of my life. [*She goes off quickly in the opposite direction to that taken by CROFTS.*]

FRANK    But I say—wait—dash it! [*He runs after her.*]

# ACT IV

*Honoria Fraser's chambers in Chancery Lane. An office at the top of New Stone Buildings, with a plate-glass window, distempered\* walls, electric light, and a patent stove. Saturday afternoon. The chimneys of Lincoln's Inn and the western sky beyond are seen through the window. There is a double writing table in the middle of the room, with a cigar box, ash pans, and a portable electric reading lamp almost snowed up in heaps of papers and books. This table has knee holes and chairs right and left and is very untidy. The clerk's desk, closed and tidy, with its high stool, is against the wall, near a door communicating with the inner rooms. In the opposite wall is the door leading to the public corridor. Its upper panel is of opaque glass, lettered in black on the outside, "Fraser and Warren." A baize† screen hides the corner between this door and the window.*

*FRANK, in a fashionable light-colored coaching suit, with his stick, gloves, and white hat in his hands, is pacing up and down the office. Somebody tries the door with a key.*

FRANK [*calling*]   Come in. It's not locked.

[*VIVIE comes in, in her hat and jacket. She stops and stares at him.*]

VIVIE [*sternly*]   What are you doing here?

FRANK   Waiting to see you. I've been here for hours. Is this the way you attend to your business? [*He puts his hat and stick on the table, and perches himself with a vault on the clerk's stool, looking at her*

---

\*Whitewashed.
†Green, felt-like fabric that covers billiard tables.

*with every appearance of being in a specially restless, teasing, flippant mood.*]

VIVIE    I've been away exactly twenty minutes for a cup of tea. [*She takes off her hat and jacket and hangs them up behind the screen.*] How did you get in?

FRANK    The staff had not left when I arrived. He's gone to play football on Primrose Hill. Why don't you employ a woman, and give your sex a chance?

VIVIE    What have you come for?

FRANK    [*springing off the stool and coming close to her*]    Viv: let's go and enjoy the Saturday half-holiday somewhere, like the staff. What do you say to Richmond, and then a music hall, and a jolly supper?

VIVIE    Can't afford it. I shall put in another six hours' work before I go to bed.

FRANK    Can't afford it, can't we? Aha! Look here. [*He takes out a handful of sovereigns and makes them chink.*] Gold, Viv, gold!

VIVIE    Where did you get it?

FRANK    Gambling, Viv, gambling. Poker.

VIVIE    Pah! It's meaner than stealing it. No: I'm not coming. [*She sits down to work at the table, with her back to the glass door, and begins turning over the papers.*]

FRANK    [*remonstrating piteously*]    But, my dear Viv, I want to talk to you ever so seriously.

VIVIE    Very well: sit down in Honoria's chair and talk here. I like ten minutes' chat after tea. [*He murmurs.*] No use groaning: I'm inexorable. [*He takes the opposite seat disconsolately.*] Pass that cigar box, will you?

FRANK    [*pushing the cigar box across*]    Nasty womanly habit. Nice men don't do it any longer.

VIVIE    Yes: they object to the smell in the office; and we've had to take to cigarets. See! [*She opens the box and takes out a cigaret, which she lights. She offers him one; but he shakes his head with a wry face. She settles herself comfortably in her chair, smoking.*] Go ahead.

FRANK     Well, I want to know what you've done—what arrangements you've made.

VIVIE     Everything was settled twenty minutes after I arrived here. Honoria has found the business too much for her this year; and she was on the point of sending for me and proposing a partnership when I walked in and told her I hadn't a farthing in the world. So I installed myself and packed her off for a fortnight's holiday. What happened at Haslemere when I left?

FRANK     Nothing at all. I said you'd gone to town on particular business.

VIVIE     Well?

FRANK     Well, either they were too flabbergastcd to say anything, or else Crofts had prepared your mother. Anyhow, she didn't say anything; and Crofts didn't say anything; and Praddy only stared. After tea they got up and went; and I've not seen them since.

VIVIE [*nodding placidly with one eye on a wreath of smoke*]     That's all right.

FRANK [*looking round disparagingly*]     Do you intend to stick in this confounded place?

VIVIE [*blowing the wreath decisively away and sitting straight up*]     Yes. These two days have given me back all my strength and self-possession. I will never take a holiday again as long as I live.

FRANK [*with a very wry face*]     Mps! You look quite happy—and as hard as nails.

VIVIE [*grimly*]     Well for me that I am!

FRANK [*rising*]     Look here, Viv: we must have an cxplanation. We parted the other day under a complete misunderstanding.

VIVIE [*putting away the cigaret*]     Well: clear it up.

FRANK     You remember what Crofts said?

VIVIE     Yes.

FRANK     That revelation was supposed to bring about a complete change in the nature of our feeling for one another. It placed us on the footing of brother and sister.

VIVIE     Yes.

FRANK    Have you ever had a brother?

VIVIE    No.

FRANK    Then you don't know what being brother and sister feels like? Now I have lots of sisters: Jessie and Georgina and the rest. The fraternal feeling is quite familiar to me; and I assure you my feeling for you is not the least in the world like it. The girls will go t h e i r way; I will go mine; and we shan't care if we never see one another again. That's brother and sister. But as to you, I can't be easy if I have to pass a week without seeing you. That's not brother and sister. It's exactly what I felt an hour before Crofts made his revelation. In short, dear Viv, it's love's young dream.

VIVIE [*bitingly*]    The same feeling, Frank, that brought your father to my mother's feet. Is that it?

FRANK [*revolted*]    I very strongly object, Viv, to have my feelings compared to any which the Reverend Samuel is capable of harboring; and I object still more to a comparison of you to your mother. Besides, I don't believe the story. I have taxed my father with it, and obtained from him what I consider tantamount to a denial.

VIVIE    What did he say?

FRANK    He said he was sure there must be some mistake.

VIVIE    Do you believe him?

FRANK    I am prepared to take his word as against Crofts'.

VIVIE    Does it make any difference? I mean in your imagination or conscience; for of course it makes no real difference.

FRANK [*shaking his head*]    None whatever to m e.

VIVIE    Nor to me.

FRANK [*staring*]    But this is ever so surprising! I thought our whole relations were altered in your imagination and conscience, as you put it, the moment those words were out of that brute's muzzle.

VIVIE    No: it was not that. I didn't believe him. I only wish I could.

FRANK    Eh?

VIVIE     I think brother and sister would be a very suitable relation for us.

FRANK     You really mean that?

VIVIE     Yes. It's the only relation I care for, even if we could afford any other. I mean that.

FRANK     [*raising his eyebrows like one on whom a new light has dawned, and speaking with quite an effusion of chivalrous sentiment*]     My dear Viv: why didn't you say so before? I am ever so sorry for persecuting you. I understand, of course.

VIVIE     [*puzzled*]     Understand what?

FRANK     Oh, I'm not a fool in the ordinary sense—only in the Scriptural sense of doing all the things the wise man declared to be folly, after trying them himself on the most extensive scale. I see I am no longer Vivvums' little boy. Don't be alarmed: I shall never call you Vivvums again—at least unless you get tired of your new little boy, whoever he may be.

VIVIE     My new little boy!

FRANK     [*with conviction*]     Must be a new little boy. Always happens that way. No other way, in fact.

VIVIE     None that you know of, fortunately for you. [*Someone knocks at the door.*]

FRANK     My curse upon yon caller, whoe'er he be!

VIVIE     It's Praed. He's going to Italy and wants to say good-bye. I asked him to call this afternoon. Go and let him in.

FRANK     We can continue our conversation after his departure for Italy. I'll stay him out. [*He goes to the door and opens it.*] How are you, Praddy? Delighted to see you. Come in. [*PRAED, dressed for travelling, comes in, in high spirits, excited by the beginning of his journey.*]

PRAED     How do you do, Miss Warren. [*She presses his hand cordially, though a certain sentimentality in his high spirits jars on her.*] I start in an hour from Holborn Viaduct. I wish I could persuade you to try Italy.

VIVIE     What for?

PRAED    Why, to saturate yourself with beauty and romance, of course. [*VIVIE, with a shudder, turns her chair to the table, as if the work waiting for her there were a consolation and support to her. PRAED sits opposite to her. FRANK places a chair just behind VIVIE, and drops lazily and carelessly into it, talking at her over his shoulder.*]

FRANK    No use, Praddy. Viv is a little Philistine. She is indifferent to my romance, and insensible to my beauty.

VIVIE    Mr. Praed: once for all, there is no beauty and no romance in life for me. Life is what it is; and I am prepared to take it as it is.

PRAED    [*enthusiastically*]    You will not say that if you come to Verona and on to Venice. You will cry with delight at living in such a beautiful world.

FRANK    This is most eloquent, Praddy. Keep it up.

PRAED    Oh, I assure you *I* have cried—I shall cry again, I hope—at fifty! At your age, Miss Warren, you would not need to go so far as Verona. Your spirits would absolutely fly up at the mere sight of Ostend. You would be charmed with the gaiety, the vivacity, the happy air of Brussels. [*VIVIE recoils.*] What's the matter?

FRANK    Hallo, Viv!

VIVIE    [*to PRAED with deep reproach*]    Can you find no better example of your beauty and romance than Brussels to talk to me about?

PRAED    [*puzzled*]    Of course it's very different from Verona. I don't suggest for a moment that—

VIVIE    [*bitterly*]    Probably the beauty and romance come to much the same in both places.

PRAED    [*completely sobered and much concerned*]    My dear Miss Warren: I—[*looking enquiringly at FRANK*] Is anything the matter?

FRANK    She thinks your enthusiasm frivolous, Praddy. She's had ever such a serious call.

VIVIE    [*sharply*]    Hold your tongue, Frank. Don't be silly.

FRANK    [*calmly*]    Do you call this good manners, Praed?

PRAED    [*anxious and considerate*]    Shall I take him away, Miss Warren? I feel sure we have disturbed you at your work. [*He is about to rise.*]

VIVIE   Sit down: I'm not ready to go back to work yet. You both think I have an attack of nerves. Not a bit of it. But there are two subjects I want dropped, if you don't mind. One of them [*to FRANK*] is love's young dream in any shape or form: the other [*to PRAED*] is the romance and beauty of life, especially as exemplified by the gaiety of Brussels. You are welcome to any illusions you may have left on these subjects: I have none. If we three are to remain friends, I must be treated as a woman of business, permanently single [*to FRANK*] and permanently unromantic [*to PRAED*].

FRANK   I also shall remain permanently single until you change your mind. Praddy: change the subject. Be eloquent about something else.

PRAED [*diffidently*]   I'm afraid there's nothing else in the world that I c a n talk about. The Gospel of Art[8] is the only one I can preach. I know Miss Warren is a great devotee of the Gospel of Getting On; but we can't discuss that without hurting your feelings, Frank, since you are determined not to get on.

FRANK   Oh, don't mind my feelings. Give me some improving advice by all means; it does me ever so much good. Have another try to make a successful man of me, Viv. Come: let's have it all: energy, thrift, foresight, self-respect, character. Don't you hate people who have no character, Viv?

VIVIE [*wincing*]   Oh, stop: stop: let us have no more of that horrible cant. Mr. Praed: if there are really only those two gospels in the world, we had better all kill ourselves; for the same taint is in both, through and through.

FRANK [*looking critically at her*]   There is a touch of poetry about you to-day, Viv, which has hitherto been lacking.

PRAED [*remonstrating*]   My dear Frank: aren't you a little unsympathetic?

VIVIE [*merciless to herself*]    No: it's good for me. It keeps me from being sentimental.

FRANK [*bantering her*]    Checks your strong natural propensity that way, don't it?

VIVIE [*almost hysterically*]    Oh, yes: go on: don't spare me. I was sentimental for one moment in my life—beautifully sentimental—by moonlight; and now—

FRANK [*quickly*]    I say, Viv: take care. Don't give yourself away.

VIVIE    Oh, do you think Mr. Praed does not know all about my mother? [*Turning on PRAED.*] You had better have told me that morning, Mr. Praed. You are very old-fashioned in your delicacies, after all.

PRAED    Surely it is you who are a little old-fashioned in your prejudices, Miss Warren. I feel bound to tell you, speaking as an artist, and believing that the most intimate human relationships are far beyond and above the scope of the law, that though I know that your mother is an unmarried woman, I do not respect her the less on that account. I respect her more.

FRANK [*airily*]    Hear, hear!

VIVIE [*staring at him*]    Is that a l l you know?

PRAED    Certainly that is all.

VIVIE    Then you neither of you know anything. Your guesses are innocence itself compared to the truth.

PRAED [*startled and indignant, preserving his politeness with an effort*]    I hope not. [*More emphatically.*] I hope not, Miss Warren. [*FRANK's face shows that he does not share PRAED's incredulity. VIVIE utters an exclamation of impatience. PRAED's chivalry droops before their conviction. He adds, slowly*] If there is anything worse—that is, anything else— are you sure you are right to tell us, Miss Warren?

VIVIE    I am sure that if I had the courage I should spend the rest of my life in telling it to everybody—in stamping and branding it into them until they felt their share in its shame and horror as I feel mine. There is nothing I despise more than the wicked convention that protects these things by forbidding a woman to mention them. And yet I can't tell you. The two infamous words that describe what my mother is are ringing in my ears and struggling on my tongue; but I can't utter them: my instinct is too strong for me. [*She buries her face in her hands. The two men, astonished, stare at one another and then at her. She raises her head again desperately and takes a sheet of paper and a pen.*] Here: let me draft you a prospectus.

FRANK   Oh, she's mad. Do you hear, Viv, mad. Come: pull yourself together.

VIVIE   You shall see. [*She writes.*] "Paid up capital: not less than £40,000 standing in the name of Sir George Crofts, Baronet, the chief shareholder." What comes next?—I forget. Oh, yes: "Premises at Brussels, Berlin, Vienna and Buda-Pesth. Managing director: Mrs. Warren;" and now don't let us forget h e r qualifications: the two words.* There! [*She pushes the paper to them.*] Oh, no: don't read it: don't! [*She snatches it back and tears it to pieces; then seizes her head in her hands and hides her face on the table. FRANK, who has watched the writing carefully over her shoulder, and opened his eyes very widely at it, takes a card from his pocket; scribbles a couple of words; and silently hands it to PRAED, who looks at it with amazement. FRANK then remorsefully stoops over VIVIE.*]

FRANK   [*whispering tenderly*]   Viv, dear: that's all right. I read what you wrote: so did Praddy. We understand. And we remain, as this leaves us at present, yours ever so devotedly. [*VIVIE slowly raises her head.*]

PRAED   We do, indeed, Miss Warren. I declare you are the most splendidly courageous woman I ever met. [*This sentimental compliment braces VIVIE. She throws it away from her with an impatient shake, and forces herself to stand up, though not without some support from the table.*]

FRANK   Don't stir, Viv, if you don't want to. Take it easy.

---

*When asked to identify the words, Shaw complied with "prostitute" and "procuress."

VIVIE    Thank you. You can always depend on me for two things, not to cry and not to faint. [*She moves a few steps towards the door of the inner rooms, and stops close to PRAED to say*] I shall need much more courage than that when I tell my mother that we have come to the parting of the ways. Now I must go into the next room for a moment to make myself neat again, if you don't mind.

PRAED    Shall we go away?

VIVIE    No: I'll be back presently. Only for a moment. [*She goes into the other room, PRAED opening the door for her.*]

PRAED    What an amazing revelation! I'm extremely disappointed in Crofts: I am indeed.

FRANK    I'm not in the least. I feel he's perfectly accounted for at last. But what a facer* for me, Praddy! I can't marry her now.

PRAED [*sternly*]    Frank! [*The two look at one another, FRANK unruffled, PRAED deeply indignant.*] Let me tell you, Gardner, that if you desert her now you will behave very despicably.

FRANK    Good old Praddy! Ever chivalrous! But you mistake: it's not the moral aspect of the case: it's the money aspect. I really can't bring myself to touch the old woman's money now!

PRAED    And was that what you were going to marry on?

FRANK    What else? *I* haven't any money, nor the smallest turn for making it. If I married Viv now she would have to support me; and I should cost her more than I am worth.

PRAED    But surely a clever, bright fellow like you can make something by your own brains.

FRANK    Oh, yes, a little. [*He takes out his money again.*] I made all that yesterday—in an hour and a half. But I made it in a highly speculative business. No, dear Praddy: even if Jessie and Georgina marry millionaires and the governor dies after cutting them off with a shilling, I shall have only four hundred a year. And he won't die until he's three score and ten: he hasn't origi-

---

*Unanticipated problem.

nality enough.[9] I shall be on short allowance for the next twenty years. No short allowance for Viv, if I can help it. I withdraw gracefully and leave the field to the gilded youth of England. So that's settled. I shan't worry her about it: I'll just send her a little note after we're gone. She'll understand.

PRAED [*grasping his hand*]   Good fellow, Frank! I heartily beg your pardon. But must you never see her again?

FRANK   Never see her again! Hang it all, be reasonable. I shall come along as often as possible, and be her brother. I cannot understand the absurd consequences you romantic people expect from the most ordinary transactions. [*A knock at the door.*] I wonder who this is. Would you mind opening the door? If it's a client it will look more respectable than if I appeared.

PRAED   Certainly. [*He goes to the door and opens it. FRANK sits down in VIVIE's chair to scribble a note.*] My dear Kitty: come in, come in.
   [*MRS. WARREN comes in, looking apprehensively round for VIVIE. She has done her best to make herself matronly and dignified. The brilliant hat is replaced by a sober bonnet, and the gay blouse covered by a costly black silk mantle. She is pitiably anxious and ill at ease—evidently panic-stricken.*]

MRS. WARREN [*to FRANK*]   What! Y o u ' r e here, are you?

FRANK [*turning in his chair from his writing, but not rising*]*   Here, and charmed to see you. You come like a breath of spring.

MRS. WARREN   Oh, get out with your nonsense. [*In a low voice.*] Where's Vivie?
   [*FRANK points expressively to the door of the inner room, but says nothing.*]

MRS. WARREN [*sitting down suddenly and almost beginning to cry*] Praddy: won't she see me, don't you think?

PRAED   My dear Kitty: don't distress yourself. Why should she not?

---

*Because Frank now knows that she is not a lady.

MRS. WARREN    Oh, you never can see why not: you're too amiable. Mr. Frank:* did she say anything to you?

FRANK [ *folding his note*]    She must see you, i f [*very expressively*] you
wait until she comes in.

MRS. WARREN [ *frightened*]    Why shouldn't I wait?
[*FRANK looks quizzically at her; puts his note carefully on the ink-bot-
tle, so that VIVIE cannot fail to find it when next she dips her pen; then
rises and devotes his attention entirely to her.*]

FRANK    My dear Mrs. Warren: suppose you were a sparrow—
ever so tiny and pretty a sparrow hopping in the roadway—and
you saw a steam roller coming in your direction, would you wait
for it?

MRS. WARREN    Oh, don't bother me with your sparrows. What
did she run away from Haslemere like that for?

FRANK    I'm afraid she'll tell you if you wait until she comes back.

MRS. WARREN    Do you want me to go away?

FRANK    No. I always want you to stay. But I  a d v i s e  you to go
away.

MRS. WARREN    What! And never see her again!

FRANK    Precisely.

MRS. WARREN [ *crying again*]    Praddy: don't let him be cruel to
me. [*She hastily checks her tears and wipes her eyes.*] She'll be so
angry if she sees I've been crying.

FRANK [*with a touch of real compassion in his airy tenderness*]    You
know that Praddy is the soul of kindness, Mrs. Warren. Praddy:
what do y o u say? Go or stay?

PRAED [*to MRS. WARREN*]    I really should be very sorry to cause
you unnecessary pain; but I think perhaps you had better not
wait. The fact is—[*VIVIE is heard at the inner door.*]

FRANK    Sh! Too late. She's coming.

MRS. WARREN    Don't tell her I was crying. [*VIVIE comes in. She*

---

*Mrs. Warren's semi-formal form of address here takes note of Frank's changed
manners.

*stops gravely on seeing MRS. WARREN, who greets her with hysterical cheerfulness.*] Well, dearie. So here you are at last.

VIVIE    I am glad you have come: I want to speak to you. You said you were going, Frank, I think.

FRANK    Yes. Will you come with me, Mrs. Warren? What do you say to a trip to Richmond, and the theatre in the evening? There is safety in Richmond. No steam roller there.

VIVIE    Nonsense, Frank. My mother will stay here.

MRS. WARREN [*scared*]    I don't know: perhaps I'd better go. We're disturbing you at your work.

VIVIE [*with quiet decision*]    Mr. Praed: please take Frank away. Sit down, mother. [*MRS. WARREN obeys helplessly.*]

PRAED    Come, Frank. Good-bye, Miss Vivie.

VIVIE [*shaking hands*]    Good-bye. A pleasant trip.

PRAED    Thank you: thank you. I hope so.

FRANK [*to MRS. WARREN*]    Good-bye: you'd ever so much better have taken my advice. [*He shakes hands with her. Then airily to VIVIE*] Bye-bye, Viv.

VIVIE    Good-bye. [*He goes out gaily without shaking hands with her. PRAED follows. VIVIE, composed and extremely grave, sits down in Honoria's chair, and waits for her mother to speak. MRS. WARREN, dreading a pause, loses no time in beginning.*]

MRS. WARREN    Well, Vivie, what did you go away like that for without saying a word to me? How could you do such a thing! And what have you done to poor George? I wanted him to come with me; but he shuffled out of it. I could see that he was quite afraid of you. Only fancy: he wanted me not to come. As if [*trembling*] I should be afraid of you, dear. [*VIVIE's gravity deepens.*] But of course I told him it was all settled and comfortable between us, and that we were on the best of terms. [*She breaks down.*] Vivie: what's the meaning of this? [*She produces a paper from an envelope; comes to the table; and hands it across.*] I got it from the bank this morning.

VIVIE    It is my month's allowance. They sent it to me as usual the other day. I simply sent it back to be placed to your credit, and asked them to send you the lodgment receipt. In future I shall support myself.

MRS. WARREN [*not daring to understand*]  Wasn't it enough? Why didn't you tell me? [*With a cunning gleam in her eye.*] I'll double it: I was intending to double it. Only let me know how much you want.

VIVIE   You know very well that that has nothing to do with it. From this time I go my own way in my own business and among my own friends. And you will go yours. [*She rises.*] Good-bye.

MRS. WARREN [*appalled*]  Good-bye?

VIVIE   Yes: good-bye. Come: don't let us make a useless scene: you understand perfectly well. Sir George Crofts has told me the whole business.

MRS. WARREN [*angrily*]  Silly old— [*She swallows an epithet, and turns white at the narrowness of her escape from uttering it.*] He ought to have his tongue cut out. But I explained it all to you; and you said you didn't mind.

VIVIE [*steadfastly*]  Excuse me: I d o mind. You explained how it came about. That does not alter it.

[*MRS. WARREN, silenced for a moment, looks forlornly at VIVIE, who waits like a statue, secretly hoping that the combat is over. But the cunning expression comes back into MRS. WARREN's face; and she bends across the table, sly and urgent, half whispering.*]

MRS. WARREN   Vivie: do you know how rich I am?

VIVIE   I have no doubt you are very rich.

MRS. WARREN   But you don't know all that that means: you're too young. It means a new dress every day; it means theatres and balls every night; it means having the pick of all the gentlemen in Europe at your feet; it means a lovely house and plenty of servants; it means the choicest of eating and drinking; it means everything you like, everything you want, everything you can think of. And what are you here? A mere drudge, toiling and moiling early and late for your bare living and two cheap dresses

a year. Think over it. [*Soothingly.*] You're shocked, I know. I can
enter into your feelings; and I think they do you credit; but trust
me, nobody will blame you: you may take my word for that. I
know what young girls are; and I know you'll think better of it
when you've turned it over in your mind.

VIVIE   So that's how it's done, is it? You must have said all that to
many a woman, mother, to have it so pat.

MRS. WARREN [*passionately*]   What harm am I asking you to do?
[*VIVIE turns away contemptuously. MRS. WARREN follows her desperately.*]
Vivie: listen to me: you don't understand: you've been taught
wrong on purpose: you don't know what the world is really like.

VIVIE [*arrested*]   Taught wrong on purpose! What do you mean?

MRS. WARREN   I mean that you're throwing away all your
chances for nothing. You think that people are what they pretend
to be—that the way you were taught at school and college to
think right and proper is the way things really are. But it's not:
it's all only a pretence, to keep the cowardly, slavish, common
run of people quiet. Do you want to find that out, like other
women, at forty, when you've thrown yourself away and lost
your chances; or won't you take it in good time now from your
own mother, that loves you and swears to you that it's truth—
gospel truth? [*Urgently.*] Vivie: the big people, the clever people,
the managing people, all know it. They do as I do, and think what
I think. I know plenty of them. I know them to speak to, to introduce you to, to make friends of for you. I don't mean anything wrong: that's what you don't understand: your head is full
of ignorant ideas about me. What do the people that taught you
know about life or about people like me? When did they ever
meet me, or speak to me, or let anyone tell them about me?—
the fools! Would they ever have done anything for you if I hadn't
paid them? Haven't I told you that I want you to be respectable?
Haven't I brought you up to be respectable? And how can you
keep it up without my money and my influence and Lizzie's

friends? Can't you see that you're cutting your own throat as well as breaking my heart in turning your back on me?

VIVIE    I recognise the Crofts philosophy of life, mother. I heard it all from him that day at the Gardners'.

MRS. WARREN    You think I want to force that played-out old sot on you! I don't, Vivie: on my oath I don't.

VIVIE    It would not matter if you did: you would not succeed. [*MRS. WARREN winces, deeply hurt by the implied indifference towards her affectionate intention. VIVIE, neither understanding this nor concerning herself about it, goes on calmly*] Mother: you don't at all know the sort of person I am. I don't object to Crofts more than to any other coarsely built man of his class. To tell you the truth, I rather admire him for being strong-minded enough to enjoy himself in his own way and make plenty of money instead of living the usual shooting, hunting, dining-out, tailoring, loafing life of his set merely because all the rest do it. And I'm perfectly aware that if I'd been in the same circumstances as my aunt Liz, I'd have done exactly what she did. I don't think I'm more prejudiced or straitlaced than you: I think I'm less. I'm certain I'm less sentimental. I know very well that fashionable morality is all a pretence: and that if I took your money and devoted the rest of my life to spending it fashionably, I might be as worthless and vicious as the silliest woman could possibly want to be without having a word said to me about it. But I don't want to be worthless. I shouldn't enjoy trotting about the park to advertise my dressmaker and carriage builder, or being bored at the opera to show off a shop windowful of diamonds.

MRS. WARREN [*bewildered*]    But—

VIVIE    Wait a moment: I've not done. Tell me why you continue your business now that you are independent of it. Your sister, you told me, has left all that behind her. Why don't you do the same?

MRS. WARREN    Oh, it's all very easy for Liz: she likes good society, and has the air of being a lady. Imagine me in a cathedral town! Why, the very rooks in the trees would find me out even if I could stand the dulness of it. I must have work and excitement, or I should go melancholy mad. And what else is there for me to do? The life suits me: I'm fit for it and not for anything else. If I didn't do it somebody else would; so I don't do any real harm by it. And then it brings in money; and I like making money. No: it's no use: I can't give it up—not for anybody. But what need you know about it? I'll never mention it. I'll keep Crofts away. I'll not trouble you much: you see I have to be constantly running about from one place to another. You'll be quit of me altogether when I die.

VIVIE    No: I am my mother's daughter. I am like you: I must have work, and must make more money than I spend. But my work is not your work, and my way not your way. We must part. It will not make much difference to us; instead of meeting one another for perhaps a few months in twenty years, we shall never meet: that's all.

MRS. WARREN [*her voice stifled in tears*]    Vivie: I meant to have been more with you: I did indeed.

VIVIE    It's no use, mother: I am not to be changed by a few cheap tears and entreaties any more than you are, I dare say.

MRS. WARREN [*wildly*]    Oh, you call a mother's tears cheap.

VIVIE    They cost you nothing; and you ask me to give you the peace and quietness of my whole life in exchange for them. What use would my company be to you if you could get it? What have we two in common that could make either of us happy together?

MRS. WARREN [*lapsing recklessly into her dialect*]    We're mother and daughter. I want my daughter. I've a right to you. Who is to care for me when I'm old? Plenty of girls have taken to me like daughters and cried at leaving me; but I let them all go because I had you to look forward to. I kept myself lonely for you. You've no right to turn on me now and refuse to do your duty as a daughter.

VIVIE [*jarred and antagonized by the echo of the slums in her mother's voice*]   My duty as a daughter! I thought we should come to that presently. Now once for all, mother, you want a daughter and Frank wants a wife. I don't want a mother; and I don't want a husband. I have spared neither Frank nor myself in sending him about his business. Do you think I will spare  y o u?

MRS. WARREN [*violently*]   Oh, I know the sort you are—no mercy for yourself or anyone else. *I* know. My experience has done that for me anyhow: I can tell the pious, canting, hard, self-ish woman when I meet her. Well, keep yourself to yourself: *I* don't want you. But listen to this. Do you know what I would do with you if you were a baby again—aye, as sure as there's a Heaven above us?

VIVIE   Strangle me, perhaps.

MRS. WARREN   No: I'd bring you up to be a real daughter to me, and not what you are now, with your pride and your preju-dices and the college education you stole from me—yes, stole: deny it if you can: what was it but stealing? I'd bring you up in my own house, so I would.

VIVIE [*quietly*]   In one of your own houses.

MRS. WARREN [*screaming*]   Listen to her! listen to how she spits on her mother's grey hairs! Oh, may you live to have your own daughter tear and trample on you as you have trampled on me. And you will: you will. No woman ever had luck with a mother's curse on her.

VIVIE   I wish you wouldn't rant, mother. It only hardens me. Come: I suppose I am the only young woman you ever had in your power that you did good to. Don't spoil it all now.

MRS. WARREN   Yes. Heaven forgive me, it's true; and you are the only one that ever turned on me. Oh, the injustice of it, the injustice, the injustice! I always wanted to be a good woman. I tried honest work; and I was slave-driven until I cursed the day I ever heard of honest work. I was a good mother; and because I made my daughter a good woman she turns me out as if I was a leper. Oh, if I only had my life to live over again! I'd talk to that lying clergyman in the school. From this time forth, so help me Heaven in my last hour, I'll do wrong and nothing but wrong. And I'll prosper on it.

VIVIE    Yes: it's better to choose your line and go through with it. If I had been you, mother, I might have done as you did; but I should not have lived one life and believed in another. You are a conventional woman at heart. That is why I am bidding you good-bye now. I am right, am I not?

MRS. WARREN [*taken aback*]    Right to throw away all my money!

VIVIE    No: right to get rid of you? I should be a fool not to? Isn't that so?

MRS. WARREN [*sulkily*]    Oh, well, yes, if you come to that, I suppose you are. But Lord help the world if everybody took to doing the right thing! And now I'd better go than stay where I'm not wanted. [*She turns to the door.*]

VIVIE [*kindly*]    Won't you shake hands?

MRS. WARREN [*after looking at her fiercely for a moment with a savage impulse to strike her*]    No, thank you. Good-bye.

VIVIE [*matter-of-factly*]    Good-bye. [*MRS. WARREN goes out, slamming the door behind her. The strain on VIVIE's face relaxes; her grave expression breaks up into one of joyous content; her breath goes out in a half sob, half laugh of intense relief. She goes buoyantly to her place at the writing-table; pushes the electric lamp out of the way; pulls over a great sheaf of papers; and is in the act of dipping her pen in the ink when she finds FRANK's note. She opens it unconcernedly and reads it quickly, giving a little laugh at some quaint turn of expression in it.*] And good-bye, Frank. [*She tears the note up and tosses the pieces into the wastepaper basket without a second thought. Then she goes at her work with a plunge, and soon becomes absorbed in her figures.*][10]

# CANDIDA

# PREFACE

READERS OF THE DISCOURSE with which the preceding volume is prefaced will remember that I turned my hand to playwriting when a great deal of talk about "the New Drama," and the actual establishment of a "New Theatre" (the Independent), threatened to end in the humiliating discovery that "the New Drama," in England at least, was a figment of the revolutionary imagination. This was not to be endured. I had rashly taken up the case; and rather than let it collapse, I manufactured the evidence.

Man is a creature of habit. You cannot write three plays and then stop. Besides, the "New" movement did not stop. In 1894, some public spirited person,* then as now unknown to me, declared that the London theatres were intolerable, and financed a season of plays of the "new" order at the Avenue Theatre. There were, as available new dramatists, myself, discovered by the Independent Theatre (at my own suggestion); and Mr. John Todhunter, who had indeed been discovered before, but whose *Black Cat* had been one of the Independent's successes. Mr. Todhunter supplied *A Comedy of Sighs.* I, having nothing but "unpleasant" plays in my desk, hastily completed a first attempt at a pleasant one, and called it *Arms and the Man.* It passed for a success: that is, the first night was as brilliant as could be desired; and it ran from the 21st April to the 7th July. To witness it the public paid precisely £1777:5:6, an average of £23:2:5 per representation (including nine matinees), the average cost of each representation being about £80. A publisher receiving £1700 for a book would

---

*In later editions identified as Miss A. E. F. Horniman, a patroness of the New Theatre.

have made a satisfactory profit on it: the loss to the Avenue management was not far from £5000. This, however, need not altogether
discourage speculators in the "new" drama. If the people who were
willing to pay £1700 to see the play had all come within a fortnight
instead of straggling in during twelve weeks—and such people can
easily be trained to understand this necessity—the result would have
been financially satisfactory to the management and at least flattering
to the author. In America, where the play, after a fortnight in New
York, took its place simply as an item in the repertory of Mr. Richard
Mansfield, it has kept alive to this day. What the feelings of the unknown benefactor of the drama were on realizing that the net cost of
running an "artistically successful" theatre on the ordinary London
system was from £400 to £500 a week, I do not know. As for me, I
opened a very modest banking account, and became comparatively
Conservative in my political opinions.

In the autumn of 1894 I spent a few weeks in Florence, where I occupied myself with the religious art of the Middle Ages and its destruction by the Renascence. From a former visit to Italy on the same
business I had hurried back to Birmingham to discharge my duties as
musical critic at the Festival there. On that occasion there was a very
remarkable collection of the works of our "pre-Raphaelite" painters at
the public gallery. I looked at these, and then went into the Birmingham churches to see the windows of William Morris and Burne-
Jones. On the whole, Birmingham was more hopeful than the Italian
cities; for the art it had to shew me was the work of living men,
whereas modern Italy had, as far as I could see, no more connection
with Giotto than Port Said has with Ptolemy. Now I am no believer in
the worth of any "taste" for art that cannot produce what it professes
to love. When my subsequent visit to Italy found me practising the
dramatist's craft, the time was ripe for the birth of a pre-Raphaelite
play; for religion was alive again, coming back upon men—even clergymen—with such power that not the Church of England itself could
keep it out. Here my activity as a Socialist had placed me on sure and
familiar ground. To me the members of the Guild of St. Matthew[1]

were no more "High Church clergymen," Dr. Clifford no more "an eminent Nonconformist divine," than I was to them "an infidel." There is only one religion, though there are a hundred versions of it. We all had the same thing to say; and though some of us cleared our throats to say it by singing Secularist poems or republican hymns, we sang them to the music of "Onward, Christian Soldiers" or Haydn's "God Preserve the Emperor." But unity, however desirable in political agitations, is fatal to drama, since every drama must be the artistic presentation of a conflict. The end may be reconciliation or destruction, or, as in life itself, there may be no end; but the conflict is indispensable: no conflict, no drama. Now it is easy enough to dramatize the prosaic conflict of Christian Socialism with vulgar Unsocialism: for instance, in *Widowers' Houses* the clergyman, who never appears on the stage at all, is the only real opponent of the slum landlord. But the obvious conflicts of unmistakeable good with unmistakeable evil can only supply the crude drama of villain and hero, in which some absolute point of view is taken, and the dissentients* are treated by the dramatist as enemies to be deliberately and piously vilified. In such cheap wares I do not deal. Even in the propagandist dramas of the previous volume I have allowed every person his or her own point of view, and have, I hope, to the full extent of my understanding of him, been as sympathetic with Sir George Crofts as with any of the more genial and popular characters in the present volume. To distil the quintessential drama from pre-Raphaelitism, medieval or modern, it must be shewn in conflict with the first broken, nervous, stumbling attempts to formulate its own revolt against itself as it develops into something higher. A coherent explanation of any such revolt, addressed intelligibly and prosaically to the intellect, can only come when the work is done, and indeed *done with:* that is to say, when the development, accomplished, admitted, and assimilated, is only a story of yesterday. But long before any such understanding is reached, the

---

*Those who disagree.

eyes of men begin to turn towards the distant light of the new age. Discernible at first only by the eyes of the man of genius, it must be concentrated by him on the speculum* of a work of art, and flashed back from that into the eyes of the common man. Nay, the artist himself has no other way of making himself conscious of the ray: it is by a blind instinct that he keeps on building up his masterpieces until their pinnacles catch the glint of the unrisen sun. Ask him to explain himself prosaically, and you find that he "writes like an angel and talks like poor Poll,"[2] and is himself the first to make that epigram at his own expense. Mr. Ruskin has told us clearly enough what is in the pictures of Carpaccio and Bellini: let him explain, if he can, where we shall be when the sun that is caught by the summits of the work of his favorite Tintoretto, of his aversion Rembrandt, of Mozart, of Beethoven and Wagner, of Blake and of Shelley, shall have reached the valleys. Let Ibsen explain, if he can, why the building of churches and happy homes is not the ultimate destiny of Man, and why, at the bidding of the younger generations, he must mount beyond it to heights that now seem unspeakably giddy and dreadful to him, and from which the first climbers must fall and dash themselves to pieces. He cannot explain it: he can only shew it to you as a vision in the magic glass of his art work; so that you may catch his presentiment and make what you can of it. And this is the function that raises dramatic art above imposture and pleasure hunting, and enables the dramatist to be something more than a skilled liar and pandar.

Here, then, was the higher, but vaguer, timider vision, and the incoherent, mischievous, and even ridiculous, unpracticalness, which offered me a dramatic antagonist for the clear, bold, sure, sensible, benevolent, salutarily shortsighted Christian Socialist idealism. I availed myself of it in my drama *Candida*, the "drunken scene" in which has been much appreciated, I am told, in Aberdeen.† I pur-

---

*Reflecting surface; mirror.

†Shaw is joking about the alleged fondness for alcohol of the people of Aberdeen.

posely contrived the play in such a way as to make the expenses of representation insignificant; so that, without pretending that I could appeal to a very wide circle of playgoers, I could reasonably sound a few of our more enlightened managers as to an experiment with half a dozen afternoon performances. They admired the play so generously that I think that if any of them had been young enough to play the poet, my proposal might have been acceded to, in spite of many incidental difficulties. Nay, if only I had made the poet a cripple, or at least blind, so as to combine an easier disguise with a larger claim for sympathy, something might have been done. Mr. Richard Mansfield, who had won distinction for my *Arms and the Man* in America by his impersonation of Captain Bluntschli, went so far as to put the play actually into rehearsal before he would confess himself beaten by the physical difficulties of the part. But they did beat him; and *Candida* did not see the footlights until last year, when my old ally the Independent Theatre, making a propagandist tour through the provinces with *A Doll's House*, added *Candida* to its repertory, to the great astonishment of its audiences.

In an idle moment in 1895 I began the little scene called *The Man of Destiny*, which is hardly more than a bravura piece to display the virtuosity of the two principal performers. Its stage rights were secured by a hasty performance at Croydon last year, when, affronting the stupefied inhabitants of that suburb in the guise of a blood-and-thunder historical drama, in which Napoleon's suggestion that the innkeeper should kill somebody to provide him with red ink was received as a serious trait of the Corsican ogre, it drove my critical colleagues to the verge of downright mendacity—in fact, one or two went over it—to conceal the worst from the public, and spare the author's feelings.

In the meantime I had devoted the spare moments of 1896 to the composition of two more plays, only the first of which appears in this volume. *You Never Can Tell* was an attempt to comply with many requests for a play in which the much paragraphed "brilliancy" of *Arms and the Man* should be tempered by some consideration for the requirements of managers in search of fashionable comedies for West End theatres. I had no difficulty in complying, as I have always cast my plays in the ordinary practical comedy form in use at all the theatres; and far from taking an unsympathetic view of the popular demand for fun, for fashionable dresses, for a pretty scene or two, a little music, and even for a great ordering of drinks by people with an expensive air from an if-possible-comic waiter, I was more than willing to shew that the drama can humanize these things as easily as they, in undramatic hands, can dehumanize the drama. But it is one thing to give the theatre what it wants, and quite another for the theatre to do what it wants. The demands of the fashionable theatre are founded on an idealization of its own resources; and the test of rehearsal proved that in making my play acceptable I had made it, for the moment at least, impracticable. And so I reached the point at which, as narrated in the preface to the first volume, I resolved to avail myself of my literary expertness to put my plays before the public in my own way.

It will be noticed that I have not been driven to this expedient by any hostility on the part of our managers. I will not pretend that the modern actor-manager's rare combination of talent as an actor with capacity as a man of business can in the nature of things be often associated with exceptional critical insight. As a rule, by the time a manager has experience enough given him to be as safe a judge of plays as a Bond Street dealer is of pictures, he begins to be thrown out in his calculations by the slow but constant change of public taste, and by his own growing Conservatism. But his need for new plays is so great, and the handful of accredited authors so little able to keep pace with their commissions, that he is always apt to overrate rather than to underrate his discoveries in the way of new pieces by new authors. An original work by a man of genius like Ibsen may, of course, baffle him as it baffles many professed critics; but in the beaten path of drama no unacted works of merit, suitable to his purposes, have been discovered; whereas the production, at great expense, of very faulty plays written by novices (not "backers") is by no means an unknown event. Indeed, to anyone who can estimate, even vaguely, the complicated trouble, the risk of heavy loss, and the initial expense and thought involved by the production of a play, the ease with which dramatic authors, known and unknown, get their works performed must needs seem a wonder.

Only, authors must not expect managers to invest many thousands of pounds in plays, however fine (or the reverse), which will clearly not attract perfectly commonplace people. Playwriting and theatrical management, on the present commercial basis, are businesses like other businesses, depending on the patronage of great numbers of very ordinary customers. If the managers and authors study the wants of those customers they will succeed: if not, they will fail. A public-spirited manager, or author with a keen artistic conscience, may choose to pursue his business with the minimum of profit and the maximum of social usefulness by keeping as close as he can to the highest marketable limit of quality, and constantly feeling for an extension of that limit through the advance of popular culture. An unscrupulous manager or author may aim simply at the maximum of profit with the minimum of risk. These are the extreme limits of our system, represented in practice by our first rate managements on the one hand, and the syndicates which exploit pornographic musical farces at the other. Between them there is plenty of room for most talents to breathe freely: at all events there is a career, no harder of access than any cognate career, for all qualified playwrights who bring the manager what his customers want and understand, or even enough of it to induce them to swallow at the same time a great deal of what they neither want nor understand (the public is touchingly humble in such matters).

For all that, the commercial limits are too narrow for our social welfare. The theatre is growing in importance as a social organ. Bad theatres are as mischievous as bad schools or bad churches; for modern civilization is rapidly multiplying the numbers to whom the theatre is both school and church. Public and private life become daily more theatrical: the modern Emperor is "the leading man" on the

stage of his country; all great newspapers are now edited dramatically; the records of our law courts show that the spread of dramatic
consciousness is affecting personal conduct to an unprecedented extent, and affecting it by no means for the worse, except in so far as
the dramatic education of the persons concerned has been romantic:
that is, spurious, cheap and vulgar. In the face of such conditions
there can be no question that the commercial limits should be over-
stepped, and that the highest prestige, with a personal position of
reasonable security and comfort, should be attainable in theatrical
management by keeping the public in constant touch with the highest achievements of dramatic art. Our managers will not dissent to
this: the best of them are so willing to get as near that position as they
can without ruining themselves, that they can all point to honorable
losses incurred through aiming "over the heads of the public," and are
quite willing to face such a loss again as soon as a few popular successes enable them to afford it, for the sake of their reputation as
artists. But even if it were possible for them to educate the nation at
their own private cost, why should they be expected to do it? There
are much stronger objections to the pauperization of the public by
private doles than were ever entertained, even by the Poor Law
Commissioners of 1834, to the pauperization of private individuals
by public doles. If we want a theatre which shall be to the drama what
the National Gallery and British Museum are to painting and literature, we can get it by endowing it in the same way. The practical
question then is, where is the State to find such a nucleus for a national theatre as was presented in the case of the National Gallery by
the Angerstein collection, and in that of the British Museum by the
Cotton and Sloane collections? No doubt this is the moment for my
old ally the Independent Theatre, and its rival the New Century Theatre, to invite attention by a modest cough. But though I appreciate
the value of both, I perceive that they will be as incapable of attracting a State endowment as they already are of even uniting the supporters of "the New Drama." The proper course is to form an
influential committee, without any actors, critics, or dramatists on

it, and with as many persons of title as possible, for the purpose of approaching one of our leading managers with a proposal that he shall, under a guarantee against loss, undertake a certain number of afternoon performances of the class required by the committee, in addition to his ordinary business. If the committee is influential enough, the offer will be accepted. In that case, the first performance will be the beginning of a classic repertory for the manager and his company which every subsequent performance will extend. The formation of the repertory will go hand in hand with the discovery and habituation of a regular audience for it, like that of the Saturday Popular Concerts; and it will eventually become profitable for the manager to multiply the number of performances at his own risk. Finally it might become worth his while to take a second theatre and establish the repertory permanently in it. In the event of any of his classic productions proving a fashionable success, he could transfer it to his fashionable house and make the most of it there. Such managership would carry a knighthood with it; and such a theatre would be the needed nucleus for municipal or national endowment. I make the suggestion quite disinterestedly; for as I am not an academic person, I should not be welcomed as an unacted classic by such a committee; and cases like mine would still leave forlorn hopes like the Independent and New Century Theatres their reason for existing. The committee plan, I may remind its critics, has been in operation in London for two hundred years in support of Italian opera.

Returning now to the actual state of things, it will be seen that I have no grievance against our theatres. Knowing quite well what I was doing, I have heaped difficulties in the way of the performance of my plays by ignoring the majority of the manager's customers—nay, by positively making war on them. To the actor I have been much more considerate, using all my cunning to enable him to make the most of his methods; but though I have facilitated his business, I have occasionally taxed his intelligence very severely, making the stage effect depend not only on *nuances* of execution quite beyond the average skill produced by the routine of the English stage, in its present condition, but upon a perfectly simple and straightforward conception of states of mind which still seem cynically perverse to most people, or on a goodhumoredly contemptuous or profoundly pitiful attitude towards ethical conceptions which seem to them validly heroic or venerable. It is inevitable that actors should suffer more than any other class from the sophistication of their consciousness by romance; and my conception of romance as the great heresy to be rooted out from art and life—as the root of modern pessimism and the bane of modern self-respect, is far more puzzling to the performers than it is to the pit. The misunderstanding is complicated by the fact that actors, in their demonstrations of emotion, have made a second nature of stage custom, which is often very much out of date as a representation of contemporary life. Sometimes the stage custom is not only obsolete, but fundamentally wrong: for instance, in the simple case of laughter and tears, in which it deals too liberally, it is certainly not based on the fact, easily enough discoverable in real life, that tears in adult life are the natural expression of happiness, as laughter is at all ages the natural recognition of destruction, confusion, and ruin. When a comedy of mine is performed, it is nothing to me that the spectators laugh— any fool can make an audience laugh. I want to see how many of them, laughing or grave, have tears in their eyes. And this result cannot be achieved, even by actors who thoroughly understand my purpose, except through an artistic beauty of execution unattainable without long and arduous practice, and an effort which my plays probably do not seem serious enough to call forth.

Beyond the difficulties thus raised by the nature and quality of my plays, I have none to complain of. I have come upon no ill will, no inaccessibility, on the part of the very few managers with whom I have discussed them. As a rule, I find that the actor-manager is oversanguine, because he has the artist's habit of underrating the force of circumstances and exaggerating the power of the talented individual to prevail against them; whilst I have acquired the politician's habit of regarding the individual, however talented, as having no choice but to make the most of his circumstances. I half suspect that those managers who have had most to do with me, if asked to name the main obstacle to the performance of my plays, would unhesitatingly and unanimously reply "The author." And I confess that though as a matter of business I wish my plays to be performed, as a matter of instinct I fight against the inevitable misrepresentation of them with all the subtlety needed to conceal my ill will from myself as well as from the manager.

The real difficulty, of course, is the incapacity for serious drama of thousands of playgoers of all classes whose shillings and half guineas will buy as much in the market as if they delighted in the highest art. But with them I must frankly take the superior position. I know that many managers are wholly dependent on them, and that no manager is wholly independent of them; but I can no more write what they want than Joachim* can put aside his fiddle and oblige a happy company of beanfeasters† with a marching tune on the German concertina. They must keep away from my plays: that is all. There is no reason, however, why I should take this haughty attitude towards those representative critics whose complaint is that my plays, though not unentertaining, lack the elevation of sentiment and seriousness of purpose of Shakespear and Ibsen. They can find, under the surface brilliancy for which they give me credit, no coherent thought or sympathy, and accuse me, in various terms and degrees, of an inhuman and freakish wantonness; of preoccupation with "the seamy side of life;" of paradox, cynicism, and eccentricity, reducible, as some contend, to a trite formula of treating bad as good, and good as bad, important as trivial, and trivial as important, serious as laughable, and laughable as serious, and so forth. As to this formula I can only say that if any gentleman is simple enough to think that even a good comic opera can be produced by it, I invite him to try his hand, and see whether anything remotely resembling one of my plays will result.

---

*Famous violinist Joseph Joachim (1831–1907); Brahms's only violin concerto was written for him.

†Workers having a picnic in the country.

I could explain the matter easily enough if I chose; but the result would be that the people who misunderstand the plays would misunderstand the explanation ten times more. The particular exceptions taken are seldom more than symptoms of the underlying fundamental disagreement between the romantic morality of the critics and the realistic morality of the plays. For example, I am quite aware that the much criticized Swiss officer in *Arms and the Man* is not a conventional stage soldier. He suffers from want of food and sleep; his nerves go to pieces after three days under fire, ending in the horrors of a rout and pursuit; he has found by experience that it is more important to have a few bits of chocolate to eat in the field than cartridges for his revolver. When many of my critics rejected these circumstances as fantastically improbable and cynically unnatural, it was not necessary to argue them into common sense: all I had to do was to brain them, so to speak, with the first half dozen military authorities at hand, beginning with the present Commander in Chief. But when it proved that such unromantic (but all the more dramatic) facts implied to them a denial of the existence of courage, patriotism, faith, hope, and charity, I saw that it was not really mere matter of fact that was at issue between us. One strongly Liberal critic, who had received my first play with the most generous encouragement, declared, when *Arms and the Man* was produced, that I had struck a wanton blow at the cause of liberty in the Balkan Peninsula by mentioning that it was not a matter of course for a Bulgarian in 1885 to wash his hands every day. My Liberal critic* no doubt saw soon afterwards the squabble, reported all through Europe, between Stambouiloff and an eminent lady of the Bulgarian court who took exception to his neglect of his fingernails. After that came the news of his ferocious assassination, and a description of the room prepared for the reception of visitors by his widow, who draped it with black, and decorated it with photographs of the mutilated body of her husband. Here was a sufficiently sensational confirmation of the accu-

---

*Identified in later editions as Moy Thomas; he reviewed Shaw's early plays favorably.

racy of my sketch of the theatrical nature of the first apings of western civilization by spirited races just emerging from slavery. But it had no bearing on the real issue between my critic and myself, which was, whether the political and religious idealism which had inspired the rescue of these Balkan principalities from the despotism of the Turk, and converted miserably enslaved provinces into hopeful and gallant little states, will survive the general onslaught on idealism which is implicit, and indeed explicit, in *Arms and the Man* and the realistic plays of the modern school. For my part I hope not; for idealism, which is only a flattering name for romance in politics and morals, is as obnoxious to me as romance in ethics or religion. In spite of a Liberal Revolution or two, I can no longer be satisfied with fictitious morals and fictitious good conduct, shedding fictitious glory on overcrowding, disease, crime, drink, war, cruelty, infant mortality, and all the other commonplaces of civilization which drive men to the theatre to make foolish pretences that these things are progress, science, morals, religion, patriotism, imperial supremacy, national greatness and all the other names the newspapers call them. On the other hand, I see plenty of good in the world working itself out as fast as the idealist will allow it; and if they would only let it alone and learn to respect reality, which would include the beneficial exercise of respecting themselves, and incidentally respecting me, we should all get along much better and faster. At all events, I do not see moral chaos and anarchy as the alternative to romantic convention; and I am not going to pretend that I do to please the less clear-sighted people who are convinced that the world is only held together by the force of unanimous, strenuous, eloquent, trumpet-tongued lying. To me the tragedy and comedy of life lie in the consequences, sometimes terrible, sometimes ludicrous, of our persistent attempts to found our institutions on the ideals suggested to our imaginations by our half-satisfied passions, instead of on a genuinely scientific natural history. And with that hint as to what I am driving at, I withdraw and ring up the curtain.

# CANDIDA

## ACT I

*A fine October morning in the north east suburbs of London, a vast district many miles away from the London of Mayfair and St. James's, much less known there than the Paris of the Rue de Rivoli and the Champs Elysées, and much less narrow, squalid, fetid and airless in its slums; strong in comfortable, prosperous middle class life; wide streeted; myriad-populated; well-served with ugly iron urinals, Radical clubs, tram lines, and a perpetual stream of yellow cars; enjoying in its main thoroughfares the luxury of grass-grown "front gardens," untrodden by the foot of man save as to the path from the gate to the hall door; but blighted by an intolerable monotony of miles and miles of graceless, characterless brick houses, black iron railings, stony pavements, slaty roofs, and respectably ill dressed or disreputably poorly dressed people, quite accustomed to the place, and mostly plodding about somebody else's work, which they would not do if they themselves could help it. The little energy and eagerness that crop up shew themselves in cockney cupidity and business "push." Even the policemen and the chapels are not infrequent enough to break the monotony. The sun is shining cheerfully; there is no fog; and though the smoke effectually prevents anything, whether faces and hands or bricks and mortar, from looking fresh and clean, it is not banging heavily enough to trouble a Londoner.*

*This desert of unattractiveness has its oasis. Near the outer end of the Hackney Road is a park of 217 acres, fenced in, not by railings, but by a wooden paling, and containing plenty of greensward, trees, a lake*

*for bathers, flower beds with the flowers arranged carefully in patterns
by the admired cockney art of carpet gardening and a sandpit,
imported from the seaside for the delight of the children, but speedily
deserted on its becoming a natural vermin preserve for all the petty
fauna of Kingsland, Hackney and Hoxton. A bandstand, an unfinished
forum for religious, anti-religious and political orators, cricket pitches,
a gymnasium, and an old fashioned stone kiosk are among its
attractions. Wherever the prospect is bounded by trees or rising green
grounds, it is a pleasant place. Where the ground stretches flat to the
grey palings, with bricks and mortar, sky signs, crowded chimneys and
smoke beyond, the prospect makes desolate and sordid.*

*The best view of Victoria Park is from the front window of St.
Dominic's Parsonage, from which not a single chimney is visible. The
parsonage is a semi-detached villa with a front garden and a porch.
Visitors go up the flight of steps to the porch: tradespeople and members
of the family go down by a door under the steps to the basement, with a
breakfast room, used for all meals, in front, and the kitchen at the back.
Upstairs, on the level of the hall door, is the drawing-room, with its
large plate glass window looking on the park. In this room, the only
sitting-room that can be spared from the children and the family
meals, the parson, the Reverend James Mavor Morell does his work. He
is sitting in a strong round backed revolving chair at the right hand
end of a long table, which stands across the window, so that he can
cheer himself with the view of the park at his elbow. At the opposite end
of the table, adjoining it, is a little table only half the width of the
other, with a typewriter on it. His typist is sitting at this machine, with
her back to the window. The large table is littered with pamphlets,
journals, letters, nests of drawers, an office diary, postage scales and the
like. A spare chair for visitors having business with the parson is in the
middle, turned to his end. Within reach of his hand is a stationery case,
and a cabinet photograph in a frame. Behind him the right hand wall,
recessed above the fireplace, is fitted with bookshelves, on which an
adept eye can measure the parson's divinity and casuistry by a complete
set of Browning's poems and Maurice's Theological Essays,[3] and guess*

at his politics from a yellow backed *Progress and Poverty,** *Fabian Essays,*[4] *a Dream of John Ball,*† *Marx's Capital,* and half a dozen other literary landmarks in Socialism. Opposite him on the left, near the typewriter, is the door. Further down the room, opposite the fireplace, a bookcase stands on a cellaret, with a sofa near it. There is a generous fire burning; and the hearth, with a comfortable armchair and a japanned flower painted coal scuttle at one side, a miniature chair for a boy or girl on the other, a nicely varnished wooden mantelpiece, with neatly moulded shelves, tiny bits of mirror let into the panels, and a travelling clock in a leather case (the inevitable wedding present), and on the wall above a large autotype of the chief figure in Titian's Virgin of the Assumption, is very inviting. Altogether the room is the room of a good housekeeper, vanquished, as far as the table is concerned, by an untidy man, but elsewhere mistress of the situation. The furniture, in its ornamental aspect, betrays the style of the advertised "drawing-room suite" of the pushing suburban furniture dealer; but there is nothing useless or pretentious in the room. The paper and panelling are dark, throwing the big cheery window and the park outside into strong relief.

The Reverend James Mavor Morell is a Christian Socialist clergyman of the Church of England, and an active member of the Guild of St. Matthew and the Christian Social Union. A vigorous, genial, popular man of forty, robust and goodlooking, full of energy, with pleasant, hearty, considerate manners, and a sound, unaffected voice, which he uses with the clean, athletic articulation of a practised orator, and with a wide range and perfect command of expression. He is a first rate clergyman, able to say what he likes to whom he likes, to lecture people without setting himself up against them, to impose his authority on them without humiliating them, and to interfere in their business without impertinence. His well spring of spiritual enthusiasm

---

*The book *Progress and Poverty* (1879) was written by Henry George, an American and a leading socialist.

†The book *A Dream of John Ball* (1888) was written by William Morris; John Ball was a fourteenth-century priest and reformer.

*and sympathetic emotion has never run dry for a moment: he still eats and sleeps heartily enough to win the daily battle between exhaustion and recuperation triumphantly. Withal, a great baby, pardonably vain of his powers and unconsciously pleased with himself. He has a healthy complexion, a good forehead, with the brows somewhat blunt, and the eyes bright and eager, a mouth resolute, but not particularly well cut, and a substantial nose, with the mobile, spreading nostrils of the dramatic orator, but, like all his features, void of subtlety.*

*The typist, MISS PROSERPINE GARNETT, is a brisk little woman of about 30, of the lower middle class, neatly but cheaply dressed in a black merino skirt and a blouse, rather pert and quick of speech, and not very civil in her manner, but sensitive and affectionate. She is clattering away busily at her machine whilst MORELL opens the last of his morning's letters. He realizes its contents with a comic groan of despair.*

PROSERPINE     Another lecture?

MORELL     Yes. The Hoxton Freedom Group want me to address them on Sunday morning [*great emphasis on "Sunday," this being the unreasonable part of the business*]. What are they?

PROSERPINE     Communist Anarchists, I think.

MORELL     Just like Anarchists not to know that they can't have a parson on Sunday! Tell them to come to church if they want to hear me: it will do them good. Say I can only come on Mondays and Thursdays. Have you the diary there?

PROSERPINE [*taking up the diary*]     Yes.

MORELL     Have I any lecture on for next Monday?

PROSERPINE [*referring to diary*]     Tower Hamlets Radical Club.

MORELL     Well, Thursday then?

PROSERPINE     English Land Restoration League.

MORELL     What next?

PROSERPINE     Guild of St. Matthew on Monday. Independent Labor Party, Greenwich Branch, on Thursday. Monday, Social-Democratic Federation, Mile End Branch. Thursday, first Confirmation class— [*Impatiently*.] Oh, I'd better tell them you can't come. They're only half a dozen ignorant and conceited coster-mongers without five shillings between them.

MORELL [*amused*]    Ah; but you see they're near relatives of mine, Miss Garnett.

PROSERPINE [*staring at him*]    Relatives of yours!

MORELL    Yes: we have the same father—in Heaven.

PROSERPINE [*relieved*]    Oh, is that all?

MORELL [*with a sadness which is a luxury to a man whose voice expresses it so finely*]    Ah, you don't believe it. Everybody says it: nobody believes it—nobody. [*Briskly, getting back to business.*] Well, well! Come, Miss Proserpine, can't you find a date for the costers? What about the 25th?: that was vacant the day before yesterday.

PROSERPINE [*referring to diary*]    Engaged—the Fabian Society.

MORELL    Bother the Fabian Society! Is the 28th gone, too?

PROSERPINE    City dinner. You're invited to dine with the Founder's Company.

MORELL    That'll do; I'll go to the Hoxton Group of Freedom instead. [*She enters the engagement in silence, with implacable disparagement of the Hoxton Anarchists in every line of her face. MORELL bursts open the cover of a copy of The Church Reformer, which has come by post, and glances through Mr. Stewart Headlam's leader and the Guild of St. Matthew news. These proceedings are presently enlivened by the appearance of MORELL's curate, the Reverend Alexander Mill, a young gentleman gathered by MORELL from the nearest University settlement,\* whither he had come from Oxford to give the east end of London the benefit of his university training. He is a conceitedly well intentioned, enthusiastic, immature person, with nothing positively unbearable about him except a habit of speaking with his lips carefully closed for half an inch from each corner, a finicking articulation, and a set of horribly corrupt vowels, notably ow for o, this being his chief means of bring-*]

---

\*Settlements were organizations of university graduates designed to improve social conditions and help educate residents of poor sections of London.

*ing Oxford refinement to bear on Hackney vulgarity. MORELL, whom he has won over by a doglike devotion, looks up indulgently from The Church Reformer as he enters, and remarks*] Well, Lexy! Late again, as usual.

LEXY    I'm afraid so. I wish I could get up in the morning.

MORELL [*exulting in his own energy*]    Ha! ha! [*Whimsically*] Watch and pray, Lexy: watch and pray.

LEXY    I know. [*Rising wittily to the occasion*] But how can I watch and pray when I am asleep? Isn't that so, Miss Prossy?

PROSERPINE [*sharply*]    Miss Garnett, if you please.

LEXY    I beg your pardon—Miss Garnett.

PROSERPINE    You've got to do all the work to-day.

LEXY    Why?

PROSERPINE    Never mind why. It will do you good to earn your supper before you eat it, for once in a way, as I do. Come: don't dawdle. You should have been off on your rounds half an hour ago.

LEXY [*perplexed*]    Is she in earnest, Morell?

MORELL [*in the highest spirits—his eyes dancing*]    Yes. *I* am going to dawdle to-day.

LEXY    You! You don't know how.

MORELL [*heartily*]    Ha! ha! Don't I? I'm going to have this day all to myself—or at least the forenoon. My wife's coming back: she's due here at 11.45.

LEXY [*surprised*]    Coming back already—with the children? I thought they were to stay to the end of the month.

MORELL    So they are: she's only coming up for two days, to get some flannel things for Jimmy, and to see how we're getting on without her.

LEXY [*anxiously*]    But, my dear Morell, if what Jimmy and Fluffy had was scarlatina, do you think it wise—

MORELL    Scarlatina!—rubbish, German measles. I brought it into the house myself from the Pycroft Street School. A parson is like a doctor, my boy: he must face infection as a soldier must face bullets. [*He rises and claps Lexy on the shoulder.*] Catch the measles if you can, Lexy: she'll nurse you; and what a piece of luck that will be for you!—eh?

LEXY [*smiling uneasily*]   It's so hard to understand you about Mrs. Morell—

MORELL [*tenderly*]   Ah, my boy, get married—get married to a good woman; and then you'll understand. That's a foretaste of what will be best in the Kingdom of Heaven we are trying to establish on earth. That will cure you of dawdling. An honest man feels that he must pay Heaven for every hour of happiness with a good spell of hard, unselfish work to make others happy. We have no more right to consume happiness without producing it than to consume wealth without producing it. Get a wife like my Candida; and you'll always be in arrear with your repayment.

[*He pats LEXY affectionately on the back, and is leaving the room when LEXY calls to him.*]

LEXY   Oh, wait a bit: I forgot. [*MORELL halts and turns with the door knob in his hand.*] Your father-in-law is coming round to see you.

[*MORELL shuts the door again, with a complete change of manner.*]

MORELL [*surprised and not pleased*]   Mr. Burgess?

LEXY   Yes. I passed him in the park, arguing with somebody. He gave me good day and asked me to let you know that he was coming.

MORELL [*half incredulous*]   But he hasn't called here for—I may almost say for years. Are you sure, Lexy? You're not joking, are you?

LEXY [*earnestly*]   No, sir, really.

MORELL [*thoughtfully*]   Hm! Time for him to take another look at Candida before she grows out of his knowledge. [*He resigns himself to the inevitable, and goes out. LEXY looks after him with beaming, foolish worship.*]

LEXY   What a good man! What a thorough, loving soul he is!

[*He takes MORELL's place at the table, making himself very comfortable as he takes out a cigaret.*]

PROSERPINE [*impatiently, pulling the letter she has been working at off the typewriter and folding it*]    Oh, a man ought to be able to be fond of his wife without making a fool of himself about her.

LEXY [*shocked*]    Oh, Miss Prossy!

PROSERPINE [*rising busily and coming to the stationery case to get an envelope, in which she encloses the letter as she speaks*]    Candida here, and Candida there, and Candida everywhere! [*She licks the envelope.*] It's enough to drive anyone out of their senses [*thumping the envelope to make it stick*] to hear a perfectly commonplace woman raved about in that absurd manner merely because she's got good hair, and a tolerable figure.

LEXY [*with reproachful gravity*]    I think her extremely beautiful, Miss Garnett. [*He takes the photograph up; looks at it; and adds, with even greater impressiveness*]    E x t r e m e l y  beautiful. How fine her eyes are!

PROSERPINE    Her eyes are not a bit better than mine—now! [*He puts down the photograph and stares austerely at her.*] And you know very well that you think me dowdy and second rate enough.

LEXY [*rising majestically*]    Heaven forbid that I should think of any of God's creatures in such a way! [*He moves softly away from her across the room to the neighbourhood of the bookcase.*]

PROSERPINE    Thank you. That's very nice and comforting.

LEXY [*saddened by her depravity*]    I had no idea you had any feeling against Mrs. Morell.

PROSERPINE [*indignantly*]    I have no feeling against her. She's very nice, very good-hearted: I'm very fond of her and can appreciate her real qualities far better than any man can. [*He shakes his head sadly and turns to the bookcase, looking along the shelves for a volume. She follows him with intense pepperiness.*] You don't believe me? [*He turns and faces her. She pounces at him with spitfire energy.*] You think I'm jealous. Oh, what a profound knowledge of the human heart you have, Mr. Lexy Mill! How well you know the weaknesses of Woman, don't you? It must be so nice to be a man and have a fine penetrating intellect instead of mere emotions like us, and to know that the reason we don't share your amorous delusions is that we're all jealous of one another! [*She abandons him with a toss of her shoulders, and crosses to the fire to warm her hands.*]

LEXY    Ah, if you women only had the same clue to Man's strength that you have to his weakness, Miss Prossy, there would be no Woman Question.[5]

PROSERPINE [*over her shoulder, as she stoops, holding her hands to the blaze*]    Where did you hear Morell say that? You didn't invent it yourself: you're not clever enough.

LEXY    That's quite true. I am not ashamed of owing him that, as I owe him so many other spiritual truths. He said it at the annual conference of the Women's Liberal Federation. Allow me to add that though they didn't appreciate it, I, a mere man, did. [*He turns to the bookcase again, hoping that this may leave her crushed.*]

PROSERPINE [*putting her hair straight at the little panel of mirror in the mantelpiece*]    Well, when you talk to me, give me your own ideas, such as they are, and not his. You never cut a poorer figure than when you are trying to imitate him.

LEXY [*stung*]    I try to follow his example, not to imitate him.

PROSERPINE [*coming at him again on her way back to her work*]    Yes, you do: you i m i t a t e him. Why do you tuck your umbrella under your left arm instead of carrying it in your hand like anyone else? Why do you walk with your chin stuck out before you, hurrying along with that eager look in your eyes—you, who never get up before half past nine in the morning? Why do you say "knoaledge" in church, though you always say "knolledge" in private conversation! Bah! do you think I don't know? [*She goes back to the typewriter.*] Here, come and set about your work: we've wasted enough time for one morning. Here's a copy of the diary for to-day. [*She hands him a memorandum.*]

LEXY [*deeply offended*]    Thank you. [*He takes it and stands at the table with his back to her, reading it. She begins to transcribe her shorthand notes on the typewriter without troubling herself about his feelings. MR.*

*BURGESS enters unannounced. He is a man of sixty, made coarse and sordid by the compulsory selfishness of petty commerce, and later on softened into sluggish bumptiousness by overfeeding and commercial success. A vulgar, ignorant, guzzling man, offensive and contemptuous to people whose labor is cheap, respectful to wealth and rank, and quite sincere and without rancour or envy in both attitudes. Finding him without talent, the world has offered him no decently paid work except ignoble work, and he has become in consequence, somewhat hoggish. But he has no suspicion of this himself, and honestly regards his commercial prosperity as the inevitable and socially wholesome triumph of the ability, industry, shrewdness and experience in business of a man who in private is easygoing, affectionate and humorously convivial to a fault. Corporeally, he is a podgy man, with a square, clean shaven face and a square beard under his chin; dust colored, with a patch of grey in the centre, and small watery blue eyes with a plaintively sentimental expression, which he transfers easily to his voice by his habit of pompously intoning his sentences.*]

BURGESS [*stopping on the threshold, and looking round*]   They told me Mr. Morell was here.

PROSERPINE [*rising*]   He's upstairs. I'll fetch him for you.

BURGESS [*staring boorishly at her*]   You're not the same young lady as hused to typewrite for him?

PROSERPINE   No.

BURGESS [*assenting*]   No: she was young-er. [*MISS GARNETT stolidly stares at him; then goes out with great dignity. He receives this quite obtusely, and crosses to the hearth-rug, where he turns and spreads himself with his back to the fire.*] Startin' on your rounds, Mr. Mill?

LEXY [*folding his paper and pocketing it*]   Yes: I must be off presently.

BURGESS [*momentously*]   Don't let me detain you, Mr. Mill. What I come about is  p r i v a t e  between me and Mr. Morell.

LEXY [*huffily*]   I have no intention of intruding, I am sure, Mr. Burgess. G o o d morning.

BURGESS [*patronizingly*]   Oh, good morning to you. [*MORELL returns as LEXY is making for the door.*]

MORELL [*to LEXY*]    Off to work?

LEXY    Yes, sir.

MORELL [*patting him affectionately on the shoulder*]    Take my silk handkerchief and wrap your throat up. There's a cold wind. Away with you.

[*LEXY brightens up, and goes out.*]

BURGESS    Spoilin' your curates, as usu'l, James. Good mornin'. When I pay a man, an' 'is livin' depen's on me, I keep him in his place.

MORELL [*rather shortly*]    I always keep my curates in their places as my helpers and comrades. If you get as much work out of your clerks and warehousemen as I do out of my curates, you must be getting rich pretty fast. Will you take your old chair?

[*He points with curt authority to the armchair beside the fireplace; then takes the spare chair from the table and sits down in front of BURGESS.*]

BURGESS [*without moving*]    Just the same as hever, James!

MORELL    When you last called—it was about three years ago, I think—you said the same thing a little more frankly. Your exact words then were: "Just as big a fool as ever, James?"[6]

BURGESS [*soothingly*]    Well, perhaps I did; but [*with conciliatory cheerfulness*] I meant no offence by it. A clorgyman is privileged to be a bit of a fool, you know: it's on'y becomin' in his profession that he should. Anyhow, I come here, not to rake up hold differences, but to let bygones be bygones. [*Suddenly becoming very solemn, and approaching MORELL.*] James: three year ago, you done me a hill turn. You done me hout of a contrac'; an' when I gev you 'arsh words in my nat'ral disappointment, you, turned my daughrter again me. Well, I've come to act the part of a Cherischin.* [*Offering his hand.*] I forgive you, James.

MORELL [*starting up*]    Confound your impudence!

BURGESS [*retreating, with almost lachrymose deprecation of this treat-

---

*Christian.

*ment*]   Is that becomin' language for a clorgyman, James?—and you so partic'lar, too?

MORELL [*hotly*]   No, sir, it is not becoming language for a clergyman. I used the wrong word. I should have said damn your impudence: that's what St. Paul, or any honest priest would have said to you. Do you think I have forgotten that tender of yours for the contract to supply clothing to the workhouse?

BURGESS [*in a paroxysm of public spirit*]   I acted in the interest of the ratepayers, James. It was the lowest tender:* you can't deny that.

MORELL   Yes, the lowest, because you paid worse wages than any other employer—starvation wages—aye, worse than starvation wages—to the women who made the clothing. Your wages would have driven them to the streets to keep body and soul together. [*Getting angrier and angrier.*] Those women were my parishioners. I shamed the Guardians out of accepting your tender: I shamed the ratepayers out of letting them do it: I shamed everybody but you. [*Boiling over.*] How dare you, sir, come here and offer to forgive me, and talk about your daughter, and—

BURGESS   Easy, James, easy, easy. Don't git hinto a fluster about nothink. I've howned I was wrong.

MORELL [*fuming about*]   Have you? I didn't hear you.

BURGESS   Of course I did. I hown it now. Come: I harsk your pardon for the letter I wrote you. Is that enough?

MORELL [*snapping his fingers*]   That's nothing. Have you raised the wages?

BURGESS [*triumphantly*]   Yes.

MORELL [*stopping dead*]   What!

BURGESS [*unctuously*]   I've turned a moddle hemployer. I don't hemploy no women now: they're all sacked; and the work is done by machinery. Not a man 'as less than sixpence a *hour*; and the skilled 'ands gits the Trade Union rate. [*Proudly.*] What 'ave you to say to me now?

---

*Bid, cost-estimate.

MORELL [*overwhelmed*]   Is it possible! Well, there's more joy in heaven over one sinner that repenteth— [*Going to BURGESS with an explosion of apologetic cordiality.*] My dear Burgess, I most heartily beg your pardon for my hard thoughts of you. [*Grasps his hand.*] And now, don't you feel the better for the change? Come, confess, you're happier. You look happier.

BURGESS [*ruefully*]   Well, p'raps I do. I s'pose I must, since you notice it. At all events, I git my contrax asseppit [accepted] by the County Council. [*Savagely.*] They dussent 'ave nothink to do with me unless I paid fair wages—curse 'em for a parcel o' meddlin' fools!

MORELL [*dropping his hand, utterly discouraged*]   So that was why you raised the wages! [*He sits down moodily.*]

BURGESS [*severely, in spreading, mounting tones*]   Why else should I do it? What does it lead to but drink and huppishness in workin' men? [*He seats himself magisterially in the easy chair.*] It's hall very well for you, James: it gits you hinto the papers and makes a great man of you; but you never think of the 'arm you do, puttin' money into the pockets of workin' men that they don't know 'ow to spend, and takin' it from people that might be makin' a good huse on it.

MORELL [*with a heavy sigh, speaking with cold politeness*]   What is your business with me this morning? I shall not pretend to believe that you are here merely out of family sentiment.

BURGESS [*obstinately*]   Yes, I ham—just family sentiment and nothink else.

MORELL [*with weary calm*]   I don't belicve you!

BURGESS [*rising threateningly*]   Don't say that to me again, James Mavor Morell.

MORELL [*unmoved*]   I'll say it just as often as may be necessary to convince you that it's true. I don't believe you.

BURGESS [*collapsing into an abyss of wounded feeling*]   Oh, well, if you're determined to be unfriendly, I s'pose I'd better go. [*He moves reluctantly towards the door. MORELL makes no sign. He lingers.*] I didn't hexpect to find a hunforgivin' spirit in you, James.

[*MORELL still not responding, he takes a few more reluctant steps door-wards. Then he comes back whining.*] We huseter git on well enough, spite of our different opinions. Why are you so changed to me? I give you my word I come here in pyorr [pure] frenliness, not wishin' to be on bad terms with my hown daughrter's 'usban'. Come, James: be a Cheristhin and shake 'ands. [*He puts his hand sentimentally on MORELL's shoulder.*]

MORELL [*looking up at him thoughtfully*]    Look here, Burgess. Do you want to be as welcome here as you were before you lost that contract?

BURGESS    I do, James. I do—honest.

MORELL    Then why don't you behave as you did then?

BURGESS [*cautiously removing his hand*]    'Ow d'y'mean?

MORELL    I'll tell you. You thought me a young fool then.

BURGESS [*coaxingly*]    No, I didn't, James. I—

MORELL [*cutting him short*]    Yes, you did. And I thought you an old scoundrel.

BURGESS [*most vehemently deprecating this gross self-accusation on MORELL's part*]    No, you didn't, James. Now you do yourself a hinjustice.

MORELL    Yes, I did. Well, that did not prevent our getting on very well together. God made you what I call a scoundrel as he made me what you call a fool. [*The effect of this observation on BURGESS is to remove the keystone of his moral arch. He becomes bod-ily weak, and, with his eyes fixed on MORELL in a helpless stare, puts out his hand apprehensively to balance himself, as if the floor had sud-denly sloped under him. MORELL proceeds in the same tone of quiet con-viction.*] It was not for me to quarrel with his handiwork in the one case more than in the other. So long as you come here hon-estly as a self-respecting, thorough, convinced scoundrel, justify-ing your scoundrelism, and proud of it, you are welcome. But [*and now MORELL's tone becomes formidable; and he rises and strikes the back of the chair for greater emphasis*] I won't have you here sniv-elling about being a model employer and a converted man when you're only an apostate with your coat turned for the sake of a County Council contract. [*He nods at him to enforce the point; then goes to the hearth-rug, where he takes up a comfortably commanding position with his back to the fire, and continues*] No: I like a man to be true to himself, even in wickedness. Come now: either take your hat and go; or else sit down and give me a good scoundrelly reason for wanting to be friends with me. [*BURGESS, whose emotions have subsided sufficiently to be expressed by a dazed grin, is relieved by this concrete proposition. He ponders it for a moment, and then, slowly and very modestly, sits down in the chair MORELL has just left.*][7] That's right. Now, out with it.

BURGESS [*chuckling in spite of himself*]   Well, you a r e a queer bird, James, and no mistake. But [*almost enthusiastically*] one carnt 'elp likin' you; besides, as I said afore, of course one don't take all a clorgyman says seriously, or the world couldn't go on. Could it now? [*He composes himself for graver discourse, and turning his eyes on MORELL proceeds with dull seriousness.*] Well, I don't mind tellin' you, since it's your wish we should be free with one another, that I did think you a bit of a fool once; but I'm beginnin' to think that p'r'aps I was be'ind the times a bit.

MORELL [*delighted*]   Aha! You're finding that out at last, are you?

BURGESS [*portentously*]   Yes, times 'as changed mor'n I could a believed. Five yorr (year) ago, no sensible man would a thought o' takin' up with your ideas. I hused to wonder you was let preach at all. Why, I know a clorgyman that 'as bin kep' hout of his job for yorrs by the Bishop of London, although the pore feller's not a bit more religious than you are. But to-day, if henyone was to offer to bet me a thousan' poun' that you'll end by bein' a bishop yourself, I shouldn't venture to take the bet. You and yore crew are gettin' hinfluential: I can see that. They'll 'ave to give you something someday, if it's only to stop yore mouth. You 'ad the right instinc' arter all, James: the line you took is the payin' line in the long run fur a man o' your sort.

MORELL [*decisively—offering his hand*]   Shake hands, Burgess.

Now you're talking honestly. I don't think they'll make me a bishop; but if they do, I'll introduce you to the biggest jobbers I can get to come to my dinner parties.

BURGESS [*who has risen with a sheepish grin and accepted the hand of friendship*]    You will 'ave your joke, James. Our quarrel's made up now, isn't it?

A WOMAN'S VOICE    Say yes, James.[8]

*Startled, they turn quickly and find that CANDIDA has just come in, and is looking at them with an amused maternal indulgence which is her characteristic expression. She is a woman of 33, well built, well nourished, likely, one guesses, to become matronly later on, but now quite at her best, with the double charm of youth and motherhood. Her ways are those of a woman who has found that she can always manage people by engaging their affection; and who does so frankly and instinctively without the smallest scruple. So far, she is like any other pretty woman who is just clever enough to make the most of her sexual attractions for trivially selfish ends; but CANDIDA's serene brow, courageous eyes, and well set mouth and chin signify largeness of mind and dignity of character to ennoble her cunning in the affections. A wisehearted observer, looking at her, would at once guess that whoever had placed the Virgin of the Assumption over her hearth did so because he fancied some spiritual resemblance between them, and yet would not suspect either her husband or herself of any such idea, or indeed of any concern with the art of Titian.*

*Just now she is in bonnet and mantle, laden with a strapped rug with her umbrella stuck through it, a handbag, and a supply of illustrated papers.*

MORELL [*shocked at his remissness*]    Candida! Why— [*looks at his watch, and is horrified to find it so late.*] My darling! [*Hurrying to her and seizing the rug strap, pouring forth his remorseful regrets all the time.*] I intended to meet you at the train. I let the time slip. [*Flinging the rug on the sofa.*] I was so engrossed by—[*returning to her*]—I forgot—oh! [*He embraces her with penitent emotion.*]

BURGESS [*a little shamefaced and doubtful of his reception*]    How orr you, Candy? [*She, still in MORELL's arms, offers him her cheek, which he kisses.*] James and me is come to a unnerstandin'——a honourable unnerstandin'. Ain' we, James?

MORELL [*impetuously*]   Oh, bother your understanding! You've kept me late for Candida. [*With compassionate fervor.*] My poor love: how did you manage about the luggage?——how——

CANDIDA [*stopping him and disengaging herself*]   There, there, there. I wasn't alone. Eugene came down yesterday; and we traveled up together.

MORELL [*pleased*]   Eugene!

CANDIDA   Yes: he's struggling with my luggage, poor boy. Go out, dear, at once; or he will pay for the cab; and I don't want that. [*MORELL hurries out. CANDIDA puts down her handbag; then takes off her mantle and bonnet and puts them on the sofa with the rug, chatting meanwhile.*] Well, papa, how are you getting on at home?

BURGESS   The 'ouse ain't worth livin' in since you left it, Candy. I wish you'd come round and give the gurl a talkin' to. Who's this Eugene that's come with you?

CANDIDA   Oh, Eugene's one of James's discoveries. He found him sleeping on the Embankment last June. Haven't you noticed our new picture [*pointing to the Virgin*]? He gave us that.

BURGESS [*incredulously*]   Garn! D'you mean to tell me——your hown father!——that cab touts or such like, orf the Embankment, buys pictur's like that? [*Severely.*] Don't deceive me, Candy: it's a 'Igh Church pictur;[9] and James chose it hisself.

CANDIDA   Guess again. Eugene isn't a cab tout.*

BURGESS   Then wot is he? [*Sarcastically.*] A nobleman, I 'spose.

CANDIDA [*delighted——nodding*]   Yes. His uncle's a peer——a real live earl.

BURGESS [*not daring to believe such good news*]   No!

CANDIDA   Yes. He had a seven day bill[†] for £55 in his pocket when

---

*Poor people who hail cabs for others in hope of a small tip.
†Financial note that can be cashed in seven days.

James found him on the Embankment. He thought he couldn't get any money for it until the seven days were up; and he was too shy to ask for credit. Oh, he's a dear boy! We are very fond of him.

BURGESS [*pretending to belittle the aristocracy, but with his eyes gleaming*]   Hm, I thort you wouldn't git a piorr's (peer's) nevvy visitin' in Victoria Park unless he were a bit of a flat. [*Looking again at the picture.*] Of course I don't 'old with that pictur, Candy; but still it's a 'igh class, fust rate work of art: I can see that. Be sure you hintroduce me to him, Candy. [*He looks at his watch anxiously.*] I can only stay about two minutes.

*MORELL comes back with EUGENE, whom BURGESS contemplates moist-eyed with enthusiasm. He is a strange, shy youth of eighteen, slight, effeminate, with a delicate childish voice, and a hunted, tormented expression and shrinking manner that shew the painful sensitiveness that very swift and acute apprehensiveness produces in youth, before the character has grown to its full strength. Yet everything that his timidity and frailty suggests is contradicted by his face. He is miserably irresolute, does not know where to stand or what to do with his hands and feet, is afraid of BURGESS, and would run away into solitude if he dared; but the very intensity with which he feels a perfectly commonplace position shews great nervous force, and his nostrils and mouth shew a fiercely petulant wilfulness, as to the quality of which his great imaginative eyes and fine brow are reassuring. He is so entirely uncommon as to be almost unearthly; and to prosaic people there is something noxious in this unearthliness, just as to poetic people there is something angelic in it. His dress is anarchic. He wears an old blue serge jacket, unbuttoned over a woollen lawn tennis shirt, with a silk handkerchief for a cravat, trousers matching the jacket, and brown canvas shoes. In these garments he has apparently lain in the heather and waded through the waters; but there is no evidence of his having ever brushed them.*

*As he catches sight of a stranger on entering, he stops, and edges along the wall on the opposite side of the room.*

MORELL [*as he enters*]   Come along: you can spare us quarter of an hour, at all events. This is my father-in-law, Mr. Burgess—Mr. Marchbanks.

MARCHBANKS [*nervously backing against the bookcase*]   Glad to meet you, sir.

BURGESS [*crossing to him with great heartiness, whilst MORELL joins CANDIDA at the fire*]   Glad to meet y o u , I'm shore, Mr. Morchbanks. [*Forcing him to shake hands.*] 'Ow do you find yore-self this weather? 'Ope you ain't lettin' James put no foolish ideas into your 'ed?

MARCHBANKS   Foolish ideas! Oh, you mean Socialism. No.

BURGESS   That's right. [*Again looking at his watch.*] Well, I must go now: there's no 'elp for it. Yo're not comin' my way, are you, Mr. Morchbanks?

MARCHBANKS   Which way is that?

BURGESS   Victawriar Pork Station. There's a city train at 1 2:2 5.

MORELL   Nonsense. Eugene will stay to lunch with us, I expect.

MARCHBANKS [*anxiously excusing himself*]   No—I—I—

BURGESS   Well, well, I shan't press you: I bet you'd rather lunch with Candy. Some night, I 'ope, you'll come and dine with me at my club, the Freeman Founders in Nortn Folgit. Come, say you will.

MARCHBANKS   Thank you, Mr. Burgess. Where is Norton Fol-gate—down in Surrey, isn't it? [*BURGESS, inexpressibly tickled, be-gins to splutter with laughter.*]

CANDIDA [*coming to the rescue*]   You'll lose your train, papa, if you don't go at once. Come back in the afternoon and tell Mr. Marchbanks where to find the club.

BURGESS [*roaring with glee*]   Down in Surrey—har, har! that's not a bad one. Well, I never met a man as didn't know Nortn Folgit before. [*Abashed at his own noisiness.*] Good-bye, Mr. Morchbanks: I know yo're too 'ighbred to take my pleasantry in bad part. [*He again offers his hand.*]

MARCHBANKS [*taking it with a nervous jerk*]   Not at all.

BURGESS    Bye, bye, Candy. I'll look in again later on. So long, James.

MORELL    Must you go?

BURGESS    Don't stir. [*He goes out with unabated heartiness.*]

MORELL    Oh, I'll see you out. [*He follows him out. EUGENE stares after them apprehensively, holding his breath until BURGESS disappears.*]

CANDIDA [*laughing*]    Well, Eugene. [*He turns with a start and comes eagerly towards her, but stops irresolutely as he meets her amused look.*] What do you think of my father?

MARCHBANKS    I—I hardly know him yet. He seems to be a very nice old gentleman.

CANDIDA [*with gentle irony*]    And you'll go to the Freeman Founders to dine with him, won't you?

MARCHBANKS [*miserably, taking it quite seriously*]    Yes, if it will please you.

CANDIDA [*touched*]    Do you know, you are a very nice boy, Eugene, with all your queerness. If you had laughed at my father I shouldn't have minded; but I like you ever so much better for being nice to him.

MARCHBANKS    Ought I to have laughed? I noticed that he said something funny; but I am so ill at ease with strangers; and I never can see a joke! I'm very sorry. [*He sits down on the sofa, his elbows on his knees and his temples between his fists, with an expression of hopeless suffering.*]

CANDIDA [*bustling him goodnaturedly*]    Oh, come! You great baby, you! You are worse than usual this morning. Why were you so melancholy as we came along in the cab?

MARCHBANKS    Oh, that was nothing. I was wondering how much I ought to give the cabman. I know it's utterly silly; but you don't know how dreadful such things are to me—how I shrink from having to deal with strange people. [*Quickly and reassuringly.*] But it's all right. He beamed all over and touched his hat when Morell gave him two shillings. I was on the point of offering him ten. [*CANDIDA laughs heartily. MORELL comes back with a few letters and newspapers which have come by the midday post.*]

CANDIDA   Oh, James, dear, he was going to give the cabman ten shillings—ten shillings for a three minutes' drive—oh, dear!

MORELL [*at the table, glancing through the letters*]   Never mind her, Marchbanks. The overpaying instinct is a generous one: better than the underpaying instinct, and not so common.

MARCHBANKS [*relapsing into dejection*]   No: cowardice, incompetence. Mrs. Morell's quite right.

CANDIDA   Of course she is. [*She takes up her handbag.*] And now I must leave you to James for the present. I suppose you are too much of a poet to know the state a woman finds her house in when she's been away for three weeks. Give me my rug. [*EUGENE takes the strapped rug from the couch, and gives it to her. She takes it in her left hand, having the bag in her right.*] Now hang my cloak across my arm. [*He obeys.*] Now my hat. [*He puts it into the hand which has the bag.*] Now open the door for me. [*He hurries up before her and opens the door.*] Thanks. [*She goes out; and MARCHBANKS shuts the door.*]

MORELL [*still busy at the table*]   You'll stay to lunch, Marchbanks, of course.

MARCHBANKS [*scared*]   I mustn't. [*He glances quickly at MORELL, but at once avoids his frank look, and adds, with obvious disingenuousness*] I can't.

MORELL [*over his shoulder*]   You mean you won't.

MARCHBANKS [*earnestly*]   No: I should like to, indeed. Thank you very much. But—but—

MORELL [*breezily, finishing with the letters and coming close to him*]   But—but—but—but—bosh! If you'd like to stay, stay. You don't mean to persuade me you have anything else to do. If you're shy, go and take a turn in the park and write poetry until half past one; and then come in and have a good feed.

MARCHBANKS   Thank you, I should like that very much. But I really mustn't. The truth is, Mrs. Morell told me not to. She said she didn't think you'd ask me to stay to lunch, but that I was to remember, if you did, that you didn't really want me to. [*Plaintively.*] She said I'd understand; but I don't. Please don't tell her I told you.

MORELL [*drolly*]   Oh, is that all? Won't my suggestion that you should take a turn in the park meet the difficulty?

MARCHBANKS   How?

MORELL [*exploding good-humoredly*]   Why, you duffer— [*But this boisterousness jars himself as well as EUGENE. He checks himself and resumes, with affectionate seriousness*] No: I won't put it in that way. My dear lad: in a happy marriage like ours, there is something very sacred in the return of the wife to her home. [*MARCHBANKS looks quickly at him, half anticipating his meaning.*] An old friend or a truly noble and sympathetic soul is not in the way on such occasions; but a chance visitor is. [*The hunted, horror-stricken expression comes out with sudden vividness in EUGENE's face as he understands. MORELL, occupied with his own thought, goes on without noticing it.*] Candida thought I would rather not have you here; but she was wrong. I'm very fond of you, my boy, and I should like you to see for yourself what a happy thing it is to be married as I am.

MARCHBANKS   Happy!—y o u r marriage! You think that! You believe that!

MORELL [*buoyantly*]   I know it, my lad. La Rochefoucauld said that there are convenient marriages, but no delightful ones. You don't know the comfort of seeing through and through a thundering liar and rotten cynic like that fellow. Ha, ha! Now off with you to the park, and write your poem. Half past one, sharp, mind: we never wait for anybody.

MARCHBANKS [*wildly*]   No: stop: you shan't. I'll force it into the light.

MORELL [*puzzled*]   Eh? Force what?

MARCHBANKS   I must speak to you. There is something that must be settled between us.

MORELL [*with a whimsical glance at the clock*]   Now?

MARCHBANKS [*passionately*]  Now. Before you leave this room. [*He retreats a few steps, and stands as if to bar MORELL's way to the door.*]

MORELL [*without moving, and gravely, perceiving now that there is something serious the matter*]  I'm not going to leave it, my dear boy: I thought y o u were. [*EUGENE, baffled by his firm tone, turns his back on him, writhing with anger. MORELL goes to him and puts his hand on his shoulder strongly and kindly, disregarding his attempt to shake it off.*] Come: sit down quietly; and tell me what it is. And remember: we are friends, and need not fear that either of us will be anything but patient and kind to the other, whatever we may have to say.

MARCHBANKS [*twisting himself round on him*]  Oh, I am not forgetting myself: I am only [*covering his face desperately with his hands*] full of horror. [*Then, dropping his hands, and thrusting his face forward fiercely at MORELL, he goes on threateningly.*] You shall see whether this is a time for patience and kindness. [*MORELL, firm as a rock, looks indulgently at him.*] Don't look at me in that self-complacent way. You think yourself stronger than I am; but I shall stagger you if you have a heart in your breast.

MORELL [*powerfully confident*]  Stagger me, my boy. Out with it.

MARCHBANKS  First—

MORELL  First?

MARCHBANKS  I love your wife.

[*MORELL recoils, and, after staring at him for a moment in utter amazement, bursts into uncontrollable laughter. EUGENE is taken aback, but not disconcerted; and he soon becomes indignant and contemptuous.*]

MORELL [*sitting down to have his laugh out*]  Why, my dear child, of course you do. Everybody loves her: they can't help it. I like it. But [*looking up whimsically at him*] I say, Eugene: do you think yours is a case to be talked about? You're under twenty: she's over thirty. Doesn't it look rather too like a case of calf love?

MARCHBANKS [*vehemently*]   You dare say that of her! You think that way of the love she inspires! It is an insult to her!

MORELL [*rising quickly, in an altered tone*]   To her! Eugene: take care. I have been patient. I hope to remain patient. But there are some things I won't allow. Don't force me to shew you the indulgence I should shew to a child. Be a man.

MARCHBANKS [*with a gesture as if sweeping something behind him*] Oh, let us put aside all that cant. It horrifies me when I think of the doses of it she has had to endure in all the weary years during which you have selfishly and blindly sacrificed her to minister to your self-sufficiency—y o u [*turning on him*] who have not one thought—one sense—in common with her.

MORELL [*philosophically*]   She seems to bear it pretty well. [*Looking him straight in the face.*] Eugene, my boy: you are making a fool of yourself—a very great fool of yourself. There's a piece of wholesome plain speaking for you.

MARCHBANKS   Oh, do you think I don't know all that? Do you think that the things people make fools of themselves about are any less real and true than the things they behave sensibly about? [*MORELL's gaze wavers for the first time. He instinctively averts his face and stands listening, startled and thoughtful.*] They are more true: they are the only things that are true. You are very calm and sensible and moderate with me because you can see that I am a fool about your wife; just as no doubt that old man who was here just now is very wise over your socialism, because he sees that y o u are a fool about it. [*MORELL's perplexity deepens markedly. EUGENE follows up his advantage, plying him fiercely with questions.*] Does that prove you wrong? Does your complacent superiority to me prove that *I* am wrong?

MORELL [*turning on EUGENE, who stands his ground*]   Marchbanks: some devil is putting these words into your mouth. It is easy— terribly easy—to shake a man's faith in himself. To take advantage of that to break a man's spirit is devil's work.[10] Take care of what you are doing. Take care.

MARCHBANKS [*ruthlessly*]   I know. I'm doing it on purpose. I told you I should stagger you.

[*They confront one another threateningly for a moment. Then MORELL recovers his dignity.*]

MORELL [*with noble tenderness*]   Eugene: listen to me. Some day, I hope and trust, you will be a happy man like me. [*EUGENE chafes intolerantly, repudiating the worth of his happiness. MORELL, deeply insulted, controls himself with fine forbearance, and continues steadily, with great artistic beauty of delivery*] You will be married; and you will be working with all your might and valor to make every spot on earth as happy as your own home. You will be one of the makers of the Kingdom of Heaven on earth; and—who knows?—you may be a pioneer and master builder where I am only a humble journeyman; for don't think, my boy, that I cannot see in you, young as you are, promise of higher powers than I can ever pretend to. I well know that it is in the poet that the holy spirit of man—the god within him—is most godlike. It should make you tremble to think of that—to think that the heavy burthen and great gift of a poet may be laid upon you.

MARCHBANKS [*unimpressed and remorseless, his boyish crudity of assertion telling sharply against MORELL's oratory*]   It does not make me tremble. It is the want of it in others that makes me tremble.

MORELL [*redoubling his force of style under the stimulus of his genuine feeling and EUGENE's obduracy*]   Then help to kindle it in them—in m e —not to extinguish it. In the future—when you are as happy as I am—I will be your true brother in the faith. I will help you to believe that God has given us a world that nothing but our own folly keeps from being a paradise. I will help you to believe that every stroke of your work is sowing happiness for the great harvest that all—even the humblest—shall one day reap. And last, but trust me, not least, I will help you to believe that your wife loves you and is happy in her home. We need such help, Marchbanks: we need it greatly and always. There are so many things to make us doubt, if once we let our understanding be troubled. Even at home, we sit as if in camp, encompassed by a hostile army of doubts. Will you play the traitor and let them in on me?

MARCHBANKS [*looking round him*]    Is it like this for her here always? A woman, with a great soul, craving for reality, truth, freedom, and being fed on metaphors, sermons, stale perorations, mere rhetoric. Do you think a woman's soul can live on your talent for preaching?

MORELL [*stung*]    Marchbanks: you make it hard for me to control myself. My talent is like yours insofar as it has any real worth at all. It is the gift of finding words for divine truth.

MARCHBANKS [*impetuously*]    It's the gift of the gab, nothing more and nothing less. What has your knack of fine talking to do with the truth, any more than playing the organ has? I've never been in your church; but I've been to your political meetings; and I've seen you do what's called rousing the meeting to enthusiasm: that is, you excited them until they behaved exactly as if they were drunk. And their wives looked on and saw clearly enough what fools they were. Oh, it's an old story: you'll find it in the Bible. I imagine King David, in his fits of enthusiasm, was very like you. [*Stabbing him with the words.*] "But his wife despised him in her heart."

MORELL [*wrathfully*]    Leave my house. Do you hear? [*He advances on him threateningly.*]

MARCHBANKS [*shrinking back against the couch*]    Let me alone. Don't touch me. [*MORELL grasps him powerfully by the lappell of his coat: he cowers down on the sofa and screams passionately.*] Stop, Morell, if you strike me, I'll kill myself: I won't bear it. [*Almost in hysterics.*] Let me go. Take your hand away.

MORELL [*with slow, emphatic scorn*]    You little snivelling, cowardly whelp. [*Releasing him.*] Go, before you frighten yourself into a fit.

MARCHBANKS [*on the sofa, gasping, but relieved by the withdrawal of MORELL's hand*]    I'm not afraid of you: it's you who are afraid of me.

MORELL [*quietly, as he stands over him*]    It looks like it, doesn't it?

MARCHBANKS [*with petulant vehemence*]    Yes, it does. [*MORELL *turns away contemptuously. EUGENE scrambles to his feet and follows him.*] You think because I shrink from being brutally handled—because [*with tears in his voice*] I can do nothing but cry with rage when I am met with violence—because I can't lift a heavy trunk down from the top of a cab like you—because I can't fight you for your wife as a navvy would: all that makes you think that I'm afraid of you. But you're wrong. If I haven't got what you call British pluck, I haven't British cowardice either: I'm not afraid of a clergyman's ideas. I'll fight your ideas. I'll rescue her from her slavery to them: I'll pit my own ideas against them. You are driving me out of the house because you daren't let her choose between your ideas and mine. You are afraid to let me see her again. [*MORELL, angered, turns suddenly on him. He flies to the door in involuntary dread.*] Let me alone, I say. I'm going.

MORELL [*with cold scorn*]   Wait a moment: I am not going to touch you: don't be afraid. When my wife comes back she will want to know why you have gone. And when she finds that you are never going to cross our threshold again, she will want to have that explained, too. Now I don't wish to distress her by telling her that you have behaved like a blackguard.

MARCHBANKS [*coming back with renewed vehemence*]   You shall—you must. If you give any explanation but the true one, you are a liar and a coward. Tell her what I said; and how you were strong and manly, and shook me as a terrier shakes a rat; and how I shrank and was terrified; and how you called me a snivelling little whelp and put me out of the house. If you don't tell her, I will: I'll write it to her.

MORELL [*taken aback*]   Why do you want her to know this?

MARCHBANKS [*with lyric rapture*]   Because she will understand me, and know that I understand her. If you keep back one word of it from her—if you are not ready to lay the truth at her feet as I am—then you will know to the end of your days that she really belongs to me and not to you. Good-bye. [*Going.*]

MORELL [*terribly disquieted*]   Stop: I will not tell her.

MARCHBANKS [*turning near the door*]   Either the truth or a lie you must tell her, if I go.

MORELL [*temporizing*]   Marchbanks: it is sometimes justifiable.

MARCHBANKS [*cutting him short*]   I know—to lie. It will be useless. Good-bye, Mr. Clergyman.

[*As he turns finally to the door, it opens and CANDIDA enters in housekeeping attire.*]

CANDIDA   Are you going, Eugene? [*Looking more observantly at him.*] Well, dear me, just look at you, going out into the street in that state! You a r e a poet, certainly. Look at him, James! [*She takes him by the coat, and brings him forward to show him to MORELL.*] Look at his collar! look at his tie! look at his hair! One would think somebody had been throttling you. [*The two men guard themselves against betraying their consciousness.*] Here! Stand still. [*She buttons his collar; ties his neckerchief in a bow; and arranges his hair.*] There! Now you look so nice that I think you'd better stay to lunch after all, though I told you you mustn't. It will be ready in half an hour. [*She puts a final touch to the bow. He kisses her hand.*] Don't be silly.

MARCHBANKS   I want to stay, of course—unless the reverend gentleman, your husband, has anything to advance to the contrary.

CANDIDA   Shall he stay, James, if he promises to be a good boy and to help me to lay the table? [*MARCHBANKS turns his head and looks steadfastly at MORELL over his shoulder, challenging his answer.*]

MORELL [*shortly*]   Oh, yes, certainly: he had better. [*He goes to the table and pretends to busy himself with his papers there.*]

MARCHBANKS [*offering his arm to CANDIDA*]   Come and lay the table. [*She takes it and they go to the door together. As they go out he adds*] I am the happiest of men.

MORELL   So was I—an hour ago.

# ACT II

*The same day. The same room. Late in the afternoon. The spare chair for visitors has been replaced at the table, which is, if possible, more untidy than before. MARCHBANKS, alone and idle, is trying to find out how the typewriter works. Hearing someone at the door, he steals guiltily away to the window and pretends to be absorbed in the view. MISS GARNETT, carrying the notebook in which she takes down MORELL's letters in shorthand from his dictation, sits down at the typewriter and sets to work transcribing them, much too busy to notice EUGENE. Unfortunately the first key she strikes sticks.*

PROSERPINE    Bother! You've been medling with my typewriter, Mr. Marchbanks; and there's not the least use in your trying to look as if you hadn't.

MARCHBANKS [*timidly*]    I'm very sorry, Miss Garnett. I only tried to make it write.

PROSERPINE    Well, you've made this key stick.

MARCHBANKS [*earnestly*]    I assure you I didn't touch the keys. I didn't, indeed. I only turned a little wheel. [*He points irresolutely at the tension wheel.*]

PROSERPINE    Oh, now I understand. [*She sets the machine to rights, talking volubly all the time.*] I suppose you thought it was a sort of barrel-organ. Nothing to do but turn the handle, and it would write a beautiful love letter for you straight off, eh?

MARCHBANKS [*seriously*]    I suppose a machine could be made to write love-letters. They're all the same, aren't they?

PROSERPINE [*somewhat indignantly: any such discussion, except by way of pleasantry, being outside her code of manners*]    How do I know? Why do you ask me?

MARCHBANKS    I beg your pardon. I thought clever people—

people who can do business and write letters, and that sort of
thing—always had love affairs.

PROSERPINE [*rising, outraged*]    Mr. Marchbanks! [*She looks severely
at him, and marches with much dignity to the bookcase.*]

MARCHBANKS [*approaching her humbly*]    I hope I haven't offended you. Perhaps I shouldn't have alluded to your love affairs.

PROSERPINE [*plucking a blue book from the shelf and turning sharply on
him*]    I haven't any love affairs. How dare you say such a thing?

MARCHBANKS [*simply*]    Really! Oh, then you are shy, like me.
Isn't that so?

PROSERPINE    Certainly I am not shy. What do you mean?

MARCHBANKS [*secretly*]    You must be: that is the reason there
are so few love affairs in the world. We all go about longing for
love: it is the first need of our natures, the loudest cry of our
hearts; but we dare not utter our longing: we are too shy. [*Very
earnestly.*] Oh, Miss Garnett, what would you not give to be
without fear, without shame—

PROSERPINE [*scandalized*]    Well, upon my word!

MARCHBANKS [*with petulant impatience*]    Ah, don't say those stupid things to me: they don't deceive me: what use are they? Why
are you afraid to be your real self with me? I am just like you.

PROSERPINE    Like me! Pray, are you flattering me or flattering
yourself? I don't feel quite sure which. [*She turns to go back to the
typewriter.*]

MARCHBANKS [*stopping her mysteriously*]    Hush! I go about in
search of love; and I find it in unmeasured stores in the bosoms
of others. But when I try to ask for it, this horrible shyness stran-
gles me; and I stand dumb, or worse than dumb, saying meaningless things—foolish lies. And I see the affection I am longing
for given to dogs and cats and pet birds, because they come and
ask for it. [*Almost whispering.*] It must be asked for: it is like a
ghost: it cannot speak unless it is first spoken to. [*At his normal
pitch, but with deep melancholy.*] All the love in the world is longing to speak; only it dare not, because it is shy, shy, shy. That is

the world's tragedy. [*With a deep sigh he sits in the spare chair and buries his face in his hands.*]

PROSERPINE [*amazed, but keeping her wits about her—her point of honor in encounters with strange young men*] Wicked people get over that shyness occasionally, don't they?

MARCHBANKS [*scrambling up almost fiercely*] Wicked people means people who have no love: therefore they have no shame. They have the power to ask for love because they don't need it: they have the power to offer it because they have none to give. [*He collapses into his seat, and adds, mournfully*] But we, who have love, and long to mingle it with the love of others: we cannot utter a word. [*Timidly.*] You find that, don't you?

PROSERPINE Look here: if you don't stop talking like this, I'll leave the room, Mr. Marchbanks: I really will. It's not proper. [*She resumes her seat at the typewriter, opening the blue book and preparing to copy a passage from it.*]

MARCHBANKS [*hopelessly*] Nothing that's worth saying is proper. [*He rises, and wanders about the room in his lost way, saying*] I can't understand you, Miss Garnett. What am I to talk about?

PROSERPINE [*snubbing him*] Talk about indifferent things. Talk about the weather.

MARCHBANKS Would you stand and talk about indifferent things if a child were by, crying bitterly with hunger.

PROSERPINE I suppose not.

MARCHBANKS Well: *I* can't talk about indifferent things with my heart crying out bitterly in i t s hunger.

PROSERPINE Then hold your tongue.

MARCHBANKS Yes: that is what it always comes to. We hold our tongues. Does that stop the cry of your heart?—for it does cry: doesn't it? It must, if you have a heart.

PROSERPINE [*suddenly rising with her hand pressed on her heart*] Oh, it's no use trying to work while you talk like that. [*She leaves her little table and sits on the sofa. Her feelings are evidently strongly worked on.*] It's no business of yours, whether my heart cries or not; but I have a mind to tell you, for all that.

MARCHBANKS     You needn't. I know already that it must.

PROSERPINE     But mind: if you ever say I said so, I'll deny it.

MARCHBANKS [*compassionately*]     Yes, I know. And so you haven't the courage to tell him?

PROSERPINE [*bouncing up*]     H i m ! Who?

MARCHBANKS     Whoever he is. The man you love. It might be anybody. The curate, Mr. Mill, perhaps.

PROSERPINE [*with disdain*]     Mr. Mill!!! A fine man to break my heart about, indeed! I'd rather have  y o u  than Mr. Mill.

MARCHBANKS [*recoiling*]     No, really—I'm very sorry; but you mustn't think of that. I—

PROSERPINE [*testily, crossing to the fire and standing at it with her back to him*]     Oh, don't be frightened: it's not you. It's not any one particular person.

MARCHBANKS     I know. You feel that you could love anybody that offered—

PROSERPINE [*exasperated*]     Anybody that offered! No, I do not. What do you take me for?

MARCHBANKS [*discouraged*]     No use. You won't make me  r e a l  answers—only those things that everybody says. [*He strays to the sofa and sits down disconsolately.*]

PROSERPINE [*nettled at what she takes to be a disparagement of her manners by an aristocrat*]     Oh, well, if you want original conversation, you'd better go and talk to yourself.

MARCHBANKS     That is what all poets do: they talk to themselves out loud; and the world overhears them. But it's horribly lonely not to hear someone else talk sometimes.

PROSERPINE     Wait until Mr. Morell comes. H e ' l l  talk to you. [*MARCHBANKS shudders.*] Oh, you needn't make wry faces over him: he can talk better than you. [*With temper.*] He'd talk your little head off. [*She is going back angrily to her place, when, suddenly enlightened, he springs up and stops her.*]

MARCHBANKS    Ah, I understand now!

PROSERPINE [*reddening*]    What do you understand?

MARCHBANKS    Your secret. Tell me: is it really and truly possible for a woman to love him?

PROSERPINE [*as if this were beyond all bounds*]    Well!!

MARCHBANKS [*passionately*]    No, answer me. I want to know: I m u s t know. *I* can't understand it. I can see nothing in him but words, pious resolutions, what people call goodness. You can't love that.

PROSERPINE [*attempting to snub him by an air of cool propriety*]    I simply don't know what you're talking about. I don't understand you.

MARCHBANKS [*vehemently*]    You do. You lie—

PROSERPINE    Oh!

MARCHBANKS    You d o understand; and you k n o w . [*Determined to have an answer.*] Is it possible for a woman to love him?

PROSERPINE [*looking him straight in the face*]    Yes. [*He covers his face with his hands.*] Whatever is the matter with you! [*He takes down his hands and looks at her. Frightened at the tragic mask presented to her, she hurries past him at the utmost possible distance, keeping her eyes on his face until he turns from her and goes to the child's chair beside the hearth, where he sits in the deepest dejection. As she approaches the door, it opens and BURGESS enters. On seeing him, she ejaculates*] Praise heaven, here's somebody! [*and sits down, reassured, at her table. She puts a fresh sheet of paper into the typewriter as BURGESS crosses to EUGENE.*]

BURGESS [*bent on taking care of the distinguished visitor*]    Well: so this is the way they leave you to yourself, Mr. Morchbanks. I've come to keep you company. [*MARCHBANKS looks up at him in consternation, which is quite lost on him.*] James is receivin' a deppitation in the dinin' room; and Candy is hupstairs educatin' of a young stitcher gurl she's hinterusted in. She's settin' there learnin' her to read out of the "'Ev'nly Twins."[11] [*Condolingly.*]

You must find it lonesome here with no one but the typist to talk to. [*He pulls round the easy chair above fire, and sits down.*]

PROSERPINE [*highly incensed*]   He'll be all right now that he has the advantage of y o u r polished conversation: that's one comfort, anyhow. [*She begins to typewrite with clattering asperity.*]

BURGESS [*amazed at her audacity*]   Hi was not addressin' myself to you, young woman, that I'm awerr of.

PROSERPINE [*tartly, to MARCHBANKS*]   Did you ever see worse manners, Mr. Marchbanks?

BURGESS [*with pompous severity*]   Mr. Morchbanks is a gentleman and knows his place, which is more than some people do.

PROSERPINE [*fretfully*]   It's well you and I are not ladies and gentlemen: I'd talk to you pretty straight if Mr. Marchbanks wasn't here. [*She pulls the letter out of the machine so crossly that it tears.*] There, now I've spoiled this letter—have to be done all over again. Oh, I can't contain myself—silly old fathead!

BURGESS [*rising, breathless with indignation*]   Ho! I'm a silly ole fat'ead, am I? Ho, indeed [*gasping*]. Hall right, my gurl! Hall right. You just wait till I tell that to your employer. You'll see. I'll teach you: see if I don't.

PROSERPINE   I—

BURGESS [*cutting her short*]   No, you've done it now. No huse a-talkin' to me. I'll let you know who I am. [*PROSERPINE shifts her paper carriage with a defiant bang, and disdainfully goes on with her work.*] Don't you take no notice of her, Mr. Morchbanks. She's beneath it. [*He sits down again loftily.*]

MARCHBANKS [*miserably nervous and disconcerted*]   Hadn't we better change the subject. I—I don't think Miss Garnett meant anything.

PROSERPINE [*with intense conviction*]   Oh, didn't I though, j u s t !

BURGESS   I wouldn't demean myself to take notice on her. [*An electric bell rings twice.*]

PROSERPINE [*gathering up her note-book and papers*]   That's for me. [*She hurries out.*]

BURGESS [*calling after her*]   Oh, we can spare you. [*Somewhat relieved by the triumph of having the last word, and yet half inclined to try to improve on it, he looks after her for a moment; then subsides into his seat by EUGENE, and addresses him very confidentially.*] Now we're alone, Mr. Morchbanks, let me give you a friendly 'int that I wouldn't give to everybody. 'Ow long 'ave you known my son-in-law James here?

MARCHBANKS   I don't know. I never can remember dates. A few months, perhaps.

BURGESS   Ever notice anything queer about him?

MARCHBANKS   I don't think so.

BURGESS [*impressively*]   No more you wouldn't. That's the danger in it. Well, he's mad.

MARCHBANKS   Mad!

BURGESS   Mad as a Morch 'are. You take notice on him and you'll see.

MARCHBANKS [*beginning*]   But surely that is only because his opinions —

BURGESS [*touching him with his forefinger on his knee, and pressing it as if to hold his attention with it*]   That's wot I used ter think, Mr. Morchbanks. H i thought long enough that it was honly 'is opinions; though, mind you, hopinions becomes vurry serious things when people takes to hactin on 'em as 'e does. But that's not wot I go on. [*He looks round to make sure that they are alone, and bends over to EUGENE's ear.*] Wot do you think he says to me this mornin' in this very room?

MARCHBANKS   What?

BURGESS   He sez to me—this is as sure as we're settin' here now—he sez: "I'm a fool," he sez; "and yore a scounderl"—as cool as possible. Me a scounderl, mind you! And then shook 'ands with me on it, as if it was to my credit! Do you mean to tell me that that man's sane?

MORELL [*outside, calling to PROSERPINE, holding the door open*]   Get all their names and addresses, Miss Garnett.

PROSERPINE [*in the distance*]    Yes, Mr. Morell.

[*MORELL comes in, with the deputation's documents in his hands.*]

BURGESS [*aside to MARCHBANKS*]    Yorr he is. Just you keep your heye on him and see. [*Rising momentously.*] I'm sorry, James, to 'ave to make a complaint to you. I don't want to do it; but I feel I oughter, as a matter o' right and dooty.

MORELL    What's the matter.

BURGESS    Mr. Morchbanks will bear me out: he was a witness. [*Very solemnly.*] Your young woman so far forgot herself as to call me a silly ole fat'ead.

MORELL [*delighted—with tremendous heartiness*]    Oh, now, isn't that e x a c t l y like Prossy? She's so frank: she can't contain herself! Poor Prossy! Ha! Ha!

BURGESS [*trembling with rage*]    And do you hexpec me to put up with it from the like of 'er?

MORELL    Pooh, nonsense! you can't take any notice of it. Never mind. [*He goes to the cellaret and puts the papers into one of the drawers.*]

BURGESS    Oh, *I* don't mind. I'm above it. But is it r i g h t ?— that's what I want to know. Is it right?

MORELL    That's a question for the Church, not for the laity. Has it done you any harm, that's the question for you, eh? Of course, it hasn't. Think no more of it. [*He dismisses the subject by going to his place at the table and setting to work at his correspondence.*]

BURGESS [*aside to MARCHBANKS*]    What did I tell you? Mad as a 'atter. [*He goes to the table and asks, with the sickly civility of a hungry man*] When's dinner, James?

MORELL    Not for half an hour yet.

BURGESS [*with plaintive resignation*]    Gimme a nice book to read over the fire, will you, James: thur's a good chap.

MORELL    What sort of book? A good one?

BURGESS [*with almost a yell of remonstrance*]    Nah-oo! Summat pleasant, just to pass the time. [*MORELL takes an illustrated paper from the table and offers it. He accepts it humbly.*] Thank yer, James.

[*He goes back to his easy chair at the fire, and sits there at his ease, reading.*]

MORELL [*as he writes*] Candida will come to entertain you presently. She has got rid of her pupil. She is filling the lamps.

MARCHBANKS [*starting up in the wildest consternation*] But that will soil her hands. I can't bear that, Morell: it's a shame. I'll go and fill them. [*He makes for the door.*]

MORELL You'd better not. [*MARCHBANKS stops irresolutely.*] She'd only set you to clean my boots, to save me the trouble of doing it myself in the morning.

BURGESS [*with grave disapproval*] Don't you keep a servant now, James?

MORELL Yes; but she isn't a slave; and the house looks as if I kept three. That means that everyone has to lend a hand. It's not a bad plan: Prossy and I can talk business after breakfast whilst we're washing up. Washing up's no trouble when there are two people to do it.

MARCHBANKS [*tormentedly*] Do you think every woman is as coarse-grained as Miss Garnett?

BURGESS [*emphatically*] That's quite right, Mr. Morchbanks. That's q u i t e right. She is corse-grained.

MORELL [*quietly and significantly*] Marchbanks!

MARCHBANKS Yes.

MORELL How many servants does your father keep?

MARCHBANKS Oh, I don't know. [*He comes back uneasily to the sofa, as if to get as far as possible from MORELL's questioning, and sits down in great agony of mind, thinking of the paraffin.*]

MORELL [*very gravely*] So many that you don't know. [*More aggressively.*] Anyhow, when there's anything coarse-grained to be done, you ring the bell and throw it on to somebody else, eh? That's one of the great facts in y o u r existence, isn't it?

MARCHBANKS Oh, don't torture me. The one great fact now is that your wife's beautiful fingers are dabbling in paraffin oil, and that you are sitting here comfortably preaching about it—ever-lasting preaching, preaching, words, words, words.

BURGESS [*intensely appreciating this retort*]   Ha, ha! Devil a better. [*Radiantly.*] 'Ad you there, James, straight.

[*CANDIDA comes in, well aproned, with a reading lamp trimmed, filled, and ready for lighting. She places it on the table near MORELL, ready for use.*]

CANDIDA [*brushing her finger tips together with a slight twitch of her nose*]   If you stay with us, Eugene, I think I will hand over the lamps to you.

MARCHBANKS   I will stay on condition that you hand over all the rough work to me.

CANDIDA   That's very gallant; but I think I should like to see how you do it first. [*Turning to MORELL.*] James: you've not been looking after the house properly.

MORELL   What have I done—or not done—my love?

CANDIDA [*with serious vexation*]   My own particular pet scrubbing brush has been used for blackleading. [*A heartbreaking wail bursts from MARCHBANKS. BURGESS looks round, amazed. CANDIDA hurries to the sofa.*] What's the matter? Are you ill, Eugene?

MARCHBANKS   No, not ill. Only horror, horror, horror! [*He bows his head on his hands.*]

BURGESS [*shocked*]   What! Got the 'orrors, Mr. Morchbanks! Oh, that's bad, at your age. You must leave it off grajally.

CANDIDA [*reassured*]   Nonsense, papa. It's only poetic horror, isn't it, Eugene? [*Petting him.*]

BURGESS [*abashed*]   Oh, poetic 'orror, is it? I beg your pordon, I'm shore. [*He turns to the fire again, deprecating his hasty conclusion.*]

CANDIDA   What is it, Eugene—the scrubbing brush? [*He shudders.*] Well, there! never mind. [*She sits down beside him.*] Wouldn't you like to present me with a nice new one, with an ivory back inlaid with mother-of-pearl?

MARCHBANKS [*softly and musically, but sadly and longingly*]   No, not a scrubbing brush, but a boat—a tiny shallop[12] to sail away in, far from the world, where the marble floors are washed by the rain and dried by the sun, where the south wind dusts the beautiful green and purple carpets. Or a chariot—to carry us up into the sky, where the lamps are stars, and don't need to be filled with paraffin oil every day.

MORELL [*harshly*]   And where there is nothing to do but to be idle, selfish and useless.

CANDIDA [*jarred*]   Oh, James, how could you spoil it all!

MARCHBANKS [*firing up*]   Yes, to be idle, selfish and useless: that is to be beautiful and free and happy: hasn't every man desired that with all his soul for the woman he loves? That's my ideal: what's yours, and that of all the dreadful people who live in these hideous rows of houses? Sermons and scrubbing brushes! With you to preach the sermon and your wife to scrub.

CANDIDA [*quaintly*]   He cleans the boots, Eugene. You will have to clean them to-morrow for saying that about him.

MARCHBANKS   Oh! don't talk about boots. Your feet should be beautiful on the mountains.*

CANDIDA   My feet would not be beautiful on the Hackney Road without boots.

BURGESS [*scandalized*]   Come, Candy, don't be vulgar. Mr. Morchbanks ain't accustomed to it. You're givin' him the 'orrors again. I mean the poetic ones.

[*MORELL is silent. Apparently he is busy with his letters: really he is puzzling with misgiving over his new and alarming experience that the surer he is of his moral thrusts, the more swiftly and effectively EUGENE parries them. To find himself beginning to fear a man whom he does not respect afflicts him bitterly.*]

[*MISS GARNETT comes in with a telegram.*]

PROSERPINE [*handing the telegram to MORELL*]   Reply paid. The

---

* An allusion to the Bible, Isaiah 52:7: "How beautiful upon the mountains are the feet of him that bringeth good tidings, that publisheth peace" (King James Version).

boy's waiting. [*To CANDIDA, coming back to her machine and sitting down.*] Maria is ready for you now in the kitchen, Mrs. Morell. [*CANDIDA rises.*] The onions have come.

MARCHBANKS [*convulsively*]  Onions!

CANDIDA    Yes, onions. Not even Spanish ones—nasty little red onions. You shall help me to slice them. Come along.

[*She catches him by the wrist and runs out, pulling him after her. BURGESS rises in consternation, and stands aghast on the hearth-rug, staring after them.*]

BURGESS    Candy didn't oughter 'andle a peer's nevvy* like that. It's goin' too fur with it. Lookee 'ere, James: do 'e often git taken queer like that?

MORELL [*shortly, writing a telegram*]    I don't know.

BURGESS [*sentimentally*]    He talks very pretty. I allus had a turn for a bit of potery. Candy takes arter me that-a-way: huse ter make me tell her fairy stories when she was on'y a little kiddy not that 'igh [*indicating a stature of two feet or thereabouts*].

MORELL [*preoccupied*]    Ah, indeed. [*He blots the telegram, and goes out.*]

PROSERPINE    Used you to make the fairy stories up out of your own head?

[*BURGESS, not deigning to reply, strikes an attitude of the haughtiest disdain on the hearth-rug.*]

PROSERPINE [*calmly*]    I should never have supposed you had it in you. By the way, I'd better warn you, since you've taken such a fancy to Mr. Marchbanks. He's mad.

BURGESS    Mad! Wot! 'Im too!!

PROSERPINE    Mad as a March hare. He did frighten me, I can tell you just before you came in that time. Haven't you noticed the queer things he says?

BURGESS    So that's wot the poetic 'orrors means. Blame me if it didn't come into my head once or twyst that he must be off his

---

*Nephew.

chump!* [*He crosses the room to the door, lifting up his voice as he goes.*] Well, this is a pretty sort of asylum for a man to be in, with no one but you to take care of him!

PROSERPINE [*as he passes her*]   Yes, what a dreadful thing it would be if anything happened to  y o u !

BURGESS [*loftily*]   Don't you address no remarks to me. Tell your hemployer that I've gone into the garden for a smoke.

PROSERPINE [*mocking*]   Oh!

[*Before BURGESS can retort, MORELL comes back.*]

BURGESS [*sentimentally*]   Goin' for a turn in the garden to smoke, James.

MORELL [*brusquely*]   Oh, all right, all right. [*BURGESS goes out pathetically in the character of the weary old man. MORELL stands at the table, turning over his papers, and adding, across to PROSERPINE, half humorously, half absently*] Well, Miss Prossy, why have you been calling my father-in-law names?

PROSERPINE [*blushing fiery red, and looking quickly up at him, half scared, half reproachful*]   I—[*She bursts into tears.*]

MORELL [*with tender gaiety, leaning across the table towards her, and consoling her*]   Oh, come, come, come! Never mind, Pross: he i s  a silly old fathead, isn't he?

[*With an explosive sob, she makes a dash at the door, and vanishes, banging it. MORELL, shaking his head resignedly, sighs, and goes wearily to his chair, where he sits down and sets to work, looking old and careworn.*]

[*CANDIDA comes in. She has finished her household work and taken off the apron. She at once notices his dejected appearance, and posts herself quietly at the spare chair, looking down at him attentively; but she says nothing.*]

MORELL [*looking up, but with his pen raised ready to resume his work*]   Well? Where is Eugene?

CANDIDA   Washing his hands in the scullery—under the tap. He

---

*Head.

will make an excellent cook if he can only get over his dread of Maria.

MORELL [*shortly*]    Ha! No doubt. [*He begins writing again.*]

CANDIDA [*going nearer, and putting her hand down softly on his to stop him, as she says*]    Come here, dear. Let me look at you. [*He drops his pen and yields himself at her disposal. She makes him rise and brings him a little away from the table, looking at him critically all the time.*] Turn your face to the light. [*She places him facing the window.*] My boy is not looking well. Has he been overworking?

MORELL    Nothing more than usual.

CANDIDA    He looks very pale, and grey, and wrinkled, and old. [*His melancholy deepens; and she attacks it with wilful gaiety.*] Here [*pulling him towards the easy chair*] you've done enough writing for to-day. Leave Prossy to finish it and come and talk to me.

MORELL    But—

CANDIDA    Yes, I  m u s t  be talked to sometimes. [*She makes him sit down, and seats herself on the carpet beside his knee.*] Now [*patting his hand*] you're beginning to look better already. Why don't you give up all this tiresome overworking—going out every night lecturing and talking? Of course what you say is all very true and very right; but it does no good: they don't mind what you say to them one little bit. Of course they agree with you; but what's the use of people agreeing with you if they go and do just the opposite of what you tell them the moment your back is turned? Look at our congregation at St. Dominic's! Why do they come to hear you talking about Christianity every Sunday? Why, just because they've been so full of business and money-making for six days that they want to forget all about it and have a rest on the seventh, so that they can go back fresh and make money harder than ever! You positively help them at it instead of hindering them.

MORELL [*with energetic seriousness*]    You know very well, Candida, that I often blow them up soundly for that. But if there is nothing in their church-going but rest and diversion, why don't they try something more amusing—more self-indulgent? There must be some good in the fact that they prefer St. Dominic's to worse places on Sundays.

CANDIDA    Oh, the worst places aren't open; and even if they were, they daren't be seen going to them. Besides, James, dear, you preach so splendidly that it's as good as a play for them. Why do you think the women are so enthusiastic?

MORELL [*shocked*]    Candida!

CANDIDA    Oh, *I* know. You silly boy: you think it's your Socialism and your religion; but if it was that, they'd do what you tell them instead of only coming to look at you. They all have Prossy's complaint.

MORELL    Prossy's complaint! What do you mean, Candida?

CANDIDA    Yes, Prossy, and all the other secretaries you ever had. Why does Prossy condescend to wash up the things, and to peel potatoes and abase herself in all manner of ways for six shillings a week less than she used to get in a city office? She's in love with you, James: that's the reason. They're all in love with you. And you are in love with preaching because you do it so beautifully. And you think it's all enthusiasm for the kingdom of Heaven on earth; and so do they. You dear silly!

MORELL    Candida: what dreadful, what soul-destroying cynicism! Are you jesting? Or——can it be?——are you jealous?

CANDIDA [*with curious thoughtfulness*]    Yes, I feel a little jealous sometimes.

MORELL [*incredulously*]    What! Of Prossy!

CANDIDA [*laughing*]    No, no, no, no. Not jealous of anybody. Jealous for somebody else, who is not loved as he ought to be.

MORELL    Me!

CANDIDA    You! Why, you're spoiled with love and worship: you get far more than is good for you. No: I mean Eugene.

MORELL [*startled*]    Eugene!

CANDIDA    It seems unfair that all the love should go to you, and none to him, although he needs it so much more than you do. [*A convulsive movement shakes him in spite of himself* ] What's the matter? Am I worrying you?

MORELL [*hastily*]   Not at all. [*Looking at her with troubled intensity.*] You know that I have perfect confidence in you, Candida.

CANDIDA   You vain thing! Are you so sure of your irresistible attractions?

MORELL   Candida: you are shocking me. I never thought of my attractions. I thought of your goodness—your purity. That is what I confide in.

CANDIDA   What a nasty, uncomfortable thing to say to me! Oh, you a r e a clergyman, James—a thorough clergyman.

MORELL [*turning away from her, heart-stricken*]   So Eugene says.

CANDIDA [*with lively interest, leaning over to him with her arms on his knee*]   Eugene's always right. He's a wonderful boy: I have grown fonder and fonder of him all the time I was away. Do you know, James, that though he has not the least suspicion of it himself, he is ready to fall madly in love with me?

MORELL [*grimly*]   Oh, he has no suspicion of it himself, hasn't he?

CANDIDA   Not a bit. [*She takes her arms from his knee, and turns thoughtfully, sinking into a more restful attitude with her hands in her lap.*] Some day he will know—when he is grown up and experienced, like you. And he will know that I must have known. I wonder what he will think of me then.

MORELL   No evil, Candida. I hope and trust, no evil.

CANDIDA [*dubiously*]   That will depend.

MORELL [*bewildered*]   Depend!

CANDIDA [*looking at him*]   Yes: it will depend on what happens to him. [*He looks vacantly at her.*] Don't you see? It will depend on how he comes to learn what love really is. I mean on the sort of woman who will teach it to him.

MORELL [*quite at a loss*]   Yes. No. I don't know what you mean.

CANDIDA [*explaining*]   If he learns it from a good woman, then it will be all right: he will forgive me.

MORELL   Forgive!

CANDIDA    But suppose he learns it from a bad woman, as so many men do, especially poetic men, who imagine all women are angels! Suppose he only discovers the value of love when he has thrown it away and degraded himself in his ignorance. Will he forgive me then, do you think?

MORELL    Forgive you for what?

CANDIDA [*realizing how stupid he is, and a little disappointed, though quite tenderly so*]   Don't you understand? [*He shakes his head. She turns to him again, so as to explain with the fondest intimacy.*] I mean, will he forgive me for not teaching him myself? For abandoning him to the bad women for the sake of my goodness—my purity, as you call it? Ah, James, how little you understand me, to talk of your confidence in my goodness and purity! I would give them both to poor Eugene as willingly as I would give my shawl to a beggar dying of cold, if there were nothing else to restrain me. Put your trust in my love for you, James, for if that went, I should care very little for your sermons—mere phrases that you cheat yourself and others with every day. [*She is about to rise.*]

MORELL    H i s words!

CANDIDA [*checking herself quickly in the act of getting up, so that she is on her knees, but upright*]   Whose words?

MORELL    Eugene's.

CANDIDA [*delighted*]   He is always right. He understands you; he understands me; he understands Prossy; and you, James—you understand nothing. [*She laughs, and kisses him to console him. He recoils as if stung, and springs up.*]

MORELL    How can you bear to do that when—oh, Candida [*with anguish in his voice*] I had rather you had plunged a grappling iron into my heart than given me that kiss.

CANDIDA [*rising, alarmed*]   My dear: what's the matter?

MORELL [*frantically waving her off*]   Don't touch me.

CANDIDA [*amazed*]   James!

[*They are interrupted by the entrance of MARCHBANKS, with*

*BURGESS, who stops near the door, staring, whilst EUGENE hurries forward between them.*]

MARCHBANKS    Is anything the matter?

MORELL [*deadly white, putting an iron constraint on himself*]    Nothing but this: that either you were right this morning, or Candida is mad.

BURGESS [*in loudest protest*]    Wot! Candy mad too! Oh, come, come, come! [*He crosses the room to the fireplace, protesting as he goes, and knocks the ashes out of his pipe on the bars. MORELL sits down desperately, leaning forward to hide his face, and interlacing his fingers rigidly to keep them steady.*]

CANDIDA [*to MORELL, relieved and laughing*]    Oh, you're only shocked! Is that all? How conventional all you unconventional people are!

BURGESS    Come: be'ave yourself, Candy. What'll Mr. Morchbanks think of you?

CANDIDA    This comes of James teaching me to think for myself, and never to hold back out of fear of what other people may think of me. It works beautifully as long as I think the same things as he does. But now, because I have just thought something different!—look at him—just look! [*She points to MORELL, greatly amused. EUGENE looks, and instantly presses his hand on his heart, as if some deadly pain had shot through it, and sits down on the sofa like a man witnessing a tragedy.*]

BURGESS [*on the hearth-rug*]    Well, James, you certainly ain't as himpressive lookin' as usu'l.

MORELL [*with a laugh which is half a sob*]    I suppose not. I beg all your pardons: I was not conscious of making a fuss. [*Pulling himself together.*] Well, well, well, well, well! [*He goes back to his place at the table, setting to work at his papers again with resolute cheerfulness.*]

CANDIDA [*going to the sofa and sitting beside MARCHBANKS, still in a bantering humor*]    Well, Eugene, why are you so sad? Did the onions make you cry?

[*MORELL cannot prevent himself from watching them.*]

MARCHBANKS [*aside to her*]   It is your cruelty. I hate cruelty. It is a horrible thing to see one person make another suffer.

CANDIDA [*petting him ironically*]   Poor boy, have I been cruel? Did I make it slice nasty little red onions?

MARCHBANKS [*earnestly*]   Oh, stop, stop: I don't mean myself. You have made him suffer frightfully. I feel his pain in my own heart. I know that it is not your fault—it is something that must happen; but don't make light of it. I shudder when you torture him and laugh.

CANDIDA [*incredulously*]   *I* torture James! Nonsense, Eugene: how you exaggerate! Silly! [*She looks round at MORELL, who hastily resumes his writing. She goes to him and stands behind his chair, bending over him.*] Don't work any more, dear. Come and talk to us.

MORELL [*affectionately but bitterly*]   Ah no: *I* can't talk. I can only preach.

CANDIDA [*caressing him*]   Well, come and preach.

BURGESS [*strongly remonstrating*]   Aw, no, Candy. 'Ang it all!

[*LEXY MILL comes in, looking anxious and important.*]

LEXY [*hastening to shake hands with CANDIDA*]   How do you do, Mrs. Morell? So glad to see you back again.

CANDIDA   Thank you, Lexy. You know Eugene, don't you?

LEXY   Oh, yes. How do you do, Marchbanks?

MARCHBANKS   Quite well, thanks.

LEXY [*to MORELL*]   I've just come from the Guild of St. Matthew. They are in the greatest consternation about your telegram. There's nothing wrong, is there?

CANDIDA   What did you telegraph about, James?

LEXY [*to CANDIDA*]   He was to have spoken for them tonight. They've taken the large hall in Mare Street and spent a lot of money on posters. Morell's telegram was to say he couldn't come. It came on them like a thunderbolt.

CANDIDA [*surprised, and beginning to suspect something wrong*]   Given up an engagement to speak!

BURGESS   First time in his life, I'll bet. Ain' it, Candy?

LEXY [to MORELL]   They decided to send an urgent telegram to you asking whether you could not change your mind. Have you received it?

MORELL [with restrained impatience]   Yes, yes: I got it.

LEXY   It was reply paid.

MORELL   Yes, I know. I answered it. I can't go.

CANDIDA   But why, James?

MORELL [almost fiercely]   Because I don't choose. These people forget that I am a man: they think I am a talking machine to be turned on for their pleasure every evening of my life. May I not have o n e night at home, with my wife, and my friends?
[They are all amazed at this outburst, except EUGENE. His expression remains unchanged.]

CANDIDA   Oh, James, you know you'll have an attack of bad conscience to-morrow; and I shall have to suffer for that.

LEXY [intimidated, but urgent]   I know, of course, that they make the most unreasonable demands on you. But they have been telegraphing all over the place for another speaker: and they can get nobody but the President of the Agnostic League.

MORELL [promptly]   Well, an excellent man. What better do they want?

LEXY   But he always insists so powerfully on the divorce of Socialism from Christianity. He will undo all the good we have been doing. Of course you know best; but—[He hesitates.]

CANDIDA [coaxingly]   Oh, d o go, James. We'll all go.

BURGESS [grumbling]   Look 'ere, Candy! I say! Let's stay at home by the fire, comfortable. He won't need to be more'n a couple-o'-hour away.

CANDIDA   You'll be just as comfortable at the meeting. We'll all sit on the platform and be great people.

EUGENE [terrified]   Oh, please don't let us go on the platform. No—everyone will stare at us—I couldn't. I'll sit at the back of the room.

CANDIDA   Don't be afraid. They'll be too busy looking at James to notice you.

MORELL [*turning his head and looking meaningly at her over his shoulder*]   Prossy's complaint, Candida! Eh?

CANDIDA [*gaily*]   Yes.

BURGESS [*mystified*]   Prossy's complaint. Wot are you talking about, James?

MORELL [*not heeding him, rises; goes to the door; and holds it open, shouting in a commanding voice*]   Miss Garnett.

PROSERPINE [*in the distance*]   Yes, Mr. Morell. Coming.

[*They all wait, except BURGESS, who goes stealthily to LEXY and draws him aside.*]

BURGESS   Listen here, Mr. Mill. Wot's Prossy's complaint? Wot's wrong with 'er?

LEXY [*confidentially*]   Well, I don't exactly know; but she spoke very strangely to me this morning. I'm afraid she's a little out of her mind sometimes.

BURGESS [*overwhelmed*]   Why, it must be catchin'! Four in the same 'ouse! [*He goes back to the hearth, quite lost before the instability of the human intellect in a clergyman's house.*]

PROSERPINE [*appearing on the threshold*]   What is it, Mr. Morell?

MORELL   Telegraph to the Guild of St. Matthew that I am coming.

PROSERPINE [*surprised*]   Don't they expect you?

MORELL [*peremptorily*]   Do as I tell you.

[*PROSERPINE frightened, sits down at her typewriter, and obeys. MORELL goes across to BURGESS, CANDIDA watching his movements all the time with growing wonder and misgiving.*]

MORELL   Burgess: you don't want to come?

BURGESS [*in deprecation*]   Oh, don't put it like that, James. It's only that it ain't Sunday, you know.

MORELL   I'm sorry. I thought you might like to be introduced to the chairman. He's on the Works Committee of the County Council and has some influence in the matter of contracts.

[*BURGESS wakes up at once. MORELL, expecting as much, waits a moment, and says*] Will you come?

BURGESS [*with enthusiasm*]    Course I'll come, James. Ain' it always a pleasure to 'ear you.

MORELL [*turning from him*]    I shall want you to take some notes at the meeting, Miss Garnett, if you have no other engagement. [*She nods, afraid to speak.*] You are coming, Lexy, I suppose.

LEXY    Certainly.

CANDIDA    We are all coming, James.

MORELL    No: you are not coming; and Eugene is not coming. You will stay here and entertain him—to celebrate your return home. [*EUGENE rises, breathless.*]

CANDIDA    But James—

MORELL [*authoritatively*]    I insist. You do not want to come; and he does not want to come. [*CANDIDA is about to protest.*] Oh, don't concern yourselves: I shall have plenty of people without you: your chairs will be wanted by unconverted people who have never heard me before.

CANDIDA [*troubled*]    Eugene: wouldn't you like to come?

MORELL    I should be afraid to let myself go before Eugene: he is so critical of sermons. [*Looking at him.*] He knows I am afraid of him: he told me as much this morning. Well, I shall shew him how much afraid I am by leaving him here in your custody, Candida.

MARCHBANKS [*to himself with vivid feeling*]    That's brave. That's beautiful. [*He sits down again listening with parted lips.*]

CANDIDA [*with anxious misgiving*]    But—but— Is anything the matter, James? [*Greatly troubled.*] I can't understand—

MORELL    Ah, I thought it was *I* who couldn't understand, dear. [*He takes her tenderly in his arms and kisses her on the forehead; then looks round quietly at MARCHBANKS.*]

# ACT III

*Late in the evening. Past ten. The curtains are drawn, and the lamps lighted. The typewriter is in its case; the large table has been cleared and tidied; everything indicates that the day's work is done.*

*CANDIDA and MARCHBANKS are seated at the fire. The reading lamp is on the mantelshelf above MARCHBANKS, who is sitting on the small chair reading aloud from a manuscript. A little pile of manuscripts and a couple of volumes of poetry are on the carpet beside him. CANDIDA is in the easy chair with the poker, a light brass one, upright in her hand. She is leaning back and looking at the point of it curiously, with her feet stretched towards the blaze and her heels resting on the fender, profoundly unconscious of her appearance and surroundings.*

MARCHBANKS [*breaking off in his recitation*]   Every poet that ever lived has put that thought into a sonnet. He must: he can't help it. [*He looks to her for assent, and notices her absorption in the poker.*] Haven't you been listening? [*No response.*] Mrs. Morell!

CANDIDA [*starting*]   Eh?

MARCHBANKS   Haven't you been listening?

CANDIDA [*with a guilty excess of politeness*]   Oh, yes. It's very nice. Go on, Eugene. I'm longing to hear what happens to the angel.

MARCHBANKS [*crushed—the manuscript dropping from his hand to the floor*]   I beg your pardon for boring you.

CANDIDA   But you are not boring me, I assure you. P l e a s e go on. Do, Eugene.

MARCHBANKS   I finished the poem about the angel quarter of an hour ago. I've read you several things since.

CANDIDA [*remorsefully*]  I'm so sorry, Eugene. I think the poker must have fascinated me. [*She puts it down.*]

MARCHBANKS  It made me horribly uneasy.

CANDIDA  Why didn't you tell me? I'd have put it down at once.

MARCHBANKS  I was afraid of making you uneasy, too. It looked as if it were a weapon. If I were a hero of old, I should have laid my drawn sword between us. If Morell had come in he would have thought you had taken up the poker because there was no sword between us.

CANDIDA [*wondering*]  What? [*With a puzzled glance at him.*] I can't quite follow that. Those sonnets of yours have perfectly addled me. Why should there be a sword between us?

MARCHBANKS [*evasively*]  Oh, never mind. [*He stoops to pick up the manuscript.*]

CANDIDA  Put that down again, Eugene. There are limits to my appetite for poetry—even your poetry. You've been reading to me for more than two hours—ever since James went out. I want to talk.

MARCHBANKS [*rising, scared*]  No: I mustn't talk. [*He looks round him in his lost way, and adds, suddenly*] I think I'll go out and take a walk in the park. [*Making for the door.*]

CANDIDA  Nonsense: it's shut long ago. Come and sit down on the hearth-rug, and talk moonshine as you usually do. I want to be amused. Don't you want to?

MARCHBANKS [*in half terror, half rapture*]  Yes.

CANDIDA  Then come along. [*She moves her chair back a little to make room. He hesitates; then timidly stretches himself on the hearth-rug, face upwards, and throws back his head across her knees, looking up at her.*]

MARCHBANKS  Oh, I've been so miserable all the evening, because I was doing right. Now I'm doing wrong; and I'm happy.

CANDIDA [*tenderly amused at him*]  Yes: I'm sure you feel a great grown up wicked deceiver—quite proud of yourself, aren't you?

MARCHBANKS [*raising his head quickly and turning a little to look *round at her*]    Take care. I'm ever so much older than you, if you only knew. [*He turns quite over on his knees, with his hands clasped and his arms on her lap, and speaks with growing impulse, his blood beginning to stir.*] May I say some wicked things to you?

CANDIDA [*without the least fear or coldness, quite nobly, and with perfect respect for his passion, but with a touch of her wise-hearted maternal humor*]    No. But you may say anything you really and truly feel. Anything at all, no matter what it is. I am not afraid, so long as it is your real self that speaks, and not a mere attitude—a gallant attitude, or a wicked attitude, or even a poetic attitude. I put you on your honor and truth. Now say whatever you want to.

MARCHBANKS [*the eager expression vanishing utterly from his lips and nostrils as his eyes light up with pathetic spirituality*]    Oh, now I can't say anything: all the words I know belong to some attitude or other—all except one.

CANDIDA    What one is that?

MARCHBANKS [*softly, losing himself in the music of the name*]    Candida, Candida, Candida, Candida, Candida. I must say that now, because you have put me on my honor and truth; and I never think or feel Mrs. Morell: it is always Candida.

CANDIDA    Of course. And what have you to say to Candida?

MARCHBANKS    Nothing, but to repeat your name a thousand times. Don't you feel that every time is a prayer to you?

CANDIDA    Doesn't it make you happy to be able to pray?

MARCHBANKS    Yes, very happy.

CANDIDA    Well, that happiness is the answer to your prayer. Do you want anything more?

MARCHBANKS [*in beatitude*]    No: I have come into heaven, where want is unknown.

[*MORELL comes in. He halts on the threshold, and takes in the scene at a glance.*]

MORELL [*grave and self-contained*]    I hope I don't disturb you.

[*CANDIDA starts up violently, but without the smallest embarrassment, laughing at herself. EUGENE, still kneeling, saves himself from falling by putting his hands on the seat of the chair, and remains there, staring open mouthed at MORELL.*]

CANDIDA [*as she rises*]   Oh, James, how you startled me! I was so taken up with Eugene that I didn't hear your latch-key. How did the meeting go off? Did you speak well?

MORELL   I have never spoken better in my life.

CANDIDA   That was first rate! How much was the collection?

MORELL   I forgot to ask.

CANDIDA [*to EUGENE*]   He must have spoken splendidly, or he would never have forgotten that. [*To MORELL.*] Where are all the others?

MORELL   They left long before I could get away: I thought I should never escape. I believe they are having supper somewhere.

CANDIDA [*in her domestic business tone*]   Oh; in that case, Maria may go to bed. I'll tell her. [*She goes out to the kitchen.*]

MORELL [*looking sternly down at MARCHBANKS*]   Well?

MARCHBANKS [*squatting cross-legged on the hearth-rug, and actually at ease with MORELL—even impishly humorous*]   Well?

MORELL   Have you anything to tell me?

MARCHBANKS   Only that I have been making a fool of myself here in private whilst you have been making a fool of yourself in public.

MORELL   Hardly in the same way, I think.

MARCHBANKS [*scrambling up—eagerly*]   The very, very, v e r y same way. I have been playing the good man just like you. When you began your heroics about leaving me here with Candida—

MORELL [*involuntarily*]   Candida?

MARCHBANKS   Oh, yes: I've got that far. Heroics are infectious: I caught the disease from you. I swore not to say a word in your absence that I would not have said a month ago in your presence.

MORELL   Did you keep your oath?

MARCHBANKS [*suddenly perching himself grotesquely on the easy chair*]   I was ass enough to keep it until about ten minutes ago.

Up to that moment I went on desperately reading to her—reading my own poems—anybody's poems—to stave off a conversation. I was standing outside the gate of Heaven, and refusing to go in. Oh, you can't think how heroic it was, and how uncomfortable! Then—

MORELL [*steadily controlling his suspense*]    Then?—

MARCHBANKS [*prosaically slipping down into a quite ordinary attitude in the chair*]    Then she couldn't bear being read to any longer.

MORELL    And you approached the gate of Heaven at last?

MARCHBANKS    Yes.

MORELL    Well? [*Fiercely.*] Speak, man: have you no feeling for me?

MARCHBANKS [*softly and musically*]    Then she became an angel; and there was a flaming sword that turned every way, so that I couldn't go in; for I saw that that gate was really the gate of Hell.

MORELL [*triumphantly*]    She repulsed you!

MARCHBANKS [*rising in wild scorn*]    No, you fool: if she had done that I should never have seen that I was in Heaven already. Repulsed me! You think that would have saved me—virtuous indignation! Oh, you are not worthy to live in the same world with her. [*He turns away contemptuously to the other side of the room.*]

MORELL [*who has watched him quietly without changing his place*]    Do you think you make yourself more worthy by reviling me, Eugene?

MARCHBANKS    Here endeth the thousand and first lesson. Morell: I don't think much of your preaching after all: I believe I could do it better myself. The man I want to meet is the man that Candida married.

MORELL    The man that—? Do you mean me?

MARCHBANKS    I don't mean the Reverend James Mavor Morell, moralist and windbag. I mean the real man that the Reverend James must have hidden somewhere inside his black coat—the man that Candida loved. You can't make a woman like Candida love you by merely buttoning your collar at the back instead of in front.

MORELL [*boldly and steadily*]   When Candida promised to marry me, I was the same moralist and windbag that you now see. I wore my black coat; and my collar was buttoned behind instead of in front. Do you think she would have loved me any the better for being insincere in my profession?

MARCHBANKS [*on the sofa hugging his ankles*]   Oh, she forgave you, just as she forgives me for being a coward, and a weakling, and what you call a snivelling little whelp and all the rest of it. [*Dreamily.*] A woman like that has divine insight: she loves our souls, and not our follies and vanities and illusions, or our collars and coats, or any other of the rags and tatters we are rolled up in. [*He reflects on this for an instant; then turns intently to question MORELL.*] What I want to know is how you got past the flaming sword that stopped me.

MORELL [*meaningly*]   Perhaps because I was not interrupted at the end of ten minutes.

MARCHBANKS [*taken aback*]   What!

MORELL   Man can climb to the highest summits; but he cannot dwell there long.

MARCHBANKS   It's false: there can he dwell for ever and there only. It's in the other moments that he can find no rest, no sense of the silent glory of life. Where would you have me spend my moments, if not on the summits?

MORELL   In the scullery, slicing onions and filling lamps.

MARCHBANKS   Or in the pulpit, scrubbing cheap earthenware souls?

MORELL   Yes, that, too. It was there that I earned my golden moment, and the right, in that moment, to ask her to love me. *I* did not take the moment on credit; nor did I use it to steal another man's happiness.

MARCHBANKS [*rather disgustedly, trotting back towards the fireplace*] I have no doubt you conducted the transaction as honestly as if you were buying a pound of cheese. [*He stops on the brink of the hearth-rug and adds, thoughtfully, to himself, with his back turned to MORELL*] I could only go to her as a beggar.

MORELL [*starting*]    A beggar dying of cold—asking for her shawl?

MARCHBANKS [*turning, surprised*]    Thank you for touching up my poetry. Yes, if you like, a beggar dying of cold asking for her shawl.

MORELL [*excitedly*]    And she refused. Shall I tell you why she refused? I can tell you, on her own authority. It was because of—

MARCHBANKS    She didn't refuse.

MORELL    Not!

MARCHBANKS    She offered me all I chose to ask for, her shawl, her wings, the wreath of stars on her head, the lilies in her hand, the crescent moon beneath her feet—*

MORELL [*seizing him*]    Out with the truth, man: my wife is my wife: I want no more of your poetic fripperies. I know well that if I have lost her love and you have gained it, no law will bind her.

MARCHBANKS [*quaintly, without fear or resistance*]    Catch me by the shirt collar, Morell: she will arrange it for me afterwards as she did this morning. [*With quiet rapture.*] I shall feel her hands touch me.

MORELL    You young imp, do you know how dangerous it is to say that to me? Or [*with a sudden misgiving*] has something made you brave?

MARCHBANKS    I'm not afraid now. I disliked you before: that was why I shrank from your touch. But I saw to-day—when she tortured you—that you love her. Since then I have been your friend: you may strangle me if you like.

MORELL [*releasing him*]    Eugene: if that is not a heartless lie—if you have a spark of human feeling left in you—will you tell me what has happened during my absence?

---

*Eugene describes the Pre-Raphaelite painting *The Blessed Damozel*, by Dante Rossetti.

MARCHBANKS    What happened! Why, the flaming sword—
[*MORELL stamps with impatience.*] Well, in plain prose, I loved her
so exquisitely that I wanted nothing more than the happiness of
being in such love. And before I had time to come down from the
highest summits, y o u  came in.

MORELL [*suffering deeply*]    So it is still unsettled—still the misery
of doubt.

MARCHBANKS    Misery! I am the happiest of men. I desire nothing now but her happiness. [*With dreamy enthusiasm.*] Oh, Morell,
let us both give her up. Why should she have to choose between
a wretched little nervous disease like me, and a pig-headed parson like you? Let us go on a pilgrimage, you to the east and I to
the west, in search of a worthy lover for her—some beautiful
archangel with purple wings—

MORELL    Some fiddlestick. Oh, if she is mad enough to leave me
for you, who will protect her? Who will help her? who will
work for her? who will be a father to her children? [*He sits down
distractedly on the sofa, with his elbows on his knees and his head
propped on his clenched fists.*]

MARCHBANKS [*snapping his fingers wildly*]    She does not ask those
silly questions. It is she who wants somebody to protect, to help,
to work for—somebody to give her children to protect, to help
and to work for. Some grown up man who has become as a little
child again. Oh, you fool, you fool, you triple fool! I am the
man, Morell: I am the man. [*He dances about excitedly, crying.*] You
don't understand what a woman is. Send for her, Morell: send
for her and let her choose between— [*The door opens and CAN-
DIDA enters. He stops as if petrified.*]

CANDIDA [*amazed, on the threshold*]    What on earth are you at,
Eugene?

MARCHBANKS [*oddly*]    James and I are having a preaching match;
and he is getting the worst of it. [*CANDIDA looks quickly round at
MORELL. Seeing that he is distressed, she hurries down to him, greatly
vexed, speaking with vigorous reproach to MARCHBANKS.*]

CANDIDA   You have been annoying him. Now I won't have it, Eugene: do you hear? [*Putting her hand on MORELL's shoulder, and quite forgetting her wifely tact in her annoyance.*] My boy shall not be worried: I will protect him.

MORELL [*rising proudly*]   Protect!

CANDIDA [*not heeding him—to EUGENE*]   What have you been saying?

MARCHBANKS [*appalled*]   Nothing—I—

CANDIDA   Eugene! Nothing?

MARCHBANKS [*piteously*]   I mean—I—I'm very sorry. I won't do it again: indeed I won't. I'll let him alone.

MORELL [*indignantly, with an aggressive movement towards EUGENE*] Let me alone! You young—

CANDIDA [*stopping him*]   Sh—no, let me deal with him, James.

MARCHBANKS   Oh, you're not angry with me, are you?

CANDIDA [*severely*]   Yes, I am—very angry. I have a great mind to pack you out of the house.

MORELL [*taken aback by CANDIDA's vigor, and by no means relishing the sense of being rescued by her from another man*]   Gently, Candida, gently. I am able to take care of myself.

CANDIDA [*petting him*]   Yes, dear: of course you are. But you mustn't be annoyed and made miserable.

MARCHBANKS [*almost in tears, turning to the door*]   I'll go.

CANDIDA   Oh, you needn't go: I can't turn you out at this time of night. [*Vehemently.*] Shame on you! For shame!

MARCHBANKS [*desperately*]   But what have I done?

CANDIDA   I know what you have done—as well as if I had been here all the time. Oh, it was unworthy! You are like a child: you cannot hold your tongue.

MARCHBANKS   I would die ten times over sooner than give you a moment's pain.

CANDIDA [*with infinite contempt for this puerility*]   Much good your dying would do me!

MORELL   Candida, my dear: this altercation is hardly quite

seemly. It is a matter between two men; and I am the right person to settle it.

CANDIDA    Two  m e n ! Do you call that a man? [*To* EUGENE.] You bad boy!

MARCHBANKS [*gathering a whimsically affectionate courage from the scolding*]    If I am to be scolded like this, I must make a boy's excuse. He began it. And he's bigger than I am.

CANDIDA [*losing confidence a little as her concern for* MORELL'*s dignity takes the alarm*]    That can't be true. [*To* MORELL.] You didn't begin it, James, did you?

MORELL [*contemptuously*]    No.

MARCHBANKS [*indignant*]    Oh!

MORELL [*to* EUGENE]    Y o u  began it—this morning. [CANDIDA, *instantly connecting this with his mysterious allusion in the afternoon to something told him by* EUGENE *in the morning, looks quickly at him, wrestling with the enigma.* MORELL *proceeds with the emphasis of offended superiority.*] But your other point is true. I am certainly the bigger of the two, and, I hope, the stronger, Candida. So you had better leave the matter in my hands.

CANDIDA [*again soothing him*]    Yes, dear; but—[*Troubled.*] I don't understand about this morning.

MORELL [*gently snubbing her*]    You need not understand, my dear.

CANDIDA    But, James, I— [*The street bell rings.*] Oh, bother! Here they all come. [*She goes out to let them in.*]

MARCHBANKS [*running to* MORELL]    Oh, Morell, isn't it dreadful? She's angry with us: she hates me. What shall I do?

MORELL [*with quaint desperation, clutching himself by the hair*]    Eugene: my head is spinning round. I shall begin to laugh presently. [*He walks up and down the middle of the room.*]

MARCHBANKS [*following him anxiously*]    No, no: she'll think I've thrown you into hysterics. Don't laugh. [*Boisterous voices and laughter are heard approaching.* LEXY MILL, *his eyes sparkling, and his bearing denoting unwonted elevation of spirit, enters with* BURGESS, *who is greasy and self-complacent, but has all his wits about him. MISS GARNETT, with her smartest hat and jacket on, follows them; but though her eyes are brighter than before, she is evidently a prey to misgiving. She places herself with her back to her typewriting table, with one hand on it to rest herself, passes the other across her forehead as if she were a little tired and giddy. MARCHBANKS relapses into shyness and edges away into the corner near the window, where MORELL's books are.]*

MILL [*exhilaratedly*]   Morell: I m u s t congratulate you. [*Grasping his hand.*] What a noble, splendid, inspired address you gave us! You surpassed yourself.

BURGESS   So you did, James. It fair kep' me awake to the last word. Didn't it, Miss Gornett?

PROSERPINE [*worriedly*]   Oh, I wasn't minding you: I was trying to make notes. [*She takes out her note-book, and looks at her stenography, which nearly makes her cry.*]

MORELL   Did I go too fast, Pross?

PROSERPINE   Much too fast. You know I can't do more than a hundred words a minute. [*She relieves her feelings by throwing her note-book angrily beside her machine, ready for use next morning.*]

MORELL [*soothingly*]   Oh, well, well, never mind, never mind, never mind. Have you all had supper?

LEXY   Mr. Burgess has been kind enough to give us a really splendid supper at the Belgrave.

BURGESS [*with effusive magnanimity*]   Don't mention it, Mr. Mill. [*Modestly.*] You're 'arty welcome to my little treat.

PROSERPINE   We had champagne! I never tasted it before. I feel quite giddy.

MORELL [*surprised*]   A champagne supper! That was very handsome. Was it my eloquence that produced all this extravagance?

MILL [*rhetorically*]   Your eloquence, and Mr. Burgess's goodness of heart. [*With a fresh burst of exhilaration.*] And what a very fine fellow the chairman is, Morell! He came to supper with us.

MORELL [*with long drawn significance, looking at BURGESS*] O-o-o-h, the chairman. N o w I understand.

[*BURGESS, covering a lively satisfaction in his diplomatic cunning with a deprecatory cough, retires to the hearth. LEXY folds his arms and leans against the cellaret in a high-spirited attitude. CANDIDA comes in with glasses, lemons, and a jug of hot water on a tray.*]

CANDIDA    Who will have some lemonade? You know our rules: total abstinence. [*She puts the tray on the table, and takes up the lemon squeezers, looking enquiringly round at them.*]

MORELL    No use, dear. They've all had champagne. Pross has broken her pledge.

CANDIDA [*to PROSERPINE*]    You don't mean to say you've been drinking champagne!

PROSERPINE [*stubbornly*]    Yes, I do. I'm only a beer teetotaller, not a champagne teetotaller. I don't like beer. Are there any letters for me to answer, Mr. Morell?

MORELL    No more to-night.

PROSERPINE    Very well. Good-night, everybody.

LEXY [*gallantly*]    Had I not better see you home, Miss Garnett?

PROSERPINE    No, thank you. I shan't trust myself with anybody to-night. I wish I hadn't taken any of that stuff. [*She walks straight out.*]

BURGESS [*indignantly*]    Stuff, indeed! That gurl dunno wot champagne is! Pommery and Greeno at twelve and six a bottle. She took two glasses a'most straight hoff.

MORELL [*a little anxious about her*]    Go and look after her, Lexy.

LEXY [*alarmed*]    But if she should really be— Suppose she began to sing in the street, or anything of that sort.

MORELL    Just so: she may. That's why you'd better see her safely home.

CANDIDA    Do, Lexy: there's a good fellow. [*She shakes his hand and pushes him gently to the door.*]

LEXY    It's evidently my duty to go. I hope it may not be necessary. Good-night, Mrs. Morell. [*To the rest.*] Good-night. [*He goes. CANDIDA shuts the door.*]

BURGESS    He was gushin' with hextra piety hisself arter two sips.

People carn't drink like they huseter. [*Dismissing the subject and bustling away from the hearth.*] Well, James: it's time to lock up. Mr. Morchbanks: shall I 'ave the pleasure of your company for a bit of the way home?

MARCHBANKS [*affrightedly*]    Yes: I'd better go. [*He hurries across to the door; but CANDIDA places herself before it, barring his way.*]

CANDIDA [*with quiet authority*]    You sit down. You're not going yet.

MARCHBANKS [*quailing*]    No: I—I didn't mean to. [*He comes back into the room and sits down abjectly on the sofa.*]

CANDIDA    Mr. Marchbanks will stay the night with us, papa.

BURGESS    Oh, well, I'll say good night. So long, James. [*He shakes hands with MORELL and goes on to EUGENE.*] Make 'em give you a night light by your bed, Mr. Morchbanks: it'll comfort you if you wake up in the night with a touch of that complaint of yores. Good-night.

MARCHBANKS    Thank you: I will. Good-night, Mr. Burgess. [*They shake hands and BURGESS goes to the door.*]

CANDIDA [*intercepting MORELL, who is following BURGESS*]    Stay here, dear: I'll put on papa's coat for him. [*She goes out with BURGESS.*]

MARCHBANKS    Morell: there's going to be a terrible scene. Aren't you afraid?

MORELL    Not in the least.

MARCHBANKS    I never envied you your courage before. [*He rises timidly and puts his hand appealingly on MORELL's forearm.*] Stand by me, won't you?

MORELL [*casting him off gently, but resolutely*]    Each for himself, Eugene. She must choose between us now. [*He goes to the other side of the room as CANDIDA returns. EUGENE sits down again on the sofa like a guilty schoolboy on his best behaviour.*]

CANDIDA [*between them, addressing EUGENE*]    Are you sorry?

MARCHBANKS [*earnestly*]    Yes, heartbroken.

CANDIDA    Well, then, you are forgiven. Now go off to bed like a good little boy: I want to talk to James about you.

MARCHBANKS [*rising in great consternation*]    Oh, I can't do that, Morell. I must be here. I'll not go away. Tell her.

CANDIDA [*with quick suspicion*]    Tell me what? [*His eyes avoid hers furtively. She turns and mutely transfers the question to MORELL.*]

MORELL [*bracing himself for the catastrophe*]    I have nothing to tell her, except [*here his voice deepens to a measured and mournful tenderness*] that she is my greatest treasure on earth—if she is really mine.

CANDIDA [*coldly, offended by his yielding to his orator's instinct and treating her as if she were the audience at the Guild of St. Matthew*]    I am sure Eugene can say no less, if that is all.

MARCHBANKS [*discouraged*]    Morell: she's laughing at us.

MORELL [*with a quick touch of temper*]    There is nothing to laugh at. Are you laughing at us, Candida?

CANDIDA [*with quiet anger*]    Eugene is very quick-witted, James. I hope I am going to laugh; but I am not sure that I am not going to be very angry. [*She goes to the fireplace, and stands there leaning with her arm on the mantelpiece, and her foot on the fender, whilst EUGENE steals to MORELL and plucks him by the sleeve.*]

MARCHBANKS [*whispering*]    Stop, Morell. Don't let us say anything.

MORELL [*pushing EUGENE away without deigning to look at him*]    I hope you don't mean that as a threat, Candida.

CANDIDA [*with emphatic warning*]    Take care, James. Eugene: I asked you to go. Are you going?

MORELL [*putting his foot down*]    He shall not go. I wish him to remain.

MARCHBANKS    I'll go. I'll do whatever you want. [*He turns to the door.*]

CANDIDA    Stop! [*He obeys.*] Didn't you hear James say he wished you to stay? James is master here. Don't you know that?

MARCHBANKS [*flushing with a young poet's rage against tyranny*]    By what right is he master?

CANDIDA [*quietly*]    Tell him, James.

MORELL [*taken aback*]   My dear: I don't know of any right that makes me master. I assert no such right.

CANDIDA [*with infinite reproach*]   You don't know! Oh, James, James! [*To EUGENE, musingly.*] I wonder do you understand, Eugene! No: you're too young. Well, I give you leave to stay—to stay and learn. [*She comes away from the hearth and places herself between them.*] Now, James: what's the matter? Come: tell me.

MARCHBANKS [*whispering tremulously across to him*]   Don't.

CANDIDA   Come. Out with it!

MORELL [*slowly*]   I meant to prepare your mind carefully, Candida, so as to prevent misunderstanding.

CANDIDA   Yes, dear: I am sure you did. But never mind: I shan't misunderstand.

MORELL   Well—er— [*He hesitates, unable to find the long explanation which he supposed to be available.*]

CANDIDA   Well?

MORELL [*baldly*]   Eugene declares that you are in love with him.

MARCHBANKS [*frantically*]   No, no, no, no, never. I did not, Mrs. Morell: it's not true. I said I loved you, and that he didn't. I said that I understood you, and that he couldn't. And it was not after what passed there before the fire that I spoke: it was not, on my word. It was this morning.

CANDIDA [*enlightened*]   This morning!

MARCHBANKS   Yes. [*He looks at her, pleading for credence, and then adds, simply*] That was what was the matter with my collar.

CANDIDA [*after a pause; for she does not take in his meaning at once*] His collar! [*She turns to MORELL, shocked.*] Oh, James: did you— [*she stops*]?

MORELL [*ashamed*]   You know, Candida, that I have a temper to struggle with. And he said [*shuddering*] that you despised me in your heart.

CANDIDA [*turning quickly on EUGENE*]   Did you say that?

MARCHBANKS [*terrified*]   No!

CANDIDA [*severely*]   Then James has just told me a falsehood. Is that what you mean?

MARCHBANKS   No, no: I—I— [*blurting out the explanation desperately*] —it was David's wife. And it wasn't at home: it was when she saw him dancing before all the people.

MORELL [*taking the cue with a debater's adroitness*]   Dancing before all the people,* Candida; and thinking he was moving their hearts by his mission when they were only suffering from—Prossy's complaint. [*She is about to protest: he raises his hand to silence her, exclaiming*] Don't try to look indignant, Candida:—

CANDIDA [*interjecting*]   Try!

MORELL [*continuing*]   Eugene was right. As you told me a few hours after, he is always right. He said nothing that you did not say far better yourself. He is the poet, who sees everything; and I am the poor parson, who understands nothing.

CANDIDA [*remorsefully*]   Do you mind what is said by a foolish boy, because I said something like it again in jest?

MORELL   That foolish boy can speak with the inspiration of a child and the cunning of a serpent. He has claimed that you belong to him and not to me; and, rightly or wrongly, I have come to fear that it may be true. I will not go about tortured with doubts and suspicions. I will not live with you and keep a secret from you. I will not suffer the intolerable degradation of jealousy. We have agreed—he and I—that you shall choose between us now. I await your decision.

CANDIDA [*slowly recoiling a step, her heart hardened by his rhetoric in spite of the sincere feeling behind it*]   Oh! I am to choose, am I? I suppose it is quite settled that I must belong to one or the other.

MORELL [*firmly*]   Quite. You must choose definitely.

MARCHBANKS [*anxiously*]   Morell: you don't understand. She means that she belongs to herself.

---

*A reference to the Bible, 2 Samuel 6:16: "Michal Saul's daughter looked through a window, and saw king David leaping and dancing before the Lord" (KJV).

CANDIDA [*turning on him*]   I mean that and a good deal more, Master Eugene, as you will both find out presently. And pray, my lords and masters, what have you to offer for my choice? I am up for auction, it seems. What do you bid, James?

MORELL [*reproachfully*]   Cand— [*He breaks down: his eyes and throat fill with tears: the orator becomes the wounded animal.*] I can't speak—

CANDIDA [*impulsively going to him*]   Ah, dearest—

MARCHBANKS [*in wild alarm*]   Stop: it's not fair. You mustn't show her that you suffer, Morell. I am on the rack, too; but I am not crying.

MORELL [*rallying all his forces*]   Yes: you are right. It is not for pity that I am bidding. [*He disengages himself from CANDIDA.*]

CANDIDA [*retreating, chilled*]   I beg your pardon, James; I did not mean to touch you. I am waiting to hear your bid.

MORELL [*with proud humility*]   I have nothing to offer you but my strength for your defence, my honesty of purpose for your surety, my ability and industry for your livelihood, and my authority and position for your dignity. That is all it becomes a man to offer to a woman.

CANDIDA [*quite quietly*]   And you, Eugene? What do you offer?

MARCHBANKS   My weakness! my desolation! my heart's need!

CANDIDA [*impressed*]   That's a good bid, Eugene. Now I know how to make my choice.

*She pauses and looks curiously from one to the other, as if weighing them. MORELL, whose lofty confidence has changed into heartbreaking dread at EUGENE's bid, loses all power of concealing his anxiety. EUGENE, strung to the highest tension, does not move a muscle.*

MORELL [*in a suffocated voice—the appeal bursting from the depths of his anguish*]   Candida!

MARCHBANKS [*aside, in a flash of contempt*]   Coward!

CANDIDA [*significantly*]   I give myself to the weaker of the two.

*EUGENE divines her meaning at once: his face whitens like steel in a furnace that cannot melt it.*

MORELL [*bowing his head with the calm of collapse*]   I accept your sentence, Candida.

CANDIDA   Do y o u understand, Eugene?

MARCHBANKS   Oh, I feel I'm lost. He cannot bear the burden.

MORELL [*incredulously, raising his head with prosaic abruptness*]   Do you mean me, Candida?

CANDIDA [*smiling a little*]   Let us sit and talk comfortably over it like three friends. [*To MORELL.*] Sit down, dear. [*MORELL takes the chair from the fireside—the children's chair.*] Bring me that chair, Eugene. [*She indicates the easy chair. He fetches it silently, even with something like cold strength, and places it next MORELL, a little behind him. She sits down. He goes to the sofa and sits there, still silent and inscrutable. When they are all settled she begins, throwing a spell of quietness on them by her calm, sane, tender tone.*] You remember what you told me about yourself, Eugene: how nobody has cared for you since your old nurse died: how those clever, fashionable sisters and successful brothers of yours were your mother's and father's pets: how miserable you were at Eton: how your father is trying to starve you into returning to Oxford: how you have had to live without comfort or welcome or refuge, always lonely, and nearly always disliked and misunderstood, poor boy!

MARCHBANKS [*faithful to the nobility of his lot*]   I had my books. I had Nature. And at last I met you.

CANDIDA   Never mind that just at present. Now I want you to look at this other boy here—m y boy—spoiled from his cradle. We go once a fortnight to see his parents. You should come with us, Eugene, and see the pictures of the hero of that household. James as a baby! the most wonderful of all babies. James holding his first school prize, won at the ripe age of eight! James as the captain of his eleven! James in his first frock coat! James under all sorts of glorious circumstances! You know how strong he is [I hope he didn't hurt you]—how clever he is—how happy! [*With deepening gravity.*] Ask James's mother and his three sisters what it cost to save James the trouble of doing anything but be strong and clever and happy. Ask m e what it costs to be James's mother and three sisters and wife and mother to his children all in one. Ask Prossy and Maria how troublesome the house is even when we have no visitors to help us to slice the onions. Ask the tradesmen who want to worry James and spoil his beautiful sermons who it is that puts them off. When there is money to give, he gives it: when there is money to refuse, I refuse it. I build a castle of comfort and indulgence and love for him, and stand sentinel always to keep little vulgar cares out. I make him master here, though he does not know it, and could not tell you a moment ago how it came to be so. [*With sweet irony.*] And when he thought I might go away with you, his only anxiety was what should become of m e ! And to tempt me to stay he offered me [*leaning forward to stroke his hair caressingly at each phrase*] h i s strength for m y defence, his industry for my livelihood, his position for my dignity, his— [*Relenting.*] Ah, I am mixing up your beautiful sentences and spoiling them, am I not, darling? [*She lays her cheek fondly against his.*]

MORELL [*quite overcome, kneeling beside her chair and embracing her with boyish ingenuousness*]   It's all true, every word. What I am you have made me with the labor of your hands and the love of your heart! You are my wife, my mother, my sisters: you are the sum of all loving care to me.

CANDIDA [*in his arms, smiling, to EUGENE*]   Am I y o u r mother and sisters to you, Eugene?

MARCHBANKS [*rising with a fierce gesture of disgust*]   Ah, never. Out, then, into the night with me!

CANDIDA [*rising quickly and intercepting him*]   You are not going like that, Eugene?

MARCHBANKS [*with the ring of a man's voice—no longer a boy's—in the words*]   I know the hour when it strikes. I am impatient to do what must be done.

MORELL [*rising from his knee, alarmed*]   Candida: don't let him do anything rash.

CANDIDA [*confident, smiling at EUGENE*]    Oh, there is no fear. He has learnt to live without happiness.

MARCHBANKS    I no longer desire happiness: life is nobler than that. Parson James: I give you my happiness with both hands: I love you because you have filled the heart of the woman I loved. Good-bye. [*He goes towards the door.*]

CANDIDA    One last word. [*He stops, but without turning to her.*] How old are you, Eugene?

MARCHBANKS    As old as the world now. This morning I was eighteen.

CANDIDA [*going to him, and standing behind him with one hand caressingly on his shoulder*]    Eighteen! Will you, for my sake, make a little poem out of the two sentences I am going to say to you? And will you promise to repeat it to yourself whenever you think of me?

MARCHBANKS [*without moving*]    Say the sentences.

CANDIDA    When I am thirty, she will be forty-five. When I am sixty, she will be seventy-five.

MARCHBANKS [*turning to her*]    In a hundred years, we shall be the same age. But I have a better secret than that in my heart. Let me go now. The night outside grows impatient.

CANDIDA    Good-bye. [*She takes his face in her hands; and as he divines her intention and bends his knee, she kisses his forehead. Then he flies out into the night. She turns to MORELL, holding out her arms to him.*] Ah, James! [*They embrace. But they do not know the secret in the poet's heart.*]

# THE DEVIL'S
# DISCIPLE

# THREE PLAYS FOR PURITANS

## WHY FOR PURITANS?

Since I gave my Plays, Pleasant and Unpleasant, to the world two years ago, many things have happened to me. I had then just entered on the fourth year of my activity as a critic of the London theatres. They very nearly killed me. I had survived seven years of London's music, four or five years of London's pictures, and about as much of its current literature, wrestling critically with them with all my force and skill. After that, the criticism of the theatre came to me as a huge relief in point of bodily exertion. The difference between the leisure of a Persian cat and the labor of a cockney cab horse is not greater than the difference between the official weekly or fortnightly* playgoings of the theatre critic and the restless daily rushing to and fro of the music critic, from the stroke of three in the afternoon, when the concerts begin, to the stroke of twelve at night, when the opera ends. The pictures were nearly as bad. An Alpinist once, noticing the massive soles of my boots, asked me whether I climbed mountains. No, I replied: these boots are for the hard floors of the London galleries. Yet I once dealt with music and pictures together in the spare time of an active young revolutionist, and wrote plays and books and other toilsome things into the bargain. But the theatre struck me down like the veriest weakling. I sank under it like a baby fed on starch. My very bones began to perish, so that I had to get them planed and gouged by ac-

---

*Every two weeks.

complished surgeons. I fell from heights and broke my limbs in pieces. The doctors said: This man has not eaten meat for twenty years: he must eat it or die. I said: This man has been going to the London theatres for three years; and the soul of him has become inane and is feeding unnaturally on his body. And I was right. I did not change my diet; but I had myself carried up into a mountain where there was no theatre; and there I began to revive. Too weak to work, I wrote books and plays; hence the second and third plays in this volume. And now I am stronger than I have been at any moment since my feet first carried me as a critic across the fatal threshold of a London playhouse.

Why was this? What is the matter with the theatre, that a strong man can die of it? Well, the answer will make a long story; but it must be told. And, to begin, why have I just called the theatre a playhouse? The well-fed Englishman, though he lives and dies a schoolboy, cannot play. He cannot even play cricket or football: he has to work at them: that is why he beats the foreigner who plays at them. To him playing means playing the fool. He can hunt and shoot and travel and fight; he can, when special holiday festivity is suggested to him, eat and drink, dice and drab,* smoke and lounge. But play he cannot. The moment you make his theatre a place of amusement instead of a place of edification, you make it, not a real playhouse, but a place of excitement for the sportsman and the sensualist.

However, this well-fed grown-up-schoolboy Englishman counts for little in the modern metropolitan audience. In the long lines of waiting playgoers lining the pavements outside our fashionable theatres every evening, the men are only the currants in the dumpling. Women are in the majority; and women and men alike belong to that least robust of all our social classes, the class which earns from eighteen to thirty shillings a week in sedentary employment, and lives in a dull lodging or with its intolerably prosaic families. These people preserve the innocence of the theatre: they have neither the philosopher's impatience to get to realities (reality being the one

---

*To frequent prostitutes (as used in Shakespeare's *Hamlet*, act 2, scene 1).

thing they want to escape from), nor the longing of the sportsman for violent action, nor the fullfed, experienced, disillusioned sensuality of the rich man, whether he be gentleman or sporting publican. They read a good deal, and are at home in the fool's paradise of popular romance. They love the pretty man and the pretty woman, and will have both of them fashionably dressed and exquisitely idle, posing against backgrounds of drawing-room and dainty garden; in love, but sentimentally, romantically; always ladylike and gentlemanlike. Jejunely insipid, all this, to the stalls, which are paid for (when they *are* paid for) by people who have their own dresses and drawingrooms, and know them to be a mere masquerade behind which there is nothing romantic, and little that is interesting to most of the masqueraders except the clandestine play of natural licentiousness.

The stalls cannot be fully understood without taking into account the absence of the rich evangelical English merchant and his family, and the presence of the rich Jewish merchant and *his* family. I can see no validity whatever in the view that the influence of the rich Jews on the theatre is any worse than the influence of the rich of any other race. Other qualities being equal, men become rich in commerce in proportion to the intensity and exclusiveness of their desire for money. It may be a misfortune that the purchasing power of men who value money above art, philosophy, and the welfare of the whole community, should enable them to influence the theatre (and everything else in the market); but there is no reason to suppose that their influence is any nobler when they imagine themselves Christians than when they know themselves Jews. All that can fairly be said of the Jewish influence on the theatre is that it is exotic, and is not only a customer's influence but a financier's influence: so much so, that the way is smoothest for those plays and those performers that appeal specially to the Jewish taste. English influence on the theatre, as far as the stalls are concerned, does not exist, because the rich purchasing-powerful Englishman prefers politics and church-going: his soul is too stubborn to be purged by an avowed make-believe. When he wants sensuality he practices it;

he does not play with voluptuous or romantic ideas. From the play of ideas—and the drama can never be anything more—he demands edification, and will not pay for anything else in that arena. Consequently the box office will never become an English influence until the theatre turns from the drama of romance and sensuality to the drama of edification.

Turning from the stalls to the whole auditorium, consider what is implied by the fact that the prices (all much too high, by the way) range from half a guinea to a shilling, the ages from eighteen to eighty, whilst every age, and nearly every price, represents a different taste. Is it not clear that this diversity in the audience makes it impossible to gratify every one of its units by the same luxury, since in that domain of infinite caprice, one man's meat is another man's poison, one age's longing another age's loathing? And yet that is just what the theatres kept trying to do almost all the time I was doomed to attend them. On the other hand, to interest people of divers ages, classes, and temperaments, by some generally momentous subject of thought, as the politicians and preachers do, would seem the most obvious course in the world. And yet the theatres avoided that as a ruinous eccentricity. Their wiseacres persisted in assuming that all men have the same tastes, fancies, and qualities of passion; that no two have the same interests; and that most playgoers have no interests at all. This being precisely contrary to the obvious facts, it followed that the majority of the plays produced were failures, recognizable as such before the end of the first act by the very wiseacres aforementioned, who, quite incapable of understanding the lesson, would thereupon set to work to obtain and produce a play applying their theory still more strictly, with proportionately more disastrous results. The sums of money I saw thus transferred from the pockets of theatrical speculators and syndicates to those of wigmakers, costumiers, scene painters, carpenters, doorkeepers, actors, theatre landlords, and all the other people for whose exclusive benefit most London theatres seem to exist, would have kept a theatre devoted exclusively to the highest drama open all the year round. If the Browning and Shelley Societies were fools, as the wiseacres said they were, for producing Strafford, Colombe's Birthday,* and The Cenci;† if the Independent Theatre, the New Century Theatre, and the Stage Society are impracticable faddists for producing the plays of Ibsen and Maeterlinck,‡ then what epithet is contemptuous enough for the people who produce the would-be popular plays?

The actor-managers were far more successful, because they produced plays that at least pleased themselves, whereas the others, with a false theory of how to please everybody, produced plays that pleased nobody. But their occasional personal successes in voluptuous plays, and, in any case, their careful concealment of failure, confirmed the prevalent error, which was only exposed fully when the plays had to stand or fall openly by their own merits. Even Shakespear was played with his brains cut out. In 1896, when Sir Henry Irving was disabled by an accident at a moment when Miss Ellen Terry was too ill to appear, the theatre had to be closed after a brief attempt to rely on the attraction of a Shakespearean play performed by the stock company. This may have been Shakespear's fault: indeed Sir Henry later on complained that he had lost a princely sum by Shakespear. But Shakespear's reply to this, if he were able to make it, would be that the princely sum was spent, not on his dramatic poetry, but on a gorgeous stage ritualism superimposed on reckless mutilations of his text, the whole being addressed to a public as to which nothing is certain except that its natural bias is towards reverence for Shakespear and dislike and distrust of ritualism. No doubt the Lyceum ritual appealed to a far more cultivated sensuousness and imaginativeness than the musical farces in which our stage Abbots of Misrule§ pontificated (with

---

*Strafford* and *Colombe's Birthday* are verse dramas by Robert Browning (1812–1889).

† Verse drama by Percy Shelley (1792–1822).

‡Maurice Maeterlinck (1862–1949), Belgian symbolist playwright, author of *Pelléas et Mélisande* (1892).

§Shaw compares theater managers of his time to medieval arrangers of crude holiday entertainments.

the same financially disastrous result); but in both there was the same intentional brainlessness, founded on the same theory that the public did not want brains, did not want to think, did not want anything but pleasure at the theatre. Unfortunately, this theory happens to be true of a certain section of the public. This section, being courted by the theatres, went to them and drove the other people out. It then discovered, as any expert could have foreseen, that the theatre cannot compete in mere pleasuremongering either with the other arts or with matter-of-fact gallantry. Stage pictures are the worst pictures, stage music the worst music, stage scenery the worst scenery within reach of the Londoner. The leading lady or gentleman may be as tempting to the admirer in the pit as the dishes in a cookshop window are to the penniless tramp on the pavement; but people do not, I presume, go to the theatre to be merely tantalized.

The breakdown on the last point was conclusive. For when the managers tried to put their principle of pleasing everybody into practice, Necessity, ever ironical towards Folly, had driven them to seek a universal pleasure to appeal to. And since many have no ear for music or eye for color, the search for universality inevitably flung the managers back on the instinct of sex as the avenue to all hearts. Of course the appeal was a vapid failure. Speaking for my own sex, I can say that the leading lady was not to everybody's taste: her pretty face often became ugly when she tried to make it expressive; her voice lost its charm (if it ever had any) when she had nothing sincere to say; and the stalls, from racial prejudice, were apt to insist on more Rebecca and less Rowena than the pit cared for. It may seem strange, even monstrous, that a man should feel a constant attachment to the hideous witches in Macbeth, and yet yawn at the prospect of spending another evening in the contemplation of a beauteous young leading lady with voluptuous contours and longlashed eyes, painted and dressed to perfection in the latest fashions. But that is just what happened to me in the theatre.

I did not find that matters were improved by the lady pretending to be "a woman with a past," violently oversexed, or the play being called a problem play, even when the manager, and sometimes, I suspect, the very author, firmly believed the word problem to be the latest euphemism for what Justice Shallow* called a bona roba,† and certainly would not either of them have staked a farthing on the interest of a genuine problem. In fact these so-called problem plays invariably depended for their dramatic interest on foregone conclusions of the most heart-wearying conventionality concerning sexual morality. The authors had no problematic views: all they wanted was to capture some of the fascination of Ibsen. It seemed to them that most of Ibsen's heroines were naughty ladies. And they tried to produce Ibsen plays by making their heroines naughty. But they took great care to make them pretty and expensively dressed. Thus the pseudo-Ibsen play was nothing but the ordinary sensuous ritual of the stage become as frankly pornographic as good manners allowed.

I found that the whole business of stage sensuousness, whether as Lyceum Shakespear, musical farce, or sham Ibsen, finally disgusted me, not because I was Pharisaical, or intolerantly refined, but because I was bored; and boredom is a condition which makes men as susceptible to disgust and irritation as headache makes them to noise and glare. Being a man, I have my share of the masculine silliness and vulgarity on the subject of sex which so astonishes women, to whom sex is a serious matter. I am not an Archbishop, and do not pretend to pass my life on one plane or in one mood, and that the highest: on the contrary, I am, I protest, as accessible to the humors of the Rogue's Comedy‡ or the Rake's Progress as to the pious decencies of The Sign of The Cross. Thus Falstaff, coarser than any of the men in our loosest plays, does not bore me: Doll Tearsheet, more abandoned than any of the women, does not shock me: I think that Romeo and Juliet would be a poorer play if it were robbed of the solitary fragment it has preserved for us of the conversation of the husband of Juliet's nurse. No: my disgust was not mere thinskinned prudery.

---

*Character in Shakespeare's *Henry IV, Part Two*.

†Good material (Italian); slang phrase for "prostitute."

‡An 1896 play by Henry Arthur Jones that Shaw reviewed.

When my moral sense revolted, as it often did to the very fibres, it was invariably at the nauseous compliances of the theatre with conventional virtue. If I despised the musical farces, it was because they never had the courage of their vices. With all their labored efforts to keep up an understanding of furtive naughtiness between the low comedian on the stage and the drunken undergraduate in the stalls, they insisted all the time on their virtue and patriotism and loyalty as pitifully as a poor girl of the pavement will pretend to be a clergyman's daughter. True, I may have been offended when a manager, catering for me with coarse frankness as a slave-dealer caters for a Pasha, invited me to forget the common bond of humanity between me and his company by demanding nothing from them but a gloatably voluptuous appearance. But this extreme is never reached at our better theatres. The shop assistants, the typists, the clerks, who, as I have said, preserve the innocence of the theatre, would not dare to let themselves be pleased by it. Even if they did, they would not get it from the managers, who, when they are brought to the only logical conclusion from their principle of making the theatre a temple of pleasure, indignantly refuse to change the dramatic profession for Mrs. Warren's. For that is what all this demand for pleasure at the theatre finally comes to; and the answer to it is, not that people ought not to desire sensuous pleasure (they cannot help it), but that the theatre cannot give it to them, even to the extent permitted by the honor and conscience of the best managers, because a theatre is so far from being a pleasant or even a comfortable place that only by making us forget ourselves can it prevent us from realizing its inconveniences. A play that does not do this for the pleasure-seeker allows him to discover that he has chosen a disagreeable and expensive way of spending an evening. He wants to drink, to smoke, to change the spectacle, to get rid of the middle-aged actor and actress who are boring him, and to see shapely young dancing girls and acrobats doing more amusing things in a more plastic manner. In short, he wants the music hall; and he goes there, leaving the managers astonished at this unexpected but quite inevitable result of the attempt to please him. Whereas, had he been enthralled by the play, even with horror, instead of himself enthralling with the dread of his displeasure the manager, the author and the actors, all had been well. And so we must conclude that the theatre is a place which people can only endure when they forget themselves: that is, when their attention is entirely captured, their interest thoroughly roused, their sympathies raised to the eagerest readiness, and their selfishness utterly annihilated. Imagine, then, the result of conducting theatres on the principle of appealing exclusively to the instinct of self-gratification in people without power of attention, without interests, without sympathy, in short, without brains or heart. That is how they were conducted whilst I was writing about them; and that is how they nearly killed me.

Yet the managers mean well. Their self-respect is in excess rather than in defect; for they are in full reaction against the Bohemianism of past generations of actors, and so bent on compelling social recognition by a blameless respectability, that the drama, neglected in the struggle, is only just beginning to stir feebly after standing stock-still in England from Robertson's time* in the sixties until the first actor was knighted in the nineties. The manager may not want good plays; but he does not want bad plays: he wants nice plays. Nice plays, with nice dresses, nice drawing-rooms and nice people, are indispensable: to be ungenteel is worse than to fail. I use the word ungenteel purposely; for the stage presents life on thirty pounds a day, not as it is, but as it is conceived by the earners of thirty shillings a week. The real thing would shock the audience exactly as the manners of the public school and university shock a Board of Guardians. In just the same way, the plays which constitute the genuine aristocracy of modern dramatic literature shock the reverence for gentility which governs our theatres today. For instance, the objection to Ibsen is not really an objection to his philosophy: it is a protest against the fact

---

*Victorian playwright Tom Robertson (1829–1871) attempted to deal with social themes.

that his characters do not behave as ladies and gentlemen are popularly supposed to behave. If you adore Hedda Gabler in real life, if you envy her and feel that nothing but your poverty prevents you from being as exquisite a creature, if you know that the accident of matrimony (say with an officer of the guards who falls in love with you across the counter whilst you are reckoning the words in his telegram) may at any moment put you in her place, Ibsen's exposure of the worthlessness and meanness of her life is cruel and blasphemous to you. This point of view is not caught by the clever ladies of Hedda's own class, who recognize the portrait, applaud its painter, and think the fuss against Ibsen means nothing more than the conventional disapproval of her discussions of a *ménage à trois* with Judge Brack. A little experience of popular plays would soon convince these clever ladies that a heroine that atones in the last act by committing suicide may do all the things that Hedda only talked about, without a word of remonstrance from the press or the public. It is not murder, not adultery, not rapine that is objected to: quite the contrary. It is an unladylike attitude towards life: in other words, a disparagement of the social ideals of the poorer middle class and of the vast reinforcements it has had from the working class during the last twenty years. Let but the attitude of the author be gentlemanlike, and his heroines may do what they please. Mrs. Tanqueray was received with delight by the public: Saint Teresa would have been hissed off the same stage for her contempt for the ideal represented by a carriage, a fashionable dressmaker, and a dozen servants.

Here, then, is a pretty problem for the manager. He is convinced that plays must depend for their dramatic force on appeals to the sex instinct: and yet he owes it to his own newly conquered social position that they shall be perfectly genteel plays, fit for churchgoers. The sex instinct must therefore proceed upon genteel assumptions. Impossible! you will exclaim. But you are wrong: nothing is more astonishing than the extent to which, in real life, the sex instinct does so proceed, even when the consequence is its lifelong starvation. Few of us have vitality enough to make any of our instincts imperious: we can be made to live on pretences, as the masterful minority well know. But the timid majority, if it rules nowhere else, at least rules in the theatre: fitly enough too, because on the stage pretence is all that can exist. Life has its realities behind its shows: the theatre has nothing but its shows. But can the theatre make a show of lovers' endearments? A thousand times no: perish the thought of such unladylike, ungentlemanlike exhibitions. You can have fights, rescues, conflagrations, trials at law, avalanches, murders and executions all directly simulated on the stage if you will. But any such realistic treatment of the incidents of sex is quite out of the question. The singer, the dramatic dancer, the exquisite declaimer of impassioned poesy, the rare artist who, bringing something of the art of all three to the ordinary work of the theatre, can enthral an audience by the expression of dramatic feeling alone, may take love for a theme on the stage; but the prosaic walking gentlemen of our fashionable theatres, realistically simulating the incidents of life, cannot touch it without indecorum.

Can any dilemma be more complete? Love is assumed to be the only theme that touches all your audience infallibly, young and old, rich and poor. And yet love is the one subject that the drawingroom drama dare not present.

Out of this dilemma, which is a very old one, has come the romantic play: that is, the play in which love is carefully kept off the stage, whilst it is alleged as the motive of all the actions presented to the audience. The result is to me, at least, an intolerable perversion of human conduct. There are two classes of stories that seem to me to be not only fundamentally false but sordidly base. One is the pseudo-religious story, in which the hero or heroine does good on strictly commercial grounds, reluctantly exercising a little virtue on earth in consideration of receiving in return an exorbitant payment in heaven: much as if an odalisque* were to allow a cadi† to whip her

---

*Harem concubine.

†Minor legal official in the Middle East.

for a couple of millions in gold. The other is the romance in which the hero, also rigidly commercial, will do nothing except for the sake of the heroine. Surely this is as depressing as it is unreal. Compare with it the treatment of love, frankly indecent according to our notions, in oriental fiction. In The Arabian Nights we have a series of stories, some of them very good ones, in which no sort of decorum is observed. The result is that they are infinitely more instructive and enjoyable than our romances, because love is treated in them as naturally as any other passion. There is no cast iron convention as to its effects; no false association of general depravity of character with its corporealities or of general elevation with its sentimentalities; no pretence that a man or woman cannot be courageous and kind and friendly unless infatuatedly in love with somebody (is no poet manly enough to sing The Old Maids of England?): rather, indeed, an insistence on the blinding and narrowing power of lovesickness to make princely heroes unhappy and unfortunate. These tales expose, further, the delusion that the interest of this most capricious, most transient, most easily baffled of all instincts, is inexhaustible, and that the field of the English romancer has been cruelly narrowed by the restrictions under which he is permitted to deal with it. The Arabian storyteller, relieved of all such restrictions, heaps character on character, adventure on adventure, marvel on marvel; whilst the English novelist, like the starving tramp who can think of nothing but his hunger, seems to be unable to escape from the obsession of sex, and will rewrite the very gospels because the originals are not written in the sensuously ecstatic style. At the instance* of Martin Luther we long ago gave up imposing celibacy on our priests; but we still impose it on our art, with the very undesirable and unexpected result that no editor, publisher, or manager, will now accept a story or produce a play without "love interest" in it. Take, for a recent example, Mr. H. G. Wells's War of Two Worlds,† a tale of the invasion of the

---

*Misprint; should be "insistence."

†Should be The War of the Worlds (1898); corrected by Shaw in later editions.

earth by the inhabitants of the planet Mars: a capital story, not to be laid down until finished. Love interest is impossible on its scientific plane: nothing could be more impertinent and irritating. Yet Mr. Wells has had to pretend that the hero is in love with a young lady manufactured for the purpose, and to imply that it is on her account alone that he feels concerned about the apparently inevitable destruction of the human race by the Martians. Another example. An American novelist,* recently deceased, made a hit some years ago by compiling a Bostonian Utopia from the prospectuses of the little bands of devout Communists who have from time to time, since the days of Fourier and Owen, tried to establish millennial colonies outside our commercial civilization. Even in this economic Utopia we find the inevitable love affair. The hero, waking up in a distant future from a miraculous sleep, meets a Boston young lady, provided expressly for him to fall in love with. Women have by that time given up wearing skirts; but she, to spare his delicacy, gets one out of a museum of antiquities to wear in his presence until he is hardened to the customs of the new age. When I came to that touching incident, I became as Paolo and Francesca: "in that book I read no more." I will not multiply examples: if such unendurable follies occur in the sort of story made by working out a meteorologic or economic hypothesis, the extent to which it is carried in sentimental romances needs no expatiation.

The worst of it is that since man's intellectual consciousness of himself is derived from the descriptions of him in books, a persistent misrepresentation of humanity in literature gets finally accepted and acted upon. If every mirror reflected our noses twice their natural size, we should live and die in the faith that we were all Punches; and we should scout a true mirror as the work of a fool, madman, or jester. Nay, I believe we should, by Lamarckian adaptation, enlarge our noses to the admired size; for I have noticed that when a certain

---

*Edward Bellamy, author of *Looking Backward* (1888).

type of feature appears in painting and is admired as beautiful, it presently becomes common in nature;* so that the Beatrices and Francescas in the picture galleries of one generation, to whom minor poets address verses entitled To My Lady, come to life as the parlor-maids and waitresses of the next. If the conventions of romance are only insisted on long enough and uniformly enough (a condition guaranteed by the uniformity of human folly and vanity), then, for the huge School Board taught masses who read romance and nothing else, these conventions will become the laws of personal honor. Jealousy, which is either an egotistical meanness or a specific mania, will become obligatory; and ruin, ostracism, breaking up of homes, duelling, murder, suicide and infanticide will be produced (often have been produced, in fact) by incidents which, if left to the operation of natural and right feeling, would produce nothing worse than an hour's soon-forgotten fuss. Men will be slain needlessly on the field of battle because officers conceive it to be their first duty to make romantic exhibitions of conspicuous gallantry. The squire who has never spared an hour from the hunting field to do a little public work on a parish council will be cheered as a patriot because he is willing to kill and be killed for the sake of conferring himself as an institution on other countries. In the courts cases will be argued, not on juridical but on romantic principles; and vindictive damages and vindictive sentences, with the acceptance of nonsensical, and the repudiation or suppression of sensible testimony, will destroy the very sense of law. Kaisers, generals, judges, and prime ministers will set the example of playing to the gallery. Finally the people, now that their Board School literacy enables every penman to play on their romantic illusions, will be led by the nose far more completely than they ever were by playing on their former ignorance and superstition. Nay, why should I say will be? they *are*. Ten years of cheap read-

---

*Shaw borrows Oscar Wilde's paradoxical aesthetic pronouncement that nature imitates art.

ing have changed the English from the most stolid nation in Europe to the most theatrical and hysterical.

Is it clear now, why the theatre was insufferable to me; why it left its black mark on my bones as it has left its black mark on the character of the nation; why I call the Puritans to rescue it again as they rescued it before when its foolish pursuit of pleasure sunk it in "profaneness and immorality"? I have, I think, always been a Puritan in my attitude towards Art. I am as fond of fine music and handsome building as Milton was, or Cromwell, or Bunyan; but if I found that they were becoming the instruments of a systematic idolatry of sensuousness, I would hold it good statesmanship to blow every cathedral in the world to pieces with dynamite, organ and all, without the least heed to the screams of the art critics and cultured voluptuaries. And when I see that the nineteenth century has crowned the idolatry of Art with the deification of Love, so that every poet is supposed to have pierced to the holy of holies when he has announced that Love is the Supreme, or the Enough, or the All, I feel that Art was safer in the hands of the most fanatical of Cromwell's major generals than it will be if ever it gets into mine. The pleasures of the senses I can sympathize with and share; but the substitution of sensuous ecstasy for intellectual activity and honesty is the very devil. It has already brought us to Flogging Bills in Parliament, and, by reaction, to androgynous heroes on the stage; and if the infection spreads until the democratic attitude becomes thoroughly Romanticist, the country will become unbearable for all realists, Philistine or Platonic. When it comes to that, the brute force of the strong-minded Bismarckian man of action, impatient of humbug, will combine with the subtlety and spiritual energy of the man of thought whom shams cannot illude or interest. That combination will be on one side; and Romanticism will be on the other. In which event, so much the worse for Romanticism, which will come down even if it has to drag Democracy down with it. For all institutions have in the long run to live by the nature of things, and not by imagination.

# ON DIABOLONIAN ETHICS

There is a foolish opinion prevalent that an author should allow his works to speak for themselves, and that he who appends and prefixes explanations to them is likely to be as bad an artist as the painter cited by Cervantes, who wrote under his picture This is a Cock, lest there should be any mistake about it. The pat retort to this thoughtless comparison is that the painter invariably does so label his picture. What is a Royal Academy catalogue but a series of statements that This is the Vale of Rest, This is The School of Athens, This is Chill October, This is The Prince of Wales, and so on? The reason most dramatists do not publish their plays with prefaces is that they cannot write them, the business of intellectually conscious philosopher and skilled critic being no part of the playwright's craft. Naturally, making a virtue of their incapacity, they either repudiate prefaces as shameful, or else, with a modest air, request some popular critic to supply one, as much as to say, Were I to tell the truth about myself I must needs seem vainglorious: were I to tell less than the truth I should do myself an injustice and deceive my readers. As to the critic thus called in from the outside, what can he do but imply that his friend's transcendent ability as a dramatist is surpassed only by his beautiful nature as a man? Now what I say is, why should I get another man to praise me when I can praise myself? I have no disabilities to plead: produce me your best critic, and I will criticize his head off. As to philosophy, I taught my critics the little they know in my Quintessence of Ibsenism; and now they turn their guns—the guns I loaded for them—on me, and proclaim that I write as if mankind had intellect without will, or heart, as they call it. Ingrates: who was it that directed your attention to the distinction between Will and Intellect? Not Schopenhauer, I think, but Shaw.

Again, they tell me that So-and-So, who does not write prefaces, is no charlatan. Well, I am. I first caught the ear of the British public on a cart in Hyde Park, to the blaring of brass bands, and this not at all as a reluctant sacrifice of my instinct of privacy to political necessity, but because, like all dramatists and mimes of genuine vocation, I am a natural-born mountebank. I am well aware that the ordinary British citizen requires a profession of shame from all mountebanks by way of homage to the sanctity of the ignoble private life to which he is condemned by his incapacity for public life. Thus Shakespear, after proclaiming that Not marble nor the gilded monuments of Princes should outlive his powerful rhyme,* would apologise, in the approved taste, for making himself a motley to the view;† and the British citizen has ever since quoted the apology and ignored the fanfare. When an actress writes her memoirs, she impresses on you in every chapter how cruelly it tried her feelings to exhibit her person to the public gaze; but she does not forget to decorate the book with a dozen portraits of herself. I really cannot respond to this demand for mock-modesty. I am ashamed neither of my work nor of the way it is done. I like explaining its merits to the huge majority who don't know good work from bad. It does them good; and it does me good, curing me of nervousness, laziness, and snobbishness. I write prefaces as Dryden did, and treatises as Wagner, because I *can*; and I would give half a dozen of Shakespear's plays for one of the prefaces he ought to have written. I leave the delicacies of retirement to those who are gentlemen first and literary workmen afterwards. The cart and trumpet for me.

This is all very well; but the trumpet is an instrument that grows on one; and sometimes my blasts have been so strident that even those who are most annoyed by them have mistaken the novelty of my shamelessness for novelty in my plays and opinions. Take, for instance, the first play in this volume, entitled The Devil's Disciple. It does not contain a single even passably novel incident. Every old patron of the Adelphi pit would, were he not beglamored in a way

---

*A near-quotation from Sonnet 55, lines 1 and 2.

†An allusion to Sonnet 110, whose first four lines are: "Alas, 'tis true I have gone here and there / And made myself a motley to the view, / Gored mine own thoughts, sold cheap what is most dear, / Made old offences of affections new."

presently to be explained, recognize the reading of the will, the oppressed orphan finding a protector, the arrest, the heroic sacrifice,
the court martial, the scaffold, the reprieve at the last moment, as he
recognizes beefsteak pudding on the bill of fare at his restaurant. Yet
when the play was produced in 1897 in New York by Mr. Richard
Mansfield, with a success that proves either that the melodrama was
built on very safe old lines, or that the American public is composed
exclusively of men of genius, the critics, though one said one thing
and another another as to the play's merits, yet all agreed that it was
novel—*original*, as they put it—to the verge of audacious eccentricity.

Now this, if it applies to the incidents, plot, construction, and
general professional and technical qualities of the play, is nonsense;
for the truth is, I am in these matters a very old-fashioned playwright. When a good deal of the same talk, both hostile and friendly,
was provoked by my last volume of plays, Mr. Robert Buchanan, a
dramatist who knows what I know and remembers what I remember
of the history of the stage, pointed out that the stage tricks by which
I gave the younger generation of playgoers an exquisite sense of
quaint unexpectedness, had done duty years ago in Cool as a Cucumber, Used Up, and many forgotten farces and comedies of the
Byron*-Robertson school, in which the imperturbably impudent comedian, afterwards shelved by the reaction to brainless sentimentality, was a stock figure. It is always so more or less: the novelties of
one generation are only the resuscitated fashions of the generation
before last.

But the stage tricks of The Devil's Disciple are not, like some of
those of Arms and the Man, the forgotten ones of the sixties, but the
hackneyed ones of our own time. Why, then, were they not recognized? Partly, no doubt, because of my trumpet and cartwheel declamation. The critics were the victims of the long course of suggestion

---

*Not the Romantic poet, but the popular Victorian playwright Henry James
Byron (1834–1884).

by which G.B.S. the journalist manufactured an unconventional reputation for Bernard Shaw the author. In England, as elsewhere the
spontaneous recognition of really original work begins with a mere
handful of people, and propagates itself so slowly that it has become
a commonplace to say that genius, demanding bread, is given a stone
after its possessor's death. The remedy for this is sedulous advertise-
ment. Accordingly, I have advertised myself so well that I find myself,
whilst still in middle life, almost as legendary a person as the Flying
Dutchman. Critics, like other people, see what they look for, not
what is actually before them. In my plays they look for my legendary
qualities, and find originality and brilliancy in my most hackneyed
claptraps. Were I to republish Buckstone's Wreck Ashore[1] as my latest comedy, it would be hailed as a masterpiece of perverse paradox
and scintillating satire. Not, of course, by the really able critics—for
example, you, my friend, now reading this sentence. The illusion that
makes *you* think me so original is far subtler than that. The Devil's
Disciple has, in truth, a genuine novelty in it. Only, that novelty is not
any invention of my own, but simply the novelty of the advanced
thought of my day. As such, it will assuredly lose its gloss with the
lapse of time, and leave the Devil's Disciple exposed as the thread-
bare popular melodrama it technically is.

Let me explain (for, as Mr. A. B. Walkley has pointed out in his
disquisitions on Frames of Mind, I am nothing if not explanatory).
Dick Dudgeon, the devil's disciple, is a Puritan of the Puritans. He is
brought up in a household where the Puritan religion has died, and
become, in its corruption, an excuse for his mother's master passion
of hatred in all its phases of cruelty and envy. This corruption has already been dramatized for us by Charles Dickens in his picture of the
Clennam household in Little Dorrit: Mrs. Dudgeon being a replica
of Mrs. Clennam with certain circumstantial variations, and perhaps
a touch of the same author's Mrs. Gargery in Great Expectations. In
such a home the young Puritan finds himself starved of religion,
which is the most clamorous need of his nature. With all his mother's
indomitable selffulness, but with Pity instead of Hatred as his master

passion, he pities the devil; takes his side; and champions him, like a true Covenanter,* against the world. He thus becomes, like all genuinely religious men, a reprobate and an outcast. Once this is understood, the play becomes straightforwardly simple. The Diabolonian position is new to the London playgoer of today, but not to lovers of serious literature. From Prometheus to the Wagnerian Siegfried, some enemy of the gods, unterrified champion of those oppressed by them, has always towered among the heroes of the loftiest poetry. Our newest idol, the Overman,† celebrating the death of godhead, may be younger than the hills; but he is as old as the shepherds. Two and a half centuries ago our greatest English dramatizer of life, John Bunyan, ended one of his stories with the remark that there is a way to hell even from the gates of heaven, and so led us to the equally true proposition that there is a way to heaven even from the gates of hell. A century ago William Blake was, like Dick Dudgeon, an avowed Diabolonian: he called his angels devils and his devils angels. His devil is a Redeemer. Let those who have praised my originality in conceiving Dick Dudgeon's strange religion read Blake's Marriage of Heaven and Hell; and I shall be fortunate if they do not rail at me for a plagiarist. But they need not go back to Blake and Bunyan. Have they not heard the recent fuss about Nietzsche and his Good and Evil Turned Inside Out? Mr. Robert Buchanan has actually written a long poem of which the Devil is the merciful hero, which poem was in my hands before a word of The Devil's Disciple was written. There never was a play more certain to be written than The Devil's Disciple at the end of the nineteenth century. The age was visibly pregnant with it.

I grieve to have to add that my old friends and colleagues the London critics for the most part shewed no sort of connoisseurship either in Puritanism or Diabolonianism when the play was performed

---

*One who is aggressively loyal to a religious sect, after the Scots who signed the Covenant in 1638 to remain loyal Protestants.

†The earliest English translation of the term "Übermensch," coined by German philosopher Friedrich Nietzsche (1844–1900). Shaw would later use "Superman."

for a few weeks at a suburban theatre (Kennington) in October 1899 by Mr. Murray Carson. They took Mrs. Dudgeon at her own valuation as a religious woman because she was detestably disagreeable. And they took Dick as a blackguard, on her authority, because he was neither detestable nor disagreeable. But they presently found themselves in a dilemma. Why should a blackguard save another man's life, and that man no friend of his, at the risk of his own? Clearly, said the critics, because he is redeemed by love. All wicked heroes are, on the stage: that is the romantic metaphysic. Unfortunately for this explanation (which I do not profess to understand) it turned out in the third act that Dick was a Puritan in this respect also: a man impassioned only for saving grace, and not to be led or turned by wife or mother, Church or State, pride of life or lust of the flesh. In the lovely home of the courageous, affectionate, practical minister who marries a pretty wife twenty years younger than himself, and turns soldier in an instant to save the man who has saved him, Dick looks round and understands the charm and the peace and the sanctity, but knows that such material comforts are not for him. When the woman nursed in that atmosphere falls in love with him and concludes (like the critics, who somehow always agree with my sentimental heroines) that he risked his life for her sake, he tells her the obvious truth that he would have done as much for any stranger—that the law of his own nature, and no interest nor lust whatsoever, forbad him to cry out that the hangman's noose should be taken off his neck only to be put on another man's.

But then, said the critics, where is the motive? *Why* did Dick save Anderson? On the stage, it appears, people do things for reasons. Off the stage they dont: that is why your penny-in-the-slot heroes, who only work when you drop a motive into them, are so oppressively automatic and uninteresting. The saving of life at the risk of the saver's own is not a common thing; but modern populations are so vast that even the most uncommon things are recorded once a week or oftener. Not one of my critics but has seen a hundred times in his paper how some policeman or fireman or nursemaid has received a medal, or the compliments of a magistrate, or perhaps a public funeral, for risking his or her life to save another's. Has he ever seen it added that the saved was the husband of the woman the saver loved, or was that woman herself, or was even known to the saver as much as by sight? Never. When we want to read of the deeds that are done for love, whither do we turn? To the murder column; and there we are rarely disappointed.

Need I repeat that the theatre critic's professional routine so discourages any association between real life and the stage, that he soon loses the natural habit of referring to the one to explain the other? The critic who discovered a romantic motive for Dick's sacrifice was no mere literary dreamer, but a clever barrister. He pointed out that Dick Dudgeon clearly did adore Mrs. Anderson; that it was for her sake that he offered his life to save her beloved husband; and that his explicit denial of his passion was the splendid mendacity of a gentleman whose respect for a married woman, and duty to her absent husband, sealed his passion-palpitating lips. From the moment that this fatally plausible explanation was launched, my play became my critic's play, not mine. Thenceforth Dick Dudgeon every night confirmed the critic by stealing behind Judith, and mutely attesting his passion by surreptitiously imprinting a heartbroken kiss on a stray lock of her hair whilst he uttered the barren denial. As for me, I was just then wandering about the streets of Constantinople, unaware of all these doings. When I returned all was over. My personal relations with the critic and the actor forbad me to curse them. I had not even a chance of publicly forgiving them. They meant well by me; but if they ever write a play, may I be there to explain!

*SURREY, 1900*

# THE DEVIL'S DISCIPLE

## ACT I

*At the most wretched hour between a black night and a wintry morning in the year 1777, Mrs. Dudgeon, of New Hampshire, is sitting up in the kitchen and general dwelling room of her farm house on the outskirts of the town of Websterbridge. She is not a prepossessing woman. No woman looks her best after sitting up all night; and Mrs. Dudgeon's face, even at its best, is grimly trenched by the channels into which the barren forms and observances of a dead Puritanism can pen a bitter temper and a fierce pride. She is an elderly matron who has worked hard and got nothing by it except dominion and detestation in her sordid home, and an unquestioned reputation for piety and respectability among her neighbors, to whom drink and debauchery are still so much more tempting than religion and rectitude, that they conceive goodness simply as self-denial. This conception is easily extended to others-denial, and finally generalized as covering anything disagreeable. So Mrs. Dudgeon, being exceedingly disagreeable, is held to be exceedingly good. Short of flat felony, she enjoys complete license except for amiable weaknesses of any sort, and is consequently, without knowing it, the most licentious woman in the parish on the strength of never having broken the seventh commandment or missed a Sunday at the Presbyterian church.*

*The year 1777 is the one in which the passions roused by the breaking-off of the American colonies from England, more by their own weight than their own will, boiled up to shooting point, the shooting being idealized to the English mind as suppression of rebellion and* maintenance of British dominion, and to the American as defence of liberty, resistance to tyranny, and self-sacrifice on the altar of the Rights of Man. Into the merits of these idealizations it is not here necessary to inquire: suffice it to say, without prejudice, that they have convinced both Americans and English that the most high minded course for them to pursue is to kill as many of one another as possible, and that military operations to that end are in full swing, morally supported by confident requests from the clergy of both sides for the blessing of God on their arms.

Under such circumstances many other women besides this disagreeable Mrs. Dudgeon find themselves sitting up all night waiting for news. Like her, too, they fall asleep towards morning at the risk of nodding themselves into the kitchen fire. Mrs. Dudgeon sleeps with a shawl over her head, and her feet on a broad fender of iron laths, the step of the domestic altar of the fireplace, with its huge bobs and boiler, and its hinged arm above the smoky mantel-shelf for roasting. The plain kitchen table is opposite the fire, at her elbow, with a candle on it in a tin sconce. Her chair, like all the others in the room, is uncushioned and unpainted; but as it has a round railed back and a seat conventionally moulded to the sitter's curves, it is comparatively a chair of state. The room has three doors, one on the same side as the fireplace, near the corner, leading to the best bedroom; one, at the opposite end of the opposite wall, leading to the scullery and washhouse; and the housedoor, with its latch, heavy lock, and clumsy wooden bar, in the front wall, between the window in its middle and the corner next the bedroom door. Between the door and the window a rack of pegs suggests to the deductive observer that the men of the house are all away, as there are no hats or coats on them.[2] On the other side of the window the clock hangs on a nail, with its white wooden dial, black iron weights, and brass pendulum. Between the clock and the corner, a big cupboard, locked, stands on a dwarf dresser full of common crockery.

On the side opposite the fireplace, between the door and the corner, a shamelessly ugly black horsehair sofa stands against the wall. An

*inspection of its stridulous surface shews that Mrs. Dudgeon is not
alone. A girl of sixteen or seventeen has fallen asleep on it. She is a
wild, timid looking creature with black hair and tanned skin. Her
frock, a scanty garment, is rent, weatherstained, berrystained, and by no
means scrupulously clean. It hangs on her with a freedom which, taken
with her brown legs and bare feet, suggests no great stock of
underclothing.*

*Suddenly there comes a tapping at the door, not loud enough to wake the
sleepers. Then knocking, which disturbs MRS. DUDGEON a little. Finally the
latch is tried, whereupon she springs up at once.*

MRS. DUDGEON [*threateningly*]  Well, why dont³ you open the
   door? [*She sees that the girl is asleep, and immediately raises a clamor
   of heartfelt vexation*]. Well, dear, dear me! Now this is—[*shaking
   her*] wake up, wake up: do you hear?

THE GIRL [*sitting up*]  What is it?

MRS. DUDGEON  Wake up; and be ashamed of yourself, you un-
   feeling sinful girl, falling asleep like that, and your father hardly
   cold in his grave.

THE GIRL [*half asleep still*]  I didn't mean to. I dropped off—

MRS. DUDGEON [*cutting her short*]  Oh yes, youve plenty of ex-
   cuses, I daresay. Dropped off! [*Fiercely, as the knocking recommences*]
   Why dont you get up and let your uncle in? after me waiting up
   all night for him! [*She pushes her rudely off the sofa*]. There: I'll
   open the door: much good you are to wait up. Go and mend that
   fire a bit.

*The girl, cowed and wretched, goes to the fire and puts a log on. MRS.
DUDGEON unbars the door and opens it, letting into the stuffy kitchen
a little of the freshness and a great deal of the chill of the dawn, also her
second son CHRISTY, a fattish, stupid, fairhaired, roundfaced man of
about 22, muffled in a plaid shawl and grey overcoat. He hurries, shivering, to the fire, leaving MRS. DUDGEON to shut the door.*

CHRISTY [*at the fire*]   F—f—f! but it is cold. [*Seeing the girl, and staring lumpishly at her*] Why, who are you?

THE GIRL [*shyly*]   Essie.

MRS. DUDGEON   Oh, you may well ask. [*To ESSIE*] Go to your room child, and lie down, since you havnt feeling enough to keep you awake. Your history isnt fit for your own ears to hear.

ESSIE   I—

MRS. DUDGEON [*peremptorily*]   Dont answer me, Miss; but shew your obedience by doing what I tell you. [*ESSIE, almost in tears, crosses the room to the door near the sofa*]. And dont forget your prayers. [*ESSIE goes out*]. She'd have gone to bed last night just as if nothing had happened if I'd let her.

CHRISTY [*phlegmatically*]   Well, she cant be expected to feel Uncle Peter's death like one of the family.

MRS. DUDGEON   What are you talking about, child? Isnt she his daughter—the punishment of his wickedness and shame? [*She assaults her chair by sitting down*].

CHRISTY [*staring*]   Uncle Peter's daughter!

MRS. DUDGEON   Why else should she be here? D'ye think Ive not had enough trouble and care put upon me bringing up my own girls, let alone you and your good-for-nothing brother, without having your uncle's bastards—

CHRISTY [*interrupting her with an apprehensive glance at the door by which ESSIE went out*] Sh! She may hear you.

MRS. DUDGEON [*raising her voice*]   Let her hear me. People who fear God dont fear to give the devil's work its right name. [*CHRISTY, soullessly indifferent to the strife of Good and Evil, stares at the fire, warming himself*]. Well, how long are you going to stare there like a stuck pig? What news have you for me?

CHRISTY [*taking off his hat and shawl and going to the rack to hang them up*]   The minister is to break the news to you. He'll be here presently.

MRS. DUDGEON   Break what news?

CHRISTY [*standing on tiptoe, from boyish habit, to hang his hat up, though he is quite tall enough to reach the peg, and speaking with callous placidity, considering the nature of the announcement*]    Father's dead too.

MRS. DUDGEON [*stupent*]    Your father!

CHRISTY [*sulkily, coming back to the fire and warming himself again, attending much more to the fire than to his mother*]    Well, it's not my fault. When we got to Nevinstown we found him ill in bed. He didnt know us at first. The minister sat up with him and sent me away. He died in the night.

MRS. DUDGEON [*bursting into dry angry tears*]    Well, I do think this is hard on me—very hard on me. His brother, that was a disgrace to us all his life, gets hanged on the public gallows as a rebel; and your father, instead of staying at home where his duty was, with his own family, goes after him and dies, leaving everything on my shoulders. After sending this girl to me to take care of, too! [*She plucks her shawl vexedly over her ears*]. It's sinful, so it is; downright sinful.

CHRISTY [*with a slow, bovine cheerfulness, after a pause*]    I think it's going to be a fine morning, after all.

MRS. DUDGEON [*railing at him*]    A fine morning! And your father newly dead! Wheres your feelings, child?

CHRISTY [*obstinately*]    Well, I didn't mean any harm. I suppose a man may make a remark about the weather even if his father's dead.

MRS. DUDGEON [*bitterly*]    A nice comfort my children are to me! One son a fool, and the other a lost sinner thats left his home to live with smugglers and gypsies and villains, the scum of the earth!

*Someone knocks.*

CHRISTY [*without moving*]    That's the minister.

MRS. DUDGEON [*sharply*]    Well, arnt you going to let Mr. Anderson in?

*CHRISTY goes sheepishly to the door. MRS. DUDGEON buries her face in her hands, as it is her duty as a widow to be overcome with grief.*

*CHRISTY opens the door, and admits the minister, ANTHONY AN-*
*DERSON, a shrewd, genial, ready Presbyterian divine of about 50, with*
*something of the authority of his profession in his bearing. But it is an*
*altogether secular authority, sweetened by a conciliatory, sensible manner*
*not at all suggestive of a quite thoroughgoing other-worldliness. He is a*
*strong, healthy man, too, with a thick, sanguine neck; and his keen, cheer-*
*ful mouth cuts into somewhat fleshy corners. No doubt an excellent par-*
*son, but still a man capable of making the most of this world, and*
*perhaps a little apologetically conscious of getting on better with it than*
*a sound Presbyterian ought.*

ANDERSON [*to CHRISTY, at the door, looking at MRS. DUDGEON*
*whilst he takes off his cloak*]    Have you told her?

CHRISTY    She made me. [*He shuts the door; yawns; and loafs across to*
*the sofa, where he sits down and presently drops off to sleep*].

*ANDERSON looks compassionately at MRS. DUDGEON.Then he hangs*
*his cloak and hat on the rack. MRS. DUDGEON dries her eyes and looks*
*up at him.*

ANDERSON    Sister: the Lord has laid his hand very heavily upon
you.

MRS. DUDGEON [*with intensely recalcitrant resignation*]    It's His
will, I suppose; and I must bow to it. But I do think it hard. What
call had Timothy to go to Springtown, and remind everybody
that he belonged to a man that was being hanged?—and [*spite-*
*fully*] that deserved it, if ever a man did.

ANDERSON [*gently*]    They were brothers, Mrs. Dudgeon.

MRS. DUDGEON    Timothy never acknowledged him as his
brother after we were married: he had too much respect for me
to insult me with such a brother. Would such a selfish wretch as
Peter have come thirty miles to see Timothy hanged, do you
think? Not thirty yards, not he. However, I must bear my cross
as best I may: least said is soonest mended.

ANDERSON [*very grave, coming down to the fire to stand with his back*
*to it*]    Your eldest son was present at the execution, Mrs.
Dudgeon.

MRS. DUDGEON [*disagreeably surprised*]   Richard?

ANDERSON [*nodding*]   Yes.

MRS. DUDGEON [*vindictively*]   Let it be a warning to him. He may end that way himself, the wicked, dissolute, godless—[*she suddenly stops; her voice fails; and she asks, with evident dread*] Did Timothy see him?

ANDERSON   Yes.

MRS. DUDGEON [*holding her breath*]   Well?

ANDERSON   He only saw him in the crowd: they did not speak. [*MRS. DUDGEON, greatly relieved, exhales the pent up breath and sits at her ease again*]. Your husband was greatly touched and impressed by his brother's awful death. [*MRS. DUDGEON sneers. ANDERSON breaks off to demand with some indignation*] Well, wasnt it only natural, Mrs. Dudgeon? He softened towards his prodigal son in that moment. He sent for him to come to see him.

MRS. DUDGEON [*her alarm renewed*]   Sent for Richard!

ANDERSON   Yes; but Richard would not come. He sent his father a message; but I'm sorry to say it was a wicked message—an awful message.

MRS. DUDGEON   What was it?

ANDERSON   That he would stand by his wicked uncle, and stand against his good parents, in this world and the next.

MRS. DUDGEON [*implacably*]   He will be punished for it. He will be punished for it—in both worlds.

ANDERSON   That is not in our hands, Mrs. Dudgeon.

MRS. DUDGEON   Did I say it was, Mr. Anderson? We are told that the wicked shall be punished. Why should we do our duty and keep God's law if there is to be no difference made between us and those who follow their own likings and dislikings, and make a jest of us and of their Maker's word?

ANDERSON   Well, Richard's earthly father has been merciful to him; and his heavenly judge is the father of us all.

MRS. DUDGEON [*forgetting herself*]   Richard's earthly father was a softheaded—

ANDERSON [*shocked*]   Oh!

MRS. DUDGEON [*with a touch of shame*]   Well, I am Richard's mother. If I am against him who has any right to be for him? [*Trying to conciliate him*] Wont you sit down, Mr. Anderson? I should have asked you before; but I'm so troubled.

ANDERSON   Thank you. [*He takes a chair from beside the fireplace, and turns it so that he can sit comfortably at the fire. When he is seated he adds, in the tone of a man who knows that he is opening a difficult subject*] Has Christy told you about the new will?

MRS. DUDGEON [*all her fears returning*]   The new will! Did Timothy——? [*She breaks off, gasping, unable to complete the question*].

ANDERSON   Yes. In his last hours he changed his mind.

MRS. DUDGEON [*white with intense rage*]   And you let him rob me?

ANDERSON   I had no power to prevent him giving what was his to his own son.

MRS. DUDGEON   He had nothing of his own. His money was the money I brought him as my marriage portion. It was for me to deal with my own money and my own son. He dare not have done it if I had been with him; and well he knew it. That was why he stole away like a thief to take advantage of the law to rob me by making a new will behind my back. The more shame on you, Mr. Anderson,—you, a minister of the gospel—to act as his accomplice in such a crime.

ANDERSON [*rising*]   I will take no offence at what you say in the first bitterness of your grief.

MRS. DUDGEON [*contemptuously*]   Grief!

ANDERSON   Well, of your disappointment, if you can find it in your heart to think that the better word.

MRS. DUDGEON   My heart! My heart! And since when, pray, have you begun to hold up our hearts as trustworthy guides for us?

ANDERSON [*rather guiltily*]   I—er——

MRS. DUDGEON [*vehemently*]   Dont lie, Mr. Anderson. We are told that the heart of man is deceitful above all things, and desperately wicked. My heart belonged, not to Timothy, but to that poor wretched brother of his that has just ended his days with a rope round his neck—aye, to Peter Dudgeon. You know it: old Eli Hawkins, the man to whose pulpit you succeeded, though you are not worthy to loose his shoe latchet,* told it you when he gave over our souls into your charge. He warned me and strengthened me against my heart, and made me marry a God-fearing man—as he thought. What else but that discipline has made me the woman I am? And you, you, who followed your heart in your marriage, you talk to me of what I find in my heart. Go home to your pretty wife, man; and leave me to my prayers. [*She turns from him and leans with her elbows on the table, brooding over her wrongs and taking no further notice of him*].

ANDERSON [*willing enough to escape*]   The lord forbid that I should come between you and the source of all comfort! [*He goes to the rack for his coat and hat*].

MRS. DUDGEON [*without looking at him*]   The Lord will know what to forbid and what to allow without your help.

ANDERSON   And whom to forgive, I hope—Eli Hawkins and myself, if we have ever set up our preaching against His law. [*He fastens his cloak, and is now ready to go*]. Just one word—on necessary business, Mrs. Dudgeon. There is the reading of the will to be gone through; and Richard has a right to be present. He is in the town; but he has the grace to say that he does not want to force himself in here.

MRS. DUDGEON   He s h a l l come here. Does he expect us to leave his father's house for his convenience? Let them all come, and come quickly, and go quickly. They shall not make the will an excuse to shirk half their day's work. I shall be ready, never fear.

---

*In the Bible, Mark 1:7, John the Baptist says of himself in relation to Christ: "There cometh one mightier than I after me, the latchet of whose shoes I am not worthy to stoop down and unloose" (KJV).

ANDERSON [*coming back a step or two*]   Mrs. Dudgeon: I used to have some little influence with you. When did I lose it?

MRS. DUDGEON [*still without turning to him*]   When you married for love. Now youre answered.

ANDERSON   Yes: I am answered. [*He goes out, musing*].

MRS. DUDGEON [*to herself, thinking of her husband*]   Thief! Thief!! [*She shakes herself angrily out of the chair; throws back the shawl from her head; and sets to work to prepare the room for the reading of the will, beginning by replacing ANDERSON's chair against the wall, and pushing back her own to the window. Then she calls, in her hard, driving, wrathful way*] Christy. [*No answer: he is fast asleep*]. Christy. [*She shakes him roughly*]. Get up out of that; and be ashamed of yourself—sleeping, and your father dead! [*She returns to the table; puts the candle on the mantelshelf; and takes from the table drawer a red table cloth which she spreads*].

CHRISTY [*rising reluctantly*]   Well, do you suppose we are never going to sleep until we are out of mourning?

MRS. DUDGEON   I want none of your sulks. Here: help me to set this table. [*They place the table in the middle of the room, with CHRISTY's end towards the fireplace and MRS. DUDGEON's towards the sofa. CHRISTY drops the table as soon as possible, and goes to the fire, leaving his mother to make the final adjustments of its position*]. We shall have the minister back here with the lawyer and all the family to read the will before you have done toasting yourself. Go and wake that girl; and then light the stove in the shed: you cant have your breakfast here. And mind you wash yourself, and make yourself fit to receive the company. [*She punctuates these orders by going to the cupboard; unlocking it; and producing a decanter of wine, which has no doubt stood there untouched since the last state occasion in the family, and some glasses, which she sets on the table. Also two green ware plates, on one of which she puts a barnbrack* with a knife beside it. On the other she shakes some biscuits out of a tin, putting back*]

---

*Plain-style country cake.

*one or two, and counting the rest*]. Now mind: there are ten biscuits there: let there be ten there when I come back after dressing myself. And keep your fingers off the raisins in that cake. And tell Essie the same. I suppose I can trust you to bring in the case of stuffed birds without breaking the glass? [*She replaces the tin in the cupboard, which she locks, pocketing the key carefully*].

CHRISTY [*lingering at the fire*]   Youd better put the inkstand instead, for the lawyer.

MRS. DUDGEON   Thats no answer to make to me, sir. Go and do as youre told. [*CHRISTY turns sullenly to obey*]. Stop: take down that shutter before you go, and let the daylight in: you cant expect me to do all the heavy work of the house with a great heavy lout like you idling about.

*CHRISTY takes the window bar out of its clamps, and puts it aside; then opens the shutter, shewing the grey morning. MRS. DUDGEON takes the sconce from the mantelshelf; blows out the candle; extinguishes the snuff by pinching it with her fingers, first licking them for the purpose; and replaces the sconce on the shelf.*

CHRISTY [*looking through the window*]   Here's the minister's wife.

MRS. DUDGEON [*displeased*]   What! Is she coming here?

CHRISTY   Yes.

MRS. DUDGEON   What does she want troubling me at this hour, before I'm properly dressed to receive people?

CHRISTY   Youd better ask her.

MRS. DUDGEON [*threateningly*]   Youd better keep a civil tongue in your head. [*He goes sulkily towards the door. She comes after him, plying him with instructions*]. Tell that girl to come to me as soon as she's had her breakfast. And tell her to make herself fit to be seen before the people. [*CHRISTY goes out and slams the door in her face*]. Nice manners, that! [*Someone knocks at the house door: she turns and cries inhospitably*] Come in. [*JUDITH ANDERSON, the minister's wife, comes in. JUDITH is more than twenty years younger than her husband, though she will never be as young as he in vitality. She is pretty and proper and ladylike, and has been admired and petted into an opinion of herself sufficiently favorable to give her a self-assurance which serves her instead of strength. She has a pretty taste in dress, and in her face the pretty lines of a sentimental character formed by dreams. Even her little self complacency is pretty, like a child's vanity. Rather a pathetic creature to any sympathetic observer who knows how rough a place the world is. One feels, on the whole, that ANDERSON might have chosen worse, and that she, needing protection, could not have chosen better*]. Oh, it's you, is it, Mrs. Anderson?

JUDITH [*very politely—almost patronizingly*]   Yes. Can I do anything for you, Mrs. Dudgeon? Can I help to get the place ready before they come to read the will?

MRS. DUDGEON [*stiffly*]   Thank you, Mrs. Anderson, my house is always ready for anyone to come into.

MRS. ANDERSON [*with complacent amiability*]   Yes, indeed it is. Perhaps you had rather I did not intrude on you just now.

MRS. DUDGEON   Oh, one more or less will make no difference this morning, Mrs. Anderson. Now that youre here, youd better stay. If you wouldnt mind shutting the door! [*JUDITH smiles, implying "How stupid of me!" and shuts it with an exasperating air of doing something pretty and becoming*]. Thats better. I must go and tidy myself a bit. I suppose you dont mind stopping here to receive anyone that comes until I'm ready.

JUDITH [*graciously giving her leave*]   Oh yes, certainly. Leave them to me, Mrs. Dudgeon; and take your time. [*She hangs her cloak and bonnet on the rack*].

MRS. DUDGEON [*half sneering*]   I thought that would be more in your way than getting the house ready. [*ESSIE comes back*]. Oh, here you are! [*Severely*] Come here: let me see you. [*ESSIE timidly goes to her. MRS. DUDGEON takes her roughly by the arm and pulls her round to inspect the results of her attempt to clean and tidy herself— results which shew little practice and less conviction*]. Mm! Thats what you call doing your hair properly, I suppose. It's easy to see what you are, and how you were brought up. [*She throws her arms away, and goes on, peremptorily*] Now you listen to me and do as youre told. You sit down there in the corner by the fire; and when the company comes dont dare to speak until youre spoken to. [*ESSIE creeps away to the fireplace*]. Your father's people had better see you and know youre there: theyre as much bound to keep you from starvation as I am. At any rate they might help. But let me have no chattering and making free with them, as if you were their equal. Do you hear?

ESSIE    Yes.

MRS. DUDGEON    Well, then go and do as youre told. [*ESSIE sits down miserably on the corner of the fender furthest from the door*]. Never mind her, Mrs. Anderson: you know who she is and what she is. If she gives you any trouble, just tell me; and I'll settle accounts with her. [*MRS. DUDGEON goes into the bedroom, shutting the door sharply behind her as if even it had to be made to do its duty with a ruthless hand*].

JUDITH [*patronizing ESSIE, and arranging the cake and wine on the table more becomingly*]    You must not mind if your aunt is strict with you. She is a very good woman, and desires your good too.

ESSIE [*in listless misery*]    Yes.

JUDITH [*annoyed with ESSIE for her failure to be consoled and edified, and to appreciate the kindly condescension of the remark*]    You are not going to be sullen, I hope, Essie.

ESSIE    No.

JUDITH    Thats a good girl! [*She places a couple of chairs at the table with their backs to the window, with a pleasant sense of being a more thoughtful housekeeper than MRS. DUDGEON*]. Do you know any of your father's relatives?

ESSIE    No. They wouldnt have anything to do with him: they were too religious. Father used to talk about Dick Dudgeon; but I never saw him.

JUDITH [*ostentatiously shocked*]    Dick Dudgeon! Essie: do you wish to be a really respectable and grateful girl, and to make a place for yourself here by steady good conduct?

ESSIE [*very half-heartedly*]    Yes.

JUDITH   Then you must never mention the name of Richard Dudgeon—never even think about him. He is a bad man.

ESSIE   What has he done?

JUDITH   You must not ask questions about him, Essie. You are too young to know what it is to be a bad man. But he is a smuggler; and he lives with gypsies; and he has no love for his mother and his family; and he wrestles and plays games on Sunday instead of going to church. Never let him into your presence, if you can help it, Essie; and try to keep yourself and all womanhood unspotted by contact with such men.

ESSIE   Yes.

JUDITH [*again displeased*]   I am afraid you say Yes and No without thinking very deeply.

ESSIE   Yes. At least I mean—

JUDITH [*severely*]   What do you mean?

ESSIE [*almost crying*]   Only—my father was a smuggler; and— [*Someone knocks*].

JUDITH   They are beginning to come. Now remember your aunt's directions, Essie; and be a good girl. [*CHRISTY comes back with the stand of stuffed birds under a glass case, and an inkstand, which he places on the table*]. Good morning, Mr. Dudgeon. Will you open the door, please: the people have come.

CHRISTY   Good morning. [*He opens the house door*].

*The morning is now fairly bright and warm; and ANDERSON, who is the first to enter, has left his cloak at home. He is accompanied by LAWYER HAWKINS, a brisk, middleaged man in brown riding gaiters and yellow breeches, looking as much squire as solicitor. He and ANDERSON are allowed precedence as representing the learned professions. After them comes the family, headed by the senior uncle, WILLIAM DUDGEON, a large, shapeless man, bottle-nosed and evidently no ascetic at table. His clothes are not the clothes, nor his anxious wife the wife, of a prosperous man. The junior uncle, TITUS DUDGEON, is a wiry little terrier of a man, with an immense and visibly purse-proud wife, both free from the cares of the WILLIAM household.*

*HAWKINS at once goes briskly to the table and takes the chair nearest the sofa, CHRISTY having left the inkstand there. He puts his hat on the floor beside him, and produces the will. UNCLE WILLIAM comes to the fire and stands on the hearth warming his coat tails, leaving MRS. WILLIAM derelict near the door. UNCLE TITUS, who is the lady's man of the family, rescues her by giving her his disengaged arm and bringing her to the sofa, where he sits down warmly between his own lady and his brother's. ANDERSON hangs up his hat and waits for a word with JUDITH.*

JUDITH    She will be here in a moment. Ask them to wait. [*She taps at the bedroom door. Receiving an answer from within, she opens it and passes through*].

ANDERSON [*taking his place at the table at the opposite end to HAWKINS*]    Our poor afflicted sister will be with us in a moment. Are we all here?

CHRISTY [*at the house door, which he has just shut*]    All except Dick.
*The callousness with which CHRISTY names the reprobate jars on the moral sense of the family. UNCLE WILLIAM shakes his head slowly and repeatedly. MRS. TITUS catches her breath convulsively through her nose. Her husband speaks.*

UNCLE TITUS    Well, I hope he will have the grace not to come. I  h o p e  so.
*The DUDGEONS all murmur assent, except CHRISTY, who goes to the window and posts himself there, looking out. HAWKINS smiles secretively as if he knew something that would change their tune if they knew it. ANDERSON is uneasy: the love of solemn family councils, especially funereal ones, is not in his nature. JUDITH appears at the bedroom door.*

JUDITH [*with gentle impressiveness*]    Friends, Mrs. Dudgeon. [*She takes the chair from beside the fireplace; and places it for MRS. DUDGEON, who comes from the bedroom in black, with a clean handkerchief to her eyes. All rise, except ESSIE. MRS. TITUS and MRS. WILLIAM produce equally clean handkerchiefs and weep. It is an affecting moment*].

UNCLE WILLIAM    Would it comfort you, sister, if we were to offer up a prayer?

UNCLE TITUS    Or sing a hymn?

ANDERSON [*rather hastily*]    I have been with our sister this morning already, friends. In our hearts we ask a blessing.

ALL [*except ESSIE*]    Amen.

*They all sit down, except JUDITH, who stands behind MRS. DUDGEON's chair.*

JUDITH [*to ESSIE*]    Essie: did you say Amen?

ESSIE [*scaredly*]    No.

JUDITH    Then say it, like a good girl.

ESSIE    Amen.

UNCLE WILLIAM [*encouragingly*]    Thats right: thats right. We know who you are; but we are willing to be kind to you if you are a good girl and deserve it. We are all equal before the Throne.

*This republican sentiment does not please the women, who are convinced that the Throne is precisely the place where their superiority, often questioned in this world, will be recognized and rewarded.*

CHRISTY [*at the window*]    Here's Dick.

*ANDERSON and HAWKINS look round sociably. ESSIE, with a gleam of interest breaking through her misery, looks up. CHRISTY grins and gapes expectantly at the door. The rest are petrified with the intensity of their sense of Virtue menaced with outrage by the approach of flaunting Vice. The reprobate appears in the doorway, graced beyond his alleged merits by the morning sunlight. He is certainly the best looking member of the family; but his expression is reckless and sardonic, his manner defiant and satirical, his dress picturesquely careless. Only, his forehead and mouth betray an extraordinary steadfastness; and his eyes are the eyes of a fanatic.*

RICHARD [*on the threshold, taking off his hat*]    Ladies and gentlemen: your servant, your very humble servant. [*With this comprehensive insult, he throws his hat to CHRISTY with a suddenness that makes him jump like a negligent wicket keeper,* * *and comes into the middle of the room, where he turns and deliberately surveys the company*].

---

*In cricket, the guard who stops balls from passing the wicket.

How happy you all look! how glad to see me! [*He turns towards MRS. DUDGEON's chair; and his lip rolls up horribly from his dog tooth as he meets her look of undisguised hatred*]. Well, mother: keeping up appearances as usual? thats right, thats right. [*JUDITH pointedly moves away from his neighborhood to the other side of the kitchen, holding her skirt instinctively as if to save it from contamination. UNCLE TITUS promptly marks his approval of her action by rising from the sofa, and placing a chair for her to sit down upon*]. What! Uncle William! I havnt seen you since you gave up drinking. [*Poor UNCLE WILLIAM, shamed, would protest; but RICHARD claps him heartily on his shoulder, adding*] you have given it up, havnt you? [*releasing him with a playful push*] of course you have: quite right too: you overdid it. [*He turns away from UNCLE WILLIAM and makes for the sofa*]. And now, where is that upright horsedealer Uncle Titus? Uncle Titus: come forth. [*He comes upon him holding the chair as JUDITH sits down*]. As usual, looking after the ladies!

UNCLE TITUS [*indignantly*]   Be ashamed of yourself, sir—

RICHARD [*interrupting him and shaking his hand in spite of him*]   I am: I am; but I am proud of my uncle—proud of all my relatives—[*again surveying them*] who could look at them and not be proud and joyful? [*UNCLE TITUS, overborne, resumes his seat on the sofa. RICHARD turns to the table*]. Ah, Mr. Anderson, still at the good work, still shepherding them. Keep them up to the mark, minister, keep them up to the mark. Come! [*with a spring he seats himself on the table and takes up the decanter*] clink a glass with me, Pastor, for the sake of old times.

ANDERSON   You know, I think, Mr. Dudgeon, that I do not drink before dinner.

RICHARD   You will, some day, Pastor: Uncle William used to drink before breakfast. Come: it will give your sermons unction. [*He smells the wine and makes a wry face*]. But do not begin on my mother's company sherry. I stole some when I was six years old; and I have been a temperate man ever since. [*He puts the decanter down and changes the subject*]. So I hear you are married, Pastor, and that your wife has a most ungodly allowance of good looks.

ANDERSON [*quietly indicating JUDITH*]   Sir: you are in the presence of my wife. [*JUDITH rises and stands with stony propriety*].

RICHARD [*quickly slipping down from the table with instinctive good manners*]   Your servant, madam: no offence. [*He looks at her earnestly*]. You deserve your reputation; but I'm sorry to see by your expression that youre a good woman. [*She looks shocked, and sits down amid a murmur of indignant sympathy from his relatives. AN-DERSON, sensible enough to know that these demonstrations can only gratify and encourage a man who is deliberately trying to provoke them, remains perfectly goodhumored*]. All the same, Pastor, I respect you more than I did before. By the way, did I hear, or did I not, that our late lamented Uncle Peter, though unmarried, was a father?

UNCLE TITUS   He had only one irregular child, sir.

RICHARD   O n l y  one! He thinks one a mere trifle! I blush for you, Uncle Titus.

ANDERSON   Mr. Dudgeon: you are in the presence of your mother and her grief.

RICHARD   It touches me profoundly, Pastor. By the way, what has become of the irregular child?

ANDERSON [*pointing to ESSIE*]   There, sir, listening to you.

RICHARD [*shocked into sincerity*]   What! Why the devil didnt you tell me that before? Children suffer enough in this house without—[*He hurries remorsefully to ESSIE*]. Come, little cousin! never mind me: it was not meant to hurt you. [*She looks up gratefully at him. Her tearstained face affects him violently, and he bursts out, in a transport of wrath*] Who has been making her cry? Who has been ill-treating her? By God—

MRS. DUDGEON [*rising and confronting him*]   Silence your blasphemous tongue. I will bear no more of this. Leave my house.

RICHARD   How do you know it's your house until the will is read? [*They look at one another for a moment with intense hatred; and then she sinks, checkmated, into her chair. RICHARD goes boldly up past*

*ANDERSON to the window, where he takes the railed chair in his hand*]. Ladies and gentlemen: as the eldest son of my late father, and the unworthy head of this household, I bid you welcome. By your leave, Minister Anderson: by your leave, Lawyer Hawkins. The head of the table for the head of the family. [*He places the chair at the table between the minister and the attorney; sits down between them; and addresses the assembly with a presidential air*]. We meet on a melancholy occasion: a father dead! an uncle actually hanged, and probably damned. [*He shakes his head deploringly. The relatives freeze with horror*]. T h a t s right: pull your longest faces [*his voice suddenly sweetens gravely as his glance lights on ESSIE*] provided only there is hope in the eyes of the child. [*Briskly*] Now then, Lawyer Hawkins: business, business. Get on with the will, man.

TITUS    Do not let yourself be ordered or hurried, Mr. Hawkins.

HAWKINS [*very politely and willingly*]    Mr. Dudgeon means no offence, I feel sure. I will not keep you one second, Mr. Dudgeon. Just while I get my glasses—[*he fumbles for them. The DUDGEONS look at one another with misgiving*].

RICHARD    Aha! They notice your civility, Mr. Hawkins. They are prepared for the worst. A glass of wine to clear your voice before you begin. [*He pours out one for him and hands it; then pours one for himself*].

HAWKINS    Thank you, Mr. Dudgeon. Your good health, sir.

RICHARD    Yours, sir. [*With the glass halfway to his lips, he checks himself, giving a dubious glance at the wine, and adds, with quaint intensity*] Will anyone oblige me with a glass of water?

*ESSIE, who has been hanging on his every word and movement, rises stealthily and slips out behind MRS. DUDGEON through the bedroom door, returning presently with a jug and going out of the house as quietly as possible.*

HAWKINS    The will is not exactly in proper legal phraseology.

RICHARD    No: my father died without the consolations of the law.

HAWKINS    Good again, Mr. Dudgeon, good again. [*Preparing to read*] Are you ready, sir?

RICHARD    Ready, aye ready. For what we are about to receive, may the Lord make us truly thankful. Go ahead.

HAWKINS [*reading*]    "This is the last will and testament of me Timothy Dudgeon on my deathbed at Nevinstown on the road from Springtown to Websterbridge on this twenty-fourth day of September, one thousand seven hundred and seventy seven. I hereby revoke all former wills made by me and declare that I am of sound mind and know well what I am doing and that this is my real will according to my own wish and affections."

RICHARD [*glancing at his mother*]    Aha!

HAWKINS [*shaking his head*]    Bad phraseology, sir, wrong phraseology. "I give and bequeath a hundred pounds to my younger son Christopher Dudgeon, fifty pounds to be paid to him on the day of his marriage to Sarah Wilkins if she will have him, and ten pounds on the birth of each of his children up to the number of five."

RICHARD    How if she wont have him?

CHRISTY    She will if I have fifty pounds.

RICHARD    Good, my brother. Proceed.

HAWKINS    "I give and bequeath to my wife Annie Dudgeon, born Annie Primrose"—you see he did not know the law, Mr. Dudgeon: your mother was not born Annie: she was christened so— "an annuity of fifty two pounds a year for life [*MRS. DUDGEON, with all eyes on her, holds herself convulsively rigid*] to be paid out of the interest on her own money"—t h e r e ' s a way to put it, Mr. Dudgeon! Her own money!

MRS. DUDGEON    A very good way to put God's truth. It was every penny my own. Fifty-two pounds a year!

HAWKINS    "And I recommend her for her goodness and piety to the forgiving care of her children, having stood between them and her as far as I could to the best of my ability."

MRS. DUDGEON    And this is my reward! [*raging inwardly*] You know what I think, Mr. Anderson: you know the word I gave to it.

ANDERSON    It cannot be helped, Mrs. Dudgeon. We must take what comes to us. [*To HAWKINS*]. Go on, sir.

HAWKINS    "I give and bequeath my house at Websterbridge with the land belonging to it and all the rest of my property soever to my eldest son and heir, Richard Dudgeon."

RICHARD    Oho! The fatted calf, Minister, the fatted calf.

HAWKINS    "On these conditions—"

RICHARD    The devil! Are there conditions?

HAWKINS    "To wit: first, that he shall not let my brother Peter's natural child starve or be driven by want to an evil life."

RICHARD [*emphatically, striking his fist on the table*]    Agreed.

*MRS. DUDGEON, turning to look malignantly at ESSIE, misses her and looks quickly round to see where she has moved to; then, seeing that she has left the room without leave, closes her lips vengefully.*

HAWKINS    "Second, that he shall be a good friend to my old horse Jim"—[*again shaking his head*] he should have written James, sir.

RICHARD    James shall live in clover. Go on.

HAWKINS    —"and keep my deaf farm laborer Prodger Feston in his service."

RICHARD    Prodger Feston shall get drunk every Saturday.

HAWKINS    "Third, that he make Christy a present on his marriage out of the ornaments in the best room."

RICHARD [*holding up the stuffed birds*]    Here you are, Christy.

CHRISTY [*disappointed*]    I'd rather have the china peacocks.

RICHARD    You shall have both. [*CHRISTY is greatly pleased*]. Go on.

HAWKINS    "Fourthly and lastly, that he try to live at peace with his mother as far as she will consent to it."

RICHARD [*dubiously*]    Hm! Anything more, Mr. Hawkins?

HAWKINS [*solemnly*]    "Finally I give and bequeath my soul into my Maker's hands, humbly asking forgiveness for all my sins and mistakes, and hoping that he will so guide my son that it may not be said that I have done wrong in trusting to him rather than to others in the perplexity of my last hour in this strange place."

ANDERSON   Amen.

THE UNCLES AND AUNTS   Amen.

RICHARD   My mother does not say Amen.

MRS. DUDGEON [*rising, unable to give up her property without a struggle*]   Mr. Hawkins: is that a proper will? Remember, I have his rightful, legal will, drawn up by yourself, leaving all to me.

HAWKINS   This is a very wrongly and irregularly worded will, Mrs. Dudgeon; though [*turning politely to RICHARD*] it contains in my judgment an excellent disposal of his property.

ANDERSON [*interposing before MRS. DUDGEON can retort*]   That is not what you are asked, Mr. Hawkins. Is it a legal will?

HAWKINS   The courts will sustain it against the other.

ANDERSON   But why, if the other is more lawfully worded?

HAWKINS   Because, sir, the courts will sustain the claim of a man —and that man the eldest son—against any woman, if they can. I warned you, Mrs. Dudgeon, when you got me to draw that other will, that it was not a wise will, and that though you might make him sign it, would never be easy until he revoked it. But you wouldn't take advice; and now Mr. Richard is cock of the walk. [*He takes his hat from the floor; rises; and begins pocketing his papers and spectacles*].

*This is the signal for the breaking-up of the party. ANDERSON takes his hat from the rack and joins UNCLE WILLIAM at the fire. UNCLE TITUS fetches JUDITH her things from the rack. The three on the sofa rise and chat with HAWKINS. MRS. DUDGEON, now an intruder in her own house, stands erect, crushed by the weight of the law on women, accepting it, as she has been trained to accept all monstrous calamities, as proofs of the greatness of the power that inflicts them, and of her own wormlike insignificance. For at this time, remember, Mary Wollstonecraft is as yet only a girl of eighteen, and her Vindication of the Rights of Women is still fourteen years off. MRS. DUDGEON is rescued from her*

*apathy by ESSIE, who comes back with the jug full of water. She is tak-
ing it to RICHARD when MRS. DUDGEON stops her.*

MRS. DUDGEON [*threatening her*]   Where have you been? [*ESSIE,
appalled, tries to answer, but cannot*]. How dare you go out by yourself after the orders I gave you?

ESSIE   He asked for a drink—[*she stops, her tongue cleaving to her
palate with terror*].

JUDITH [*with gentler severity*]   Who asked for a drink? [*ESSIE,
speechless, points to RICHARD*].

RICHARD   What! I!

JUDITH [*shocked*]   Oh Essie, Essie!

RICHARD   I believe I did. [*He takes a glass and holds it to ESSIE to
be filled. Her hand shakes*].   What! afraid of me?

ESSIE [*quickly*]   No. I—[*She pours out the water*].

RICHARD [*tasting it*]   Ah, youve been up the street to the market
gate spring to get that. [*He takes a draught*]. Delicious! Thank you.
[*Unfortunately, at this moment he chances to catch sight of JUDITH's
face, which expresses the most prudish disapproval of his evident attraction for ESSIE, who is devouring him with her grateful eyes. His mocking expression returns instantly. He puts down the glass; deliberately
winds his arm round ESSIE's shoulders; and brings her into the middle
of the company. MRS. DUDGEON being in ESSIE's way as they come
past the table, he says*] By your leave, mother [*and compels her to
make way for them*]. What do they call you? Bessie?

ESSIE   Essie.

RICHARD   Essie, to be sure. Are you a good girl, Essie?

ESSIE [*greatly disappointed that he, of all people, should begin at her in
this way*]   Yes. [*She looks doubtfully at JUDITH*]. I think so. I mean
I—I hope so.

RICHARD   Essie: did you ever hear of a person called the devil?

ANDERSON [*revolted*]   Shame on you, sir, with a mere child—

RICHARD   By your leave, Minister: I do not interfere with your
sermons: do not you interrupt mine. [*To ESSIE*] Do you know
what they call me, Essie?

ESSIE   Dick.

RICHARD [*amused: patting her on the shoulder*]   Yes, Dick; but something else too. They call me the Devil's Disciple.

ESSIE   Why do you let them?

RICHARD [*seriously*]   Because it's true. I was brought up in the other service; but I knew from the first that the Devil was my natural master and captain and friend. I saw that he was in the right, and that the world cringed to his conqueror only through fear. I prayed secretly to him; and he comforted me, and saved me from having my spirit broken in this house of children's tears. I promised him my soul, and swore an oath that I would stand up for him in this world and stand by him in the next. [*Solemnly*] That promise and that oath made a man of me. From this day this house is his home; and no child shall cry in it: this hearth is his altar; and no soul shall ever cower over it in the dark evenings and be afraid. Now [*turning forcibly on the rest*] which of you good men will take this child and rescue her from the house of the devil?

JUDITH [*coming to ESSIE and throwing a protecting arm about her*]   I will. You should be burnt alive.

ESSIE   But I dont want to. [*She shrinks back, leaving RICHARD and JUDITH face to face*].

RICHARD [*to JUDITH*]   Actually doesnt want to, most virtuous lady!

UNCLE TITUS   Have a care, Richard Dudgeon. The law—

RICHARD [*turning threateningly on him*]   Have a care, you. In an hour from this there will be no law here but martial law. I passed the soldiers within six miles on my way here: before noon Major Swindon's gallows for rebels will be up in the market place.

ANDERSON [*calmly*]   What have we to fear from that, sir?

RICHARD   More than you think. He hanged the wrong man at Springtown: he thought Uncle Peter was respectable, because the Dudgeons had a good name. But his next example will be the best man in the town to whom he can bring home a rebellious word. Well, we're all rebels; and you know it.

ALL THE MEN [*except ANDERSON*]   No, no, no!

RICHARD    Yes, you are. You havnt damned King George up hill and down dale as I have; but youve prayed for his defeat; and you, Anthony Anderson, have conducted the service, and sold your family bible to buy a pair of pistols. They maynt hang me, perhaps; because the moral effect of the Devil's Disciple dancing on nothing wouldnt help them. But a Minister! [*JUDITH, dismayed, clings to ANDERSON*] or a lawyer! [*HAWKINS smiles like a man able to take care of himself*] or an upright horsedealer! [*UNCLE TITUS snarls at him in rage and terror*] or a reformed drunkard! [*UNCLE WILLIAM, utterly unnerved, moans and wobbles with fear*] eh? Would that shew that King George meant business——ha?

ANDERSON [*perfectly self-possessed*]    Come, my dear: he is only trying to frighten you. There is no danger. [*He takes her out of the house. The rest crowd to the door to follow him, except ESSIE, who remains near RICHARD*].

RICHARD [*boisterously derisive*]    Now then: how many of you will stay with me; run up the American flag on the devil's house; and make a fight for freedom? [*They scramble out, CHRISTY among them, hustling one another in their haste*] Ha ha! Long live the devil! [*To MRS. DUDGEON, who is following them*] What, mother! Are you off too?

MRS. DUDGEON [*deadly pale, with her hand on her heart as if she had received a deathblow*]    My curse on you! My dying curse! [*She goes out*].

RICHARD [*calling after her*]    It will bring me luck. Ha ha ha!

ESSIE [*anxiously*]    Maynt I stay?

RICHARD [*turning to her*]    What! Have they forgotten to save your soul in their anxiety about their own bodies? Oh yes: you may stay. [*He turns excitedly away again and shakes his fist after them. His left fist, also clenched, hangs down. ESSIE seizes it and kisses it, her tears falling on it. He starts and looks at it*]. Tears! The devil's baptism! [*She falls on her knees, sobbing. He stoops goodnaturedly to raise her, saying*] Oh yes, you may cry that way, Essie, if you like.

# ACT II

*Minister Anderson's house is in the main street of Websterbridge, not far
from the town hall. To the eye of the eighteenth century New
Englander, it is much grander than the plain farmhouse of the
Dudgeons; but it is so plain itself that a modern house agent would let
both at about the same rent. The chief dwelling room has the same sort
of kitchen fireplace, with boiler, toaster hanging on the bars, movable
iron griddle socketed to the hob, hook above for roasting, and broad
fender, on which stand a kettle and a plate of buttered toast. The door,
between the fireplace and the corner, has neither panels, fingerplates
nor handles: it is made of plain boards, and fastens with a latch. The
table is a kitchen table, with a treacle colored cover of American cloth,
chapped\* at the corners by draping. The tea service on it consists of two
thick cups and saucers of the plainest ware, with milk jug and bowl to
match, each large enough to contain nearly a quart, on a black
japanned tray, and, in the middle of the table, a wooden trencher with
a big loaf upon it, and a square half pound block of butter in a crock.
The big oak press facing the fire from the opposite side of the room, is
for use and storage, not for ornament; and the minister's house coat
hangs on a peg from its door, shewing that he is out; for when he is in,
it is his best coat that hangs there. His big riding boots stand beside
the press, evidently in their usual place, and rather proud of themselves.
In fact, the evolution of the minister's kitchen, dining room and
drawing room into three separate apartments has not yet taken place;
and so, from the point of view of our pampered period, he is no better
off than the Dudgeons.*

---

\*Worn (from covering the corners of the table).

But there is a difference, for all that. To begin with, Mrs. Anderson is a pleasanter person to live with than Mrs. Dudgeon. To which Mrs. Dudgeon would at once reply, with reason, that Mrs. Anderson has no children to look after; no poultry, pigs nor cattle; a steady and sufficient income not directly dependent on harvests and prices at fairs; an affectionate husband who is a tower of strength to her: in short, that life is as easy at the minister's house as it is hard at the farm. This is true; but to explain a fact is not to alter it; and however little credit Mrs. Anderson may deserve for making her home happier, she has certainly succeeded in doing it. The outward and visible signs of her superior social pretensions are, a drugget* on the floor, a plaster ceiling between the timbers, and chairs which, though not upholstered, are stained and polished. The fine arts are represented by a mezzotint portrait of some Presbyterian divine, a copperplate of Raphael's St Paul preaching at Athens, a rococo presentation clock on the mantelshelf, flanked by a couple of miniatures, a pair of crockery dogs with baskets in their mouths, and, at the corners, two large cowrie shells.† A pretty feature of the room is the low wide latticed window, nearly its whole width, with little red curtains running on a rod half way up it to serve as a blind. There is no sofa; but one of the seats, standing near the press, has a railed back and is long enough to accommodate two people easily. On the whole, it is rather the sort of room that the nineteenth century has ended in struggling to get back to under the leadership of Mr. Philip Webb‡ and his disciples in domestic architecture, though no genteel clergyman would have tolerated it fifty years ago.

The evening has closed in; and the room is dark except for the cosy firelight and the dim oil lamps seen through the window in the wet street, where there is a quiet, steady, warm, windless downpour of rain. As the town clock strikes the quarter, Judith comes in with a couple of

---

*Coarse rug.

†Highly polished, colorful shells.

‡English architect (1831–1915) who worked with the socialist William Morris (1834–1896).

*candles in earthenware candlesticks, and sets them on the table. Her*
*self-conscious airs of the morning are gone: she is anxious and*
*frightened. She goes to the window and peers into the street. The first*
*thing she sees there is her husband, hurrying home through the rain.*
*She gives a little gasp of relief, not very far removed from a sob, and*
*turns to the door. Anderson comes in, wrapped in a very wet cloak.*

JUDITH [*running to him*]   Oh, here you are at last, at last! [*She attempts to embrace him*].

ANDERSON [*keeping her off*]   Take care, my love: I'm wet. Wait
till I get my cloak off. [*He places a chair with its back to the fire;
hangs his cloak on it to dry; shakes the rain from his hat and puts it on
the fender; and at last turns with his hands outstretched to JUDITH*].
Now! [*She flies into his arms*]. I am not late, am I? The town clock
struck the quarter as I came in at the front door. And the town
clock is always fast.

JUDITH   I'm sure it's slow this evening. I'm so glad youre back.

ANDERSON [*taking her more closely in his arms*]   Anxious, my dear?

JUDITH   A little.

ANDERSON   Why, youve been crying.

JUDITH   Only a little. Never mind: it's all over now. [*A bugle call is
heard in the distance. She starts in terror and retreats to the long seat,
listening.*] Whats that?

ANDERSON [*following her tenderly to the seat and making her sit down
with him*]   Only King George, my dear. He's returning to bar-
racks, or having his roll called, or getting ready for tea, or boot-
ing or saddling or something. Soldiers dont ring the bell or call
over the banisters when they want anything: they send a boy out
with a bugle to disturb the whole town.

JUDITH   Do you think there is really any danger?

ANDERSON   Not the least in the world.

JUDITH   You say that to comfort me, not because you believe it.

ANDERSON   My dear: in this world there is always danger for
those who are afraid of it. There's a danger that the house will

catch fire in the night; but we shant sleep any the less soundly for that.

JUDITH     Yes, I know what you always say; and youre quite right. Oh, quite right: I know it. But—I suppose I'm not brave: thats all. My heart shrinks every time I think of the soldiers.

ANDERSON     Never mind that, dear: bravery is none the worse for costing a little pain.

JUDITH     Yes, I suppose so. [*Embracing him again*] Oh how brave you are, my dear! [*With tears in her eyes*] Well, I'll be brave too: you shant be ashamed of your wife.

ANDERSON     Thats right. Now you make me happy. Well, well! [*He rises and goes cheerily to the fire to dry his shoes*]. I called on Richard Dudgeon on my way back; but he wasn't in.

JUDITH [*rising in consternation*]     You called on that man!

ANDERSON [*reassuring her*]     Oh, nothing happened, dearie. He was out.

JUDITH [*almost in tears, as if the visit were a personal humiliation to her*] But why did you go there?

ANDERSON [*gravely*]     Well, it is all the talk that Major Swindon is going to do what he did in Springtown—make an example of some notorious rebel, as he calls us. He pounced on Peter Dudgeon as the worst character there; and it is the general belief that he will pounce on Richard as the worst here.

JUDITH     But Richard said—

ANDERSON [*goodhumoredly cutting her short*]     Pooh! Richard said! He said what he thought would frighten you and frighten me, my dear. He said what perhaps (God forgive him!) he would like to believe. It's a terrible thing to think of what death must mean for a man like that. I felt that I must warn him. I left a message for him.

JUDITH [*querulously*]     What message?

ANDERSON     Only that I should be glad to see him for a moment on a matter of importance to himself; and that if he would look in here when he was passing he would be welcome.

JUDITH [*aghast*]    You asked that man to come here!

ANDERSON    I did.

JUDITH [*sinking on the seat and clasping her hands*]    I hope he wont come! Oh, I pray that he may not come!

ANDERSON    Why? Dont you want him to be warned?

JUDITH    He must know his danger. Oh, Tony, is it wrong to hate a blasphemer and a villain? I do hate him. I cant get him out of my mind: I know he will bring harm with him. He insulted you: he insulted me: he insulted his mother.

ANDERSON [*quaintly*]    Well, dear, let's forgive him; and then it wont matter.

JUDITH    Oh, I know it's wrong to hate anybody; but—

ANDERSON [*going over to her with humorous tenderness*]    Come, dear, youre not so wicked as you think. The worst sin towards our fellow creatures is not to hate them, but to be indifferent to them: that's the essence of inhumanity. After all, my dear, if you watch people carefully, youll be surprised to find how like hate is to love. [*She starts, strangely touched—even appalled. He is amused at her*]. Yes: I'm quite in earnest. Think of how some of our married friends worry one another, tax one another, are jealous of one another, cant bear to let one another out of sight for a day, are more like jailers and slave-owners than lovers. Think of those very same people with their enemies, scrupulous, lofty, self-respecting, determined to be independent of one another, careful of how they speak of one another—pooh! havent you often thought that if they only knew it, they were better friends to their enemies than to their own husbands and wives? Come: depend on it, my dear, you are really fonder of Richard than you are of me, if you only knew it. Eh?

JUDITH    Oh, dont say that: dont say that, Tony, even in jest. You don't know what a horrible feeling it gives me.

ANDERSON [*laughing*]    Well, well: never mind, pet. He's a bad man; and you hate him as he deserves. And youre going to make the tea, arnt you?

JUDITH [*remorsefully*]   Oh yes, I forgot. Ive been keeping you waiting all this time. [*She goes to the fire and puts on the kettle*].

ANDERSON [*going to the press and taking his coat off*]   Have you
stitched up the shoulder of my old coat?

JUDITH   Yes, dear. [*She goes to the table, and sets about putting the tea
into the teapot from the caddy*].

ANDERSON [*as he changes his coat for the older one hanging on the
press, and replaces it by the one he has just taken off*]   Did anyone
call when I was out?

JUDITH   No, only——[*Someone knocks at the door. With a start which
betrays her intense nervousness, she retreats to the further end of the table
with the tea caddy and spoon in her hands, exclaiming*] Who's that?

ANDERSON [*going to her and patting her encouragingly on the shoulder*]   All right, pet, all right. He wont eat you, whoever he is.
[*She tries to smile, and nearly makes herself cry. He goes to the door and
opens it. RICHARD is there, without overcoat or cloak*]. You might
have raised the latch and come in, Mr. Dudgeon. Nobody stands
on much ceremony with us. [*Hospitably*] Come in. [*RICHARD
comes in carelessly and stands at the table, looking round the room with
a slight pucker of his nose at the mezzotinted divine on the wall. JU-
DITH keeps her eyes on the tea caddy*]. Is it still raining? [*He shuts the
door*].

RICHARD   Raining like the very [*his eye catches JUDITH's as she
looks quickly and haughtily up*]——I beg your pardon; but [*shewing
that his coat is wet*] you see——!

ANDERSON   Take it off, sir; and let it hang before the fire a
while: my wife will excuse your shirtsleeves. Judith: put in another spoonful of tea for Mr. Dudgeon.

RICHARD [*eyeing him cynically*]   The magic of property, Pastor! Are
even y o u civil to me now that I have succeeded to my father's
estate?

*JUDITH throws down the spoon indignantly.*

ANDERSON [*quite unruffled, and helping RICHARD off with his coat.*]
I think, sir, that since you accept my hospitality, you cannot have

so bad an opinion of it. Sit down. [*With the coat in his hand, he points to the railed seat. RICHARD, in his shirtsleeves, looks at him half quarrelsomely for a moment; then, with a nod, acknowledges that the minister has got the better of him, and sits down on the seat. ANDERSON pushes his cloak into a heap on the seat of the chair at the fire, and hangs RICHARD's coat on the back in its place*].

RICHARD    I come, sir, on your own invitation. You left word you had something important to tell me.

ANDERSON    I have a warning which it is my duty to give you.

RICHARD [*quickly rising*]    You want to preach to me. Excuse me: I prefer a walk in the rain [*he makes for his coat*].

ANDERSON [*stopping him*]    Dont be alarmed, sir; I am no great preacher. You are quite safe. [*RICHARD smiles in spite of himself. His glance softens: he even makes a gesture of excuse. ANDERSON, seeing that he has tamed him, now addresses him earnestly*]. Mr. Dudgeon: you are in danger in this town.

RICHARD    What danger?

ANDERSON    Your uncle's danger. Major Swindon's gallows.

RICHARD    It is you who are in danger. I warned you—

ANDERSON [*interrupting him goodhumoredly but authoritatively*] Yes, yes, Mr. Dudgeon; but they do not think so in the town. And even if I were in danger, I have duties here which I must not forsake. But you are a free man. Why should you run any risk?

RICHARD    Do you think I should be any great loss, Minister?

ANDERSON    I think that a man's life is worth saving, whoever it belongs to. [*RICHARD makes him an ironical bow. ANDERSON returns the bow humorously*]. Come: youll have a cup of tea, to prevent you catching cold?

RICHARD    I observe that Mrs. Anderson is not quite so pressing as you are, Pastor.

JUDITH [*almost stifled with resentment, which she has been expecting her husband to share and express for her at every insult of RICHARD's*] You are welcome for my husband's sake. [*She brings the teapot to the fireplace and sets it on the hob*].

RICHARD  I know I am not welcome for my own, madam. [*He rises*]. But I think I will not break bread here, Minister.

ANDERSON [*cheerily*]  Give me a good reason for that.

RICHARD  Because there is something in you that I respect, and that makes me desire to have you for my enemy.

ANDERSON  Thats well said. On those terms, sir, I will accept your enmity or any man's. Judith: Mr. Dudgeon will stay to tea. Sit down: it will take a few minutes to draw by the fire. [*RICHARD glances at him with a troubled face; then sits down with his head bent, to hide a convulsive swelling of his throat*]. I was just saying to my wife, Mr. Dudgeon, that enmity— [*She grasps his hand and looks imploringly at him, doing both with an intensity that checks him at once*]. Well, well, I mustnt tell you, I see; but it was nothing that need leave us worse friend—enemies, I mean. Judith is a great enemy of yours.

RICHARD  If all my enemies were like Mrs. Anderson, I should be the best Christian in America.

ANDERSON [*gratified, patting her hand*]  You hear that, Judith? Mr. Dudgeon knows how to turn a compliment.

*The latch is lifted from without.*

JUDITH [*starting*]  Who is that?

*CHRISTY comes in.*

CHRISTY [*stopping and staring at RICHARD*]  Oh, are you here?

RICHARD  Yes. Begone, you fool: Mrs. Anderson doesnt want the whole family to tea at once.

CHRISTY [*coming further in*]  Mother's very ill.

RICHARD  Well, does she want to see me?

CHRISTY  No.

RICHARD  I thought not.

CHRISTY  She wants to see the minister—at once.

JUDITH [*to ANDERSON*]  Oh, not before youve had some tea.

ANDERSON  I shall enjoy it more when I come back, dear. [*He is about to take up his cloak*].

CHRISTY  The rain's over.

ANDERSON [*dropping the cloak and picking up his hat from the fender*]
Where is your mother, Christy?

CHRISTY   At Uncle Titus's.

ANDERSON   Have you fetched the doctor?

CHRISTY   No: she didnt tell me to.

ANDERSON   Go on there at once: I'll overtake you on his
doorstep. [*CHRISTY turns to go*]. Wait a moment. Your brother
must be anxious to know the particulars.

RICHARD   Psha! not I: he doesnt know; and I dont care. [*Violently*]
Be off, you oaf. [*CHRISTY runs out. RICHARD adds, a little shamefacedly*] We shall know soon enough.

ANDERSON   Well, perhaps you will let me bring you the news
myself. Judith: will you give Mr. Dudgeon his tea, and keep him
here until I return.

JUDITH [*white and trembling*]   Must I—

ANDERSON [*taking her hands and interrupting her to cover her agita-
tion*]   My dear: I can depend on you?

JUDITH [*with a piteous effort to be worthy of his trust*]   Yes.

ANDERSON [*pressing her hand against his cheek*]   You will not mind
two old people like us, Mr. Dudgeon. [*Going*] I shall not say good
evening: you will be here when I come back. [*He goes out*].[4]
*They watch him pass the window, and then look at each other dumbly,
quite disconcerted. RICHARD, noting the quiver of her lips, is the first to
pull himself together.*

RICHARD   Mrs. Anderson: I am perfectly aware of the nature of
your sentiments towards me. I shall not intrude on you. Good
evening. [*Again he starts for the fireplace to get his coat*].

JUDITH [*getting between him and the coat*]   No, no. Dont go: please
dont go.

RICHARD [*roughly*]   Why? You dont want me here.

JUDITH   Yes, I— [*Wringing her hands in despair*] Oh, if I tell you the
truth, you will use it to torment me.

RICHARD [*indignantly*]   Torment! What right have you to say
that? Do you expect me to stay after that?

JUDITH   I want you to stay; but [*suddenly raging at him like an angry child*] it is not because I like you.

RICHARD   Indeed!

JUDITH   Yes: I had rather you did go than mistake me about that. I hate and dread you; and my husband knows it. If you are not here when he comes back, he will believe that I disobeyed him and drove you away.

RICHARD [*ironically*]   Whereas, of course, you have really been so kind and hospitable and charming to me that I only want to go away out of mere contrariness, eh?

*JUDITH, unable to bear it, sinks on the chair and bursts into tears.*

RICHARD   Stop, stop, stop, I tell you. Dont do that. [*Putting his hand to his breast as if to a wound*] He wrung my heart by being a man. Need you tear it by being a woman? Has he not raised you above my insults, like himself? [*She stops crying, and recovers herself somewhat, looking at him with a scared curiosity*]. There: thats right. [*Sympathetically*] Youre better now, arnt you? [*He puts his hand encouragingly on her shoulder. She instantly rises haughtily, and stares at him defiantly. He at once drops into his usual sardonic tone*]. Ah, thats better. You are yourself again: so is Richard.[5] Well, shall we go to tea like a quiet respectable couple, and wait for your husband's return?

JUDITH [*rather ashamed of herself*]   If you please. I——I am sorry to have been so foolish. [*She stoops to take up the plate of toast from the fender*].

RICHARD   I am sorry, for your sake, that I am——what I am. Allow me. [*He takes the plate from her and goes with it to the table*].

JUDITH [*following with the teapot*]   Will you sit down? [*He sits down at the end of the table nearest the press. There is a plate and knife laid there. The other plate is laid near it; but JUDITH stays at the opposite end of the table, next the fire, and takes her place there, drawing the tray towards her*]. Do you take sugar.

RICHARD   No; but plenty of milk. Let me give you some toast. [*He puts some on the second plate, and hands it to her, with the knife.*

*The action shews quietly how well he knows that she has avoided her usual place so as to be as far from him as possible].*

JUDITH [*consciously*]    Thanks. [*She gives him his tea*]. Wont you help yourself?

RICHARD    Thanks. [*He puts a piece of toast on his own plate; and she pours out tea for herself*].

JUDITH [*observing that he tastes nothing*]    Dont you like it? You are not eating anything?

RICHARD    Neither are you.

JUDITH [*nervously*]    I never care much for my tea. Please dont mind me.

RICHARD [*looking dreamily round*]    I am thinking. It is all so strange to me. I can see the beauty and peace of this home: I think I have never been more at rest in my life than at this moment; and yet I know quite well I could never live here. It's not in my nature, I suppose, to be domesticated. But it's very beautiful: it's almost holy. [*He muses a moment, and then laughs softly*].

JUDITH [*quickly*]    Why do you laugh?

RICHARD    I was thinking that if any stranger came in here now, he would take us for man and wife.

JUDITH [*taking offence*]    You mean, I suppose, that you are more my age than he is.

RICHARD [*staring at this unexpected turn*]    I never thought of such a thing. [*Sardonic again*]. I see there is another side to domestic joy.

JUDITH [*angrily*]    I would rather have a husband whom everybody respects than—than—

RICHARD    Than the devil's disciple. You are right; but I daresay your love helps him to be a good man, just as your hate helps me to be a bad one.

JUDITH    My husband has been very good to you. He has forgiven you for insulting him, and is trying to save you. Can you not forgive him for being so much better than you are? How dare you belittle him by putting yourself in his place?

RICHARD    Did I?

JUDITH    Yes, you did. You said that if anybody came in they would take us for man and— [*She stops, terror-stricken, as a squad of soldiers tramps past the window*]. The English soldiers! Oh, what do they—

RICHARD [*listening*]    Sh!

A VOICE [*outside*]    Halt! Four outside: two in with me.

*JUDITH half rises, listening and looking with dilated eyes at RICHARD, who takes up his cup prosaically, and is drinking his tea when the latch goes up with a sharp click, and an English sergeant walks into the room with two privates, who post themselves at the door. He comes promptly to the table between them.*

THE SERGEANT    Sorry to disturb you, mum! duty! Anthony Anderson: I arrest you in King George's name as a rebel.

JUDITH [*pointing at RICHARD*]    But that is not— [*He looks up quickly at her, with a face of iron. She stops her mouth hastily with the hand she has raised to indicate him, and stands staring affrightedly*].

THE SERGEANT    Come, parson: put your coat on and come along.

RICHARD    Yes: I'll come. [*He rises and takes a step towards his own coat; then recollects himself, and, with his back to the sergeant, moves his gaze slowly round the room without turning his head until he sees AN-DERSON's black coat hanging up on the press. He goes composedly to it; takes it down; and puts it on. The idea of himself as a parson tickles him: he looks down at the black sleeve on his arm, and then smiles slyly at JU-DITH, whose white face shews him that what she is painfully struggling to grasp is not the humor of the situation but its horror. He turns to the sergeant, who is approaching him with a pair of handcuffs hidden behind him, and says lightly*] Did you ever arrest a man of my cloth before, Sergeant?

THE SERGEANT [*instinctively respectful, half to the black coat, half to RICHARD's good breeding*]    Well, no sir. At least, only an army chaplain. [*Shewing the handcuffs*]. I'm sorry, sir; but duty—

RICHARD    Just so, Sergeant. Well, I'm not ashamed of them: thank you kindly for the apology. [*He holds out his hands*].

SERGEANT [*not availing himself of the offer*]    One gentleman to another, sir. Wouldnt you like to say a word to your missis, sir, before you go?

RICHARD [*smiling*]   Oh, we shall meet again before——eh? [*meaning "before you hang me."*].

SERGEANT [*loudly, with ostentatious cheerfulness*]   Oh, of course, of course. No call for the lady to distress herself. Still——[*in a lower voice, intended for RICHARD alone*] your last chance, sir.

*They look at one another significantly for a moment. Then RICHARD exhales a deep breath and turns towards JUDITH.*

RICHARD [*very distinctly*]   My love. [*She looks at him, pitiably pale, and tries to answer, but cannot——tries also to come to him, but cannot trust herself to stand without the support of the table*]. This gallant gentleman is good enough to allow us a moment of leavetaking. [*The SERGEANT retires delicately and joins his men near the door*]. He is trying to spare you the truth; but you had better know it. Are you listening to me? [*She signifies assent*]. Do you understand that I am going to my death? [*She signifies that she understands*]. Remember, you must find our friend who was with us just now. Do you understand? [*She signifies yes*]. See that you get him safely out of harm's way. Dont for your life let him know of my danger; but if he finds it out, tell him that he cannot save me: they would hang him; and they would not spare me. And tell him that I am steadfast in my religion as he is in his, and that he may depend on me to the death. [*He turns to go, and meets the eye of the SERGEANT, who looks a little suspicious. He considers a moment, and then, turning roguishly to JUDITH with something of a smile breaking through his earnestness, says*] And now, my dear, I am afraid the sergeant will not believe that you love me like a wife unless you give one kiss before I go.

*He approaches her and holds out his arms. She quits the table and almost falls into them.*

JUDITH [*the words choking her*]   I ought to——it's murder——

RICHARD   No: only a kiss [*softly to her*] for his sake.

JUDITH   I cant. Y o u  must——

RICHARD [*folding her in his arms with an impulse of compassion for her distress*]   My poor girl!

> JUDITH, *with a sudden effort, throws her arms round him; kisses him; and swoons away, dropping from his arms to the ground as if the kiss had killed her.*

RICHARD [*going quickly to the sergeant*]   Now, Sergeant: quick before she comes to. The handcuffs. [*He puts out his hands*].

SERGEANT [*pocketing them*]   Never mind, sir: I'll trust you. Youre a game one. You ought to a bin a soldier, sir. Between them two, please. [*The soldiers place themselves one before RICHARD and one behind him. The sergeant opens the door*].

RICHARD [*taking a last look round him*]   Goodbye, wife: goodbye, home. Muffle the drums, and quick march!

> *The sergeant signs to the leading soldier to march. They file out quickly.* \* \* \* \* \* \* \* \* \* \* \* \* *When ANDERSON returns from MRS. DUD-GEON's he is astonished to find the room apparently empty and almost in darkness except for the glow from the fire; for one of the candles has burnt out, and the other is at its last flicker.*

ANDERSON   Why, what on earth——? [*Calling*] Judith, Judith! [*He listens: there is no answer*]. Hm! [*He goes to the cupboard; takes a candle from the drawer; lights it at the flicker of the expiring one on the table; and looks wonderingly at the untasted meal by its light. Then he sticks it in the candlestick; takes off his hat; and scratches his head, much puzzled. This action causes him to look at the floor for the first time; and there he sees JUDITH lying motionless with her eyes closed. He runs to her and stoops beside her, lifting her head*]. Judith.

JUDITH [*waking; for her swoon has passed into the sleep of exhaustion after suffering*]   Yes. Did you call? Whats the matter?

ANDERSON   Ive just come in and found you lying here with the candles burnt out and the tea poured out and cold. What has happened?

JUDITH [*still astray*]   I dont know. Have I been asleep? I suppose—— [*She stops blankly*]. I dont know.

ANDERSON [*groaning*]   Heaven forgive me, I left you alone with that scoundrel. [*JUDITH remembers. With an agonized cry, she clutches his shoulders and drags herself to her feet as he rises with her. He clasps her tenderly in his arms*]. My poor pet!

JUDITH [*frantically clinging to him*]    What shall I do? Oh my God, what shall I do?

ANDERSON    Never mind, never mind, my dearest dear: it was my fault. Come: youre safe now; and youre not hurt, are you? [*He takes his arms from her to see whether she can stand*]. There: thats right, thats right. If only you are not hurt, nothing else matters.

JUDITH    No, no, no: I'm not hurt.

ANDERSON    Thank Heaven for that! Come now: [*leading her to the railed seat and making her sit down beside him*] sit down and rest: you can tell me about it to-morrow. Or [*misunderstanding her distress*] you shall not tell me at all if it worries you. There, there! [*Cheerfully*] I'll make you some fresh tea: that will set you up again. [*He goes to the table, and empties the teapot into the slop bowl*].

JUDITH [*in a strained tone*]    Tony.

ANDERSON    Yes, dear?

JUDITH    Do you think we are only in a dream now?

ANDERSON [*glancing round at her for a moment with a pang of anxiety, though he goes on steadily and cheerfully putting fresh tea into the pot*]    Perhaps so, pet. But you may as well dream a cup of tea when youre about it.

JUDITH    Oh stop, stop. You dont know—[*Distracted, she buries her face in her knotted hands*].

ANDERSON [*breaking down and coming to her*]    My dear, what is it? I cant bear it any longer: you must tell me. It was all my fault: I was mad to trust him.

JUDITH    No: dont say that. You mustnt say that. He—oh no, no: I cant. Tony: dont speak to me. Take my hands—both my hands. [*He takes them, wondering*]. Make me think of you, not of him. There's danger, frightful danger; but it is your danger; and I cant keep thinking of it; I cant, I cant: my mind goes back to his danger. He must be saved—no: you must be saved: you, you, you. [*She springs up as if to do something or go somewhere, exclaiming] Oh, Heaven help me!

ANDERSON [*keeping his seat and holding her hands with resolute composure*]   Calmly, calmly, my pet. Youre quite distracted.

JUDITH   I may well be. I dont know what to do. I dont know what to do. [*Tearing her hands away*]. I must save him. [*ANDERSON rises in alarm as she runs wildly to the door. It is opened in her face by ESSIE, who hurries in full of anxiety. The surprise is so disagreeable to JUDITH that it brings her to her senses. Her tone is sharp and angry as she demands*] What do you want?

ESSIE   I was to come to you.

ANDERSON   Who told you to?

ESSIE [*staring at him, as if his presence astonished her*]   Are you here?

JUDITH   Of course. Dont be foolish, child.

ANDERSON   Gently, dearest: youll frighten her. [*Going between them*]. Come here, Essie. [*She comes to him*]. Who sent you?

ESSIE   Dick. He sent me word by a soldier. I was to come here at once and do whatever Mrs. Anderson told me.

ANDERSON [*enlightened*]   A soldier! Ah, I see it all now! They have arrested Richard. [ *JUDITH makes a gesture of despair*].

ESSIE   No. I asked the soldier. Dick's safe. But the soldier said you had been taken.

ANDERSON   I! [*Bewildered, he turns to JUDITH for an explanation*].

JUDITH [*coaxingly*]   All right, dear: I understand. [*To ESSIE*] Thank you, Essie, for coming; but I dont need you now. You may go home.

ESSIE [*suspicious*]   Are you sure Dick has not been touched? Perhaps he told the soldier to say it was the minister. [*Anxiously*] Mrs. Anderson: do you think it can have been that?

ANDERSON   Tell her the truth if it is so, Judith. She will learn it from the first neighbor she meets in the street. [*JUDITH turns away and covers her eyes with her hands*].

ESSIE [*wailing*]   But what will they do to him? Oh, what will they do to him? Will they hang him? [ *JUDITH shudders convulsively, and throws herself into the chair in which RICHARD sat at the tea table*].

ANDERSON [*patting ESSIE's shoulder and trying to comfort her*]    I hope not. I hope not. Perhaps if youre very quiet and patient, we may be able to help him in some way.

ESSIE    Yes—help him—yes, yes, yes. I'll be good.

ANDERSON    I must go to him at once, Judith.

JUDITH [*springing up*]    Oh no. You must go away—far away, to some place of safety.

ANDERSON    Pooh!

JUDITH [*passionately*]    Do you want to kill me? Do you think I can bear to live for days and days with every knock at the door— every footstep—giving me a spasm of terror? to lie awake for nights and nights in an agony of dread, listening for them to come and arrest you?

ANDERSON    Do you think it would be better to know that I had run away from my post at the first sign of danger?

JUDITH [*bitterly*]    Oh, you wont go. I know it. Youll stay; and I shall go mad.

ANDERSON    My dear, your duty—

JUDITH [*fiercely*]    What do I care about my duty?

ANDERSON [*shocked*]    Judith!

JUDITH    I am doing my duty. I am clinging to my duty. My duty is to get you away, to save you, to leave him to his fate [*ESSIE utters a cry of distress and sinks on the chair at the fire, sobbing silently*]. My instinct is the same as hers—to save him above all things, though it would be so much better for him to die! so much greater! But I know you will take your own way as he took it. I have no power. [*She sits down sullenly on the railed seat*]. I'm only a woman: I can do nothing but sit here and suffer. Only, tell him I tried to save you—that I did my best to save you.

ANDERSON    My dear, I am afraid he will be thinking more of his own danger than of mine.

JUDITH    Stop; or I shall hate you.

ANDERSON [*remonstrating*]  Come, come, come! How am I to leave you if you talk like this! You are quite out of your senses. [*He turns to ESSIE*] Essie.

ESSIE [*eagerly rising and drying her eyes*]  Yes?

ANDERSON  Just wait outside a moment, like a good girl: Mrs. Anderson is not well. [*ESSIE looks doubtful*]. Never fear: I'll come to you presently; and I'll go to Dick.

ESSIE  You are sure you will go to him? [*Whispering*]. You wont let her prevent you?

ANDERSON [*smiling*]  No, no: it's all right. All right. [*She goes*]. Thats a good girl. [*He closes the door, and returns to JUDITH*].

JUDITH [*seated—rigid*]  You are going to your death.

ANDERSON [*quaintly*]  Then I shall go in my best coat, dear. [*He turns to the press, beginning to take off his coat*]. Where—? [*He stares at the empty nail for a moment; then looks quickly round to the fire; strides across to it; and lifts RICHARD's coat*]. Why, my dear, it seems that he has gone in my best coat.

JUDITH [*still motionless*]  Yes.

ANDERSON  Did the soldiers make a mistake?

JUDITH  Yes: they made a mistake.

ANDERSON  He might have told them. Poor fellow, he was too upset, I suppose.

JUDITH  Yes: he might have told them. So might I.

ANDERSON  Well, it's all very puzzling—almost funny. It's curious how these little things strike us even in the most— [*He breaks off and begins putting on RICHARD's coat*]. I'd better take him his own coat. I know what he'll say— [*imitating RICHARD's sardonic manner*] "Anxious about my soul, Pastor, and also about your best coat." Eh?

JUDITH  Yes, that is just what he will say to you. [*Vacantly*] It doesnt matter: I shall never see either of you again.

ANDERSON [*rallying her*]  Oh pooh, pooh, pooh! [*He sits down beside her*]. Is this how you keep your promise that I shant be ashamed of my brave wife?

JUDITH    No: this is how I break it. I cannot keep my promises to
him: why should I keep my promises to you?

ANDERSON    Dont speak so strangely, my love. It sounds insincere to me. [*She looks unutterable reproach at him*]. Yes, dear, nonsense is always insincere; and my dearest is talking nonsense. Just
nonsense. [*Her face darkens into dumb obstinacy. She stares straight before her, and does not look at him again, absorbed in RICHARD's fate.
He scans her face; sees that his rallying has produced no effect; and gives
it up, making no further effort to conceal his anxiety*]. I wish I knew
what has frightened you so. Was there a struggle? Did he fight?

JUDITH    No. He smiled.

ANDERSON    Did he realise his danger, do you think?

JUDITH    He realised yours.

ANDERSON    Mine!

JUDITH [*monotonously*]    He said, "See that you get him safely out of
harm's way." I promised: I cant keep my promise. He said, "Dont
for your life let him know of my danger." Ive told you of it. He
said that if you found it out, you could not save him—that they
will hang him and not spare you.

ANDERSON [*rising in generous indignation*]    And you think that I
will let a man with that much good in him die like a dog, when
a few words might make him die like a Christian. I'm ashamed
of you, Judith.

JUDITH    He will be steadfast in his religion as you are in yours;
and you may depend on him to the death. He said so.

ANDERSON    God forgive him! What else did he say?

JUDITH    He said goodbye.

ANDERSON [*fidgeting nervously to and fro in great concern*]    Poor
fellow, poor fellow! You said goodbye to him in all kindness and
charity, Judith, I hope.

JUDITH    I kissed him.

ANDERSON    What! Judith!

JUDITH    Are you angry?

ANDERSON    No, no. You were right: you were right. Poor fellow, poor fellow! [*Greatly distressed*] To be hanged like that at his age! And then did they take him away?

JUDITH [*wearily*]   Then you were here: thats the next thing I remember. I suppose I fainted. Now bid me goodbye, Tony. Perhaps I shall faint again. I wish I could die.

ANDERSON   No, no, my dear: you must pull yourself together and be sensible. I am in no danger—not the least in the world.

JUDITH [*solemnly*]   You are going to your death, Tony—your sure death, if God will let innocent men be murdered. They will not let you see him: they will arrest you the moment you give your name. It was for you the soldiers came.

ANDERSON [*thunderstruck*]   For me!!! [*His fists clinch; his neck thickens; his face reddens; the fleshy purses under his eyes become injected with hot blood; the man of peace vanishes, transfigured into a choleric and formidable man of war. Still, she does not come out of her absorption to look at him: her eyes are steadfast with a mechanical reflection of RICHARD's steadfastness.*]

JUDITH   He took your place: he is dying to save you. That is why he went in your coat. That is why I kissed him.

ANDERSON [*exploding*]   Blood an' owns!* [*His voice is rough and dominant, his gesture full of brute energy*]. Here! Essie, Essie!

ESSIE [*running in*]   Yes.

ANDERSON [*impetuously*]   Off with you as hard as you can run, to the inn. Tell them to saddle the fastest and strongest horse they have [*JUDITH rises breathless, and stares at him incredulously*]—the chestnut mare, if she's fresh—without a moment's delay. Go into the stable yard and tell the black man there that I'll give him a silver dollar if the horse is waiting for me when I come, and that I am close on your heels. Away with you. [*His energy sends ESSIE flying from the room. He pounces on his riding boots; rushes with them to the chair at the fire; and begins pulling them on*].

---

*[Christ's] blood and wounds; an indecorous oath for a minister.

JUDITH [*unable to believe such a thing of him*]    You are not going to him!

ANDERSON [*busy with the boots*]    Going to him! What good would that do? [*Growling to himself as he gets the first boot on with a wrench*] I'll go to them, so I will. [*To JUDITH peremptorily*] Get me the pistols: I want them. And money, money: I want money—all the money in the house. [*He stoops over the other boot, grumbling*] A great satisfaction it would be to him to have my company on the gallows. [*He pulls on the boot*].

JUDITH    You are deserting him, then?

ANDERSON    Hold your tongue, woman; and get me the pistols. [*She goes to the press and takes from it a leather belt with two pistols, a powder horn, and a bag of bullets attached to it. She throws it on the table. Then she unlocks a drawer in the press and takes out a purse. AN-DERSON grabs the belt and buckles it on, saying*] If they took him for me in my coat, perhaps theyll take me for him in his. [*Hitching the belt into its place*] Do I look like him?

JUDITH [*turning with the purse in her hand*]    Horribly unlike him.

ANDERSON [*snatching the purse from her and emptying it on the table*] Hm! We shall see.

JUDITH [*sitting down helplessly*]    Is it of any use to pray, do you think, Tony?

ANDERSON [*counting the money*]    Pray! Can we pray Swindon's rope off Richard's neck?

JUDITH    God may soften Major Swindon's heart.

ANDERSON [*contemptuously—pocketing a handful of money*]    Let him, then. I am not God; and I must go to work another way. [*JUDITH gasps at the blasphemy. He throws the purse on the table*]. Keep that. Ive taken 25 dollars.

JUDITH    Have you forgotten even that you are a minister?

ANDERSON    Minister be—faugh! My hat: wheres my hat? [*He snatches up hat and cloak, and puts both on in hot haste*]. Now listen, you. If you can get a word with him by pretending youre his wife, tell him to hold his tongue until morning: that will give me all the start I need.

JUDITH [*solemnly*]    You may depend on him to the death.

ANDERSON    Youre a fool, a fool, Judith [*for a moment checking the torrent of his haste, and speaking with something of his old quiet and impressive conviction*] You dont know the man youre married to. [*ESSIE returns. He swoops at her at once*]. Well: is the horse ready?

ESSIE [*breathless*]    It will be ready when you come.

ANDERSON    Good. [*He makes for the door*].

JUDITH [*rising and stretching out her arms after him involuntarily*] Wont you say goodbye?

ANDERSON    And waste another half minute! Psha! [*He rushes out like an avalanche*].

ESSIE [*hurrying to JUDITH*]    He has gone to save Richard, hasnt he?

JUDITH    To save Richard! No: Richard has saved him. He has gone to save himself. Richard must die.

*ESSIE screams with terror and falls on her knees, hiding her face. JUDITH, without heeding her, looks rigidly straight in front of her, at the vision of RICHARD, dying.*

# ACT III

*Early next morning the sergeant, at the British headquarters in the Town Hall, unlocks the door of a little empty panelled waiting room, and invites Judith to enter. She has had a bad night, probably a rather delirious one; for even in the reality of the raw morning, her fixed gaze comes back at moments when her attention is not strongly held.*

*The SERGEANT considers that her feelings do her credit, and is sympathetic in an encouraging military way. Being a fine figure of a man, vain of his uniform and of his rank, he feels specially qualified, in a respectful way, to console her.*

SERGEANT    You can have a quiet word with him here, mum.

JUDITH    Shall I have long to wait?

SERGEANT    No, mum, not a minute. We kep him in the Bridewell* for the night; and he's just been brought over here for the court martial. Dont fret, mum: he slep like a child, and has made a rare good breakfast.

JUDITH [*incredulously*]    He is in good spirits!

SERGEANT    Tip top, mum. The chaplain looked in to see him last night; and he won seventeen shillings off him at spoil five. He spent it among us like the gentleman he is. Duty's duty, mum, of course; but youre among friends here. [*The tramp of a couple of soldiers is heard approaching*]. There: I think he's coming. [*RICHARD comes in, without a sign of care or captivity in his bearing.*

---

*That is, the jail; a generic term derived from the name of a notorious London prison.

*The sergeant nods to the two soldiers, and shews them the key of the room in his hand. They withdraw].* Your good lady, sir.

RICHARD [*going to her*]    What! My wife. My adored one. [*He takes her hand and kisses it with a perverse, raffish\* gallantry*]. How long do you allow a brokenhearted husband for leave-taking, Sergeant?

SERGEANT    As long as we can, sir. We shall not disturb you til the court sits.

RICHARD    But it has struck the hour.

SERGEANT    So it has, sir; but there's a delay. General Burgoyne's just arrived—Gentlemanly Johnny we call him, sir—and he wont have done finding fault with everything this side of half past. I know him, sir: I served with him in Portugal. You may count on twenty minutes, sir; and by your leave I wont waste any more of them. [*He goes out, locking the door. RICHARD immediately drops his raffish manner and turns to JUDITH with considerate sincerity*].

RICHARD    Mrs. Anderson: this visit is very kind of you. And how are you after last night? I had to leave you before you recovered; but I sent word to Essie to go and look after you. Did she understand the message?

JUDITH [*breathless and urgent*]    Oh, dont think of me: I havent come here to talk about myself. Are they going to—to—[*meaning "to hang you"*]?

RICHARD [*whimsically*]    At noon, punctually. At least, that was when they disposed of Uncle Peter. [*She shudders*]. Is your husband safe? Is he on the wing?

JUDITH    He is no longer my husband.

RICHARD [*opening his eyes wide*]    Eh?

JUDITH    I disobeyed you. I told him everything. I expected him to come here and save you. I wanted him to come here and save you. He ran away instead.

---

\*Devil-may-care.

RICHARD    Well, thats what I meant him to do. What good would his staying have done? Theyd only have hanged us both.

JUDITH [*with reproachful earnestness*]    Richard Dudgeon: on your honour, what would you have done in his place?

RICHARD    Exactly what he has done, of course.

JUDITH    Oh, why will you not be simple with me—honest and straightforward? If you are so selfish as that, why did you let them take you last night?

RICHARD [*gaily*]    Upon my life, Mrs. Anderson, I dont know. Ive been asking myself that question ever since; and I can find no manner of reason for acting as I did.

JUDITH    You know you did it for his sake, believing he was a more worthy man than yourself.

RICHARD [*laughing*]    Oho! No: thats a very pretty reason, I must say; but I'm not so modest as that. No: it wasnt for his sake.

JUDITH [*after a pause, during which she looks shamefacedly at him, blushing painfully*]    Was it for my sake?

RICHARD [*gallantly*]    Well, you had a hand in it. It must have been a little for your sake. You let them take me, at all events.

JUDITH    Oh, do you think I have not been telling myself that all night? Your death will be at my door. [*Impulsively, she gives him her hand, and adds, with intense earnestness*]. If I could save you as you saved him, I would do it, no matter how cruel the death was.

RICHARD [*holding her hand and smiling, but keeping her almost at arms length*]    I am very sure I shouldnt let you.

JUDITH    Dont you see that I can save you?

RICHARD    How? By changing clothes with me, eh?

JUDITH [*disengaging her hand to touch his lips with it*]    Dont [*meaning "Dont jest"*]. No: by telling the Court who you really are.

RICHARD [*frowning*]    No use: they wouldnt spare me; and it would spoil half of his chance of escaping. They are determined to cow us by making an example of somebody on that gallows today. Well, let us cow them by showing that we can stand by one another to the death. That is the only force that can send Burgoyne back across the Atlantic and make America a nation.

JUDITH [*impatiently*]   Oh, what does all that matter?

RICHARD [*laughing*]   True: what does it matter? what does anything matter? You see, men have these strange notions, Mrs. Anderson; and women see the folly of them.

JUDITH   Women have to lose those they love through them.

RICHARD   They can easily get fresh lovers.

JUDITH [*revolted*]   Oh! [*Vehemently*] Do you realise that you are going to kill yourself?

RICHARD   The only man I have any right to kill, Mrs. Anderson. Dont be concerned: no woman will lose her lover through my death. [*Smiling*] Bless you, nobody cares for me. Have you heard that my mother is dead?

JUDITH   Dead!

RICHARD   Of heart disease——in the night. Her last word to me was her curse: I dont think I could have borne her blessing. My other relatives will not grieve much on my account. Essie will cry for a day or two; but I have provided for her: I made my own will last night.

JUDITH [*stonily, after a moment's silence*]   And I!

RICHARD [*surprised*]   You?

JUDITH   Yes, I. Am I not to care at all?

RICHARD [*gaily and bluntly*]   Not a scrap. Oh, you expressed your feelings towards me very frankly yesterday. What happened may have softened you for the moment; but believe me, Mrs. Anderson, you dont like a bone in my skin or a hair on my head. I shall be as good a riddance at 12 to-day as I should have been at 12 yesterday.

JUDITH [*her voice trembling*]   What can I do to shew you that you are mistaken.

RICHARD   Dont trouble. I'll give you credit for liking me a little better than you did. All I say is that my death will not break your heart.

JUDITH [*almost in a whisper*]   How do you know? [*She puts her hands on his shoulders and looks intently at him*].

RICHARD [*amazed—divining the truth*]   Mrs. Anderson!!! [*The bell of the town clock strikes the quarter. He collects himself, and removes her hands, saying rather coldly*] Excuse me: they will be here for me presently. It is too late.

JUDITH   It is not too late. Call me as witness: they will never kill you when they know how heroically you have acted.

RICHARD [*with some scorn*]   Indeed! But if I dont go through with it, where will the heroism be? I shall simply have tricked them; and theyll hang me for that like a dog. Serve me right too!

JUDITH [*wildly*]   Oh, I believe you w a n t to die.

RICHARD [*obstinately*]   No I dont.

JUDITH   Then why not try to save yourself? I implore you—listen. You said just now that you saved him for my sake—yes [*clutching him as he recoils with a gesture of denial*] a little for my sake. Well, save yourself for my sake. And I will go with you to the end of the world.

RICHARD [*taking her by the wrists and holding her a little way from him, looking steadily at her*]   Judith.

JUDITH [*breathless—delighted at the name*]   Yes.

RICHARD   If I said—to please you—that I did what I did ever so little for your sake, I lied as men always lie to women. You know how much I have lived with worthless men—aye, and worthless women too. Well, they could all rise to some sort of goodness and kindness when they were in love [*the word love comes from him with true Puritan scorn*]. That has taught me to set very little store by the goodness that only comes out red hot. What I did last night, I did in cold blood, caring not half so much for your husband, or [*ruthlessly*] for you [*she droops, stricken*] as I do for myself. I had no motive and no interest: all I can tell you is that when it came to the point whether I would take my neck out of the noose and put another man's into it, I could not do it. I dont know why not: I see myself as a fool for my pains; but I could not and I cannot. I have been brought up standing by the law of my own nature; and I may not go against it, gallows or no gallows. [*She has slowly raised her head and is now looking full at him*]. I should have done the same for any other man in the town, or any other man's wife. [*Releasing her*]. Do you understand that?

JUDITH    Yes: you mean that you do not love me.

RICHARD [*revolted—with fierce contempt*]    Is that all it means to you?

JUDITH    What more—what worse—can it mean to me? [*The SERGEANT knocks. The blow on the door jars on her heart*]. Oh, one moment more. [*She throws herself on her knees*]. I pray to you—

RICHARD    Hush! [*Calling*] Come in. [*The SERGEANT unlocks the door and opens it. The guard is with him*].

SERGEANT [*coming in*]    Time's up, sir.

RICHARD    Quite ready, Sergeant. Now, my dear. [*He attempts to raise her*].

JUDITH [*clinging to him*]    Only one thing more—I entreat, I implore you. Let me be present in the court. I have seen Major Swindon: he said I should be allowed if you asked it. You will ask it. It is my last request: I shall never ask you anything again. [*She clasps his knee*]. I beg and pray it of you.

RICHARD    If I do, will you be silent?

JUDITH    Yes.

RICHARD    You will keep faith?

JUDITH    I will keep— [*She breaks down, sobbing*].

RICHARD [*taking her arm to lift her*]    Just—her other arm, Sergeant. *They go out, she sobbing convulsively, supported by the two men.*

*Meanwhile, the Council Chamber is ready for the court martial. It is a large, lofty room, with a chair of state in the middle under a tall canopy with a gilt crown, and maroon curtains with the royal monogram G. R.\* In front of the chair is a table, also draped in maroon, with a bell, a heavy inkstand, and writing materials on it. Several chairs are set at the table. The*

---

\*Georgius Rex (Latin for "George the King").

*door is at the right hand of the occupant of the chair of state when it has an occupant: at present it is empty. MAJOR SWINDON, a pale, sandy haired, very conscientious looking man of about 45, sits at the end of the table with his back to the door, writing. He is alone until the SERGEANT announces the GENERAL in a subdued manner which suggests that GEN-TLEMANLY JOHNNY has been making his presence felt rather heavily.*

SERGEANT    The General, sir.

*SWINDON rises hastily. The general comes in: the SERGEANT goes out. GENERAL BURGOYNE is 55, and very well preserved. He is a man of fashion, gallant enough to have made a distinguished marriage by an elopement, witty enough to write successful comedies, aristocratically-connected enough to have had opportunities of high military distinction. His eyes, large, brilliant, apprehensive, and intelligent, are his most re-markable feature: without them his fine nose and small mouth would suggest rather more fastidiousness and less force than go to the making of a first rate general. Just now the eyes are angry and tragic, and the mouth and nostrils tense.*

BURGOYNE    Major Swindon, I presume.

SWINDON    Yes. General Burgoyne, if I mistake not. [*They bow to one another ceremoniously*]. I am glad to have the support of your presence this morning. It is not particularly lively business, hanging this poor devil of a minister.

BURGOYNE [*throwing himself into SWINDON's chair*]    No, sir, it is not. It is making too much of the fellow to execute him: what more could you have done if he had been a member of the Church of England? Martyrdom, sir, is what these people like: it is the only way in which a man can become famous without abil-ity.* However, you have committed us to hanging him: and the sooner he is hanged the better.

SWINDON    We have arranged it for 12 o'clock. Nothing remains to be done except to try him.

BURGOYNE [*looking at him with suppressed anger*]    Nothing—ex-

---

*One of Shaw's best epigrams.

cept to save our own necks, perhaps. Have you heard the news from Springtown?

SWINDON   Nothing special. The latest reports are satisfactory.

BURGOYNE [*rising in amazement*]   Satisfactory, sir! Satisfactory!! [*He stares at him for a moment, and then adds, with grim intensity*] I am glad you take that view of them.

SWINDON [*puzzled*]   Do I understand that in your opinion—

BURGOYNE   I do not express my opinion. I never stoop to that habit of profane language which unfortunately coarsens our profession. If I did, sir, perhaps I should be able to express my opinion of the news from Springtown—the news which  y o u [*severely*] have apparently not heard. How soon do you get news from your supports here?—in the course of a month, eh?

SWINDON [*turning sulky*]   I suppose the reports have been taken to you, sir, instead of to me. Is there anything serious?

BURGOYNE [*taking a report from his pocket and holding it up*] Springtown's in the hands of the rebels. [*He throws the report on the table*].

SWINDON [*aghast*]   Since yesterday!

BURGOYNE   Since two o'clock this morning. Perhaps  w e  shall be in their hands before two o'clock to-morrow morning. Have you thought of that?

SWINDON [*confidently*]   As to that, General, the British soldier will give a good account of himself.

BURGOYNE [*bitterly*]   And therefore, I suppose, sir, the British officer need not know his business: the British soldier will get him out of all his blunders with the bayonet. In future, sir, I must ask you to be a little less generous with the blood of your men, and a little more generous with your own brains.

SWINDON   I am sorry I cannot pretend to your intellectual eminence, sir. I can only do my best, and rely on the devotion of my countrymen.

BURGOYNE [*suddenly becoming suavely sarcastic*]   May I ask are you writing a melodrama, Major Swindon?

SWINDON [*flushing*]   No, sir.

BURGOYNE   What a pity! W h a t a pity! [*Dropping his sarcastic tone and facing him suddenly and seriously*] Do you at all realize, sir, that we have nothing standing between us and destruction but our own bluff and the sheepishness of these colonists? They are men of the same English stock as ourselves: six to one of us [*repeating it emphatically*] six to one, sir; and nearly half our troops are Hessians, Brunswickers, German dragoons, and Indians with scalping knives. These are the countrymen on whose devotion you rely! Suppose the colonists find a leader! Suppose the news from Springtown should turn out to mean that they have already found a leader! What shall we do then? Eh?

SWINDON [*sullenly*]   Our duty, sir, I presume.

BURGOYNE [*again sarcastic—giving him up as a fool*]   Quite so, quite so. Thank you, Major Swindon, thank you. Now youve settled the question, sir—thrown a flood of light on the situation. What a comfort to me to feel that I have at my side so devoted and able an officer to support me in this emergency! I think, sir, it will probably relieve both our feelings if we proceed to hang this dissenter* without further delay [*he strikes the bell*] especially as I am debarred by my principles from the customary military vent for my feelings. [*The SERGEANT appears*]. Bring your man in.

SERGEANT   Yes, sir.

BURGOYNE   And mention to any officer you may meet that the court cannot wait any longer for him.

SWINDON [*keeping his temper with difficulty*]   The staff is perfectly ready, sir. They have been waiting your convenience for fully half an hour. P e r f e c t l y ready, sir.

BURGOYNE [*blandly*]   So am I. [*Several officers come in and take their seats. One of them sits at the end of the table furthest from the door, and*

---

*That is, from the Church of England; here used metaphorically to mean a rebel.

*acts throughout as clerk to the court, making notes of the proceedings. The uniforms are those of the 9th, 20th, 21st, 24th, 47th, 53rd, and 62nd British Infantry. One officer is a Major General of the Royal Artillery. There are also German officers of the Hessian Rifles, and of German dragoon and Brunswicker regiments].* Oh, good morning, gentlemen. Sorry to disturb you, I am sure. Very good of you to spare us a few moments.

SWINDON    Will you preside, sir?

BURGOYNE [*becoming additionally polished, lofty, sarcastic and urbane now that he is in public*]    No, sir: I feel my own deficiencies too keenly to presume so far. If you will kindly allow me, I will sit at the feet of Gamaliel. [*He takes the chair at the end of the table next the door, and motions SWINDON to the chair of state, waiting for him to be seated before sitting down himself*].

SWINDON [*greatly annoyed*]    As you please, sir. I am only trying to do my duty under excessively trying circumstances. [*He takes his place in the chair of state*].

*BURGOYNE, relaxing his studied demeanor for the moment, sits down and begins to read the report with knitted brows and careworn looks, reflecting on his desperate situation and SWINDON's uselessness. RICHARD is brought in. JUDITH walks beside him. Two soldiers precede and two follow him, with the SERGEANT in command. They cross the room to the wall opposite the door; but when RICHARD has just passed before the chair of state the SERGEANT stops him with a touch on the arm, and posts himself behind him, at his elbow. JUDITH stands timidly at the wall. The four soldiers place themselves in a squad near her.*

BURGOYNE [*looking up and seeing JUDITH*]    Who is that woman?

SERGEANT    Prisoner's wife, sir.

SWINDON [*nervously*]    She begged me to allow her to be present; and I thought—

BURGOYNE [*completing the sentence for him ironically*]    You thought it would be a pleasure for her. Quite so, quite so. [*blandly*] Give the lady a chair; and make her thoroughly comfortable.

*The SERGEANT fetches a chair and places it near RICHARD.*

JUDITH    Thank you, sir. [*She sits down after an awestricken curtsy to BURGOYNE, which he acknowledges by a dignified bend of his head*].

SWINDON [*to RICHARD, sharply*]    Your name, sir?

RICHARD [*affable, but obstinate*]    Come: you dont mean to say that youve brought me here without knowing who I am?

SWINDON    As a matter of form, sir, give your name.

RICHARD    As a matter of form then, my name is Anthony Anderson, Presbyterian minister in this town.

BURGOYNE [*interested*]    Indeed! Pray, Mr. Anderson, what do you gentlemen believe?

RICHARD    I shall be happy to explain if time is allowed me. I cannot undertake to complete your conversion in less than a fortnight.

SWINDON [*snubbing him*]    We are not here to discuss your views.

BURGOYNE [*with an elaborate bow to the unfortunate SWINDON*]    I stand rebuked.

SWINDON [*embarrassed*]    Oh, not you, I as—

BURGOYNE    Dont mention it. [*To RICHARD, very politely*] Any political views, Mr. Anderson?

RICHARD    I understand that that is just what we are here to find out.

SWINDON [*severely*]    Do you mean to deny that you are a rebel?

RICHARD    I am an American, sir.

SWINDON    What do you expect me to think of that speech, Mr. Anderson?

RICHARD    I never expect a soldier to think, sir.

*BURGOYNE is boundlessly delighted by this retort, which almost reconciles him to the loss of America.*

SWINDON [*whitening with anger*]    I advise you not to be insolent, prisoner.

RICHARD    You cant help yourself, General. When you make up your mind to hang a man, you put yourself at a disadvantage with him. Why should I be civil to you? I may as well be hanged for a sheep as a lamb.

SWINDON   You have no right to assume that the court has made up its mind without a fair trial. And you will please not address me as General. I am Major Swindon.

RICHARD   A thousand pardons. I thought I had the honor of addressing Gentlemanly Johnny.

*Sensation among the officers. The sergeant has a narrow escape from a guffaw.*

BURGOYNE [*with extreme suavity*]   I believe I am Gentlemanly Johnny, sir, at your service. My more intimate friends call me General Burgoyne. [*RICHARD bows with perfect politeness*]. You will understand, sir, I hope, since you seem to be a gentleman and a man of some spirit in spite of your calling, that if we should have the misfortune to hang you, we shall do so as a mere matter of political necessity and military duty, without any personal ill-feeling.

RICHARD   Oh, quite so. That makes all the difference in the world, of course.

*They all smile in spite of themselves; and some of the younger officers burst out laughing.*

JUDITH [*her dread and horror deepening at every one of these jests and compliments*]   How c a n you?

RICHARD   You promised to be silent.

BURGOYNE [*to JUDITH, with studied courtesy*]   Believe me, Madam, your husband is placing us under the greatest obligation by taking this very disagreeable business so thoroughly in the spirit of a gentleman. Sergeant: give Mr. Anderson a chair. [*The SERGEANT does so. RICHARD sits down*]. Now, Major Swindon: we are waiting for you.

SWINDON   You are aware, I presume, Mr. Anderson, of your obligations as a subject of His Majesty King George the Third.

RICHARD   I am aware, sir, that His Majesty King George the Third is about to hang me because I object to Lord North's robbing me.

SWINDON   That is a treasonable speech, sir.

RICHARD [*briefly*]    Yes. I meant it to be.

BURGOYNE [*strongly deprecating this line of defence, but still polite*] Dont you think, Mr. Anderson, that this is rather—if you will excuse the word—a vulgar line to take? Why should you cry out robbery because of a stamp duty and a tea duty and so forth? After all, it is the essence of your position as a gentleman that you pay with a good grace.

RICHARD    It is not the money, General. But to be swindled by a pig-headed lunatic like King George—

SWINDON [*scandalised*]    Chut, sir—silence!

SERGEANT [*in stentorian tones, greatly shocked*]    Silence!

BURGOYNE [*unruffled*]    Ah, that is another point of view. My position does not allow of my going into that, except in private. But [*shrugging his shoulders*] of course, Mr. Anderson, if you are determined to be hanged [*JUDITH flinches*] there's nothing more to be said. An unusual taste! however [*with a final shrug*]—!

SWINDON [*to BURGOYNE*]    Shall we call witnesses?

RICHARD    What need is there of witnesses? If the townspeople here had listened to me, you would have found the streets barricaded, the houses loopholed, and the people in arms to hold the town against you to the last man. But you arrived, unfortunately, before we had got out of the talking stage; and then it was too late.

SWINDON [*severely*]    Well, sir, we shall teach you and your townspeople a lesson they will not forget. Have you anything more to say?

RICHARD    I think you might have the decency to treat me as a prisoner of war, and shoot me like a man instead of hanging me like a dog.

BURGOYNE [*sympathetically*]    Now there, Mr. Anderson, you talk like a civilian, if you will excuse my saying so. Have you any idea of the average marksmanship of the army of His Majesty King George the Third? If we make you up a firing party, what will happen? Half of them will miss you: the rest will make a mess of the business and leave you to the provo-marshal's pistol. Whereas we can hang you in a perfectly workmanlike and agreeable way. [*Kindly*] Let me persuade you to be hanged, Mr. Anderson?

JUDITH [*sick with horror*]   My God!

RICHARD [*to JUDITH*]   Your promise! [*to BURGOYNE*] Thank you, General: that view of the case did not occur to me before. To oblige you, I withdraw my objection to the rope. Hang me, by all means.

BURGOYNE [*smoothly*]   Will 12 o'clock suit you, Mr. Anderson?

RICHARD   I shall be at your disposal then, General.

BURGOYNE [*rising*]   Nothing more to be said, gentlemen. [*They all rise*].

JUDITH [*rushing to the table*]   Oh, you are not going to murder a man like that, without a proper trial—without thinking of what you are doing—without— [*she cannot find words*].

RICHARD   Is this how you keep your promise?

JUDITH   If I am not to speak, you must. Defend yourself: save yourself: tell them the truth.

RICHARD [*worriedly*]   I have told them truth enough to hang me ten times over. If you say another word you will risk other lives; but you will not save mine.

BURGOYNE   My good lady, our only desire is to save unpleasantness. What satisfaction would it give you to have a solemn fuss made, with my friend Swindon in a black cap and so forth? I am sure we are greatly indebted to the admirable tact and gentlemanly feeling shewn by your husband.

JUDITH [*throwing the words in his face*]   Oh, you are mad. Is it nothing to you what wicked thing you do if only you do it like a gentleman? Is it nothing to you whether you are a murderer or not, if only you murder in a red coat? [*Desperately*] You shall not hang him: that man is not my husband.

*The officers look at one another, and whisper: some of the Germans asking their neighbors to explain what the woman has said. BURGOYNE, who has been visibly shaken by JUDITH's reproach, recovers himself promptly at this new development. RICHARD meanwhile raises his voice above the buzz.*

RICHARD    I appeal to you, gentlemen, to put an end to this. She will not believe that she cannot save me. Break up the court.

BURGOYNE [*in a voice so quiet and firm that it restores silence at once*] One moment, Mr. Anderson. One moment, gentlemen. [*He resumes his seat. SWINDON and the officers follow his example*]. Let me understand you clearly, madam. Do you mean that this gentleman is not your husband, or merely—I wish to put this with all delicacy—that you are not his wife?

JUDITH    I dont know what you mean. I say that he is not my husband—that my husband has escaped. This man took his place to save him. Ask anyone in the town—send out into the street for the first person you find there, and bring him in as a witness. He will tell you that the prisoner is not Anthony Anderson.

BURGOYNE [*quietly, as before*]    Sergeant.

SERGEANT    Yes sir.

BURGOYNE    Go out into the street and bring in the first townsman you see there.

SERGEANT [*making for the door*]    Yes sir.

BURGOYNE [*as the SERGEANT passes*]    The first clean, sober townsman you see.

SERGEANT    Yes, sir. [*He goes out*].

BURGOYNE    Sit down, Mr. Anderson—if I may call you so for the present. [*RICHARD sits down*]. Sit down, madam, whilst we wait. Give the lady a newspaper.

RICHARD [*indignantly*]    Shame!

BURGOYNE [*keenly, with a half smile*]    If you are not her husband, sir, the case is not a serious one—for her. [*RICHARD bites his lip, silenced*].

JUDITH [*to RICHARD, as she returns to her seat*]    I couldnt help it. [*He shakes his head. She sits down*].

BURGOYNE    You will understand of course, Mr. Anderson, that you must not build on this little incident. We are bound to make an example of somebody.

RICHARD    I quite understand. I suppose there's no use in my explaining.

BURGOYNE    I think we should prefer independent testimony, if you dont mind.

*The SERGEANT, with a packet of papers in his hand, returns conducting CHRISTY, who is much scared.*

SERGEANT [*giving BURGOYNE the packet*]    Dispatches, sir. Delivered by a corporal of the 53rd. Dead beat with hard riding, sir.

*BURGOYNE opens the dispatches, and presently becomes absorbed in them. They are so serious as to take his attention completely from the court martial.*

THE SERGEANT [*to CHRISTY*]    Now then. Attention; and take your hat off. [*He posts himself in charge of CHRISTY, who stands on BURGOYNE's side of the court*].

RICHARD [*in his usual bullying tone to CHRISTY*]    Dont be frightened, you fool: youre only wanted as a witness. Theyre not going to hang you.

SWINDON    What's your name?

CHRISTY    Christy.

RICHARD [*impatiently*]    Christopher Dudgeon, you blatant idiot. Give your full name.

SWINDON    Be silent, prisoner. You must not prompt the witness.

RICHARD    Very well. But I warn you youll get nothing out of him unless you shake it out of him. He has been too well brought up by a pious mother to have any sense or manhood left in him.

BURGOYNE [*springing up and speaking to the SERGEANT in a startling voice*]    Where is the man who brought these?

SERGEANT    In the guard-room, sir.

*BURGOYNE goes out with a haste that sets the officers exchanging looks.*

SWINDON [*to CHRISTY*]    Do you know Anthony Anderson, the Presbyterian minister?

CHRISTY    Of course I do [*implying that SWINDON must be an ass not to know it*].

SWINDON    Is he here?

CHRISTY [*staring round*]    I dont know.

SWINDON    Do you see him?

CHRISTY    No.

SWINDON    You seem to know the prisoner?

CHRISTY    Do you mean Dick?

SWINDON    Which is Dick?

CHRISTY [*pointing to RICHARD*]    Him.

SWINDON    What is his name?

CHRISTY    Dick.

RICHARD    Answer properly, you jumping jackass. What do they know about Dick?

CHRISTY    Well, you a r e Dick, aint you? What am I to say?

SWINDON    Address me, sir; and do you, prisoner, be silent. Tell us who the prisoner is.

CHRISTY    He's my brother Dick—Richard—Richard Dudgeon.

SWINDON    Your brother!

CHRISTY    Yes.

SWINDON    You are sure he is not Anderson.

CHRISTY    Who?

RICHARD [*exasperatedly*]    Me, me, me, you—

SWINDON    Silence, sir.

SERGEANT [*shouting*]    Silence.

RICHARD [*impatiently*]    Yah! [*To CHRISTY*] He wants to know am I Minister Anderson. Tell him, and stop grinning like a zany.

CHRISTY [*grinning more than ever*]    Y o u Pastor Anderson! [*To SWINDON*] Why, Mr. Anderson's a minister—a very good man; and Dick's a bad character: the respectable people wont speak to him. He's the bad brother: I'm the good one. [*The officers laugh outright. The soldiers grin*].

SWINDON    Who arrested this man?

SERGEANT    I did, sir. I found him in the minister's house, sitting at tea with the lady with his coat off, quite at home. If he isnt married to her, he ought to be.

SWINDON    Did he answer to the minister's name?

SERGEANT    Yes sir, but not to a minister's nature. You ask the chaplain, sir.

SWINDON [*to RICHARD, threateningly*]    So, sir you have attempted to cheat us. And your name is Richard Dudgeon?

RICHARD    Youve found it out at last, have you?

SWINDON    Dudgeon is a name well known to us, eh?

RICHARD    Yes: Peter Dudgeon, whom you murdered, was my uncle.

SWINDON    Hm! [*He compresses his lips, and looks at RICHARD with vindictive gravity*].

CHRISTY    Are they going to hang you, Dick?

RICHARD    Yes. Get out: theyve done with you.

CHRISTY    And I may keep the china peacocks?

RICHARD [*jumping up*]    Get out. Get out, you blithering baboon, you. [*CHRISTY flies, panicstricken*].

SWINDON [*rising—all rise*]    Since you have taken the minister's place, Richard Dudgeon, you shall go through with it. The execution will take place at 12 o'clock as arranged; and unless Anderson surrenders before then you shall take his place on the gallows. Sergeant: take your man out.

JUDITH [*distracted*]    No, no—

SWINDON [*fiercely, dreading a renewal of her entreaties*]    Take that woman away.

RICHARD [*springing across the table with a tiger-like bound, and seizing SWINDON by the throat*]    You infernal scoundrel—

*The SERGEANT rushes to the rescue from one side, the soldiers from the other. They seize RICHARD and drag him back to his place. SWINDON, who has been thrown supine on the table, rises, arranging his stock. He is about to speak, when he is anticipated by BURGOYNE, who has just appeared at the door with two papers in his hand: a white letter and a blue dispatch.*

BURGOYNE [*advancing to the table, elaborately cool*]    What is this? Whats happening? Mr. Anderson: I'm astonished at you.

RICHARD    I am sorry I disturbed you, General. I merely wanted to strangle your understrapper there. [*Breaking out violently at SWINDON*] Why do you raise the devil in me by bullying the woman like that? You oatmeal faced dog, I'd twist your cursed head off with the greatest satisfaction. [*He puts out his hands to the SERGEANT*] Here: handcuff me, will you; or I'll not undertake to keep my fingers off him.

*The SERGEANT takes out a pair of handcuffs and looks to BURGOYNE for instructions.*

BURGOYNE    Have you addressed profane language to the lady, Major Swindon?

SWINDON [*very angry*]    No, sir, certainly not. That question should not have been put to me. I ordered the woman to be removed, as she was disorderly; and the fellow sprang at me. Put away those handcuffs. I am perfectly able to take care of myself.

RICHARD    Now you talk like a man, I have no quarrel with you.

BURGOYNE    Mr. Anderson—

SWINDON    His name is Dudgeon, sir, Richard Dudgeon. He is an impostor.

BURGOYNE [*brusquely*]    Nonsense, sir; you hanged Dudgeon at Springtown.

RICHARD    It was my uncle, General.

BURGOYNE    Oh, your uncle. [*To SWINDON, handsomely*] I beg your pardon, Major Swindon. [*SWINDON acknowledges the apology stiffly. BURGOYNE turns to RICHARD*]. We are somewhat unfortunate in our relations with your family. Well, Mr. Dudgeon, what I wanted to ask you is this: Who is [*reading the name from the letter*] William Maindeck Parshotter?

RICHARD    He is the Mayor of Springtown.

BURGOYNE    Is William—Maindeck and so on—a man of his word?

RICHARD    Is he selling you anything?

BURGOYNE   No.

RICHARD   Then you may depend on him.

BURGOYNE   Thank you, Mr——'m Dudgeon. By the way, since you are not Mr. Anderson, do we still——eh, Major Swindon? [*meaning "do we still hang him?"*]

RICHARD   The arrangements are unaltered, General.

BURGOYNE   Ah, indeed. I am sorry. Good morning, Mr. Dudgeon. Good morning, madam.

RICHARD [*interrupting JUDITH almost fiercely as she is about to make some wild appeal, and taking her arm resolutely*]   Not one word more. Come.

> She looks imploringly at him, but is overborne by his determination. They are marched out by the four soldiers: the SERGEANT, very sulky, walking between SWINDON and RICHARD, whom he watches as if he were a dangerous animal.

BURGOYNE   Gentlemen: we need not detain you. Major Swindon: a word with you. [*The officers go out. BURGOYNE waits with unruffled serenity until the last of them disappears. Then he becomes very grave, and addresses SWINDON for the first time without his title*]. Swindon: do you know what this is [*shewing him the letter*]?

SWINDON   What?

BURGOYNE   A demand for a safe-conduct for an officer of their militia to come here and arrange terms with us.

SWINDON   Oh, they are giving in.

BURGOYNE   They add that they are sending the man who raised Springtown last night and drove us out; so that we may know that we are dealing with an officer of importance.

SWINDON   Pooh!

BURGOYNE   He will be fully empowered to arrange the terms of——guess what.

SWINDON   Their surrender, I hope.

BURGOYNE   No: our evacuation of the town. They offer us just six hours to clear out.

SWINDON   What monstrous impudence!

BURGOYNE    What shall we do, eh?

SWINDON    March on Springtown and strike a decisive blow at once.

BURGOYNE [*quietly*]    Hm! [*Turning to the door*] Come to the adjutant's office.

SWINDON    What for?

BURGOYNE    To write out that safe-conduct. [*He puts his hand to the door knob to open it*].

SWINDON [*who has not budged*]    General Burgoyne.

BURGOYNE [*returning*]    Sir?

SWINDON    It is my duty to tell you, sir, that I do not consider the threats of a mob of rebellious tradesmen a sufficient reason for our giving way.

BURGOYNE [*imperturbable*]    Suppose I resign my command to you, what will you do?

SWINDON    I will undertake to do what we have marched south from Boston to do, and what General Howe has marched north from New York to do: effect a junction at Albany and wipe out the rebel army with our united forces.

BURGOYNE [*enigmatically*]    And will you wipe out our enemies in London, too?

SWINDON    In London! What enemies?

BURGOYNE [*forcibly*]    Jobbery and snobbery, incompetence and Red Tape. [*He holds up the dispatch and adds, with despair in his face and voice*] I have just learnt, sir, that General Howe is still in New York.

SWINDON [*thunderstruck*]    Good God! He has disobeyed orders!

BURGOYNE [*with sardonic calm*]    He has received no orders, sir. Some gentleman in London forgot to dispatch them: he was leaving town for his holiday, I believe. To avoid upsetting his arrangements, England will lose her American colonies; and in a few days you and I will be at Saratoga with 5,000 men to face 16,000 rebels in an impregnable position.

SWINDON [*appalled*]    Impossible!

BURGOYNE [*coldly*]    I beg your pardon!

SWINDON    I cant believe it! What will History say?

BURGOYNE    History, sir, will tell lies, as usual. Come: we must send the safe-conduct. [*He goes out*].

SWINDON [*following distractedly*]    My God, my God! We shall be wiped out.

*As noon approaches there is excitement in the marketplace. The gallows which hangs there permanently for the terror of evildoers, with such minor advertizers and examples of crime as the pillory, the whipping post, and the stocks, has a new rope attached, with the noose hitched up to one of the uprights, out of reach of the boys. Its ladder, too, has been brought out and placed in position by the town beadle, who stands by to guard it from unauthorized climbing. The Websterbridge townsfolk are present in force, and in high spirits; for the news has spread that it is the devil's disciple and not the minister that the Continentals [so they call BURGOYNE's forces] are about to hang: consequently the execution can be enjoyed without any misgiving as to its righteousness, or to the cowardice of allowing it to take place without a struggle. There is even some fear of a disappointment as midday approaches and the arrival of the beadle with the ladder remains the only sign of preparation. But at last reassuring shouts of Here they come: Here they are, are heard, and a company of soldiers with fixed bayonets, half British infantry, half HESSIANS, tramp quickly into the middle of the marketplace, driving the crowd to the sides.*

THE SERGEANT    Halt. Front. Dress. [*The soldiers change their column into a square enclosing the gallows, their petty officers, energetically led by the SERGEANT, hustling the persons who find themselves inside the square out at the corners*]. Now then! Out of it with you: out of it. Some o, youll get strung up yourselves presently. Form that square there, will you, you damned Hoosians. No use talkin German to them: talk to their toes with the butt ends of your muskets: theyll understand that. Get out of it, will you. [*He comes upon JUDITH, standing near the gallows*]. Now then: y o u v e  no call here.

JUDITH    May I not stay? What harm am I doing?

SERGEANT   I want none of your argufying. You ought to be ashamed of yourself, running to see a man hanged thats not your husband. And he's no better than yourself. I told my major he was a gentleman; and then he goes and tries to strangle him, and calls his blessed Majesty a lunatic. So out of it with you, double quick.

JUDITH   Will you take these two silver dollars and let me stay?

*The SERGEANT, without an instant's hesitation, looks quickly and furtively round as he shoots the money dexterously into his pocket. Then he raises his voice in virtuous indignation.*

THE SERGEANT   M e take money in the execution of my duty! Certainly not. Now I'll tell you what I'll do, to teach you to corrupt the King's officer. I'll put you under arrest until the execution's over. You just stand there; and dont let me see you as much as move from that spot until youre let. [*With a swift wink at her he points to the corner of the square behind the gallows on his right, and turns noisily away, shouting*] Now then, dress up and keep em back, will you.

*Cries of Hush and Silence are heard among the townsfolk; and the sound of a military band, playing the Dead March from Saul,\* is heard. The crowd becomes quiet at once; and the SERGEANT and petty officers, hurrying to the back of the square, with a few whispered orders and some stealthy hustling cause it to open and admit the funeral procession, which is protected from the crowd by a double file of soldiers. First come BUR-GOYNE and SWINDON, who, on entering the square, glance with distaste at the gallows, and avoid passing under it by wheeling a little to the right and stationing themselves on that side. Then MR. BRU-DENELL, the chaplain, in his surplice, with his prayer book open in his hand, walking beside RICHARD, who is moody and disorderly. He walks doggedly through the gallows framework, and posts himself a little in front of it. Behind him comes the executioner, a stalwart soldier in his shirtsleeves. Following him, two soldiers haul a light military waggon. Fi-*

---

*Solemn music from the oratorio *Saul* (1739), by George Frideric Handel (1685–1759).

*nally comes the band, which posts itself at the back of the square, and finishes the Dead March. JUDITH, watching RICHARD painfully, steals down to the gallows, and stands leaning against its right post. During the conversation which follows, the two soldiers place the cart under the gallows, and stand by the shafts, which point backwards. The executioner takes a set of steps from the cart and places it ready for the prisoner to mount. Then he climbs the tall ladder which stands against the gallows, and cuts the string by which the rope is hitched up; so that the noose drops dangling over the cart, into which he steps as he descends.*

RICHARD [*with suppressed impatience, to BRUDENELL*]   Look here, sir: this is no place for a man of your profession. Hadnt you better go away?

SWINDON   I appeal to you, prisoner, if you have any sense of decency left, to listen to the ministrations of the chaplain, and pay due heed to the solemnity of the occasion.

THE CHAPLAIN [*gently reproving RICHARD*]   Try to control yourself, and submit to the divine will. [*He lifts his book to proceed with the service*].

RICHARD   Answer for your own will, sir, and those of your accomplices here [*indicating BURGOYNE and SWINDON*]: I see little divinity about them or you. You talk to me of Christianity when you are in the act of hanging your enemies. Was there ever such blasphemous nonsense! [*To SWINDON, more rudely*] Youve got up the solemnity of the occasion, as you call it, to impress the people with your own dignity—Handel's music and a clergyman to make murder look like piety! Do you suppose *I* am going to help you? Youve asked me to choose the rope because you dont know your own trade well enough to shoot me properly. Well, hang away and have done with it.

SWINDON [*to the CHAPLAIN*]   Can you do nothing with him, Mr. Brudenell?

CHAPLAIN   I will try, sir. [*Beginning to read*] Man that is born of woman hath—

RICHARD [*fixing his eyes on him*]   "Thou shalt not kill."

*The book drops in BRUDENELL's hands.*

CHAPLAIN [*confessing his embarrassment*]    What am I to say, Mr. Dudgeon?

RICHARD    Let me alone, man, cant you?

BURGOYNE [*with extreme urbanity*]    I think, Mr. Brudenell, that as the usual professional observations seem to strike Mr. Dudgeon as incongruous under the circumstances, you had better omit them until—er—until Mr. Dudgeon can no longer be inconvenienced by them. [*BRUDENELL, with a shrug, shuts his book and retires behind the gallows*]. Y o u seem in a hurry, Mr. Dudgeon.

RICHARD [*with the horror of death upon him*]    Do you think this is a pleasant sort of thing to be kept waiting for? You've made up your mind to commit murder: well, do it and have done with it.

BURGOYNE    Mr. Dudgeon: we are only doing this—

RICHARD    Because youre paid to do it.

SWINDON    You insolent— [*he swallows his rage*].

BURGOYNE [*with much charm of manner*]    Ah, I am really sorry that you should think that, Mr. Dudgeon. If you knew what my commission cost me, and what my pay is, you would think better of me. I should be glad to part from you on friendly terms.

RICHARD    Hark ye, General Burgoyne. If you think that I like being hanged, youre mistaken. I dont like it; and I dont mean to pretend that I do. And if you think I'm obliged to you for hanging me in a gentlemanly way, youre wrong there too. I take the whole business in devilish bad part; and the only satisfaction I have in it is that youll feel a good deal meaner than I'll look when it's over. [*He turns away, and is striding to the cart when JUDITH advances and interposes with her arms stretched out to him. RICHARD, feeling that a very little will upset his self-possession, shrinks from her, crying*] What are you doing here? This is no place for you. [*She makes a gesture as if to touch him. He recoils impatiently.*] No: go away, go away; youll unnerve me. Take her away, will you.

JUDITH    Wont you bid me good-bye?

RICHARD [*allowing her to take his hand*]    Oh good-bye, good-bye.

Now go—go—quickly. [*She clings to his hand—will not be put off with so cold a last farewell—at last, as he tries to disengage himself, throws herself on his breast in agony*].

SWINDON [*angrily to the SERGEANT, who, alarmed at JUDITH's movement, has come from the back of the square to pull her back, and stopped irresolutely on finding that he is too late*]    How is this? Why is she inside the lines?

SERGEANT [*guiltily*]    I dunno, sir. She's that artful—cant keep her away.

BURGOYNE    You were bribed.

SERGEANT [*protesting*]    No, sir—

SWINDON [*severely*]    Fall back. [*He obeys*].

RICHARD [*imploringly to those around him, and finally to BURGOYNE, as the least stolid of them*]    Take her away. Do you think I want a woman near me now?

BURGOYNE [*going to JUDITH and taking her hand*]    Here, madam: you had better keep inside the lines; but stand here behind us; and dont look.

*RICHARD, with a great sobbing sigh of relief as she releases him and turns to BURGOYNE, flies for refuge to the cart and mounts into it. The executioner takes off his coat and pinions him.*

JUDITH [*resisting BURGOYNE quietly and drawing her hand away*]    No: I must stay. I wont look. [*She goes to the right of the gallows. She tries to look at RICHARD, but turns away with a frightful shudder, and falls on her knees in prayer. BRUDENELL comes towards her from the back of the square*].

BURGOYNE [*nodding approvingly as she kneels*]    Ah, quite so. Do not disturb her, Mr. Brudenell: that will do very nicely. [*BRUDENELL nods also, and withdraws a little, watching her sympathetically. BURGOYNE resumes his former position, and takes out a handsome gold chronometer*]. Now then, are those preparations made? We must not detain Mr. Dudgeon.

*By this time RICHARD's hands are bound behind him; and the noose is round his neck. The two soldiers take the shaft of the waggon, ready to pull it away. The executioner, standing in the cart behind RICHARD, makes a sign to the SERGEANT.*

SERGEANT [*to BURGOYNE*]   Ready, sir.

BURGOYNE   Have you anything more to say, Mr. Dudgeon? It wants two minutes of twelve still.

RICHARD [*in the strong voice of a man who has conquered the bitterness of death*]   Your watch is two minutes slow by the town clock, which I can see from here, General, [*The town clock strikes the first stroke of twelve. Involuntarily the people flinch at the sound, and a subdued groan breaks from them*]. Amen! my life for the world's future!

ANDERSON [*shouting as he rushes into the marketplace*]   Amen; and stop the execution. [*He bursts through the line of soldiers opposite BURGOYNE, and rushes, panting, to the gallows*]. I am Anthony Anderson, the man you want.

*The crowd, intensely excited, listens with all its ears. JUDITH, half rising, stares at him; then lifts her hands like one whose dearest prayer has been granted.*

SWINDON   Indeed. Then you are just in time to take your place on the gallows. Arrest him.

*At a sign from the SERGEANT, two soldiers come forward to seize ANDERSON.*

ANDERSON [*thrusting a paper under SWINDON's nose*]   There's my safe-conduct, sir.

SWINDON [*taken aback*]   Safe-conduct! Are you—!

ANDERSON [*emphatically*]   I am. [*The two soldiers take him by the elbows*]. Tell these men to take their hands off me.

SWINDON [*to the men*]   Let him go.

SERGEANT   Fall back.

*The two men return to their places. The townsfolk raise a cheer; and begin to exchange exultant looks, with a presentiment of triumph as they see their Pastor speaking with their enemies in the gate.*

ANDERSON [*exhaling a deep breath of relief, and dabbing his perspiring brow with his handkerchief*]   Thank God, I was in time!

BURGOYNE [*calm as ever, and still watch in hand*]   Ample time, sir.

Plenty of time. I should never dream of hanging any gentleman by an American clock. [*He puts up his watch*].

ANDERSON   Yes: we are some minutes ahead of you already, General. Now tell them to take the rope from the neck of that American citizen.

BURGOYNE [*to the executioner in the cart—very politely*]   Kindly undo Mr. Dudgeon.

*The executioner takes the rope from RICHARD's neck, unties his hands, and helps him on with his coat.*

JUDITH [*stealing timidly to ANDERSON*]   Tony.

ANDERSON [*putting his arm round her shoulders and bantering her affectionately*]   Well, what do you think of your husband now, eh?—eh??—eh???

JUDITH   I am ashamed—[*she hides her face against his breast.*]

BURGOYNE [*to SWINDON*]   You look disappointed, Major Swindon.

SWINDON   You look defeated, General Burgoyne.

BURGOYNE   I am, sir; and I am humane enough to be glad of it. [*RICHARD jumps down from the cart, BRUDENELL offering his hand to help him, and runs to ANDERSON, whose left hand he shakes heartily, the right being occupied by JUDITH*]. By the way, Mr. Anderson, I do not quite understand. The safe-conduct was for a commander of the militia. I understand you are a—[*He looks as pointedly as his good manners permit at the riding boots, the pistols, and RICHARD's coat, and adds*]—a clergyman.

ANDERSON [*between JUDITH and RICHARD*]   Sir: it is in the hour of trial that a man finds his true profession. This foolish young man [*placing his hand on RICHARD's shoulder*] boasted himself the Devil's Disciple; but when the hour of trial came to him, he found that it was his destiny to suffer and be faithful to the death. I thought myself a decent minister of the gospel of peace; but when the hour of trial came to me, I found that it was my destiny to be a man of action and that my place was amid the thunder of the captains and the shouting. So I am starting life at fifty as Captain Anthony Anderson of the Springtown militia; and the Devil's Disciple here will start presently as the Reverend Richard Dudgeon, and wag his pow* in my old pulpit, and give good advice to this silly sentimental little wife of mine [*putting his other hand on her shoulder. She steals a glance at RICHARD to see how the prospect pleases him*]. Your mother told me, Richard, that I should never have chosen Judith if I'd been born for the ministry. I am afraid she was right; so, by your leave, you may keep my coat and I'll keep yours.

RICHARD    Minister—I should say Captain. I have behaved like a fool.

JUDITH    Like a hero.

RICHARD    Much the same thing, perhaps. [*With some bitterness towards himself*] But no: if I had been any good, I should have done for you what you did for me, instead of making a vain sacrifice.

ANDERSON    Not vain, my boy. It takes all sorts to make a world—saints as well as soldiers. [*Turning to BURGOYNE*] And now, General, time presses; and America is in a hurry. Have you realized that though you may occupy towns and win battles, you cannot conquer a nation?

BURGOYNE    My good sir, without a Conquest you cannot have an aristocracy. Come and settle the matter at my quarters.

ANDERSON    At your service, sir. [*To RICHARD*] See Judith home for me, will you, my boy. [*He hands her over to him*]. Now General. [*He goes busily up the marketplace towards the Town Hall, leaving JUDITH and RICHARD together. BURGOYNE follows him a step or two; then checks himself and turns to RICHARD*].

BURGOYNE    Oh, by the way, Mr. Dudgeon, I shall be glad to see you at lunch at half-past one. [*He pauses a moment, and adds, with politely veiled slyness*] Bring Mrs. Anderson, if she will be so good. [*To SWINDON, who is fuming*] Take it quietly, Major Swindon:

---

*Head.

your friend the British soldier can stand up to anything except the British War Office. [*He follows ANDERSON*].

SERGEANT [*to SWINDON*]    What orders, sir?

SWINDON [*savagely*]    Orders! What use are orders now? There's no army. Back to quarters; and be d— [*He turns on his heel and goes*].

SERGEANT [*pugnacious and patriotic, repudiating the idea of defeat*] 'Tention. Now then: cock up your chins, and shew em you dont care a damn for em. Slope arms! Fours! Wheel! Quick march!

*The drum marks time with a tremendous bang; the band strikes up British Grenadiers; and the sergeant, BRUDENELL, and the English troops march off defiantly to their quarters. The townsfolk press in behind, and follow them up the market, jeering at them; and the town band, a very primitive affair, brings up the rear, playing Yankee Doodle. ESSIE, who comes in with them, runs to RICHARD.*

ESSIE    Oh, Dick!

RICHARD [*good-humoredly, but wilfully*]    Now, now: come, come! I dont mind being hanged; but I will not be cried over.

ESSIE    No, I promise. I'll be good. [*She tries to restrain her tears, but cannot*]. I—I want to see where the soldiers are going to. [*She goes a little way up the market, pretending to look after the crowd*].

JUDITH    Promise me you will never tell him.

RICHARD    Dont be afraid.

*They shake hands on it.*

ESSIE [*calling to them*]    Theyre coming back. They want you.

*Jubilation in the market. The townsfolk surge back again in wild enthusiasm with their band, and hoist RICHARD on their shoulders, cheering him.*

# SHAW'S NOTES TO THE DEVIL'S DISCIPLE

## BURGOYNE

General John Burgoyne, who is presented in this play for the first time (as far as I am aware) on the English stage, is not a conventional stage soldier, but as faithful a portrait as it is in the nature of stage portraits to be. His objection to profane swearing is not borrowed from Mr. Gilbert's H.M.S. Pinafore: it is taken from the Code of Instructions drawn up by himself for his officers when he introduced Light Horse into the English army. His opinion that English soldiers should be treated as thinking beings was no doubt as unwelcome to the military authorities of his time, when nothing was thought of ordering a soldier a thousand lashes, as it will be to those modern victims of the flagellation neurosis who are so anxious to revive that discredited sport. His military reports are very clever as criticisms, and are humane and enlightened within certain aristocratic limits, best illustrated perhaps by his declaration, which now sounds so curious, that he should blush to ask for promotion on any other ground than that of family influence. As a parliamentary candidate, Burgoyne took our common expression "fighting an election" so very literally that he led his supporters to the poll at Preston in 1768 with a loaded pistol in each hand, and won the seat, though he was fined £1,000, and denounced by Junius, for the pistols.

It is only within quite recent years that any general recognition has become possible for the feeling that led Burgoyne, a professed enemy of oppression in India and elsewhere, to accept his American command when so many other officers threw up their commissions rather than serve in a civil war against the Colonies. His biographer De Fonblanque, writing in 1876, evidently regarded his position as indefensible. Nowadays, it is sufficient to say that Burgoyne was an Imperialist. He sympathized with the colonists; but when they proposed as a remedy the disruption of the Empire, he regarded that as a step backward in civilization. As he put it to the House of Commons, "while we remember that we are contending against brothers and fellow subjects, we must also remember that we are contending in this crisis for the fate of the British Empire." Eighty-four years after his defeat, his republican conquerors themselves engaged in a civil war for the integrity of their Union. In 1885 the Whigs who represented the anti-Burgoyne tradition of American Independence in English politics, abandoned Gladstone and made common cause with their political opponents in defence of the Union between England and Ireland. Only the other day England sent 200,000 men into the field south of the equator to fight out the question whether South Africa should develop as a Federation of British Colonies or as an independent Afrikander United States. In all these cases the Unionists who were detached from their parties were called renegades, as Burgoyne was. That, of course, is only one of the unfortunate consequences of the fact that mankind, being for the most part incapable of politics, accepts vituperation as an easy and congenial substitute. Whether Burgoyne or Washington, Lincoln or Davis, Gladstone or Bright, Mr. Chamberlain or Mr. Leonard Courtney was in the right will never be settled, because it will never be possible to prove that the government of the victor has been better for mankind than the government of the vanquished would have been. It is true that the victors have no doubt on the point; but to the dramatist, that certainty of theirs is only part of the human comedy. The American Unionist is often a Separatist as to Ireland; the English Unionist often sympathizes with the Polish Home Ruler; and both English and American Unionists are apt to be Disruptionists as regards that Imperial Ancient of Days, the Empire of China. Both are Unionists concerning Canada, but with a difference as to the precise application to it of the Monroe doctrine. As for me, the dramatist, I smile, and lead the conversation back to Burgoyne.

Burgoyne's surrender at Saratoga made him that occasionally necessary part of our British system, a scapegoat. The explanation of his defeat given in the play (p. 282) is founded on a passage quoted by De Fonblanque from Fitzmaurice's Life of Lord Shelburne, as follows: "Lord George Germain, having among other peculiarities a particular dislike to be put out of his way on any occasion, had arranged to call at his office on his way to the country to sign the dispatches; but as those addressed to Howe had not been fair-copied, and he was not disposed to be balked of his projected visit to Kent, they were not signed then and were forgotten on his return home." These were the dispatches instructing Sir William Howe, who was in New York, to effect a junction at Albany with Burgoyne, who had marched from Boston for that purpose. Burgoyne got as far as Saratoga, where, failing the expected reinforcement, he was hopelessly outnumbered, and his officers picked off, Boer fashion, by the American farmer-sharpshooters. His own collar was pierced by a bullet. The publicity of his defeat, however, was more than compensated at home by the fact that Lord George's trip to Kent had not been interfered with, and that nobody knew about the oversight of the dispatch. The policy of the English Government and Court for the next two years was simply concealment of Germain's neglect. Burgoyne's demand for an inquiry was defeated in the House of Commons by the court party; and when he at last obtained a committee, the king got rid of it by a prorogation. When Burgoyne realized what had happened about the instructions to Howe (the scene in which I have represented him as learning it before Saratoga is not historical: the truth did not dawn on him until many months afterwards) the king actually took advantage of his being a prisoner of war in England on parole, and ordered him to return to America into captivity. Burgoyne immediately resigned all his appointments; and this practically closed his military career, though he was afterwards made

Commander of the Forces in Ireland for the purpose of banishing him from parliament.

The episode illustrates the curious perversion of the English sense of honor when the privileges and prestige of the aristocracy are at stake. Mr. Frank Harris said, after the disastrous battle of Modder River, that the English, having lost America a century ago because they preferred George III, were quite prepared to lose South Africa to-day because they preferred aristocratic commanders to successful ones. Horace Walpole, when the parliamentary recess came at a critical period of the War of Independence, said that the Lords could not be expected to lose their pheasant shooting for the sake of America. In the working class, which, like all classes, has its own official aristocracy, there is the same reluctance to discredit an institution or to "do a man out of his job." At bottom, of course, this apparently shameless sacrifice of great public interests to petty personal ones, is simply the preference of the ordinary man for the things he can feel and understand to the things that are beyond his capacity. It is stupidity, not dishonesty.

Burgoyne fell a victim to this stupidity in two ways. Not only was he thrown over, in spite of his high character and distinguished services, to screen a court favorite who had actually been cashiered for cowardice and misconduct in the field fifteen years before; but his peculiar critical temperament and talent, artistic, satirical, rather histrionic, and his fastidious delicacy of sentiment, his fine spirit and humanity, were just the qualities to make him disliked by stupid people because of their dread of ironic criticism. Long after his death, Thackeray, who had an intense sense of human character, but was typically stupid in valuing and interpreting it, instinctively sneered at him and exulted in his defeat. That sneer represents the common English attitude towards the Burgoyne type. Every instance in which the critical genius is defeated, and the stupid genius (for both temperaments have their genius) "muddles through all right," is popular in England. But Burgoyne's failure was not the work of his own temperament, but of the stupid temperament. What man could do under the circumstances he did, and did handsomely and loftily. He fell, and his ideal empire was dismembered, not through his own misconduct, but because Sir George Germain overestimated the importance of his Kentish holiday, and underestimated the difficulty of conquering those remote and inferior creatures, the colonists. And King George and the rest of the nation agreed, on the whole, with Germain. It is a significant point that in America, where Burgoyne was an enemy and an invader, he was admired and praised. The climate there is no doubt more favorable to intellectual vivacity.

I have described Burgoyne's temperament as rather histrionic; and the reader will have observed that the Burgoyne of the Devil's Disciple is a man who plays his part in life, and makes all its points, in the manner of a born high comedian. If he had been killed at Saratoga, with all his comedies unwritten, and his plan for turning As You Like It into a Beggar's Opera unconceived, I should still have painted the same picture of him on the strength of his reply to the

| PROPOSITION. | ANSWER. |
|---|---|
| 1. General Burgoyne's army being reduced by repeated defeats, by desertion, sickness, etc., their provisions exhausted, their military horses, tents and baggage taken or destroyed, their retreat cut off, and their camp invested, they can only be allowed to surrender as prisoners of war. | Lieut-General Burgoyne's army, however reduced, will never admit that their retreat is cut off while they have arms in their hands. |
| 2. The officers and soldiers may keep the baggage belonging to them. The Generals of the United States never permit individuals to be pillaged. | Noted. |
| 3. The troops under his Excellency General Burgoyne will be conducted by the most convenient route to New England, marching by easy marches, and sufficiently provided for by the way. | Agreed. |

4. The officers will be admitted on parole and will be treated with the liberality customary in such cases, so long as they, by proper behaviour, continue to deserve it; but those who are apprehended having broke their parole, as some British officers have done, must expect to be close confined.

There being no officer in this army under, or capable of being under, the description of breaking parole, this article needs no answer.

5. All public stores, artillery, arms, ammunition, carriages, horses, etc., etc., must be delivered to commissaries appointed to receive them.

All public stores may be delivered, arms excepted.

6. These terms being agreed to and signed, the troops under his Excellency's, General Burgoyne's command, may be drawn up in their encampments, where they will be ordered to ground their arms, and may thereupon be marched to the riverside on their way to Bennington.

This article is inadmissable in any extremity. Sooner than this army will consent to ground their arms in their encampments, they will rush on the enemy determined to take no quarter.

articles of capitulation proposed to him by his American conqueror General Gates. Here they are:

And, later on, "If General Gates does not mean to recede from the 6th article, the treaty ends at once: the army will to a man proceed to any act of desperation sooner than submit to that article."

Here you have the man at his Burgoynest. Need I add that he had his own way; and that when the actual ceremony of surrender came, he would have played poor General Gates off the stage, had not that commander risen to the occasion by handing him back his sword.

In connection with the reference to Indians with scalping knives who, with the troops hired from Germany, made up about half Burgoyne's force, I may mention that Burgoyne offered two of them a reward to guide a Miss McCrea, betrothed to one of the English officers, into the English lines. The two braves quarrelled about the reward; and the more sensitive of them, as a protest against the u

fairness of the other, tomahawked the young lady. The usual retalia-
tions were proposed under the popular titles of justice and so forth;
but as the tribe of the slayer would certainly have followed suit by a
massacre of whites on the Canadian frontier, Burgoyne was compelled to forgive the crime, to the intense disgust of indignant Chris-
tendom.

## BRUDENELL

Brudenell is also a real person. At least an artillery chaplain of that
name distinguished himself at Saratoga by reading the burial service
over Major Fraser under fire, and by a quite readable adventure,
chronicled by Burgoyne, with Lady Harriet Ackland. Lady Harriet's
husband achieved the remarkable feat of killing himself, instead of his
adversary, in a duel. He overbalanced himself in the heat of his
swordsmanship, and fell with his head against a pebble. Lady Harriet
then married the warrior chaplain, who, like Anthony Anderson in
the play, seems to have mistaken his natural profession.

The rest of the Devil's Disciple may have actually occurred, like
most stories invented by dramatists; but I cannot produce any documents. Major Swindon's name is invented; but the man, of course, is
real. There are dozens of him extant to this day.

# MAN AND
# SUPERMAN

# TO ARTHUR BINGHAM WALKLEY*

MY DEAR WALKLEY

You once asked me why I did not write a Don Juan play. The levity with which you assumed this frightful responsibility has probably by this time enabled you to forget it; but the day of reckoning has arrived: here is your play! I say y o u r play, because q u i f a c i t p e r a l i u m f a c i t p e r s e.† Its profits, like its labor, belong to me: its morals, its manners, its philosophy, its influence on the young, are for you to justify. You were of mature age when you made the suggestion; and you knew your man. It is hardly fifteen years since, as twin pioneers of the New Journalism of that time, we two, cradled in the same new sheets, made an epoch in the criticism of the theatre and the opera house by making it a pretext for a propaganda of our own views of life. So you cannot plead ignorance of the character of the force you set in motion. You meant me to épater le bourgeois; and if he protests, I hereby refer him to you as the accountable party.

I warn you that if you attempt to repudiate your responsibility, I shall suspect you of finding the play too decorous for your taste. The fifteen years have made me older and graver. In you I can detect no such becoming change. Your levities and audacities are like the loves and comforts prayed for by Desdemona: they increase, even as your days do grow. No mere pioneering journal dares meddle with them now: the stately Times itself is alone sufficiently above suspicion to

---

*Shaw fondly portrayed his fellow critic as Mr. Trotter in *Fanny's First Play* (1911).

†He who acts through an agent acts for himself (Latin).

act as your chaperone; and even the Times must sometimes thank its stars that new plays are not produced every day, since after each such event its gravity is compromised, its platitude turned to epigram, its portentousness to wit, its propriety to elegance, and even its decorum into naughtiness by criticisms which the traditions of the paper do not allow you to sign at the end, but which you take care to sign with the most extravagant flourishes between the lines. I am not sure that this is not a portent of Revolution. In eighteenth century France the end was at hand when men bought the Encyclopedia and found Diderot there. When I buy the Times and find you there, my prophetic ear catches a rattle of twentieth century tumbrils.

However, that is not my present anxiety. The question is, will you not be disappointed with a Don Juan play in which not one of that hero's m i l l e   e   t r e* adventures is brought upon the stage? To propitiate you, let me explain myself. You will retort that I never do anything else: it is your favorite jibe at me that what I call drama is nothing but explanation. But you must not expect me to adopt your inexplicable, fantastic, petulant, fastidious ways: you must take me as I am, a reasonable, patient, consistent, apologetic, laborious person, with the temperament of a schoolmaster and the pursuits of a vestryman. No doubt that literary knack of mine which happens to amuse the British public distracts attention from my character; but the character is there none the less, solid as bricks. I have a conscience; and conscience is always anxiously explanatory. You, on the contrary, feel that a man who discusses his conscience is much like a woman who discusses her modesty. The only moral force you condescend to parade is the force of your wit: the only demand you make in public is the demand of your artistic temperament for symmetry, elegance, style, grace, refinement, and the cleanliness which comes next to godliness if not before it. But my conscience is the genuine pulpit article: it annoys me to see people comfortable when they ought to be

---

*One thousand and three (Italian); in Mozart's *Don Giovanni* (1787), the Don's servant Leporello claims for his master this number of amorous conquests in Spain.

uncomfortable; and I insist on making them think in order to bring them to conviction of sin. If you dont like my preaching you must lump it. I really cannot help it.

In the preface to my Plays for Puritans I explained the predicament of our contemporary English drama, forced to deal almost exclusively with cases of sexual attraction, and yet forbidden to exhibit the incidents of that attraction or even to discuss its nature. Your suggestion that I should write a Don Juan play was virtually a challenge to me to treat this subject myself dramatically. The challenge was difficult enough to be worth accepting, because, when you come to think of it, though we have plenty of dramas with heroes and heroines who are in love and must accordingly marry or perish at the end of the play, or about people whose relations with one another have been complicated by the marriage laws, not to mention the looser sort of plays which trade on the tradition that illicit love affairs are at once vicious and delightful, we have no modern English plays in which the natural attraction of the sexes for one another is made the mainspring of the action. That is why we insist on beauty in our performers, differing herein from the countries our friend William Archer holds up as examples of seriousness to our childish theatres. There the Juliets and Isoldes, the Romeos and Tristans, might be our mothers and fathers. Not so the English actress. The heroine she impersonates is not allowed to discuss the elemental relations of men and women: all her romantic twaddle about novelet-made love, all her purely legal dilemmas as to whether she was married or "betrayed," quite miss our hearts and worry our minds. To console ourselves we must just look at her. We do so; and her beauty feeds our starving emotions. Sometimes we grumble ungallantly at the lady because she does not act as well as she looks. But in a drama which, with all its preoccupation with sex, is really void of sexual interest, good looks are more desired than histrionic skill.

Let me press this point on you, since you are too clever to raise the fool's cry of paradox whenever I take hold of a stick by the right instead of the wrong end. Why are our occasional attempts to deal with the sex problem on the stage so repulsive and dreary that even those who are most determined that sex questions shall be held open and their discussion kept free, cannot pretend to relish these joyless attempts at social sanitation? Is it not because at bottom they are utterly sexless? What is the usual formula for such plays? A woman has, on some past occasion, been brought into conflict with the law which regulates the relations of the sexes. A man, by falling in love with her, or marrying her, is brought into conflict with the social convention which discountenances the woman. Now the conflicts of individuals with law and convention can be dramatized like all other human conflicts; but they are purely judicial; and the fact that we are much more curious about the suppressed relations between the man and the woman than about the relations between both and our courts of law and private juries of matrons, produces that sensation of evasion, of dissatisfaction, of fundamental irrelevance, of shallowness, of useless disagreeableness, of total failure to edify and partial failure to interest, which is as familiar to you in the theatres as it was to me when I, too, frequented those uncomfortable buildings, and found our popular playwrights in the mind to (as they thought) emulate Ibsen.

I take it that when you asked me for a Don Juan play you did not want that sort of thing. Nobody does: the successes such plays sometimes obtain are due to the incidental conventional melodrama with which the experienced popular author instinctively saves himself from failure. But what did you want? Owing to your unfortunate habit—you now, I hope, feel its inconvenience—of not explaining yourself, I have had to discover this for myself. First, then, I have had to ask myself, what is a Don Juan? Vulgarly, a libertine. But your dislike of vulgarity is pushed to the length of a defect (universality of character is impossible without a share of vulgarity); and even if you could acquire the taste, you would find yourself overfed from ordinary sources without troubling me. So I took it that you demanded a Don Juan in the philosophic sense.

Philosophically, Don Juan is a man who, though gifted enough to be exceptionally capable of distinguishing between good and evil, follows his own instincts without regard to the common, statute, or canon law; and therefore, whilst gaining the ardent sympathy of our rebellious instincts (which are flattered by the brilliancies with which Don Juan associates them) finds himself in mortal conflict with existing institutions, and defends himself by fraud and force as unscrupulously as a farmer defends his crops by the same means against vermin. The prototypic Don Juan, invented early in the XVI century by a Spanish monk,* was presented, according to the ideas of that time, as the enemy of God, the approach of whose vengeance is felt throughout the drama, growing in menace from minute to minute. No anxiety is caused on Don Juan's account by any minor antagonist: he easily eludes the police, temporal and spiritual; and when an indignant father seeks private redress with the sword, Don Juan kills him without an effort. Not until the slain father returns from heaven as the agent of God, in the form of his own statue, does he prevail against his slayer and cast him into hell. The moral is a monkish one: repent and reform now; for to-morrow it may be too late. This is really the only point on which Don Juan is sceptical; for he is a devout believer in an ultimate hell, and risks damnation only because, as he is young, it seems so far off that repentance can be postponed until he has amused himself to his heart's content.

But the lesson intended by an author is hardly ever the lesson the world chooses to learn from his book. What attracts and impresses us in El Burlador de Sevilla† is not the immediate urgency of repentance, but the heroism of daring to be the enemy of God. From Prometheus to my own Devil's Disciple, such enemies have always been popular. Don Juan became such a pet that the world could not bear his damnation. It reconciled him sentimentally to God in a second version, and clamored for his canonization for a whole century, thus treating him as English journalism has treated that comic foe of

---

*Fray Gabriel Téllez (Tirso de Molina), a dramatist who lived in the early seventeenth (not sixteenth) century.

†The Trickster (Deceiver, Gamester) of Seville.

the gods, Punch. Molière's Don Juan casts back to the original in point of impenitence; but in piety he falls off greatly. True, he also proposes to repent; but in what terms! "Oui, ma foi? il faut s'amender. Encore vingt ou trente ans de cette vie-ci, et puis nous songerons à nous."[1] After Molière comes the artist-enchanter, the master of masters, Mozart, who reveals the hero's spirit in magical harmonies, elfin tones, and elate darting rhythms as of summer lightning made audible. Here you have freedom in love and in morality mocking exquisitely at slavery to them, and interesting you, attracting you, tempting you, inexplicably forcing you to range the hero with his enemy the statue on a transcendant plane, leaving the prudish daughter and her priggish lover on a crockery shelf below to live piously ever after.

After these completed works Byron's fragment* does not count for much philosophically. Our vagabond libertines are no more interesting from that point of view than the sailor who has a wife in every port; and Byron's hero is, after all, only a vagabond libertine. And he is dumb: he does not discuss himself with a Sganarelle-Leporello[†] or with the fathers or brothers of his mistresses: he does not even, like Casanova, tell his own story. In fact he is not a true Don Juan at all; for he is no more an enemy of God than any romantic and adventurous young sower of wild oats. Had you and I been in his place at his age, who knows whether we might not have done as he did, unless indeed your fastidiousness had saved you from the empress Catherine.[‡] Byron was as little of a philosopher as Peter the Great: both were instances of that rare and useful, but unedifying variation, an energetic genius born without the prejudices or superstitions of his contemporaries. The resultant unscrupulous freedom

---

*Don Juan (1824), a comic-epic poem.

†Don Juan's servant in works by Molière (Don Juan, 1665) and Mozart (Don Giovanni, 1787), respectively.

‡Of eighteenth-century Russia; reputedly most amorous, she was the subject of Shaw's Great Catherine (1913).

of thought made Byron a greater poet than Wordsworth just as it
made Peter a greater king than George III; but as it was, after all, only
a negative qualification, it did not prevent Peter from being an appalling blackguard and an arrant poltroon, nor did it enable Byron to
become a religious force like Shelley. Let us, then, leave Byron's Don
Juan out of account. Mozart's is the last of the true Don Juans; for by
the time he was of age, his cousin Faust had, in the hands of Goethe,
taken his place and carried both his warfare and his reconciliation
with the gods far beyond mere lovemaking into politics, high art,
schemes for reclaiming new continents from the ocean, and recognition of an eternal womanly principle in the universe. Goethe's Faust
and Mozart's Don Juan were the last words of the XVIII century on
the subject; and by the time the polite critics of the XIX century, ignoring William Blake as superficially as the XVIII had ignored Hogarth or the XVII Bunyan, had got past the Dickens-Macaulay
Dumas-Guizot* stage and the Stendhal-Meredith-Turgenieff stage,
and were confronted with philosophic fiction by such pens as Ibsen's
and Tolstoy's, Don Juan had changed his sex and become Doña Juana,
breaking out of the Doll's House and asserting herself as an individual instead of a mere item in a moral pageant.

Now it is all very well for you at the beginning of the XX century
to ask me for a Don Juan play; but you will see from the foregoing
survey that Don Juan is a full century out of date for you and for me;
and if there are millions of less literate people who are still in the
eighteenth century, have they not Molière and Mozart, upon whose
art no human hand can improve? You would laugh at me if at this
time of day I dealt in duels and ghosts and "womanly" women. As to
mere libertinism, you would be the first to remind me that the Fes-
tin de Pierre† of Molière is not a play for amorists, and that one bar
of the voluptuous sentimentality of Gounod or Bizet would appear as
a licentious stain on the score of Don Giovanni. Even the more ab-

---

*François Guizot was a nineteenth-century Protestant historian.

†The Stony Dinner-Party (French).

stract parts of the Don Juan play are dilapidated past use: for instance, Don Juan's supernatural antagonist hurled those who refuse
to repent into lakes of burning brimstone, there to be tormented by
devils with horns and tails. Of that antagonist, and of that conception
of repentance, how much is left that could be used in a play by me
dedicated to you? On the other hand, those forces of middle class
public opinion which hardly existed for a Spanish nobleman in the
days of the first Don Juan, are now triumphant everywhere. Civilized
society is one huge bourgeoisie: no nobleman dares now shock his
greengrocer. The women, "marchesane, principesse, cameriere, cittadine"[2] and all, are become equally dangerous: the sex is aggressive,
powerful: when women are wronged they do not group themselves
pathetically to sing "Protegga il giusto cielo":* they grasp formidable
legal and social weapons, and retaliate. Political parties are wrecked
and public careers undone by a single indiscretion. A man had better
have all the statues in London to supper with him, ugly as they are,
than be brought to the bar of the Nonconformist Conscience by
Donna Elvira. Excommunication has become almost as serious a
business as it was in the X century.

As a result, Man is no longer, like Don Juan, victor in the duel of
sex. Whether he has ever really been may be doubted: at all events
the enormous superiority of Woman's natural position in this matter
is telling with greater and greater force. As to pulling the Nonconformist Conscience by the beard as Don Juan plucked the beard of
the Commandant's statue in the convent of San Francisco, that is out
of the question nowadays: prudence and good manners alike forbid it
to a hero with any mind. Besides, it is Don Juan's own beard that is
in danger of plucking. Far from relapsing into hypocrisy, as Sganarelle
feared, he has unexpectedly discovered a moral in his immorality.
The growing recognition of his new point of view is heaping responsibility on him. His former jests he has had to take as seriously as I

---

*Let a just heaven protect (Italian); sung by Anna and Ottavio in Mozart's *Don
Giovanni*.

have had to take some of the jests of Mr. W. S. Gilbert. His scepticism, once his least tolerated quality, has now triumphed so completely that he can no longer assert himself by witty negations, and
must, to save himself from cipherdom, find an affirmative position.
His thousand and three affairs of gallantry, after becoming, at most,
two immature intrigues leading to sordid and prolonged complications and humiliations, have been discarded altogether as unworthy
of his philosophic dignity and compromising to his newly acknowledged position as the founder of a school. Instead of pretending to
read Ovid he does actually read Schopenhaur and Nietzsche, studies
Westermarck,* and is concerned for the future of the race instead of
for the freedom of his own instincts. Thus his profligacy and his dare-
devil airs have gone the way of his sword and mandoline into the rag
shop of anachronisms and superstitions. In fact, he is now more
Hamlet than Don Juan; for though the lines put into the actor's
mouth to indicate to the pit that Hamlet is a philosopher are for the
most part mere harmonious platitude which, with a little debasement of the word-music, would be properer to Pecksniff,† yet if you
separate the real hero, inarticulate and unintelligible to himself except in flashes of inspiration, from the performer who has to talk at
any cost through five acts; and if you also do what you must always
do in Shakespear's tragedies: that is, dissect out the absurd sensational incidents and physical violences of the borrowed story from
the genuine Shakespearian tissue, you will get a true Promethean foe
of the gods, whose instinctive attitude towards women much resembles that to which Don Juan is now driven. From this point of view
Hamlet was a developed Don Juan whom Shakespear palmed off as a
reputable man just as he palmed poor Macbeth off as a murderer. To-
day the palming off is no longer necessary (at least on your plane and
mine) because Don Juanism is no longer misunderstood as mere

---

*Edward Alexander Westermarck (1862–1939), Finnish anthropologist of mar-
riage.

†Hypocritical character in Charles Dickens's *Martin Chuzzlewit* (1844).

Casanovism. Don Juan himself is almost ascetic in his desire to avoid that misunderstanding; and so my attempt to bring him up to date by launching him as a modern Englishman into a modern English environment has produced a figure superficially quite unlike the hero of Mozart.

And yet I have not the heart to disappoint you wholly of another glimpse of the Mozartian dissoluto punito* and his antagonist the statue. I feel sure you would like to know more of that statue—to draw him out when he is off duty, so to speak. To gratify you, I have resorted to the trick of the strolling theatrical manager who advertizes the pantomime of Sinbad the Sailor with a stock of second-hand picture posters designed for Ali Baba. He simply thrusts a few oil jars into the valley of diamonds, and so fulfils the promise held out by the hoardings to the public eye. I have adapted this simple device to our occasion by thrusting into my perfectly modern three-act play a totally extraneous act in which my hero, enchanted by the air of the Sierra, has a dream in which his Mozartian ancestor appears and philosophizes at great length in a Shavio-Socratic dialogue with the lady, the statue, and the devil.

But this pleasantry is not the essence of the play. Over this essence I have no control. You propound a certain social substance, sexual attraction to wit, for dramatic distillation; and I distil it for you. I do not adulterate the product with aphrodisiacs nor dilute it with romance and water; for I am merely executing your commission, not producing a popular play for the market. You must therefore (unless, like most wise men, you read the play first and the preface afterwards) prepare yourself to face a trumpery story of modern London life, a life in which, as you know, the ordinary man's main business is to get means to keep up the position and habits of a gentleman, and the ordinary woman's business is to get married. In 9,999 cases out of 10,000, you can count on their doing nothing, whether noble or base, that conflicts with these ends; and

---

*The libertine punished (Italian); subtitle of Mozart's *Don Giovanni* (1787).

that assurance is what you rely on as their religion, their morality, their principles, their patriotism, their reputation, their honor and so forth.

On the whole, this is a sensible and satisfactory foundation for society. Money means nourishment and marriage means children; and that men should put nourishment first and women children first is, broadly speaking, the law of Nature and not the dictate of personal ambition. The secret of the prosaic man's success, such as it is, is the simplicity with which he pursues these ends: the secret of the artistic man's failure, such as that is, is the versatility with which he strays in all directions after secondary ideals. The artist is either a poet or a scallawag: as poet, he cannot see, as the prosaic man does, that chivalry is at bottom only romantic suicide: as scallawag, he cannot see that it does not pay to spunge and beg and lie and brag and neglect his person. Therefore do not misunderstand my plain statement of the fundamental constitution of London society as an Irishman's reproach to your nation. From the day I first set foot on this foreign soil I knew the value of the prosaic qualities of which Irishmen teach Englishmen to be ashamed as well as I knew the vanity of the poetic qualities of which Englishmen teach Irishmen to be proud. For the Irishman instinctively disparages the quality which makes the Englishman dangerous to him; and the Englishman instinctively flatters the fault that makes the Irishman harmless and amusing to him. What is wrong with the prosaic Englishman is what is wrong with the prosaic men of all countries: stupidity. The vitality which places nourishment and children first, heaven and hell a somewhat remote second, and the health of society as an organic whole nowhere, may muddle successfully through the comparatively tribal stages of gregariousness; but in nineteenth century nations and twentieth century empires the determination of every man to be rich at all costs, and of every woman to be married at all costs, must, without a highly scientific social organization, produce a ruinous development of poverty, celibacy, prostitution, infant mortality, adult degeneracy, and everything that wise men most dread. In short, there is no future

312 GEORGE BERNARD SHAW

for men, however brimming with crude vitality, who are neither intelligent nor politically educated enough to be Socialists. So do not misunderstand me in the other direction either: if I appreciate the vital qualities of the Englishman as I appreciate the vital qualities of the bee, I do not guarantee the Englishman against being, like the bee (or the Canaanite) smoked out and unloaded of his honey by beings inferior to himself in simple acquisitiveness, combativeness, and fecundity, but superior to him in imagination and cunning.

The Don Juan play, however, is to deal with sexual attraction, and not with nutrition, and to deal with it in a society in which the serious business of sex is left by men to women, as the serious business of nutrition is left by women to men. That the men, to protect themselves against a too aggressive prosecution of the women's business, have set up a feeble romantic convention that the initiative in sex business must always come from the man, is true; but the pretence is so shallow that even in the theatre, that last sanctuary of unreality, it imposes only on the inexperienced. In Shakespear's plays the woman always takes the initiative. In his problem plays and his popular plays alike the love interest is the interest of seeing the woman hunt the man down. She may do it by blandishment, like Rosalind, or by stratagem, like Mariana; but in every case the relation between the woman and the man is the same: she is the pursuer and contriver, he the pursued and disposed of. When she is baffled, like Ophelia, she goes mad and commits suicide; and the man goes straight from her funeral to a fencing match. No doubt Nature, with very young creatures, may save the woman the trouble of scheming: Prospero knows that he has only to throw Ferdinand and Miranda together and they will mate like a pair of doves; and there is no need for Perdita to capture Florizel as the lady doctor in All's Well That Ends Well (an early Ibsenite heroine) captures Bertram. But the mature cases all illustrate the Shakespearian law. The one apparent exception, Petruchio, is not a real one: he is most carefully characterized as a purely commercial matrimonial adventurer. Once he is assured that Katharine has money, he undertakes to marry her before he has seen her. In real life we find not only Petruchios, but Mantalinis and Dobbins* who pursue women with appeals to their pity or jealousy or vanity, or cling to them in a romantically infatuated way. Such effeminates do not count in the world scheme: even Bunsby dropping like a fascinated bird into the jaws of Mrs. MacStinger[†] is by comparison a true tragic object of pity and terror. I find in my own plays that Woman, projecting herself dramatically by my hands (a process over which I assure you I have no more real control than I have over my wife),[3] behaves just as Woman did in the plays of Shakespear.

And so your Don Juan has come to birth as a stage projection of the tragi-comic love chase of the man by the woman; and my Don Juan is the quarry instead of the huntsman. Yet he is a true Don Juan, with a sense of reality that disables convention, defying to the last the fate which finally overtakes him. The woman's need of him to enable her to carry on Nature's most urgent work, does not prevail against him until his resistance gathers her energy to a climax at which she dares to throw away her customary exploitations of the conventional affectionate and dutiful poses, and claim him by natural right for a purpose that far transcends their mortal personal purposes.

Among the friends to whom I have read this play in manuscript are some of our own sex who are shocked at the "unscrupulousness," meaning the total disregard of masculine fastidiousness, with which the woman pursues her purpose. It does not occur to them that if women were as fastidious as men, morally or physically, there would be an end of the race. Is there anything meaner than to throw necessary work upon other people and then disparage it as unworthy and indelicate. We laugh at the haughty American nation because it makes the negro clean its boots and then proves the moral and physical inferiority of the negro by the fact that he is a shoeblack; but we ourselves throw the whole drudgery of creation on one sex, and then

---

*In Thackeray's *Vanity Fair* (1848), a type of the faithful, devoted suitor.

†Bunsby and Mrs. MacStinger are characters in Dickens's *Dombey and Son* (1848).

imply that no female of any womanliness or delicacy would initiate any effort in that direction. There are no limits to male hypocrisy in this matter. No doubt there are moments when man's sexual immunities are made acutely humiliating to him. When the terrible moment of birth arrives, its supreme importance and its superhuman effort and peril, in which the father has no part, dwarf him into the meanest insignificance: he slinks out of the way of the humblest petticoat, happy if he be poor enough to be pushed out of the house to outface his ignominy by drunken rejoicings. But when the crisis is over he takes his revenge, swaggering as the breadwinner, and speaking of Woman's "sphere" with condescension, even with chivalry, as if the kitchen and the nursery were less important than the office in the city. When his swagger is exhausted he drivels into erotic poetry or sentimental uxoriousness; and the Tennysonian King Arthur posing at Guinevere becomes Don Quixote grovelling before Dulcinea. You must admit that here Nature beats Comedy out of the field: the wildest hominist or feminist farce is insipid after the most commonplace "slice of life." The pretence that women do not take the initiative is part of the farce. Why, the whole world is strewn with snares, traps, gins and pitfalls for the capture of men by women. Give women the vote, and in five years there will be a crushing tax on bachelors. Men, on the other hand, attach penalties to marriage, depriving women of property, of the franchise, of the free use of their limbs, of that ancient symbol of immortality, the right to make oneself at home in the house of God by taking off the hat, of everything that he can force Woman to dispense with without compelling himself to dispense with her. All in vain. Woman must marry because the race must perish without her travail: if the risk of death and the certainty of pain, danger and unutterable discomforts cannot deter her, slavery and swaddled ankles will not. And yet we assume that the force that carries women through all these perils and hardships, stops abashed before the primnesses of our behavior for young ladies. It is assumed that the woman must wait, motionless, until she is wooed. Nay, she often does wait motionless. That is how the spider waits for the fly. But the spider spins her web. And if the fly, like my hero, shews a strength that promises to extricate him, how swiftly does she abandon her pretence of passiveness, and openly fling coil after coil about him until he is secured for ever!

If the really impressive books and other art-works of the world were produced by ordinary men, they would express more fear of women's pursuit than love of their illusory beauty. But ordinary men cannot produce really impressive art-works. Those who can are men of genius: that is, men selected by Nature to carry on the work of building up an intellectual consciousness of her own instinctive purpose. Accordingly, we observe in the man of genius all the unscrupulousness and all the "self-sacrifice" (the two things are the same) of Woman. He will risk the stake and the cross; starve, when necessary, in a garret all his life; study women and live on their work and care as Darwin studied worms and lived upon sheep; work his nerves into rags without payment, a sublime altruist in his disregard of himself, an atrocious egotist in his disregard of others. Here Woman meets a purpose as impersonal, as irresistible as her own; and the clash is sometimes tragic. When it is complicated by the genius being a woman, then the game is one for a king of critics: your George Sand* becomes a mother to gain experience for the novelist and to develop her, and gobbles up men of genius, Chopins, Mussets and the like, as mere hors d'œuvres.

I state the extreme case, of course; but what is true of the great man who incarnates the philosophic consciousness of Life and the woman who incarnates its fecundity, is true in some degree of all geniuses and all women. Hence it is that the world's books get written, its pictures painted, its statues modelled, its symphonies composed, by people who are free of the otherwise universal dominion of the tyranny of sex. Which leads us to the conclusion, astonishing to the vulgar, that art, instead of being before all things the expression of

---

*Amandine Dupin, Baronne Dudevant (1804–1876) published novels under this name.

the normal sexual situation, is really the only department in which sex is a superseded and secondary power, with its consciousness so confused and its purpose so perverted, that its ideas are mere fantasy to common men. Whether the artist becomes poet or philosopher, moralist or founder of a religion, his sexual doctrine is nothing but a barren special pleading for pleasure, excitement, and knowledge when he is young, and for contemplative tranquillity when he is old and satiated. Romance and Asceticism, Amorism and Puritanism are equally unreal in the great Philistine world. The world shewn us in books, whether the books be confessed epics or professed gospels, or in codes, or in political orations, or in philosophic systems, is not the main world at all: it is only the self-consciousness of certain abnormal people who have the specific artistic talent and temperament. A serious matter this for you and me, because the man whose consciousness does not correspond to that of the majority is a madman; and the old habit of worshipping madmen is giving way to the new habit of locking them up. And since what we call education and culture is for the most part nothing but the substitution of reading for experience, of literature for life, of the obsolete fictitious for the contemporary real, education, as you no doubt observed at Oxford, destroys, by supplantation, every mind that is not strong enough to see through the imposture and to use the great Masters of Arts as what they really are and no more: that is, patentees of highly questionable methods of thinking, and manufacturers of highly questionable, and for the majority but half valid representations of life. The schoolboy who uses his Homer to throw at his fellow's head makes perhaps the safest and most rational use of him; and I observe with reassurance that you occasionally do the same, in your prime, with your Aristotle.

Fortunately for us, whose minds have been so overwhelmingly sophisticated by literature, what produces all these treatises and poems and scriptures of one sort or another is the struggle of Life to become divinely conscious of itself instead of blindly stumbling hither and thither in the line of least resistance. Hence there is a driving towards truth in all books on matters where the writer, though exceptionally gifted, is normally constituted, and has no private axe to grind. Copernicus had no motive for misleading his fellowmen as to the place of the sun in the solar system: he looked for it as honestly as a shepherd seeks his path in a mist. But Copernicus would not have written love stories scientifically. When it comes to sex relations, the man of genius does not share the common man's danger of capture, nor the woman of genius the common woman's overwhelming specialization. And that is why our scriptures and other art works, when they deal with love, turn from honest attempts at science in physics to romantic nonsense, erotic ecstasy, or the stern asceticism of satiety ("the road of excess leads to the palace of wisdom" said William Blake; for "you never know what is enough unless you know what is more than enough").*

There is a political aspect of this sex question which is too big for my comedy, and too momentous to be passed over without culpable frivolity. It is impossible to demonstrate that the initiative in sex transactions remains with Woman, and has been confirmed to her, so far, more and more by the suppression of rapine and discouragement of importunity, without being driven to very serious reflections on the fact that this initiative is politically the most important of all the initiatives, because our political experiment of democracy, the last refuge of cheap misgovernment, will ruin us if our citizens are ill bred.

When we two were born, this country was still dominated by a selected class bred by political marriages. The commercial class had not then completed the first twenty-five years of its new share of political power; and it was itself selected by money qualification, and bred, if not by political marriage, at least by a pretty rigorous class marriage. Aristocracy and plutocracy still furnish the figureheads of politics; but they are now dependent on the votes of the promiscuously bred masses. And this, if you please, at the very moment when the political problem, having suddenly ceased to mean a very limited and occa-

---

*In *The Marriage of Heaven and Hell* (c. 1790).

sional interference, mostly by way of jobbing public appointments, in the mismanagement of a tight but parochial little island, with occasional meaningless prosecution of dynastic wars, has become the industrial reorganization of Britain, the construction of a practically international Commonwealth, and the partition of the whole of Africa and perhaps the whole of Asia by the civilized Powers. Can you believe that the people whose conceptions of society and conduct, whose power of attention and scope of interest, are measured by the British theatre as you know it to-day, can either handle this colossal task themselves, or understand and support the sort of mind and character that is (at least comparatively) capable of handling it? For remember: what our voters are in the pit and gallery they are also in the polling booth. We are all now under what Burke called "the hoofs of the swinish multitude." Burke's language gave great offence because the implied exceptions to its universal application made it a class insult; and it certainly was not for the pot to call the kettle black. The aristocracy he defended, in spite of the political marriages by which it tried to secure breeding for itself, had its mind undertrained by silly schoolmasters and governesses, its character corrupted by gratuitous luxury, its self-respect adulterated to complete spuriousness by flattery and flunkeyism. It is no better to-day and never will be any better: our very peasants have something morally hardier in them that culminates occasionally in a Bunyan, a Burns, or a Carlyle. But observe, this aristocracy, which was overpowered from 1832 to 1885 by the middle class, has come back to power by the votes of "the swinish multitude." Tom Paine has triumphed over Edmund Burke; and the swine are now courted electors. How many of their own class have these electors sent to parliament? Hardly a dozen out of 670, and these only under the persuasion of conspicuous personal qualifications and popular eloquence. The multitude thus pronounces judgment on its own units: it admits itself unfit to govern, and will vote only for a man morphologically and generically transfigured by palatial residence and equipage, by transcendent tailoring, by the glamor of aristocratic kinship. Well, we two know these transfigured persons, these college passmen, these well groomed monocular Algys and Bobbies, these cricketers to whom age brings golf instead of wisdom, these plutocratic products of "the nail and sarspan* business as he got his money by." Do you know whether to laugh or cry at the notion that they, poor devils! will drive a team of continents as they drive a four-in-hand; turn a jostling anarchy of casual trade and speculation into an ordered productivity; and federate our colonies into a world-Power of the first magnitude? Give these people the most perfect political constitution and the soundest political program that benevolent omniscience can devise for them, and they will interpret it into mere fashionable folly or canting charity as infallibly as a savage converts the philosophical theology of a Scotch missionary into crude African idolatry.

I do not know whether you have any illusions left on the subject of education, progress, and so forth. I have none. Any pamphleteer can shew the way to better things; but when there is no will there is no way. My nurse was fond of remarking that you cannot make a silk purse out of a sow's ear, and the more I see of the efforts of our churches and universities and literary sages to raise the mass above its own level, the more convinced I am that my nurse was right. Progress can do nothing but make the most of us all as we are, and that most would clearly not be enough even if those who are already raised out of the lowest abysses would allow the others a chance. The bubble of Heredity has been pricked: the certainty that acquirements are negligible as elements in practical heredity has demolished the hopes of the educationists as well as the terrors of the degeneracy mongers; and we know now that there is no hereditary "governing class" any more than a hereditary hooliganism. We must either breed political capacity or be ruined by Democracy, which was forced on us by the failure of the older alternatives. Yet if Despotism failed only for want of a capable benevolent despot, what chance has Democracy, which requires a whole population of capable voters: that is, of political critics who, if they cannot govern in

---

*Saucepan.

person for lack of spare energy or specific talent for administration, can at least recognize and appreciate capacity and benevolence in others, and so govern through capably benevolent representatives? Where are such voters to be found to-day? Nowhere. Promiscuous breeding has produced a weakness of character that is too timid to face the full stringency of a thoroughly competitive struggle for existence and too lazy and petty to organize the commonwealth co-operatively. Being cowards, we defeat natural selection under cover of philanthropy: being sluggards, we neglect artificial selection under cover of delicacy and morality.

Yet we must get an electorate of capable critics or collapse as Rome and Egypt collapsed. At this moment the Roman decadent phase of p a n e m   e t   c i r c e n s e s* is being inaugurated under our eyes. Our newspapers and melodramas are blustering about our imperial destiny; but our eyes and hearts turn eagerly to the American millionaire. As his hand goes down to his pocket, our fingers go up to the brims of our hats by instinct. Our ideal prosperity is not the prosperity of the industrial north, but the prosperity of the Isle of Wight, of Folkestone and Ramsgate, of Nice and Monte Carlo. That is the only prosperity you see on the stage, where the workers are all footmen, parlourmaids, comic lodging-letters and fashionable professional men, whilst the heroes and heroines are miraculously provided with unlimited dividends, and eat gratuitously, like the knights in Don Quixote's books of chivalry. The city papers prate of the competition of Bombay with Manchester and the like. The real competition is the competition of Regent Street with the Rue de Rivoli, of Brighton and the south coast with the Riviera, for the spending money of the American Trusts. What is all this growing love of pageantry, this effusive loyalty, this officious rising and uncovering at a wave from a flag or a blast from a brass band? Imperialism? Not a bit of it. Obsequiousness, servility, cupidity roused by the prevailing smell of money. When Mr. Carnegie rat-

---

*Bread and games (Latin); from one of Juvenal's *Satires*.

tled his millions in his pockets all England became one rapacious cringe. Only, when Rhodes (who had probably been reading my Socialism for Millionaires) left word that no idler was to inherit his estate, the bent backs straightened mistrustfully for a moment. Could it be that the Diamond King was no gentleman after all? However, it was easy to ignore a rich man's solecism. The ungentlemanly clause was not mentioned again; and the backs soon bowed themselves back into their natural shape.

But I hear you asking me in alarm whether I have actually put all this tub thumping into a Don Juan comedy. I have not. I have only made my Don Juan a political pamphleteer, and given you his pamphlet in full by way of appendix. You will find it at the end of the book. I am sorry to say that it is a common practice with romancers to announce their hero as a man of extraordinary genius, and to leave his works entirely to the reader's imagination; so that at the end of the book you whisper to yourself ruefully that but for the author's solemn preliminary assurance you should hardly have given the gentleman credit for ordinary good sense. You cannot accuse me of this pitiable barrenness, this feeble evasion. I not only tell you that my hero wrote a revolutionists' handbook: I give you the handbook* at full length for your edification if you care to read it. And in that handbook you will find the politics of the sex question as I conceive Don Juan's descendant to understand them. Not that I disclaim the fullest responsibility for his opinions and for those of all my characters, pleasant and unpleasant. They are all right from their several points of view; and their points of view are, for the dramatic moment, mine also. This may puzzle the people who believe that there is such a thing as an absolutely right point of view, usually their own. It may seem to them that nobody who doubts this can be in a state of grace. However that may be, it is certainly true that nobody who agrees with them can possibly be a dramatist, or indeed anything else that turns

---

*Shaw appended Tanner's Revolutionist's Handbook to *Man and Superman*.

upon a knowledge of mankind. Hence it has been pointed out that Shakespear had no conscience. Neither have I, in that sense.[4]

You may, however, remind me that this digression of mine into politics was preceded by a very convincing demonstration that the artist never catches the point of view of the common man on the question of sex, because he is not in the same predicament. I first prove that anything I write on the relation of the sexes is sure to be misleading; and then I proceed to write a Don Juan play. Well, if you insist on asking me why I behave in this absurd way, I can only reply that you asked me to, and that in any case my treatment of the subject may be valid for the artist, amusing to the amateur, and at least intelligible and therefore possibly suggestive to the Philistine. Every man who records his illusions is providing data for the genuinely scientific psychology which the world still waits for. I plank down my view of the existing relations of men to women in the most highly civilized society for what it is worth. It is a view like any other view and no more, neither true nor false, but, I hope, a way of looking at the subject which throws into the familiar order of cause and effect a sufficient body of fact and experience to be interesting to you, if not to the playgoing public of London. I have certainly shewn little consideration for that public in this enterprise; but I know that it has the friendliest disposition towards you and me as far as it has any consciousness of our existence, and quite understands that what I write for you must pass at a considerable height over its simple romantic head. It will take my books as read and my genius for granted, trusting me to put forth work of such quality as shall bear out its verdict. So we may disport ourselves on our own plane to the top of our bent; and if any gentleman points out that neither this epistle dedicatory nor the dream of Don Juan in the third act of the ensuing comedy is suitable for immediate production at a popular theatre we need not contradict him. Napoleon provided Talma with a pit of kings, with what effect on Talma's acting is not recorded. As for me, what I have always wanted is a pit of philosophers; and this is a play for such a pit.

I should make formal acknowledgment to the authors whom I have pillaged in the following pages if I could recollect them all. The

theft of the brigand-poetaster from Sir Arthur Conan Doyle* is deliberate; and the metamorphosis of Leporello into Enry Straker,
motor engineer and New Man, is an intentional dramatic sketch for
the contemporary embryo of Mr. H. G. Wells's anticipation of the efficient engineering class which will, he hopes, finally sweep the jab-
berers out of the way of civilization. Mr. Barrie has also, whilst I am
correcting my proofs, delighted London with a servant who knows
more than his masters.† The conception of Mendoza Limited I trace
back to a certain West Indian colonial secretary, who, at a period
when he and I and Mr. Sidney Webb were sowing our political wild
oats as a sort of Fabian Three Musketeers, without any prevision of
the surprising respectability of the crop that followed, recommended
Webb, the encyclopedic and inexhaustible, to form himself into a
company for the benefit of the shareholders. Octavius I take over unaltered from Mozart; and I hereby authorize any actor who impersonates him, to sing "Dalla sua pace"‡ (if he can) at any convenient
moment during the representation. Ann was suggested to me by the
fifteenth century Dutch morality called Everyman, which Mr.
William Poel has lately resuscitated so triumphantly. I trust he will
work that vein further, and recognize that Elizabethan Renascence
fustian is no more bearable after medieval poesy than Scribe after
Ibsen. As I sat watching Everyman at the Charterhouse, I said to myself Why not Everywoman? Ann was the result: every woman is not
Ann; but Ann is Everywoman.

That the author of Everyman was no mere artist, but an artist-
philosopher, and that the artist-philosophers are the only sort of
artists I take quite seriously, will be no news to you. Even Plato and
Boswell, as the dramatists who invented Socrates and Dr Johnson,
impress me more deeply than the romantic playwrights. Ever since,

---

*Shaw's Mendoza derives from Doyle's El Cuchillo in *The Exploits of Brigadier Gerard* (1896).

†Shaw is referring to J. M. Barrie's *The Admirable Crichton* (1902).

‡On her peace (Italian).

as a boy, I first breathed the air of the transcendental regions at a performance of Mozart's Zauberflöte, I have been proof against the garish splendors and alcoholic excitements of the ordinary stage combinations of Tappertitian* romance with the police intelligence. Bunyan, Blake, Hogarth and Turner (these four apart and above all the English classics), Goethe, Shelley, Schopenhaur, Wagner, Ibsen, Morris, Tolstoy, and Nietzsche are among the writers whose peculiar sense of the world I recognize as more or less akin to my own. Mark the word peculiar. I read Dickens and Shakespear without shame or stint; but their pregnant observations and demonstrations of life are not co-ordinated into any philosophy or religion: on the contrary, Dickens's sentimental assumptions are violently contradicted by his observations; and Shakespear's pessimism is only his wounded humanity. Both have the specific genius of the fictionist and the common sympathies of human feeling and thought in pre-eminent degree. They are often saner and shrewder than the philosophers just as Sancho-Panza was often saner and shrewder than Don Quixote. They clear away vast masses of oppressive gravity by their sense of the ridiculous, which is at bottom a combination of sound moral judgment with lighthearted good humor. But they are concerned with the diversities of the world instead of with its unities: they are so irreligious that they exploit popular religion for professional purposes without delicacy or scruple (for example, Sydney Carton and the ghost in Hamlet!): they are anarchical, and cannot balance their exposures of Angelo and Dogberry, Sir Leicester Dedlock and Mr. Tite Barnacle,† with any portrait of a prophet or a worthy leader: they have no constructive ideas: they regard those who have them as dangerous fanatics: in all their fictions there is no leading thought or inspiration for which any man could conceivably risk the spoiling of

---

*Simon Tappertit, in Dickens's *Barnaby Rudge* (1841), schemes to marry above his station.

†Sir Leicester Dedlock and Mr. Tite Barnicle are characters in Dickens's *Bleak House* (1853) and *Little Dorrit* (1857), respectively.

his hat in a shower, much less his life. Both are alike forced to borrow motives for the more strenuous actions of their personages from the common stockpot of melodramatic plots; so that Hamlet has to be stimulated by the prejudices of a policeman and Macbeth by the cupidities of a bushranger. Dickens, without the excuse of having to manufacture motives for Hamlets and Macbeths, superfluously punts his crew down the stream of his monthly parts by mechanical devices which I leave you to describe, my own memory being quite baffled by the simplest question as to Monks in Oliver Twist, or the long lost parentage of Smike, or the relations between the Dorrit and Clennam families so inopportunely discovered by Monsieur Rigaud Blandois. The truth is, the world was to Shakespear a great "stage of fools" on which he was utterly bewildered. He could see no sort of sense in living at all; and Dickens saved himself from the despair of the dream in The Chimes by taking the world for granted and busying himself with its details. Neither of them could do anything with a serious positive character: they could place a human figure before you with perfect verisimilitude; but when the moment came for making it live and move, they found, unless it made them laugh, that they had a puppet on their hands, and had to invent some artificial external stimulus to make it work. This is what is the matter with Hamlet all through: he has no will except in his bursts of temper. Foolish Bardolaters make a virtue of this after their fashion: they declare that the play is the tragedy of irresolution; but all Shakespear's projections of the deepest humanity he knew have the same defect: their characters and manners are lifelike; but their actions are forced on them from without, and the external force is grotesquely inappropriate except when it is quite conventional, as in the case of Henry V. Falstaff is more vivid than any of these serious reflective characters, because he is self-acting: his motives are his own appetites and instincts and humors. Richard III, too, is delightful as the whimsical comedian who stops a funeral to make love to the corpse's widow; but when, in the next act, he is replaced by a stage villain who smothers babies and offs with people's heads, we are revolted at the imposture and repudiate the changeling. Faulconbridge, Coriolanus, Leontes are admirable descriptions of instinctive temperaments: indeed the play of Coriolanus is the greatest of Shakespear's comedies;[5] but description is not philosophy; and comedy neither compromises the author nor reveals him. He must be judged by those characters into which he puts what he knows of himself, his Hamlets and Macbeths and Lears and Prosperos. If these characters are agonizing in a void about factitious melodramatic murders and revenges and the like, whilst the comic characters walk with their feet on solid ground, vivid and amusing, you know that the author has much to shew and nothing to teach. The comparison between Falstaff and Prospero is like the comparison between Micawber and David Copperfield. At the end of the book you know Micawber, whereas you only know what has happened to David, and are not interested enough in him to wonder what his politics or religion might be if anything so stupendous as a religious or political idea, or a general idea of any sort, were to occur to him. He is tolerable as a child; but he never becomes a man, and might be left out of his own biography altogether but for his usefulness as a stage confidant, a Horatio or "Charles his friend"—what they call on the stage a feeder.

Now you cannot say this of the works of the artist-philosophers. You cannot say it, for instance, of The Pilgrim's Progress. Put your Shakespearian hero and coward, Henry V and Pistol or Parolles, beside Mr. Valiant and Mr. Fearing, and you have a sudden revelation of the abyss that lies between the fashionable author who could see nothing in the world but personal aims and the tragedy of their disappointment or the comedy of their incongruity, and the field preacher who achieved virtue and courage by identifying himself with the purpose of the world as he understood it. The contrast is enormous: Bunyan's coward stirs your blood more than Shakespear's hero, who actually leaves you cold and secretly hostile. You suddenly see that Shakespear, with all his flashes and divinations, never understood virtue and courage, never conceived how any man who was not a fool could, like Bunyan's hero, look back from the brink of the river of death over the strife and labor of his pilgrimage, and say "yet do I not repent me"; or, with the panache of a millionaire, bequeath "my sword to him that shall succeed me in my pilgrimage, and my courage and skill to him that can get it." This is the true joy in life, the being used for a purpose recognized by yourself as a mighty one; the being thoroughly worn out before you are thrown on the scrap heap; the being a force of Nature instead of a feverish selfish little clod of ailments and grievances complaining that the world will not devote itself to making you happy. And also the only real tragedy in life is the being used by personally minded men for purposes which you recognize to be base. All the rest is at worst mere misfortune or mortality: this alone is misery, slavery, hell on earth; and the revolt against it is the only force that offers a man's work to the poor artist, whom our personally minded rich people would so willingly employ as pandar, buffoon, beauty monger, sentimentalizer and the like.

It may seem a long step from Bunyan to Nietzsche; but the difference between their conclusions is purely formal. Bunyan's perception that righteousness is filthy rags, his scorn for Mr. Legality in the village of Morality, his defiance of the Church as the supplanter of religion, his insistence on courage as the virtue of virtues, his estimate of the career of the conventionally respectable and sensible Worldly Wiseman as no better at bottom than the life and death of Mr. Badman: all this, expressed by Bunyan in the terms of a tinker's theology, is what Nietzsche has expressed in terms of post-Darwinian, post-Schopenhaurian philosophy; Wagner in terms of polytheistic mythology; and Ibsen in terms of mid-XIX century Parisian dramaturgy. Nothing is new in these matters except their novelties: for instance, it is a novelty to call Justification by Faith "Wille," and Justification by Works "Vorstellung." The sole use of the novelty is that you and I buy and read Schopenhaur's treatise on Will and Representation when we should not dream of buying a set of sermons on Faith versus Works. At bottom the controversy is the same, and the dramatic results are the same. Bunyan makes no attempt to present his pilgrims as more sensible or better conducted than Mr. Worldly Wiseman. Mr. W. W.'s worst enemies, as Mr. Embezzler, Mr. Never-go-to-Church-on-Sunday, Mr. Bad Form, Mr. Murderer, Mr. Burglar, Mr. Co-respondent, Mr. Blackmailer, Mr. Cad, Mr. Drunkard, Mr. Labor Agitator and so forth, can read the Pilgrim's Progress without finding a word said against them; whereas the respectable people who snub them and put them in prison, such as Mr. W. W. himself and his young friend Civility; Formalist and Hypocrisy; Wildhead, Inconsiderate, and Pragmatick (who were clearly young university men of good family and high feeding); that brisk lad Ignorance, Talkative, By-Ends of Fair-speech and his mother-in-law Lady Feigning, and other reputable gentlemen and citizens, catch it very severely. Even Little Faith, though he gets to heaven at last, is given to understand that it served him right to be mobbed by the brothers Faint Heart, Mistrust, and Guilt, all three recognized members of respectable society and veritable pillars of the law. The whole allegory is a consistent attack on morality and respectability, without a word that one can remember against vice and crime. Exactly what is complained of in Nietzsche and Ibsen, is it not? And also exactly what would be complained of in all the literature which is great enough and old enough to have attained canonical rank, officially or unofficially, were it not that books are admitted to the canon by a compact which confesses their greatness in consideration of abrogating their meaning; so that the reverend rector can agree with the prophet Micah as to his inspired style without being committed to any complicity in Micah's furiously Radical opinions. Why, even I, as I force myself, pen in hand, into recognition and civility, find all the force of my onslaught destroyed by a simple policy of non-resistance. In vain do I redouble the violence of the language in which I proclaim my heterodoxies. I rail at the theistic credulity of Voltaire, the amoristic superstition of Shelley, the revival of tribal soothsaying and idolatrous rites which Huxley called Science and mistook for an advance on the Pentateuch, no less than at the welter of ecclesiastical and professional humbug which saves the face of the stupid system of violence and robbery which we call Law and Industry. Even atheists reproach me with infidelity and anarchists with nihilism because I can-

not endure their moral tirades. And yet, instead of exclaiming "Send this inconceivable Satanist to the stake," the respectable newspapers pith me by announcing "another book by this brilliant and thoughtful writer." And the ordinary citizen, knowing that an author who is well spoken of by a respectable newspaper must be all right, reads me, as he reads Micah, with undisturbed edification from his own point of view. It is narrated that in the eighteenseventies an old lady, a very devout Methodist, moved from Colchester to a house in the neighborhood of the City Road, in London, where, mistaking the Hall of Science for a chapel, she sat at the feet of Charles Bradlaugh for many years, entranced by his eloquence, without questioning his orthodoxy or moulting a feather of her faith. I fear I shall be defrauded of my just martyrdom in the same way.

However, I am digressing, as a man with a grievance always does. And after all, the main thing in determining the artistic quality of a book is not the opinions it propagates, but the fact that the writer has opinions. The old lady from Colchester was right to sun her simple soul in the energetic radiance of Bradlaugh's genuine beliefs and disbeliefs rather than in the chill of such mere painting of light and heat as elocution and convention can achieve. My contempt for belles lettres, and for amateurs who become the heroes of the fanciers of literary virtuosity, is not founded on any illusion of mind as to the permanence of those forms of thought (call them opinions) by which I strive to communicate my bent to my fellows. To younger men they are already outmoded; for though they have no more lost their logic than an eighteenth century pastel has lost its drawing or its color, yet, like the pastel, they grow indefinably shabby, and will grow shabbier until they cease to count at all, when my books will either perish, or, if the world is still poor enough to want them, will have to stand, with Bunyan's, by quite amorphous qualities of temper and energy. With this conviction I cannot be a bellettrist. No doubt I must recognize, as even the Ancient Mariner did, that I must tell my story entertainingly if I am to hold the wedding guest spellbound in spite of the siren sounds of the loud bassoon. But " for art's sake" alone I

would not face the toil of writing a single sentence. I know that there are men who, having nothing to say and nothing to write, are nevertheless so in love with oratory and with literature that they keep desperately repeating as much as they can understand of what others have said or written aforetime. I know that the leisurely tricks which their want of conviction leaves them free to play with the diluted and misapprehended message supply them with a pleasant parlor game which they call style. I can pity their dotage and even sympathize with their fancy. But a true original style is never achieved for its own sake: a man may pay from a shilling to a guinea, according to his means, to see, hear, or read another man's act of genius; but he will not pay with his whole life and soul to become a mere virtuoso in literature, exhibiting an accomplishment which will not even make money for him, like fiddle playing. Effectiveness of assertion is the Alpha and Omega of style. He who has nothing to assert has no style and can have none: he who has something to assert will go as far in power of style as its momentousness and his conviction will carry him. Disprove his assertion after it is made, yet its style remains. Darwin has no more destroyed the style of Job nor of Handel than Martin Luther destroyed the style of Giotto. All the assertions get disproved sooner or later; and so we find the world full of a magnificent débris of artistic fossils, with the matter-of-fact credibility gone clean out of them, but the form still splendid. And that is why the old masters play the deuce with our mere susceptibles. Your Royal Academician thinks he can get the style of Giotto without Giotto's beliefs, and correct his perspective into the bargain. Your man of letters thinks he can get Bunyan's or Shakespear's style without Bunyan's conviction or Shakespear's apprehension, especially if he takes care not to split his infinitives. And so with your Doctors of Music, who, with their collections of discords duly prepared and resolved or retarded or anticipated in the manner of the great composers, think they can learn the art of Palestrina from Cherubini's treatise. All this academic art is far worse than the trade in sham antique furniture; for the man who sells me an oaken chest which he swears was made

in the XIII century, though as a matter of fact he made it himself only yesterday, at least does not pretend that there are any modern ideas in it, whereas your academic copier of fossils offers them to you as the latest outpouring of the human spirit, and, worst of all, kidnaps young people as pupils and persuades them that his limitations are rules, his observances dexterities, his timidities good taste, and his emptinesses purities. And when he declares that art should not be didactic, all the people who have nothing to teach and all the people who dont want to learn agree with him emphatically.

I pride myself on not being one of these susceptibles. If you study the electric light with which I supply you in that Bumbledonian public capacity of mine over which you make merry from time to time, you will find that your house contains a great quantity of highly susceptible copper wire which gorges itself with electricity and gives you no light whatever. But here and there occurs a scrap of intensely insusceptible, intensely resistant material; and that stubborn scrap grapples with the current and will not let it through until it has made itself useful to you as those two vital qualities of literature, light and heat. Now if I am to be no mere copper wire amateur but a luminous author, I must also be a most intensely refractory person, liable to go out and to go wrong at inconvenient moments, and with incendiary possibilities. These are the faults of my qualities; and I assure you that I sometimes dislike myself so much that when some irritable reviewer chances at that moment to pitch into me with zest, I feel unspeakably relieved and obliged. But I never dream of reforming, knowing that I must take myself as I am and get what work I can out of myself. All this you will understand; for there is community of material between us: we are both critics of life as well as of art; and you have perhaps said to yourself when I have passed your windows "There, but for the grace of God, go I." An awful and chastening reflection, which shall be the closing cadence of this immoderately long letter from yours faithfully,

G. BERNARD SHAW.
Woking, 1903.

# MAN AND SUPERMAN

## ACT I

*Roebuck Ramsden is in his study, opening the morning letters. The
study, handsomely and solidly furnished, proclaims the man of means.
Not a speck of dust is visible: it is clear that there are at least two
housemaids and a parlormaid downstairs, and a housekeeper upstairs
who does not let them spare elbow-grease. Even the top of Roebuck's
head is polished: on a sunshiny day he could heliograph his orders to
distant camps by merely nodding. In no other respect, however, does he
suggest the military man. It is in active civil life that men get his broad
air of importance, his dignified expectation of deference, his
determinate mouth disarmed and refined since the hour of his success
by the withdrawal of opposition and the concession of comfort and
precedence and power. He is more than a highly respectable man: he is
marked out as a president of highly respectable men, a chairman
among directors, an alderman among councillors, a mayor among
aldermen. Four tufts of iron-grey hair, which will soon be as white as
isinglass, and are in other respects not at all unlike it, grow in two
symmetrical pairs above his ears and at the angles of his spreading
jaws. He wears a black frock coat, a white waistcoat (it is bright spring
weather), and trousers, neither black nor perceptibly blue, of one of
those indefinitely mixed hues which the modern clothier has produced
to harmonize with the religions of respectable men. He has not been
out of doors yet to-day; so he still wears his slippers, his boots being
ready for him on the hearthrug. Surmising that he has no valet, and
seeing that he has no secretary with a shorthand notebook and a*

*typewriter, one meditates on how little our great burgess domesticity
has been disturbed by new fashions and methods, or by the enterprise of
the railway and hotel companies which sell you a Saturday to Monday
of life at Folkestone as a real gentleman for two guineas, first class fares
both ways included.*

*How old is Roebuck? The question is important on the threshold of
a drama of ideas; for under such circumstances everything depends on
whether his adolescence belonged to the sixties or to the eighties. He
was born, as a matter of fact, in 1839, and was a Unitarian and Free
Trader from his boyhood, and an Evolutionist from the publication of
the Origin of Species. Consequently he has always classed himself as an
advanced thinker and fearlessly outspoken reformer.*

*Sitting at his writing table, he has on his right the windows giving
on Portland Place. Through these, as through a proscenium, the curious
spectator may contemplate his profile as well as the blinds will permit.
On his left is the inner wall, with a stately bookcase, and the door not
quite in the middle, but somewhat further from him. Against the wall
opposite him are two busts on pillars: one, to his left, of John Bright;
the other, to his right, of Mr. Herbert Spencer. Between them hang an
engraved portrait of Richard Cobden; enlarged photographs of
Martineau, Huxley, and George Eliot; autotypes of allegories by Mr.
G. F. Watts (for Roebuck believes in the fine arts with all the
earnestness of a man who does not understand them), and an
impression of Dupont's engraving of Delaroche's Beaux Arts hemicycle,
representing the great men of all ages. On the wall behind him, above
the mantelshelf, is a family portrait of impenetrable obscurity.*

*A chair stands near the writing table for the convenience of business
visitors. Two other chairs are against the wall between the busts.*

*A parlormaid enters with a visitor's card. ROEBUCK takes it, and nods,
pleased. Evidently a welcome caller.*

RAMSDEN     Shew him up.

*The parlormaid goes out and returns with the visitor.*

THE MAID    Mr. Robinson.

*MR. ROBINSON is really an uncommonly nice looking young fellow. He must, one thinks, be the jeune premier;\* for it is not in reason to suppose that a second such attractive male figure should appear in one story. The slim, shapely frame, the elegant suit of new mourning, the small head and regular features, the pretty little moustache, the frank clear eyes, the wholesome bloom on the youthful complexion, the well brushed glossy hair, not curly, but of fine texture and good dark color, the arch of good nature in the eyebrows, the erect forehead and neatly pointed chin, all announce the man who will love and suffer later on. And that he will not do so without sympathy is guaranteed by an engaging sincerity and eager modest serviceableness which stamp him as a man of amiable nature. The moment he appears, RAMSDEN's face expands into fatherly liking and welcome, an expression which drops into one of decorous grief as the young man approaches him with sorrow in his face as well as in his black clothes. RAMSDEN seems to know the nature of the bereavement. As the visitor advances silently to the writing table, the old man rises and shakes his hand across it without a word: a long, affectionate shake which tells the story of a recent sorrow common to both.*

RAMSDEN [*concluding the handshake and cheering up*]    Well, well, Octavius, it's the common lot. We must all face it some day. Sit down.

*OCTAVIUS takes the visitor's chair. RAMSDEN replaces himself in his own.*

OCTAVIUS    Yes: we must face it, Mr. Ramsden. But I owed him a great deal. He did everything for me that my father could have done if he had lived.

RAMSDEN    He had no son of his own, you see.

OCTAVIUS    But he had daughters; and yet he was as good to my sister as to me. And his death was so sudden! I always intended to thank him—to let him know that I had not taken all his care of me as a matter of course, as any boy takes his father's care. But I waited for an opportunity; and now he is dead—dropped with-

---

*French theatrical term for the young male lead.

out a moment's warning. He will never know what I felt. [*He takes out his handkerchief and cries unaffectedly*].

RAMSDEN    How do we know that, Octavius? He may know it: we cannot tell. Come! dont grieve. [*OCTAVIUS masters himself and puts up his handkerchief*]. Thats right. Now let me tell you something to console you. The last time I saw him—it was in this very room—he said to me: "Tavy is a generous lad and the soul of honor; and when I see how little consideration other men get from their sons, I realize how much better than a son hes been to me." There! Doesnt that do you good?

OCTAVIUS    Mr. Ramsden: he used to say to me that he had met only one man in the world who was the soul of honor, and that was Roebuck Ramsden.

RAMSDEN    Oh, that was his partiality: we were very old friends, you know. But there was something else he used to say about you. I wonder whether I ought to tell you or not!

OCTAVIUS    You know best.

RAMSDEN    It was something about his daughter.

OCTAVIUS [*eagerly*]    About Ann! Oh, do tell me that, Mr. Ramsden.

RAMSDEN    Well, he said he was glad, after all, you were not his son, because he thought that someday Annie and you—[*OCTAVIUS blushes vividly*]. Well, perhaps I shouldn't have told you. But he was in earnest.

OCTAVIUS    Oh, if only I thought I had a chance! You know, Mr. Ramsden, I don't care about money or about what people call position; and I can't bring myself to take an interest in the business of struggling for them. Well, Ann has a most exquisite nature; but she is so accustomed to be in the thick of that sort of thing that she thinks a man's character incomplete if he is not ambitious. She knows that if she married me she would have to reason herself out of being ashamed of me for not being a big success of some kind.

RAMSDEN [*getting up and planting himself with his back to the fire-*

*place*] Nonsense, my boy, nonsense! You're too modest. What does she know about the real value of men at her age? [*More seriously*] Besides, she's a wonderfully dutiful girl. Her father's wish would be sacred to her. Do you know that since she grew up to years of discretion, I don't believe she has ever once given her own wish as a reason for doing anything or not doing it. It's always "Father wishes me to," or "Mother wouldn't like it." It's really almost a fault in her. I have often told her she must learn to think for herself.

OCTAVIUS [*shaking his head*]   I couldn't ask her to marry me because her father wished it, Mr. Ramsden.

RAMSDEN   Well, perhaps not. No: of course not. I see that. No: you certainly couldn't. But when you win her on your own merits, it will be a great happiness to her to fulfil her father's desire as well as her own. Eh? Come! you'll ask her, won't you?

OCTAVIUS [*with sad gaiety*]   At all events I promise you I shall never ask anyone else.

RAMSDEN   Oh, you shan't need to. She'll accept you, my boy— although [*here he suddenly becomes very serious indeed*] you have one great drawback.

OCTAVIUS [*anxiously*]   What drawback is that, Mr. Ramsden? I should rather say which of my many drawbacks?

RAMSDEN   I'll tell you, Octavius. [*He takes from the table a book bound in red cloth*]. I have in my hand a copy of the most infamous, the most scandalous, the most mischievous, the most blackguardly book that ever escaped burning at the hands of the common hangman. I have not read it: I would not soil my mind with such filth; but I have read what the papers say of it. The title is quite enough for me. [*He reads it*]. The Revolutionist's Handbook and Pocket Companion. By John Tanner, M.I.R.C., Member of the Idle Rich Class.

OCTAVIUS [*smiling*]   But Jack—

RAMSDEN [*testily*]   For goodness' sake, don't call him Jack under my roof [*he throws the book violently down on the table. Then, some-*

*what relieved, he comes past the table to OCTAVIUS, and addresses him at close quarters with impressive gravity*]. Now, Octavius, I know that my dead friend was right when he said you were a generous lad. I know that this man was your schoolfellow, and that you feel bound to stand by him because there was a boyish friendship between you. But I ask you to consider the altered circumstances. You were treated as a son in my friend's house. You lived there; and your friends could not be turned from the door. This man Tanner was in and out there on your account almost from his childhood. He addresses Annie by her Christian name as freely as you do. Well, while her father was alive, that was her father's business, not mine. This man Tanner was only a boy to him: his opinions were something to be laughed at, like a man's hat on a child's head. But now Tanner is a grown man and Annie a grown woman. And her father is gone. We don't as yet know the exact terms of his will; but he often talked it over with me; and I have no more doubt than I have that you're sitting there that the will appoints me Annie's trustee and guardian. [*Forcibly*] Now I tell you, once for all, I can't and I won't have Annie placed in such a position that she must, out of regard for you, suffer the intimacy of this fellow Tanner. It's not fair: it's not right: it's not kind. What are you going to do about it?

OCTAVIUS    But Ann herself has told Jack that whatever his opinions are, he will always be welcome because he knew her dear father.

RAMSDEN [*out of patience*]    That girl's mad about her duty to her parents. [*He starts off like a goaded ox in the direction of John Bright, in whose expression there is no sympathy for him. As he speaks he fumes down to Herbert Spencer, who receives him still more coldly*]. Excuse me, Octavius; but there are limits to social toleration. You know that I am not a bigoted or prejudiced man. You know that I am plain Roebuck Ramsden when other men who have done less have got handles to their names, because I have stood for equality and liberty of conscience while they were truckling to the

Church and to the aristocracy. Whitefield and I lost chance after chance through our advanced opinions. But I draw the line at Anarchism and Free Love and that sort of thing. If I am to be Annie's guardian, she will have to learn that she has a duty to me. I won't have it: I will n o t have it. She must forbid John Tanner the house; and so must you.

*The parlormaid returns.*

OCTAVIUS   But—

RAMSDEN [*calling his attention to the servant*]   Ssh! Well?

THE MAID   Mr. Tanner wishes to see you, sir.

RAMSDEN   Mr. Tanner!

OCTAVIUS   Jack!

RAMSDEN   How dare Mr. Tanner call on me! Say I cannot see him.

OCTAVIUS [*hurt*]   I am sorry you are turning my friend from your door like that.

THE MAID [*calmly*]   He's not at the door, sir. He's upstairs in the drawingroom with Miss Ramsden. He came with Mrs. Whitefield and Miss Ann and Miss Robinson, sir.

*RAMSDEN's feelings are beyond words.*

OCTAVIUS [*grinning*]   That's very like Jack, Mr. Ramsden. You must see him, even if it's only to turn him out.

RAMSDEN [*hammering out his words with suppressed fury*]   Go upstairs and ask Mr. Tanner to be good enough to step down here. [*The parlormaid goes out; and RAMSDEN returns to the fireplace, as to a fortified position*]. I must say that of all the confounded pieces of impertinence—well, if these are Anarchist manners, I hope you like them. And Annie with him! Annie! A—[*he chokes*].

OCTAVIUS   Yes: that's what surprises m e . He's so desperately afraid of Ann. There must be something the matter.

*MR. JOHN TANNER suddenly opens the door and enters. He is too young to be described simply as a big man with a beard. But it is already plain that middle life will find him in that category. He has still some of the slimness of youth; but youthfulness is not the effect he aims at: his frock coat would befit a prime minister; and a certain high chested car-*

*riage of the shoulders, a lofty pose of the head, and the Olympian majesty with which a mane, or rather a huge wisp, of hazel colored hair is thrown back from an imposing brow, suggest Jupiter rather than Apollo. He is prodigiously fluent of speech, restless, excitable (mark the snorting nostril and the restless blue eye, just the thirty-secondth of an inch too wide open), possibly a little mad. He is carefully dressed, not from the vanity that cannot resist finery, but from a sense of the importance of everything he does which leads him to make as much of paying a call as other men do of getting married or laying a foundation stone. A sensitive, susceptible, exaggerative, earnest man: a megalomaniac, who would be lost without a sense of humor.*

*Just at present the sense of humor is in abeyance. To say that he is excited is nothing: all his moods are phases of excitement. He is now in the panic-stricken phase; and he walks straight up to RAMSDEN as if with the fixed intention of shooting him on his own hearthrug. But what he pulls from his breast pocket is not a pistol, but a foolscap document which he thrusts under the indignant nose of RAMSDEN as he exclaims—*

TANNER    Ramsden: do you know what that is?

RAMSDEN [*loftily*]    No, sir.

TANNER    It's a copy of Whitefield's will. Ann got it this morning.

RAMSDEN    When you say Ann, you mean, I presume, Miss Whitefield.

TANNER    I mean our Ann, your Ann, Tavy's Ann, and now, Heaven help me, m y Ann!

OCTAVIUS [*rising, very pale*]    What do you mean?

TANNER    Mean! [*He holds up the will*]. Do you know who is appointed Ann's guardian by this will?

RAMSDEN [*coolly*]    I believe I am.

TANNER    You! You and I, man. I! I!! I!!! Both of us! [*He flings the will down on the writing table*].

RAMSDEN    You! Impossible.

TANNER    It's only too hideously true. [*He throws himself into OCTAVIUS's chair*]. Ramsden: get me out of it somehow. You don't know Ann as well as I do. She'll commit every crime a respectable woman can; and she'll justify everyone of them by saying that it was the wish of her guardians. She'll put everything on us; and we shall have no more control over her than a couple of mice over a cat.

OCTAVIUS    Jack: I wish you wouldn't talk like that about Ann.

TANNER    This chap's in love with her: that's another complication. Well, she'll either jilt him and say I didn't approve of him, or marry him and say you ordered her to. I tell you, this is the most staggering blow that has ever fallen on a man of my age and temperament.

RAMSDEN    Let me see that will, sir. [*He goes to the writing table and picks it up*]. I cannot believe that my old friend Whitefield would have shewn such a want of confidence in me as to associate me with— [*His countenance falls as he reads*].

TANNER    It's all my own doing: that's the horrible irony of it. He told me one day that you were to be Ann's guardian; and like a fool I began arguing with him about the folly of leaving a young woman under the control of an old man with obsolete ideas.

RAMSDEN [*stupended*]    My ideas obsolete!!!!!!!

TANNER    Totally. I had just finished an essay called Down with Government by the Greyhaired; and I was full of arguments and illustrations. I said the proper thing was to combine the experience of an old hand with the vitality of a young one. Hang me if he didn't take me at my word and alter his will—it's dated only a fortnight after that conversation—appointing me as joint guardian with you!

RAMSDEN [*pale and determined*]    I shall refuse to act.

TANNER    What's the good of that? I've been refusing all the way from Richmond; but Ann keeps on saying that of course she's only an orphan; and that she can't expect the people who were glad to come to the house in her father's time to trouble much about her now. That's the latest game. An orphan! It's like hearing an ironclad talk about being at the mercy of the winds and waves.

OCTAVIUS    This is not fair, Jack. She is an orphan. And you ought
to stand by her.

TANNER    Stand by her! What danger is she in? She has the law on
her side; she has popular sentiment on her side; she has plenty of
money and no conscience. All she wants with me is to load up all
her moral responsibilities on me, and do as she likes at the
expense of my character. I can't control her; and she can compromise me as much as she likes. I might as well be her husband.

RAMSDEN    You can refuse to accept the guardianship. *I* shall certainly refuse to hold it jointly with you.

TANNER    Yes; and what will she say to that? what d o e s she say
to it? Just that her father's wishes are sacred to her, and that she
shall always look up to me as her guardian whether I care to face
the responsibility or not. Refuse! You might as well refuse to accept the embraces of a boa constrictor when once it gets round
your neck.

OCTAVIUS    This sort of talk is not kind to me, Jack.

TANNER [*rising and going to* OCTAVIUS *to console him, but still lament-
ing*]    If he wanted a young guardian, why didn't he appoint Tavy?

RAMSDEN    Ah! why indeed?

OCTAVIUS    I will tell you. He sounded me about it; but I refused
the trust because I loved her. I had no right to let myself be
forced on her as a guardian by her father. He spoke to her about
it; and she said I was right. You know I love her, Mr. Ramsden;
and Jack knows it too. If Jack loved a woman, I would not compare her to a boa constrictor in his presence, however much I
might dislike her [*he sits down between the busts and turns his face to
the wall*].

RAMSDEN    I do not believe that Whitefield was in his right senses
when he made that will. You have admitted that he made it under
your influence.

TANNER    You ought to be pretty well obliged to me for my influence. He leaves you two thousand five hundred for your trouble.

He leaves Tavy a dowry for his sister and five thousand for him-self.

OCTAVIUS [*his tears flowing afresh*]   Oh, I can't take it. He was too good to us.

TANNER   You won't get it, my boy, if Ramsden upsets the will.

RAMSDEN   Ha! I see. You have got me in a cleft stick.

TANNER   He leaves m e nothing but the charge of Ann's morals, on the ground that I have already more money than is good for me. That shews that he had his wits about him, doesn't it?

RAMSDEN [*grimly*]   I admit that.

OCTAVIUS [*rising and coming from his refuge by the wall*]   Mr. Rams-den: I think you are prejudiced against Jack. He is a man of honor, and incapable of abusing——

TANNER   Don't, Tavy: you'll make me ill. I am not a man of honor: I am a man struck down by a dead hand. Tavy: you must marry her after all and take her off my hands. And I had set my heart on saving you from her!

OCTAVIUS   Oh, Jack, you talk of saving me from my highest hap-piness.

TANNER   Yes, a lifetime of happiness. If it were only the first half hour's happiness, Tavy, I would buy it for you with my last penny. But a lifetime of happiness! No man alive could bear it: it would be hell on earth.

RAMSDEN [*violently*]   Stuff, sir. Talk sense; or else go and waste someone else's time: I have something better to do than listen to your fooleries [*he positively kicks his way to his table and resumes his seat*].

TANNER   You hear him, Tavy! Not an idea in his head later than eighteensixty. We can't leave Ann with no other guardian to turn to.

RAMSDEN   I am proud of your contempt for my character and opinions, sir. Your own are set forth in that book, I believe.

TANNER [*eagerly going to the table*]   What! You've got my book! What do you think of it?

RAMSDEN    Do you suppose I would read such a book, sir?

TANNER    Then why did you buy it?

RAMSDEN    I did n o t buy it, sir. It has been sent me by some foolish lady who seems to admire your views. I was about to dispose of it when Octavius interrupted me. I shall do so now, with your permission. [*He throws the book into the waste paper basket with such vehemence that TANNER recoils under the impression that it is being thrown at his head*].

TANNER    You have no more manners than I have myself. However, that saves ceremony between us. [*He sits down again*]. What do you intend to do about this will?

OCTAVIUS    May I make a suggestion?

RAMSDEN    Certainly, Octavius.

OCTAVIUS    Arn't we forgetting that Ann herself may have some wishes in this matter?

RAMSDEN    I quite intend that Annie's wishes shall be consulted in every reasonable way. But she is only a woman, and a young and inexperienced woman at that.

TANNER    Ramsden: I begin to pity you.

RAMSDEN    [*hotly*]    I don't want to know how you feel towards me, Mr. Tanner.

TANNER    Ann will do just exactly what she likes. And what's more, she'll force us to advise her to do it; and she'll put the blame on us if it turns out badly. So, as Tavy is longing to see her—

OCTAVIUS    [*shyly*]    I am not, Jack.

TANNER    You lie, Tavy: you are. So let's have her down from the drawingroom and ask her what she intends us to do. Off with you, Tavy, and fetch her. [*TAVY turns to go*]. And don't be long; for the strained relations between myself and Ramsden will make the interval rather painful [*RAMSDEN compresses his lips, but says nothing*].

OCTAVIUS    Never mind him, Mr. Ramsden. He's not serious. [*He goes out*].

RAMSDEN [*very deliberately*]   Mr. Tanner: you are the most impudent person I have ever met.

TANNER [*seriously*]   I know it, Ramsden. Yet even I cannot wholly conquer shame. We live in an atmosphere of shame. We are ashamed of everything that is real about us; ashamed of ourselves, of our relatives, of our incomes, of our accents, of our opinions, of our experience, just as we are ashamed of our naked skins. Good Lord, my dear Ramsden, we are ashamed to walk, ashamed to ride in an omnibus, ashamed to hire a hansom instead of keeping a carriage, ashamed of keeping one horse instead of two and a groom-gardener instead of a coachman and footman. The more things a man is ashamed of, the more respectable he is. Why, you're ashamed to buy my book, ashamed to read it: the only thing you're not ashamed of is to judge me for it without having read it; and even that only means that you're ashamed to have heterodox opinions. Look at the effect I produce because my fairy godmother withheld from me this gift of shame. I have every possible virtue that a man can have except—

RAMSDEN   I am glad you think so well of yourself.

TANNER   All you mean by that is that you think I ought to be ashamed of talking about my virtues. You don't mean that I havn't got them: you know perfectly well that I am as sober and honest a citizen as yourself, as truthful personally, and much more truthful politically and morally.

RAMSDEN [*touched on his most sensitive point*]   I deny that. I will not allow you or any man to treat me as if I were a mere member of the British public. I detest its prejudices; I scorn its narrowness; I demand the right to think for myself. You pose as an advanced man. Let me tell you that I was an advanced man before you were born.

TANNER   I knew it was a long time ago.

RAMSDEN   I am as advanced as ever I was. I defy you to prove that

I have ever hauled down the flag. I am m o r e advanced than ever I was. I grow more advanced every day.

TANNER    More advanced in years, Polonius.

RAMSDEN    Polonius! So you are Hamlet, I suppose.

TANNER    No: I am only the most impudent person you've ever met. That's your notion of a thoroughly bad character. When you want to give me a piece of your mind, you ask yourself, as a just and upright man, what is the worst you can fairly say of me. Thief, liar, forger, adulterer, perjurer, glutton, drunkard? Not one of these names fit me. You have to fall back on my deficiency in shame. Well, I admit it. I even congratulate myself; for if I were ashamed of my real self I should cut as stupid a figure as any of the rest of you. Cultivate a little impudence, Ramsden; and you will become quite a remarkable man.

RAMSDEN    I have no—

TANNER    You have no desire for that sort of notoriety. Bless you, I knew that answer would come as well as I know that a box of matches will come out of an automatic machine when I put a penny in the slot: you would be ashamed to say anything else.

*The crushing retort for which RAMSDEN has been visibly collecting his forces is lost for ever; for at this point OCTAVIUS returns with MISS ANN WHITEFIELD and her mother; and RAMSDEN springs up and hurries to the door to receive them. Whether ANN is good-looking or not depends upon your taste; also and perhaps chiefly on your age and sex. To OC-TAVIUS she is an enchantingly beautiful woman, in whose presence the world becomes transfigured, and the puny limits of individual conscious-ness are suddenly made infinite by a mystic memory of the whole life of the race to its beginnings in the east, or even back to the paradise from which it fell. She is to him the reality of romance, the inner good sense of nonsense, the unveiling of his eyes, the freeing of his soul, the aboli-tion of time, place and circumstance, the etherealization of his blood into rapturous rivers of the very water of life itself, the revelation of all the mysteries and the sanctification of all the dogmas. To her mother she is, to put it as moderately as possible, nothing whatever of the kind. Not* that OCTAVIUS's admiration is in any way ridiculous or discreditable. ANN is a well formed creature, as far as that goes; and she is perfectly ladylike, graceful, and comely, with ensnaring eyes and hair. Besides, instead of making herself an eyesore, like her mother, she has devised a mourning costume of black and violet silk which does honor to her late father and reveals the family tradition of brave unconventionality by which RAMSDEN sets such store.

But all this is beside the point as an explanation of ANN's charm. Turn up her nose, give a cast to her eye, replace her black and violet confection by the apron and feathers of a flower girl, strike all the aitches out of her speech, and ANN would still make men dream. Vitality is as common as humanity; but, like humanity, it sometimes rises to genius; and ANN is one of the vital geniuses. Not at all, if you please, an oversexed person: that is a vital defect, not a true excess. She is a perfectly respectable, perfectly self-controlled woman, and looks it; though her pose is fashionably frank and impulsive. She inspires confidence as a person who will do nothing she does not mean to do; also some fear, perhaps, as a woman who will probably do everything she means to do without taking more account of other people than may be necessary and what she calls right. In short, what the weaker of her own sex sometimes call a cat.

Nothing can be more decorous than her entry and her reception by RAMSDEN, whom she kisses. The late MR. WHITEFIELD would be gratified almost to impatience by the long faces of the men (except TANNER, who is fidgety), the silent handgrasps, the sympathetic placing of chairs, the sniffing of the widow, and the liquid eye of the daughter, whose heart, apparently, will not let her control her tongue to speech. RAMSDEN and OCTAVIUS take the two chairs from the wall, and place them for the two ladies; but ANN comes to TANNER and takes his chair, which he offers with a brusque gesture, subsequently relieving his irritation by sitting down on the corner of the writing table with studied indecorum. OCTAVIUS gives MRS. WHITEFIELD a chair next ANN, and himself takes the vacant one which RAMSDEN has placed under the nose of the effigy of MR. HERBERT SPENCER.

MRS. WHITEFIELD, by the way, is a little woman, whose faded flaxen

*hair looks like straw on an egg. She has an expression of muddled shrewd-*
*ness, a squeak of protest in her voice, and an odd air of continually el-*
*bowing away some larger person who is crushing her into a corner. One*
*guesses her as one of those women who are conscious of being treated as*
*silly and negligible, and who, without having strength enough to assert*
*themselves effectually, at any rate never submit to their fate. There is a*
*touch of chivalry in OCTAVIUS's scrupulous attention to her, even whilst*
*his whole soul is absorbed by ANN.*

    *RAMSDEN goes solemnly back to his magisterial seat at the writing*
*table, ignoring TANNER, and opens the proceedings.*

RAMSDEN   I am sorry, Annie, to force business on you at a sad
time like the present. But your poor dear father's will has raised
a very serious question. You have read it, I believe?

*ANN assents with a nod and a catch of her breath, too much affected to*
*speak.*

    I must say I am surprised to find Mr. Tanner named as joint
guardian and trustee with myself of you and Rhoda. [*A pause. They*
*all look portentous; but they have nothing to say. RAMSDEN, a little*
*ruffled by the lack of any response, continues*] I don't know that I can
consent to act under such conditions. Mr. Tanner has, I understand, some objection also; but I do not profess to understand its
nature: he will no doubt speak for himself. But we are agreed
that we can decide nothing until we know your views. I am afraid
I shall have to ask you to choose between my sole guardianship
and that of Mr. Tanner; for I fear it is impossible for us to undertake a joint arrangement.

ANN [*in a low musical voice*]   Mamma—

MRS. WHITEFIELD [*hastily*]   Now, Ann, I do beg you not to put
it on me. I have no opinion on the subject; and if I had, it would
probably not be attended to. I am quite content with whatever
you three think best.

*TANNER turns his head and looks fixedly at RAMSDEN, who angrily*
*refuses to receive this mute communication.*

ANN [*resuming in the same gentle voice, ignoring her mother's bad taste*]

Mamma knows that she is not strong enough to bear the whole responsibility for me and Rhoda without some help and advice. Rhoda must have a guardian; and though I am older, I do not think any young unmarried woman should be left quite to her own guidance. I hope you agree with me, Granny?

TANNER [*starting*]   Granny! Do you intend to call your guardians Granny?

ANN   Don't be foolish, Jack. Mr. Ramsden has always been Grandpapa Roebuck to me: I am Granny's Annie; and he is Annie's Granny. I christened him so when I first learned to speak.

RAMSDEN [*sarcastically*]   I hope you are satisfied, Mr. Tanner. Go on, Annie: I quite agree with you.

ANN   Well, if I am to have a guardian, c a n I set aside anybody whom my dear father appointed for me?

RAMSDEN [*biting his lip*]   You approve of your father's choice, then?

ANN   It is not for me to approve or disapprove. I accept it. My father loved me and knew best what was good for me.

RAMSDEN   Of course I understand your feeling, Annie. It is what I should have expected of you; and it does you credit. But it does not settle the question so completely as you think. Let me put a case to you. Suppose you were to discover that I had been guilty of some disgraceful action—that I was not the man your poor dear father took me for! Would you still consider it right that I should be Rhoda's guardian?

ANN   I can't imagine you doing anything disgraceful, Granny.

TANNER [*to RAMSDEN*]   You havn't done anything of the sort, have you?

RAMSDEN [*indignantly*]   No sir.

MRS. WHITEFIELD [*placidly*]   Well, then, why suppose it?

ANN   You see, Granny, Mamma would not like me to suppose it.

RAMSDEN [*much perplexed*]   You are both so full of natural and affectionate feeling in these family matters that it is very hard to put the situation fairly before you.

TANNER    Besides, my friend, you are not putting the situation fairly before them.

RAMSDEN [*sulkily*]    Put it yourself, then.

TANNER    I will. Ann: Ramsden thinks I am not fit to be your guardian; and I quite agree with him. He considers that if your father had read my book, he wouldn't have appointed me. That book is the disgraceful action he has been talking about. He thinks it's your duty for Rhoda's sake to ask him to act alone and to make me withdraw. Say the word; and I will.

ANN    But I havn't read your book, Jack.

TANNER [*diving at the waste-paper basket and fishing the book out for her*]    Then read it at once and decide.

RAMSDEN [*vehemently*]    If I am to be your guardian, I positively forbid you to read that book, Annie. [*He smites the table with his fist and rises*].

ANN    Of course not if you don't wish it. [*She puts the book on the table*].

TANNER    If one guardian is to forbid you to read the other guardian's book, how are we to settle it? Suppose I order you to read it! What about your duty to me?

ANN [*gently*]    I am sure you would never purposely force me into a painful dilemma, Jack.

RAMSDEN [*irritably*]    Yes, yes, Annie: this is all very well, and, as I said, quite natural and becoming. But you must make a choice one way or the other. We are as much in a dilemma as you.

ANN    I feel that I am too young, too inexperienced, to decide. My father's wishes are sacred to me.

MRS. WHITEFIELD    If you two men won't carry them out I must say it is rather hard that you should put the responsibility on Ann. It seems to me that people are always putting things on other people in this world.

RAMSDEN    I am sorry you take it in that way.

ANN [*touchingly*]    Do you refuse to accept me as your ward, Granny?

RAMSDEN   No: I never said that. I greatly object to act with Mr.
Tanner: that's all.

MRS. WHITEFIELD   Why? What's the matter with poor Jack?

TANNER   My views are too advanced for him.

RAMSDEN [*indignantly*]   They are not. I deny it.

ANN   Of course not. What nonsense! Nobody is more advanced
than Granny. I am sure it is Jack himself who has made all the difficulty. Come, Jack! be kind to me in my sorrow. You don't refuse to accept me as your ward, do you?

TANNER [*gloomily*]   No. I let myself in for it; so I suppose I must
face it. [*He turns away to the bookcase, and stands there, moodily studying the titles of the volumes*].

ANN [*rising and expanding with subdued but gushing delight*]   Then we
are all agreed; and my dear father's will is to be carried out. You
don't know what a joy that is to me and to my mother! [*She goes
to RAMSDEN and presses both his hands, saying*] And I shall have my
dear Granny to help and advise me. [*She casts a glance at TANNER
over her shoulder*]. And Jack the Giant Killer. [*She goes past her
mother to OCTAVIUS*] And Jack's inseparable friend Ricky-ticky-
tavy* [*he blushes and looks inexpressibly foolish*].

MRS. WHITEFIELD [*rising and shaking her widow's weeds straight*]
Now that you are Ann's guardian, Mr. Ramsden, I wish you
would speak to her about her habit of giving people nicknames.
They can't be expected to like it. [*She moves towards the door*].

ANN   How can you say such a thing, Mamma! [*Glowing with affectionate remorse*] Oh, I wonder can you be right! H a v e I been inconsiderate? [*She turns to Octavius, who is sitting astride his chair with
his elbows on the back of it. Putting her hand on his forehead she turns
his face up suddenly*]. Do you want to be treated like a grown up
man? Must I call you Mr. Robinson in future?

OCTAVIUS [*earnestly*]   Oh please call me Ricky-ticky-tavy. "Mr.

---

*In *The Jungle Book* (1894), Rudyard Kipling's brave mongoose, which kills a
cobra to save a baby.

Robinson" would hurt me cruelly. [*She laughs and pats his cheek with her finger; then comes back to RAMSDEN*]. You know I'm beginning to think that Granny is rather a piece of impertinence. But I never dreamt of its hurting you.

RAMSDEN [*breezily, as he pats her affectionately on the back*]    My dear Annie, nonsense. I insist on Granny. I won't answer to any other name than Annie's Granny.

ANN [*gratefully*]    You all spoil me, except Jack.

TANNER [*over his shoulder, from the bookcase*]    I think you ought to call me Mr. Tanner.

ANN [*gently*]    No you don't, Jack. That's like the things you say on purpose to shock people: those who know you pay no attention to them. But, if you like, I'll call you after your famous ancestor Don Juan.

RAMSDEN    Don Juan!

ANN [*innocently*]    Oh, is there any harm in it? I didn't know. Then I certainly won't call you that. May I call you Jack until I can think of something else?

TANNER    Oh, for Heaven's sake don't try to invent anything worse. I capitulate. I consent to Jack. I embrace Jack. Here endeth my first and last attempt to assert my authority.

ANN    You see, Mamma, they all really like to have pet names.

MRS. WHITEFIELD    Well, I think you might at least drop them until we are out of mourning.

ANN [*reproachfully, stricken to the soul*]    Oh, how could you remind me, mother? [*She hastily leaves the room to conceal her emotion*].

MRS. WHITEFIELD    Of course. My fault as usual! [*She follows ANN*].

TANNER [*coming from the bookcase*]    Ramsden: we're beated—smashed—nonentitized, like her mother.

RAMSDEN    Stuff, sir. [*He follows MRS. WHITEFIELD out of the room*].

TANNER [*left alone with OCTAVIUS, stares whimsically at him*]    Tavy: do you want to count for something in the world?

OCTAVIUS   I want to count for something as a poet: I want to write a great play.

TANNER   With Ann as the heroine?

OCTAVIUS   Yes: I confess it.

TANNER   Take care, Tavy. The play with Ann as the heroine is all right; but if you're not very careful, by Heaven she'll marry you.

OCTAVIUS [*sighing*]   No such luck, Jack!

TANNER   Why, man, your head is in the lioness's mouth: you are half swallowed already—in three bites—Bite One, Ricky; Bite Two, Ticky; Bite Three, Tavy; and down you go.

OCTAVIUS   She is the same to everybody, Jack: you know her ways.

TANNER   Yes: she breaks everybody's back with the stroke of her paw; but the question is, which of us will she eat? My own opinion is that she means to eat you.

OCTAVIUS [*rising, pettishly*]   It's horrible to talk like that about her when she is upstairs crying for her father. But I do so want her to eat me that I can bear your brutalities because they give me hope.

TANNER   Tavy; that's the devilish side of a woman's fascination: she makes you will your own destruction.

OCTAVIUS   But it's not destruction: it's fulfilment.

TANNER   Yes, of h e r purpose; and that purpose is neither her happiness nor yours, but Nature's. Vitality in a woman is a blind fury of creation. She sacrifices herself to it: do you think she will hesitate to sacrifice you?

OCTAVIUS   Why, it is just because she is self-sacrificing that she will not sacrifice those she loves.

TANNER   That is the profoundest of mistakes, Tavy. It is the self-sacrificing women that sacrifice others most recklessly. Because they are unselfish, they are kind in little things. Because they have a purpose which is not their own purpose, but that of the whole universe, a man is nothing to them but an instrument of that purpose.

OCTAVIUS   Don't be ungenerous, Jack. They take the tenderest care of us.

TANNER   Yes, as a soldier takes care of his rifle or a musician of his violin. But do they allow us any purpose or freedom of our own? Will they lend us to one another? Can the strongest man escape from them when once he is appropriated? They tremble when we are in danger, and weep when we die; but the tears are not for us, but for a father wasted, a son's breeding thrown away. They accuse us of treating them as a mere means to our pleasure; but how can so feeble and transient a folly as a man's selfish pleasure enslave a woman as the whole purpose of Nature embodied in a woman can enslave a man?

OCTAVIUS   What matter, if the slavery makes us happy?

TANNER   No matter at all if you have no purpose of your own, and are, like most men, a mere breadwinner. But you, Tavy, are an artist: that is, you have a purpose as absorbing and as unscrupulous as a woman's purpose.

OCTAVIUS   Not unscrupulous.

TANNER   Quite unscrupulous. The true artist will let his wife starve, his children go barefoot, his mother drudge for his living at seventy, sooner than work at anything but his art. To women he is half vivisector, half vampire. He gets into intimate relations with them to study them, to strip the mask of convention from them, to surprise their inmost secrets, knowing that they have the power to rouse his deepest creative energies, to rescue him from his cold reason, to make him see visions and dream dreams, to inspire him, as he calls it. He persuades women that they may do this for their own purpose whilst he really means them to do it for his. He steals the mother's milk and blackens it to make printer's ink to scoff at her and glorify ideal women with. He pretends to spare her the pangs of child-bearing so that he may have for himself the tenderness and fostering that belong of right to her children. Since marriage began, the great artist has been known as a bad husband. But he is worse: he is a child-robber, a blood-sucker, a hypocrite and a cheat. Perish the race and wither a thousand women if only the sacrifice of them enable him to act Hamlet better, to paint a finer picture, to write a deeper poem, a greater play, a profounder philosophy! For mark you, Tavy, the artist's work is to shew us ourselves as we really are. Our minds are nothing but this knowledge of ourselves; and he who adds a jot to such knowledge creates new mind as surely as any woman creates new men. In the rage of that creation he is as ruthless as the woman, as dangerous to her as she to him, and as horribly fascinating. Of all human struggles there is none so treacherous and remorseless as the struggle between the artist man and the mother woman. Which shall use up the other? that is the issue between them. And it is all the deadlier because, in your romanticist cant, they love one another.

OCTAVIUS   Even if it were so—and I don't admit it for a moment—it is out of the deadliest struggles that we get the noblest characters.

TANNER   Remember that the next time you meet a grizzly bear or a Bengal tiger, Tavy.

OCTAVIUS   I meant where there is love, Jack.

TANNER   Oh, the tiger will love you. There is no love sincerer than the love of food. I think Ann loves you that way: she patted your cheek as if it were a nicely under done chop.

OCTAVIUS   You know, Jack, I should have to run away from you if I did not make it a fixed rule not to mind anything you say. You come out with perfectly revolting things sometimes.

*RAMSDEN returns, followed by ANN. They come in quickly, with their former leisurely air of decorous grief changed to one of genuine concern, and, on RAMSDEN's part, of worry. He comes between the two men, intending to address OCTAVIUS, but pulls himself up abruptly as he sees TANNER.*

RAMSDEN   I hardly expected to find you still here, Mr. Tanner.

TANNER   Am I in the way? Good morning, fellow guardian [*he goes towards the door*].

ANN    Stop, Jack. Granny: he must know, sooner or later.

RAMSDEN    Octavius: I have a very serious piece of news for you. It is of the most private and delicate nature—of the most painful nature too, I am sorry to say. Do you wish Mr. Tanner to be present whilst I explain?

OCTAVIUS [*turning pale*]    I have no secrets from Jack.

RAMSDEN    Before you decide that finally, let me say that the news concerns your sister, and that it is t e r r i b l e news.

OCTAVIUS    Violet! What has happened? Is she—dead?

RAMSDEN    I am not sure that it is not even worse than that.

OCTAVIUS    Is she badly hurt? Has there been an accident?

RAMSDEN    No: nothing of that sort.

TANNER    Ann: will y o u have the common humanity to tell us what the matter is?

ANN [*half whispering*]    I can't. Violet has done something dreadful. We shall have to get her away somewhere. [*She flutters to the writing table and sits in RAMSDEN's chair, leaving the three men to fight it out between them*].

OCTAVIUS [*enlightened*]    Is t h a t what you meant, Mr. Ramsden?

RAMSDEN    Yes. [*OCTAVIUS sinks upon a chair, crushed*]. I am afraid there is no doubt that Violet did not really go to Eastbourne three weeks ago when we thought she was with the Parry Whitefields. And she called on a strange doctor yesterday with a wedding ring on her finger. Mrs. Parry Whitefield met her there by chance; and so the whole thing came out.

OCTAVIUS [*rising with his fists clenched*]    Who is the scoundrel?

ANN    She won't tell us.

OCTAVIUS [*collapsing into the chair again*]    What a frightful thing!

TANNER [*with angry sarcasm*]    Dreadful. Appalling. Worse than death, as Ramsden says. [*He comes to OCTAVIUS*]. What would you not give, Tavy, to turn it into a railway accident, with all her bones broken, or something equally respectable and deserving of sympathy?

OCTAVIUS    Don't be brutal, Jack.

TANNER    Brutal! Good Heavens, man, what are you crying for? Here is a woman whom we all supposed to be making bad water color sketches, practising Grieg and Brahms, gadding about to concerts and parties, wasting her life and her money. We suddenly learn that she has turned from these sillinesses to the fulfilment of her highest purpose and greatest function—to increase, multiply and replenish the earth. And instead of admiring her courage and rejoicing in her instinct; instead of crowning the completed womanhood and raising the triumphal strain of "Unto us a child is born: unto us a son is given,"* here you are— you who have been as merry as grigs† in your mourning for the dead—all pulling long faces and looking as ashamed and disgraced as if the girl had committed the vilest of crimes.

RAMSDEN [*roaring with rage*]    I will not have these abominations uttered in my house [*he smites the writing table with his fist*].

TANNER    Look here: if you insult me again I'll take you at your word and leave your house. Ann: where is Violet now?

ANN    Why? Are you going to her?

TANNER    Of course I am going to her. She wants help; she wants money; she wants respect and congratulation; she wants every chance for her child. She does not seem likely to get it from you: she shall from me. Where is she?

ANN    Don't be so headstrong, Jack. She's upstairs.

TANNER    What! Under Ramsden's sacred roof! Go and do your miserable duty, Ramsden. Hunt her out into the street. Cleanse your threshold from her contamination. Vindicate the purity of your English home. I'll go for a cab.

ANN [*alarmed*]    Oh, Granny, you mustn't do that.

OCTAVIUS [*broken-heartedly, rising*]    I'll take her away, Mr. Ramsden. She had no right to come to your house.

RAMSDEN [*indignantly*]    But I am only too anxious to help her.

---

*A chorus from Handel's *Messiah* (1742).

†Lighthearted youngsters.

[*Turning on TANNER*] How dare you, sir, impute such monstrous intentions to me? I protest against it. I am ready to put down my last penny to save her from being driven to run to you for protection.

TANNER [*subsiding*]   It's all right, then. He's not going to act up to his principles. It's agreed that we all stand by Violet.

OCTAVIUS   But who is the man? He can make reparation by marrying her; and he shall, or he shall answer for it to me.

RAMSDEN   He shall, Octavius. There you speak like a man.

TANNER   Then you don't think him a scoundrel, after all?

OCTAVIUS   Not a scoundrel! He is a heartless scoundrel.

RAMSDEN   A damned scoundrel. I beg your pardon, Annie; but I can say no less.

TANNER   So we are to marry your sister to a damned scoundrel by way of reforming her character! On my soul, I think you are all mad.

ANN   Don't be absurd, Jack. Of course you are quite right, Tavy; but we don't know who he is: Violet won't tell us.

TANNER   What on earth does it matter who he is? He's done his part; and Violet must do the rest.

RAMSDEN [*beside himself*]   Stuff! lunacy! There is a rascal in our midst, a libertine, a villain worse than a murderer; and we are not to learn who he is! In our ignorance we are to shake him by the hand; to introduce him into our homes; to trust our daughters with him; to—to—

ANN [*coaxingly*]   There, Granny, don't talk so loud. It's most shocking: we must all admit that; but if Violet won't tell us, what can we do? Nothing. Simply nothing.

RAMSDEN   Hmph! I'm not so sure of that. If any man has paid Violet any special attention, we can easily find that out. If there is any man of notoriously loose principles among us—

TANNER   Ahem!

RAMSDEN [*raising his voice*]   Yes sir, I repeat, if there is any man of notoriously loose principles among us—

TANNER   Or any man notoriously lacking in self-control.

RAMSDEN [*aghast*]   Do you dare to suggest that *I* am capable of such an act?

TANNER   My dear Ramsden, this is an act of which every man is capable. That is what comes of getting at cross purposes with Nature. The suspicion you have just flung at me clings to us all. It's a sort of mud that sticks to the judge's ermine or the cardinal's robe as fast as to the rags of the tramp. Come, Tavy: don't look so bewildered: it might have been me: it might have been Ramsden; just as it might have been anybody. If it had, what could we do but lie and protest—as Ramsden is going to protest.

RAMSDEN [*choking*]   I—I—I—

TANNER   Guilt itself could not stammer more confusedly. And yet you know perfectly well he's innocent, Tavy.

RAMSDEN [*exhausted*]   I am glad you admit that, sir. I admit, myself, that there is an element of truth in what you say, grossly as you may distort it to gratify your malicious humor. I hope, Octavius, no suspicion of me is possible in your mind.

OCTAVIUS   Of you! No, not for a moment.

TANNER [*drily*]   I think he suspects me just a little.

OCTAVIUS   Jack: you couldn't—you wouldn't—

TANNER   Why not?

OCTAVIUS [*appalled*]   Why not!

TANNER   Oh, well, I'll tell you why not. First, you would feel bound to quarrel with me. Second, Violet doesn't like me. Third, if I had the honor of being the father of Violet's child, I should boast of it instead of denying it. So be easy: our friendship is not in danger.

OCTAVIUS   I should have put away the suspicion with horror if only you would think and feel naturally about it. I beg your pardon.

TANNER   M y pardon! nonsense! And now let's sit down and have a family council. [*He sits down. The rest follow his example, more or less under protest*]. Violet is going to do the State a service; consequently she must be packed abroad like a criminal until it's over. What's happening upstairs?

ANN    Violet is in the housekeeper's room—by herself, of course.

TANNER    Why not in the drawingroom?

ANN    Don't be absurd, Jack. Miss Ramsden is in the drawingroom with my mother, considering what to do.

TANNER    Oh! the housekeeper's room is the penitentiary, I suppose; and the prisoner is waiting to be brought before her judges. The old cats!

ANN    Oh, Jack!

RAMSDEN    You are at present a guest beneath the roof of one of the old cats, sir. My sister is the mistress of this house.

TANNER    She would put me in the housekeeper's room, too, if she dared, Ramsden. However, I withdraw cats. Cats would have more sense. Ann: as your guardian, I order you to go to Violet at once and be particularly kind to her.

ANN    I h a v e seen her, Jack. And I am sorry to say I am afraid she is going to be rather obstinate about going abroad. I think Tavy ought to speak to her about it.

OCTAVIUS    How can I speak to her about such a thing [*he breaks down*]?

ANN    Don't break down, Ricky. Try to bear it for all our sakes.

RAMSDEN    Life is not all plays and poems, Octavius. Come! face it like a man.

TANNER [*chafing again*]    Poor dear brother! Poor dear friends of the family! Poor dear Tabbies and Grimalkins! Poor dear everybody except the woman who is going to risk her life to create another life! Tavy: don't you be a selfish ass. Away with you and talk to Violet; and bring her down here if she cares to come. [*Octavius rises*]. Tell her we'll stand by her.

RAMSDEN [*rising*]    No, sir—

TANNER [*rising also and interrupting him*]    Oh, we understand: it's against your conscience; but still you'll do it.

OCTAVIUS    I assure you all, on my word, I never meant to be self-ish. It's so hard to know what to do when one wishes earnestly to do right.

TANNER    My dear Tavy, your pious English habit of regarding the world as a moral gymnasium built expressly to strengthen your character in, occasionally leads you to think about your own con-founded principles when you should be thinking about other people's necessities. The need of the present hour is a happy mother and a healthy baby. Bend your energies on that; and you will see your way clearly enough.

*OCTAVIUS, much perplexed, goes out.*

RAMSDEN [*facing TANNER impressively*]    And Morality, sir? What is to become of that?

TANNER    Meaning a weeping Magdalen and an innocent child branded with her shame. Not in our circle, thank you. Morality can go to its father the devil.

RAMSDEN    I thought so, sir. Morality sent to the devil to please our libertines, male and female. That is to be the future of En-gland, is it?

TANNER    Oh, England will survive your disapproval. Meanwhile, I understand that you agree with me as to the practical course we are to take?

RAMSDEN    Not in your spirit, sir. Not for your reasons.

TANNER    You can explain that if anybody calls you to account, here or hereafter. [*He turns away, and plants himself in front of Mr. Herbert Spencer, at whom he stares gloomily*].

ANN [*rising and coming to RAMSDEN*]    Granny: hadn't you better go up to the drawingroom and tell them what we intend to do?

RAMSDEN [*looking pointedly at TANNER*]    I hardly like to leave you alone with this gentleman. Will you not come with me?

ANN    Miss Ramsden would not like to speak about it before me, Granny. I ought not to be present.

RAMSDEN    You are right: I should have thought of that. You are a good girl, Annie.

*He pats her on the shoulder. She looks up at him with beaming eyes; and he goes out, much moved. Having disposed of him, she looks at TANNER. His back being turned to her, she gives a moment's attention to her personal appearance, then softly goes to him and speaks almost into his ear.*

ANN     Jack [*he turns with a start*]: are you glad that you are my guardian? You don't mind being made responsible for me, I hope.

TANNER     The latest addition to your collection of scapegoats, eh?

ANN     Oh, that stupid old joke of yours about me! Do please drop it. Why do you say things that you know must pain me? I do my best to please you, Jack: I suppose I may tell you so now that you are my guardian. You will make me so unhappy if you refuse to be friends with me.

TANNER [*studying her as gloomily as he studied the bust*]     You need not go begging for my regard. How unreal our moral judgments are! You seem to me to have absolutely no conscience—only hypocrisy; and you can't see the difference—yet there is a sort of fascination about you. I always attend to you, somehow. I should miss you if I lost you.

ANN [*tranquilly slipping her arm into his and walking about with him*] But isn't that only natural, Jack? We have known each other since we were children. Do you remember—

TANNER [*abruptly breaking loose*]     Stop! I remember e v e r y t h i n g.

ANN     Oh, I daresay we were often very silly; but—

TANNER     I won't have it, Ann. I am no more that schoolboy now than I am the dotard of ninety I shall grow into if I live long enough. It is over: let me forget it.

ANN     Wasn't it a happy time? [*She attempts to take his arm again*].

TANNER     Sit down and behave yourself. [*He makes her sit down in the chair next the writing table*]. No doubt it was a happy time for you. You were a good girl and never compromised yourself. And yet the wickedest child that ever was slapped could hardly have had a better time. I can understand the success with which you bullied the other girls: your virtue imposed on them. But tell me this: did you ever know a good boy?

ANN    Of course. All boys are foolish sometimes; but Tavy was always a really good boy.

TANNER [*struck by this*]    Yes: you're right. For some reason you never tempted Tavy.

ANN    Tempted! Jack!

TANNER    Yes, my dear Lady Mephistopheles, tempted.[6] You were insatiably curious as to what a boy might be capable of, and diabolically clever at getting through his guard and surprising his inmost secrets.

ANN    What nonsense! All because you used to tell me long stories of the wicked things you had done—silly boys' tricks! And you call such things inmost secrets! Boys' secrets are just like men's; and you know what t h e y are!

TANNER [*obstinately*]    No I don't. What are they, pray?

ANN    Why, the things they tell everybody, of course.

TANNER    Now I swear I told you things I told no one else. You lured me into a compact by which we were to have no secrets from one another. We were to tell one another everything. I didn't notice that you never told me anything.

ANN    You didn't want to talk about me, Jack. You wanted to talk about yourself.

TANNER    Ah, true, horribly true. But what a devil of a child you must have been to know that weakness and to play on it for the satisfaction of your own curiosity! I wanted to brag to you, to make myself interesting. And I found myself doing all sorts of mischievous things simply to have something to tell you about. I fought with boys I didn't hate; I lied about things I might just as well have told the truth about; I stole things I didn't want; I kissed little girls I didn't care for. It was all bravado: passionless and therefore unreal.

ANN    I never told of you, Jack.

TANNER    No; but if you had wanted to stop me you would have told of me. You wanted me to go on.

ANN [ *flashing out*]    Oh, that's not true: it's n o t true, Jack. I never wanted you to do those dull, disappointing, brutal, stupid, vulgar things. I always hoped that it would be something really heroic at last. [*Recovering herself*] Excuse me, Jack; but the things you did were never a bit like the things I wanted you to do. They often gave me great uneasiness; but I could not tell on you and get you into trouble. And you were only a boy. I knew you would grow out of them. Perhaps I was wrong.

TANNER [*sardonically*]    Do not give way to remorse, Ann. At least nineteen twentieths of the exploits I confessed to you were pure lies. I soon noticed that you didn't like the true stories.

ANN    Of course I knew that some of the things couldn't have happened. But—

TANNER    You are going to remind me that some of the most disgraceful ones did.

ANN [ *fondly, to his great terror*]    I don't want to remind you of anything. But I knew the people they happened to, and heard about them.

TANNER    Yes; but even the true stories were touched up for telling. A sensitive boy's humiliations may be very good fun for ordinary thickskinned grown-ups; but to the boy himself they are so acute, so ignominious, that he cannot confess them—cannot but deny them passionately. However, perhaps it was as well for me that I romanced a bit; for, on the one occasion when I told you the truth, you threatened to tell of me.

ANN    Oh, never. Never once.

TANNER    Yes, you did. Do you remember a dark-eyed girl named Rachel Rosetree? [*Ann's brows contract for an instant involuntarily*]. I got up a love affair with her; and we met one night in the garden and walked about very uncomfortably with our arms round one another, and kissed at parting, and were most conscientiously romantic. If that love affair had gone on, it would have bored me to death; but it didn't go on; for the next thing that happened was that Rachel cut me because she found out that I had told you. How did she find it out? From you. You went to her and held the guilty secret over her head, leading her a life of abject terror and humiliation by threatening to tell on her.

ANN   And a very good thing for her, too. It was my duty to stop her misconduct; and she is thankful to me for it now.

TANNER   Is she?

ANN   She ought to be, at all events.

TANNER   It was not your duty to stop my misconduct, I suppose.

ANN   I did stop it by stopping her.

TANNER   Are you sure of that? You stopped my telling you about my adventures; but how do you know that you stopped the adventures?

ANN   Do you mean to say that you went on in the same way with other girls?

TANNER   No. I had enough of that sort of romantic tomfoolery with Rachel.

ANN [*unconvinced*]   Then why did you break off our confidences and become quite strange to me?

TANNER [*enigmatically*]   It happened just then that I got something that I wanted to keep all to myself instead of sharing it with you.

ANN   I am sure I shouldn't have asked for any of it if you had grudged it.

TANNER   It wasn't a box of sweets, Ann. It was something you'd never have let me call my own.

ANN [*incredulously*]   What?

TANNER   My soul.

ANN   Oh, do be sensible, Jack. You know you're talking nonsense.

TANNER   The most solemn earnest, Ann. You didn't notice at that time that you were getting a soul too. But you were. It was not for nothing that you suddenly found you had a moral duty to chastise and reform Rachel. Up to that time you had traded pretty extensively in being a good child; but you had never set up a sense of duty to others. Well, I set one up too. Up to that time I had played the boy buccaneer with no more conscience than a fox in a poultry farm. But now I began to have scruples, to feel obligations, to find that veracity and honor were no longer goody-goody expressions in the mouths of grown up people, but compelling principles in myself.

ANN [*quietly*]   Yes, I suppose you're right. You were beginning to be a man, and I to be a woman.

TANNER   Are you sure it was not that we were beginning to be something more? What does the beginning of manhood and womanhood mean in most people's mouths? You know: it means the beginning of love. But love began long before that for me. Love played its part in the earliest dreams and follies and romances I can remember—may I say the earliest follies and romances we can remember?—though we did not understand it at the time. No: the change that came to me was the birth in me of moral passion; and I declare that according to my experience moral passion is the only real passion.

ANN   All passions ought to be moral, Jack.

TANNER   Ought! Do you think that anything is strong enough to impose oughts on a passion except a stronger passion still?

ANN   Our moral sense controls passion, Jack. Don't be stupid.

TANNER   Our moral sense! And is that not a passion? Is the devil to have all the passions as well as all the good tunes? If it were not a passion—if it were not the mightiest of the passions, all the other passions would sweep it away like a leaf before a hurricane. It is the birth of that passion that turns a child into a man.

ANN   There are other passions, Jack. Very strong ones.

TANNER   All the other passions were in me before; but they were idle and aimless—mere childish greedinesses and cruelties, curiosities and fancies, habits and superstitions, grotesque and ridiculous to the mature intelligence. When they suddenly began to shine like newly lit flames it was by no light of their own, but by the radiance of the dawning moral passion. That passion dignified them, gave them conscience and meaning, found them a mob of appetites and organized them into an army of purposes and principles. My soul was born of that passion.

ANN    I noticed that you got more sense. You were a dreadfully destructive boy before that.

TANNER    Destructive! Stuff! I was only mischievous.

ANN    Oh Jack, you were very destructive. You ruined all the young fir trees by chopping off their leaders with a wooden sword. You broke all the cucumber frames with your catapult. You set fire to the common: the police arrested Tavy for it because he ran away when he couldn't stop you. You—

TANNER    Pooh! pooh! pooh! these were battles, bombardments, stratagems to save our scalps from the red Indians. You have no imagination, Ann. I am ten times more destructive now than I was then. The moral passion has taken my destructiveness in hand and directed it to moral ends. I have become a reformer, and, like all reformers, an iconoclast. I no longer break cucumber frames and burn gorse bushes: I shatter creeds and demolish idols.

ANN [*bored*]    I am afraid I am too feminine to see any sense in destruction. Destruction can only destroy.

TANNER    Yes. That is why it is so useful. Construction cumbers the ground with institutions made by busybodies. Destruction clears it and gives us breathing space and liberty.

ANN    It's no use, Jack. No woman will agree with you there.

TANNER    That's because you confuse construction and destruction with creation and murder. They're quite different: I adore creation and abhor murder. Yes: I adore it in tree and flower, in bird and beast, even in you. [*A flush of interest and delight suddenly chases the growing perplexity and boredom from her face*]. It was the creative instinct that led you to attach me to you by bonds that have left their mark on me to this day. Yes, Ann; the old childish compact between us was an unconscious love compact—

ANN    Jack!

TANNER   Oh, don't be alarmed—

ANN   I am not alarmed.

TANNER [*whimsically*]   Then you ought to be: where are your principles?

ANN   Jack: are you serious or are you not?

TANNER   Do you mean about the moral passion?

ANN   No, no; the other one. [*Confused*] Oh! you are so silly: one never knows how to take you.

TANNER   You must take me quite seriously. I am your guardian; and it is my duty to improve your mind.

ANN   The love compact is over, then, is it? I suppose you grew tired of me?

TANNER   No; but the moral passion made our childish relations impossible. A jealous sense of my new individuality arose in me—

ANN   You hated to be treated as a boy any longer. Poor Jack!

TANNER   Yes, because to be treated as a boy was to be taken on the old footing. I had become a new person; and those who knew the old person laughed at me. The only man who behaved sensibly was my tailor: he took my measure anew every time he saw me, whilst all the rest went on with their old measurements and expected them to fit me.

ANN   You became frightfully self-conscious.

TANNER   When you go to heaven, Ann, you will be frightfully conscious of your wings for the first year or so. When you meet your relatives there, and they persist in treating you as if you were still a mortal, you will not be able to bear them. You will try to get into a circle which has never known you except as an angel.

ANN   So it was only your vanity that made you run away from us after all?

TANNER   Yes, only my vanity, as you call it.

ANN   You need not have kept away from m e on that account.

TANNER    From you above all others. You fought harder than anybody against my emancipation.

ANN [*earnestly*]    Oh, how wrong you are! I would have done anything for you.

TANNER    Anything except let me get loose from you. Even then you had acquired by instinct that damnable woman's trick of heaping obligations on a man, of placing yourself so entirely and helplessly at his mercy that at last he dare not take a step without running to you for leave. I know a poor wretch whose one desire in life is to run away from his wife. She prevents him by threatening to throw herself in front of the engine of the train he leaves her in. That is what all women do. If we try to go where you do not want us to go there is no law to prevent us; but when we take the first step your breasts are under our foot as it descends: your bodies are under our wheels as we start. No woman shall ever enslave me in that way.

ANN    But, Jack, you cannot get through life without considering other people a little.

TANNER    Ay; but what other people? It is this consideration of other people—or rather this cowardly fear of them which we call consideration—that makes us the sentimental slaves we are. To consider you, as you call it, is to substitute your will for my own. How if it be a baser will than mine? Are women taught better than men or worse? Are mobs of voters taught better than statesmen or worse? Worse, of course, in both cases. And then what sort of world are you going to get, with its public men considering its voting mobs, and its private men considering their wives? What does Church and State mean nowadays? The Woman and the Ratepayer.

ANN [*placidly*]    I am so glad you understand politics, Jack: it will be most useful to you if you go into parliament [*he collapses like a pricked bladder*]. But I am sorry you thought my influence a bad one.

TANNER    I don't say it was a bad one. But bad or good, I didn't choose to be cut to your measure. And I won't be cut to it.

ANN    Nobody wants you to, Jack. I assure you—really on my word—I don't mind your queer opinions one little bit. You know we have all been brought up to have advanced opinions. Why do you persist in thinking me so narrow minded?

TANNER    That's the danger of it. I know you don't mind, because you've found out that it doesn't matter. The boa constrictor doesn't mind the opinions of a stag one little bit when once she has got her coils round it.

ANN [*rising in sudden enlightenment*]    O-o-o-o-oh! now I understand why you warned Tavy that I am a boa constrictor. Granny told me. [*She laughs and throws her boa round his neck*]. Doesn't it feel nice and soft, Jack?

TANNER [*in the toils*]    You scandalous woman, will you throw away even your hypocrisy?

ANN    I am never hypocritical with you, Jack. Are you angry? [*She withdraws the boa and throws it on a chair*]. Perhaps I shouldn't have done that.

TANNER [*contemptuously*]    Pooh, prudery! Why should you not, if it amuses you?

ANN [*shyly*]    Well, because—because I suppose what you really meant by the b o a constrictor was this [*she puts her arms round his neck*].

TANNER [*staring at her*]    Magnificent audacity! [*She laughs and pats his cheeks*]. Now just to think that if I mentioned this episode not a soul would believe me except the people who would cut me for telling, whilst if you accused me of it nobody would believe my denial!

ANN [*taking her arms away with perfect dignity*]    You are incorrigible, Jack. But you should not jest about our affection for one another. Nobody could possibly misunderstand it. Y o u do not misunderstand it, I hope.

TANNER My blood interprets for me, Ann. Poor Ricky Ticky Tavy!

ANN [*looking quickly at him as if this were a new light*] Surely you are not so absurd as to be jealous of Tavy.

TANNER Jealous! Why should I be? But I don't wonder at your grip of him. I feel the coils tightening round my very self, though you are only playing with me.

ANN Do you think I have designs on Tavy?

TANNER I know you have.

ANN [*earnestly*] Take care, Jack. You may make Tavy very unhappy if you mislead him about me.

TANNER Never fear: he will not escape you.

ANN I wonder are you really a clever man!

TANNER Why this sudden misgiving on the subject?

ANN You seem to understand all the things I don't understand; but you are a perfect baby in the things I do understand.

TANNER I understand how Tavy feels for you, Ann: you may depend on that, at all events.

ANN And you think you understand how I feel for Tavy, don't you?

TANNER I know only too well what is going to happen to poor Tavy.

ANN I should laugh at you, Jack, if it were not for poor papa's death. Mind! Tavy will be very unhappy.

TANNER Yes; but he won't know it, poor devil. He is a thousand times too good for you. That's why he is going to make the mistake of his life about you.

ANN I think men make more mistakes by being too clever than by being too good [*she sits down, with a trace of contempt for the whole male sex in the elegant carriage of her shoulders*].

TANNER Oh, I know you don't care very much about Tavy. But there is always one who kisses and one who only allows the kiss. Tavy will kiss; and you will only turn the cheek. And you will throw him over if anybody better turns up.

ANN [*offended*] You have no right to say such things, Jack. They are not true, and not delicate. If you and Tavy choose to be stupid about me, that is not my fault.

TANNER [*remorsefully*]   Forgive my brutalities, Ann. They are levelled at this wicked world, not at you. [*She looks up at him, pleased and forgiving. He becomes cautious at once*]. All the same, I wish Ramsden would come back. I never feel safe with you: there is a devilish charm—or no: not a charm, a subtle interest [*she laughs*]—Just so: you know it; and you triumph in it. Openly and shamelessly triumph in it!

ANN   What a shocking flirt you are, Jack!

TANNER   A flirt!! I!!!

ANN   Yes, a flirt. You are always abusing and offending people; but you never really mean to let go your hold of them.

TANNER   I will ring the bell. This conversation has already gone further than I intended.

*RAMSDEN and OCTAVIUS come back with MISS RAMSDEN, a hard-headed old maiden lady in a plain brown silk gown, with enough rings, chains and brooches to shew that her plainness of dress is a matter of principle, not of poverty. She comes into the room very determinedly: the two men, perplexed and downcast, following her. ANN rises and goes eagerly to meet her. TANNER retreats to the wall between the busts and pretends to study the pictures. RAMSDEN goes to his table as usual; and OCTAVIUS clings to the neighborhood of TANNER.*

MISS RAMSDEN [*almost pushing ANN aside as she comes to MRS. WHITEFIELD's chair and plants herself there resolutely*]   I wash my hands of the whole affair.

OCTAVIUS [*very wretched*]   I know you wish me to take Violet away, Miss Ramsden. I will. [*He turns irresolutely to the door*].

RAMSDEN   No no—

MISS RAMSDEN   What is the use of saying no, Roebuck? Octavius knows that I would not turn any truly contrite and repentant woman from your doors. But when a woman is not only wicked, but intends to go on being wicked, she and I part company.

ANN   Oh, Miss Ramsden, what do you mean? What has Violet said?

RAMSDEN   Violet is certainly very obstinate. She won't leave London. I don't understand her.

MISS RAMSDEN   I do. It's as plain as the nose on your face, Roebuck, that she won't go because she doesn't want to be separated from this man, whoever he is.

ANN   Oh, surely, surely! Octavius: did y o u speak to her?

OCTAVIUS   She won't tell us anything. She won't make any arrangement until she has consulted somebody. It can't be anybody else than the scoundrel who has betrayed her.

TANNER [*to Octavius*]   Well, let her consult him. He will be glad enough to have her sent abroad. Where is the difficulty?

MISS RAMSDEN [*taking the answer out of OCTAVIUS's mouth*]   The difficulty, Mr. Jack, is that when I offered to help her I didn't offer to become her accomplice in her wickedness. She either pledges her word never to see that man again, or else she finds some new friends; and the sooner the better.

*The parlormaid appears at the door. ANN hastily resumes her seat, and looks as unconcerned as possible. OCTAVIUS instinctively imitates her.*

THE MAID   The cab is at the door, ma'am.

MISS RAMSDEN   What cab?

THE MAID   For Miss Robinson.

MISS RAMSDEN   Oh! [*Recovering herself*] All right. [*The maid withdraws*]. She has sent for a cab.

TANNER   *I* wanted to send for that cab half an hour ago.

MISS RAMSDEN   I am glad she understands the position she has placed herself in.

RAMSDEN   I don't like her going away in this fashion, Susan. We had better not do anything harsh.

OCTAVIUS   No: thank you again and again; but Miss Ramsden is quite right. Violet cannot expect to stay.

ANN   Hadn't you better go with her, Tavy?

OCTAVIUS   She won't have me.

MISS RAMSDEN    Of course she won't. She's going straight to that man.

TANNER    As a natural result of her virtuous reception here.

RAMSDEN [*much troubled*]    There, Susan! You hear! and there's some truth in it. I wish you could reconcile it with your principles to be a little patient with this poor girl. She's very young; and there's a time for everything.

MISS RAMSDEN    Oh, she will get all the sympathy she wants from the men. I'm surprised at you, Roebuck.

TANNER    So am I, Ramsden, most favorably.

*VIOLET appears at the door. She is as impenitent and self-possessed a young lady as one would desire to see among the best behaved of her sex. Her small head and tiny resolute mouth and chin; her haughty crispness of speech and trimness of carriage; the ruthless elegance of her equipment, which includes a very smart hat with a dead bird in it, mark a personality which is as formidable as it is exquisitely pretty. She is not a siren, like ANN: admiration comes to her without any compulsion or even interest on her part; besides, there is some fun in ANN, but in this woman none, perhaps no mercy either: if anything restrains her, it is intelligence and pride, not compassion. Her voice might be the voice of a schoolmistress addressing a class of girls who had disgraced themselves, as she proceeds with complete composure and some disgust to say what she has come to say.*

VIOLET    I have only looked in to tell Miss Ramsden that she will find her birthday present to me, the filagree bracelet, in the housekeeper's room.

TANNER    Do come in, Violet, and talk to us sensibly.

VIOLET    Thank you: I have had quite enough of the family conversation this morning. So has your mother, Ann: she has gone home crying. But at all events, I have found out what some of my pretended friends are worth. Good bye.

TANNER    No, no: one moment. I have something to say which I beg you to hear. [*She looks at him without the slightest curiosity, but waits, apparently as much to finish getting her glove on as to hear what he has to say*]. I am altogether on your side in this matter. I congratulate you, with the sincerest respect, on having the courage to do what you have done. You are entirely in the right; and the family is entirely in the wrong.

*Sensation. ANN and MISS RAMSDEN rise and turn towards the two. VIOLET, more surprised than any of the others, forgets her glove, and comes forward into the middle of the room, both puzzled and displeased. OCTAVIUS alone does not move or raise his head: he is overwhelmed with shame.*

ANN [*pleading to TANNER to be sensible*]    Jack!

MISS RAMSDEN [*outraged*]    Well, I must say!

VIOLET [*sharply to TANNER*]    Who told you?

TANNER    Why, Ramsden and Tavy of course. Why should they not?

VIOLET    But they don't know.

TANNER    Don't know what?

VIOLET    They don't know that I am in the right, I mean.

TANNER    Oh, they know it in their hearts, though they think themselves bound to blame you by their silly superstitions about morality and propriety and so forth. But I know, and the whole world really knows, though it dare not say so, that you were right to follow your instinct; that vitality and bravery are the greatest qualities a woman can have, and motherhood her solemn initiation into womanhood; and that the fact of your not being legally married matters not one scrap either to your own worth or to our real regard for you.

VIOLET [*flushing with indignation*]    Oh! You think me a wicked woman, like the rest. You think I have not only been vile, but that I share your abominable opinions. Miss Ramsden: I have borne your hard words because I knew you would be sorry for them when you found out the truth. But I won't bear such a horrible insult as to be complimented by Jack on being one of the wretches of whom he approves. I have kept my marriage a secret for my husband's sake. But now I claim my right as a married woman not to be insulted.

OCTAVIUS [*raising his head with inexpressible relief*]    You are married!

VIOLET    Yes; and I think you might have guessed it. What business had you all to take it for granted that I had no right to wear my wedding ring? Not one of you even asked me: I cannot forget that.

TANNER [*in twits*]    I am utterly crushed. I meant well. I apologize—abjectly apologize.

VIOLET    I hope you will be more careful in future about the things you say. Of course one does not take them seriously; but they are very disagreeable, and rather in bad taste, I think.

TANNER [*bowing to the storm*]    I have no defence: I shall know better in future than to take any woman's part. We have all disgraced ourselves in your eyes, I am afraid, except Ann. S h e befriended you. For Ann's sake, forgive us.

VIOLET    Yes: Ann has been very kind; but then Ann knew.

TANNER    Oh!

MISS RAMSDEN [*stiffly*]    And who, pray, is the gentleman who does not acknowledge his wife?

VIOLET [*promptly*]    That is my business, Miss Ramsden, and not yours. I have my reasons for keeping my marriage a secret for the present.

RAMSDEN    All I can say is that we are extremely sorry, Violet. I am shocked to think of how we have treated you.

OCTAVIUS [*awkwardly*]    I beg your pardon, Violet. I can say no more.

MISS RAMSDEN [*still loth to surrender*]    Of course what you say puts a very different complexion on the matter. All the same, I owe it to myself—

VIOLET [*cutting her short*]    You owe me an apology, Miss Ramsden: that's what you owe both to yourself and to me. If you were a married woman you would not like sitting in the housekeeper's room and being treated like a naughty child by young girls and old ladies without any serious duties and responsibilities.

TANNER    Don't hit us when we're down, Violet. We seem to have made fools of ourselves; but really it was you who made fools of us.

VIOLET    It was no business of yours, Jack, in any case.

TANNER    No business of mine! Why, Ramsden as good as accused me of being the unknown gentleman.

*RAMSDEN makes a frantic demonstration; but VIOLET's cool keen anger extinguishes it.*

VIOLET    You! Oh, how infamous! how abominable! how disgracefully you have all been talking about me! If my husband knew it he would never let me speak to any of you again. [*To RAMSDEN*] I think you might have spared me that, at least.

RAMSDEN    But I assure you I never—at least it is a monstrous perversion of something I said that—

MISS RAMSDEN    You needn't apologize, Roebuck. She brought it all on herself. It is for her to apologize for having deceived us.

VIOLET    I can make allowances for you, Miss Ramsden: you cannot understand how I feel on this subject, though I should have expected rather better taste from people of greater experience. However, I quite feel that you have all placed yourselves in a very painful position; and the most truly considerate thing for me to do is to go at once. Good morning.

*She goes, leaving them staring.*

MISS RAMSDEN    Well, I must say!

RAMSDEN [*plaintively*]    I don't think she is quite fair to us.

TANNER    You must cower before the wedding ring like the rest of us, Ramsden. The cup of our ignominy is full.

# ACT II

*On the carriage drive in the park of a country house near Richmond a motor car has broken down. It stands in front of a clump of trees round which the drive sweeps to the house, which is partly visible through them: indeed Tanner, standing in the drive with the car on his right hand, could get an unobstructed view of the west corner of the house on his left were he not far too much interested in a pair of supine legs in blue serge trousers which protrude from beneath the machine. He is watching them intently with bent back and hands supported on his knees. His leathern overcoat and peaked cap proclaim him one of the dismounted passengers.*

THE LEGS   Aha! I got him.

TANNER   All right now?

THE LEGS   Aw right now.

*TANNER stoops and takes the legs by the ankles, drawing their owner forth like a wheelbarrow, walking on his hands, with a hammer in his mouth. He is a young man in a neat suit of blue serge, clean shaven, dark eyed, square fingered, with short well brushed black hair and rather irregular sceptically turned eyebrows. When he is manipulating the car his movements are swift and sudden, yet attentive and deliberate. With TANNER and TANNER's friends his manner is not in the least deferential, but cool and reticent, keeping them quite effectually at a distance whilst giving them no excuse for complaining of him. Nevertheless he has a vigilant eye on them always, and that, too, rather cynically, like a man who knows the world well from its seamy side. He speaks slowly and with a touch of sarcasm; and as he does not at all affect the gentleman in his speech, it may be inferred that his smart appearance is a mark of respect to himself and his own class, not to that which employs him.*

*He now gets into the car to test his machinery and put his cap and overcoat on again. TANNER takes off his leathern overcoat and pitches it into the car. THE CHAUFFEUR (or automobilist or motoreer or whatever England may presently decide to call him) looks round inquiringly in the act of stowing away his hammer.*[7]

THE CHAUFFEUR    Had enough of it, eh?

TANNER    I may as well walk to the house and stretch my legs and calm my nerves a little. [*Looking at his watch*] I suppose you know that we have come from Hyde Park Corner to Richmond in twenty-one minutes.

THE CHAUFFEUR    I'd ha done it under fifteen if I'd had a clear road all the way.

TANNER    Why do you do it? Is it for love of sport or for the fun of terrifying your unfortunate employer?

THE CHAUFFEUR    What are you afraid of?

TANNER    The police, and breaking my neck.

THE CHAUFFEUR    Well, if you like easy going, you can take a bus, you know. It's cheaper. You pay me to save your time and give you the value of your thousand pound car. [*He sits down calmly*].

TANNER    I am the slave of that car and of you too. I dream of the accursed thing at night.

THE CHAUFFEUR    You'll get over that. If you're going up to the house, may I ask how long you're goin to stay there? Because if you mean to put in the whole morning talkin to the ladies, I'll put the car in the stables and make myself comfortable. If not, I'll keep the car on the go about here til you come.

TANNER    Better wait here. We shan't be long. There's a young American gentleman, a Mr. Malone, who is driving Mr. Robinson down in his new American steam car.

THE CHAUFFEUR [*springing up and coming hastily out of the car to TANNER*]    American steam car! Wot! racin us down from London!

TANNER    Perhaps they're here already.

THE CHAUFFEUR   If I'd known it! [*With deep reproach*] Why didn't you tell me, Mr. Tanner?

TANNER   Because I've been told that this car is capable of 84 miles an hour; and I already know what y o u are capable of when there is a rival car on the road. No, Henry: there are things it is not good for you to know; and this was one of them. However, cheer up: we are going to have a day after your own heart. The American is to take Mr. Robinson and his sister and Miss White-field. We are to take Miss Rhoda.

THE CHAUFFEUR [*consoled, and musing on another matter*]   That's Miss Whitefield's sister, isn't it?

TANNER   Yes.

THE CHAUFFEUR   And Miss Whitefield herself is goin in the other car? Not with you?

TANNER   Why the devil should she come with me? Mr. Robinson will be in the other car. [*THE CHAUFFEUR looks at TANNER with cool incredulity, and turns to the car, whistling a popular air softly to himself. TANNER, a little annoyed, is about to pursue the subject when he hears the footsteps of OCTAVIUS on the gravel. OCTAVIUS is coming from the house, dressed for motoring, but without his overcoat*]. We've lost the race, thank Heaven: here's Mr. Robinson. Well, Tavy, is the steam car a success?

OCTAVIUS   I think so. We came from Hyde Park Corner here in seventeen minutes. [*THE CHAUFFEUR, furious, kicks the car with a groan of vexation*]. How long were you?

TANNER   Oh, about three quarters of an hour or so.

THE CHAUFFEUR [*remonstrating*]   Now, now, Mr. Tanner, come now! We could ha done it easy under fifteen.

TANNER   By the way, let me introduce you. Mr. Octavius Robin-son: Mr. Enry Straker.

STRAKER   Pleased to meet you, sir. Mr. Tanner is gittin at you with is Enry Straker, you know. You call it Henery. But I don't mind, bless you.

TANNER   You think it's simply bad taste in me to chaff him, Tavy.

But you're wrong. This man takes more trouble to drop his aitches than ever his father did to pick them up. It's a mark of caste to him. I have never met anybody more swollen with the pride of class than Enry is.

STRAKER   Easy, easy! A little moderation, Mr. Tanner.

TANNER   A little moderation, Tavy, you observe. Y o u would tell me to draw it mild. But this chap has been educated. What's more, he knows that we havn't. What was that Board School* of yours, Straker?

STRAKER   Sherbrooke Road.

TANNER   Sherbrooke Road! Would any of us say Rugby! Harrow! Eton! in that tone of intellectual snobbery? Sherbrooke Road is a place where boys learn something: Eton is a boy farm where we are sent because we are nuisances at home, and because in after life, whenever a Duke is mentioned, we can claim him as an old schoolfellow.

STRAKER   You don't know nothing about it, Mr. Tanner. It's not the Board School that does it: it's the Polytechnic.

TANNER   His university, Octavius. Not Oxford, Cambridge, Durham, Dublin or Glasgow. Not even those Nonconformist holes† in Wales. No, Tavy. Regent Street, Chelsea, the Borough——I don't know half their confounded names: these are h i s universities, not mere shops for selling class limitations like ours. You despise Oxford, Enry, don't you?

STRAKER   No, I don't. Very nice sort of place, Oxford, I should think, for people that like that sort of place. They teach you to be a gentleman there. In the Polytechnic they teach you to be an engineer or such like. See?

TANNER   Sarcasm, Tavy, sarcasm! Oh, if you could only see into Enry's soul, the depth of his contempt for a gentleman, the arrogance of his pride in being an engineer, would appal you. He pos-

---

*Analogous to a U.S. public school.

†Religious (but not Church of England) universities.

itively likes the car to break down because it brings out my gentlemanly helplessness and his workmanlike skill and resource.

STRAKER    Never you mind him, Mr. Robinson. He likes to talk. We know him, don't we?

OCTAVIUS [*earnestly*]    But there's a great truth at the bottom of what he says. I believe most intensely in the dignity of labor.

STRAKER [*unimpressed*]    That's because you never done any, Mr. Robinson. My business is to do away with labor. You'll get more out of me and a machine than you will out of twenty laborers, and not so much to drink either.

TANNER    For Heaven's sake, Tavy, don't start him on political economy. He knows all about it; and we don't. You're only a poetic Socialist, Tavy: he's a scientific one.

STRAKER [*unperturbed*]    Yes. Well, this conversation is very improvin; but I've got to look after the car; and you two want to talk about your ladies. *I* know. [*He retires to busy himself about the car; and presently saunters off towards the house*].

TANNER    That's a very momentous social phenomenon.

OCTAVIUS    What is?

TANNER    Straker is. Here have we literary and cultured persons been for years setting up a cry of the New Woman whenever some unusually old fashioned female came along; and never noticing the advent of the New Man. Straker's the New Man.

OCTAVIUS    I see nothing new about him, except your way of chaffing him. But I don't want to talk about him just now. I want to speak to you about Ann.

TANNER    Straker knew even that. He learnt it at the Polytechnic, probably. Well, what about Ann? Have you proposed to her?

OCTAVIUS [*self-reproachfully*]    I was brute enough to do so last night.

TANNER    Brute enough! What do you mean?

OCTAVIUS [*dithyrambically*]    Jack: we men are all coarse: we never understand how exquisite a woman's sensibilities are. How could I have done such a thing!

TANNER   Done what, you maudlin idiot?

OCTAVIUS   Yes, I am an idiot. Jack: if you had heard her voice! if you had seen her tears! I have lain awake all night thinking of them. If she had reproached me, I could have borne it better.

TANNER   Tears! that's dangerous. What did she say?

OCTAVIUS   She asked me how she could think of anything now but her dear father. She stifled a sob— [*he breaks down*].

TANNER [*patting him on the back*]   Bear it like a man, Tavy, even if you feel it like an ass. It's the old game: she's not tired of playing with you yet.

OCTAVIUS [*impatiently*]   Oh, don't be a fool, Jack. Do you suppose this eternal shallow cynicism of yours has any real bearing on a nature like hers?

TANNER   Hm! Did she say anything else?

OCTAVIUS   Yes; and that is why I expose myself and her to your ridicule by telling you what passed.

TANNER [*remorsefully*]   No, dear Tavy, not ridicule, on my honor! However, no matter. Go on.

OCTAVIUS   Her sense of duty is so devout, so perfect, so—

TANNER   Yes: I know. Go on.

OCTAVIUS   You see, under this new arrangement, you and Ramsden are her guardians; and she considers that all her duty to her father is now transferred to you. She said she thought I ought to have spoken to you both in the first instance. Of course she is right; but somehow it seems rather absurd that I am to come to you and formally ask to be received as a suitor for your ward's hand.

TANNER   I am glad that love has not totally extinguished your sense of humor, Tavy.

OCTAVIUS   That answer won't satisfy her.

TANNER   My official answer is, obviously, Bless you, my children: may you be happy!

OCTAVIUS   I wish you would stop playing the fool about this. If it is not serious to you, it is to me, and to her.

TANNER    You know very well that she is as free to choose as you are.

OCTAVIUS    She does not think so.

TANNER    Oh, doesn't she! j u s t! However, say what you want me to do?

OCTAVIUS    I want you to tell her sincerely and earnestly what you think about me. I want you to tell her that you can trust her to me—that is, if you feel you can.

TANNER    I have no doubt that I can trust her to you. What worries me is the idea of trusting you to her. Have you read Maeterlinck's book about the bee?*

OCTAVIUS [*keeping his temper with difficulty*]    I am not discussing literature at present.

TANNER    Be just a little patient with me. *I* am not discussing literature: the book about the bee is natural history. It's an awful lesson to mankind. You think that you are Ann's suitor; that you are the pursuer and she the pursued; that it is your part to woo, to persuade, to prevail, to overcome. Fool: it is you who are the pursued, the marked down quarry, the destined prey. You need not sit looking longingly at the bait through the wires of the trap: the door is open, and will remain so until it shuts behind you for ever.

OCTAVIUS    I wish I could believe that, vilely as you put it.

TANNER    Why, man, what other work has she in life but to get a husband? It is a woman's business to get married as soon as possible, and a man's to keep unmarried as long as he can. You have your poems and your tragedies to work at: Ann has nothing.

OCTAVIUS    I cannot write without inspiration. And nobody can give me that except Ann.

TANNER    Well, hadn't you better get it from her at a safe distance? Petrarch didn't see half as much of Laura, nor Dante of Beatrice, as you see of Ann now; and yet they wrote first-rate poetry—at least so I'm told. They never exposed their idolatry to the test of domestic familiarity; and it lasted them to their

---

*The Life of the Bee (1901).

graves. Marry Ann; and at the end of a week you'll find no more inspiration in her than in a plate of muffins.

OCTAVIUS    You think I shall tire of her!

TANNER    Not at all: you don't get tired of muffins. But you don't find inspiration in them; and you won't in her when she ceases to be a poet's dream and becomes a solid eleven stone wife. You'll be forced to dream about somebody else; and then there will be a row.

OCTAVIUS    This sort of talk is no use, Jack. You don't understand. You have never been in love.

TANNER    I! I have never been out of it. Why, I am in love even with Ann. But I am neither the slave of love nor its dupe. Go to the bee, thou poet: consider her ways and be wise.* By Heaven, Tavy, if women could do without our work, and we ate their children's bread instead of making it, they would kill us as the spider kills her mate or as the bees kill the drone. And they would be right if we were good for nothing but love.

OCTAVIUS    Ah, if we were only good enough for Love! There is nothing like Love: there is nothing else but Love: without it the world would be a dream of sordid horror.

TANNER    And this—t h i s is the man who asks me to give him the hand of my ward! Tavy: I believe we were changed in our cradles, and that you are the real descendant of Don Juan.

OCTAVIUS    I beg you not to say anything like that to Ann.

TANNER    Don't be afraid. She has marked you for her own; and nothing will stop her now. You are doomed. [*STRAKER comes back with a newspaper*]. Here comes the New Man, demoralizing himself with a halfpenny paper as usual.

STRAKER    Now would you believe it, Mr. Robinson, when we're out motoring we take in two papers, the Times for him, the Leader or the Echo for me. And do you think I ever see my

---

*In this reference to the Bible, Tanner adapts Proverbs 6:6: "Go to the ant, thou sluggard; consider her ways, and be wise" (KJV).

paper? Not much. He grabs the Leader and leaves me to stodge myself with his Times.

OCTAVIUS    Are there no winners in the Times?

TANNER    Enry don't old with bettin, Tavy. Motor records are his weakness. What's the latest?

STRAKER    Paris to Biskra at forty mile an hour average, not countin the Mediterranean.

TANNER    How many killed?

STRAKER    Two silly sheep. What does it matter? Sheep don't cost such a lot: they were glad to ave the price without the trouble o sellin em to the butcher. All the same, d'y'see, there'll be a clamor agin it presently; and then the French Government'll stop it; an our chance'll be gone, see? That's what makes me fairly mad: Mr. Tanner won't do a good run while he can.

TANNER    Tavy: do you remember my uncle James?

OCTAVIUS    Yes. Why?

TANNER    Uncle James had a first rate cook: he couldn't digest anything except what she cooked. Well, the poor man was shy and hated society. But his cook was proud of her skill, and wanted to serve up dinners to princes and ambassadors. To prevent her from leaving him, that poor old man had to give a big dinner twice a month, and suffer agonies of awkwardness. Now here am I; and here is this chap Enry Straker, the New Man. I loathe travelling; but I rather like Enry. He cares for nothing but tearing along in a leather coat and goggles, with two inches of dust all over him, at sixty miles an hour and the risk of his life and mine. Except, of course, when he is lying on his back in the mud under the machine trying to find out where it has given way. Well, if I don't give him a thousand mile run at least once a fortnight I shall lose him. He will give me the sack and go to some American millionaire; and I shall have to put up with a nice respectful groom-gardener-amateur, who will touch his hat and know his place. I am Enry's slave, just as Uncle James was his cook's slave.

STRAKER [*exasperated*]   Garn! I wish I had a car that would go as fast as you can talk, Mr. Tanner. What I say is that you lose money by a motor car unless you keep it workin. Might as well ave a pram and a nussmaid to wheel you in it as that car and me if you don't git the last inch out of us both.

TANNER [*soothingly*]   All right, Henry, all right. We'll go out for half an hour presently.

STRAKER [*in disgust*]   Arf an ahr! [*He returns to his machine; seats himself in it; and turns up a fresh page of his paper in search of more news*].

OCTAVIUS   Oh, that reminds me. I have a note for you from Rhoda. [*He gives TANNER a note*].

TANNER [*opening it*]   I rather think Rhoda is heading for a row with Ann. As a rule there is only one person an English girl hates more than she hates her mother; and that's her eldest sister. But Rhoda positively prefers her mother to Ann. She—[*indignantly*] Oh, I say!

OCTAVIUS   What's the matter?

TANNER   Rhoda was to have come with me for a ride in the motor car. She says Ann has forbidden her to go out with me.
*STRAKER suddenly begins whistling his favorite air with remarkable deliberation. Surprised by this burst of larklike melody, and jarred by a sardonic note in its cheerfulness, they turn and look inquiringly at him. But he is busy with his paper; and nothing comes of their movement.*

OCTAVIUS [*recovering himself*]   Does she give any reason?

TANNER   Reason! An insult is not a reason. Ann forbids her to be alone with me on any occasion. Says I am not a fit person for a young girl to be with. What do you think of your paragon now?

OCTAVIUS   You must remember that she has a very heavy responsibility now that her father is dead. Mrs. Whitefield is too weak to control Rhoda.

TANNER [*staring at him*]   In short, you agree with Ann.

OCTAVIUS   No; but I think I understand her. You must admit that your views are hardly suited for the formation of a young girl's mind and character.

TANNER   I admit nothing of the sort. I admit that the formation of a young lady's mind and character usually consists in telling her lies; but I object to the particular lie that I am in the habit of abusing the confidence of girls.

OCTAVIUS   Ann doesn't say that, Jack.

TANNER   What else does she mean?

STRAKER [*catching sight of ANN coming from the house*]   Miss Whitefield, gentlemen. [*He dismounts and strolls away down the avenue with the air of a man who knows he is no longer wanted*].

ANN [*coming between OCTAVIUS and TANNER*]   Good morning, Jack. I have come to tell you that poor Rhoda has got one of her headaches and cannot go out with you to-day in the car. It is a cruel disappointment to her, poor child!

TANNER   What do you say now, Tavy.

OCTAVIUS   Surely you cannot misunderstand, Jack. Ann is shewing you the kindest consideration, even at the cost of deceiving you.

ANN   What do you mean?

TANNER   Would you like to cure Rhoda's headache, Ann?

ANN   Of course.

TANNER   Then tell her what you said just now; and add that you arrived about two minutes after I had received her letter and read it.

ANN   Rhoda has written to you!

TANNER   With full particulars.

OCTAVIUS   Never mind him, Ann. You were right—quite right. Ann was only doing her duty, Jack; and you know it. Doing it in the kindest way, too.

ANN [*going to OCTAVIUS*]   How kind you are, Tavy! How helpful! How well you understand!

*OCTAVIUS beams.*

TANNER   Ay: tighten the coils. You love her, Tavy, don't you?

OCTAVIUS   She knows I do.

ANN   Hush. For shame, Tavy!

TANNER   Oh, I give you leave. I am your guardian; and I commit you to Tavy's care for the next hour. I am off for a turn in the car.

ANN   No, Jack. I must speak to you about Rhoda. Ricky: will you go back to the house and entertain your American friend. He's rather on Mamma's hands so early in the morning. She wants to finish her housekeeping.

OCTAVIUS   I fly, dearest Ann [*he kisses her hand*].

ANN [*tenderly*]   Ricky Ticky Tavy!

*He looks at her with an eloquent blush, and runs off.*

TANNER [*bluntly*]   Now look here, Ann. This time you've landed yourself; and if Tavy were not in love with you past all salvation he'd have found out what an incorrigible liar you are.

ANN   You misunderstand, Jack. I didn't dare tell Tavy the truth.

TANNER   No: your daring is generally in the opposite direction. What the devil do you mean by telling Rhoda that I am too vicious to associate with her? How can I ever have any human or decent relations with her again, now that you have poisoned her mind in that abominable way?

ANN   I know you are incapable of behaving badly—

TANNER   Then why did you lie to her?

ANN   I had to.

TANNER   Had to!

ANN   Mother made me.

TANNER [*his eye flashing*]   Ha! I might have known it. The mother! Always the mother!

ANN   It was that dreadful book of yours. You know how timid mother is. All timid women are conventional: we m u s t be conventional, Jack, or we are so cruelly, so vilely misunderstood. Even you, who are a man, cannot say what you think without being misunderstood and vilified—yes: I admit it: I have had to vilify you. Do you want to have poor Rhoda misunderstood and vilified in the same way? Would it be right for mother to let her expose herself to such treatment before she is old enough to judge for herself?

TANNER   In short, the way to avoid misunderstanding is for everybody to lie and slander and insinuate and pretend as hard as they can. That is what obeying your mother comes to.

ANN   I love my mother, Jack.

TANNER [*working himself up into a sociological rage*]   Is that any reason why you are not to call your soul your own? Oh, I protest against this vile abjection of youth to age! Look at fashionable society as you know it. What does it pretend to be? An exquisite dance of nymphs. What i s it? A horrible procession of wretched girls, each in the claws of a cynical, cunning, avaricious, disillusioned, ignorantly experienced, foul-minded old woman whom she calls mother, and whose duty it is to corrupt her mind and sell her to the highest bidder. Why do these unhappy slaves marry anybody, however old and vile, sooner than not marry at all? Because marriage is their only means of escape from these decrepit fiends who hide their selfish ambitions, their jealous hatreds of the young rivals who have supplanted them, under the mask of maternal duty and family affection. Such things are abominable: the voice of nature proclaims for the daughter a father's care and for the son a mother's. The law for father and son and mother and daughter is not the law of love: it is the law of revolution, of emancipation, of final supersession of the old and worn-out by the young and capable. I tell you, the first duty of manhood and womanhood is a Declaration of Independence: the man who pleads his father's authority is no man: the woman who pleads her mother's authority is unfit to bear citizens to a free people.

ANN [*watching him with quiet curiosity*]   I suppose you will go in seriously for politics some day, Jack.[8]

TANNER [*heavily let down*]   Eh? What? Wh——? [*Collecting his scattered wits*] What has that got to do with what I have been saying?

ANN   You talk so well.

TANNER   Talk! Talk! It means nothing to you but talk. Well, go back to your mother, and help her to poison Rhoda's imagination as she has poisoned yours. It is the tame elephants who enjoy capturing the wild ones.

ANN   I am getting on. Yesterday I was a boa constrictor: to-day I am an elephant.

TANNER   Yes. So pack your trunk and begone: I have no more to say to you.

ANN   You are so utterly unreasonable and impracticable. What c a n I do?

TANNER   Do! Break your chains. Go your way according to your own conscience and not according to your mother's. Get your mind clean and vigorous; and learn to enjoy a fast ride in a motor car instead of seeing nothing in it but an excuse for a detestable intrigue. Come with me to Marseilles and across to Algiers and to Biskra, at sixty miles an hour. Come right down to the Cape if you like. That will be a Declaration of Independence with a vengeance. You can write a book about it afterwards. That will finish your mother and make a woman of you.

ANN   [*thoughtfully*]   I don't think there would be any harm in that, Jack. You are my guardian: you stand in my father's place, by his own wish. Nobody could say a word against our travelling together. It would be delightful: thank you a thousand times, Jack. I'll come.

TANNER   [*aghast*]   You'll come!!!

ANN   Of course.

TANNER   But—[*he stops, utterly appalled; then resumes feebly*] No: look here, Ann: if there's no harm in it there's no point in doing it.

ANN   How absurd you are! You don't want to compromise me,* do you?

TANNER   Yes: that's the whole sense of my proposal.

---

*That is, undermine my reputation as a chaste woman.

ANN   You are talking the greatest nonsense; and you know it. You would never do anything to hurt me.

TANNER   Well, if you don't want to be compromised, don't come.

ANN [*with simple earnestness*]   Yes, I will come, Jack, since you wish it. You are my guardian; and I think we ought to see more of one another and come to know one another better. [*Gratefully*] It's very thoughtful and very kind of you, Jack, to offer me this lovely holiday, especially after what I said about Rhoda. You really are good—much better than you think. When do we start?

TANNER   But—

*The conversation is interrupted by the arrival of MRS. WHITEFIELD from the house. She is accompanied by the American gentleman, and followed by RAMSDEN and OCTAVIUS.*

*HECTOR MALONE is an Eastern American; but he is not at all ashamed of his nationality. This makes English people of fashion think well of him, as of a young fellow who is manly enough to confess to an obvious disadvantage without any attempt to conceal or extenuate it. They feel that he ought not to be made to suffer for what is clearly not his fault, and make a point of being specially kind to him. His chivalrous manners to women, and his elevated moral sentiments, being both gratuitous and unusual, strike them as being a little unfortunate; and though they find his vein of easy humor rather amusing when it has ceased to puzzle them (as it does at first), they have had to make him understand that he really must not tell anecdotes unless they are strictly personal and scandalous, and also that oratory is an accomplishment which belongs to a cruder stage of civilization than that in which his migration has landed him. On these points HECTOR is not quite convinced: he still thinks that the British are apt to make merits of their stupidities, and to represent their various incapacities as points of good breeding. English life seems to him to suffer from a lack of edifying rhetoric (which he calls moral tone); English behavior to shew a want of respect for womanhood; English pronunciation to fail very vulgarly in tackling such words as world, girl, bird, etc.; English society to be plain spoken to an extent which stretches occa-*

*sionally to intolerable coarseness; and English intercourse to need en-
livening by games and stories and other pastimes; so he does not feel called
upon to acquire these defects after taking great pains to cultivate himself
in a first rate manner before venturing across the Atlantic. To this culture
he finds English people either totally indifferent, as they very commonly
are to all culture, or else politely evasive, the truth being that HECTOR's
culture is nothing but a state of saturation with our literary exports of
thirty years ago, reimported by him to be unpacked at a moment's notice
and hurled at the head of English literature, science and art, at every con-
versational opportunity. The dismay set up by these sallies encourages him
in his belief that he is helping to educate England. When he finds people
chattering harmlessly about Anatole France and Nietzsche, he devastates
them with Matthew Arnold, the Autocrat of the Breakfast Table,\* and even
Macaulay; and as he is devoutly religious at bottom, he first leads the un-
wary, by humorous irreverences, to leave popular theology out of account
in discussing moral questions with him, and then scatters them in confusion by demanding whether the carrying out of his ideals of conduct was
not the manifest object of God Almighty in creating honest men and pure
women. The engaging freshness of his personality and the dumbfounder-
ing staleness of his culture make it extremely difficult to decide whether
he is worth knowing; for whilst his company is undeniably pleasant and
enlivening, there is intellectually nothing new to be got out of him, especially as he despises politics, and is careful not to talk commercial shop, in
which department he is probably much in advance of his English capitalist friends. He gets on best with romantic Christians of the amoristic sect:
hence the friendship which has sprung up between him and OCTAVIUS.*

*In appearance HECTOR is a neatly built young man of twenty-four,
with a short, smartly trimmed black beard, clear, well shaped eyes, and an
ingratiating vivacity of expression. He is, from the fashionable point of
view, faultlessly dressed. As he comes along the drive from the house with
MRS. WHITEFIELD he is sedulously making himself agreeable and entertaining, and thereby placing on her slender wit a burden it is unable to*

---

\*A book (1858) of essays by Oliver Wendell Holmes.

*bear. An Englishman would let her alone, accepting boredom and indif-ference as their common lot; and the poor lady wants to be either let alone or let prattle about the things that interest her.*

*RAMSDEN strolls over to inspect the motor car. OCTAVIUS joins HECTOR.*

ANN [*pouncing on her mother joyously*]   Oh, mamma, what do you think! Jack is going to take me to Nice in his motor car. Isn't it lovely? I am the happiest person in London.

TANNER [*desperately*]   Mrs. Whitefield objects. I am sure she ob-jects. Doesn't she, Ramsden?

RAMSDEN   I should think it very likely indeed.

ANN   You don't object, do you, mother?

MRS. WHITEFIELD   *I* object! Why should I? I think it will do you good, Ann. [*Trotting over to TANNER*] I meant to ask you to take Rhoda out for a run occasionally: she is too much in the house; but it will do when you come back.

TANNER   Abyss beneath abyss of perfidy!

ANN [*hastily, to distract attention from this outburst*]   Oh, I forgot: you have not met Mr. Malone. Mr. Tanner, my guardian: Mr. Hector Malone.

HECTOR   Pleased to meet you, Mr. Tanner. I should like to sug-gest an extension of the travelling party to Nice, if I may.

ANN   Oh, we're all coming. That's understood, isn't it?

HECTOR   I also am the modest\* possessor of a motor car. If Miss Robinson will allow me the privilege of taking her, my car is at her service.

OCTAVIUS   Violet!

*General constraint.*

ANN [*subduedly*]   Come, mother: we must leave them to talk over the arrangements. I must see to my travelling kit.

---

\*In a later edition, Shaw changed this to "mawdest," to indicate Hector's Amer-ican accent.

*MRS. WHITEFIELD looks bewildered; but ANN draws her discreetly away; and they disappear round the corner towards the house.*

HECTOR    I think I may go so far as to say that I can depend on Miss Robinson's consent.

*Continued embarrassment.*

OCTAVIUS    I'm afraid we must leave Violet behind. There are circumstances which make it impossible for her to come on such an expedition.

HECTOR [*amused and not at all convinced*]    Too American, eh? Must the young lady have a chaperone?

OCTAVIUS    It's not that, Malone—at least not altogether.

HECTOR    Indeed! May I ask what other objection applies?

TANNER [*impatiently*]    Oh, tell him, tell him. We shall never be able to keep the secret unless everybody knows what it is. Mr. Malone: if you go to Nice with Violet, you go with another man's wife. She is married.

HECTOR [*thunderstruck*]    You don't tell me so!

TANNER    We do. In confidence.

RAMSDEN [*with an air of importance, lest MALONE should suspect a misalliance*]    Her marriage has not yet been made known: she desires that it shall not be mentioned for the present.

HECTOR    I shall respect the lady's wishes. Would it be indiscreet to ask who her husband is, in case I should have an opportunity of consulting him about this trip?

TANNER    We don't know who he is.

HECTOR [*retiring into his shell in a very marked manner*]    In that case, I have no more to say.

*They become more embarrassed than ever.*

OCTAVIUS    You must think this very strange.

HECTOR    A little singular. Pardon me for saying so.

RAMSDEN [*half apologetic, half buffy*]    The young lady was married secretly; and her husband has forbidden her, it seems, to declare his name. It is only right to tell you, since you are interested in Miss—er—in Violet.

OCTAVIUS [*sympathetically*]　I hope this is not a disappointment to you.

HECTOR [*softened, coming out of his shell again*]　Well: it is a blow. I can hardly understand how a man can leave his wife in such a position. Surely it's not customary. It's not manly. It's not considerate.

OCTAVIUS　We feel that, as you may imagine, pretty deeply.

RAMSDEN [*testily*]　It is some young fool who has not enough experience to know what mystifications of this kind lead to.

HECTOR [*with strong symptoms of moral repugnance*]　I hope so. A man need be very young and pretty foolish too to be excused for such conduct. You take a very lenient view, Mr. Ramsden. Too lenient to my mind. Surely marriage should ennoble a man.

TANNER [*sardonically*]　Ha!

HECTOR　Am I to gather from that cacchination* that you don't agree with me, Mr. Tanner?

TANNER [*drily*]　Get married and try. You m a y find it delightful for a while: you certainly won't find it ennobling. The greatest common measure of a man and a woman is not necessarily greater than the man's single measure.

HECTOR　Well, we think in America that a woman's morl number is higher than a man's, and that the purer nature of a woman lifts a man right out of himself, and makes him better than he was.

OCTAVIUS [*with conviction*]　So it does.

TANNER　No wonder American women prefer to live in Europe! It's more comfortable than standing all their lives on an altar to be worshipped. Anyhow, Violet's husband has not been ennobled. So what's to be done?

HECTOR [*shaking his head*]　I can't dismiss that man's conduct as lightly as you do, Mr. Tanner. However, I'll say no more. Whoever he is, he's Miss Robinson's husband; and I should be glad for her sake to think better of him.

---

*Unpleasant-sounding laughter.

OCTAVIUS [*touched; for he divines a secret sorrow*]    I'm very sorry, Malone. Very sorry.

HECTOR [*gratefully*]    You're a good fellow, Robinson. Thank you.

TANNER    Talk about something else. Violet's coming from the house.

HECTOR    I should esteem it a very great favor, gentlemen, if you would take the opportunity to let me have a few words with the lady alone. I shall have to cry off this trip; and it's rather a delicate—

RAMSDEN [*glad to escape*]    Say no more. Come, Tanner. Come, Tavy. [*He strolls away into the park with OCTAVIUS and TANNER, past the motor car*].

*VIOLET comes down the avenue to HECTOR.*

VIOLET    Are they looking?

HECTOR    No.

*She kisses him.*

VIOLET    Have you been telling lies for my sake?

HECTOR    Lying! Lying hardly describes it. I overdo it. I get carried away in an ecstacy of mendacity. Violet: I wish you'd let me own up.

VIOLET [*instantly becoming serious and resolute*]    No, no, Hector: you promised me not to.

HECTOR    I'll keep my promise until you release me from it. But I feel mean, lying to those men, and denying my wife. Just dastardly.

VIOLET    I wish your father were not so unreasonable.

HECTOR    He's not unreasonable. He's right from his point of view. He has a prejudice against the English middle class.

VIOLET    It's too ridiculous. You know how I dislike saying such things to you, Hector; but if I were to—oh, well, no matter.

HECTOR    I know. If you were to marry the son of an English manufacturer of office furniture, your friends would consider it a misalliance. And here's my silly old dad, who is the biggest office furniture man in the world, would shew me the door for marrying the most perfect lady in England merely because she has no handle to her name. Of course it's just absurd. But I tell you, Violet, I don't like deceiving him. I feel as if I was stealing his money. Why won't you let me own up?

VIOLET    We can't afford it. You can be as romantic as you please about love, Hector; but you mustn't be romantic about money.

HECTOR [*divided between his uxoriousness and his habitual elevation of moral sentiment*]    That's very English. [*Appealing to her impulsively*] Violet: dad's bound to find us out someday.

VIOLET    Oh yes, later on of course. But don't let's go over this every time we meet, dear. You promised——

HECTOR    All right, all right, I——

VIOLET [*not to be silenced*]    It is I and not you who suffer by this concealment; and as to facing a struggle and poverty and all that sort of thing I simply will not do it. It's too silly.

HECTOR    You shall not. I'll sort of borrow the money from my dad until I get on my own feet; and then I can own up and pay up at the same time.

VIOLET [*alarmed and indignant*]    Do you mean to work? Do you want to spoil our marriage?

HECTOR    Well, I don't mean to let marriage spoil my character. Your friend Mr. Tanner has got the laugh on me a bit already about that; and——

VIOLET    The beast! I hate Jack Tanner.

HECTOR [*magnanimously*]    Oh, h e ' s all right: he only needs the love of a good woman to ennoble him. Besides, he's proposed a motoring trip to Nice; and I'm going to take you.

VIOLET    How jolly!

HECTOR    Yes; but how are we going to manage? You see, they've warned me off going with you, so to speak. They've told me in confidence that you're married. That's just the most overwhelming confidence I've ever been honored with.

*TANNER returns with STRAKER, who goes to his car.*

TANNER    Your car is a great success, Mr. Malone. Your engineer is showing it off to Mr. Ramsden.

HECTOR [*eagerly—forgetting himself*]    Let's come, Vi.

VIOLET [*coldly, warning him with her eyes*]    I beg your pardon, Mr. Malone, I did not quite catch—

HECTOR [*recollecting himself*]    I ask to be allowed the pleasure of shewing you my little American steam car, Miss Robinson.

VIOLET    I shall be very pleased. [*They go off together down the avenue*].

TANNER    About this trip, Straker.

STRAKER [*preoccupied with the car*]    Yes?

TANNER    Miss Whitefield is supposed to be coming with me.

STRAKER    So I gather.

TANNER    Mr. Robinson is to be one of the party.

STRAKER    Yes.

TANNER    Well, if you can manage so as to be a good deal occupied with me, and leave Mr. Robinson a good deal occupied with Miss Whitefield, he will be deeply grateful to you.

STRAKER [*looking round at him*]    Evidently.

TANNER    "Evidently"! Your grandfather would have simply winked.

STRAKER    My grandfather would have touched his at.

TANNER    And I should have given your good nice respectful grandfather a sovereign.

STRAKER    Five shillins, more likely. [*He leaves the car and approaches TANNER*]. What about the lady's views?

TANNER    She is just as willing to be left to Mr. Robinson as Mr. Robinson is to be left to her. [*STRAKER looks at his principal with cool scepticism; then turns to the car whistling his favorite air*]. Stop that aggravating noise. What do you mean by it? [*STRAKER calmly resumes the melody and finishes it. TANNER politely hears it out before he again addresses STRAKER, this time with elaborate seriousness*]. Enry: I have ever been a warm advocate of the spread of music among the masses; but I object to your obliging the company whenever Miss Whitefield's name is mentioned. You did it this morning, too.

STRAKER [*obstinately*]   It's not a bit o use. Mr. Robinson may as well give it up first as last.

TANNER   Why?

STRAKER   Garn! You know why. Course it's not my business; but you needn't start kiddin me about it.

TANNER   I am not kidding. I don't know why.

STRAKER [*cheerfully sulky*]   Oh, very well. All right. It ain't my business.

TANNER [*impressively*]   I trust, Enry, that, as between employer and engineer, I shall always know how to keep my proper distance, and not intrude my private affairs on you. Even our business arrangements are subject to the approval of your Trade Union. But don't abuse your advantages. Let me remind you that Voltaire said that what was too silly to be said could be sung.

STRAKER   It wasn't Voltaire: it was Bow Mar Shay.

TANNER   I stand corrected: Beaumarchais* of course. Now y o u seem to think that what is too delicate to be said can be whistled. Unfortunately your whistling, though melodious, is unintelligible. Come! there's nobody listening: neither my genteel relatives nor the secretary of your confounded Union. As man to man, Enry, why do you think that my friend has no chance with Miss Whitefield?

STRAKER   Cause she's arter summun else.

TANNER   Bosh! who else?

STRAKER   You.

TANNER   Me!!!

STRAKER   Mean to tell me you didn't know? Oh, come, Mr. Tanner!

---

*Pierre de Beaumarchais was an eighteenth-century playwright whose *Marriage of Figaro* (1784) criticized aristocratic privilege.

TANNER [*in fierce earnest*]   Are you playing the fool, or do you mean it?

STRAKER [*with a flash of temper*]   I'm not playin no fool. [*More coolly*] Why, it's as plain as the nose on your face. If you ain't spotted that, you don't know much about these sort of things. [*Serene again*] Ex-cuse me, you know, Mr. Tanner; but you asked me as man to man; and I told you as man to man.

TANNER [*wildly appealing to the heavens*]   Then I——I am the bee, the spider, the marked down victim, the destined prey.

STRAKER   I dunno about the bee and the spider. But the marked down victim, that's what you are and no mistake; and a jolly good job for you, too, I should say.

TANNER [*momentously*]   Henry Straker: the golden moment of your life has arrived.

STRAKER   What d'y'mean?

TANNER   That record to Biskra.

STRAKER [*eagerly*]   Yes?

TANNER   Break it.

STRAKER [*rising to the height of his destiny*]   D'y' mean it?

TANNER   I do.

STRAKER   When?

TANNER   Now. Is that machine ready to start?

STRAKER [*quailing*]   But you can't——

TANNER [*cutting him short by getting into the car*]   Off we go. First to the bank for money; then to my rooms for my kit; then to your rooms for your kit; then break the record from London to Dover or Folkestone; then across the channel and away like mad to Marseilles, Gibraltar, Genoa, any port from which we can sail to a Mahometan country where men are protected from women.

STRAKER   Garn! you're kiddin.

TANNER [*resolutely*]   Stay behind then. If you won't come I'll do it alone. [*He starts the motor*].

STRAKER [*running after him*]   Here! Mister! arf a mo! steady on! [*he scrambles in as the car plunges forward*].

# ACT III

*Evening in the Sierra Nevada. Rolling slopes of brown, with olive trees instead of apple trees in the cultivated patches, and occasional prickly pears instead of gorse and bracken in the wilds. Higher up, tall stone peaks and precipices, all handsome and distinguished. No wild nature here: rather a most aristocratic mountain landscape made by a fastidious artist-creator. No vulgar profusion of vegetation: even a touch of aridity in the frequent patches of stones: Spanish magnificence and Spanish economy everywhere.*

*Not very far north of a spot at which the high road over one of the passes crosses a tunnel on the railway from Malaga to Granada, is one of the mountain amphitheatres of the Sierra. Looking at it from the wide end of the horse-shoe, one sees, a little to the right, in the face of the cliff, a romantic cave which is really an abandoned quarry, and towards the left a little hill, commanding a view of the road, which skirts the amphitheatre on the left, maintaining its higher level on embankments and an occasional stone arch. On the hill, watching the road, is a man who is either a Spaniard or a Scotchman. Probably a Spaniard, since he wears the dress of a Spanish goatherd and seems at home in the Sierra Nevada, but very like a Scotchman for all that. In the hollow, on the slope leading to the quarry-cave, are about a dozen men who, as they recline at their ease round a heap of smouldering white ashes of dead leaf and brushwood, have an air of being conscious of themselves as picturesque scoundrels honoring the Sierra by using it as an effective pictorial background. As a matter of artistic fact they are not picturesque; and the mountains tolerate them as lions tolerate lice. An English policeman or Poor Law Guardian would recognize them as a selected band of tramps and ablebodied paupers.*

*This description of them is not wholly contemptuous. Whoever has*

*intelligently observed the tramp, or visited the ablebodied ward of a
workhouse, will admit that our social failures are not all drunkards
and weaklings. Some of them are men who do not fit the class they were
born into. Precisely the same qualities that make the educated
gentleman an artist may make an uneducated manual laborer an
ablebodied pauper. There are men who fall helplessly into the workhouse
because they are good for nothing; but there are also men who are there
because they are strongminded enough to disregard the social
convention (obviously not a disinterested one on the part of the
ratepayer) which bids a man live by heavy and badly paid drudgery
when he has the alternative of walking into the workhouse, announcing
himself as a destitute person, and legally compelling the Guardians to
feed, clothe and house him better than he could feed, clothe and house
himself without great exertion. When a man who is born a poet refuses
a stool in a stockbroker's office, and starves in a garret, spunging on a
poor landlady or on his friends and relatives sooner than work against
his grain; or when a lady, because she is a lady, will face any extremity
of parasitic dependence rather than take a situation as cook or
parlormaid, we make large allowances for them. To such allowances the
ablebodied pauper, and his nomadic variant the tramp, are equally
entitled.*

*Further, the imaginative man, if his life is to be tolerable to him,
must have leisure to tell himself stories, and a position which lends
itself to imaginative decoration. The ranks of unskilled labor offer no
such positions. We misuse our laborers horribly; and when a man refuses
to be misused, we have no right to say that he is refusing honest work.
Let us be frank in this matter before we go on with our play; so that we
may enjoy it without hypocrisy. If we were reasoning, farsighted people,
four fifths of us would go straight to the Guardians for relief, and
knock the whole social system to pieces with most beneficial
reconstructive results. The reason we do not do this is because we work
like bees or ants, by instinct or habit, not reasoning about the matter at
all. Therefore when a man comes along who can and does reason, and
who, applying the Kantian test to his conduct, can truly say to us, If*

everybody did as I do, the world would be compelled to reform itself industrially, and abolish slavery and squalor, which exist only because everybody does as you do, let us honor that man and seriously consider the advisability of following his example. Such a man is the able-bodied, able-minded pauper. Were he a gentleman doing his best to get a pension or a sinecure instead of sweeping a crossing, nobody would blame him for deciding that so long as the alternative lies between living mainly at the expense of the community and allowing the community to live mainly at his, it would be folly to accept what is to him personally the greater of the two evils.

We may therefore contemplate the tramps of the Sierra without prejudice, admitting cheerfully that our objects—briefly, to be gentlemen of fortune—are much the same as theirs, and the difference in our position and methods merely accidental. One or two of them, perhaps, it would be wiser to kill without malice in a friendly and frank manner; for there are bipeds, just as there are quadrupeds, who are too dangerous to be left unchained and unmuzzled; and these cannot fairly expect to have other men's lives wasted in the work of watching them. But as society has not the courage to kill them, and, when it catches them, simply wreaks on them some superstitious expiatory rites of torture and degradation, and then lets them loose with heightened qualifications for mischief, it is just as well that they are at large in the Sierra, and in the hands of a chief who looks as if he might possibly, on provocation, order them to be shot.

This chief, seated in the centre of the group on a squared block of stone from the quarry, is a tall strong man, with a striking cockatoo nose, glossy black hair, pointed beard, upturned moustache, and a Mephistophelean affectation which is fairly imposing, perhaps because the scenery admits of a larger swagger than Piccadilly, perhaps because of a certain sentimentality in the man which gives him that touch of grace which alone can excuse deliberate picturesquesness. His eyes and mouth are by no means rascally; he has a fine voice and a ready wit; and whether he is really the strongest man in the party or not, he looks it. He is certainly the best fed, the best dressed, and the best trained.

*The fact that he speaks English is not unexpected, in spite of the*
*Spanish landscape; for with the exception of one man who might be*
*guessed as a bullfighter ruined by drink, and one unmistakable*
*Frenchman, they are all cockney or American; therefore, in a land of*
*cloaks and sombreros, they mostly wear seedy overcoats, woollen*
*mufflers, hard hemispherical hats, and dirty brown gloves. Only a very*
*few dress after their leader, whose broad sombrero with a cock's feather*
*in the band, and voluminous cloak descending to his high boots, are as*
*un-English as possible. None of them are armed; and the ungloved ones*
*keep their hands in their pockets because it is their national belief that*
*it must be dangerously cold in the open air with the night coming on.*
*(It is as warm an evening as any reasonable man could desire).*

*Except the bullfighting inebriate there is only one person in the*
*company who looks more than, say, thirty-three. He is a small man*
*with reddish whiskers, weak eyes, and the anxious look of a small*
*tradesman in difficulties. He wears the only tall hat visible: it shines in*
*the sunset with the sticky glow of some sixpenny patent hat reviver,*
*often applied and constantly tending to produce a worse state of the*
*original surface than the ruin it was applied to remedy. He has a collar*
*and cuffs of celluloid; and his brown Chesterfield overcoat, with velvet*
*collar, is still presentable. He is pre-eminently the respectable man of*
*the party, and is certainly over forty, possibly over fifty. He is the corner*
*man on the leader's right, opposite three men in scarlet ties on his left.*
*One of these three is the Frenchman. Of the remaining two, who are*
*both English, one is argumentative, solemn, and obstinate; the other*
*rowdy and mischievous.*

*THE CHIEF, with a magnificent fling of the end of his cloak across his left*
*shoulder, rises to address them. The applause which greets him shews that he*
*is a favorite orator.*

THE CHIEF  Friends and fellow brigands. I have a proposal to
make to this meeting. We have now spent three evenings in discussing the question Have Anarchists or Social-Democrats the

most personal courage? We have gone into the principles of Anarchism and Social-Democracy at great length. The cause of Anarchy has been ably represented by our one Anarchist, who
doesn't know what Anarchism means [*laughter*]—

THE ANARCHIST [*rising*]    A point of order, Mendoza—

MENDOZA [*forcibly*]    No, by thunder: your last point of order
took half an hour. Besides, Anarchists don't believe in order.

THE ANARCHIST [*mild, polite but persistent: he is, in fact, the respectable looking elderly man in the celluloid collar and cuffs*]    That is
a vulgar error. I can prove—

MENDOZA    Order, order.

THE OTHERS [*shouting*]    Order, order. Sit down. Chair! Shut up.
*THE ANARCHIST is suppressed.*

MENDOZA    On the other hand we have three Social-Democrats
among us. They are not on speaking terms; and they have put
before us three distinct and incompatible views of Social-
Democracy.

THE THREE MEN IN SCARLET TIES    1. Mr. Chairman, I
protest. A personal explanation. 2. It's a lie. I never said so. Be
fair, Mendoza. 3. Je demande la parole. C'est absolument faux.
C'est faux! faux!! faux!!! Assas-s-s-s-sin!!!!!!*

MENDOZA    Order, order.

THE OTHERS    Order, order, order! Chair!
*The Social-Democrats are suppressed.*

MENDOZA    Now, we tolerate all opinions here. But after all,
comrades, the vast majority of us are neither Anarchists nor
Socialists, but gentlemen and Christians.

THE MAJORITY [*shouting assent*]    Hear, hear! So we are. Right.

THE ROWDY SOCIAL-DEMOCRAT [*smarting under suppression*]
You ain't no Christian. You're a Sheeny, you are.

MENDOZA [*with crushing magnanimity*]    My friend: *I* am an excep-

---

*I demand to speak. It is completely false. It's false! false!! false!!! Mur-r-r-r-
derer! (French).

tion to all rules. It is true that I have the honor to be a Jew; and when the Zionists need a leader to reassemble our race on its historic soil of Palestine, Mendoza will not be the last to volunteer [*sympathetic applause—hear, hear, & c.*]. But I am not a slave to any superstition. I have swallowed all the formulas, even that of Socialism; though, in a sense, once a Socialist, always a Socialist.

THE SOCIAL-DEMOCRATS     Hear, hear!

MENDOZA     But I am well aware that the ordinary man—even the ordinary brigand, who can scarcely be called an ordinary man [*Hear, hear!*]—is not a philosopher. Common sense is good enough for him; and in our business affairs common sense is good enough for me. Well, what is our business here in the Sierra Nevada, chosen by the Moors as the fairest spot in Spain? Is it to discuss abstruse questions of political economy? No: it is to hold up motor cars and secure a more equitable distribution of wealth.

THE SULKY SOCIAL-DEMOCRAT     All made by labor, mind you.

MENDOZA [*urbanely*]     Undoubtedly. All made by labor, and on its way to be squandered by wealthy vagabonds in the dens of vice that disfigure the sunny shores of the Mediterranean. We intercept that wealth. We restore it to circulation among the class that produced it and that chiefly needs it—the working class. We do this at the risk of our lives and liberties, by the exercise of the virtues of courage, endurance, foresight, and abstinence—especially abstinence. I myself have eaten nothing but prickly pears and broiled rabbit for three days.

THE SULKY SOCIAL-DEMOCRAT [*stubbornly*]     No more ain't we.

MENDOZA [*indignantly*]     Have I taken more than my share?

THE SULKY SOCIAL-DEMOCRAT [*unmoved*]     Why should you?

THE ANARCHIST     Why should he not? To each according to his needs: from each according to his means.

THE FRENCHMAN [*shaking his fist at the ANARCHIST*]    Fumiste!*

MENDOZA [*diplomatically*]    I agree with both of you.

THE GENUINELY ENGLISH BRIGANDS    Hear, hear! Bravo, Mendoza!

MENDOZA    What I say is, let us treat one another as gentlemen, and strive to excel in personal courage only when we take the field.

THE ROWDY SOCIAL-DEMOCRAT [*derisively*]    Shikespear.

*A whistle comes from the goatherd on the hill. He springs up and points excitedly forward along the road to the north.*

THE GOATHERD    Automobile! Automobile! [*He rushes down the hill and joins the rest, who all scramble to their feet*].

MENDOZA [*in ringing tones*]    To arms! Who has the gun?

THE SULKY SOCIAL-DEMOCRAT [*handing a rifle to MENDOZA*]    Here.

MENDOZA    Have the nails been strewn in the road?

THE ROWDY SOCIAL-DEMOCRAT    Two ahnces of em.

MENDOZA    Good! [*To the Frenchman*] With me, Duval. If the nails fail, puncture their tires with a bullet. [*He gives the rifle to DUVAL, who follows him up the hill. MENDOZA produces an opera glass. The others hurry across to the road and disappear to the north*].

MENDOZA [*on the hill, using his glass*]    Two only, a capitalist and his chauffeur. They look English.

DUVAL    Angliche! Aoh yess. Cochons! [*Handling the rifle*] Faut tirer, n'est-ce-pas?†

MENDOZA    No: the nails have gone home. Their tire is down: they stop.

DUVAL [*shouting to the others*]    Fondez sur eux, nom de Dieu!‡

MENDOZA [*rebuking his excitement*]    Du calme,§ Duval: keep your hair on. They take it quietly. Let us descend and receive them.

---

*Phony (French).

†Pigs! . . . We have to shoot, right? (French).

‡Fall on them, for God's sake (French).

§Calm down (French).

*MENDOZA descends, passing behind the fire and coming forward, whilst TANNER and STRAKER, in their motoring goggles, leather coats, and caps, are led in from the road by the brigands.*

TANNER    Is this the gentleman you describe as your boss? Does he speak English?

THE ROWDY SOCIAL-DEMOCRAT    Course he does. Y' downt suppowz we Hinglishmen lets ahrselves be bossed by a bloomin Spenniard, do you?

MENDOZA [*with dignity*]    Allow me to introduce myself: Mendoza, President of the League of the Sierra! [*Posing loftily*] I am a brigand: I live by robbing the rich.

TANNER [*promptly*]    I am a gentleman: I live by robbing the poor. Shake hands.

THE ENGLISH SOCIAL-DEMOCRATS    Hear, hear!

*General laughter and good humor. TANNER and MENDOZA shake hands. The BRIGANDS drop into their former places.*

STRAKER    Ere! where do I come in?

TANNER [*introducing*]    My friend and chauffeur.

THE SULKY SOCIAL-DEMOCRAT [*suspiciously*]    Well, which is he? friend or show-foor? It makes all the difference, you know.

MENDOZA [*explaining*]    We should expect ransom for a friend. A professional chauffeur is free of the mountains. He even takes a trifling percentage of his principal's ransom if he will honor us by accepting it.

STRAKER    I see. Just to encourage me to come this way again. Well, I'll think about it.

DUVAL [*impulsively rushing across to STRAKER*]    Mon frère!* [*He embraces him rapturously and kisses him on both cheeks*].

STRAKER [*disgusted*]    Ere, git out: don't be silly. Who are you, pray?

DUVAL    Duval: Social-Democrat.

STRAKER    Oh, you're a Social-Democrat, are you?

---

*My brother (French).

THE ANARCHIST   He means that he has sold out to the parliamentary humbugs and the bourgeoisie. Compromise! that is his faith.

DUVAL [*furiously*]   I understand what he say. He say Bourgeois. He say Compromise. Jamais de la vie! Misérable menteur——*

STRAKER   See here, Captain Mendoza, ow much o this sort o thing do you put up with here? Are we avin a pleasure trip in the mountains, or are we at a Socialist meetin?

THE MAJORITY   Hear, hear! Shut up. Chuck it. Sit down, &c. &c. [*The Social-Democrats and the ANARCHIST are bustled into the background. STRAKER, after superintending this proceeding with satisfaction, places himself on MENDOZA's left, TANNER being on his right*].

MENDOZA   Can we offer you anything? Broiled rabbit and prickly pears——

TANNER   Thank you: we have dined.

MENDOZA [*to his followers*]   Gentlemen: business is over for the day. Go as you please until morning.

*The BRIGANDS disperse into groups lazily. Some go into the cave. Others sit down or lie down to sleep in the open. A few produce a pack of cards and move off towards the road; for it is now starlight; and they know that motor cars have lamps which can be turned to account for lighting a card party.*

STRAKER [*calling after them*]   Don't none of you go fooling with that car, d'ye hear?

MENDOZA   No fear, Monsieur le Chauffeur. The first one we captured cured us of that.

STRAKER [*interested*]   What did it do?

MENDOZA   It carried three brave comrades of ours, who did not know how to stop it, into Granada, and capsized them opposite the police station. Since then we never touch one without sending for the chauffeur. Shall we chat at our ease?

TANNER   By all means.

---

*Never in my life! Rotten liar (French).

*TANNER, MENDOZA, and STRAKER sit down on the turf by the fire. MENDOZA delicately waives his presidential dignity, of which the right to sit on the squared stone block is the appanage, by sitting on the ground like his guests, and using the stone only as a support for his back.*

MENDOZA   It is the custom in Spain always to put off business until to-morrow. In fact, you have arrived out of office hours. However, if you would prefer to settle the question of ransom at once, I am at your service.

TANNER   To-morrow will do for me. I am rich enough to pay anything in reason.

MENDOZA [*respectfully, much struck by this admission*]   You are a remarkable man, sir. Our guests usually describe themselves as miserably poor.

TANNER   Pooh! Miserably poor people don't own motor cars.

MENDOZA   Precisely what we say to them.

TANNER   Treat us well: we shall not prove ungrateful.

STRAKER   No prickly pears and broiled rabbits, you know. Don't tell me you can't do us a bit better than that if you like.

MENDOZA   Wine, kids, milk, cheese and bread can be procured for ready money.

STRAKER [*graciously*]   Now you're talking.

TANNER   Are you all Socialists here, may I ask?

MENDOZA [*repudiating this humiliating misconception*]   Oh no, no, no: nothing of the kind, I assure you. We naturally have modern views as to the justice of the existing distribution of wealth: otherwise we should lose our self-respect. But nothing that you could take exception to, except two or three faddists.

TANNER   I had no intention of suggesting anything discreditable. In fact, I am a bit of a Socialist myself.

STRAKER [*drily*]   Most rich men are, I notice.

MENDOZA   Quite so. It has reached us, I admit. It is in the air of the century.

STRAKER   Socialism must be looking up a bit if your chaps are taking to it.

MENDOZA    That is true, sir. A movement which is confined to philosophers and honest men can never exercise any real political influence: there are too few of them. Until a movement shews itself capable of spreading among brigands, it can never hope for a political majority.

TANNER    But are your brigands any less honest than ordinary citizens?

MENDOZA    Sir: I will be frank with you. Brigandage is abnormal. Abnormal professions attract two classes: those who are not good enough for ordinary bourgeois life and those who are too good for it. We are dregs and scum, sir: the dregs very filthy, the scum very superior.

STRAKER    Take care! some o the dregs'll hear you.

MENDOZA    It does not matter: each brigand thinks himself scum, and likes to hear the others called dregs.

TANNER    Come! you are a wit. [*MENDOZA inclines his head, flattered*]. May one ask you a blunt question?

MENDOZA    As blunt as you please.

TANNER    How does it pay a man of your talent to shepherd such a flock as this on broiled rabbit and prickly pears? I have seen men less gifted, and I'll swear less honest, supping at the Savoy on foie gras and champagne.

MENDOZA    Pooh! they have all had their turn at the broiled rabbit, just as I shall have my turn at the Savoy. Indeed, I have had a turn there already—as waiter.

TANNER    A waiter! You astonish me!

MENDOZA    [*reflectively*]    Yes: I, Mendoza of the Sierra, was a waiter. Hence, perhaps, my cosmopolitanism. [*With sudden intensity*] Shall I tell you the story of my life?

STRAKER [*apprehensively*]    If it ain't too long, old chap—

TANNER [*interrupting him*]    Tsh-sh: you are a Philistine, Henry: you have no romance in you. [*To MENDOZA*] You interest me extremely, President. Never mind Henry: he can go to sleep.

MENDOZA    The woman I loved—

STRAKER   Oh, this is a love story, is it? Right you are. Go on: I was only afraid you were going to talk about yourself.

MENDOZA   Myself! I have thrown myself away for her sake: that is why I am here. No matter: I count the world well lost for her. She had, I pledge you my word, the most magnificent head of hair I ever saw. She had humor; she had intellect; she could cook to perfection; and her highly strung temperament made her uncertain, incalculable, variable, capricious, cruel, in a word, enchanting.

STRAKER   A six shillin novel sort o woman, all but the cookin. Er name was Lady Gladys Plantagenet, wasn't it?

MENDOZA   No, sir: she was not an earl's daughter. Photography, reproduced by the half-tone process, has made me familiar with the appearance of the daughters of the English peerage; and I can honestly say that I would have sold the lot, faces, dowries, clothes, titles, and all, for a smile from this woman. Yet she was a woman of the people, a worker: otherwise—let me reciprocate your bluntness—I should have scorned her.

TANNER   Very properly. And did she respond to your love?

MENDOZA   Should I be here if she did? She objected to marry a Jew.

TANNER   On religious grounds?

MENDOZA   No: she was a freethinker.* She said that every Jew considers in his heart that English people are dirty in their habits.

TANNER [*surprised*]   Dirty!

MENDOZA   It shewed her extraordinary knowledge of the world; for it is undoubtedly true. Our elaborate sanitary code makes us unduly contemptuous of the Gentile.

TANNER   Did you ever hear that, Henry?

---

* Atheist.

STRAKER    I've heard my sister say so. She was cook in a Jewish family once.

MENDOZA    I could not deny it; neither could I eradicate the impression it made on her mind. I could have got round any other objection; but no woman can stand a suspicion of indelicacy as to her person. My entreaties were in vain: she always retorted that she wasn't good enough for me, and recommended me to marry an accursed barmaid named Rebecca Lazarus, whom I loathed. I talked of suicide: she offered me a packet of beetle poison to do it with. I hinted at murder: she went into hysterics; and as I am a living man I went to America so that she might sleep without dreaming that I was stealing upstairs to cut her throat. In America I went out west and fell in with a man who was wanted by the police for holding up trains. It was he who had the idea of holding up motor cars in the South of Europe: a welcome idea to a desperate and disappointed man. He gave me some valuable introductions to capitalists of the right sort. I formed a syndicate; and the present enterprise is the result. I became leader, as the Jew always becomes leader, by his brains and imagination. But with all my pride of race I would give everything I possess to be an Englishman. I am like a boy: I cut her name on the trees and her initials on the sod. When I am alone I lie down and tear my wretched hair and cry Louisa—

STRAKER [*startled*]    Louisa!

MENDOZA    It is her name—Louisa—Louisa Straker—

TANNER    Straker!

STRAKER [*scrambling up on his knees most indignantly*]    Look here: Louisa Straker is my sister, see? Wot do you mean by gassin about her like this? Wotshe got to do with you?

MENDOZA    A dramatic coincidence! You are Enry, her favorite brother!

STRAKER    Oo are you callin Enry? What call have you to take a liberty with my name or with hers? For two pins I'd punch your fat ed, so I would.

MENDOZA [*with grandiose calm*]    If I let you do it, will you promise to brag of it afterwards to her? She will be reminded of her Mendoza: that is all I desire.

TANNER    This is genuine devotion, Henry. You should respect it.

STRAKER [*fiercely*]    Funk,* more likely.

MENDOZA [*springing to his feet*]    Funk! Young man: I come of a famous family of fighters; and as your sister well knows, you would have as much chance against me as a perambulator against your motor car.

STRAKER [*secretly daunted, but rising from his knees with an air of reckless pugnacity*]    I ain't afraid of you. With your Louisa! Louisa! Miss Straker is good enough for you, I should think.

MENDOZA    I wish you could persuade her to think so.

STRAKER [*exasperated*]    Here—

TANNER [*rising quickly and interposing*]    Oh come, Henry: even if you could fight the President you can't fight the whole League of the Sierra. Sit down again and be friendly. A cat may look at a king; and even a President of brigands may look at your sister. All this family pride is really very old fashioned.

STRAKER [*subdued, but grumbling*]    Let him look at her. But wot does he mean by makin out that she ever looked at im? [*Reluctantly resuming his couch on the turf* ] Ear him talk, one ud think she was keepin company with him. [*He turns his back on them and composes himself to sleep*].

MENDOZA [*to TANNER, becoming more confidential as he finds himself virtually alone with a sympathetic listener in the still starlight of the mountains; for all the rest are asleep by this time*]    It was just so with her, sir. Her intellect reached forward into the twentieth century: her social prejudices and family affections reached back

---

*Cold feet.

into the dark ages. Ah, sir, how the words of Shakespear seem to fit every crisis in our emotions!

> I loved Louisa: 40,000 brothers
> Could not with all their quantity of love
> Make up my sum.*

And so on. I forget the rest. Call it madness if you will—infatuation. I am an able man, a strong man: in ten years I should have owned a first-class hotel. I met her; and—you see!—I am a brigand, an outcast. Even Shakespear cannot do justice to what I feel for Louisa. Let me read you some lines that I have written about her myself. However slight their literary merit may be, they express what I feel better than any casual words can. [*He produces a packet of hotel bills scrawled with manuscript, and kneels at the fire to decipher them, poking it with a stick to make it glow*].

TANNER [*slapping him rudely on the shoulder*]    Put them in the fire, President.

MENDOZA [*startled*]    Eh?

TANNER    You are sacrificing your career to a monomania.

MENDOZA    I know it.

TANNER    No you don't. No man would commit such a crime against himself if he really knew what he was doing. How can you look round at these august hills, look up at this divine sky, taste this finely tempered air, and then talk like a literary hack on a second floor in Bloomsbury?

MENDOZA [*shaking his head*]    The Sierra is no better than Bloomsbury when once the novelty has worn off. Besides, these mountains make you dream of women—of women with magnificent hair.

TANNER    Of Louisa, in short. They will not make me dream of women, my friend: I am heartwhole.

---

*Quotation from *Hamlet* (act 5, scene 1), with "Louisa" substituted for "Ophelia."

MENDOZA   Do not boast until morning, sir. This is a strange
country for dreams.

TANNER   Well, we shall see. Goodnight. [*He lies down and composes
himself to sleep*].

*MENDOZA, with a sigh, follows his example; and for a few moments
there is peace in the Sierra. Then MENDOZA sits up suddenly and says
pleadingly to TANNER—*

MENDOZA   Just allow me to read a few lines before you go to
sleep. I should really like your opinion of them.

TANNER [*drowsily*]   Go on. I am listening.

MENDOZA   I saw thee first in Whitsun week*

Louisa, Louisa—

TANNER [*rousing himself*]   My dear President, Louisa is a very
pretty name; but it really doesn't rhyme well to Whitsun week.

MENDOZA   Of course not. Louisa is not the rhyme, but the refrain.

TANNER [*subsiding*]   Ah, the refrain. I beg your pardon. Go on.

MENDOZA   Perhaps you do not care for that one: I think you will
like this better. [*He recites, in rich soft tones, and in slow time*]

Louisa, I love thee.
I love thee, Louisa.
Louisa, Louisa, Louisa, I love thee.
One name and one phrase make my music, Louisa.
Louisa, Louisa, Louisa, I love thee.

Mendoza thy lover,
Thy lover, Mendoza,
Mendoza adoringly lives for Louisa.
There's nothing but that in the world for Mendoza.
Louisa, Louisa, Mendoza adores thee.

---

*White Sunday (Pentecost) week, a solemn period in the Christian calendar.

[*Affected*] There is no merit in producing beautiful lines upon such a name. Louisa is an exquisite name, is it not?

TANNER [*all but asleep, responds with a faint groan*].

MENDOZA    O wert thou, Louisa,
> The wife of Mendoza,
> Mendoza's Louisa, Louisa Mendoza,
> How blest were the life of Louisa's Mendoza!
> How painless his longing of love for Louisa!

That is real poetry—from the heart—from the heart of hearts. Don't you think it will move her?

*No answer.*

[*Resignedly*] Asleep, as usual. Doggrel to all the world: heavenly music to me! Idiot that I am to wear my heart on my sleeve! [*He composes himself to sleep, murmuring*] Louisa, I love thee; I love thee, Louisa; Louisa, Louisa, Louisa, I—

*STRAKER snores; rolls over on his side; and relapses into sleep. Stillness settles on the Sierra; and the darkness deepens. The fire has again buried itself in white ash and ceased to glow. The peaks shew unfathomably dark against the starry firmament; but now the stars dim and vanish; and the sky seems to steal away out of the universe. Instead of the Sierra there is nothing; omnipresent nothing. No sky, no peaks, no light, no sound, no time nor space, utter void. Then somewhere the beginning of a pallor, and with it a faint throbbing buzz as of a ghostly violoncello palpitating on the same note endlessly. A couple of ghostly violins presently take advantage of this bass*

*and therewith the pallor reveals a man in the void, an incorporeal but visible man, seated, absurdly enough, on nothing. For a moment he raises his head as the music passes him by. Then, with a heavy sigh, he droops in utter dejection; and the violins, discouraged, retrace their melody in despair and at last give it up, extinguished by wailings from uncanny wind instruments, thus:—*

It is all very odd. One recognizes the Mozartian strain; and on this hint, and by the aid of certain sparkles of violet light in the pallor, the man's costume explains itself as that of a Spanish nobleman of the XV–XVI century. DON JUAN, of course; but where? why? how? Besides, in the brief lifting of his face, now hidden by his hat brim, there was a curious suggestion of TANNER. A more critical, fastidious, handsome face, paler and colder, without TANNER's impetuous credulity and enthusiasm, and without a touch of his modern plutocratic vulgarity, but still a resemblance, even an identity. The name too: DON JUAN TENORIO, JOHN TANNER. Where on earth—or elsewhere—have we got to from the XX century and the Sierra?

Another pallor in the void, this time not violet, but a disagreeable smoky yellow. With it, the whisper of a ghostly clarionet turning this tune into infinite sadness:

The yellowish pallor moves: there is an old crone wandering in the void, bent and toothless; draped, as well as one can guess, in the coarse brown frock of some religious order. She wanders and wanders in her slow hopeless way, much as a wasp flies in its rapid busy way, until she blunders against the thing she seeks: companionship. With a sob of relief the poor

*old creature clutches at the presence of the man and addresses him in her
dry unlovely voice, which can still express pride and resolution as well as
suffering.*

THE OLD WOMAN    Excuse me; but I am so lonely; and this
place is so awful.

DON JUAN    A new comer?

THE OLD WOMAN    Yes: I suppose I died this morning. I confessed; I had extreme unction; I was in bed with my family about
me and my eyes fixed on the cross. Then it grew dark; and when
the light came back it was this light by which I walk seeing nothing. I have wandered for hours in horrible loneliness.

DON JUAN [sighing]    Ah! you have not yet lost the sense of time.
One soon does, in eternity.

THE OLD WOMAN    Where are we?

DON JUAN    In hell.

THE OLD WOMAN [proudly]    Hell! I in hell! How dare you?

DON JUAN [unimpressed]    Why not, Señora?

THE OLD WOMAN    You do not know to whom you are speaking. I am a lady, and a faithful daughter of the Church.

DON JUAN    I do not doubt it.

THE OLD WOMAN    But how then can I be in hell? Purgatory,
perhaps: I have not been perfect: who has? But hell! oh, you are
lying.

DON JUAN    Hell, Señora, I assure you; hell at its best: that is, its
most solitary—though perhaps you would prefer company.

THE OLD WOMAN    But I have sincerely repented; I have confessed—

DON JUAN    How much?

THE OLD WOMAN    More sins than I really committed. I loved
confession.

DON JUAN    Ah, that is perhaps as bad as confessing too little. At
all events, Señora, whether by oversight or intention, you are
certainly damned, like myself; and there is nothing for it now
but to make the best of it.

THE OLD WOMAN [*indignantly*]    Oh! and I might have been so much wickeder! All my good deeds wasted! It is unjust.

DON JUAN    No: you were fully and clearly warned. For your bad deeds, vicarious atonement, mercy without justice. For your good deeds, justice without mercy. We have many good people here.

THE OLD WOMAN    Were you a good man?

DON JUAN    I was a murderer.

THE OLD WOMAN    A murderer! Oh, how dare they send me to herd with murderers! I was not as bad as that: I was a woman. There is some mistake: where can I have to set right?

DON JUAN    I do not know whether mistakes can be corrected here. Probably they will not admit a mistake even if they have made one.

THE OLD WOMAN    But whom can I ask?

DON JUAN    I should ask the Devil, Señora: he understands the ways of this place, which is more than I ever could.

THE OLD WOMAN    The Devil! *I* speak to the Devil!

DON JUAN    In hell, Señora, the Devil is the leader of the best society.

THE OLD WOMAN    I tell you, wretch, I know I am not in hell.

DON JUAN    How do you know?

THE OLD WOMAN    Because I feel no pain.

DON JUAN    Oh, then there is no mistake: you are intentionally damned.

THE OLD WOMAN    Why do you say that?

DON JUAN    Because hell, Señora, is a place for the wicked. The wicked are quite comfortable in it: it was made for them. You tell me you feel no pain. I conclude you are one of those for whom Hell exists.

THE OLD WOMAN    Do y o u feel no pain?

DON JUAN    I am not one of the wicked, Señora; therefore it bores me, bores me beyond description, beyond belief.

THE OLD WOMAN  Not one of the wicked! You said you were a murderer.

DON JUAN  Only a duel. I ran my sword through an old man who was trying to run his through me.

THE OLD WOMAN  If you were a gentleman, that was not a murder.

DON JUAN  The old man called it murder, because he was, he said, defending his daughter's honor. By this he meant that because I foolishly fell in love with her and told her so, she screamed; and he tried to assassinate me after calling me insulting names.

THE OLD WOMAN  You were like all men. Libertines and murderers all, all, all!

DON JUAN  And yet we meet here, dear lady.

THE OLD WOMAN  Listen to me. My father was slain by just such a wretch as you, in just such a duel, for just such a cause. I screamed: it was my duty. My father drew on my assailant: his honor demanded it. He fell: that was the reward of honor. I am here: in hell, you tell me: that is the reward of duty. Is there justice in heaven?

DON JUAN  No; but there is justice in hell: heaven is far above such idle human personalities. You will be welcome in hell, Señora. Hell is the home of honor, duty, justice, and the rest of the seven deadly virtues. All the wickedness on earth is done in their name: where else but in hell should they have their reward? Have I not told you that the truly damned are those who are happy in hell?

THE OLD WOMAN  And are you happy here?

DON JUAN [springing to his feet]  No; and that is the enigma on which I ponder in darkness. Why am I here? I, who repudiated all duty, trampled honor underfoot, and laughed at justice!

THE OLD WOMAN  Oh, what do I care why you are here? Why am I here? I, who sacrificed all my inclinations to womanly virtue and propriety!

DON JUAN   Patience, lady: you will be perfectly happy and at home here. As saith the poet, "Hell is a city much like Seville."*

THE OLD WOMAN   Happy! here! where I am nothing! where I am nobody!

DON JUAN   Not at all: you are a lady; and wherever ladies are is hell. Do not be surprised or terrified: you will find everything here that a lady can desire, including devils who will serve you from sheer love of servitude, and magnify your importance for the sake of dignifying their service—the best of servants.

THE OLD WOMAN   My servants will be devils!

DON JUAN   Have you ever had servants who were not devils?

THE OLD WOMAN   Never: they were devils, perfect devils, all of them. But that is only a manner of speaking. I thought you meant that my servants here would be real devils.

DON JUAN   No more real devils than you will be a real lady. Nothing is real here. That is the horror of damnation.

THE OLD WOMAN   Oh, this is all madness. This is worse than fire and the worm.

DON JUAN   For you, perhaps, there are consolations. For instance: how old were you when you changed from time to eternity?

THE OLD WOMAN   Do not ask me how old I w a s—as if I were a thing of the past. I a m 77.

DON JUAN   A ripe age, Señora. But in hell old age is not tolerated. It is too real. Here we worship Love and Beauty. Our souls being entirely damned, we cultivate our hearts. As a lady of 77, you would not have a single acquaintance in hell.

THE OLD WOMAN   How can I help my age, man?

DON JUAN   You forget that you have left your age behind you in the realm of time. You are no more 77 than you are 7 or 17 or 27.

THE OLD WOMAN   Nonsense!

---

*A paraphrase of Percy Bysshe Shelley's *Peter Bell the Third* (1819; part 3, stanza 1), which has "London" in place of "Seville."

DON JUAN   Consider, Señora: was not this true even when you lived on earth? When you were 70, were you really older underneath your wrinkles and your grey hairs than when you were 30?

THE OLD WOMAN   No, younger: at 30 I was a fool. But of what use is it to feel younger and look older?

DON JUAN   You see, Señora, the look was only an illusion. Your wrinkles lied, just as the plump smooth skin of many a stupid girl of 17, with heavy spirits and decrepit ideas, lies about her age? Well, here we have no bodies: we see each other as bodies only because we learnt to think about one another under that aspect when we were alive, and we still think in that way, knowing no other. But we can appear to one another at what age we choose. You have but to will any of your old looks back, and back they will come.

THE OLD WOMAN   It cannot be true.

DON JUAN   Try.

THE OLD WOMAN   Seventeen!

DON JUAN   Stop. Before you decide, I had better tell you that these things are a matter of fashion. Occasionally we have a rage for 17; but it does not last long. Just at present the fashionable age is 40—or say 37; but there are signs of a change. If you were at all good-looking at 27, I should suggest your trying that, and setting a new fashion.

THE OLD WOMAN   I do not believe a word you are saying. However, 27 be it. [*Whisk! the old woman becomes a young one, and so handsome that in the radiance into which her dull yellow halo has suddenly lightened one might almost mistake her for ANN WHITE-FIELD*].

DON JUAN   Doña Ana de Ulloa!

ANA   What? You know me!

DON JUAN   And you forget me!

ANA   I cannot see your face. [*He raises his hat*]. Don Juan Tenorio! Monster! You who slew my father! even here you pursue me.

DON JUAN    I protest I do not pursue you. Allow me to withdraw [*going*].

ANA [*seizing his arm*]    You shall not leave me alone in this dreadful place.

DON JUAN    Provided my staying be not interpreted as pursuit.

ANA [*releasing him*]    You may well wonder how I can endure your presence. My dear, dear father!

DON JUAN    Would you like to see him?

ANA    My father  h e r e !!!

DON JUAN    No: he is in heaven.

ANA    I knew it. My noble father! He is looking down on us now. What must he feel to see his daughter in this place, and in conversation with his murderer!

DON JUAN    By the way, if we should meet him—

ANA    How can we meet him? He is in heaven.

DON JUAN    He condescends to look in upon us here from time to time. Heaven bores him. So let me warn you that if you meet him he will be mortally offended if you speak of me as his murderer! He maintains that he was a much better swordsman than I, and that if his foot had not slipped he would have killed me. No doubt he is right: I was not a good fencer. I never dispute the point; so we are excellent friends.

ANA    It is no dishonor to a soldier to be proud of his skill in arms.

DON JUAN    You would rather not meet him, probably.

ANA    How dare you say that?

DON JUAN    Oh, that is the usual feeling here. You may remember that on earth—though of course we never confessed it—the death of anyone we knew, even those we liked best, was always mingled with a certain satisfaction at being finally done with them.

ANA    Monster! Never, never.

DON JUAN [*placidly*]    I see you recognize the feeling. Yes: a funeral was always a festivity in black, especially the funeral of a relative. At all events, family ties are rarely kept up here. Your father is quite accustomed to this: he will not expect any devotion from you.

ANA    Wretch: I wore mourning for him all my life.

DON JUAN    Yes: it became you. But a life of mourning is one thing: an eternity of it quite another. Besides, here you are as dead as he. Can anything be more ridiculous than one dead person mourning for another? Do not look shocked, my dear Ana; and do not be alarmed: there is plenty of humbug in hell (indeed there is hardly anything else); but the humbug of death and age and change is dropped because here we are all dead and all eternal. You will pick up our ways soon.

ANA    And will all the men call me their dear Ana?

DON JUAN    No. That was a slip of the tongue. I beg your pardon.

ANA [*almost tenderly*]    Juan: did you really love me when you behaved so disgracefully to me?

DON JUAN [*impatiently*]    Oh, I beg you not to begin talking about love. Here they talk of nothing else but love—its beauty, its holiness, its spirituality, its devil knows what!—excuse me; but it does so bore me. They don't know what they're talking about. I do. They think they have achieved the perfection of love because they have no bodies. Sheer imaginative debauchery! Faugh!

ANA    Has even death failed to refine your soul, Juan? Has the terrible judgment of which my father's statue was the minister taught you no reverence?

DON JUAN    How is that very flattering statue, by the way? Does it still come to supper with naughty people and cast them into this bottomless pit?

ANA    It has been a great expense to me. The boys in the monastery school would not let it alone: the mischievous ones broke it; and the studious ones wrote their names on it. Three new noses in two years, and fingers without end. I had to leave it to its fate at last; and now I fear it is shockingly mutilated. My poor father!

DON JUAN    Hush! Listen! [*Two great chords rolling on syncopated waves of sound break forth: D minor and its dominant: a sound of dread-*

*ful joy to all musicians*]. Ha! Mozart's statue music. It is your father. You had better disappear until I prepare him. [*She vanishes*].
*From the void comes a living statue of white marble, designed to repre-
sent a majestic old man. But he waives his majesty with infinite grace;
walks with a feather-like step; and makes every wrinkle in his war worn
visage brim over with holiday joyousness. To his sculptor he owes a perfectly trained figure, which he carries erect and trim; and the ends of his
moustache curl up, elastic as watchsprings, giving him an air which, but
for its Spanish dignity, would be called jaunty. He is on the pleasantest
terms with DON JUAN. His voice, save for a much more distinguished intonation, is so like the voice of ROEBUCK RAMSDEN that it calls attention to the fact that they are not unlike one another in spite of their
very different fashions of shaving*].

DON JUAN    Ah, here you are, my friend. Why don't you learn to
sing the splendid music Mozart has written for you?

THE STATUE    Unluckily he has written it for a bass voice. Mine
is a counter tenor. Well: have you repented yet?

DON JUAN    I have too much consideration for you to repent,
Don Gonzalo. If I did, you would have no excuse for coming
from Heaven to argue with me.

THE STATUE    True. Remain obdurate, my boy. I wish I had killed
you, as I should have done but for an accident. Then I should
have come here; and you would have had a statue and a reputation for piety to live up to. Any news?

DON JUAN    Yes: your daughter is dead.

THE STATUE [*puzzled*]    My daughter? [*Recollecting*] Oh! the one
you were taken with. Let me see: what was her name?

DON JUAN    Ana.

THE STATUE    To be sure: Ana. A goodlooking girl, if I recollect
aright. Have you warned Whatshisname—her husband?

DON JUAN    My friend Ottavio? No: I have not seen him since Ana
arrived.

*Ana comes indignantly to light.*

ANA    What does this mean? Ottavio here and y o u r friend! And you, father, have forgotten my name. You are indeed turned to stone.

THE STATUE    My dear: I am so much more admired in marble than I ever was in my own person that I have retained the shape the sculptor gave me. He was one of the first men of his day: you must acknowledge that.

ANA    Father! Vanity! personal vanity! from you!

THE STATUE    Ah, you outlived that weakness, my daughter: you must be nearly 80 by this time. I was cut off [by an accident] in my 64th year, and am considerably your junior in consequence. Besides, my child, in this place, what our libertine friend here would call the farce of parental wisdom is dropped. Regard me, I beg, as a fellow creature, not as a father.

ANA    You speak as this villain speaks.

THE STATUE    Juan is a sound thinker, Ana. A bad fencer, but a sound thinker.

ANA [horror creeping upon her]    I begin to understand. These are devils, mocking me. I had better pray.

THE STATUE [consoling her]    No, no, no, my child: do not pray. If you do, you will throw away the main advantage of this place. Written over the gate here are the words "Leave every hope behind, ye who enter." Only think what a relief that is! For what is hope? A form of moral responsibility. Here there is no hope, and consequently no duty, no work, nothing to be gained by praying, nothing to be lost by doing what you like. Hell, in short, is a place where you have nothing to do but amuse yourself. [DON JUAN sighs deeply]. You sigh, friend Juan; but if you dwelt in heaven, as I do, you would realize your advantages.

DON JUAN    You are in good spirits to-day, Commander. You are positively brilliant. What is the matter?

THE STATUE    I have come to a momentous decision, my boy. But first, where is our friend the Devil? I must consult him in the matter. And Ana would like to make his acquaintance, no doubt.

ANA    You are preparing some torment for me.

DON JUAN    All that is superstition, Ana. Reassure yourself. Remember: the devil is not so black as he is painted.

THE STATUE    Let us give him a call.

*At the wave of THE STATUE's hand the great chords roll out again; but this time Mozart's music gets grotesquely adulterated with Gounod's.*[9] *A scarlet halo begins to glow; and into it the DEVIL rises, very Mephistophelean, and not at all unlike MENDOZA, though not so interesting. He looks older; is getting prematurely bald; and, in spite of an effusion of goodnature and friendliness, is peevish and sensitive when his advances are not reciprocated. He does not inspire much confidence in his powers of hard work or endurance, and is, on the whole, a disagreeably self-indulgent looking person; but he is clever and plausible, though perceptibly less well bred than the two other men, and enormously less vital than the woman.*

THE DEVIL [*heartily*]    Have I the pleasure of again receiving a visit from the illustrious Commander of Calatrava? [*Coldly*] Dun Juan, your servant. [*Politely*] And a strange lady? My respects, Señora.

ANA    Are you—

THE DEVIL [*bowing*]    Lucifer, at your service.

ANA    I shall go mad.

THE DEVIL [*gallantly*]    Ah, Señora, do not be anxious. You come to us from earth, full of the prejudices and terrors of that priest-ridden place. You have heard me ill spoken of; and yet, believe me, I have hosts of friends there.

ANA    Yes: you reign in their hearts.

THE DEVIL [*shaking his head*]    You flatter me, Señora; but you are mistaken. It is true that the world cannot get on without me; but it never gives me credit for that: in its heart it mistrusts and hates me. Its sympathies are all with misery, with poverty, with starvation of the body and of the heart. I call on it to sympathize with joy, with love, with happiness, with beauty—[10]

DON JUAN [*nauseated*]    Excuse me: I am going. You know I cannot stand this.

THE DEVIL [*angrily*]    Yes: I know that you are no friend of mine.

THE STATUE    What harm is he doing you, Juan? It seems to me that he was talking excellent sense when you interrupted him.

THE DEVIL [*warmly shaking THE STATUE's hand*]    Thank you, my friend: thank you. You have always understood me: he has always disparaged and avoided me.

DON JUAN    I have treated you with perfect courtesy.

THE DEVIL    Courtesy! What is courtesy? I care nothing for mere courtesy. Give me warmth of heart, true sincerity, the bond of sympathy with love and joy—

DON JUAN    You are making me ill.

THE DEVIL    There! [*Appealing to THE STATUE*] You hear, sir! Oh, by what irony of fate was this cold selfish egotist sent to my kingdom, and you taken to the icy mansions of the sky!

THE STATUE    I can't complain. I was a hypocrite; and it served me right to be sent to heaven.

THE DEVIL    Why, sir, do you not join us, and leave a sphere for which your temperament is too sympathetic, your heart too warm, your capacity for enjoyment too generous?

THE STATUE    I have this day resolved to do so. In future, excellent Son of the Morning, I am yours. I have left Heaven for ever.

THE DEVIL [*again grasping his hand*]    Ah, what an honor for me! What a triumph for our cause! Thank you, thank you. And now, my friend—I may call you so at last—could you not persuade h i m to take the place you have left vacant above?

THE STATUE [*shaking his head*]    I cannot conscientiously recommend anybody with whom I am on friendly terms to deliberately make himself dull and uncomfortable.

THE DEVIL    Of course not; but are you sure h e would be uncomfortable? Of course you know best: you brought him here originally; and we had the greatest hopes of him. His sentiments were in the best taste of our best people. You remember how he sang? [*He begins to sing in a nasal operatic baritone, tremulous from an eternity of misuse in the French manner*]

Vivan le feminine!
Viva il buon vino!*


THE STATUE [*taking up the tune an octave higher in his counter tenor*]


Sostegno e gloria
D'umanità.†


THE DEVIL     Precisely. Well, he never sings for us now.

DON JUAN     Do you complain of that? Hell is full of musical amateurs: music is the brandy of the damned. May not one lost soul
be permitted to abstain?

THE DEVIL     You dare blaspheme against the sublimest of the arts!

DON JUAN [*with cold disgust*]     You talk like a hysterical woman
fawning on a fiddler.

THE DEVIL     I am not angry. I merely pity you. You have no soul;
and you are unconscious of all that you lose. Now you, Señor
Commander, are a born musician. How well you sing! Mozart
would be delighted if he were still here; but he moped and went
to heaven. Curious how these clever men, whom you would
have supposed born to be popular here, have turned out social
failures, like Don Juan!

DON JUAN     I am really very sorry to be a social failure.

THE DEVIL     Not that we don't admire your intellect, you know.
We do. But I look at the matter from your own point of view.
You don't get on with us. The place doesn't suit you. The truth
is, you have—I won't say no heart; for we know that beneath all
your affected cynicism you have a warm one—

DON JUAN [*shrinking*]     Don't, please don't.

---

*Long live the females! / Long live good wine! (Italian); from Mozart's *Don
Giovanni*.

†Sustenance and glory / Of humankind (Italian); from Mozart's *Don Giovanni*.

THE DEVIL [*nettled*]  Well, you've no capacity for enjoyment. Will that satisfy you?

DON JUAN   It is a somewhat less insufferable form of cant than the other. But if you'll allow me, I'll take refuge, as usual, in solitude.

THE DEVIL   Why not take refuge in Heaven? That's the proper place for you. [*To ANA*] Come, Señora! could you not persuade him for his own good to try change of air?

ANA   But can he go to Heaven if he wants to?

THE DEVIL   What's to prevent him?

ANA   Can anybody—can *I* go to Heaven if I want to?

THE DEVIL [*rather contemptuously*]   Certainly, if your taste lies that way.

ANA   But why doesn't everybody go to Heaven, then?

THE STATUE [*chuckling*]   *I* can tell you that, my dear. It's because heaven is the most angelically dull place in creation: that's why.

THE DEVIL   His excellency the Commander puts it with military bluntness; but the strain of living in Heaven is intolerable. There is a notion that I was turned out of it; but as a matter of fact nothing could have induced me to stay there. I simply left it and organized this place.

THE STATUE   I don't wonder at it. Nobody could stand an eternity of heaven.

THE DEVIL   Oh, it suits some people. Let us be just, Commander: it is a question of temperament. I don't admire the heavenly temperament: I don't understand it: I don't know that I particularly want to understand it; but it takes all sorts to make a universe. There is no accounting for tastes: there are people who like it. I think Don Juan would like it.

DON JUAN   But—pardon my frankness—could you really go back there if you desired to; or are the grapes sour?

THE DEVIL   Back there! I often go back there. Have you never read the book of Job? Have you any canonical authority for assuming that there is any barrier between our circle and the other one?

ANA   But surely there is a great gulf fixed.

THE DEVIL   Dear lady: a parable must not be taken literally. The gulf is the difference between the angelic and the diabolic temperament. What more impassable gulf could you have? Think of what you have seen on earth. There is no physical gulf between the philosopher's class room and the bull ring; but the bull fighters do not come to the class room for all that. Have you ever been in the country where I have the largest following—England? There they have great racecourses, and also concert rooms where they play the classical compositions of his Excellency's friend Mozart. Those who go to the racecourses can stay away from them and go to the classical concerts instead if they like: there is no law against it; for Englishmen never will be slaves: they are free to do whatever the Government and public opinion allow them to do. And the classical concert is admitted to be a higher, more cultivated, poetic, intellectual, ennobling place than the racecourse. But do the lovers of racing desert their sport and flock to the concert room? Not they. They would suffer there all the weariness the Commander has suffered in heaven. There is the great gulf of the parable between the two places. A mere physical gulf they could bridge; or at least I could bridge it for them (the earth is full of Devil's Bridges); but the gulf of dislike is impassable and eternal. And that is the only gulf that separates my friends here from those who are invidiously called the blest.

ANA   I shall go to heaven at once.

THE STATUE   My child: one word of warning first. Let me complete my friend Lucifer's similitude of the classical concert. At every one of those concerts in England you will find rows of weary people who are there, not because they really like classical music, but because they think they ought to like it. Well, there is the same thing in heaven. A number of people sit there in glory, not because they are happy, but because they think they owe it to their position to be in heaven. They are almost all English.

THE DEVIL   Yes: the Southerners give it up and join me just as you have done. But the English really do not seem to know when they are thoroughly miserable. An Englishman thinks he is moral when he is only uncomfortable.

THE STATUE   In short, my daughter, if you go to Heaven without being naturally qualified for it, you will not enjoy yourself there.

ANA   And who dares say that I am not naturally qualified for it? The most distinguished princes of the Church have never questioned it. I owe it to myself to leave this place at once.

THE DEVIL [offended]   As you please, Señora. I should have expected better taste from you.

ANA   Father: I shall expect you to come with me. You cannot stay here. What will people say?

THE STATUE   People! Why, the best people are here—princes of the church and all. So few go to Heaven, and so many come here, that the blest, once called a heavenly host, are a continually dwindling minority. The saints, the fathers, the elect of long ago are the cranks, the faddists, the outsiders of to-day.

THE DEVIL   It is true. From the beginning of my career I knew that I should win in the long run by sheer weight of public opinion, in spite of the long campaign of misrepresentation and calumny against me. At bottom the universe is a constitutional one; and with such a majority as mine I cannot be kept permanently out of office.

DON JUAN   I think, Ana, you had better stay here.

ANA [jealously]   You do not want me to go with you.

DON JUAN   Surely you do not want to enter Heaven in the company of a reprobate like me.

ANA   All souls are equally precious. You repent, do you not?

DON JUAN   My dear Ana, you are silly. Do you suppose heaven is like earth, where people persuade themselves that what is done can be undone by repentance; that what is spoken can be unspoken by withdrawing it; that what is true can be annihilated by a general agreement to give it the lie? No: heaven is the home of the masters of reality: that is why I am going thither.

ANA    Thank you: I am going to heaven for happiness. I have had quite enough of reality on earth.

DON JUAN    Then you must stay here; for hell is the home of the unreal and of the seekers for happiness. It is the only refuge from heaven, which is, as I tell you, the home of the masters of reality, and from earth, which is the home of the slaves of reality. The earth is a nursery in which men and women play at being heros and heroines, saints and sinners; but they are dragged down from their fool's paradise by their bodies: hunger and cold and thirst, age and decay and disease, death above all, make them slaves of reality: thrice a day meals must be eaten and digested: thrice a century a new generation must be engendered: ages of faith, of romance, and of science are all driven at last to have but one prayer "Make me a healthy animal." But here you escape this tyranny of the flesh; for here you are not an animal at all: you are a ghost, an appearance, an illusion, a convention, deathless, age-less: in a word, bodiless. There are no social questions here, no political questions, no religious questions, best of all, perhaps, no sanitary questions. Here you call your appearance beauty, your emotions love, your sentiments heroism, your aspirations virtue, just as you did on earth; but here there are no hard facts to contradict you, no ironic contrast of your needs with your pretensions, no human comedy, nothing but a perpetual ro-mance, a universal melodrama. As our German friend put it in his poem, "the poetically nonsensical here is good sense; and the Eternal Feminine draws us ever upward and on"—*without get-ting us a step farther. And yet you want to leave this paradise!

---

*The quote is from Goethe's *Faust, Part Two*, the final chorus; the lines describe Heaven.

ANA    But if Hell be so beautiful as this, how glorious must heaven be!

*THE DEVIL, THE STATUE, and DON JUAN all begin to speak at once in violent protest; then stop, abashed.*

DON JUAN    I beg your pardon.

THE DEVIL    Not at all. I interrupted you.

THE STATUE    You were going to say something.

DON JUAN    After you, gentlemen.

THE DEVIL [*to DON JUAN*]    You have been so eloquent on the advantages of my dominions that I leave you to do equal justice to the drawbacks of the alternative establishment.

DON JUAN    In Heaven, as I picture it, dear lady, you live and work instead of playing and pretending. You face things as they are; you escape nothing but glamor; and your steadfastness and your peril are your glory. If the play still goes on here and on earth, and all the world is a stage, Heaven is at least behind the scenes. But Heaven cannot be described by metaphor. Thither I shall go presently, because there I hope to escape at last from lies and from the tedious, vulgar pursuit of happiness, to spend my eons in contemplation—

THE STATUE    Ugh!

DON JUAN    Señor Commander: I do not blame your disgust: a picture gallery is a dull place for a blind man. But even as you enjoy the contemplation of such romantic mirages as beauty and pleasure; so would I enjoy the contemplation of that which interests me above all things: namely, Life: the force that ever strives to attain greater power of contemplating itself. What made this brain of mine, do you think? Not the need to move my limbs; for a rat with half my brains moves as well as I. Not merely the need to do, but the need to know what I do, lest in my blind efforts to live I should be slaying myself.

THE STATUE    You would have slain yourself in your blind efforts to fence but for my foot slipping, my friend.

DON JUAN     Audacious ribald: your laughter will finish in hideous boredom before morning.

THE STATUE     Ha ha! Do you remember how I frightened you when I said something like that to you from my pedestal in Seville? It sounds rather flat without my trombones.

DON JUAN     They tell me it generally sounds flat with them, Commander.

ANA     Oh, do not interrupt with these frivolities, father. Is there nothing in Heaven but contemplation, Juan?

DON JUAN     In the Heaven I seek, no other joy. But there is the work of helping Life in its struggle upward. Think of how it wastes and scatters itself, how it raises up obstacles to itself and destroys itself in its ignorance and blindness. It needs a brain, this irresistible force, lest in its ignorance it should resist itself. What a piece of work is man! says the poet.* Yes: but what a blunderer! Here is the highest miracle of organization yet attained by life, the most intensely alive thing that exists, the most conscious of all the organisms; and yet, how wretched are his brains! Stupidity made sordid and cruel by the realities learnt from toil and poverty: Imagination resolved to starve sooner than face these realities, piling up illusions to hide them, and calling itself cleverness, genius! And each accusing the other of its own defect: Stupidity accusing Imagination of folly, and Imagination accusing Stupidity of ignorance: whereas, alas! Stupidity has all the knowledge, and Imagination all the intelligence.

THE DEVIL     And a pretty kettle of fish they make of it between them. Did I not say, when I was arranging that affair of Faust's, that all Man's reason has done for him is to make him beastlier than any beast. One splendid body is worth the brains of a hundred dyspeptic, flatulent philosophers.

DON JUAN     You forget that brainless magnificence of body has been tried. Things immeasurably greater than man in every re-

---

*Shakespeare is the poet, *Hamlet* the speaker (act 2, scene 2).

spect but brain have existed and perished. The megatherium, the icthyosaurus have paced the earth with seven-league steps and hidden the day with cloud vast wings. Where are they now? Fossils in museums, and so few and imperfect at that, that a knuckle bone or a tooth of one of them is prized beyond the lives of a thousand soldiers. These things lived and wanted to live; but for lack of brains they did not know how to carry out their purpose, and so destroyed themselves.

THE DEVIL    And is Man any the less destroying himself for all this boasted brain of his? Have you walked up and down upon the earth lately? I have; and I have examined Man's wonderful inventions. And I tell you that in the arts of life man invents nothing; but in the arts of death he outdoes Nature herself, and produces by chemistry and machinery all the slaughter of plague, pestilence and famine. The peasant I tempt to-day eats and drinks what was eaten and drunk by the peasants of ten thousand years ago; and the house he lives in has not altered as much in a thousand centuries as the fashion of a lady's bonnet in a score of weeks. But when he goes out to slay, he carries a marvel of mechanism that lets loose at the touch of his finger all the hidden molecular energies, and leaves the javelin, the arrow, the blowpipe of his fathers far behind. In the arts of peace Man is a bungler. I have seen his cotton factories and the like, with machinery that a greedy dog could have invented if it had wanted money instead of food. I know his clumsy typewriters and bungling locomotives and tedious bicycles: they are toys compared to the Maxim gun, the submarine torpedo boat. There is nothing in Man's industrial machinery but his greed and sloth: his heart is in his weapons. This marvellous force of Life of which you boast is a force of Death: Man measures his strength by his destructiveness. What is his religion? An excuse for hating me. What is his law? An excuse for hanging y o u. What is his morality? Gentility! an excuse for consuming without producing. What is his art? An excuse for gloating over pictures of slaugh-

ter. What are his politics? Either the worship of a despot because
a despot can kill, or parliamentary cockfighting. I spent an
evening lately in a certain celebrated legislature, and heard the
pot lecturing the kettle for its blackness, and ministers answer-
ing questions. When I left I chalked up on the door the old nursery saying "Ask no questions and you will be told no lies." I
bought a sixpenny family magazine, and found it full of pictures
of young men shooting and stabbing one another. I saw a man
die: he was a London bricklayer's laborer with seven children.
He left seventeen pounds club money;* and his wife spent it all
on his funeral and went into the workhouse with the children
next day. She would not have spent sevenpence on her children's
schooling: the law had to force her to let them be taught gratuitously; but on death she spent all she had. Their imagination
glows, their energies rise up at the idea of death, these people:
they love it; and the more horrible it is the more they enjoy it.
Hell is a place far above their comprehension: they derive their
notion of it from two of the greatest fools that ever lived, an Italian and an Englishman.[11] The Italian described it as a place of
mud, frost, filth, fire, and venomous serpents: all torture. This
ass, when he was not lying about me, was maundering about
some woman whom he saw once in the street. The Englishman
described me as being expelled from Heaven by cannons and
gunpowder; and to this day every Briton believes that the whole
of his silly story is in the Bible. What else he says I do not know;
for it is all in a long poem which neither I nor anyone else ever
succeeded in wading through. It is the same in everything. The
highest form of literature is the tragedy, a play in which everybody is murdered at the end. In the old chronicles you read of
earthquakes and pestilences, and are told that these shewed the
power and majesty of God and the littleness of Man. Nowadays
the chronicles describe battles. In a battle two bodies of men

---

*Short-term savings account.

shoot at one another with bullets and explosive shells until one body runs away, when the others chase the fugitives on horse-back and cut them to pieces as they fly. And this, the chronicle concludes, shews the greatness and majesty of empires, and the littleness of the vanquished. Over such battles the people run about the streets yelling with delight, and egg their Govern-ments on to spend hundreds of millions of money in the slaugh-ter, whilst the strongest Ministers dare not spend an extra penny in the pound against the poverty and pestilence through which they themselves daily walk. I could give you a thousand in-stances; but they all come to the same thing: the power that gov-erns the earth is not the power of Life but of Death; and the inner need that has nerved Life to the effort of organizing itself into the human being is not the need for higher life but for a more efficient engine of destruction. The plague, the famine, the earthquake, the tempest were too spasmodic in their action; the tiger and crocodile were too easily satiated and not cruel enough: something more constantly, more ruthlessly, more in-geniously destructive was needed; and that something was Man, the inventor of the rack, the stake, the gallows, and the electro-cutor;* of the sword and gun; above all, of justice, duty, patrio-tism and all the other isms by which even those who are clever enough to be humanely disposed are persuaded to become the most destructive of all the destroyers.

DON JUAN  Pshaw! all this is old. Your weak side, my diabolic friend, is that you have always been a gull: you take Man at his own valuation. Nothing would flatter him more than your opin-ion of him. He loves to think of himself as bold and bad. He is neither one nor the other: he is only a coward. Call him tyrant, murderer, pirate, bully; and he will adore you, and swagger about with the consciousness of having the blood of the old sea kings in his veins. Call him liar and thief; and he will only take an

---

*Shaw updated this to "the electric chair" in a later edition.

action against you for libel. But call him coward; and he will go mad with rage: he will face death to outface that stinging truth. Man gives every reason for his conduct save one, every excuse for his crimes save one, every plea for his safety save one; and that one is his cowardice. Yet all his civilization is founded on his cowardice, on his abject tameness, which he calls his respectability. There are limits to what a mule or an ass will stand; but Man will suffer himself to be degraded until his vileness becomes so loathsome to his oppressors that they themselves are forced to reform it.

THE DEVIL    Precisely. And these are the creatures in whom you discover what you call a Life Force!

DON JUAN    Yes; for now comes the most surprising part of the whole business.

THE STATUE    What's that?

DON JUAN    Why, that you can make any of these cowards brave by simply putting an idea into his head.

THE STATUE    Stuff! As an old soldier I admit the cowardice: it's as universal as sea sickness, and matters just as little. But that about putting an idea into a man's head is stuff and nonsense. In a battle all you need to make you fight is a little hot blood and the knowledge that it's more dangerous to lose than to win.

DON JUAN    That is perhaps why battles are so useless. But men never really overcome fear until they imagine they are fighting to further a universal purpose—fighting for an idea, as they call it. Why was the Crusader braver than the pirate? Because he fought, not for himself, but for the Cross. What force was it that met him with a valor as reckless as his own? The force of men who fought, not for themselves, but for Islam. They took Spain from us, though we were fighting for our very hearths and homes; but when we, too, fought for that mighty idea, a Catholic Church, we swept them back to Africa.

THE DEVIL [*ironically*]    What! you a Catholic, Señor Don Juan! A devotee! My congratulations.

THE STATUE [*seriously*]  Come come! as a soldier, I can listen to nothing against the Church.

DON JUAN  Have no fear, Commander: this idea of a Catholic Church will survive Islam, will survive the Cross, will survive even that vulgar pageant of incompetent schoolboyish gladiators which you call the Army.

THE STATUE  Juan: you will force me to call you to account for this.

DON JUAN  Useless: I cannot fence. Every idea for which Man will die will be a Catholic idea. When the Spaniard learns at last that he is no better than the Saracen, and his prophet no better than Mahomet, he will arise, more Catholic than ever, and die on a barricade across the filthy slum he starves in, for universal liberty and equality.

THE STATUE  Bosh!

DON JUAN  What you call bosh is the only thing men dare die for. Later on, Liberty will not be Catholic enough: men will die for human perfection, to which they will sacrifice all their liberty gladly.

THE DEVIL  Ay: they will never be at a loss for an excuse for killing one another.

DON JUAN  What of that? It is not death that matters, but the fear of death. It is not killing and dying that degrades us, but base living, and accepting the wages and profits of degradation. Better ten dead men than one live slave or his master. Men shall yet rise up, father against son and brother against brother, and kill one another for the great Catholic idea of abolishing slavery.

THE DEVIL  Yes, when the Liberty and Equality of which you prate shall have made free white Christians cheaper in the labor market than black heathen slaves sold by auction at the block.

DON JUAN  Never fear! the white laborer shall have his turn too. But I am not now defending the illusory forms the great ideas take. I am giving you examples of the fact that this creature Man, who in his own selfish affairs is a coward to the backbone, will fight for an idea like a hero. He may be abject as a citizen; but he is dangerous as a fanatic. He can only be enslaved whilst he is spiritually weak enough to listen to reason. I tell you, gentlemen, if you can shew a man a piece of what he now calls God's work to do, and what he will later on call by many new names, you can make him entirely reckless of the consequences to himself personally.

ANA    Yes: he shirks all his responsibilities, and leaves his wife to grapple with them.

THE STATUE    Well said, daughter. Do not let him talk you out of your common sense.

THE DEVIL    Alas! Señor Commander, now that we have got on to the subject of Woman, he will talk more than ever. However, I confess it is for me the one supremely interesting subject.

DON JUAN    To a woman, Señora, man's duties and responsibilities begin and end with the task of getting bread for her children. To her, Man is only a means to the end of getting children and rearing them.

ANA    Is that your idea of a woman's mind? I call it cynical and disgusting materialism.*

DON JUAN    Pardon me, Ana: I said nothing about a woman's whole mind. I spoke of her view of Man as a separate sex. It is no more cynical than her view of herself as above all things a Mother. Sexually, Woman is Nature's contrivance for perpetuating its highest achievement. Sexually, Man is Woman's contrivance for fulfilling Nature's behest in the most economical way. She knows by instinct that far back in the evolutional process she invented him, differentiated him, created him in order to produce something better than the single-sexed process can produce. Whilst he fulfils the purpose for which she made him, he is welcome to his dreams, his follies, his ideals, his heroisms, provided that the keystone of them all is the worship of

---

*Shaw changed this to "animalism" in a later edition.

woman, of motherhood, of the family, of the hearth. But how rash and dangerous it was to invent a separate creature whose sole function was her own impregnation! For mark what has happened. First, Man has multiplied on her hands until there are as many men as women; so that she has been unable to employ for her purposes more than a fraction of the immense energy she has left at his disposal by saving him the exhausting labor of gestation. This superfluous energy has gone to his brain and to his muscle. He has become too strong to be controlled by her bodily, and too imaginative and mentally vigorous to be content with mere self-reproduction. He has created civilization without consulting her, taking her domestic labor for granted as the foundation of it.

ANA    That is true, at all events.

THE DEVIL    Yes; and this civilization! what is it, after all?

DON JUAN    After all, an excellent peg to hang your cynical commonplaces on; but b e f o r e all, it is an attempt on Man's part to make himself something more than the mere instrument of Woman's purpose. So far, the result of Life's continual effort not only to maintain itself, but to achieve higher and higher organization and completer self-consciousness, is only, at best, a doubtful campaign between its forces and those of Death and Degeneration. The battles in this campaign are mere blunders, mostly won, like actual military battles, in spite of the commanders.

THE STATUE    That is a dig at me. No matter: go on, go on.

DON JUAN    It is a dig at a much higher power than you, Commander. Still, you must have noticed in your profession that even a stupid general can win battles when the enemy's general is a little stupider.

THE STATUE [*very seriously*]    Most true, Juan, most true. Some donkeys have amazing luck.

DON JUAN    Well, the Life Force is stupid; but it is not so stupid as the forces of Death and Degeneration. Besides, these are in its

pay all the time. And so Life wins, after a fashion. What mere co-
piousness of fecundity can supply and mere greed preserve, we
possess. The survival of whatever form of civilization can produce the best rifle and the best fed riflemen is assured.

THE DEVIL    Exactly! the survival, not of the most effective means
of Life but of the most effective means of Death. You always
come back to my point, in spite of your wrigglings and evasions
and sophistries, not to mention the intolerable length of your
speeches.

DON JUAN    Oh come! who began making long speeches? However, if I overtax your intellect, you can leave us and seek the society of love and beauty and the rest of your favorite boredoms.

THE DEVIL [*much offended*]    This is not fair, Don Juan, and not
civil. I am also on the intellectual plane. Nobody can appreciate
it more than I do. I am arguing fairly with you, and, I think, utterly refuting you. Let us go on for another hour if you like.

DON JUAN    Good: let us.

THE STATUE    Not that I see any prospect of your coming to any
point in particular, Juan. Still, since in this place, instead of
merely killing time we have to kill eternity, go ahead by all
means.

DON JUAN [*somewhat impatiently*]    My point, you marbleheaded
old masterpiece, is only a step ahead of you. Arc we agreed that
Life is a force which has made innumerable experiments in organizing itself; that the mammoth and the man, the mouse and
the megatherium, the flies and the fleas and the Fathers of the
Church, are all more or less successful attempts to build up that
raw force into higher and higher individuals, the ideal individual
being omnipotent, omniscient, infallible, and withal completely,
unilludedly self-conscious: in short, a god?

THE DEVIL    I agree, for the sake of argument.

THE STATUE    I agree, for the sake of avoiding argument.

ANA    I most emphatically disagree as regards the Fathers of the
Church; and I must beg you not to drag them into the argument.

DON JUAN   I did so purely for the sake of alliteration, Ana; and I shall make no further allusion to them. And now, since we are, with that exception, agreed so far, will you not agree with me further that Life has not measured the success of its attempts at godhead by the beauty or bodily perfection of the result, since in both these respects the birds, as our friend Aristophanes* long ago pointed out, are so extraordinarily superior, with their power of flight and their lovely plumage, and, may I add, the touching poetry of their loves and nestings, that it is inconceivable that Life, having once produced them, should, if love and beauty were her object, start off on another line and labor at the clumsy elephant and the hideous ape, whose grandchildren we are?

ANA   Aristophanes was a heathen; and you, Juan, I am afraid, are very little better.

THE DEVIL   You conclude, then, that Life was driving at clumsiness and ugliness?

DON JUAN   No, perverse devil that you are, a thousand times no. Life was driving at brains—at its darling object: an organ by which it can attain not only self-consciousness but self-understanding.

THE STATUE   This is metaphysics, Juan. Why the devil should— [to THE DEVIL] I b e g your pardon.

THE DEVIL   Pray don't mention it. I have always regarded the use of my name to secure additional emphasis as a high compliment to me. It is quite at your service, Commander.

THE STATUE   Thank you: that's very good of you. Even in heaven, I never quite got out of my old military habits of speech. What I was going to ask Juan was why Life should bother itself about getting a brain. Why should it want to understand itself? Why not be content to enjoy itself?

DON JUAN   Without a brain, Commander, you would enjoy yourself without knowing it, and so lose all the fun.

---

*Greek comic dramatist (c.448–380 B.C.), in his play *The Birds*.

THE STATUE    True, most true. But I am quite content with brain enough to know that I'm enjoying myself. I don't want to understand why. In fact, I'd rather not. My experience is that one's pleasures don't bear thinking about.

DON JUAN    That is why intellect is so unpopular. But to Life, the force behind the Man, intellect is a necessity, because without it he blunders into death. Just as Life, after ages of struggle, evolved that wonderful bodily organ the eye, so that the living organism could see where it was going and what was coming to help or threaten it, and thus avoid a thousand dangers that formerly slew it, so it is evolving to-day a mind's eye that shall see, not the physical world, but the purpose of Life, and thereby enable the individual to work for that purpose instead of thwarting and baffling it by setting up shortsighted personal aims as at present. Even as it is, only one sort of man has ever been happy, has ever been universally respected among all the conflicts of interests and illusions.

THE STATUE    You mean the military man.

DON JUAN    Commander: I do not mean the military man. When the military man approaches, the world locks up its spoons and packs off its womankind. No: I sing, not arms and the hero, but the philosophic man: he who seeks in contemplation to discover the inner will of the world, in invention to discover the means of fulfilling that will, and in action to do that will by the so-discovered means. Of all other sorts of men I declare myself tired. They are tedious failures. When I was on earth, professors of all sorts prowled round me feeling for an unhealthy spot in me on which they could fasten. The doctors of medicine bade me consider what I must do to save my body, and offered me quack cures for imaginary diseases. I replied that I was not a hypochondriac; so they called me Ignoramus and went their way. The doctors of divinity bade me consider what I must do to save my soul; but I was not a spiritual hypochondriac any more than a bodily one, and would not trouble myself about that either; so they called me Atheist and went their way. After them came the politician, who said there was only one purpose in Nature, and that was to get him into parliament. I told him I did not care whether he got into parliament or not; so he called me Mugwump* and went his way. Then came the romantic man, the Artist, with his love songs and his paintings and his poems; and with him I had great delight for many years, and some profit; for I cultivated my senses for his sake; and his songs taught me to hear better, his paintings to see better, and his poems to feel more deeply. But he led me at last into the worship of Woman.

ANA    Juan!

DON JUAN    Yes: I came to believe that in her voice was all the music of the song, in her face all the beauty of the painting, and in her soul all the emotion of the poem.

ANA    And you were disappointed, I suppose. Well, was it her fault that you attributed all these perfections to her?

DON JUAN    Yes, partly. For with a wonderful instinctive cunning, she kept silent and allowed me to glorify her; to mistake my own visions, thoughts, and feelings for hers. Now my friend the romantic man was often too poor or too timid to approach those women who were beautiful or refined enough to seem to realize his ideal; and so he went to his grave believing in his dream. But I was more favored by nature and circumstance. I was of noble birth and rich; and when my person did not please, my conversation flattered, though I generally found myself fortunate in both.

THE STATUE    Coxcomb!

DON JUAN    Yes; but even my coxcombry pleased. Well, I found that when I had touched a woman's imagination, she would allow me to persuade myself that she loved me; but when my suit was granted she never said "I am happy: my love is satisfied": she always said, first, "At last, the barriers are down," and second, "When will you come again?"

---

*Apolitical person; political fence-sitter.

ANA     That is exactly what men say.

DON JUAN     I protest I never said it. But all women say it. Well, these two speeches always alarmed me; for the first meant that the lady's impulse had been solely to throw down my fortifications and gain my citadel; and the second openly announced that henceforth she regarded me as her property, and counted my time as already wholly at her disposal.

THE DEVIL     That is where your want of heart came in.

THE STATUE [*shaking his head*]     You shouldn't repeat what a woman says, Juan.

ANA [*severely*]     It should be sacred to you.

THE STATUE     Still, they certainly do always say it. I never minded the barriers; but there was always a slight shock about the other, unless one was very hard hit indeed.

DON JUAN     Then the lady, who had been happy and idle enough before, became anxious, preoccupied with me, always intriguing, conspiring, pursuing, watching, waiting, bent wholly on making sure of her prey—I being the prey, you understand. Now this was not what I had bargained for. It may have been very proper and very natural; but it was not music, painting, poetry and joy incarnated in a beautiful woman. I ran away from it. I ran away from it very often: in fact I became famous for running away from it.

ANA     Infamous, you mean.

DON JUAN     I did not run away from you. Do you blame me for running away from the others?

ANA     Nonsense, man. You are talking to a woman of 77 now. If you had had the chance, you would have run away from me too—if I had let you. You would not have found it so easy with me as with some of the others. If men will not be faithful to their home and their duties, they must be made to be. I daresay you all want to marry lovely incarnations of music and painting and poetry. Well, you can't have them, because they don't exist. If flesh and blood is not good enough for you you must go without: that's all.

Women have to put up with flesh-and-blood husbands—and little enough of that too, sometimes; and you will have to put up with flesh-and-blood wives. [*THE DEVIL looks dubious. THE STATUE makes a wry face*]. I see you don't like that, any of you; but it's true, for all that; so if you don't like it you can lump it.

DON JUAN    My dear lady, you have put my whole case against romance into a few sentences. That is just why I turned my back on the romantic man with the artist nature, as he called his infatuation. I thanked him for teaching me to use my eyes and ears; but I told him that his beauty worshipping and happiness hunting and woman idealizing was not worth a dump as a philosophy of life; so he called me Philistine and went his way.

ANA    It seems that Woman taught you something, too, with all her defects.

DON JUAN    She did more: she interpreted all the other teaching for me. Ah, my friends, when the barriers were down for the first time, what an astounding illumination! I had been prepared for infatuation, for intoxication, for all the illusions of love's young dream; and lo! never was my perception clearer, nor my criticism more ruthless. The most jealous rival of my mistress never saw every blemish in her more keenly than I. I was not duped: I took her without chloroform.

ANA    But you did take her.

DON JUAN    That was the revelation. Up to that moment I had never lost the sense of being my own master; never consciously taken a single step until my reason had examined and approved it. I had come to believe that I was a purely rational creature: a thinker! I said, with the foolish philosopher, "I think; therefore I am." It was Woman who taught me to say "I am; therefore I think." And also "I would think more; therefore I must be more."

THE STATUE    This is extremely abstract and metaphysical, Juan. If you would stick to the concrete, and put your discoveries in the form of entertaining anecdotes about your adventures with women, your conversation would be easier to follow.

DON JUAN    Bah! what need I add? Do you not understand that
when I stood face to face with Woman, every fibre in my clear
critical brain warned me to spare her and save myself. My morals
said No. My conscience said No. My chivalry and pity for her
said No. My prudent regard for myself said No. My ear, practised
on a thousand songs and symphonies; my eye, exercised on a
thousand paintings; tore her voice, her features, her color to
shreds. I caught all those tell-tale resemblances to her father and
mother by which I knew what she would be like in thirty years
time. I noted the gleam of gold from a dead tooth in the laughing mouth: I made curious observations of the strange odors of
the chemistry of the nerves. The visions of my romantic rever-
ies, in which I had trod the plains of heaven with a deathless, age-
less creature of coral and ivory, deserted me in that supreme
hour. I remembered them and desperately strove to recover their
illusion; but they now seemed the emptiest of inventions: my
judgment was not to be corrupted: my brain still said No on
every issue. And whilst I was in the act of framing my excuse to
the lady, Life seized me and threw me into her arms as a sailor
throws a scrap of fish into the mouth of a seabird.

THE STATUE    You might as well have gone without thinking such
a lot about it, Juan. You are like all the clever men: you have
more brains than is good for you.

THE DEVIL    And were you not the happier for the experience,
Señor Don Juan?

DON JUAN    The happier, no: the wiser, yes. That moment introduced me for the first time to myself, and, through myself, to the
world. I saw then how useless it is to attempt to impose conditions on the irresistible force of Life; to preach prudence, careful selection, virtue, honor, chastity—

ANA    Don Juan: a word against chastity is an insult to me.

DON JUAN    I say nothing against your chastity, Señora, since it
took the form of a husband and twelve children. What more

could you have done had you been the most abandoned of women?

ANA   I could have had twelve husbands and no children: that's what I could have done, Juan. And let me tell you that that would have made all the difference to the earth which I replenished.

THE STATUE   Bravo Ana! Juan: you are floored, quelled, annihilated.

DON JUAN   No; for though that difference is the true essential difference—Doña Ana has, I admit, gone straight to the real point—yet it is not a difference of love or chastity, or even constancy; for twelve children by twelve different husbands would have replenished the earth perhaps more effectively. Suppose my friend Ottavio had died when you were thirty, you would never have remained a widow: you were too beautiful. Suppose the successor of Ottavio had died when you were forty, you would still have been irresistible; and a woman who marries twice marries three times if she becomes free to do so. Twelve lawful children borne by one highly respectable lady to three different fathers is not impossible nor condemned by public opinion. That such a lady may be more law abiding than the poor girl whom we used to spurn into the gutter for bearing one unlawful infant is no doubt true; but dare you say she is less self-indulgent?

ANA   She is less virtuous: that is enough for me.

DON JUAN   In that case, what is virtue but the Trade Unionism of the married? Let us face the facts, dear Ana. The Life Force respects marriage only because marriage is a contrivance of its own to secure the greatest number of children and the closest care of them. For honor, chastity and all the rest of your moral figments it cares not a rap. Marriage is the most licentious of human institutions—

ANA   Juan!

THE STATUE [protesting]   Really!—

DON JUAN [determinedly]   I say the most licentious of human institutions: that is the secret of its popularity. And a woman seeking a husband is the most unscrupulous of all the beasts of prey. The confusion of marriage with morality has done more to destroy the conscience of the human race than any other single error. Come, Ana! do not look shocked: you know better than any of us that marriage is a mantrap baited with simulated accomplishments and delusive idealizations. When your sainted mother, by dint of scoldings and punishments, forced you to learn how to play half a dozen pieces on the spinet—which she hated as much as you did—had she any other purpose than to delude your suitors into the belief that your husband would have in his home an angel who would fill it with melody, or at least play him to sleep after dinner? You married my friend Ottavio: well, did you ever open the spinet from the hour when the Church united him to you?

ANA    You are a fool, Juan. A young married woman has something else to do than sit at the spinet without any support for her back; so she gets out of the habit of playing.

DON JUAN    Not if she loves music. No: believe me, she only throws away the bait when the bird is in the net.

ANA [*bitterly*]    And men, I suppose, never throw off the mask when their bird is in the net. The husband never becomes negligent, selfish, brutal—oh never!

DON JUAN    What do these recriminations prove, Ana? Only that the hero is as gross an imposture as the heroine.

ANA    It is all nonsense: most marriages are perfectly comfortable.

DON JUAN    "Perfectly" is a strong expression, Ana. What you mean is that sensible people make the best of one another. Send me to the galleys and chain me to the felon whose number happens to be next before mine; and I must accept the inevitable and make the best of the companionship. Many such companionships, they tell me, are touchingly affectionate; and most are at least tolerably friendly. But that does not make a chain a desirable ornament nor the galleys an abode of bliss. Those who talk most about the blessings of marriage and the constancy of its vows are the very people who declare that if the chain were broken and the prisoners left free to choose, the whole social fabric would fly asunder. You cannot have the argument both ways. If the prisoner is happy, why lock him in? If he is not, why pretend that he is?

ANA    At all events, let me take an old woman's privilege again, and tell you flatly that marriage peoples the world and debauchery does not.

DON JUAN    How if a time come when this shall cease to be true? Do you not know that where there is a will there is a way—that whatever Man really wishes to do he will finally discover a means of doing? Well, you have done your best, you virtuous ladies, and others of your way of thinking, to bend Man's mind wholly towards honorable love as the highest good, and to understand by honorable love romance and beauty and happiness in the possession of beautiful, refined, delicate, affectionate women. You have taught women to value their own youth, health, shapeliness, and refinement above all things. Well, what place have squalling babies and household cares in this exquisite paradise of the senses and emotions? Is it not the inevitable end of it all that the human will shall say to the human brain: Invent me a means by which I can have love, beauty, romance, emotion, passion without their wretched penalties, their expenses, their worries, their trials, their illnesses and agonies and risks of death, their retinue of servants and nurses and doctors and schoolmasters.

THE DEVIL    All this, Señor Don Juan, is realized here in my realm.

DON JUAN    Yes, at the cost of death. Man will not take it at that price: he demands the romantic delights of your hell whilst he is still on earth. Well, the means will be found: the brain will not fail when the will is in earnest. The day is coming when great nations will find their numbers dwindling from census to census; when the six roomed villa will rise in price above the family mansion; when the viciously reckless poor and the stupidly pious rich will delay the extinction of the race only by degrading it; whilst the boldly prudent, the thriftily selfish and ambitious, the imaginative and poetic, the lovers of money and solid comfort, the worshippers of success, art, and of love, will all oppose to the Force of Life the device of sterility.

THE STATUE   That is all very eloquent, my young friend; but if you had lived to Ana's age, or even to mine, you would have learned that the people who get rid of the fear of poverty and children and all the other family troubles, and devote themselves to having a good time of it, only leave their minds free for the fear of old age and ugliness and impotence and death. The childless laborer is more tormented by his wife's idleness and her constant demands for amusement and distraction than he could be by twenty children; and his wife is more wretched than he. I have had my share of vanity; for as a young man I was admired by women; and as a statue I am praised by art critics. But I confess that had I found nothing to do in the world but wallow in these delights I should have cut my throat. When I married Ana's mother—or perhaps, to be strictly correct, I should rather say when I at last gave in and allowed Ana's mother to marry me— I knew that I was planting thorns in my pillow, and that marriage for me, a swaggering young officer thitherto unvanquished, meant defeat and capture.

ANA [*scandalized*]   Father!

THE STATUE   I am sorry to shock you, my love; but since Juan has stripped every rag of decency from the discussion I may as well tell the frozen truth.

ANA   Hmf! I suppose I was one of the thorns.

THE STATUE   By no means: you were often a rose. You see, your mother had most of the trouble you gave.

DON JUAN   Then may I ask, Commander, why you have left Heaven to come here and wallow, as you express it, in sentimental beatitudes which you confess would once have driven you to cut your throat?

THE STATUE [*struck by this*]   Egad, that's true.

THE DEVIL [*alarmed*]   What! You are going back from your word! [*To DON JUAN*] And all your philosophizing has been nothing but a mask for proselytizing! [*To THE STATUE*] Have you forgotten already the hideous dulness from which I am offering you a refuge here? [*To DON JUAN*] And does your demonstration of the approaching sterilization and extinction of mankind lead to anything better than making the most of those pleasures of art and love which you yourself admit refined you, elevated you, developed you?

DON JUAN   I never demonstrated the extinction of mankind. Life cannot will its own extinction either in its blind amorphous state or in any of the forms into which it has organized itself. I had not finished when His Excellency interrupted me.

THE STATUE   I begin to doubt whether you ever will finish, my friend. You are extremely fond of hearing yourself talk.

DON JUAN   True; but since you have endured so much, you may as well endure to the end. Long before this sterilization which I described becomes more than a clearly foreseen possibility, the reaction will begin. The great central purpose of breeding the race, ay, breeding it to heights now deemed superhuman: that purpose which is now hidden in a mephitic cloud of love and romance and prudery and fastidiousness, will break through into clear sunlight as a purpose no longer to be confused with the gratification of personal fancies, the impossible realization of boys' and girls' dreams of bliss, or the need of older people for companionship or money. The plain-spoken marriage services of the vernacular Churches will no longer be abbreviated and half suppressed as indelicate. The sober decency, earnestness and authority of their declaration of the real purpose of marriage will be honored and accepted, whilst their romantic vowings and pledgings and until-death-do-us-partings and the like will be expunged as unbearable frivolities. Do my sex the justice to admit, Señora, that we have always recognized that the sex relation is not a personal or friendly relation at all.

ANA    Not a personal or friendly relation! What relation is more personal? more sacred? more holy?

DON JUAN    Sacred and holy, if you like, Ana, but not personally friendly. Your relation to God is sacred and holy: dare you call it personally friendly? In the sex relation the universal creative energy, of which the parties are both the helpless agents, over-rides and sweeps away all personal considerations and dispenses with all personal relations. The pair may be utter strangers to one another, speaking different languages, differing in race and color, in age and disposition, with no bond between them but a possibility of that fecundity for the sake of which the Life Force throws them into one another's arms at the exchange of a glance. Do we not recognize this by allowing marriages to be made by parents without consulting the woman? Have you not often expressed your disgust at the immorality of the English nation, in which women and men of noble birth become acquainted and court each other like peasants? And how much does even the peasant know of his bride or she of him before he engages himself? Why, you would not make a man your lawyer or your family doctor on so slight an acquaintance as you would fall in love with and marry him!

ANA    Yes, Juan: we know the libertine's philosophy. Always ignore the consequences to the woman.

DON JUAN    The consequences, yes: they justify her fierce grip of the man. But surely you do not call that attachment a sentimental one. As well call the policeman's attachment to his prisoner a love relation.

ANA    You see you have to confess that marriage is necessary, though, according to you, love is the slightest of all the relations.

DON JUAN    How do you know that it is not the greatest of all the relations? far too great to be a personal matter. Could your father have served his country if he had refused to kill any enemy of Spain unless he personally hated him? Can a woman serve her country if she refuses to marry any man she does not personally love? You know it is not so: the woman of noble birth marries as the man of noble birth fights, on political and family grounds, not on personal ones.

THE STATUE [*impressed*]   A very clever point that, Juan: I must think it over. You are really full of ideas. How did you come to think of this one?

DON JUAN   I learnt it by experience. When I was on earth, and made those proposals to ladies which, though universally condemned, have made me so interesting a hero of legend, I was not infrequently met in some such way as this. The lady would say that she would countenance my advances, provided they were honorable. On inquiring what that proviso meant, I found that it meant that I proposed to get possession of her property if she had any, or to undertake her support for life if she had not; that I desired her continual companionship, counsel and conversation to the end of my days, and would bind myself under penalties to be always enraptured by them; and, above all, that I would turn my back on all other women for ever for her sake. I did not object to these conditions because they were exorbitant and inhuman: it was their extraordinary irrelevance that prostrated me. I invariably replied with perfect frankness that I had never dreamt of any of these things; that unless the lady's character and intellect were equal or superior to my own, her conversation must degrade and her counsel mislead me; that her constant companionship might, for all I knew, become intolerably tedious to me; that I could not answer for my feelings for a week in advance, much less to the end of my life; that to cut me off from all natural and unconstrained relations with the rest of my fellow creatures would narrow and warp me if I submitted to it, and, if not, would bring me under the curse of clandestinity; that, finally, my proposals to her were wholly unconnected with any of these matters, and were the outcome of a perfectly simple impulse of my manhood towards her womanhood.

ANA   You mean that it was an immoral impulse.

DON JUAN   Nature, my dear lady, is what you call immoral. I blush for it; but I cannot help it. Nature is a pandar, Time a wrecker, and Death a murderer. I have always preferred to stand up to those facts and build institutions on their recognition. You prefer to propitiate the three devils by proclaiming their chastity, their thrift, and their loving kindness; and to base your institutions on these flatteries. Is it any wonder that the institutions do not work smoothly?

THE STATUE   What used the ladies to say, Juan?

DON JUAN   Oh come! Confidence for confidence. First tell me what you used to say to the ladies.

THE STATUE   I! Oh, I swore that I would be faithful to the death; that I should die if they refused me; that no woman could ever be to me what she was—

ANA   She! Who?

THE STATUE   Whoever it happened to be at the time, my dear. I had certain things I always said. One of them was that even when I was eighty, one white hair of the woman I loved would make me tremble more than the thickest gold tress from the most beautiful young head. Another was that I could not bear the thought of anyone else being the mother of my children.

DON JUAN [*revolted*]   You old rascal!

THE STATUE [*stoutly*]   Not a bit; for I really believed it with all my soul at the moment. I had a heart: not like you. And it was this sincerity that made me successful.

DON JUAN   Sincerity! To be fool enough to believe a ramping, stamping, thumping lie: that is what you call sincerity! To be so greedy for a woman that you deceive yourself in your eagerness to deceive her: sincerity, you call it!

THE STATUE   Oh, damn your sophistries! I was a man in love, not a lawyer. And the women loved me for it, bless them!

DON JUAN   They made you think so. What will you say when I tell you that though I played the lawyer so callously, they made me think so too? I also had my moments of infatuation in which

I gushed nonsense and believed it. Sometimes the desire to give pleasure by saying beautiful things so rose in me on the flood of emotion that I said them recklessly. At other times I argued against myself with a devilish coldness that drew tears. But I found it just as hard to escape in the one case as in the others. When the lady's instinct was set on me, there was nothing for it but lifelong servitude or flight.

ANA    You dare boast, before me and my father, that every woman found you irresistible.

DON JUAN    Am I boasting? It seems to me that I cut the most pitiable of figures. Besides, I said "when the lady's instinct was set on me." It was not always so; and then, heavens! what transports of virtuous indignation! what overwhelming defiance to the dastardly seducer! what scenes of Imogen and Iachimo!*

ANA    I made no scenes. I simply called my father.

DON JUAN    And he came, sword in hand, to vindicate outraged honor and morality by murdering me.

THE STATUE    Murdering! What do you mean? Did I kill you or did you kill me?

DON JUAN    Which of us was the better fencer?

THE STATUE    I was.

DON JUAN    Of course you were. And yet you, the hero of those scandalous adventures you have just been relating to us, y o u had the effrontery to pose as the avenger of outraged morality and condemn me to death! You would have slain me but for an accident.

THE STATUE    I was expected to, Juan. That is how things were arranged on earth. I was not a social reformer; and I always did what it was customary for a gentleman to do.

DON JUAN    That may account for your attacking me, but not for the revolting hypocrisy of your subsequent proceedings as a statue.

---

*In Shakespeare's *Cymbeline*, the latter falsely claims to have seduced the former.

THE STATUE   That all came of my going to Heaven.

THE DEVIL   I still fail to see, Señor Don Juan, that these episodes in your earthly career and in that of the Señor Commander in any way discredit my view of life. Here, I repeat, you have all that you sought without anything that you shrank from.

DON JUAN   On the contrary, here I have everything that disappointed me without anything that I have not already tried and found wanting. I tell you that as long as I can conceive something better than myself I cannot be easy unless I am striving to bring it into existence or clearing the way for it. That is the law of my life. That is the working within me of Life's incessant aspiration to higher organization, wider, deeper, intenser self-consciousness, and clearer self-understanding. It was the supremacy of this purpose that reduced love for me to the mere pleasure of a moment, art for me to the mere schooling of my faculties, religion for me to a mere excuse for laziness, since it had set up a God who looked at the world and saw that it was good, against the instinct in me that looked through my eyes at the world and saw that it could be improved. I tell you that in the pursuit of my own pleasure, my own health, my own fortune, I have never known happiness. It was not love for Woman that delivered me into her hands: it was fatigue, exhaustion. When I was a child, and bruised my head against a stone, I ran to the nearest woman and cried away my pain against her apron. When I grew up, and bruised my soul against the brutalities and stupidities with which I had to strive, I did again just what I had done as a child. I have enjoyed, too, my rests, my recuperations, my breathing times, my very prostrations after strife; but rather would I be dragged through all the circles of the foolish Italian's Inferno than through the pleasures of Europe. That is what has made this place of eternal pleasures so deadly to me. It is the absence of this instinct in you that makes you that strange monster called a Devil. It is the success with which you have diverted the attention of men from their real purpose, which in one degree or another is the same as mine to yours, that has earned you the name of The Tempter.* It is the fact that they are doing your will, or rather drifting with your want of will, instead of doing their own, that makes them the uncomfortable, false, restless, artificial, petulant, wretched creatures they are.

THE DEVIL [*mortified*]    Señor Don Juan: you are uncivil to my friends.

DON JUAN    Pooh! Why should I be civil to them or to you? In this Palace of Lies a truth or two will not hurt you. Your friends are all the dullest dogs I know. They are not beautiful: they are only decorated. They are not clean: they are only shaved and starched. They are not dignified: they are only fashionably dressed. They are not educated: they are only college passmen. They are not religious: they are only pewrenters. They are not moral: they are only conventional. They are not virtuous: they are only cowardly. They are not even vicious: they are only "frail." They are not artistic: they are only lascivious. They are not prosperous: they are only rich. They are not loyal, they are only servile; not dutiful, only sheepish; not public spirited, only patriotic; not courageous, only quarrelsome; not determined, only obstinate; not masterful, only domineering; not self-controlled, only obtuse; not self-respecting, only vain; not kind, only sentimental; not social, only gregarious; not considerate, only polite; not intelligent, only opinionated; not progressive, only factious; not imaginative, only superstitious; not just, only vindictive; not generous, only propitiatory; not disciplined, only cowed; and not truthful at all——liars every one of them, to the very backbone of their souls.

THE STATUE    Your flow of words is simply amazing, Juan. How I wish I could have talked like that to my soldiers.

THE DEVIL    It is mere talk, though. It has all been said before; but

---

*In these lines, Shaw lays out his sense of the Devil as the destroyer of will and purpose.

what change has it ever made? What notice has the world ever taken of it?

DON JUAN    Yes, it is mere talk. But why is it mere talk? Because, my friend, beauty, purity, respectability, religion, morality, art, patriotism, bravery and the rest are nothing but words which I or anyone else can turn inside out like a glove. Were they realities, you would have to plead guilty to my indictment; but fortunately for your self-respect, my diabolical friend, they are not realities. As you say, they are mere words, useful for duping barbarians into adopting civilization, or the civilized poor into submitting to be robbed and enslaved. That is the family secret of the governing caste; and if we who are of that caste aimed at more Life for the world instead of at more power and luxury for our miserable selves, that secret would make us great. Now, since I, being a nobleman, am in the secret too, think how tedious to me must be your unending cant about all these moralistic figments, and how squalidly disastrous your sacrifice of your lives to them! If you even believed in your moral game enough to play it fairly, it would be interesting to watch; but you don't: you cheat at every trick; and if your opponent outcheats you, you upset the table and try to murder him.

THE DEVIL    On earth there may be some truth in this, because the people are uneducated and cannot appreciate my religion of love and beauty; but here—

DON JUAN    Oh yes: I know. Here there is nothing but love and beauty. Ugh! it is like sitting for all eternity at the first act of a fashionable play, before the complications begin. Never in my worst moments of superstitious terror on earth did I dream that Hell was so horrible. I live, like a hairdresser, in the continual contemplation of beauty, toying with silken tresses. I breathe an atmosphere of sweetness, like a confectioner's shopboy. Commander: are there any beautiful women in Heaven?

THE STATUE    None. Absolutely none. All dowdies. Not two pennorth of jewellery among a dozen of them. They might be men of fifty.

DON JUAN    I am impatient to get there. Is the word beauty ever mentioned; and are there any artistic people?

THE STATUE    I give you my word they won't admire a fine statue even when it walks past them.

DON JUAN    I go.

THE DEVIL    Don Juan: shall I be frank with you?

DON JUAN    Were you not so before?

THE DEVIL    As far as I went, yes. But I will now go further, and confess to you that men get tired of everything, of heaven no less than of hell; and that all history is nothing but a record of the oscillations of the world between these two extremes. An epoch is but a swing of the pendulum; and each generation thinks the world is progressing because it is always moving. But when you are as old as I am; when you have a thousand times wearied of heaven, like myself and the Commander, and a thousand times wearied of hell, as you are wearied now, you will no longer imagine that every swing from heaven to hell is an emancipation, every swing from hell to heaven an evolution. Where you now see reform, progress, fulfilment of upward tendency, continual ascent by Man on the stepping stones of his dead selves to higher things,* you will see nothing but an infinite comedy of illusion. You will discover the profound truth of the saying of my friend Koheleth, that there is nothing new under the sun.† Vanitas vanitatum—‡

---

*Adapted from the first stanza of Alfred, Lord Tennyson's *In Memoriam* (1850): "I held it truth, with him who sings / To one clear harp in divers tones, / That men may rise on stepping-stones / Of their dead selves to higher things."

†"Koheleth" is the Hebrew word, translated into Greek as Ecclesiastes (the Preacher), which names the Old Testament book from which the saying comes (Ecclesiastes 1:9): "The thing that hath been, it is that which shall be; and that which is done is that which shall be done: and there is no new thing under the sun" (KJV).

‡Vanity of vanities (Latin), a key phrase in the biblical book Ecclesiastes (chapters 1 and 12).

DON JUAN [*out of all patience*]   By Heaven, this is worse than your
cant about love and beauty. Clever dolt that you are, is a man no
better than a worm, or a dog than a wolf, because he gets tired
of everything? Shall he give up eating because he destroys his appetite in the act of gratifying it? Is a field idle when it is fallow?
Can the Commander expend his hellish energy here without ac-
cumulating heavenly energy for his next term of blessedness?
Granted that the great Life Force has hit on the device of the
clockmaker's pendulum, and uses the earth for its bob; that the
history of each oscillation, which seems so novel to us the actors,
is but the history of the last oscillation repeated; nay more, that
in the unthinkable infinitude of time the sun throws off the earth
and catches it again a thousand times as a circus rider throws up
a ball, and that the total of all our epochs is but the moment between the toss and the catch, has the colossal mechanism no
purpose?

THE DEVIL   None, my friend. You think, because you have a purpose, Nature must have one. You might as well expect it to have
fingers and toes because you have them.

DON JUAN   But I should not have them if they served no purpose. And I, my friend, am as much a part of Nature as my own
finger is a part of me. If my finger is the organ by which I grasp
the sword and the mandoline,  m y  brain is the organ by which
Nature strives to understand itself. My dog's brain serves only
my dog's purposes; but m y brain labors at a knowledge which
does nothing for me personally but make my body bitter to me
and my decay and death a calamity. Were I not possessed with a
purpose beyond my own I had better be a ploughman than a
philosopher; for the ploughman lives as long as the philosopher,
eats more, sleeps better, and rejoices in the wife of his bosom
with less misgiving. This is because the philosopher is in the grip
of the Life Force. This Life Force says to him "I have done a thousand wonderful things unconsciously by merely willing to live
and following the line of least resistance: now I want to know

myself and my destination, and choose my path; so I have made a special brain—a philosopher's brain—to grasp this knowledge for me as the husbandman's hand grasps the plough for me. And this" says the Life Force to the philosopher "must thou strive to do for me until thou diest, when I will make another brain and another philosopher to carry on the work."

THE DEVIL    What is the use of knowing?

DON JUAN    Why, to be able to choose the line of greatest advantage instead of yielding in the direction of the least resistance. Does a ship sail to its destination no better than a log drifts nowhither? The philosopher is Nature's pilot. And there you have our difference: to be in hell is to drift: to be in heaven is to steer.

THE DEVIL    On the rocks, most likely.

DON JUAN    Pooh! which ship goes oftenest on the rocks or to the bottom—the drifting ship or the ship with a pilot on board?

THE DEVIL    Well, well, go your way, Señor Don Juan. I prefer to be my own master and not the tool of any blundering universal force. I know that beauty is good to look at; that music is good to hear; that love is good to feel; and that they are all good to think about and talk about. I know that to be well exercised in these sensations, emotions, and studies is to be a refined and cultivated being. Whatever they may say of me in churches on earth, I know that it is universally admitted in good society that the Prince of Darkness is a gentleman;* and that is enough for me. As to your Life Force, which you think irresistible, it is the most resistible thing in the world for a person of any character. But if you are naturally vulgar and credulous, as all reformers are, it will thrust you first into religion, where you will sprinkle water on babies to save their souls from me; then it will drive you from religion into science, where you will snatch the babies from the water sprinkling and inoculate them with disease to

*Said by Edgar in *King Lear* (act 3, scene 4).

save them from catching it accidentally; then you will take to politics, where you will become the catspaw of corrupt functionaries and the henchman of ambitious humbugs; and the end will be despair and decrepitude, broken nerve and shattered hopes, vain regrets for that worst and silliest of wastes and sacrifices, the waste and sacrifice of the power of enjoyment: in a word, the punishment of the fool who pursues the better before he has secured the good.

DON JUAN    But at least I shall not be bored. The service of the Life Force has that advantage, at all events. So fare you well, Señor Satan.

THE DEVIL [*amiably*]    Fare you well, Don Juan. I shall often think of our interesting chats about things in general. I wish you every happiness: Heaven, as I said before, suits some people. But if you should change your mind, do not forget that the gates are always open here to the repentant prodigal. If you feel at any time that warmth of heart, sincere unforced affection, innocent enjoyment, and warm, breathing, palpitating reality—

DON JUAN    Why not say flesh and blood at once, though we have left those two greasy commonplaces behind us?

THE DEVIL [*angrily*]    You throw my friendly farewell back in my teeth, then, Don Juan?

DON JUAN    By no means. But though there is much to be learnt from a cynical devil, I really cannot stand a sentimental one. Señor Commander: you know the way to the frontier of hell and heaven. Be good enough to direct me.

THE STATUE    Oh, the frontier is only the difference between two ways of looking at things. Any road will take you across it if you really want to get there.

DON JUAN    Good. [*Saluting Doña ANA*] Señora: your servant.

ANA    But I am going with you.

DON JUAN    I can find my own way to heaven, Ana; but I cannot find yours [*he vanishes*].

ANA    How annoying!

THE STATUE [*calling after him*]   Bon voyage, Juan! [*He wafts a final blast of his great rolling chords after him as a parting salute. A faint echo of the first ghostly melody comes back in acknowledgment*]. Ah! there he goes. [*Puffing a long breath out through his lips*] Whew! How he does talk! They'll never stand it in heaven.

THE DEVIL [*gloomily*]   His going is a political defeat. I cannot keep these Life Worshippers: they all go. This is the greatest loss I have had since that Dutch painter went—a fellow who would paint a hag of 70 with as much enjoyment as a Venus of 20.

THE STATUE   I remember: he came to heaven. Rembrandt.

THE DEVIL   Ay, Rembrandt. There is something unnatural about these fellows. Do not listen to their gospel, Señor Commander: it is dangerous. Beware of the pursuit of the Superhuman: it leads to an indiscriminate contempt for the Human. To a man, horses and dogs and cats are mere species, outside the moral world. Well, to the Superman, men and women are a mere species too, also outside the moral world. This Don Juan was kind to women and courteous to men as your daughter here was kind to her pet cats and dogs; but such kindness is a denial of the exclusively human character of the soul.

THE STATUE   And who the deuce is the Superman?

THE DEVIL   Oh, the latest fashion among the Life Force fanatics. Did you not meet in Heaven, among the new arrivals, that German Polish madman—what was his name? Nietzsche?

THE STATUE   Never heard of him.

THE DEVIL   Well, he came here first, before he recovered his wits. I had some hopes of him; but he was a confirmed Life Force worshipper. It was he who raked up the Superman, who is as old as Prometheus; and the 20th century will run after this newest of the old crazes when it gets tired of the world, the flesh, and your humble servant.

THE STATUE   Superman is a good cry; and a good cry is half the battle. I should like to see this Nietzsche.

THE DEVIL     Unfortunately he met Wagner here, and had a quarrel with him.

THE STATUE     Quite right, too. Mozart for me!

THE DEVIL     Oh, it was not about music. Wagner once drifted into Life Force worship, and invented a Superman called Siegfried. But he came to his senses afterwards. So when they met here, Nietzsche denounced him as a renegade; and Wagner wrote a pamphlet to prove that Nietzsche was a Jew; and it ended in Nietzsche's going to heaven in a huff. And a good riddance too. And now, my friend, let us hasten to my palace and celebrate your arrival with a grand musical service.

THE STATUE     With pleasure: you're most kind.

THE DEVIL     This way, Commander. We go down the old trap [*he places himself on the grave trap*].

THE STATUE     Good. [*Reflectively*] All the same, the Superman is a fine conception. There is something statuesque about it. [*He places himself on the grave trap beside THE DEVIL. It begins to descend slowly. Red glow from the abyss*]. Ah, this reminds me of old times.

THE DEVIL     And me also.

ANA     Stop! [*The trap stops*].

THE DEVIL     You, Señora, cannot come this way. You will have an apotheosis. But you will be at the palace before us.

ANA     That is not what I stopped you for. Tell me: where can I find the Superman?

THE DEVIL     He is not yet created, Señora.

THE STATUE     And never will be, probably. Let us proceed: the red fire will make me sneeze. [*They descend*].

ANA     Not yet created! Then my work is not yet done. [*Crossing herself devoutly*] I believe in the Life to Come. [*Crying to the universe*] A father—a father for the Superman!

*She vanishes into the void; and again there is nothing: all existence seems suspended infinitely. Then, vaguely, there is a live human voice crying somewhere. One sees, with a shock, a mountain peak shewing faintly against a lighter background. The sky has returned from afar; and w*

*suddenly remember where we were. The cry becomes distinct and urgent: it says* Automobile, Automobile. *The complete reality comes back with a rush: in a moment it is full morning in the Sierra; and the brigands are scrambling to their feet and making for the road as the goatherd runs down from the hill, warning them of the approach of another motor. TANNER and MENDOZA rise amazedly and stare at one another with scattered wits. STRAKER sits up to yawn for a moment before he gets on his feet, making it a point of honor not to shew any undue interest in the excitement of the bandits. MENDOZA gives a quick look to see that his followers are attending to the alarm; then exchanges a private word with TANNER.*

MENDOZA    Did you dream?

TANNER    Damnably. Did you?

MENDOZA    Yes. I forget what. You were in it.

TANNER    So were you. Amazing!

MENDOZA    I warned you. [*A shot is heard from the road*]. Dolts! they w i l l play with that gun. [*The brigands come running back scared*]. Who fired that shot? [*to DUVAL*] was it you?

DUVAL [*breathless*] I have not shoot. Dey shoot first.

ANARCHIST    I told you to begin by abolishing the State. Now we are all lost.

THE ROWDY SOCIAL-DEMOCRAT [*stampeding across the amphitheatre*]    Run, everybody.

MENDOZA [*collaring him; throwing him on his back; and drawing a knife*]    I stab the man who stirs. [*He blocks the way. The stampede is checked*]. What has happened?

THE SULKY SOCIAL-DEMOCRAT    A motor—

THE ANARCHIST    Three men—

DUVAL    Deux femmes—

MENDOZA    Three men and two women! Why have you not brought them here? Are you afraid of them?

THE ROWDY ONE [*getting up*]    Thyve a hescort. Ow, de-ooh lut's ook it, Mendowza.

THE SULKY ONE    Two armored cars full o soldiers at the ed o
   the valley.

ANARCHIST    The shot was fired in the air. It was a signal.
   *STRAKER whistles his favorite air, which falls on the ears of the brig-
   ands like a funeral march.*

TANNER    It is not an escort, but an expedition to capture you. We
   were advised to wait for it; but I was in a hurry.

THE ROWDY ONE [*in an agony of apprehension*]    And Ow my
   good Lord, ere we are, w y t i n for em! Lut's tike to the
   mahntns.

MENDOZA    Idiot, what do you know about the mountains? Are
   you a Spaniard? You would be given up by the first shepherd you
   met. Besides, we are already within range of their rifles.

THE ROWDY ONE    Bat—

MENDOZA    Silence. Leave this to me. [*To TANNER*] Comrade:
   you will not betray us.

STRAKER    Oo are you callin comrade?

MENDOZA    Last night the advantage was with me. The robber of
   the poor was at the mercy of the robber of the rich. You offered
   your hand: I took it.

TANNER    I bring no charge against you, comrade. We have spent
   a pleasant evening with you: that is all.

STRAKER    I gev my and to nobody, see?

MENDOZA [*turning on him impressively*]    Young man, if I am tried,
   I shall plead guilty, and explain what drove me from England,
   home and duty. Do you wish to have the respectable name of
   Straker dragged through the mud of a Spanish criminal court?
   The police will search me. They will find Louisa's portrait. It
   will be published in the illustrated papers. You blench. It will be
   your doings remember.

STRAKER [*with baffled rage*]    I don't care about the court. It's avin
   our name mixed up with yours that I object to, you blackmailin
   swine, you.

MENDOZA    Language unworthy of Louisa's brother! But no matter: you are muzzled: that is enough for us. [*He turns to face his own men, who back uneasily across the amphitheatre towards the cave to take refuge behind him, as a fresh party, muffled for motoring, comes from the road in riotous spirits. ANN, who makes straight for TANNER, comes first; then VIOLET, helped over the rough ground by HECTOR holding her right hand and RAMSDEN her left. MENDOZA goes to his presidential block and seats himself calmly with his rank and file grouped behind him, and his Staff, consisting of DUVAL and the ANARCHIST on his right and the two Social-Democrats on his left, supporting him in flank.*]

ANN    It's Jack!

TANNER    Caught!

HECTOR    Why, certainly it is. I said it was you, Tanner. We've just been stopped by a puncture: the road is full of nails.

VIOLET    What are you doing here with all these men?

ANN    Why did you leave us without a word of warning?

HECTOR    I want that bunch of roses, Miss Whitefield. [*To TANNER*] When we found you were gone, Miss Whitefield bet me a bunch of roses my car would not overtake yours before you reached Monte Carlo.

TANNER    But this is not the road to Monte Carlo.

HECTOR    No matter. Miss Whitefield tracked you at every stopping place: she is a regular Sherlock Holmes.

TANNER    The Life Force! I am lost.

OCTAVIUS [*bounding gaily down from the road into the amphitheatre, and coming between TANNER and STRAKER*]    I am so glad you are safe, old chap. We were afraid you had been captured by brigands.

RAMSDEN [*who has been staring at MENDOZA*]    I seem to remember the face of your friend here. [*MENDOZA rises politely and advances with a smile between ANN and RAMSDEN*].

HECTOR    Why, so do I.

OCTAVIUS    I know you perfectly well, sir; but I can't think where I have met you.

MENDOZA [*to VIOLET*]    Do you remember me, madam?

VIOLET    Oh, quite well; but I am so stupid about names.

MENDOZA   It was at the Savoy Hotel. [*To HECTOR*] You, sir, used to come with this lady [*VIOLET*] to lunch. [*To OCTAVIUS*] You, sir, often brought this lady [*ANN*] and her mother to dinner on your way to the Lyceum Theatre. [*To RAMSDEN*] You, sir, used to come to supper, with [*dropping his voice to a confidential but perfectly audible whisper*] several different ladies.

RAMSDEN [*angrily*]   Well, what is that to you, pray?

OCTAVIUS   Why, Violet, I thought you hardly knew one another before this trip, you and Malone!

VIOLET [*vexed*]   I suppose this person was the manager.

MENDOZA   The waiter, madam. I have a grateful recollection of you all. I gathered from the bountiful way in which you treated me that you all enjoyed your visits very much.

VIOLET   What impertinence! [*She turns her back on him, and goes up the hill with HECTOR*].

RAMSDEN   That will do, my friend. You do not expect these ladies to treat you as an acquaintance, I suppose, because you have waited on them at table.

MENDOZA   Pardon me: it was you who claimed my acquaintance. The ladies followed your example. However, this display of the unfortunate manners of your class closes the incident. For the future, you will please address me with the respect due to a stranger and fellow traveller. [*He turns haughtily away and resumes his presidential seat*].

TANNER   There! I have found one man on my journey capable of reasonable conversation; and you all instinctively insult him. Even the New Man is as bad as any of you. Enry: you have behaved just like a miserable gentleman.

STRAKER   Gentleman! Not me.

RAMSDEN   Really, Tanner, this tone—

ANN   Don't mind him, Granny: you ought to know him by this time [*she takes his arm and coaxes him away to the hill to join VIOLET and HECTOR. OCTAVIUS follows her, dog-like*].

VIOLET [*calling from the hill*]    Here are the soldiers. They are getting out of their motors.

DUVAL [*panicstricken*]    Oh, nom de Dieu!

THE ANARCHIST    Fools: the State is about to crush you because you spared it at the prompting of the political hangers-on of the bourgeoisie.

THE SULKY SOCIAL-DEMOCRAT [*argumentative to the last*] On the contrary, only by capturing the State machine—

THE ANARCHIST    It is going to capture you.

THE ROWDY SOCIAL-DEMOCRAT [*his anguish culminating*] Ow, chack it. Wot are we ere for? W o t are we wytin for?

MENDOZA [*between his teeth*]    Go on. Talk politics, you idiots: nothing sounds more respectable. Keep it up, I tell you.

*The soldiers line the road, commanding the amphitheatre with their rifles. The brigands, struggling with an overwhelming impulse to hide behind one another, look as unconcerned as they can. MENDOZA rises superbly, with undaunted front. The officer in command steps down from the road into the amphitheatre; looks hard at the brigands; and then inquiringly at TANNER.*

THE OFFICER    Who are these men, Señor Ingles?

TANNER    My escort.

*MENDOZA, with a Mephistophelean smile, bows profoundly. An irrepressible grin runs from face to face among the brigands. They touch their hats, except the ANARCHIST, who defies the State with folded arms.*

# ACT IV

*The garden of a villa in Granada. Whoever wishes to know what it is like must go to Granada and see. One may prosaically specify a group of hills dotted with villas, the Alhambra on the top of one of the hills, and a considerable town in the valley, approached by dusty white roads in which the children, no matter what they are doing or thinking about, automatically whine for halfpence and reach out little clutching brown palms for them; but there is nothing in this description except the Alhambra, the begging, and the color of the roads, that does not fit Surrey as well as Spain. The difference is that the Surrey hills are comparatively small and ugly, and should properly be called the Surrey Protuberances; but these Spanish hills are of mountain stock: the amenity which conceals their size does not compromise their dignity.*

*This particular garden is on a hill opposite the Alhambra; and the villa is as expensive and pretentious as a villa must be if it is to be let furnished by the week to opulent American and English visitors. If we stand on the lawn at the foot of the garden and look uphill, our horizon is the stone balustrade of a flagged platform on the edge of infinite space at the top of the hill. Between us and this platform is a flower garden with a circular basin and fountain in the centre, surrounded by geometrical flower beds, gravel paths, and clipped yew trees in the genteelest order. The garden is higher than our lawn; so we reach it by a few steps in the middle of its embankment. The platform is higher again than the garden, from which we mount a couple more steps to look over the balustrade at a fine view of the town up the valley and of the hills that stretch away beyond it to where, in the remotest distance, they become mountains. On our left is the villa, accessible by steps from the left hand corner of the garden. Returning from the platform through the garden and down again to the lawn (a*

*movement which leaves the villa behind us on our right) we find
evidence of literary interests on the part of the tenants in the fact that
there is no tennis net nor set of croquet hoops, but, on our left, a little
iron garden table with books on it, mostly yellow-backed, and a chair
beside it. A chair on the right has also a couple of open books upon it.
There are no newspapers, a circumstance which, with the absence of
games, might lead an intelligent spectator to the most far reaching
conclusions as to the sort of people who live in the villa. Such
speculations are checked, however, on this delightfully fine afternoon,
by the appearance at a little gate in a paling on our left, of Henry
Straker in his professional costume. He opens the gate for an elderly
gentleman, and follows him on to the lawn.*

*This elderly gentleman defies the Spanish sun in a black frock coat,
tall silk hat, trousers in which narrow stripes of dark grey and lilac
blend into a highly respectable color, and a black necktie tied into a
bow over spotless linen. Probably therefore a man whose social position
needs constant and scrupulous affirmation without regard to climate:
one who would dress thus for the middle of the Sahara or the top of
Mont Blanc. And since he has not the stamp of the class which accepts
as its life-mission the advertizing and maintenance of first rate
tailoring and millinery, he looks vulgar in his finery, though in a
working dress of any kind he would look dignified enough. He is a
bullet cheeked man with a red complexion, stubbly hair, smallish eyes, a
hard mouth that folds down at the corners, and a dogged chin. The
looseness of skin that comes with age has attacked his throat and the
laps of his cheeks; but he is still hard as an apple above the mouth; so
that the upper half of his face looks younger than the lower. He has the
self-confidence of one who has made money, and something of the
truculence of one who has made it in a brutalizing struggle, his civility
having under it a perceptible menace that he has other methods in
reserve if necessary. Withal, a man to be rather pitied when he is not to
be feared; for there is something pathetic about him at times, as if the
huge commercial machine which has worked him into his frock coat
had allowed him very little of his own way and left his affections*

*hungry and baffled. At the first word that falls from him it is clear that he is an Irishman whose native intonation has clung to him through many changes of place and rank. One can only guess that the original material of his speech was perhaps the surly Kerry brogue; but the degradation of speech that occurs in London, Glasgow, Dublin and big cities generally has been at work on it so long that nobody but an arrant cockney would dream of calling it a brogue now; for its music is almost gone, though its surliness is still perceptible. Straker, as a very obvious cockney, inspires him with implacable contempt, as a stupid Englishman who cannot even speak his own language properly. Straker, on the other hand, regards the old gentleman's accent as a joke thoughtfully provided by Providence expressly for the amusement of the British race, and treats him normally with the indulgence due to an inferior and unlucky species, but occasionally with indignant alarm when the old gentleman shews signs of intending his Irish nonsense to be taken seriously.*

STRAKER    I'll go tell the young lady. She said you'd prefer to stay here [*he turns to go up through the garden to the villa*].

MALONE [*who has been looking round him with lively curiosity*]    The young lady? That's Miss Violet, eh?

STRAKER [*stopping on the steps with sudden suspicion*]    Well, you know, don't you?

MALONE    Do I?

STRAKER [*his temper rising*]    Well, do you or don't you?

MALONE    What business is that of yours?

     *STRAKER, now highly indignant, comes back from the steps and confronts the visitor.*

STRAKER    I'll tell you what business it is of mine. Miss Robinson—

MALONE [*interrupting*]    Oh, her name is Robinson, is it? Thank you.

STRAKER    Why, you don't know even her name?

MALONE    Yes I do, now that you've told me.

STRAKER [*after a moment of stupefaction at the old man's readiness in repartee*]    Look here: what do you mean by gittin into my car and lettin me bring you here if you're not the person I took that note to?

MALONE    Who else did you take it to, pray?

STRAKER    I took it to Mr. Ector Malone, at Miss Robinson's request, see? Miss Robinson is not my principal: I took it to oblige her. I know Mr. Malone; and he ain't you, not by a long chalk. At the hotel they told me that your name is Ector Malone—

MALONE    Hector Malone.

STRAKER [*with calm superiority*]    Hector in your own country: that's what comes o livin in provincial places like Ireland and America. Over here you're Ector: if you avn't noticed it before you soon will.

*The growing strain of the conversation is here relieved by VIOLET, who has sallied from the villa and through the garden to the steps, which she now descends, coming very opportunely between MALONE and STRAKER.*

VIOLET [*to STRAKER*]    Did you take my message?

STRAKER    Yes, miss. I took it to the hotel and sent it up, expecting to see young Mr. Malone. Then out walks this gent, and says it's all right and he'll come with me. So as the hotel people said he was Mr. Ector Malone, I fetched him. And now he goes back on what he said. But if he isn't the gentleman you meant, say the word: it's easy enough to fetch him back again.

MALONE    I should esteem it a great favor if I might have a short conversation with you, madam. I am Hector's father, as this bright Britisher would have guessed in the course of another hour or so.

STRAKER [*coolly defiant*]    No, not in another year or so. When we've ad you as long to polish up as we've ad im, perhaps you'll begin to look a little bit up to is mark. At present you fall a long way short. You've got too many aitches, for one thing. [*To VIOLET, amiably*] All right, Miss: you want to talk to him: I shan't intrude. [*He nods affably to MALONE and goes out through the little gate in the paling*].

VIOLET [*very civilly*]   I am so sorry, Mr. Malone, if that man has been rude to you. But what can we do? He is our chauffeur.

MALONE   Your hwat?

VIOLET   The driver of our automobile. He can drive a motor car at seventy miles an hour, and mend it when it breaks down. We are dependent on our motor cars; and our motor cars are dependent on him; so of course w e are dependent on him.

MALONE   I've noticed, madam, that every thousand dollars an Englishman gets seems to add one to the number of people he's dependent on. However, you needn't apologize for your man: I made him talk on purpose. By doing so I learnt that you're staying here in Grannida with a party of English, including my son Hector.

VIOLET [*conversationally*]   Yes. We intended to go to Nice; but we had to follow a rather eccentric member of our party who started first and came here. Won't you sit down? [*She clears the nearest chair of the two books on it*].

MALONE [*impressed by this attention*]   Thank you. [*He sits down, examining her curiously as she goes to the iron table to put down the books. When she turns to him again, he says*] Miss Robinson, I believe?

VIOLET [*sitting down*]   Yes.

MALONE [*taking a letter from his pocket*]   Your note to Hector runs as follows [*VIOLET is unable to repress a start. He pauses quietly to take out and put on his spectacles, which have gold rims*]: "Dearest: they have all gone to the Alhambra for the afternoon. I have shammed headache and have the garden all to myself. Jump into Jack's motor: Straker will rattle you here in a jiffy. Quick, quick, quick. Your loving Violet." [*He looks at her; but by this time she has recovered herself, and meets his spectacles with perfect composure. He continues slowly*] Now I don't know on what terms young people associate in English society; but in America that note would be considered to imply a very considerable degree of affectionate intimacy between the parties.

VIOLET    Yes: I know your son very well, Mr. Malone. Have you any objection?

MALONE [*somewhat taken aback*]    No, no objection exactly. Provided it is understood that my son is altogether dependent on me, and that I have to be consulted in any important step he may propose to take.

VIOLET    I am sure you would not be unreasonable with him, Mr. Malone.

MALONE    I hope not, Miss Robinson; but at your age you might think many things unreasonable that don't seem so to me.

VIOLET [*with a little shrug*]    Oh well, I suppose there's no use our playing at cross purposes, Mr. Malone. Hector wants to marry me.

MALONE    I inferred from your note that he might. Well, Miss Robinson, he is his own master; but if he marries you he shall not have a rap from me. [*He takes off his spectacles and pockets them with the note*].

VIOLET [*with some severity*]    That is not very complimentary to me, Mr. Malone.

MALONE    I say nothing against you, Miss Robinson: I daresay you are an amiable and excellent young lady. But I have other views for Hector.

VIOLET    Hector may not have other views for himself, Mr. Malone.

MALONE    Possibly not. Then he does without me: that's all. I daresay you are prepared for that. When a young lady writes to a young man to come to her quick, quick, quick, money seems nothing and love seems everything.

VIOLET [*sharply*]    I beg your pardon, Mr. Malone: I do not think anything so foolish. Hector must have money.

MALONE [*staggered*]    Oh, very well, very well. No doubt he can work for it.

VIOLET    What is the use of having money if you have to work for it? [*She rises impatiently*]. It's all nonsense, Mr. Malone: you must enable your son to keep up his position. It is his right.

MALONE [*grimly*]   I should not advise you to marry him on the strength of that right, Miss Robinson.

*VIOLET, who has almost lost her temper, controls herself with an effort; unclenches her fingers; and resumes her seat with studied tranquillity and reasonableness.*

VIOLET   What objection have you to me, pray? My social position is as good as Hector's, to say the least. He admits it.

MALONE [*shrewdly*]   You tell him so from time to time, eh? Hector's social position in England, Miss Robinson, is just what I choose to buy for him. I have made him a fair offer. Let him pick out the most historic house, castle or abbey that England contains. The day that he tells me he wants it for a wife worthy of its traditions, I buy it for him, and give him the means of keeping it up.

VIOLET   What do you mean by a wife worthy of its traditions? Cannot any well bred woman keep such a house for him?

MALONE   No: she must be born to it.

VIOLET   Hector was not born to it, was he?

MALONE   His granmother was a barefooted Irish girl that nursed me by a turf fire. Let him marry another such, and I will not stint her marriage portion. Let him raise himself socially with my money or raise somebody else: so long as there is a social profit somewhere, I'll regard my expenditure as justified. But there must be a profit for someone. A marriage with you would leave things just where they are.

VIOLET   Many of my relations would object very much to my marrying the grandson of a common woman, Mr. Malone. That may be prejudice; but so is your desire to have him marry a title prejudice.

MALONE [*rising, and approaching her with a scrutiny in which there is a good deal of reluctant respect*]   You seem a pretty straightforward downright sort of a young woman.

VIOLET   I do not see why I should be made miserably poor because I cannot make profits for you. Why do you want to make Hector unhappy?

MALONE   He will get over it all right enough. Men thrive better on disappointments in love than on disappointments in money. I daresay you think that sordid; but I know what I'm talking about. My father died of starvation in Ireland in the black 47. Maybe you've heard of it.

VIOLET   The Famine?

MALONE [*with smouldering passion*]   No, the starvation. When a country is full of food, and exporting it, there can be no famine. My father was starved dead; and I was starved out to America in my mother's arms. English rule drove me and mine out of Ireland. Well, you can keep Ireland. I and my like are coming back to buy England; and we'll buy the best of it. I want no middle class properties and no middle class women for Hector. That's straightforward, isn't it, like yourself?

VIOLET [*icily pitying his sentimentality*]   Really, Mr. Malone, I am astonished to hear a man of your age and good sense talking in that romantic way. Do you suppose English noblemen will sell their places to you for the asking?

MALONE   I have the refusal of two of the oldest family mansions in England. One historic owner can't afford to keep all the rooms dusted: the other can't afford the death duties. What do you say now?

VIOLET   Of course it is very scandalous; but surely you know that the Government will sooner or later put a stop to all these Socialistic attacks on property.

MALONE [*grinning*]   D'y' think they'll be able to get that done before I buy the house—or rather the abbey? They're both abbeys.

VIOLET [*putting that aside rather impatiently*]   Oh, well, let us talk sense, Mr. Malone. You must feel that we havn't been talking sense so far.

MALONE   I can't say I do. I mean all I say.

VIOLET    Then you don't know Hector as I do. He is romantic and faddy—he gets it from you, I fancy—and he wants a certain sort of wife to take care of him. Not a faddy sort of person, you know.

MALONE    Somebody like you, perhaps?

VIOLET [*quietly*]    Well, yes. But you cannot very well ask me to undertake this with absolutely no means of keeping up his position.

MALONE [*alarmed*]    Stop a bit, stop a bit. Where are we getting to? I'm not aware that I'm asking you to undertake anything.

VIOLET    Of course, Mr. Malone, you can make it very difficult for me to speak to you if you choose to misunderstand me.

MALONE [*half bewildered*]    I don't wish to take any unfair advantage; but we seem to have got off the straight track somehow.
*STRAKER, with the air of a man who has been making haste, opens the little gate, and admits HECTOR, who, snorting with indignation, comes upon the lawn, and is making for his father when VIOLET, greatly dismayed, springs up and intercepts him. STRAKER does not wait; at least he does not remain visibly within earshot.*

VIOLET    Oh, how unlucky! Now please, Hector, say nothing. Go away until I have finished speaking to your father.

HECTOR [*inexorably*]    No, Violet I mean to have this thing out, right away. [*He puts her aside; passes her by; and faces his father, whose cheeks darken as his Irish blood begins to simmer*]. Dad: you've not played this hand straight.

MALONE    Hwat d'y'mean?

HECTOR    You've opened a letter addressed to me. You've impersonated me and stolen a march on this lady. That's dishonorable.

MALONE [*threateningly*]    Now you take care what you're saying, Hector. Take care, I tell you.

HECTOR    I have taken care. I am taking care. I'm taking care of my honor and my position in English society.

MALONE [*hotly*]    Your position has been got by my money: do you know that?

HECTOR    Well, you've just spoiled it all by opening that letter. A letter from an English lady, not addressed to you—a confidential letter! a delicate letter! a private letter! opened by my father! That's a sort of thing a man can't struggle against in England. The sooner we go back together the better. [*He appeals mutely to the heavens to witness the shame and anguish of two outcasts*].

VIOLET [*snubbing him with an instinctive dislike for scene making*] Don't be unreasonable, Hector. It was quite natural of Mr. Malone to open my letter: his name was on the envelope.

MALONE    There! You've no common sense, Hector. I thank you, Miss Robinson.

HECTOR    I thank you, too. It's very kind of you. My father knows no better.

MALONE [*furiously clenching his fists*]    Hector—

HECTOR [*with undaunted moral force*]    Oh, it's no use hectoring me. A private letter's a private letter, dad: you can't get over that.

MALONE [*raising his voice*]    I won't be talked back to by you, d'y'-hear?

VIOLET    Ssh! please, p l e a s e. Here they all come.

*Father and son, checked, glare mutely at one another as TANNER comes in through the little gate with RAMSDEN, followed by OCTAVIUS and ANN.*

VIOLET    Back already!

TANNER    The Alhambra is not open this afternoon.

VIOLET    What a sell!

*TANNER passes on, and presently finds himself between HECTOR and a strange elder, both apparently on the verge of personal combat. He looks from one to the other for an explanation. They sulkily avoid his eye, and nurse their wrath in silence.*

RAMSDEN    Is it wise for you to be out in the sunshine with such a headache, Violet?

TANNER    Have you recovered too, Malone?

VIOLET    Oh, I forgot. We have not all met before. Mr. Malone: won't you introduce your father?

HECTOR [*with Roman firmness*]    No I will not. He is no father of mine.

MALONE [*very angry*]    You disown your dad before your English friends, do you?

VIOLET    Oh please don't make a scene.

*ANN and OCTAVIUS, lingering near the gate, exchange an astonished glance, and discreetly withdraw up the steps to the garden, where they can enjoy the disturbance without intruding. On their way to the steps ANN sends a little grimace of mute sympathy to VIOLET, who is standing with her back to the little table, looking on in helpless annoyance as her husband soars to higher and higher moral eminences without the least regard to the old man's millions.*

HECTOR    I'm very sorry, Miss Robinson; but I'm contending for a principle. I am a son, and, I hope, a dutiful one; but before everything I'm a Man!!! And when dad treats my private letters as his own, and takes it on himself to say that I shan't marry you if I am happy and fortunate enough to gain your consent, then I just snap my fingers and go my own way.

TANNER    Marry Violet!

RAMSDEN    Are you in your senses?

TANNER    Do you forget what we told you?

HECTOR [*recklessly*]    I don't care what you told me.

RAMSDEN [*scandalized*]    Tut tut, sir! Monstrous! [*he flings away towards the gate, his elbows quivering with indignation*].

TANNER    Another madman! These men in love should be locked up. [*He gives HECTOR up as hopeless, and turns away towards the garden; but MALONE, taking offence in a new direction, follows him and compels him, by the aggressiveness of his tone, to stop*].

MALONE    I don't understand this. Is Hector not good enough for this lady, pray?

TANNER    My dear sir, the lady is married already. Hector knows it; and yet he persists in his infatuation. Take him home and lock him up.

MALONE [*bitterly*]    So this is the high-born social tone I've spoilt be me ignorant, uncultivated behavior! Makin love to a married woman! [*He comes angrily between HECTOR and VIOLET, and almost bawls into HECTOR's left ear*] You've picked up that habit of the British aristocracy, have you?

HECTOR    That's all right. Don't you trouble yourself about that. I'll answer for the morality of what I'm doing.

TANNER [*coming forward to HECTOR's right hand with flashing eyes*] Well said, Malone! You also see that mere marriage laws are not morality! I agree with you; but unfortunately Violet does not.

MALONE    I take leave to doubt that, sir. [*Turning on VIOLET*] Let me tell you, Mrs. Robinson, or whatever your right name is, you had no right to send that letter to my son when you were the wife of another man.

HECTOR [*outraged*]    This is the last straw. Dad: you have insulted my wife.

MALONE    Y o u r  wife!

TANNER    Y o u  the missing husband! Another moral impostor! [*He smites his brow, and collapses into MALONE's chair*].

MALONE    You've married without my consent!

RAMSDEN    You have deliberately humbugged us, sir!

HECTOR    Here: I have had just about enough of being badgered. Violet and I are married: that's the long and the short of it. Now what have you got to say—any of you?

MALONE    I know what I've got to say. She's married a beggar.

HECTOR    No; she's married a Worker [*his American pronunciation imparts an overwhelming intensity to this simple and unpopular word*]. I start to earn my own living this very afternoon.

MALONE [*sneering angrily*]    Yes: you're very plucky now, because you got your remittance from me yesterday or this morning, I reckon; Wait til it's spent. You won't be so full of cheek then.

HECTOR [*producing a letter from his pocketbook*]    Here it is [*thrusting it on his father*]. Now you just take your remittance and yourself out of my life. I'm done with remittances; and I'm done with you. I don't sell the privilege of insulting my wife for a thousand dollars.

MALONE [*deeply wounded and full of concern*]   Hector: you don't know what poverty is.

HECTOR [*fervidly*]   Well, I want to know what it is. I want'be a Man. Violet: you come along with me, to your own home: I'll see you through.

OCTAVIUS [*jumping down from the garden to the lawn and running to HECTOR's left hand*]   I hope you'll shake hands with me before you go, Hector. I admire and respect you more than I can say. [*He is affected almost to tears as they shake hands*].

VIOLET [*also almost in tears, but of vexation*]   Oh don't be an idiot, Tavy. Hector's about as fit to become a workman as you are.

TANNER [*rising from his chair on the other side of HECTOR*]   Never fear: there's no question of his becoming a navvy, Mrs. Malone. [*To HECTOR*] There's really no difficulty about capital to start with. Treat me as a friend: draw on me.

OCTAVIUS [*impulsively*]   Or on me.

MALONE [*with fierce jealousy*]   Who wants your durty money? Who should he draw on but his own father? [*TANNER and OCTAVIUS recoil, OCTAVIUS rather hurt, TANNER consoled by the solution of the money difficulty. VIOLET looks up hopefully*]. Hector: don't be rash, my boy. I'm sorry for what I said: I never meant to insult Violet: I take it all back. She's just the wife you want: there!

HECTOR [*patting him on the shoulder*]   Well, that's all right, dad. Say no more: we're friends again. Only, I take no money from anybody.

MALONE [*pleading abjectly*]   Don't be hard on me, Hector. I'd rather you quarrelled and took the money than made friends and starved. You don't know what the world is: I do.

HECTOR   No, n o, NO. That's fixed: that's not going to change. [*He passes his father inexorably by, and goes to VIOLET*]. Come, Mrs. Malone: you've got to move to the hotel with me, and take your proper place before the world.

VIOLET    But I must go in, dear, and tell Davis to pack. Won't you go on and make them give you a room overlooking the garden for me? I'll join you in half an hour.

HECTOR    Very well. You'll dine with us, Dad, won't you?

MALONE [*eager to conciliate him*]    Yes, yes.

HECTOR    See you all later. [*He waves his hand to ANN, who has now been joined by TANNER, OCTAVIUS, and RAMSDEN in the garden, and goes out through the little gate, leaving his father and VIOLET together on the lawn*].

MALONE    You'll try to bring him to his senses, Violet: I know you will.

VIOLET    I had no idea he could be so headstrong. If he goes on like that, what can I do?

MALONE    Don't be discurridged: domestic pressure may be slow; but it's sure. You'll wear him down. Promise me you will.

VIOLET    I will do my best. Of course I think it's the greatest nonsense deliberately making us poor like that.

MALONE    Of course it is.

VIOLET [*after a moment's reflection*]    You had better give me the remittance. He will want it for his hotel bill. I'll see whether I can induce him to accept it. Not now, of course, but presently.

MALONE [*eagerly*]    Yes, yes, yes: that's just the thing [*he hands her the thousand dollar bill, and adds cunningly*] Y'understand that this is only a bachelor allowance.

VIOLET [*coolly*]    Oh, quite. [*She takes it*]. Thank you. By the way, Mr. Malone, those two houses you mentioned—the abbeys.

MALONE    Yes?

VIOLET    Don't take one of them until I've seen it. One never knows what may be wrong with these places.

MALONE    I won't. I'll do nothing without consulting you, never fear.

VIOLET [*politely, but without a ray of gratitude*]    Thanks: that will be much the best way. [*She goes calmly back to the villa, escorted obsequiously by MALONE to the upper end of the garden*].

TANNER [*drawing RAMSDEN's attention to MALONE's cringing attitude as he takes leave of VIOLET*]     And that poor devil is a billionaire! one of the master spirits of the age! Led in a string like a pug dog by the first girl who takes the trouble to despise him. I wonder will it ever come to that with me. [*He comes down to the lawn*].

RAMSDEN [*following him*]     The sooner the better for you.

MALONE [*slapping his hands as he returns through the garden*]     That'll be a grand woman for Hector. I wouldn't exchange her for ten duchesses. [*He descends to the lawn and comes between TANNER and RAMSDEN*].

RAMSDEN [*very civil to the billionaire*]     It's an unexpected pleasure to find you in this corner of the world, Mr. Malone. Have you come to buy up the Alhambra?

MALONE     Well, I don't say I mightn't. I think I could do better with it than the Spanish government. But that's not what I came about. To tell you the truth, about a month ago I overheard a deal between two men over a bundle of shares. They differed about the price: they were young and greedy, and didn't know that if the shares were worth what was bid for them they must be worth what was asked, the margin being too small to be of any account, you see. To amuse meself, I cut in and bought the shares. Well, to this day I havn't found out what the business is. The office is in this town; and the name is Mendoza, Limited. Now whether Mendoza's a mine, or a steamboat line, or a bank or a patent article—

TANNER     He's a man. I know him: his principles are thoroughly commercial. Let us take you round the town in our motor, Mr. Malone, and call on him on the way.

MALONE     If you'll be so kind, yes. And may I ask who—

TANNER     Mr. Roebuck Ramsden, a very old friend of your daughter-in-law.

MALONE     Happy to meet you, Mr. Ramsden.

RAMSDEN     Thank you. Mr. Tanner is also one of our circle.

MALONE     Glad to know you also, Mr. Tanner.

TANNER   Thanks. [*MALONE and RAMSDEN go out very amicably through the little gate. TANNER calls to OCTAVIUS, who is wandering in the garden with ANN*] Tavy! [*TAVY comes to the steps, TANNER whispers loudly to him*] Violet has married a financier of brigands. [*TANNER hurries away to overtake MALONE and RAMSDEN. ANN strolls to the steps with an idle impulse to torment OCTAVIUS*].

ANN   Won't you go with them, Tavy?

OCTAVIUS [*tears suddenly flushing his eyes*]   You cut me to the heart, Ann, by wanting me to go [*he comes down on the lawn to hide his face from her. She follows him caressingly*].

ANN   Poor Ricky Ticky Tavy! Poor heart!

OCTAVIUS   It belongs to you, Ann. Forgive me: I must speak of it. I love you. You know I love you.

ANN   What's the good, Tavy? You know that my mother is determined that I shall marry Jack.

OCTAVIUS [*amazed*]   Jack!

ANN   It seems absurd, doesn't it?

OCTAVIUS [*with growing resentment*]   Do you mean to say that Jack has been playing with me all this time? That he has been urging me not to marry you because he intends to marry you himself?

ANN [*alarmed*]   No no: you mustn't lead him to believe that I said that: I don't for a moment think that Jack knows his own mind. But it's clear from my father's will that he wished me to marry Jack. And my mother is set on it.

OCTAVIUS   But you are not bound to sacrifice yourself always to the wishes of your parents.

ANN   My father loved me. My mother loves me. Surely their wishes are a better guide than my own selfishness.

OCTAVIUS   Oh, I know how unselfish you are, Ann. But believe me—though I know I am speaking in my own interest—there is another side to this question. Is it fair to Jack to marry him if you do not love him? Is it fair to destroy my happiness as well as your own if you can bring yourself to love me?

ANN [*looking at him with a faint impulse of pity*]   Tavy, my dear, you are a nice creature—a good boy.

OCTAVIUS [*humiliated*]   Is that all?

ANN [*mischievously in spite of her pity*]   That's a great deal, I assure you. You would always worship the ground I trod on, wouldn't you?

OCTAVIUS   I do. It sounds ridiculous; but it's no exaggeration. I do; and I always shall.

ANN   Always is a long word, Tavy. You see, I shall have to live up always to your idea of my divinity; and I don't think I could do that if we were married. But if I marry Jack, you'll never be disillusioned—at least not until I grow too old.

OCTAVIUS   I too shall grow old, Ann. And when I am eighty, one white hair of the woman I love will make me tremble more than the thickest gold tress from the most beautiful young head.

ANN [*quite touched*]   Oh, that's poetry, Tavy, real poetry. It gives me that strange sudden sense of an echo from a former existence which always seems to me such a striking proof that we have immortal souls.

OCTAVIUS   Do you believe that it is true?

ANN   Tavy: if it is to come true, you must lose me as well as love me.

OCTAVIUS   Oh! [*he hastily sits down at the little table and covers his face with his hands*].

ANN [*with conviction*]   Tavy: I wouldn't for worlds destroy your illusions. I can neither take you nor let you go. I can see exactly what will suit you. You must be a sentimental old bachelor for my sake.

OCTAVIUS [*desperately*]   Ann: I'll kill myself.

ANN   Oh no you won't: that wouldn't be kind. You won't have a bad time. You will be very nice to women; and you will go a good deal to the opera. A broken heart is a very pleasant complaint for a man in London if he has a comfortable income.

OCTAVIUS [*considerably cooled, but believing that he is only recovering his self-control*]    I know you mean to be kind, Ann. Jack has persuaded you that cynicism is a good tonic for me. [*He rises with quiet dignity*].

ANN [*studying him slyly*]    You see, I'm disillusionizing you already. That's what I dread.

OCTAVIUS    You do not dread disillusionizing Jack.

ANN [*her face lighting up with mischievous ecstasy—whispering*]    I can't: he has no illusions about me. I shall surprise Jack the other way. Getting over an unfavorable impression is ever so much easier than living up to an ideal. Oh, I shall enrapture Jack sometimes!

OCTAVIUS [*resuming the calm phase of despair, and beginning to enjoy his broken heart and delicate attitude without knowing it*]    I don't doubt that. You will enrapture him always. And he—the fool!— thinks you would make him wretched.

ANN    Yes: that's the difficulty, so far.

OCTAVIUS [*heroically*]    Shall *I* tell him that you love him?

ANN [*quickly*]    Oh no: he'd run away again.

OCTAVIUS [*shocked*]    Ann: would you marry an unwilling man?

ANN    What a queer creature you are, Tavy! There's no such thing as a willing man when you really go for him. [*She laughs naughtily*]. I'm shocking you, I suppose. But you know you are really getting a sort of satisfaction already in being out of danger yourself.

OCTAVIUS [*startled*]    Satisfaction! [*Reproachfully*] You say that to me!

ANN    Well, if it were really agony, would you ask for more of it?

OCTAVIUS    H a v e I asked for more of it?

ANN    You have offered to tell Jack that I love him. That's self-sacrifice, I suppose; but there must be some satisfaction in it. Perhaps it's because you're a poet. You are like the bird that presses its breast against the sharp thorn to make itself sing.

OCTAVIUS    It's quite simple. I love you; and I want you to be happy. You don't love me; so I can't make you happy myself; but I can help another man to do it.

ANN  Yes: it seems quite simple. But I doubt if we ever know why we do things. The only really simple thing is to go straight for what you want and grab it. I suppose I don't love you, Tavy; but sometimes I feel as if I should like to make a man of you somehow. You are very foolish about women.

OCTAVIUS [*almost coldly*]  I am content to be what I am in that respect.

ANN  Then you must keep away from them, and only dream about them. I wouldn't marry you for worlds, Tavy.

OCTAVIUS  I have no hope, Ann: I accept my ill luck. But I don't think you quite know how much it hurts.

ANN  You are so softhearted! It's queer that you should be so different from Violet. Violet's as hard as nails.

OCTAVIUS  Oh no. I am sure Violet is thoroughly womanly at heart.

ANN [*with some impatience*]  Why do you say that? Is it unwomanly to be thoughtful and businesslike and sensible? Do you want Violet to be an idiot—or something worse, like me?

OCTAVIUS  Something worse—like y o u! What do you mean, Ann?

ANN  Oh well, I don't mean that, of course. But I have a great respect for Violet. She gets her own way always.

OCTAVIUS [*sighing*]  So do you.

ANN  Yes; but somehow she gets it without coaxing—without having to make people sentimental about her.

OCTAVIUS [*with brotherly callousness*]  Nobody could get very sentimental about Violet, I think, pretty as she is.

ANN  Oh yes they could, if she made them.

OCTAVIUS  But surely no really nice woman would deliberately practise on men's instincts in that way.

ANN [*throwing up her hands*]  Oh Tavy, Tavy, Ricky Ticky Tavy, heaven help the woman who marries you!

OCTAVIUS [*his passion reviving at the name*]   Oh why, why, why do you say that? Don't torment me. I don't understand.

ANN   Suppose she were to tell fibs, and lay snares for men?

OCTAVIUS   Do you think *I* could marry such a woman—I, who have known and loved y o u?

ANN   Hm! Well, at all events, she wouldn't let you if she were wise. So that's settled. And now I can't talk any more. Say you forgive me, and that the subject is closed.

OCTAVIUS   I have nothing to forgive; and the subject is closed. And if the wound is open, at least you shall never see it bleed.

ANN   Poetic to the last, Tavy. Goodbye, dear. [*She pats his cheek; has an impulse to kiss him and then another impulse of distaste which prevents her; finally runs away through the garden and into the villa*].

   *OCTAVIUS again takes refuge at the table, bowing his head on his arms and sobbing softly. MRS. WHITEFIELD, who has been pottering round the Granada shops, and has a net full of little parcels in her hand, comes in through the gate and sees him.*

MRS. WHITEFIELD [*running to him and lifting his head*]   What's the matter, Tavy? Are you ill?

OCTAVIUS   No, nothing, nothing.

MRS. WHITEFIELD [*still holding his head, anxiously*]   But you're crying. Is it about Violet's marriage?

OCTAVIUS   No, no. Who told you about Violet?

MRS. WHITEFIELD [*restoring the head to its owner*]   I met Roebuck and that awful old Irishman. Are you sure you're not ill? What's the matter?

OCTAVIUS [*affectionately*]   It's nothing—only a man's broken heart. Doesn't that sound ridiculous?

MRS. WHITEFIELD   But what is it all about? Has Ann been doing anything to you?

OCTAVIUS   It's not Ann's fault. And don't think for a moment that I blame you.

MRS. WHITEFIELD [*startled*]   For what?

OCTAVIUS [*pressing her hand consolingly*]  For nothing. I said I didn't blame you.

MRS. WHITEFIELD  But I haven't done anything. What's the matter?

OCTAVIUS [*smiling sadly*]  Can't you guess? I daresay you are right to prefer Jack to me as a husband for Ann; but I love Ann; and it hurts rather. [*He rises and moves away from her towards the middle of the lawn*].

MRS. WHITEFIELD [*following him hastily*]  Does Ann say that I want her to marry Jack?

OCTAVIUS  Yes: she has told me.

MRS. WHITEFIELD [*thoughtfully*]  Then I'm very sorry for you, Tavy. It's only her way of saying she wants to marry Jack. Little she cares what *I* say or what *I* want!

OCTAVIUS  But she would not say it unless she believed it. Surely you don't suspect Ann of—of d e c e i t !!

MRS. WHITEFIELD  Well, never mind, Tavy. I don't know which is best for a young man: to know too little, like you, or too much, like Jack.

*TANNER returns.*

TANNER  Well, I've disposed of old Malone. I've introduced him to Mendoza, Limited; and left the two brigands together to talk it out. Hullo, Tavy! anything wrong?

OCTAVIUS  I must go wash my face, I see. [*To MRS. WHITEFIELD*] Tell him what you wish. [*To TANNER*] You may take it from me, Jack, that Ann approves of it.

TANNER [*puzzled by his manner*]  Approves of what?

OCTAVIUS  Of what Mrs. Whitefield wishes. [*He goes his way with sad dignity to the villa*].

TANNER [*to MRS. WHITEFIELD*]  This is very mysterious. What is it you wish? It shall be done, whatever it is.

MRS. WHITEFIELD [*with snivelling gratitude*]  Thank you, Jack. [*She sits down. TANNER brings the other chair from the table and sits close to her with his elbows on his knees, giving her his whole attention*].

I don't know why it is that other people's children are so nice to me, and that my own have so little consideration for me. It's no wonder I don't seem able to care for Ann and Rhoda as I do for you and Tavy and Violet. It's a very queer world. It used to be so straightforward and simple; and now nobody seems to think and feel as they ought. Nothing has been right since that speech that Professor Tyndall* made at Belfast.

TANNER    Yes: life is more complicated than we used to think. But what am I to do for you?

MRS. WHITEFIELD    That's just what I want to tell you. Of course you'll marry Ann whether I like it or not—

TANNER [*starting*]    It seems to me that I shall presently be married to Ann whether I like it myself or not.

MRS. WHITEFIELD [*peacefully*]    Oh, very likely you will: you know what she is when she has set her mind on anything. But don't put it on me: that's all I ask. Tavy has just let out that she's been saying that I am making her marry you; and the poor boy is breaking his heart about it; for he is in love with her himself, though what he sees in her so wonderful, goodness knows: *I* don't. It's no use telling Tavy that Ann puts things into people's heads by telling them that I want them when the thought of them never crossed my mind. It only sets Tavy against me. But you know better than that. So if you marry her, don't put the blame on me.

TANNER [*emphatically*]    I havn't the slightest intention of marrying her.

MRS. WHITEFIELD [*slyly*]    She'd suit you better than Tavy. She'd meet her match in you, Jack. I'd like to see her meet her match.

TANNER    No man is a match for a woman, except with a poker and a pair of hobnailed boots. Not always even then. Anyhow, *I* can't take the poker to her. I should be a mere slave.

MRS. WHITEFIELD    No: she's afraid of you. At all events, you

---

*John Tyndall delivered a heterodox speech on religion and evolution in 1874.

would tell her the truth about herself. She wouldn't be able to slip out of it as she does with me.

TANNER    Everybody would call me a brute if I told Ann the truth about herself in terms of her own moral code. To begin with, Ann says things that are not strictly true.

MRS. WHITEFIELD    I'm glad somebody sees she is not an angel.

TANNER    In short—to put it as a husband would put it when exasperated to the point of speaking out—she is a liar. And since she has plunged Tavy head over ears in love with her without any intention of marrying him, she is a coquette, according to the standard definition of a coquette as a woman who rouses passions she has no intention of gratifying. And as she has now reduced you to the point of being willing to sacrifice me at the altar for the mere satisfaction of getting me to call her a liar to her face, I may conclude that she is a bully as well. She can't bully men as she bullies women; so she habitually and unscrupulously uses her personal fascination to make men give her whatever she wants. That makes her almost something for which I know no polite name.

MRS. WHITEFIELD [*in mild expostulation*]    Well, you can't expect perfection, Jack.

TANNER    I don't. But what annoys me is that Ann does. I know perfectly well that all this about her being a liar and a bully and a coquette and so forth is a trumped-up moral indictment which might be brought against anybody. We all lie; we all bully as much as we dare; we all bid for admiration without the least intention of earning it; we all get as much rent as we can out of our powers of fascination. If Ann would admit this I shouldn't quarrel with her. But she won't. If she has children she'll take advantage of their telling lies to amuse herself by whacking them. If another woman makes eyes at me, she'll refuse to know a coquette. She will do just what she likes herself whilst insisting on everybody else doing what the conventional code prescribes. In

short, I can stand everything except her confounded hypocrisy.
That's what beats me.

MRS. WHITEFIELD [*carried away by the relief of hearing her own
opinion so eloquently expressed*]   Oh, she i s a hypocrite. She is: she
is. Isn't she?

TANNER   Then why do you want to marry me to her?

MRS. WHITEFIELD [*querulously*]   There now! put it on me, of
course. I never thought of it until Tavy told me she said I did.
But, you know, I'm very fond of Tavy: he's a sort of son to me;
and I don't want him to be trampled on and made wretched.

TANNER   Whereas I don't matter, I suppose.

MRS. WHITEFIELD   Oh, you are different, somehow: you are
able to take care of yourself. You'd serve her out. And anyhow,
she must marry somebody.

TANNER   Aha! there speaks the life instinct. You detest her; but
you feel that you must get her married.

MRS. WHITEFIELD [*rising, shocked*]   Do you mean that I detest
my own daughter! Surely you don't believe me to be so wicked
and unnatural as that, merely because I see her faults.

TANNER [*cynically*]   You love her, then?

MRS. WHITEFIELD   Why, of course I do. What queer things
you say, Jack! We can't help loving our own blood relations.

TANNER   Well, perhaps it saves unpleasantness to say so. But for
my part, I suspect that the tables of consanguinity have a natural
basis in a natural repugnance [*he rises*].

MRS. WHITEFIELD   You shouldn't say things like that, Jack. I
hope you won't tell Ann that I have been speaking to you. I only
wanted to set myself right with you and Tavy. I couldn't sit mum-
chance and have everything put on me.

TANNER [*politely*]   Quite so.

MRS. WHITEFIELD [*dissatisfied*]   And now I've only made matters worse. Tavy's angry with me because I don't worship Ann.
And when it's been put into my head that Ann ought to marry
you, what can I say except that it would serve her right?

TANNER    Thank you.

MRS. WHITEFIELD    Now don't be silly and twist what I say into something I don't mean. I ought to have fair play—

*ANN comes from the villa, followed presently by VIOLET, who is dressed for driving.*

ANN [*coming to her mother's right hand with threatening suavity*]    Well, mamma darling, you seem to be having a delightful chat with Jack. We can hear you all over the place.

MRS. WHITEFIELD [*appalled*]    Have you overhcard—

TANNER    Never fear: Ann is only—well, we were discussing that habit of hers just now. She hasn't heard a word.

MRS. WHITEFIELD [*stoutly*]    I don't care whether she has or not: I have a right to say what I please.

VIOLET [*arriving on the lawn and coming between MRS. WHITEFIELD and TANNER*]    I've come to say goodbye. I'm off for my honeymoon.

MRS. WHITEFIELD [*crying*]    Oh don't say that, Violet. And no wedding, no breakfast, no clothes, nor anything.

VIOLET [*petting her*]    It won't be for long.

MRS. WHITEFIELD    Don't let him take you to America. Promise me that you won't.

VIOLET [*very decidedly*]    I should think not, indeed. Don't cry, dear: I'm only going to thc hotel.

MRS. WHITEFIELD    But going in that dress, with your luggage, makes one realize—[*she chokes, and then breaks out again*] How I wish you were my daughter, Violet!

VIOLET [*soothing her*]    There, there: so I am. Ann will be jealous.

MRS. WHITEFIELD    Ann doesn't care a bit for me.

ANN    Fie, mother! Come, now: you mustn't cry any more: you know Violet doesn't like it [*MRS. WHITEFIELD dries her eyes, and subsides*].

VIOLET    Goodbye, Jack.

TANNER    Goodbye, Violet.

VIOLET    The sooner you get married too, the better. You will be much less misunderstood.

TANNER [*restively*]    I quite expect to get married in the course of the afternoon. You all seem to have set your minds on it.

VIOLET    You might do worse. [*To MRS. WHITEFIELD: putting her arm round her*] Let me take you to the hotel with me: the drive will do you good. Come in and get a wrap. [*She takes her towards the villa*].

MRS. WHITEFIELD [*as they go up through the garden*]    I don't know what I shall do when you are gone, with no one but Ann in the house; and she always occupied with the men! It's not to be expected that your husband will care to be bothered with an old woman like me. Oh, you needn't tell me: politeness is all very well; but I know what people think— [*She talks herself and VIOLET out of sight and hearing*]

*ANN, musing on VIOLET's opportune advice, approaches TANNER; examines him humorously for a moment from toe to top and finally delivers her opinion.*

ANN    Violet is quite right. You ought to get married.

TANNER [*explosively*]    Ann: I will not marry you. Do you hear? I won't, won't, won't, won't, WON'T marry you.

ANN [*placidly*]    Well, nobody axd you, sir she said, sir she said, sir she said. So that's settled.

TANNER    Yes, nobody has asked me; but everybody treats the thing as settled. It's in the air. When we meet, the others go away on absurd pretexts to leave us alone together. Ramsden no longer scowls at me: his eye beams, as if he were already giving you away to me in church, Tavy refers me to your mother and gives me his blessing. Straker openly treats you as his future employer: it was he who first told me of it.

ANN    Was that why you ran away?

TANNER    Yes, only to be stopped by a lovesick brigand and run down like a truant schoolboy.

ANN    Well, if you don't want to be married, you needn't be. [*she turns away from him and sits down, much at her ease*].

TANNER [*following her*]    Does any man want to be hanged? Yet men let themselves be hanged without a struggle for life, though they could at least give the chaplain a black eye. We do the world's will, not our own. I have a frightful feeling that I shall let myself be married because it is the world's will that you should have a husband.

ANN   I daresay I shall, someday.

TANNER   But why m e—me of all men? Marriage is to me apostasy, profanation of the sanctuary of my soul, violation of my manhood, sale of my birthright, shameful surrender, ignominious capitulation, acceptance of defeat. I shall decay like a thing that has served its purpose and is done with; I shall change from a man with a future to a man with a past; I shall see in the greasy eyes of all the other husbands their relief at the arrival of a new prisoner to share their ignominy. The young men will scorn me as one who has sold out: to the young women I, who have always been an enigma and a possibility, shall be merely somebody else's property—and damaged goods at that: a secondhand man at best.

ANN   Well, your wife can put on a cap and make herself ugly to keep you in countenance, like my grandmother.

TANNER   So that she may make her triumph more insolent by publicly throwing away the bait the moment the trap snaps on the victim!

ANN   After all, though, what difference would it make? Beauty is all very well at first sight; but who ever looks at it when it has been in the house three days? I thought our pictures very lovely when papa bought them; but I havn't looked at them for years. You never bother about my looks: you are too well used to me. I might be the umbrella stand.

TANNER   You lie, you vampire: you lie.

ANN   Flatterer. Why are you trying to fascinate me, Jack, if you don't want to marry me?

TANNER   The Life Force. I am in the grip of the Life Force.

ANN   I don't understand in the least: it sounds like the Life Guards.*

---

*Cavalry regiment charged with guarding the British monarch's life.

TANNER   Why don't you marry Tavy? He is willing. Can you not be satisfied unless your prey struggles?

ANN [*turning to him as if to let him into a secret*]   Tavy will never marry. Havn't you noticed that that sort of man never marries?

TANNER   What! a man who idolizes women! who sees nothing in nature but romantic scenery for love duets! Tavy, the chivalrous, the faithful, the tenderhearted and true! Tavy never marry! Why, he was born to be swept up by the first pair of blue eyes he meets in the street.

ANN   Yes, I know. All the same, Jack, men like that always live in comfortable bachelor lodgings with broken hearts, and are adored by their landladies, and never get married. Men like you always get married.

TANNER [*smiting his brow*]   How frightfully, horribly true! It has been staring me in the face all my life; and I never saw it before.

ANN   Oh, it's the same with women. The poetic temperament's a very nice temperament, very amiable, very harmless and poetic, I daresay; but it's an old maid's temperament.

TANNER   Barren. The Life Force passes it by.

ANN   If that's what you mean by the Life Force, yes.

TANNER   You don't care for Tavy?

ANN [*looking round carefully to make sure that TAVY is not within earshot*] No.

TANNER   And you do care for me?

ANN [*rising quietly and shaking her finger at him*]   Now Jack! Behave yourself.

TANNER   Infamous, abandoned woman! Devil!

ANN   Boa-constrictor! Elephant!

TANNER   Hypocrite!

ANN [*softly*]   I must be, for my future husband's sake.

TANNER   For mine! [*Correcting himself savagely*] I mean for his.

ANN [*ignoring the correction*]   Yes, for yours. You had better marry what you call a hypocrite, Jack. Women who are not hypocrites go about in rational dress and are insulted and get into all sorts of hot water. And then their husbands get dragged in too, and live in continual dread of fresh complications. Wouldn't you prefer a wife you could depend on?

TANNER    No, a thousand times no: hot water is the revolutionist's element. You clean men as you clean milk-pails, by scalding them.

ANN    Cold water has its uses too. It's healthy.

TANNER [*despairingly*]    Oh, you are witty: at the supreme moment the Life Force endows you with every quality. Well, I too can be a hypocrite. Your father's will appointed me your guardian, not your suitor. I shall be faithful to my trust.

ANN [*in low siren tones*]    He asked me who would I have as my guardian before he made that will. I chose you!

TANNER    The will is yours then! The trap was laid from the beginning.

ANN [*concentrating all her magic*]    From the beginning—from our childhood—for both of us—by the Life Force.

TANNER    I will not marry you. I will not marry you.

ANN    Oh, you will, you will.

TANNER    I tell you, no, no, no.

ANN    I tell you, yes, yes, yes.

TANNER    No.

ANN [*coaxing—imploring—almost exhausted*]    Yes. Before it is too late for repentance. Yes.

TANNER [*struck by the echo from the past*]*    When did all this happen to me before? Are we two dreaming?

ANN [*suddenly losing her courage, with an anguish that she does not conceal*]    No. We are awake; and you have said no: that is all.

TANNER [*brutally*]    Well?

ANN    Well, I made a mistake: you do not love me.

TANNER [*seizing her in his arms*]    It is false: I love you. The Life

---

*From Mozart's *Don Giovanni*, when the Statue commands the Don to repent three times and is thrice refused.

Force enchants me: I have the whole world in my arms when I clasp you. But I am fighting for my freedom, for my honor, for my self, one and indivisible.

ANN    Your happiness will be worth them all.

TANNER    You would sell freedom and honor and self for happiness?

ANN    It will not be all happiness for me. Perhaps death.

TANNER [*groaning*]    Oh, that clutch holds and hurts. What have you grasped in me? Is there a father's heart[12] as well as a mother's?

ANN    Take care, Jack: if anyone comes while we are like this, you will have to marry me.

TANNER    If we two stood now on the edge of a precipice, I would hold you tight and jump.

ANN [*panting, failing more and more under the strain*]    Jack: let me go. I have dared so frightfully—it is lasting longer than I thought. Let me go: I can't bear it.[13]

TANNER    Nor I. Let it kill us.

ANN    Yes: I don't care. I am at the end of my forces. I don't care. I think I am going to faint.

*At this moment VIOLET and OCTAVIUS come from the villa with Mrs. Whitefield, who is wrapped up for driving. Simultaneously MALONE and RAMSDEN, followed by MENDOZA and STRAKER, come in through the little gate in the paling. TANNER shamefacedly releases ANN, who raises her hand giddily to her forehead.*

MALONE    Take care. Something's the matter with the lady.

RAMSDEN    What does this mean?

VIOLET [*running between ANN and TANNER*]    Are you ill?

ANN [*reeling, with a supreme effort*]    I have promised to marry Jack.

[*She swoons. VIOLET kneels by her and chafes her hand. TANNER runs round to her other hand, and tries to lift her head. OCTAVIUS goes to VIOLET's assistance, but does not know what to do. MRS. WHITEFIELD hurries back into the villa. OCTAVIUS, MALONE and RAMSDEN run to ANN and crowd round her, stooping to assist. STRAKER coolly comes to ANN's feet, and MENDOZA to her head, both upright and self-pos-sessed*].

STRAKER   Now then, ladies and gentlemen: she don't want a crowd round her: she wants air—all the air she can git. If you please, gents— [*MALONE and RAMSDEN allow him to drive them gently past ANN and up the lawn towards the garden, where OCTAVIUS, who has already become conscious of his uselessness, joins them. STRAKER, following them up, pauses for a moment to instruct TAN-NER*]. Don't lift er ed, Mr. Tanner: let it go flat so's the blood can run back into it.

MENDOZA   He is right, Mr. Tanner. Trust to the air of the Sierra. [*He withdraws delicately to the garden steps*].

TANNER [*rising*]   I yield to your superior knowledge of physiology, Henry. [*He withdraws to the corner of the lawn; and OCTAVIUS immediately hurries down to him*].

TAVY [*aside to TANNER, grasping his hand*]   Jack: be very happy.

TANNER [*aside to TAVY*]   I never asked her. It is a trap for me. [*He goes up the lawn towards the garden. OCTAVIUS remains petrified*].

MENDOZA [*intercepting MRS. WHITEFIELD, who comes from the villa with a glass of brandy*]   What is this, madam [*he takes it from her*]?

MRS. WHITEFIELD   A little brandy.

MENDOZA   The worst thing you could give her. Allow me. [*He swallows it*]. Trust to the air of the Sierra, madam.

*For a moment the men all forget ANN and stare at MENDOZA.*

ANN [*in VIOLET's ear, clutching her round the neck*]   Violet: did Jack say anything when I fainted?

VIOLET   No.

ANN   Ah! [*with a sigh of intense relief she relapses*].

MRS. WHITEFIELD   Oh, she's fainted again.

*They are about to rush back to her; but MENDOZA stops them with a warning gesture.*

ANN [*supine*]   No I havn't. I'm quite happy.

TANNER [*suddenly walking determinedly to her, and snatching her hand from VIOLET to feel her pulse*]   Why, her pulse is positively bounding. Come, get up. What nonsense! Up with you. [*He gets her up summarily*].

ANN    Yes: I feel strong enough now. But you very nearly killed me, Jack, for all that.

MALONE    A rough wooer, eh? They're the best sort, Miss White-field. I congratulate Mr. Tanner; and I hope to meet you and him as frequent guests at the Abbey.

ANN    Thank you. [*She goes past MALONE to OCTAVIUS*] Ricky Ticky Tavy: congratulate me. [*Aside to him*] I want to make you cry for the last time.

TAVY [*steadfastly*]    No more tears. I am happy in your happiness. And I believe in you in spite of everything.

RAMSDEN [*coming between MALONE and TANNER*]    You are a happy man, Jack Tanner. I envy you.

MENDOZA [*advancing between VIOLET and TANNER*]    Sir: there are two tragedies in life. One is not to get your heart's desire. The other is to get it. Mine and yours, sir.

TANNER    Mr. Mendoza: I have no heart's desires. Ramsden: it is very easy for you to call me a happy man: you are only a specta-tor. I am one of the principals; and I know better. Ann: stop tempting Tavy, and come back to me.

ANN [*complying*]    You are absurd, Jack. [*She takes his proffered arm*].

TANNER [*continuing*]    I solemnly say that I am not a happy man. Ann looks happy; but she is only triumphant, successful, victori-ous. That is not happiness, but the price for which the strong sell their happiness. What we have both done this afternoon is to re-nounce happiness, renounce freedom, renounce tranquillity, above all renounce the romantic possibilities of an unknown fu-ture, for the cares of a household and a family. I beg that no man may seize the occasion to get half drunk and utter imbecile speeches and coarse pleasantries at my expense. We propose to furnish our own house according to our own taste; and I hereby give notice that the seven or eight travelling clocks, the four or five dressing cases, the salad bowls, the carvers and fish slices, the copy of Tennyson* in extra morocco, and all the other articles you are preparing to heap upon us, will be instantly sold, and the proceeds devoted to circulating free copies of the Revolutionist's Handbook. The wedding will take place three days after our return to England, by special license, at the office of the district superintendent registrar, in the presence of my solicitor and his clerk, who, like his clients, will be in ordinary walking dress—

VIOLET [*with intense conviction*]   You a r e a brute, Jack.

ANN [*looking at him with fond pride and caressing his arm*]   Never mind her, dear. Go on talking.

TANNER   Talking!

*Universal laughter.*†

---

*Shaw later revised this to Coventry Patmore's "Angel in the House," a poem that idealized woman.

†Not only the characters but the audience and the cosmos as well are laughing at Tanner's destiny.

# EXCERPTS FROM

## THE REVOLUTIONIST'S HANDBOOK AND POCKET COMPANION

## BY JOHN TANNER, M.I.R.C.

**********

### FOREWORD

A revolutionist is one who desires to discard the existing social order and try another.

**********

### MAXIMS FOR REVOLUTIONISTS (*SELECTED*)

The golden rule is that there are no golden rules.

**********

Democracy substitutes election by the incompetent many for appointment by the corrupt few.

**********

He who confuses political liberty with freedom and political equality with similarity has never thought for more than five minutes about either.

**********

Liberty means responsibility. That is why most men dread it.

**********

When a man teaches something he does not know to somebody who has no aptitude for it, and gives him a certificate of proficiency, the latter has completed the education of a gentleman.

A fool's brain digests philosophy into folly, science into superstition, and art into pedantry. Hence University education.

The best brought-up children are those who have seen their parents as they are.

Hypocrisy is not the parent's first duty.

The vilest abortionist is he who attempts to mold a child's character.

**********

He who can, does. He who cannot, teaches.

A learned man is an idler who kills time with study. Beware of his false knowledge: it is more dangerous than ignorance.

Activity is the only road to knowledge.

**********

Marriage is popular because it combines the maximum of temptation with the maximum of opportunity.

**********

The essential function of marriage is the continuance of the race, as stated in the Book of Common Prayer.

The accidental function of marriage is the gratification of the amoristic sentiment of mankind.

The artificial sterilization of marriage makes it possible for marriage to fulfill its accidental function whilst neglecting its essential one.

*********

Polygamy, when tried under modern democratic conditions, as by the Mormons, is wrecked by the revolt of the mass of inferior men who are condemned to celebacy by it; for the maternal instinct leads a woman to prefer a tenth share in a first rate man to the exclusive possession of a third rate one. Polyandry has not been tried under these conditions.

*********

It is the deed that teaches, not the name we give it. Murder and capital punishment are not opposites that cancel one another, but similars that breed their kind.

*********

When a man wants to murder a tiger he calls it sport; when the tiger wants to murder him he calls it ferocity. The distinction between Crime and Justice is no greater.

Whilst we have prisons it matters little which of us occupy the cells.

*********

Ladies and gentlemen are permitted to have friends in the kennel, but not in the kitchen.

*********

What a man believes may be ascertained, not from his creed, but from the assumptions on which he habitually acts.

*********

Virtue consists, not in abstaining from vice, but in not desiring it.

**********

The man with toothache thinks everyone happy whose teeth are sound. The poverty stricken man makes the same mistake about the rich man.

The more a man possesses over and above what he uses, the more careworn he becomes.

**********

In an ugly and unhappy world the richest man can purchase nothing but ugliness and unhappiness.

**********

The unconscious self is the real genius. Your breathing goes wrong the moment your conscious self meddles with it.

**********

The reasonable man adapts himself to the world: the unreasonable one persists in trying to adapt the world to himself. Therefore all progress depends on the unreasonable man.

**********

Decency is Indecency's Conspiracy of Silence.

**********

Hell is paved with good intentions, not with bad ones.

All men mean well.

**********

Life levels all men: death reveals the eminent.

**********

Home is the girl's prison and the woman's workhouse.

**********

The most popular method of distributing wealth is the method of the roulette table.

**********

We are told that when Jehovah created the world he saw that it was good. What would he say now?

The conversion of a savage to Christianity is the conversion of Christianity to savagery.

**********

Every man over forty is a scoundrel.

Youth, which is forgiven everything, forgives itself nothing; age, which forgives itself everything, is forgiven nothing.

**********

The Chinese tame fowls by clipping their wings, and women by deforming their feet. A petticoat round the ankles serves equally well.

**********

If you begin by sacrificing yourself to those you love, you will end by hating those to whom you have sacrificed yourself.

# ENDNOTES

Acknowledgments: For many of the footnotes and endnotes of this edition, and especially when I have not been able to track a reference myself, I have relied mainly on two sources: the series of selected Shaw plays annotated by A. C. Ward, *Candida, Man and Superman* (1956), and *The Devil's Disciple* (1958), and *The Complete Prefaces*, vols. 1 and 2, annotated by Dan H. Laurence and Daniel J. Leary, London and New York: Allen Lane, Penguin Press, 1993, 1995.

## MRS. WARREN'S PROFESSION

1. (p. 29) *Summer afternoon in a cottage garden. . . . He looks over the paling; takes stock of the place; and sees the young lady:* Contemporary readers may note with surprise the length and elaborateness of Shaw's stage directions. Shaw wanted the reading of his plays to be free from professional theater jargon. Hence, no technical stage directions (for example, *crosses stage right*). Instead he describes the action and introduces the characters somewhat in the manner of a novelist.

2. (p. 30) *THE GENTLEMAN:* Shaw does not identify his speakers by name until they are so identified in the dialogue. Thus readers learn the characters' names as audiences do. Shaw is trying to make the experience of reading the play replicate in the imagination the experience of attending a performance.

3. (p. 36) *"I shall use that advantage over her if necessary":* Shaw generally depicts the struggle of children to become independent of their parents as ruthless and unsentimental, as is the case here. In his own life, he was more or less financially dependent on his

mother until he was almost thirty. As he put it himself: "I did not throw myself into the struggle for life: I threw my mother into it" (Preface to *The Irrational Knot*, 1905).

4. (p. 62) *"The people who get on in this world are the people who get up and look for the circumstances they want, and, if they can't find them, make them":* In reviews of the 2002 London revival of the play, some critics identified Vivie's position here on self-help and choosing one's destiny as "Thatcherite" (after the conservative prime minister of the 1980s, Margaret Thatcher), assuming that all right-thinking persons would dismiss her views but thus displaying a political partisanship that Shaw himself eschewed vigorously.

5. (p. 65) *"Yes, saving money. . . . Not likely":* Shaw gives Mrs. Warren a Marxist rationale to articulate—namely, that the essence of capitalism is to exploit the laborer without allowing him or her an equitable share in the profits.

6. (pp. 65–67) *"Why, of course. Everybody dislikes having to work and make money. . . . That's all the difference:* Over the course of these three speeches, Mrs. Warren articulates a clear feminist position: Women are not allowed equal access to different ways of earning a living. Yet she does so while justifying prostitution. It is characteristic of Shaw not to let his audience smugly applaud a social principle—like equal access to jobs for men and women, which he himself espoused—but instead to make the audience think about it in a complex fashion.

7. (p. 75) *"The babes in the wood":* Frank refers to a legend in which a greedy uncle arranges for his orphaned nephew and niece to be murdered so that he may obtain the property they inherited from their father, his brother. Their would-be assassin abandons them in the wood, where they starve to death. In pity, the birds cover their bodies with strawberry leaves. (See the Introduction to this volume for discussion of this allusion.)

8. (p. 91) *"The Gospel of Art is the only one I can preach":* Praed is the first in a series of figures to whom Shaw attributes an allegiance

to Aestheticism (a movement associated with Oscar Wilde and J. M. Whistler), a belief in the redemptive power of beauty and the autonomy of art, as an alternative to belief in religion.

9. (pp. 94–95) *"And he won't die until he's three score and ten: he hasn't originality enough"*: Frank's observation echoes one spoken by Algernon in act 1 of Oscar Wilde's *The Importance of Being Earnest* (1895): "Relations are simply a tedious pack of people, who haven't got . . . the smallest instinct about when to die."

10. (p. 103) Mrs. Warren goes out. . . . [Vivie] soon becomes absorbed in her figures: The language and imagery in these final stage directions—*"goes buoyantly," "dipping her pen in the ink," "with a plunge"*—suggest that by immersing herself in her actuarial calculations. Vivie may be drowning her humanity. On the other hand, she has become an independent woman, not dependent on family (she sends her mother away), not dependent on men (she sends Frank away).

# CANDIDA

1. (p. 108) *the Guild of St. Matthew:* Stewart Headlam, good friend of Shaw and fellow Fabian, founded this Christian Socialist organization in 1877, and as such has been put forth by Shaw scholars as a likely model for the Reverend James Morell.

2. (p. 110) *"writes like an angel and talks like poor Poll"*: David Garrick, the leading actor of his time, devised this epitaph in 1774 for his friend, the playwright and novelist Oliver Goldsmith, in recognition of his talent for written expression, but also of Goldsmith's poor conversation (he could only parrot what others said).

3. (p. 122) Browning's poems and Maurice's Theological Essays: The poet Robert Browning and John Frederick Denison Maurice were Victorian thinkers who grappled with issues of religious faith and doubt. Their presence in Morell's library indicates that he thinks progressively.

4. (p. 123) Fabian Essays: Shaw is referring to a volume of eco-

nomic, social, and political essays, *Fabian Essays in Socialism* (1889), written by members of the Fabian Society, which advocated the gradual adoption of socialism by peaceful, not revolutionary, means—hence the name of the society, after Fabius Cunctator (the Delayer), so called for his tactic of postponing battle with Hannibal. Shaw edited and contributed to this volume, and its presence on stage represents the first of several explicit self-references in the fictional world of his plays.

5. (p. 129) *Woman Question:* The issue of equal rights for women was becoming more urgent and would reach fruition in the suffrage movement of the following decade.

6. (p. 131) *"Just as big a fool as ever, James?":* Morell's recollection of this formulaic insult from three years ago both indicates his sensitivity to being called a fool and prepares for the way Eugene's version of the same insult will deeply affect him. Shaw is usually—and unjustly—not credited for such attention to psychological nuance.

7. (p. 135) sits down in the chair Morell has just left: With this stage direction Shaw begins to play with the seating arrangements—that is, which characters sit in which chairs—as a way of helping to express shifts in power and changes in relationships.

8. (p. 136) *"Say yes, James":* Candida makes a powerful entrance (similar to Tartuffe's delayed entrance in Moliére's play) as an offstage voice, which seems to make her mysterious, and therefore strong. Moreover, she asserts control over her husband's language, the thing that makes him so influential in the public arena. Lexy copies Morell's language by repeating things he says, and Prossy copies it by typing his sermons and letters, but Eugene offers a counter-language to Morell's public speech, for Eugene speaks the private language of inner feeling, his true poetry. Candida—her name means truth, honesty—mediates between her husband's public language and Eugene's private language. She enters the play as a peacemaker between her hus-

band and her father, and she ends the play by making peace between her husband and his would-be replacement.

9. (p. 137) *"Igh Church pictur"*: By referring to the mezzotint reproduction of Titian's Assumption (which Eugene has given to Candida) as a High Church painting, Burgess means a style of representing religious subjects favored by the part of the Church of England that retained Roman Catholic rituals without retaining allegiance to the Bishop of Rome—that is, the Pope.

10. (p. 144) *"It is easy . . . to shake a man's faith in himself. To take advantage of that . . . is devil's work"*: Shaw's model for Eugene's shaking of Morell's confidence in himself and in his wife's love for him is Iago's shaking of Othello's confidence in the nobility of human nature and in his wife's fidelity to him—notable especially in the way Shaw follows Shakespeare in identifying such a process as the devil's work.

11. (p. 153) *"Ev'nly Twins"*: *The Heavenly Twins* (1893), by Sarah Grand (Mrs. Frances McFall), was a feminist novel several times alluded to by Shaw and drawn on extensively by him for his 1896 "pleasant play" *You Never Can Tell*. In later editions of *Candida*, Shaw excised this reference to the novel.

12. (p. 158) *"a tiny shallop to sail away in"*: Shaw has given Marchbanks a self-consciously "poetic" vocabulary in this speech; it is meant to show his immaturity and the derivativeness of his style at this stage of his literary development.

# THE DEVIL'S DISCIPLE

1. (p. 211) *Buckstone's Wreck Ashore:* John Baldwin Buckstone (1802–1879) was yet another popular and prolific Victorian playwright with whose work Shaw was familiar from his youth. Readers who wish to understand both Shaw's fondness for Victorian melodramas and farces and the uses to which he put that fondness in his own plays should consult Martin Meisel's *Shaw and the Nineteenth-Century Theater* (see "For Further Reading").

2. (p. 216) a rack of pegs suggests to the deductive observer that

the men of the house are all away, as there are no hats or coats on them: A skilled crafter of plays, Shaw here directs the reader's attention to the presence or absence of men's coats, clothing that will assume both practical and symbolic importance as the play unfolds.

3. (p. 217) *dont:* Throughout the text of *The Devil's Disciple* presented here, Shaw has omitted apostrophes in contractions (except where doing so would create ambiguity). It was Shaw's practice whenever his plays were reprinted to make changes and emendations, to update references and clarify stage business, etc. He was intensely interested in reform of orthography and in the appearance of the printed page. At a certain point in his career he became convinced that apostrophes in contractions were an eyesore and unnecessary. And as his plays came up for reprinting he would omit them in the new editions. In the present volume, three of the plays are reprinted from early editions antedating Shaw's new practice: *Mrs. Warren's Profession, Candida,* and *Man and Superman.* The edition we have used for *The Devil's Disciple,* however, has been revised by Shaw to omit the apostrophes in contractions.

4. (p. 248) He goes out: With Minister Anderson's departure, Shaw replicates the basic situation in *Candida* at the end of act II, where the clergyman-husband leaves his wife alone with a man to whom the husband believes his wife is attracted, but Shaw does so with certain variations: Here the wife, instead of being wise and unconventional, is silly and complacent; the husband is older than the wife; and the intruder on the hearth, instead of being physically weak and awkward, is physically impressive and full of self-confidence. As much as anything in Shaw's plays, such variation on a situation marks Shaw as a dramatic artist: Having configured his characters in a certain relation and situation in one play, he frequently takes the same configuration and alters the angle from which he displays it, or shifts the postures of the characters in regard to one another; he will do so from play to

play until he is satisfied that he has gotten everything to be had artistically from varying the configuration.

5. (p. 249) *"You are yourself again: so is Richard"*: This is a sly, joking allusion to a line from *Richard III*—though not Shakespeare's play. In 1700 actor and dramatist College Cibber (1671–1757) wrote a popular adaptation of Shakespeare's text, which at the time was considered unstageable. In act 5 of Cibber's play, the title character says: "No, never be it said, / That Fate it self could awe the Soul of Richard. /. . . Richard's himself again. / Hark! the shrill Trumpet sounds, to Horse: Away! / My Soul's in Arms, and eager for the Fray." The line was so memorable that Laurence Olivier preserved it in his classic 1955 film version of the play.

# MAN AND SUPERMAN

1. (p. 306) *"Oui, ma foi . . . songerons à nous"*: "Yes, to be sure! I must reform. Another twenty or thirty years of this kind of life, and then we'll give it some thought." Molière's Don Juan (in act 4, scene 7 of *Don Juan*, 1665) here retains the crude postponement of repentance that Tirso de Molina made part of Don Juan's youthful bravado in the face of mortality. Don Juan's desire to live an eternal life of sexual conquests betrays the anxiety he feels over his individual mortality, for his sexual seeding of so many women suggests a frantic counterattack on death with an abundance of aggressive vitality. In *Man and Superman*, Shaw will rework this confrontation with mortality into Don Juan's rejection of the Devil's invitation to a death-in-life pursuit of pleasure and beauty; Shaw will also transform it into Tanner's embrace of fatherhood as a way of defeating death.

2. (p. 308) *"marchesane, principesse, cameriere, cittadine"*: "Marchionesses, princesses, maids, townswomen"—in Mozart's *Don Giovanni* (1787), Leporello catalogues all the types and nationalities of women the Don has seduced, making the point that Don Giovanni's erotic appetite and vitality are, like the male sexual

drive itself, of comic-epic proportions in recognizing neither class barriers nor national ones. In Shaw this becomes Tanner's political and social rebellion against artificial class distinctions and his flight from Ann across a foreign border into Spain.

3. (p. 313) *a process over which I assure you I have no more real control than I have over my wife:* Like all men who have been married only a few years—Shaw had married an Irish millionairess, Charlotte Payne-Townshend, in 1898—Shaw here notes his own bewilderment at how he came to be in the married state. His own account of the wedding, which he wrote as a publicity release for a newspaper, the *Star* (June 2), confirms the idea: "As a lady and gentleman were out driving in Henrietta-st., Covent Garden yesterday, a heavy shower drove them to take shelter in the office of the Superintendant Registrar there, and in the confusion of the moment he married them."

4. (p. 322) *Not that I disclaim the fullest responsibility for his opinions. . . . it has been pointed out that Shakespear had no conscience. Neither have I, in that sense:* Here Shaw states a cardinal principle of playwriting: that the dramatist must not propagandize for a partisan point of view. The playwright must allow each character his or her say and from their point of view: "their points of view are, for the dramatic moment, mine also." Stacking the deck against characters with whose ideas the playwright disagrees does not produce drama; it produces partisan politics. For this reason, Shaw's plays rarely lend themselves to exploitation for partisan ends—as do, say, some of Brecht's plays and indeed so much of what passes for drama now.

5. (p. 326) *the play of Coriolanus is the greatest of Shakespear's comedies:* This is one of Shaw's most puzzling pronouncements. I believe he means that Coriolanus, with his obsessive fear of still being a boy tied to his mother and not a man, resembles the great humorous characters created by Molière or Ben Jonson, characters who are so defined by a single trait—avarice, lust, and so on—

that they become comical through their seemingly mechanical behavior.

6. (p. 363) *"Yes, my dear Lady Mephistopheles, tempted"*: At this stage of the drama, Jack unconsciously thinks of marrying Ann as an obstacle to fulfilling his destiny as a revolutionary thinker and social reformer, one who will contribute to the human race's progress through writing and politics; consequently, he associates her with the Devil, who, according to Tanner's dream self, Don Juan, diverts man from his true purpose to find the heaven of the real. Only when Jack realizes that Ann is the way to the real, through marriage and fatherhood, can he agree to marry her.

7. (p. 379) *He now gets into the car. . . . stowing away his hammer*: Shaw revised this paragraph for a later edition to read: *"He now gets into the car to stow away his tools and divest himself of his overalls. Tanner takes off his leathern overcoat and pitches it into the car with a sigh of relief, glad to be rid of it. The chauffeur, noting this, tosses his head contemptuously, and surveys his employer sardonically."* The changes reflect Shaw's practical experience with the actual staging of the play.

8. (p. 390) *"I suppose you will go in seriously for politics some day, Jack"*: In a letter to Harley Granville-Barker (May 24, 1907) about staging this scene between Ann and Tanner, Shaw explained how the suggestion of Robert Lorraine (the actor playing Tanner)—that he deliver his "great speech about the tyranny of mothers enthroned in the motor car, with Lillah (McCarthy, the actress playing Ann) somewhere under the wheels with her back to the audience"—made Shaw realize that he must put Ann in the car instead, but in the driver's seat "in a fascinating attitude with her breast on the driving wheel." In that way Shaw could use the staging to help express the meaning of the scene: Tanner, in the fashion of courting males, displays his oratorical powers to impress the female, while the female audience of one, Ann, completely controls the situation.

9. (p. 429) But this time Mozart's music gets grotesquely adulterated with Gounod's: Shaw means the music Charles Gounod wrote for Mephistopheles in *Faust* (1859), an opera Shaw in his role as music critic was compelled to hear so many times that he declared himself tired of it and done with it.

10. (p. 429) *"Its sympathies are all with misery, with poverty, with starvation. . . . I call on it to sympathize with joy, with love, with happiness, with beauty"*: The Devil's sentiments here strongly resemble those expressed by Lord Henry Wotton in Oscar Wilde's *The Picture of Dorian Gray* (1891): "I cannot sympathize with [suffering]. It is too ugly, too horrible, too distressing. There is something terribly morbid in the modern sympathy with pain. One should sympathize with the colour, the beauty, the joy of life" (chapter 5). Shaw has made the Devil echo Wilde's Dandy, Sir Henry, in order to identify the Devil as an exponent of Aestheticism, one who views art as separate from moral teaching and as existing for its own sake.

11. (p. 439) *an Italian and an Englishman:* The allusion to two epic poets is not idle humor. Shaw means *Man and Superman* to stand alongside Dante Alighieri's *Divine Comedy* (c. 1320) and John Milton's *Paradise Lost* (1667)—and Johann Wolfgang von Goethe's *Faust* (1808, 1832), likewise alluded to in humorous fashion—as accounts of humankind's purpose and destiny within a cosmic framework. Like the pilgrim Dante, Shaw's Don Juan makes a literal and psychological journey from Hell to Heaven. And Tanner and Ann, like Adam and Eve in *Paradise Lost*, though they are individual characters, are also projections of maleness and femaleness uniting in marriage in order to procreate and renew the world. In this same speech the Devil goes on to criticize *Paradise Lost* for being so long that no one has ever finished it; he also constantly criticizes Don Juan's speeches for their excessive length. Thus does Shaw parallel his own writing with Milton's— both are found boring by the Devil!

12. (p. 504) *"Is there a father's heart as well as a mother's?":* Here the

originality of Shaw's conception becomes apparent as he imagines a paternal instinct that matches the intensity of the maternal instinct, and then makes its discovery and recognition the
turning point in Tanner's resistance to his destiny.

13. (p. 504) [*panting . . .*] *"Jack: let me go. . . . I can't bear it"*: Shaw
makes Ann mime simultaneously having an orgasm and giving
birth (she had a few moments before pointed out to Jack that
marriage brings for the woman the risk of death in childbirth).
In designing the climax of Ann and Jack's courtship in this way,
Shaw has in mind Arthur Schopenhauer's essay "The Metaphysics
of Sexual Love" (1844), in which the philosopher argues that
sexual attraction between a man and a woman embodies the will
to live of the future child the couple can produce.

# INSPIRED BY THE PLAYS OF GEORGE BERNARD SHAW

> The theatre may survive as a place where people are taught to act, but apart from that there will be nothing but "talkies" soon.
>
> —George Bernard Shaw

Shaw's dramatic canon continues to be produced, entire theater festivals are dedicated to his work, and the classical theatrical repertoire now includes Shaw's plays alongside those of Shakespeare, Chekhov, and Ibsen. Nevertheless, it would seem that Shaw was right in pointing out the burgeoning dominance of film in human culture. Luckily for the playwright, movie-makers have been more than happy to embrace him.

In 1959 Guy Hamilton directed an all-star production of *The Devil's Disciple*, featuring Burt Lancaster, Kirk Douglas, and Laurence Olivier. The film retains much of Shaw's dialogue and wit. Hamilton, who went on to direct four James Bond films, brings a distinctly British sensibility to Shaw's satire of the American Revolution. The British soldiers are represented not as caricatures of evil, like the "Redcoats" in many American films, but as dedicated men who simply commit the folly of forgetting to tell Lord North to join forces with General "Gentleman" Johnny Burgoyne (Olivier), who, it seems, could have taken care of all the rebels himself. Lancaster and Douglas—that legendary duo of American action-adventure—are the rebels. Lancaster plays the Reverend Anthony Anderson, a pacifist who makes a startling conversion in becoming the quintessential American firebrand. Douglas plays a revolutionary rogue, the Devil's

Disciple, who takes the reverse tack and becomes a minister. Together they whip patriotic fervor to a fever pitch. Yet Olivier steals the show with his underplayed performance of the cynical Burgoyne. Although Olivier never felt he had done Shaw's masterpiece justice, several critics have lamented that there is not more of him in the picture.

American playwright Robert Anderson is best known for his 1953 Broadway play *Tea and Sympathy*, which is in effect a retelling of Shaw's *Candida*. Anderson's play revolves around a persecuted homosexual schoolboy who becomes attached to a protective older woman. In 1956 Vincente Minnelli directed a film of *Tea and Sympathy*, featuring Deborah Kerr and John Kerr (no relation), who both appeared in the original stage production. The film, bowdlerized by the Hays Office (Hollywood's self-censor), takes pains not to reference homosexuality explicitly—"Sissy Boy" (John Kerr) is merely an effeminate but decidedly heterosexual college student. Deborah Kerr, who also appeared in *The King and I* that same year, plays the part of Laura Reynolds, a teacher's wife who eventually offers her body to the young boy. Kerr closes the action of the film with the devastating line: "When you speak of this in future years—and you will—be kind." Interestingly, Deborah Kerr had made one of her first film appearances in Shaw's *Major Barbara* (1941) and went on to play the role of Candida on the stage.

# COMMENTS & QUESTIONS

*In this section, we aim to provide the reader with an array of perspectives on the text, as well as questions that challenge those perspectives. The commentary has been culled from sources as diverse as reviews contemporaneous with the work, letters written by the author, literary criticism of later generations, and appreciations written throughout the works' history. Following the commentary, a series of questions seeks to filter George Bernard Shaw's* Man and Superman and Three Other Plays *through a variety of points of view and bring about a richer understanding of these enduring works.*

## COMMENTS

### George Bernard Shaw

> The fairness of criticism is one thing, its adequacy quite another.
>
> —*The Star* (December 19, 1892)

### H. L. Mencken

Mrs. Warren, despite her ingenious reasoning, is a vulgar, ignorant woman, little capable of analyzing her own motives. Vivie, on the other hand, is a girl of quick intelligence and extraordinary education—a Cambridge scholar, a mathematician and a student of the philosophies. As the play opens Mrs. Warren seems to have all the best of it. She is the rebel and Vivie is the slave. But in the course of the strangely searching action, there is a readjustment. Convention overcomes the mother and crushes her; her daughter, on the other hand, strikes off her shackles and is free. . . .

"Candida" is a latter-day essay in feminine psychology after the fashion of "A Doll's House," "Monna Vanna," and "Hedda Gabler." Candida Morell, the heroine, is a clergyman's wife, who, lacking an acquaintance with the philosophies and face to face with the problem of earning her daily bread, might have gone the muddy way of Mrs. Warren. As it is, she exercises her fascinations upon a moony poet, arouses him to the mad-dog stage of passion, drives her husband to the verge of suicide—and then, with bland complacency and unanswerable logic, reads both an excellent lecture, turns the poet out of doors, and falls into her husband's arms, still chemically pure. It is an edifying example of the influence of mind over matter. . . .

Measured with rule, plumb-line or hayscales, "Man and Superman" is easily Shaw's *magnum opus*. In bulk it is brobdignagian; in scope it is stupendous; in purpose it is one with the *Odyssey*. Like a full-rigged ship before a spanking breeze, it cleaves deep into the waves, sending ripples far to port and starboard, and its giant canvases rise half way to the clouds, with resplendent jibs, skysails, staysails and studdingsails standing out like quills upon the fretful porcupine. It has a preface as long as a campaign speech; an interlude in three scenes, with music and red fire; and a complete digest of the German philosophers as an appendix. With all its rings and satellites it fills a tome of 281 closely-printed pages. Its epigrams, quips, jests, and quirks are multitudinous; it preaches treason to all the schools; its hero has one speech of 350 words. No one but a circus press agent could rise to an adequate description of its innumerable marvels. It is a three-ring circus, with Ibsen doing running jumps; Schopenhauer playing the calliope and Nietzsche selling peanuts in the reserved seats. And all the while it is the most entertaining play of its generation.

—*George Bernard Shaw: His Plays* (1905)


## A. B. Walkley

The stage-presentation of *Candida* adds nothing to what is the chief delight of the play—the chief delight of every one of Mr. Shaw's plays—its brilliant dialectic. And in one respect the spectator is actually deprived of a pleasure enjoyed by the reader. The book gives characteristic fragments of exegesis which necessarily disappear on the stage. One example is the account—as good as any "portrait" of La Bruyère—of the father-in-law, Mr. Burgess. Another occurs at the fall of the curtain. The stage direction is "They (husband and wife) embrace. But they do not know the secret in the poet's heart." On the stage the actors can, and do, embrace; but they have no possible means of telling the spectator, by their actions, whether they do or do not know the secret in the poet's heart. On the whole, however, *Candida* on the stage is a capital sport. Mr. Shaw maintains that he is quite serious, an out and out realist; in short, that in saluting him as a merry sportsman one is like the young lady who, when Sydney Smith said grace, shook him by the hand with a "Thank you very much, Mr. Smith; you are always so amusing." If so, one is evidently in the ignorant position of Candida and her husband when they embrace at the fall of the curtain; one does not know the secret in the playwright's heart.

—*Drama and Life* (1907)

## P. P. Howe

Mr. Bernard Shaw confronts his age not so much a dramatist as a writer possessed of a philosophy and a trick of the stage, who has employed the one to expound the other. He has said so himself, on more than one occasion. At the outset of his career as a dramatist he defined the impulse which moved him as the "philosopher's impatience to get to realities," and he went on to state, "I fight the theater, not with pamphlets and sermons and treatises, but with plays." Now the dramatist by vocation does not fight the theater at all. It is always a pity for the artist to quarrel with his medium, for if the artist wins, he will despise the medium, and if the medium wins, he will still despise it. . . .

Quite the most complete expression of Mr. Shaw's "philosophy" is to be found in *Man and Superman*, the "comedy" of which is a very easy-going affair. Its third act, in Hell, the "home of the unreal," with Heaven, the "home of the masters of reality," just round the corner, is the Quintessence of Shavianism; but it has so little to do with the theater that when the play is given there it is found necessary to omit it. *Man and Superman*, while the most characteristic product of Mr. Shaw's genius, is thus not one of the best of his plays, because it does not carry its burden. To put the case another way, its comic vision and its philosophic vision are not in alignment. The struggle between the Philosopher and the Playwright has been fearful, but the playwright has not won.

—*Fortnightly Review* (July 1913)

## QUESTIONS

1. Is Shaw relevant today?

2. Does Shaw's socialism get in the way? Does it interfere with the action? Does it lead Shaw to create scenes and characters whose function is only to make a point?

3. The poet W. B. Yeats felt ambivalent about Shaw's work. On the one hand, he said that he "stood aghast at its energy" the way he did before certain works of modern art, that such work provoked for him a nightmare of "a sewing machine, that clicked and shone, but . . . that smiled, smiled perpetually." On the other hand, Yeats spoke of Shaw's "generosity and courage," which he [Yeats] "could not fathom." Does Yeats do justice to Shaw?

4. Could a case be made that Shaw's female characters are more convincing, or at least more interesting, than his male characters?

# FOR FURTHER READING

## WORKS BY SHAW

*Collected Plays with Their Prefaces: Vols. 1–7.* Edited by Dan H. Laurence. New York: Dodd, Mead, 1975.

*The Collected Screenplays of Bernard Shaw.* Edited by Bernard F. Dukore. Athens: University of Georgia Press, 1980.

*Collected Letters.* Edited by Dan H. Laurence. Vol. 1, 1874–1897, New York: Dodd, Mead, 1965; Vol. 2, 1898–1910, New York: Dodd, Mead, 1972; Vol. 3, 1911–1925, New York: Viking Press, 1985; Vol. 4, 1926–1950, New York: Viking Press, 1988.

*The Drama Observed.* Edited by Bernard F. Dukore. Vol. 1: 1880–1895; Vol. 2: 1895–1897; Vol. 3: 1897–1911; Vol. 4: 1911–1950. University Park: Pennsylvania State University Press, 1993. An invaluable collection of all Shaw's writings about theater.

*Shaw's Music: The Complete Musical Criticism in Three Volumes.* Edited by Dan H. Laurence. Vol. 1: 1876–1890; Vol. 2: 1890–1893; Vol. 3: 1893–1950. New York: Dodd, Mead, 1981.

## BIOGRAPHICAL

Ervine, St. John G. *Bernard Shaw: His Life, Work, and Friends.* New York: William Morrow, 1956. The most sympathetic and fair biography of Shaw.

Henderson, Archibald. *George Bernard Shaw: Man of the Century.* New York: Appleton-Century-Crofts, 1956.

Holroyd, Michael. *Bernard Shaw, Vol. 1, 1856–1898: The Search for Love,* New York: Random House 1988. *Bernard Shaw, Vol. 2,*

*1898–1918: The Pursuit of Power*, New York: Random House, 1989. *Bernard Shaw, Vol. 3, 1918–1950: The Lure of Fantasy*, New York: Random House, 1991. *Bernard Shaw, Vol. 4, 1950–1991: The Last Laugh*, New York: Random House, 1992. The most detailed and comprehensive biography. A condensed version is available: *Bernard Shaw: The One-Volume Definitive Edition*, New York: Random House, 1998.

Shaw, George Bernard. *Interviews and Recollections*. Edited by A. M. Gibbs. Iowa City: University of Iowa Press, 1990. An indispensable record of first-hand personal views of and by Shaw.

## CRITICAL WORKS

Bentley, Eric. *Bernard Shaw*. New York: New Directions, 1947.

Berst, Charles A. *Bernard Shaw and the Art of Drama*. Champaign-Urbana: University of Illinois Press, 1973.

Crompton, Louis. *Shaw the Dramatist*. Lincoln: University of Nebraska Press, 1969.

Evans, T. F., ed. *Shaw: The Critical Heritage*. London: Routledge, 1976.

Meisel, Martin. *Shaw and the Nineteenth-Century Theater*. Princeton, NJ: Princeton University Press, 1963. A brilliant and delightful account of Shaw's relationship to the theater of his youth.

Morgan, Margery M. *The Shavian Playground*. London: Methuen, 1972.

Turco, Alfred, Jr. *Shaw's Moral Vision*. Ithaca, NY: Cornell University Press, 1976.

Valency, Maurice. *The Cart and the Trumpet*. New York: Oxford University Press, 1973.

Watson, Barbara Bellow. *A Shavian Guide to the Intelligent Woman*. New York: W. W. Norton, 1972. Still the best case for Shaw as a feminist.

Wisenthal, J. L. *The Marriage of Contraries*. Cambridge, MA: Harvard University Press, 1974.

# PRESENTATION AND ANALYSIS OF SHAW'S IDEAS

Bertolini, John A. *The Playwrighting Self of Bernard Shaw.* Carbondale and Edwardsville: University of Southern Illinois Press, 1991.

Dukore, Bernard. *Shaw's Theatre.* Gainesville: University Press of Florida, 2000.

Gibbs, A. M. *The Art and Mind of Shaw.* New York: Macmillan, 1983.

Gordon, David J. *Bernard Shaw and the Comic Sublime.* New York: St. Martin's Press, 1990.

Holroyd, Michael, ed. *The Genius of Shaw.* New York: Holt, Rinehart and Winston, 1979.

*Shaw: The Annual of Bernard Shaw Studies:* Vols. 1–22 successive. General editors: Stanley Weintraub, Fred D. Crawford, Gale K. Larson. University Park: Pennsylvania State University Press, 1981–2003.